THE WOLF & THE DOE

REBECCA MAUREEN

The Wolf and the Doe

Copyright © 2025 by Rebecca Maureen.

MILTON & HUGO L.L.C.
4407 Park Ave., Suite 5
Union City, NJ 07087, USA

Website: *www. miltonandhugo.com*
Hotline: *1- 888-778-0033*
Email: *info@miltonandhugo.com*

Ordering Information:
Quantity sales. Special discounts are granted to corporations, associations, and other organizations. For more information on these discounts, please reach out to the publisher using the contact information provided above.

Library of Congress Control Number: IN-PROCESS
ISBN-13:   979-8-89285-723-9   [Paperback Edition]
                  979-8-89285-724-6   [Digital Edition]

Rev. date: 10/24/2025

MELANIE (January 10)

"I remember going to the movies with Tim. He had talked me into going to see the new Batman movie with him. It was the 3rd day of its release, so the room wasn't packed, but it wasn't empty either. The top row was full, so I picked a spot for us to sit in the second row from the top. About halfway through the movie there was a couple in the lower left corner of the room that started arguing. The female was whisper yelling at the guy; we could hear her but couldn't make out what she was saying. First popcorn went flying across the room then there was a loud BANG."

I took a deep breath and drank some water that the therapist had gotten for me. I looked at my hands and started to pick at my nails as I continued, "At first, I thought I was seeing a cherry slushie being tossed into the air, but looking back now it was definitely not a slushie. I was just sitting there in shock, all around me were people running in sporadic chaos. It was dark but in the glow of the screen I could see people shoving other people over the seats to get them out of the way. The clap of the gun was so loud and clear it was disorienting to hear it over the recorded sound of the action scene going on in the movie."

I took a breath and swallowed, my mouth felt so dry, "Tim was pulling my arm, trying to get me to move. As I stood up, I felt something push my head to the side, I stumbled back into the seat and looked around for what hit me, blinking liquid from my eyes." I trailed off and just stared at my hands.

After a moment, the therapist asked, "What happened next?"

I hate talking about this next part, it still haunts me. I touched the scar on my forehead, "Tim was on his back across the seats, there was a glistening black hole under his chin. I scrambled backwards screaming. After that it's just a blur." I picked the water back up but didn't drink it.

It was silent for a moment, I could feel her eyes burning holes into me, "I think that's enough today," I heard papers shuffling around, "Are you still having trouble sleeping? How are the nightmares?" she asked.

I shook my head, "I don't sleep much these days," the sleeping meds were giving me reoccurring nightmares, the dreams over all were different but they all ended the same. Right before I'd wake up, covered in sweat with my heart beating out of my chest, a gun would go off. Last night the shooter from the night was walking next to me. We stopped walking and he said to me, 'I gave her the world and she never appreciated it,' then he wiped something off my cheek with his thumb and continued, 'you women just take and take, you never love us like we love you.' He looked over to the side. I followed his gaze and seen that he was looking at Tim, in the nightmare Tim was sitting against a tree, blood covered the front of his shirt, and his head was hanging to the side. Horrified, I forced my eyes back to the shooter. But he wasn't the shooter anymore, he morphed into Tim, when he opened his mouth to speak, I could see daylight through the hole in the roof of his mouth. 'It took you 5 months to go out with me,' I took a step back but realized he had a grip on my arm, and then he put a gun to my head. The cold metal pressed against my temple and slipped down to my jaw, 'why didn't you give me a chance sooner?' I shook my head and tears started running down my face, WHY?!' he screamed. In some nightmares he'd kiss me before the gun went off. In others he'd just pull the trigger. But I always woke up with the gun shot still ringing in my ears.

"I see," her tone was flat, "I'm upping your trazadone, but the Lexapro will stay the same." She took out her prescription pad and scribbled out my refills. She sighed and took her glasses off. "Melanie, you've been making great progress in these last 4 months but if you keep avoiding sleep all this work will be for nothing," she folded her arms on the table and looked at me. "I really hope you've reconsidered moving. I don't think right now is the right time for such a dramatic change."

I flicked my eyes up to her. We've been discussing life changes lately and I mentioned that I wanted to move to a different city. She didn't like that idea, she was thinking more about finding a job where I would interact with the public more, and to make new friends, and maybe even start dating again. I brought my attention back down to the bottle of water in my hands and nodded.

"How's your schooling going? Are you still taking online classes? I know last time we talked your grades were starting to slip. Has it gotten any better?" She asked.

I dropped out last week. I couldn't keep up with the curriculum with the insane work load that my boss threw on me. I was suffocating and no one seemed to care, so I got rid of school, but I was still in rough waters. Work was the last thing to go. I just needed to collect the last paycheck and put in my resignation. I'm not sure if I'll be able to find another comfy work from home job but I've always hated it, the boss was a heartless jerk. I sighed and answered, "School is good. Juggling work and class has never been easier." I said sarcastically.

The doctor sighed, "Melanie, I know things are difficult, but you need to try to stay positive. I'm making an appointment for 2 weeks out. Does that work for you?"

"Yeah, that's fine." I lied. I had no real intention of keeping the appointment, I was determined that this was my last meeting with her. I've had this suffocating feeling for a while now, like my skin doesn't fit right and the walls are closing in. I need to change something in my life but not knowing what needed to be changed I decided to change it all. I hate how my therapist doesn't see it that way.

I've been living with my sister for the past year and it's time I moved out and gave her back her house. Throughout the year I've been saving and looking for a place of my own. The only thing available and realistic was in a town called Troy that was a few hours away. My sister, Kendra, at first wasn't too keen on the idea of me uprooting my whole life to move to a town where I didn't know anyone. But this will be good for me, I know it.

There's been times when I thought I was crazy for going through with this. During the first initial drive, to sign the lease, I was talking myself down, it would have been so easy to turn around and forget the entire thing, but this is what's best. I forced myself to continue the drive. I signed the lease, got the keys, checked the place out, hung curtains on the windows, and left feeling lighter than I have in a long while. Driving home I knew I had made the right decision; in 3 days I'm moving.

I walked out of the office and called an uber to pick me up and drop me off at my sisters. I was nervous about this weekend, going over all the things I still needed to do. I have already found a job; I start in 2 weeks, so I don't have to worry about paying my rent without completely draining my savings. All my things were packed and ready for the movers to take to my new apartment. A car pulled up, and I checked to make sure it was my uber, it was.

GRIFFIN (January 10)

I woke up to harsh rays of sunlight across my face. Groaning, I rolled over and buried my face into the pillow. My head was pounding. I reached my arm across the bed feeling for you, but you're gone. Squeezing my outreached hand into a fist the memories came flooding back. I couldn't remember why you were so angry with me, Ellie, but you wouldn't stop screaming and throwing things at me. "GET AWAY FROM ME!" You kept yelling, why would you want me away from you so badly? I thought you loved me.

Every muscle in my body ached when I rolled onto my back and sat up. Looking around confused; *this isn't my room* I thought. When I looked out the window and seen the endless forest I relaxed. I was at Grandpa's old house. I got up and walked over to the window, I could barely see the well from here. I rolled my shoulders, they were stiff from carrying you, I never thought of you as fat Ellie, but you weren't exactly light. It took some effort, but I was able to lift you up and over the edge, so I didn't accidentally knock over the wall of the well.

I was going to miss you, Ellie but, in a way I always knew things between us wouldn't work out, and the more I think about it I'm surprised things lasted this long. Turning my back to the window I made my way to the door and walked down the creaky stairs, every step I felt pain shoot through me. I couldn't remember how much I drank but I didn't think it was enough to cause a hangover and if I wasn't hung over then last night took more out of me than I thought.

It was cold this morning, I could use a hot cup of coffee, but we don't keep food out here, so that will have to wait. I sat down at the kitchen table anyway. I had to flip the table back over; I remember throwing it out of the way last night when you tried to run out the door. Thinking you could ever outrun me made me want to laugh but my head ached too much. I looked around, the place looked like a bear tore through here. I'm glad Grandpa is long gone; the condition of the kitchen would be more than enough for a 'trip to the cellar' as he liked to call it. Thinking of Grandpa sent a wave of panic crashing through me, I looked behind me expecting to see him charging at me with those boney hands stretched out reaching for me.

I put my head in my hands and took some deep breaths to try to subdue the headache, I didn't think I drank that much to have this bad of a hangover. I could picture the bottle of aspirin that Ellie kept in her bag, which was still in my car. Dragging myself out of the kitchen was rough, I couldn't wait to go home and go back to sleep. Somehow, I managed to drag myself across the lawn and to my car. Opening the front passenger door, I fell inside, the world started to spin, and I had just enough time to make sure I was leaning out of the car before I started throwing up. God, I felt like shit.

The purse was sitting on the floorboard. I picked it up and went straight for the aspirin. I went through the rest of the contents; a brush, some loose mints, a handful of receipts, some keys which had more charms than keys on it, and lastly the wallet, in it I found Ellies driver's license, debit card, 3 credit cards, a couple random punch cards to local restaurants, and $87 in cash. I took the cash but everything else went back into the purse.

I was tempted to dump the bag on my way home but if I didn't do it now, I'd risk getting caught with it. I pulled myself out of the car and grabbed the bag, my legs screamed at me every step, I just wanted to lie down. It took longer than it should have to get to the well, but it was a sweet relief when I sat down on the edge of it. I slumped my shoulders, I was drained. Out loud I said, "Why are you so exhausting to put up with?" *Can you hear me down there Ellie?* I thought, testing the weight of the purse, debating if it would sink. Being on the safe side I decided to walk around the well picking up bigger sized rocks and throwing them into the bag. Zipping it closed, I leaned over to look down into the well. There she was face down floating on top of the water. I dropped the purse into the well and watched it hit her back before sliding down and disappearing into the water. I leaned on the wall and looked down at Ellie for a while, I still couldn't understand why it came to this, I loved you and yet that wasn't enough for you. I looked around the yard and spotted the brush pile. *Just in case.* I sighed and went over to the pile of branches. Picking two limbs the size of my leg out I pulled them over to the well. Heaving them over the waist high wall I threw them one at a time into the well. Hearing the splash as they hit the water I looked down. It had the desired effect, looking down you just seen some tree limbs.

Smiling to myself I went to my car. I wanted more sleep but there was no way I could sleep here alone. When I slid into the driver's seat my whole body drooped, I was so tired I thought about taking a quick nap in the car. I shook my head and slapped myself in the face a few times to wake myself up. I put the key in the ignition and turned it. One more look at the well I put the car in drive and drove away, glad to see Grandpa's old house in the review mirror.

MELANIE (January 13)

When I walked through the door Kendra was in the kitchen, she asked if I was still going through with what she called 'the big move.'

"Fuck yes, I'm so ready to get out of this shit hole." I said, tossing my bag on the counter. One thing I wouldn't miss about this town is that I couldn't go anywhere without someone bringing up what happened in the theater. I was eager to go to a place where people weren't saying comments like how awful it must be to live through something like that. "I need to move on; and I can't do that when the cashier brings up how good of a guy Tim was and that it's crazy how they are still using that room to show movies." It was people like her who encouraged me to stop going into the local stores when I managed to drag myself out of the house. I just wish people would leave me alone and try to move on themselves.

There was a brief awkward silence, I leaned over to see what she was working on, it was a lamp that had a round wooden base that she's painting to look like an underwater paradise, complete with mermaids and krakens. Kendra put her paintbrush in a cup of water and got up. Going over to the sink with the paint water she dumped it out and rinsed off the paintbrushes. Turning to me she said "Fuck her. I'm going to miss you, but I understand. We still need to stop by the store after we get to your new place." She had agreed to help me unload the moving van. We were going to make a girls night out of it.

"That's fine, we can do it before, the movers said that they'd be running late anyway." I had rented one of those moving containers that the company comes by and picks up to move it for you. We got our things together and grabbed something to eat from the kitchen before we left.

For the next 3 hours we switched on and off between singing with the radio and talking about random things over a true crime podcast. Stopping only once for a bathroom break and to fill the gas tank back up.

Before we knew it, we were pulling off of the highway and driving into my new town. I pulled up the address to my apartment so we could drive by and check it out before going to the store. I had already made this trip twice a few weeks ago; once to look at the place and sign the lease and a few days later to hang some curtains and drop off some of the less important things, things that I never use but I'm not willing to let go of just yet. The last of my belongings were in the back of Kendra's car. I didn't have a vehicle at the moment, but I have enough in savings to go get a cheap one.

We pulled up to the brick building. It was 4 stories high, 4 apartments on each floor, it was a fairly standard apartment complex. We both got out and grabbed a box out of the back. "Please tell me we don't have to climb any stairs." Kendra said as we made our way to the front door.

I laughed, "No, I'm on the first floor, last one on the left."

There was a lock on the door to get into the building, but it's been busted for 5 years, and the landlord has no plans to fix it. That fact did concern me a little, but he assured me the crime rate for this area was low. If I keep my door locked, I'll be fine, he said. I sat the box in my hands down to fish the keys out of my jacket pocket to unlocked the door. It didn't take long to show off my new apartment, there was only the kitchen/living room, a bathroom/laundry room, and bedroom with a walk-in closet. There was a small, enclosed porch connected to the bedroom which is what sold me on the apartment in the first place.

I checked my phone for the time 11:24 am, "We still have about 4 hours until the movers get here."

Kendra let out a groan, forever the impatient one, "4 hours?! That's ridiculous, you should ask for a discount or something. That is completely unprofessional."

I shrugged, "At least it's still kind of early in the day, come on let's go find the store."

—⚈—

The radio was playing as we pulled up to the Target parking lot. Kendra was going over the night's plans as she put the car in park. "Ok, so we need 2 bottles of wine, chips, dip, and a pizza."

"Can we bake some cookies too?" I asked as I gathered my phone and wallet. She said something as she picked up her purse, but I was lost in thought looking out the window. I took a deep breath; being in big crowds always freaked me out, too many things happening all at once, it was hard to feel at ease when so many strangers were packed into the same place.

"Hey, are you ok?" She put her hand on my arm. "We can do something else."

I haven't been out of the house much since the shooting. Everyone told me it was normal, I just had to take it slow. 'It takes time after such a traumatic event to feel comfortable enough to step outside' yeah well, it's been over a year. It's time to move on with my life, I don't want to spend the rest of my days waiting to hear a soft *knock, knock*, letting me know that my groceries arrived cause I'm too busy cowering under the blankets to make the trip in person. Grow up and go outside, I tell myself. Enough playing the victim, go out and get your own fucking cheerios.

I shook my head, we made plans to have a girl's night, complete with plenty of wine, shitty food, and scary movies. "No, I got this." I hesitated for a moment longer before opening the door. The wind blew my hair in my face. I tucked it behind my ear and walked around the car to catch up to Kendra who was already heading towards the store.

When I fell in step beside her she gently slapped me on the arm "Melanie, knock it off. You look like an owl."

My head is on a constant swivel when I'm outside the house, I want to know what is going on around me at all times. If something bad is about to happen I would like to have a heads up. I 'hoo'ed at her and did one more look around the parking lot, a mother pushing a cart with a small child hanging off the handle; an elderly couple, the husband helping his wife out of the car, a younger couple fighting, there so many people coming and going I felt lost in a sea of bodies. My eyes landed on a guy who was walking out of the store, he was tall, slim, wearing a Tool band tee, clean shaven and had his lip pierced on the right-side bottom lip. *I have that same shirt* I thought taking a last look at him as a blast of cold air hit me in the face.

—⁓—

We've been in the store for a while now; just walking up and down aisles at this point, picking up random things we might need tonight. We ended up in the wine and spirit section. From the corner of my eye, I seen a tall figure dressed in black. It seemed like they were just standing at the end of the aisle, staring perhaps? At us? No that's crazy. I'm just paranoid. I swallowed the lump in my throat and nodded absent mindedly as Kendra asked if the wine she had chosen sounded good. I looked at her and nodded, then turned my head back to the end of the aisle. No one was standing there; I shrugged it off and followed Kendra down the aisle.

We were heading down the chip aisle going in for Lays queso chips and mild cheder cheese dip. I chanced a look behind us just in time to see a tall figure in black walking by the end cap. Seeing the eye printed on the back of the shirt I narrowed my eyes and shook my head. My mind started going into overdrive.

There is no way that was the same guy I had seen in the parking lot. He was walking out, not in. What kind of psycho goes back into a store they just came out of? Maybe he forgot something? Take a deep breath you're acting crazy, I told myself.

Someone gently shoved me from behind, I felt my heart jump into my throat. My hands started to shake as my whole body went cold. I jerked my body around trying to prepare myself for the worst… but it was only Kendra.

"Mel, are you even listening to me? I've been trying to talk to you." She said crossing her arms.

"I'm sorry, this is just a lot to take in at the moment. What were you saying?" She repeated the question about what sounded better tonight, movies or painting. "Why can't we do both? If we get too caught up in the movie, we can finish painting later."

She agreed and we grabbed the rest of the items on the list and headed for the registers. As we walked by the clothes section, my mouth went dry, and I stopped. Kendra stopped too and gave me a funny look, but I couldn't look away. There, dressed in a black Tool band tee, tall and slim, trying and failing to seem casual as he looked at the long sleeve shirts. Our eyes locked, if I wasn't so freaked out, I would have thought he was handsome. Blue eyes, smooth shave, his arms were toned and covered in tattoos. But I was freaking out, this wasn't right, something is off. I seen this man walking out of the store, I also seen him around the store the entire time we've been in here, a couple of steps behind us, dodging around corners when I tried to get a better look. He had no basket, didn't look like he was carrying anything, so what was he doing other than following us around?

"Did you want to stop and check out some clothes before we go? I could use some more pants." Kendra started heading towards the clothes and the guy smirked at me before he walked away. I felt the blood drain from my face and followed Kendra towards the jeans.

20 minutes later we were heading for the car, I wanted to tell Kendra about the weird guy I thought was stalking us, but I already thought I was over thinking and didn't want to ruin our night by dragging her down my paranoid rabbit hole. I decided to push the whole encounter to the back of my head and put on a smile. "That wasn't too horrible, in a few months I might be able to pass for normal." I said as we unloaded the bags into her car.

Kendra laughed and handed me her vape, "Here, maybe this will calm your crazy. Honestly, I didn't think that was too bad, you made it through an entire shopping trip." Her voice faded out into the background.

As she was talking, I took a hit off her pen and rolled the window down. I exhaled a cloud of smoke, and through that smoke I could see something that made my adrenaline start pumping. It was that guy again, he was sitting in a car, a black dodge charger. The windows were tinted but I could see the word "Tool" through the windshield. From here it definitely seemed like he was looking right at us.

What in the fuck, I thought, then I took a breath and tried to talk myself down, *I'm just being paranoid.* I took another hit, trying like hell to rip my eyes off his band tee. Ice ran through me, my mind was going around in circles, I didn't know what to think. I should probably tell Kendra now. I took a bigger hit off her pen before handing it back. I could make out his features now, and my paranoia was right, not only was this man staring at us, but he was also smiling.

"Kendra," I started taking a breath, "I think someone was following us around the store." I told her about passing the guy wearing a Tool shirt in the parking lot and how I kept seeing the same guy all throughout the store. I told her about the way he smirked at me in the clothing section and that he's now watching us in his car. She asked me where and I told her. We both turned our heads to find an empty parking space.

"That is fucking spooky, you should have told me sooner. Let's just get you home. The sooner we're out of here the sooner you'll feel better," smoke escaped her mouth when she was talking. Turning her into a hookah smoking caterpillar for a moment.

GRIFFIN (January 13)

I was walking out of the store carrying my dinner for the night, a 12 pack of beer and pizza rolls. I was trying to think of what to do when I got home other than drinking myself to sleep, maybe I'll get the paint out. I haven't painted anything since…no, thinking of her just ignites my anger.

Fuck, I hated being single. Things in my head were ok when I was at work, but once it was time to leave and I shut myself in my car I could feel the headache start to come on. When I wasn't at work the only place left for me to go was home, and when I was at home the place was so quiet I could feel myself going mad, and I was getting lonely. Alex was always talking about the multiple dating apps he's on, maybe I should give that a chance, see what all the hype is about.

I could go over to Levi's house, but then again his sister still going through that breakup and I don't want to deal with that disaster.

When the automated doors opened and the fresh air hit me, I took a deep breath and tried to push my negative thoughts away. I blinked a few times from the sudden brightness, but it didn't take long for my eyes to adjust; and when they did, I had to do a double take. Walking towards me was one of the most beautiful women I had the pleasure of laying my eyes on. She was a little short, her hair was put up in a messy bun, and those thighs; I could bury my face between them and never come up for air.

We caught each other's eye, but only for a moment, a moment that didn't last long enough but was enough to spark something in me that I didn't even know existed. I made a move to follow you back inside but realized I still had the bag and beer in my hand. Nearly running to my car, I fished the keys out of my pocket; but my hands were shaking so bad I almost dropped them when I pulled the keys out and went to unlock the door. I took a deep breath and put the beer, and pizza rolls in the backseat.

I had to get another look at you. I knew I was boarding stalker territory, but I didn't care. When a wolf sees a doe, he doesn't just walk away from her; no, he follows her. Waits for that perfect opportunity, creeps up behind her, and in one swift movement she's all his.

I was worried I wouldn't find you again, but the store isn't that big. I took a lap around the store and walked through a few isles when I finally caught a glimpse of you. You were disappearing down the alcohol section. I stopped at the end cap of the alcohol aisle, and I know I shouldn't be standing here as long as I am, just watching; but oh man, you make it so easy.

You don't seem comfortable; you're twitchy, nervous. You didn't strike me as someone with a drug addiction, you looked more worried than strung out. I wish I could go up to you and wrap you in my arms-oh fuck you almost saw me. I ducked out of the aisle and made myself blend into the crowd.

It's easy to lose someone in a store, but if you're paying close attention, you can find them just as fast. Walking past some empty aisles and a few crowded ones with no sign of you, I was about to call it and go home, then I walked by the chips and seen your friend shove you. Fire ran through me, and it took all I had not to run down there to punch her square in the face. *Stop that*, if I go down there right now and hit your friend in front of you, you're more likely to call the police than to go home with me. I tend to get attached too quickly, but do you blame me? When I find something that I care about I want to protect it, it's not my fault if that goes left unappreciated.

I lost sight of you again, confused on how this keeps happening and if this is even worth the effort, I ran a hand through my hair and figured I should just try to get you out of my head and go home. I walked by the long-sleeved shirts and went to find one or two. Might as well get something while I'm back in the store, following around an attractive woman like a fucking creep, what is wrong with me? I told myself I would stop after that second time, that one was a little too messy and it almost landed me in some major trouble. But here I am plotting my next attempt at love. This would be what, lucky number seven? I laughed and I grabbed 2 long sleeved shirts, one black and one dark blue, and it was there in that moment when I had just given up and was turning around to leave when my eyes landed on you. This time our eyes locked. Those green eyes could make me do anything. You teased your bottom lip with your teeth, oh what I would do to be able to bite your lip, you looked adorable, so small and frightened. I smirked and winked at you, *I'll be seeing you around* I thought and headed back to the registers.

On the way to my car, I had a huge smile on my face. I felt like I was walking on air. I sat down in the driver's seat and turned the car on. I want to try to figure out who that was. That beautiful woman who grabbed my attention and wrapped around me like a constrictor. I pulled out my phone along with a pack of cigarettes, not really sure where to begin I sent Alex a text asking him for some technical help, using only a name he could find out anything on anyone.

I was lighting a cigarette as 2 women walked in front of my car. My eyes followed them as they walked by. I was watching the shorter one walk, not believing what I was seeing. What the fuck, it couldn't be.

Of all the places in the parking lot you guys parked 4 cars away from mine, this is a sign, right? It has to be. I watched as you walked away, your hips swinging side to side. I want to grab onto those hips and ram myself inside you. My jaw dropped and my cigarette fell out of my mouth landing into my lap, good thing it wasn't lit. *Stop it,* I thought, *you don't even know this girl.* I couldn't help but smile as you two laughed. I want to be there with you, I want to be the one making you laugh.

I watched your lips part as you put a vape pen up to your mouth. You look so at ease as you turn your head to blow smoke out the window. Do you know how beautiful you are? Your green eyes drifted over to me and then they widened; and I realized a moment too late that I've been staring at you, grinning. When you looked away, I took that as my queue to leave. I put the car in drive and pulled out of the parking lot. I didn't want to scare you into calling the police.

The drive home was quiet despite the radio being on, my thoughts drowned out the music, all I could think of was you, your eyes, your thighs, your hips, your lips, fuck those lips. They would feel so good around my cock. Stop it stop it. This is one spiral I shouldn't be on but when the fixation is this desirable how can I help it?

I decided not to fight the urges. I know what I said that I was done after the last time, but this is different. I can feel it. The first thing I did when I got home and sat down was get on Facebook. I heard that girl call you "Mel" so hopefully that'll get me somewhere. Hopefully, your profile picture is you, hopefully you're on Facebook. This would be a lot better if she had called you by your full name. Looking someone up using a nickname was like trying to start a fire using a dead lighter. I didn't know that "Mel" was short for so many different names.

I was going through different "Mel's" on Instagram when Alex sent me a message, he couldn't find anything on you either. I kept searching through the night.

Before I knew it my alarm was going off, and I was no closer to finding out who you were. But there was no need to worry, I'm patient. I'll find you again; soon.

MELANIE (January 14)

My apartment was a maze of boxes. Kendra and I had put the furniture in place and moved the boxes to the respected rooms. It was odd when she left this morning, I felt a little hollow, but I pushed that aside and got on Facebook to see if I could find a car for sale close by. I didn't want to have to uber everywhere that would get expensive. As luck would have it, I found a pretty nice car nearby, the asking price was $2,000 which would take half of my savings. I messaged the seller, and we set up a time for me to come by and check out the car. I went to the guy's profile but all I could see was his profile picture and name. Ryan Sherwood was blowing smoke at the camera, so it was hard to see what he actually looked like, I guess I'll find out in 4 hours.

I put the address he had listed in google maps and it was only a 30-minute walk from here, luckily for me the winter has been pretty mild so the walk wouldn't be too bad. I put on a belt so I could carry a small belt knife for protection, I had a canister of pepper spray on my key chain, but I like to have a backup plan. I had texted Kendra and told her where I was going and who I was meeting in case something happened. I watch too many horror movies, but it never hurts to be cautious.

When it was time to head out, I put in one earbud to put on some music to help pass the time and pulled a beanie over my head to keep my ears warm. Grabbing my keys and putting on my coat I went over to the mirror to make sure that you couldn't tell I was carrying a knife and a large amount of cash on me. Taking a hit off of my vape pen I walked out the door.

Kendra and I had made for each other charms to hang on our doors last night, we decided on crafting them over painting. She made me a really awesome moon phase charm to hang on my apartment door, and I made her geometric butterfly that she's going to hang up in her beauty salon Beautiful You. After locking the door, I looked at the charm and noticed that the middle moon had flipped over when I opened and closed the door. I flipped it over and set out to hopefully buy a car.

The sky was clear today, so the sun was shining brightly, taking the chill out of the air but the wind was still brisk. Not a horrible day for a walk, but I quickly decided that if the location of the car was any further

15

away, I would have messaged the guy to cancel and go back home. But it wasn't that far, and I needed a car. Besides, exercise is good for you, and this is a good way to start to familiarize myself with the city I moved to.

The address led me to a trailer park, I felt my anxiety starting to prickle as I pulled my phone out and messaged the guy that I was there. He said he was outside and seen me. I looked up and seen some guys standing outside the back trailer. Keeping a firm hold on my keys I took a big hit off my vape and put on a brave front. When I got to the trailer the group got quiet, there were 2 guys and 1 girl, she looked me up and down sneered and walked inside, pulling one of the guys with her. "Y-y-you must be Melanie." The last guy said. "I'm Ryan" he extended his hand out to me.

I shook his hand firmly, "Nice to meet you," He was thin with a patchy beard, he kept scratching at his arms through the sleeves of his jacket. I looked at the car he was standing in front of. "This must be the car." I said walking around him. It looked to be in good condition.

"Sure is." He said, "I-I-I-I have the keys here i-i-if you want to go for a test drive."

I agreed, not wanting to pay for a car before I had a chance to actually drive it, so I took the key and got in the driver's seat. I was slightly nervous when he got in the passenger seat, but I reminded myself that I had my belt knife in case he tried to do anything. The car started right up and as I drove the car around the block, I was pleased to find out it ran well. I wasn't a mechanic but I didn't hear any weird noises so that was good. When we got back to his trailer Ryan took his seatbelt off and turned to me. "So, what do you think?" he asked. His tone was light, but my guard was still up.

"It's a nice car." I said looking around at the inside. It was cleaned out, but the seats were stained. Nothing I couldn't scrub out. I turned the car off and we both got out.

A black dodge charger pulled up as Ryan, and I were completing the sale. 2 guys stepped out of the car. A tall guy in a black hoodie stepped out of the driver seat, he had a clean shave and a pierced lip, wearing sunglasses and a beanie, he looked over in my direction. I narrowed my eyes, he seemed familiar, but I couldn't remember where I had seen him before. The other guy was slightly shorter, stark black hair, naturally tan,

16

with a neatly trimmed beard. Ryan nodded over to the guys, "H-h-hey guys. We-we-we're just finishing up here," he shouted to them. To me he said, "Wait here, I need to get the title."

When the 2 guys walked up, I expected them both to follow Ryan inside. But the guy with the beard stayed back. "Hey, I'm Alex." He said stepping up next to me.

The smell that came off him would have been pleasant if it wasn't so overwhelming, he had put way too much body spray on. "Mel." I replied with a forced smile, shifting my weight to my other leg to lean away from him.

"Is Mel short for something?" He asked.

I looked over at him, and he smirked back. "Just Mel." I said, keeping my answers short. I was getting more nervous by the moment. I just had to keep calm until I got the title then I could leave.

"Ryan is a good friend of mine. If you haven't paid for the car yet, I can get you a good discount."

I looked at the door to the trailer, impatiently waiting for Ryan to come back and give me the title so I could leave. "No that's ok." I said with a smile, gripping my keys tighter in my hand. I was growing pretty uncomfortable.

Alex raised his hands, "Ok I was just trying to help." Putting his hands down he asked, "So *Mel*, are you new around here? I haven't seen you before." He was looking me up and down.

Just then the door to the trailer slammed open and Ryan stumbled out, the tall guy with the lip piercing walked out shortly after. As they walked up, I felt the tall guy's eyes on me. Ryan came up to me and held his hand out. "I-i-if you don't mind, the cash for the title." His smile was greasy, but his tone was still disarming. I didn't like the 3 men standing around me as I took out the $2000 in cash and handed it over. When I tried to take the title, Ryan tightened his grip. I looked up at him, and he was grinning down at me, "It was a pleasure doing business with you."

I forced a smile and yanked the title out of his grip. When I opened the car door to get in, I overheard whom I'm assuming was the tall guy say, "If you sold her a shit vehicle, you'll be spitting your teeth out for a week." As odd as that was, I brushed it off, eager to get out this trailer court and away from their prying eyes.

It felt good to drive away in a car, but I felt more unsettled than excited. Looking in the review mirror I seen the guy who introduced himself as Alex and Ryan walking back inside. But the tall guy was standing in the middle of the road, watching me drive away.

Griffin (January 14)

I was sitting in my car waiting for Alex so we could go get our money from Ryan. He owed my dad 50k and so far, he has only paid 40. Normally dad doesn't bother with collecting debts but since this one was so high and most of it was due to gambling he decided that now was the time to get his money back. Ryan said he'd have the rest by the end of the day, and it was up to us to collect. When Alex finally got in, I nearly gagged. "Dude, you fucking reek." I said rolling his window down. "Never wear that shit when you're getting in my car again."

"Fuck off man. This cologne is proven to get me laid. Evey time I wear this I'm crawling with pussy." Alex was obsessed with his look. He spent more on a haircut than I do on tires for my car.

"Let's go pay Ol' Ryan a visit. It's been too long." I put the car in drive and drove off. "I hope he doesn't pull any bullshit. I'm not in the mood to fight."

Alex laughed, "Lucky for you I'm down for one. I'm kind of hoping he does something stupid." When we pulled up to the trailer park I watched as Ryan stepped out of the passenger side of his car. I felt like I was dreaming when I saw who got out of the driver's side. It was you, Mel. I didn't think I'd run into you this soon. This is fate, it has to be. Alex started laughing harder, "That desperate junkie is selling his car! Oh man this is going to be fun."

"Remember that chick from the store I asked you to help me find?"

Alex looked over at me, "Don't fucking tell me," He trailed off and looked out the window at you standing next to Ryan. "Bro is that really her?"

I nodded, "Stay out here with her while I go inside and deal with Ryan."

When we got out Ryan yelled something at us, but I was too fixated on you. I wanted to scoop you up and take you out of here, a Goddess like you shouldn't be dealing with scum like Ryan. We walked up and Ryan was saying something about going to get the title. I followed him as he went inside motioning for Alex to stay behind. I didn't want you out here alone, but I didn't trust myself to be out here with you. I knew I would grab you up and steal you away before we could get the money. So, I did the right thing and put business before pleasure.

I waited until the door closed, I didn't want you to see this, I slammed Ryan against the wall. "Where's the money Ryan?" I asked, already bored of this. I wanted to go back outside and see what you were doing. As much as I hated that Alex was out there alone with you, at least I knew you weren't being bothered by any of the crackheads that live here. You are way too pretty to be left alone in this trailer park.

"I-I-I-I have it. I just need to get the last 2,000 and it's yours. I-I-I sold my car! Come on man the dumb bitch is out there now–"

He didn't get to finish. I slammed my fist into his stomach. "Get the money." I growled. I watched as he pathetically grabbed the car title. When it was in his hand, I took him and shoved him out of the door. "Hurry up!"

Walking back up to you I felt the world go in slow motion. I watched as you unzipped your jacket and pulled a stack of cash to hand to Ryan. That's way too much money for someone like you to be carrying around, do you know how much danger you put yourself in walking into this part of town with that much cash on you, I'm glad nothing bad happened to you. My whole body tensed, this is wrong, you shouldn't be here Mel. You're too good for this kind of deal. I'll buy you a car worthy of your beauty.

I studied you as you got in the car. "If you sold her a shit vehicle, you'll be spitting your teeth out for a week." I said, I'll be keeping an eye out for this vehicle and if I see it on the side of the road or in at a mechanic, I'm coming back to make good on my promise. When the car turned the corner, I went inside to see that Alex was already collecting

19

the money. Ryans nose was bleeding. "Who did you sell your car to?" I wanted my tone to come out light, but it was full of hate.

"Some bitch off Face-"

I cut him off by punching him in the jaw, putting a hand on his shoulder to hold him there, I slammed my fist into his stomach. "Try that again." I didn't like how he's been talking about you.

Ryan took a few deep breaths and swallowed a couple times. "Her name set as Mel Cross. But you know how easy it is to fake a name on Facebook. H-h-her profile is private I only talked to her about the car. I swear check my phone."

I ripped his phone out of his outstretched hand. He already had the conversation pulled up and it was only about the car. I tried going to your profile, but I couldn't see anything other than your profile picture and name. *Smart girl* I thought throwing the phone back at Ryan. "Alex, you about ready to leave?" I asked.

"Yeah, let's go. I'm hungry." Alex said as he walked up behind Ryan and clapped him aggressively on the shoulder causing him to flinch. "Always nice to see you, Ryan."

Melanie (January 24)

Today was my first day at my job. It was a pretty standard printing job. The station I was going to be at printed on napkins, cards, and placemats. I had to make sure whatever was going into the printer was lined up with the stencil, and that whatever came out wasn't all jacked up. It was kind of boring, but we were allowed one headphone, and it was quiet enough that we could talk and actually hear each other while we work. There was only one other girl at the station I was working at. Her name was Hillary, she seemed nice enough. By the time the workday was over she had sent me a friend request on Facebook.

After work I stopped by the gas station, there were 12 pumps, and they were all full except for the two at the end. I pulled up to pump 12, leaving the one behind me open. I turned the car off at. When I got the gas going, I leaned against the car waiting for the tank to fill up. A black dodge charger pulled up and a tall guy with a lip piercing stepped out. He took his sunglasses off and smiled over at me.

The gas clicked off letting me know my tank was full, pulling my attention away from the guy I've been seeing around every time that I go out. I shook my head, although this town wasn't small it wasn't very big either. Running into the same person multiple times during the week was bound to happen. I hung the hose up and looked over at the black dodge, but the guy was gone. He must have gone inside. I got in the car and went home.

I was glad to be home, walking through the door of my own apartment after my first day at my new job felt like a huge achievement. I dropped onto the sofa and let the past couple weeks sink in. Moving to a new town, living on my own, obtaining my own vehicle, now all I had to do was make it through my first week and things would be set.

The next day at work Hillary was telling me about the wild night she had. There was a dating app that she keeps telling me to download, she met up with a guy she matched with, and they went to the local bar for a drink. I stopped listening after a while, she told me the same story but with a different guy yesterday. I kept one headphone in, so it wasn't hard to tune her out. A few minutes later it was break time. I got on Facebook and checked the one notification, a friend request from Ryan Sherwood. I ignored the request and sent Kendra a message asking her if I was being paranoid or if that was really out of the ordinary.

Then he sent me a message. 'Hey, how's the car?'

I wanted to believe in the best in people, hoping that he was just being friendly and checking in on the car only I responded, 'still running.'

'that's good to hear' then he sent me a number and told me to call it the moment anything went wrong with the car.

To Ryan I sent 'thank you. I'll keep that in mind.'

'don't let your boyfriend smoke in it lol' I was mid sip and almost spit my coffee out when I read that. I took a screen shot of the conversation and sent it to Kendra.

'Well, is he cute?' she asked.

I rolled my eyes and answered, 'if Jessie from Breaking Bad is your thing, then sure.'

'lol'

Before I knew it, it was time to go back to work. My phone went off a few times, but I chose to ignore it because I was still new here and didn't want to be caught playing on my phone. A couple minutes went by, and my phone went off a few more times so I yelled down to Hillary that I was going to the bathroom. When I got to the stall, I took my phone out to see why it was going off. I had 6 messages, all from Ryan.

'It's your car now so do what you want.'

'I didn't mean to come across as hostile I'm sorry.'

'What are you doing?'

'hey'

'Are you alone?'

'Please stop ignoring me.'

Yeah, this isn't good I thought. Trying to shut this down as quickly as possible I sent 'I'm at work. The car is great, I'll save that number. Thank you for checking but I got it from here.' I thought about looking up the number to see if it would be worth saving but decided against it. I deleted the messages then blocked him.

The rest of the day drug by. Hillary mostly kept to herself staying at the end of the line checking the product that came out the printer but mainly played on her phone. At the end of the day Hillary came up and asked if I wanted to go to the bar with her. "They have really good food." She said to try to sweeten the deal.

I shook my head drinking on a work night didn't sound like fun to me. "Maybe on the weekend. But not tonight, I don't like drinking on work nights."

Hillary laughed, "Aww your so cute. I'm holding you up to that. Friday night we're going drinking."

—⁂—

When I got home, I fell onto the sofa and looked around the room. I really don't know why it was taking so long to unpack. I had some boxes unpacked but I've been spending more time staring at the tv than anything else. Getting up I decide to do something with the kitchen. There was a dishwasher, thankfully, so I was able to unpack most of my dishes and get them washed in no time.

Once I got the load of dishes started my stomach growled, there was no food, so I had to make a run to the store down the street. It was close so I decided to walk, I was able to pick up a few things to last the rest of the week and made it home in under 40 minutes. On the way home, I saw a black dodge charger driving down the street. As it got closer to me it slowed down. I felt my body start to tense; I readied myself in case I had to use the grocery bags as a weapon. The car slowed down as it passed me but whoever was in the driver seat didn't pull over, they just crept by me and then drove off. Letting out the breath I was holding I kicked my walking pace up a notch, eager to get home.

When I walked through the door, I made sure to lock it before I put my groceries up. The dishwasher was still running so I had to eat my meal off of a paper towel, which works for me this way I won't have to wash another dish. When the dishwasher was finally done, I dried and put up the dishes. Getting the boxes of pans unpacked and loaded in the dishwasher felt like that was enough for the night. Once I got the load of pans started, I changed into pajamas and zoned out on a tv show until it was time for bed.

Griffin (January 24)

I couldn't get that woman out of my mind. Who are you 'Mel'? You looked jumpy when I spotted you at the gas station, and Alex told me how hesitant you were when he was talking to you outside of Ryans. I'm not completely mad at you for that, I don't want you to fall for his game. We were over at Ryans again, he was in the back room with some of the local drug addicts. You'd think after last time he wouldn't make any more deals through us but since he got his debt paid, here we are.

Alex was sitting on the sofa next to me looking at his phone. I looked around, the place was greasy but for the most part it was clean, my eyes landed on the phone that Ryan left on the table. I leaned over and picked it up, the dumb fuck doesn't have a lock on his phone.

Alex looked at me and gave me a 'what the fuck' look.

"I'm bored." I said and opened his Facebook messenger and scrolled until I seen your name…. There you are.

I felt like a kid at Christmas looking at your profile picture. Fuck you are so beautiful. It wouldn't let me view your profile but since you were already connected on messenger, I was able to send you a request. I sent a random message, one that was for sure going to grab your attention. 'Hey, how's the car?' I wasn't really expecting an answer but when one came back, I was over the moon.

'Still running' That was a short response. I told you that it was good to hear then I gave you my number to call if anything went wrong. 'Thank you I'll keep that in mind.' You said.

I smirked; you try to come across as assertive but we both know you're too polite to be mean. I sent a message hoping to bait you into giving some more information about yourself. 'don't let your boyfriend smoke in it lol' I watched as the status of the message went from delivered to read. The little bubble with the three dots popped up. Then it went away. And there was no new message. "What the fuck?" I said out loud.

Alex looked up at me, "What?"

"This fucking bitch left me on read." I couldn't believe you'd be so rude to me.

"Why do you care? That's not even your phone. I'm going to see what's taking so long." Alex got up and walked to the back room where Ryan disappeared with his 2 ever changing druggie roommates.

I forgot I wasn't using my phone. Laughing, I sent you some more messages. You'd have to answer me at some point; otherwise, I'll just keep sending messages until I decide to give Ryan his phone back. 'It's your car now, do what you want.' Rereading that it sounded like I was being a dick. Even if I wasn't talking to you as me, I still didn't want you to think I was a dick, so I sent, 'I didn't mean to come across as hostile I'm sorry.' I stared at the phone waiting for a response. When none came. I clicked on your profile picture to make it full screen. God, you are so sexy. I saved your picture to Ryans phone and sent it to mine, then removed the picture out of Ryans gallery, because I didn't want him to use it later. You still haven't answered yet, so I sent a 'Hey' when that went unread, I asked you if you were alone. I waited a few more minutes and sent 'Please stop ignoring me.'

Just when I was about to send another message you wrote back, 'I'm at work. The car is great I'll save that number. Thank you for checking but I got it from here.' Then that notification popped up that I was no longer able to send messages to you.

Smart Girl. I thought as I threw the phone back on the coffee table. When I stood up Alex was walking out counting some money. I nodded at him, and he nodded back going for the door. I saw Ryan watching us leave, "We'll see you next week." I said walking out the door pulling it shut behind me. As we were walking to the car I asked Alex, "He didn't try to fuck us over again, did he?"

"Count it for yourself if you want, besides his pattern is full payment, full payment, full payment, tries and fails to short us. Ryan's dumb but he's not dumb enough to short us right after we just collected his debt." Alex made a good point. "Is there anything else after this? I have plans tonight. I found this bitch off Tender; I'm telling ya man it's easier getting laid this way."

I got in and started my car, waiting for him to get in the passenger seat before answering, "Too many catfishes are on those apps. I prefer to just let things happen. You see a more realistic version of someone when you run into them by chance at the store than you do interacting with them through a screen."

I thought of your profile picture; you weren't by any means a catfish but in your picture you had your hair curled with almost too much eye makeup; if I'm being honest. Your black low-cut shirt showed off a chest tattoo that I'm aching to start kissing on, but it also showed way too much cleavage for a public profile picture, we'll have to talk about that. When I passed you in the store you had no makeup and was wearing an outfit you can relax in. I loved both versions of you Mel, but I prefer the one I had seen at the store.

Alex laughed, "Calm down Romeo, I'm not looking for love, I just want a good fuck. Kara is great and all but lately she's been holding back; and I have needs." He shrugged.

I laughed with him, "I'm still looking, but I think I finally found it. But after we drop the money off to Dad we're done for the week."

—⧼⧽—

After I dropped Alex off at his place, I decided to take the long way home. I wasn't ready to go home just yet; so, I put on some heavy music and drove around for a bit, smoking a cigarette or two. Flipping the butt out the window I made a right turn. Someone was walking on the sidewalk carrying a couple bags from the dollar store down the street. Seeing the long hair blow in the wind made me slow down. A grin crept on my face as I slowed down more to get a better view of you. You didn't bother looking over at me, my windows were so dark you wouldn't be able to see me anyway.

I drove up to the dollar store and parked so I could watch where you went. You were carrying bags so you couldn't live too far away, my theory was proven correct as I watched you walk into the apartment building that was a couple blocks down the road. Smiling, I put the car in drive and drove home. Now that I know where you live it'll be easier to find more about you. It'll be simple to find out what apartment is yours, all I have to do is go through the mailboxes and find your name. This is all falling together so nicely, we'll be together soon Mel.

Melanie (January 27 5:32)

I was scrolling through Facebook stopping to watch the random video when they popped up when my coworker Hillary called. "Hey bitch, what are you doing?" I tried not to let out the sigh that threatened to spill from my lips. "Don't even try to say that you are busy cause we both know that you ain't got shit going on. Get cute we're going drinking." Then she hung up. I rolled my eyes and called her back.

"What if I don't want to go drinking?" I asked her, the bar was never really my scene. I don't hate it, but I can think of a million other things that I'd rather be doing, "I still have a lot of unpacking to do." Both literally and metaphorically. I moved out of my sister's house not too long ago and into a small one-bedroom apartment 5 hours away for a 'fresh start'. The place was still overflowing with boxes; a pile of broken-down boxes, half unpacked boxes with clothes and towels draped over the edges, and more boxes still tightly taped shut than I care to admit. And I also need to work on my journaling. My therapist recommended that I pick up journaling as a way to help me heal from… I shook my head, sometimes it was still hard to think about, I touched the scar on my forehead and took a breath.

"Oh, come on." She whined, "It's been a week from hell at work, and we made it to Friday!! We deserve to go out and have some fun! Do you have makeup and clothes unpacked or do you need to borrow something?" She had a point; work was rough but if I keep unpacking 1 item a day I'll be living out of boxes for the rest of my life, and I told her so. "It's just for one night. It's not like I'm asking for the whole weekend. Besides, there's all day tomorrow and Sunday to do all of that. We've been saying that we'll hang out outside of work since you started. No more excuses."

"Ok. Fine." I said with a sigh, "I have enough to get by for one night out. Do you want me to meet you at the bar or are you picking me up?" she said she'd pick me up around 9 because 'that's when the bar gets fun' as Hillary put it. When I hung up the phone, I texted her my address. She was right, I deserved a night out. I looked at the time, I still had 4 hours to get ready.

To pass the time I went to the bathroom and unpacked the boxes in there to help getting ready easier. When the bathroom was in order I had about 2 hours left to do my hair and makeup. I kept the jeans I had on and put on cut up faded black Resident Evil t-shirt, there were rips on the back that made the shape of a skull, the neckline was low enough to expose some cleavage.

I sat down in front of the mirror to do my makeup. I started by putting my hair in a side braid to keep it out of my face and as an attempt at making it cute. I didn't bother with too much makeup, not only because my selection was limited; but if I tried to get too intricate with it, I'd eat up all the time I had left to get ready covering up the 3-inch scar above my left eye. I settled on shaping up my eyebrows and doing a smoky eye to bring out the green in my eyes.

There were 30 minutes left, so I made a sandwich and put Big Bang Theory on until, *KNOCK, KNOCK, KNOCK.* I looked through the peep hole before unlocking and opening the door. There in tight blue jeans and a light blue very low v neck t-shirt under a white hoodie was Hillary. She had her blonde hair curled and pinned up, makeup on point as usual and confidence oozing out of every pore. She gave me a hard look up and down "yeah, I guess that's cute enough to go out in. Alright grab your shit and let's go!" I picked up my wallet and put my phone in my back pocket. Once my apartment door was locked, I flipped over the charm. Then I tucked the key in my wallet and turned to follow Hillary out to her car. It was a nice car, bright red with tinted windows. The inside, however, was a disaster. Fast food bags and water bottles filled the back seat, and she had to clear off the passenger seat so I could sit down. "Dude, you're gonna love this bar." She said as I closed the door. "It's in the next town over, so you won't have any of the local creeps lurking around" she was always going on about the guys who try to hit on her at the bar she frequents every weekend. "I'm so excited you're finally getting out of that drab little apartment. Chill out, it's going to be fun."

We were driving for half an hour, Hillary was going on about work, just recently 2nd shift decided they were going to send of list of complaints to the boss about us. We had a meeting in the morning about it then to rub salt in the wound, we had to stay over so both shifts could get a lecture about teamwork. The thing is, we didn't realize there was an issue, we thought we were all on good terms with each other, and half of the shit they were complaining about, they did the same thing. "Fuck them," I said checking my make up in the mirror. "Let's not let it ruin our night."

Pretty soon we were pulling up to the bar. It was in a small town, located across the street from the city hall. It was a 2-story brick building with a wall of windows in the front so you could see in. They had a band playing on one side and the bar was on the other.

I took off my seatbelt when Hillary put the car in park and waited while she checked her makeup in the visor mirror. She was taking longer than I expected so I took out my phone and started scrolling on the top news headlines. 5 minutes later when Hillary was done messing with her makeup, she took off her jacket and opened the door.

"What are you doing?" Hillary asked suddenly.

I looked over at her confused, "going inside, are you coming?"

She shook her head, "nu-uh the jacket stays here."

"What? Why? It's freezing out there." I protested.

Hillary rolled her eyes, "guys will be more open to talk to you if they know what you're hiding under all those layers. Now loose the coat and let's go. You'll be fine, it's just a quick walk through the parking lot."

I sighed and gave into defeat. I took out the tube of Beeswax chapstick and put it back in the left pocket before shrugging it off and running after Hillary who was now halfway to the door. I caught up with her just as she entered the bar.

"Come on, let's get some drinks and go find some guys to dance with." Hillary shimmied her body as she said so. As we walked through the door half of the people's heads turned toward us. "It's a small-town thing. Don't take offense." Hillary led us to the bar and waved the bartender down. She got us both a Midori and monster. The drink was bright green and sweet, it went down a little too smoothly. If I didn't pace myself, I could end up shitfaced.

"Hey Wednesday!" A deep voice called to my left; it sounded like he was right next to me, so I looked. It was a guy in a dark blue polo who was sitting at the bar, he was turned towards us and said, "Let me buy you a drink, and maybe later I can put a smile on that face," he winked. I rolled my eyes and turned around, taking a drink of out of my glass as I did.

Hillary was walking towards the doors that opened up to the dance floor where we had seen the band playing outside. I followed her, not wanting to lose her; the place was packed. I finally caught up to her at a table along the wall that separated the dance floor from the bar. "Hey! I thought you were gonna stay up there, that guy was pretty cute." she said when I sat down.

I shrugged, "He wasn't really my type," as in sleezy guys at the bar isn't my thing and I should have stayed home. I spent most of the time listening to Hillary talk about everything that crossed her mind and drinking this wonderful green drink.

The band that was playing was amazing, and Hillary said she wanted to get up and dance; so, I tossed the rest of my drink back and followed her to the dance floor. We got to a spot near the stage and started moving to the beat. Hillary leaned in a shouted over the music, "The guitar player is so hot," she looked up at the stage, "do you want to be a groupie with me?" I gave her sideways glance, and she started laughing, "You don't have to sleep with them, just be my wing-girl." She said shimmying her body.

I shook my head and smiled at her, "If we hang out with them after they get done playing, they'll want someone to do more than just 'hang out' with them." I replied, using air quotes.

She elbowed me, "You need to loosen up. Check out the singer, he looks like your type."

I rubbed my side where her boney elbow dug into me. I looked up to the stage. The singer was in a dirty white T-shirt and ripped-up black jeans. He was of average build, and his right arm was covered in tattoos; the left one was bare. His hair was shaggy and was starting to stick to his forehead. I grimaced, trying not to imagine how bad he must smell right now.

Then the drummer started spinning one of his drumsticks and went into a solo. Pounding out a hypnotic beat that overtook me. He was gorgeous. A chiseled jawline, muscular arms. He was in a light grey shirt that was loose fitting, tattoos peaked out from the sleeves, and he had one on the side of his neck. He looked out into the crowd with the biggest grin, you could tell he was having the time of his life up there. I started jumping up and down with Hillary and the drummer looked over at us and winked.

I threw up my devil horns and got more into the music, the drummer laughed and returned the gesture. It might have been the alcohol but I'm fairly sure we had a moment. Maybe being a groupie wouldn't be so bad.

We were moving with the beat and having a lot of fun, laughing at how awful we danced. I didn't notice the guys who kept getting closer until one of them started dancing on Hillary, she easily accepted and started dancing with him. His buddy grabbed my waist and tried to get me to dance with him, but I wasn't in the mood anymore. "I'm gonna go get a drink," I shouted at Hillary, hoping she heard me over the music. She nodded at me and turned her focus back to the guy who was grinding on her.

I went up to the bar and ordered a whiskey sour. Declining a tab, I paid with the last of my money, a ten-dollar bill and told her to keep the change. That was my attempt at not getting any more drinks tonight. I made my way back to our table, which was thankfully still empty.

Hillary was still dancing with the guys, and I found myself thinking that I should have stayed home again. I took a sip of my drink and pulled out my phone to play Lily's Garden. My phone was at 30%.

A few songs later Hillary came up to me, "Oh good you kept the table! Hey, I'm going to go get us some drinks, I'll be right back, ok?"

"Ok, sure!" I said and looked down to continue my game., there wasn't much else to do.

"Hey Wednesday, how about that drink now?" I looked up, and it was that fucking asshole from the bar. He was grinning at me and pushed a glass towards me. "If I told you, it was my birthday, would you grant me a wish?"

I sat up, "No, I'm good." I said with a smile. Pushing the glass back towards him I added, "besides, I already have a drink."

"Mmm, I've been waiting all night to see that smile." Polo shirt guy reached up as if he wanted to touch me, I took that as my queue to get the fuck away. "Hey honey, don't be like that; give me a chance and I swear I can make you the happiest woman alive." With that he slapped my ass. A shock wave pulsed through my body; the world slowed down as I turned towards him. I wasn't aware of my hand swinging up and colliding with his face. I had no intention of slapping him, I wasn't sure exactly what I was planning on doing but as soon as the SMACK registered in my ears I turned back around, and bee lined for the bathroom.

I sat down on the toilet and rubbed my eyes. There was no use crying, that wouldn't help. I took a few deep breaths and pulled my phone out, but of course it was dead. I got up and walked out of the bathroom, that guy was still sitting at the table I had left. I looked around but there was nowhere else to sit. I didn't see Hillary anywhere and my phone was of no use.

I was walking toward the bar when a guy sitting down at a table nearby called out, "Excuse me miss, I just wanted to say that was one hell of a slap."

I looked over at him. He had dark hair, long enough on top that I could run my fingers through. He was clean shaven with a lip ring.

Nice, toned arms covered in tattoos. His smile lured me in, but it was his blue eyes that held me. He was so beautiful. I laughed and walked over to him, "Thank you, he was asking for it ya know?"

"Oh, for sure." He said and took a drink of his beer. "Would you mind if I buy you a drink?" he asked. "I was just about to go get another; I don't brining back two if you don't mind keeping the table."

I smiled at him, that was so kind to offer. I said that I would have what he was having, I didn't want to be a bother. "Umm, would you mind letting me know if you see a blonde in a blue shirt up there?"

He nodded at me and said he would be right back. I busied myself by inspecting the end of my hair. I was so bored, I just wanted to go home. But right now, I am kind of stuck. When the guy came back, he sat down with a beer bottle in front of me.

I took the bottle and looked up at him. "Thank you," I said before taking a drink. Still looking at him there was a voice in the back of my head that told me something was wrong. I narrowed my eyes, something about him seemed so familiar. He was looking down at me, even sitting he towered over me, the lights from the stage glinted off his lip ring as he smirked at me. The little voice in the back of my head reminded me of the stalker at the store, how blue his eyes were, and he had his lip pierced in the same place as this guy. "Have we met?" I asked.

He chuckled and took a drink. "Yeah, I know what you're thinking, and yes I was that creep following you in the store." My heart leapt up into my throat, I sat up straight and looked around. I was about to stand up when, "You look a lot like a friend I used to have in college," he blurted, "but as I got closer, I wasn't sure if you two were the same person." I blinked at him; the voice was telling me he was full of shit. I was still on alert but waited to hear him out. He went on to say, "And instead of approaching the beautiful girl in the store, I chickened out."

I bit my lip; *he called me beautiful*. Maybe it was the alcohol, but I relaxed a little, taking a long drink, to drown the voice in my head. This guy was attractive, and he was being nice, and after the perv slapped my ass I felt more comfortable with this nice guy in front of me than wondering around the bar by myself looking for Hillary.

"And after seeing you slap the shit out of that guy, I'm glad I backed off." He laughed and took another drink of his beer.

I laughed and took a drink myself. "Just don't piss me off." I joked. Something in me had me questioning him still. Yes, sure he was handsome, but he was also kind of creepy. I mean he was following me around the store, and I swear I have seen him lurking around town watching me. I had to make sure. I leaned forward so I could hear him better. "Where did you go to college?"

"There's a community college Goldstien University." He said, then pulled out his phone and showed me a picture of a gorgeous woman wearing a Goldstien U t-shirt. I looked back up at him when he said, "I missed out on asking her out on a date back then and thought, 'Why not now?' But then when I got a good look at you and realized you weren't who I thought you were." I looked him up and down, he didn't give any signs that he was lying. "I'm really sorry, I know I freaked you out but let's forget all of that and start over." He said with a big toothy grin. In the light red lights coming from the stage he looked like a wolf, his head slightly tilted, eyes fully trained on me like I was all he seen; it was almost sinister. My breath caught in my throat for a moment. Then the lights flashed to a blue, and his eyes softened, and he licked his lips, "Please?" he added, almost begging.

I looked him over again and leaned back in the chair. The little voice was quiet, not sure what else to do I took a drink and said, "Ok fine, but only because you're cute." Then to bring the mood down I asked, "So did you see her?"

"Yeah, she was talking to a guy at the bar." He responded.

I raised an eyebrow and sat back in the chair, picking at my nails, *so much for being a groupie,* I thought. I really hope Hillary doesn't ditch me here, I should have thought this through.

The guy cleared his throat getting my attention. "I'm Griffin by the way." He said.

I smiled up at him and sat up, "Melanie." I answered.

Griffin looked me up and down and leaned forward, "Lovely name for a lovely woman."

I could feel my cheeks redden at the compliment. I bit my lip, "You flirt."

He put his hands up and smiled, "You got me. Want me to stop?"

"No, keep going." I said with a laugh, taking a drink of beer. The warm fuzzy effects taking the edge off of the situation I was in.

Griffin looked me in the eye and said, "I'm not sure what's more alluring, your smile or your confidence?"

Yeah, there was no doubt I was blushing now. This guy was smooth, and the way he looked at me made it hard to breathe. "That was a good one." I said, smiling. "Hey, show me that girl again." I said. There was no way that woman looked like me, she was way too pretty. I had to see the picture again, something in me was still telling me that he was full of shit. Griffin pulled his phone out and showed me the girl's profile one more time. I noticed the spider tattoo he had on his hand when he held his phone out. She was beautiful, no argument there, but there was no way someone could mistake me for her. "You really think I look like her?" I asked, looking up at him.

Griffin shook his head, laughing a little and took his phone back, when our hands brushed against each other it was like electric shot up my arm. "You are far more beautiful than she is."

I scoffed and took a drink. *That is clearly a lie, but I'll take it.* "Well thank you, she is very pretty." I said, playing with the bottle.

"So, are you from around here?" He asked. "I don't think I've seen you before."

I shook my head 'no' and explained how I just moved here from a town 5 hours away. Griffin asked if my boyfriend minded me being out alone. I laughed and called him out. "That was subtle. Since I don't have a boyfriend; no, he doesn't mind me drinking at the bar, although I'd rather be doing anything else. And besides, I didn't come here alone." I reminded him. Even though Hillary was nowhere to be found, she was my ride here.

The way he licked his lips was mesmerizing. "Yeah, I know the feeling. If I had a girlfriend, I'd be home watching a movie, eating junk food, cuddled up on the sofa with her."

"That sounds really nice," I said, "Now I'm jealous of your nonexistent girlfriend." I said, taking a drink. It's either the alcohol or I'm feeling a connection with this guy. He is charming. But so is the alcohol.

"Maybe we can meet up for a movie sometime? We can make our imaginary partners jealous," he said with a wink.

I smiled and studied his face for a moment. A flash of blue and blonde hair outside the window behind Griffin caught my attention. Griffin turned around to see what I was looking at. Hillary was climbing in some guys truck. I pulled my phone out to text her, but I forgot the stupid thing was dead. "Well, there goes my ride," I tried to make it sound like a joke, but it fell short. I went to take a drink of beer, but it was empty. I shook my head and laughed, "I'll buy the next round," I said, standing up.

Griffin put his hand on my arm, I looked down at it and back up at him. He pulled his hand away and said, "I got it, want something else or do you want to stick with beer?" He asked.

I asked for a rum and coke, putting my hand on his elbow I brushed my fingers down his arm, dropping off at the wrist, "Thank you." I said, just now realizing that if he hadn't offered to buy the drinks instead there was no way I could cover the cost. I don't have my debit card on me. I put my head in my hands feeling stupid and buzzed.

GRIFFEN (January 27 9:46)

I was at the bar over in the town about a half an hour away. My buddy Levi is in a band, and they have a gig here tonight. So, being the good friend that I am, I drug myself out of the house to support my friend and his band. Besides, it's not like I had anything else going on. I was trying to get the bartender's attention when the door opened, and I saw a familiar face walking in.

It felt like the world had stopped and it was just us in the room. I wish I could have seen my face at that moment, I wish I could have taken a picture of you in that moment. You are so gorgeous, your dark brown hair is done in a side braid, ending at your chest, speaking of which the amount of cleavage you're showing is definitely leaving me wanting more. I'll be thinking of the way your jeans hug your waist all week, *please turn around* I think, getting a look at your ass would make my night. I kept my eyes on you as you took a drink from your friend. The bartender came up to me and got my order, taking my attention away from you. When I looked back it took me a moment to find you in the crowd. You were following the girl you came in with, a tall blonde in a blue shirt and jeans that were too tight, into the joining room which opens up into the dance club.

The bartender sat my bottle of beer down in front of me, I picked it up with a smile and opened a tab. I settled down in the corner of the bar, I didn't want to scare you like I did at the store, I wanted you to come to me. I know you're interested in me, I seen the way you bit your lip and smiled when you first seen me in the parking lot. I could tell you liked my shirt, and that's how you knew I was following you in the store. I admit that was a dumb fucking move, I'm glad I left when I did, you look like you could throw a punch if needed. I really like that in- well anyone really. No one will save you but you. We've ran into each other a few times since the store and I've tried to keep you at a distance, but fate has put you in my path once again. Who am I to ignore that?

I got on to the bars Facebook page, scrolling to see if you or your friend had tagged your location. No such luck but as it happens when I looked up, I seen you walk over to the bar. You seemed slightly annoyed, and I noted how you only got one drink. Maybe your friend left you alone to twerk on the dance floor? Can't say I wouldn't mind watching you dance, but only if we're alone. I don't want anyone else watching you dance. I should wait a little while before I hunt you down. I didn't want you to be in a defensive mood when I approached you.

A group of bitches walked in front of me, their high-pitched voices threatening to give me a headache if they didn't leave soon. One of them glanced over at me and whispered something to her friend, they started giggling and kept looking over at me with lopsided smiles. I glared at them until they moved on to something else, no longer interested in me.

When they moved out the way, you were no longer in sight. Scanning the room but not seeing your face in the crowd I sat back in my seat and kept drinking my beer. I'll see you again eventually, I can be patient when I want to be.

Levi's band was doing a cover of Bullet for My Valentine's 'Your Betrayal.' By this time, the place was getting more crowded than usual. Live bands typically do that. I watched as the blonde girl you came in with walked out of the dance floor and over to the bar and noticed that you didn't follow her. Did she leave you alone? To keep the table maybe or guard the purses? Is it crazy to be jealous the hypothetical guy you're talking to instead of accompanying your friend to the bar? I took a drink and decided that yes, that is completely psychotic.

I watched as your friend ordered two drinks. She started talking to the guy she was standing next to, and she was still talking to him as the bartender put two full glasses in front of her. It wasn't too long after that when your friend started drinking one of those drinks. She was laughing and touching the guys arm. I figured she was going to be there for a while. I downed the rest of my beer.

I got up and went to the bar. If I was going to walk around the dance floor, I didn't want to go empty handed. I got a bottle and put it on the tab. I looked down at the bar to make sure that your friend was still busy flirting. She was laughing and by this time she had taken the stool next to the guy. I glanced at the clock that hung above the bar 10:11. I smiled and tipped the bartender when she put the bottle in front of me and went to see if I could at least see what was going on with you in the other room.

There weren't too many empty tables, but I found one near the bathrooms and sat down. From here, I could see the whole room. People were dancing, most were having a good time, some guys were celebrating a recent sports victory and there was a bridal shower. A couple was fighting a little too loudly, apparently the guy was dancing with another girl. Over by the wall to my right is where I finally found you. You were sitting alone playing on your phone, it seemed like your friend went to get drinks and got distracted along the way. I smiled and took a drink, and since I'm by the bathroom it's only a matter of time before you walk by me.

I could feel my blood pressure rise as a guy in a light blue polo sat in front of you and offered one of the drinks he had. You straightened your back and shook your head 'no' with a small smile. *Oh 'Mel' you don't have to be nice. Take that drink and throw it in that mother fuckers face.* The guy offered the drink again and leaned in closer to you reaching up to brush some hair out of your face probably, you leaned back slightly and got up, you pulled your phone off the table and stood up. The guy smacked your ass as you walked away. I was both jealous that he got to touch you and enraged that he touched you. I made a move to stand up when you swung around and slapped him open handed across the face. Without missing a beat, you turned back around and continued on your way, which was to the bathroom, towards me. When we finally get the chance to talk, I'm going to bring that up, and how much I admire you for standing up for yourself. This might seem odd, but Mel I'm proud of you, few people would have done that; and who doesn't like a woman with some fight in her. I shifted in my seat, now aware of the growing erection.

When you walked by no one would have guessed you slapped the shit out of a handsy pervert. You brushed pass me on your way with a quick, "Excuse me," you were so close I could have put my arm out to stop you. The confidence that trailed after you was almost as enticing as the perfume that followed you. God, you smell so good. I slid into the chair that was on my left, so that I had a better view of the woman's bathroom door. I wanted to be able to see when you came out of the bathroom.

It was almost 10 minutes later before the door swung open. I took a drink of beer and watched as you looked around the room. You swallowed hard and looked at your phone. Rolling your eyes, you put it in your back pocket and leaned against the wall, scanning the room again. Is your phone dead? I have a charger in the car. What kind? It doesn't matter; I have an adapter. Looking for your friend? She's at the bar trying to get free drinks. See, Mel? I have all the answers. I looked around the room, the creepy guy was still over at the table you had left, and the rest were taken. As you got within ear shot, I heard someone say, "Excuse me miss, I just wanted to say that was one hell of a slap." What lucky son of a bitch got to say that before I could? Oh fuck, that son of a bitch was me! So much for playing it cool.

You looked up at me with these brilliant green eyes, your makeup was slightly smudged, but you did an excellent job of covering up the fact that you've been crying; without taking all your make-up off. God you're beautiful. You laughed and walked up to me. "Thank you, he was asking for it ya know?"

I agreed and took the last drink of my beer. I can't believe that you're over here talking to me, and you seem relaxed. I need to play it cool. "Would you mind if I buy you a drink? I was just about to go get another one, I don't mind bringing back two if you don't mind keeping the table."

You smiled, God you're so polite, "Sure, I'll have what you're having." I bit back my excitement and asked if beer was ok. "Yeah, that's fine." You said, "Hey, would you let me know if you see a blonde in a blue shirt up there?" You almost looked sad, but I knew you wanted to seem casual.

I nodded and went back up to the bar, eager to sit back down and talk to you. I almost have you, I knew if I could keep you relaxed and laughing with me, you'd come home with me. When I got up to the bar, I ordered two beers when the bartender came up to me. I glanced over to the spot where I last seen your friend, she was still talking and drinking with that guy, I smiled and thanked the bartender as she sat down the beers and headed back to the most beautiful woman in the bar.

I was ready to smash one of the bottles over someone's head if I saw anyone sitting in my spot talking to my girl. But luckily you were still alone. You looked adorably bored playing with your braid, and you looked so happy when you looked up and took the beer from me. I couldn't stop the smile that spread across my face. Then the smile slipped from your face and your eyes narrowed slightly, "Have we met?" you asked.

Oh fuck, my heart stopped. There is no doubt that you recognized me, I've been careless following you around, you're too smart not to recognize me. *How smart are you?* I wondered. I chuckled and took a long drink of my beer, buying myself sometime trying to come up with something that was halfway believable, "yeah I know what you're thinking, and yes I was that creep following you in the store." Where the fuck am I going with this? You sat up straight, you looked like you were about to leave. The words just fell out of my mouth, "You look a lot like a friend I used to have back in college, but as I got closer, I wasn't sure if you two were the same person. And instead of approaching the beautiful girl in the store, I chickened out. And after seeing you slap the shit out of that guy, I'm glad I backed off." Did you buy any of that? I took another drink of beer, ok maybe that was more convincing than I expected.

39

I could almost see your guard fall down as you laughed, and I watched as you took a drink. I imagined what it would be like if it were the tip of my dick your lips were on instead of the bottle. I'm glad we're sitting down; I didn't want you to notice that I was getting stiff, "Just don't piss me off," you said with a giggle, oh I'm going to have so much fun with you. A switched must have flipped in your head because you then leaned forward and most of the playfulness evaporated from you as you asked, "Where did you go to college?"

I had play this smart. You weren't dumb, and I'm not sure if you're just being extra cautious, or if you're just not buying my bullshit; but either way, I have to step up my game before you start seeing too many red flags and walk away. The smell of your perfume was making it hard to come up with something, I did my best. There was a community college an hour away, and for good measure I brought up a girl I used to work with who looked similar to you from across the room. I took my phone out and looked her up on Facebook, choking back a laugh when I saw that she was wearing an alumni tee shirt from the community college that was an hour away. I grinned sheepishly when you looked at my phone and back up to me, "I missed out on asking her on a date back then and thought 'why not now?' but then I got a good look at you, and realized you weren't who I thought you were. I'm really sorry, I know I freaked you out but let's forget all that and start over. You were taking your time responding to me and so for good measure I added "Please?" with a toothy smile.

You looked me over and leaned back in your chair, "ok fine, but only because you're cute" I felt so invincible when you said that. "So did you see her?" you asked. The concern in your voice was noticeable.

"Yeah, she was talking to a guy at the bar." You had a go figure look on your face and leaned back in your chair and started picking at your nails. I decided to take the conversation over. "I'm Griffin, by the way."

You looked back up at me and smiled. "Melanie." So, there it is. It was then that I knew I had you in my hand.

I tried to bite back a moan as I looked you up and down, I leaned on the table, "Lovely name for a lovely woman" I took a drink of beer to hide my smile as your cheeks reddened, how are you not used to people giving you compliments? You called me a flirt, "You got me. Want me to stop?" I said, putting my hands up.

You laughed, "No keep going," you said before taking another drink of beer.

I smirked and used a common pickup line that's worked for me a few times, "I'm not sure what's more alluring, your smile or your confidence?"

Your cheeks reddened again, I smiled at how adorable you are, "That was a good one," you said with a shy smile. I thought I was in the clear with you, and that we could move on to something more personal, when you suddenly asked, "Hey, show me that girl again?"

I froze; I don't like where this is going. My heart was beating out of my chest as I pulled my phone back out and went to the Facebook app. I focused on keeping my breathing even, but I was freaking out as I brought up Amy Krumm's page again. I starting making some mental notes of her face that I could use in an argument on why I thought you two look alike. Almond shaped eyes, slender nose. Both of you have long hair, Melanie's hair is darker, much darker. But girls dye their hair all the time.

My heart pounded and my mouth was bone dry as I watched you study Amy's picture. What does that look on your face mean? "You really think I look like her?" You asked, looked up and meeting my eyes.

I shook my head, chuckling a bit I took my phone back from you. I let my fingers linger on yours for a moment. "You are far more beautiful than she is."

You laughed and took another drink of beer; I could feel the anxiety that was building up melting away. "Well thank you, she is very pretty." You said, then started playing with the bottle, tilting it in circles on the table.

If there was an interest meter above your head, I imagine it would be measuring at 'bored.' I wanted to know more about you but since you're not talking much, you're either not interested in me at all, or you're shy. And since you already said I was cute, I'm betting on the second one; and lucky for me I know how to work with shy women. "So, are you from here? I don't think I've seen you before." No, I know I haven't.

I would have remembered such a beautiful face. Besides, few people around here have as many tattoos as you do.

"Um, no. I'm not from around here. I moved here not too long ago." You took a drink and shifted in your chair. "I used to live in a small-town bout 5 hours away."

I wanted to ask more about that, but you're obviously not ready to go that far into it yet. I've learned over the years that the shy ones are tricky, easy to charm them into letting you in but if you push them too soon, they tend to run away. "Your boyfriend doesn't mind that you're here alone, does he?" I took a drink waiting for the answer. That line is smoother than sandpaper. But it got the job done.

A huge smile broke out on your face, and you laughed. "That was subtle. Since I don't have a boyfriend; no, he doesn't mind me drinking at the bar. And I didn't come here alone," Soon I hope to fill the position of boyfriend, and we could drink at home by ourselves. I know I can make you happy, just look at how much I'm making you laugh. Even though you didn't come here alone, you're alone with me now.

I licked my lips. "Yeah, I know the feeling. If I had a girlfriend, I'd be home watching a movie, eating junk food with her."

You sighed, "That sounds really nice. Now I'm jealous of your nonexistent girlfriend." You went to take a drink.

"Maybe we can meet up for a movie sometime? We can make our imaginary partners jealous." I said with a wink. You studied my face for a moment then something behind me caught your attention. Through the club's windows to the outside, we watched, as your friend stumbled into a black truck. The guy she was chatting with at the bar was laughing, trying to help her into the passenger seat. I turned back around, and you had your phone out.

You sat your phone on its back and spun it in circles. "Well, there goes my ride." You went to take a drink, but it was empty. Laughing you shook your head. "I'll buy the next round." You went to stand up, but I put my hand on your arm. You looked like you were about to spiral out, and I wanted to make sure your attention was on me.

You looked down at my hand, and I pulled it away, not quite sure how to handle this situation, "I got it, want something else or do you want to stick with beer?" I asked.

"I'll take a rum and coke." You touched my elbow and ran your fingers down my arm dropping off at my wrist leaving a livewire in my arm where you touched me, "Thank you." You sat back down and watched me walk away.

MELANIE (January 27 10:24)

I watched Griffin walk away and let out a slow but shaky breath. I couldn't fucking believe this is happening. This wouldn't be such a big problem but I'm pretty screwed at the moment. I'm not upset that Hillary is leaving with a random guy she just met, but she was my ride. She could have found me and told me she was leaving. My phone is dead which doesn't help my situation at all; and the cherry on top of this shit sundae is that my address doesn't match my driver's license. I've only lived there for 2 weeks so I don't have the address memorized yet, I know it's apartment 1 D, but the street? Was the complex called fox run or was it fox trot? It's saved in my phone, but my phone is fucking dead and the girl that brought me here left me stranded and I want to scream and throw my phone across the room!

I let out a heavy sigh and tried to center myself. Losing my shit isn't going to help. I need to get a hold on my anxiety before I let it spin me out of control. I heard someone sit down a glass down. I felt relaxed, thinking that it was Griffin. "You look like you could use a drink." I froze and looked up, this can't be fucking happing again At least this wasn't that creepy perv who smacked my ass, I hope my handprint is still visible on his face. This guy had long blond hair under a black beanie, he wore a denim vest over a white shirt and ripped up jeans. The smell coming from him was awful, he needed a shower, bad.

I shook my head no, "Thanks, but I'm good." I pushed the drink back towards him. That's when I saw something powdery dissolving on the bottom of the glass.

He pushed the glass back towards me and leaned in closer, "Come on, a gothic beauty like you shouldn't sit alone. Drink with me." His breath made me gag.

I pushed the glass back to him, "My friend just went for some drinks, he should be back any minute."

The guy started laughing, but it sounded angry. "That's a classic excuse, why don't you bitches just say you're not interested, huh? Oh, I get it, you're a lesbian, right?" He was swaying a little and took a half step closer to me. He grabbed ahold of the front of his jeans, "I have a cure for that."

I stood up. If he were to come at me, I didn't want to be sitting down. "I'd rather fuck a goat."

Probably should have just kept my mouth shut on that. "You're a fucking bitch," He pointed at me and then picked up the glass, "You know, all you fucking sluts are the same. I was trying to be nice; but I guess, I'll go fuck myself then, huh?" He took a step towards me.

An arm was then slung over my shoulder, making me jump. I looked at the hand of the arm around me, it was holding a rum and coke, there was a spider tattooed on the fleshy part of the back of his hand, and I felt myself relaxing, knowing that this time it was Griffin. "Sounds like a good idea, why don't you get on that." His deep voice vibrated against me. The guy picked up his drinks and walked away, throwing meaningless insults at me as he did. Griffin pulled a chair close to me and sat down, "I want to apologize on the behalf of my gender for being such sleezy assholes. We're not all bad I promise." When he handed me my rum and coke, I brushed my fingers against his hand. Putting more alcohol in my system probably isn't a good thing right now, but I like the fuzzy feeling it gives me; like everything is going to be fine. Griffin is smiling at me, studying me with those piercing blue eyes. I took a long drink, feeling the burn of rum flow down my throat and spread through my body, but nothing made me feel more alive than when he pressed me against his side.

You said something to me, but I was too busy listening to the band play. I laughed, "I'm sorry, what did you say?" I took a sip and enjoyed the vanilla aftertaste of the drink. My words were slurring together by this time.

I had my elbow on the table and my chin resting in my palm. Griffin laughed, "I asked if your drink is good." I could feel his eyes on me, and I sat up straight, suddenly self-conscious.

"It's amazing, thank you." I turned my attention back to the stage. "These guys are really good," I said moving around a little trying to see if there was a band name anywhere around the stage, but I couldn't tell from here. They played a few original songs, but it seemed to be mostly all covers, which isn't a bad thing because they killed every song they played. "Did you catch the band name?" I asked, looking back at him.

"Yeah, they're not bad. They're called 'Yesteryear,' I'm friends with the drummer and bought one of their albums a while back. You can borrow if it you want." Griffin is turning out to be such a sweetheart.

"That would be great." I took a drink, "Um hey, do you by chance have a car charger for an android?" I hate asking him for help, he's already been buying me drinks all night and now he offered to let me borrow a CD. I just met this guy, he's super fine and he chased off that weirdo for me earlier. I took another drink and waited for an answer.

"There's a possibility, but there's something I'll need in return." He looked at me over his glass as he took a drink. A million things ran through my head, he's flirting again, and I narrowed my eyes waiting to see what he had to say. "I want a dance before we go charge your phone."

My eyebrows shot up, and I started laughing, "A dance it is, but I'm warning you. I ain't that good at dancin'." We both finished our drinks and Griffin stood up extending his hand to me. He told me not to worry about it, and he couldn't dance either, but that soon turned out to be a lie. Griffin spun me and pulled me into him, then he dipped me. It must have been the alcohol, or the music, maybe the way he was looking at me, but when Griffin brought me back up, I kissed him. His fingers were then in my hair, and he kissed me back.

Griffin pulled away first, breaking off the kiss he put his forehead on mine. "Let's go charge your phone." He whispered. I felt myself leaning back in for another kiss, but he was already turning to lead me to the door, our hands still clasped together. As we walked by the stage Griffin nodded to the drummer, I noted how the drummer clenched his jaw as he nodded back.

It was getting pretty cold and windy, I left my jacket in Hillary's car, not expecting her to take off and leave me stranded, and it was dark. I

45

shouldn't have come out tonight. Agreeing to go drinking with Hillary was a huge mistake. I pulled my phone out to check the time, I keep forgetting it's dead, it's funny how easily our life gets thrown off when our phone dies.

I paused for a moment when we got to his car, the black dodge charger I'm convinced had been following me around. The little voice spoke up again, telling me this isn't right. I couldn't help but think back when I first saw it at the store the day I moved into the town. I thought Griffin was a total creep following me around the store, and it didn't help that I've seen him and this car I was about to get into every time I went out of the apartment. Something about getting into the car felt foreboding, ominous even. Like I was wandering into a wolfs den.

I laughed at myself, and got in, sitting down in the passenger seat. I got Griffin all wrong, he was such a gentleman, he even opened the car door for me. And it wasn't like the town I moved to was a huge city. I run into the same five people every day outside of work, and Griffin doesn't seem like the stalker type, but I had to remind myself to keep my guard up. I didn't know Griffin, I don't know where I am, and I'm drunk. Really drunk.

Being shut off from the rest of the world, alone in a car with a stranger, never should have happened in the first place, I should be back in my apartment unpacking boxes. What is my fucking address, 1285 north drive apartment 1D. No that's not it, 1825 west avenue apartment 1D. That doesn't sound right either. It's saved in my phone, but the piece of shit thing is deader than a door nail. "Hey, do you mind if I smoke while your phone is charging?" Griffin asked, pulling a hand rolled joint from seemingly out of nowhere.

I pulled on my braid trying not to lose my shit in a stranger's car. "By all means, go for it. I could use a contact high." I said laughing. Griffin reached into his pocket and drew out a lighter and a set of keys. After starting the car, he lit the joint, the cabin light came on momentarily blinding me. After walking in the dark, the bright light made my eyes hurt. Griffin handed me a charger for my phone. "Thank you." I said, when I got my phone plugged in, he then handed me the joint. "Now I'm forever in debt to you." I said laughing taking it and enjoying how just one inhale made the chaotic circus in my head settle down. Griffin offered to give me a ride home which made me laugh a little and then I passed him back the joint. "That would be incredible of you, but I don't have my address memorized yet. It's saved in my phone, but the fucking thing is useless at the moment. Besides, I don't live in this town. I live over in Troy."

He was quiet, I looked over at him, and he was studying me, "that's ok," he said after a moment, "we can hang here until your phone is back on. And if it makes you feel better, I live over in Troy too." He took a hit and turned his head to blow smoke out of the window. "SO, you said that you moved recently, how's that going for you?"

How's that going? I thought of all the boxes I still had left to unpack. In apartment 1D, wherever the fuck that is. I sighed, "It's stressful, but I'm working on making it work." I swallowed and checked my phone, 5% isn't enough to turn it on.

"Hey," I looked up he was still looking over at me, has he looked away since we've been in his car? "Your friend shouldn't have ditched you like that. That was pretty low of her."

I let out a bitter laugh. I wanted to cry so badly. "Yeah well, Monday should be interesting. I'm glad I only left my jacket in her car." I brought a small wallet with me that was in my back pocket, it had my ID, some cash I had already spent and the key to my apartment. So, thankfully whenever I do make it back to Apartment 1D, I can get in. We talked for a little while longer, passing the joint back and forth.

Griffin asked how my phone was coming along, so I tried to turn it on again, which it did but "Why the fuck does this piece of shit choose now to update?" I hit update now, but an error message came up, "I need Wi-Fi to download the update, and my phone won't turn on until it does." I put my phone down and looked over at Griffin. "Can you drop me off at a McDonalds?"

Griffin shook his head. "No way am I dropping you off anywhere by yourself at this time of night." He drummed his fingers on the steering wheel. "If you want, we can go back to my place. Just to use the Wi-Fi so your phone can update. Then I'll take you home."

I looked him up and down, there were a lot of red flags, but the warm fuzzy hug of alcohol was still around me and I found myself agreeing. I nodded my head, "Ok, sure."

I was looking out the window waiting for Griffin to put the car in drive, "Are you hungry?" he asked, "I know a taco truck that's open late, they have the best nachos."

The mention of food had my stomach growling, I smiled over at him about to agree but then I remembered that I don't have any money on me. And as much as I hated it and how embarrassing it was to admit, I told him as much.

Griffin reached his arm up and then put it on the shifter. "No worries," he said, "I got you." I shook my head no and opened my mouth to protest but he quickly cut me off, "honestly it's fine." He went on to explain that he didn't live too far away from the truck so it wouldn't be out of the way.

I took a deep breath, "Ok, let's go get some nachos." I said laughing.

Griffin put his seatbelt on and waited until I put mine on before putting the car in reverse. "Ready?" he asked, shifting gears, and taking off, driving us to get some food.

I tucked some hair back in place, "I'm at your mercy."

Griffin chuckled and turned on to the freeway. I looked back out the window hoping this wasn't the second mistake I made tonight.

GRIFFIN (January 27 10:55)

I walked up to the bar to get our drinks. I kept it simple and got what you ordered, rum and coke don't sound bad. The bar was packed, more people kept coming and going. Levi's band was drawing quite the crowd tonight. Just when I was about to lose my patience a bartender came up and took my order. I got the drinks and closed my tab.

Pushing my way back through the crowd of sweaty drunk bodies had my anger starting to bubble. It didn't help when I saw that a guy was at the table trying to steal you away from me. His advances must not have been working, I heard him call you a bitch over the noise around me and it took all I had not to toss one of the drinks in his face, closely followed by a closed fist. "-I'll just go fuck myself then, huh?" I heard him say over the music as I got closer.

I threw my arm over you to keep me from pulverizing this fuck. I felt you trembling under my arm, and I pulled you in closer. *I won't let him harm you.* I thought. "Sounds like a good idea, why don't you get on that." I growled at the guy. My body tense waiting for a fight.

I eyed the guy, he was scrawny; maybe as big as my thigh and I'm not a huge guy myself. I could easily fold this bitch in half if I had to. The guy started to square up, considering whether or not this was worth it. Instead, he did the smart thing and backed off. Grabbing the glasses, he backed down and calling you every name possible as he walked away. I watched the guy as he walked into the crowd and disappeared.

What did you say to make that guy so mad? I shook my head and pulled a chair over so I could sit close to you. I charmed my way back to you by apologizing for the sleezy assholes, "We're not all bad, I promise." I finished. Truly, I'm not a bad guy. I'm just passionate.

When I handed you your drink, I made sure to linger as long as possible without coming across as weird, but when you brushed your fingers along mine, all I could think of getting us somewhere private. Your skin is so soft, I want to touch more of you. Your eyes were already starting to get heavy. You've long since passed the point of being drunk. Even sitting still you were swaying, I smiled and asked, "How's your drink?"

It took a moment for you to realize that I was talking to you. Laughing you said, "I'm sorry, what did you say?" and picked your glass up, chasing the straw around before taking a sip. Your words slurred together; you were so fucking adorable. So vulnerable and trusting.

Laughing I said, "I asked if your drink is good." I took you in, as you sat relaxed enjoying the music.

You sat up straight, "It's amazing thank you," then you started talking about the band.

I brought up my personal ties with the drummer, which could work in my favor. If you're really into the band, I can set up a meet and greet. For someone like you that is a huge panty dropper. And just as I suspected I had you hooked with the promise of a CD, you even felt comfortable enough at this point to ask if I had a charger out in my car. *Oh, little Mel, are you sure you want to go out to a stranger's car? I could be dangerous,* I thought as I watched you take a drink. "There's a possibility," I said, enjoying the look of hesitation that crossed your face for a moment, "but there's something I'll need in return." I stated coyly, taking a drink, and looking at you over the rim of the glass. You narrowed your eyes at me, waiting to see what I was going to say next. I was tempted to ask for a blow job but that send you running away, "I want a dance before we go charge your phone."

You raised your eyebrows and started laughing, I love making you laugh. "A dance it is, but I'm warning you, I ain't that good at dancin'."

I chuckled and tossed back the rest of my drink; you finished most of yours. I stood up and held out my hand to you. When you slipped your hand into mine, I noticed how tiny it was compared to mine. "Don't worry, I'm not very good either," I lied, enjoying how good it felt to touch you.

I laced my fingers through yours and pulled you out to the dance floor. As we walked up to the dance floor Levi caught my eye from the stage, he looked down at us with jealousy written all over his face, but like the good drummer he is, he never missed a beat.

I lifted my arm up and spun you in a circle, then I pulled you into me. Wrapping my other arm around to rest my palm on the small of your back I dipped you, bringing you back up we swayed to the music for a half a second before you stood on your tip toes to kiss me. My heart stopped, were you really kissing me? I melted; your lips were so soft against mine. I grabbed you by the back of your head and held you there for a second longer, I didn't want you to realize in that moment you just sealed your fate with me. I didn't want you to pull away before I had the chance to kiss you back.

The world stopped in the moment. I didn't want the kiss to end. But we were in a very public place and if we don't leave now, I will start ripping your clothes off. I pulled myself away from you, bending over slightly so I could rest my forehead against yours, I loved how little you were. "Let's go charge your phone." I whispered.

Don't think for a moment I didn't see how you went in for another kiss. I kept our hands locked together; I wasn't letting go now that I finally have you. I pulled you through the dance floor, as we passed the stage Levi gave me a head nod and held up his hand in a devil horn gesture. I nodded back with a smirk plastered on my face. I had no doubt that if he got to you first, he would be the one leading you back to his vehicle.

—ᴍᴍ—

The night was windy and cold. I looked down at you, you were trying not to shiver when the wind blew past us. I felt bad that I didn't have a coat that I could give you. I didn't let go of your hand until we got to my car. I took my keys out and unlocked the car, it's then that I let you go to open the door for you. You had suspicion in your eyes for a moment as you took in my car, I swallowed as you took a small step backwards.

I gripped the door waiting to chase after you if you decided that it would be in your best interest to run. But then you relaxed and laughed a little as you pushed past the warning signs you picked up on. I grinned ear to ear as you slid into my passenger seat. I pushed the door shut, sealing you off from the world and trapping you in mine.

When I got into the driver seat, I looked over at you. It felt like a dream, seeing you sitting in my car. I wanted to reach out and touch you again. You almost seemed like you were starting to spiral out of control, I don't blame you it's been a wild night. I tapped my thumb on the steering wheel contemplating my next move. "Hey, do you mind if I smoke while your phone is charging?" I asked, taking the joint that I had put behind the visor.

You played with your braid, which I'm noticing is a nervous tick that you seemed to have. I wanted to tell you that you don't need to be anxious around me, but that's what a psychopath would say. You forced a laugh and told me to go for it, then you said, "I could use a contact high."

I smirked; I was hoping it would be like that. I took my keys and lighter out of my pocket, I should have done that outside, but I wasn't thinking straight. I started the car then lit the joint, taking a big hit. I got out the car charger you needed and handed it to you, waiting until you got your phone plugged in to hand you the joint.

I admire the way you say thank you after everything I do for you, it makes me feel appreciated; wanted. You made a joke about how you were forever in my debt now. Fighting a smirk, I inhaled slowly through my nose, taking in the smell of your perfume. "I'd be happy to give you a ride home if you want." I hope your defenses are down enough to let me drive you home. Hell, getting you back to my place would be a huge win for the night, but I'd love to see the inside of your apartment. I already know which apartment is yours. Thankfully, the mailboxes are in the outside of the building so all I had to do was wait and see which one you opened.

You let out a bitter laugh and handed me back the joint, "That would be incredible of you, but I don't have my address memorized yet..." I didn't hear what else you were saying.

I took a drag off the joint to stop myself from saying *I know where you live, I'll drive us there now*. What a happy ending that would bring. I was admiring how well you looked in my passenger seat, I was especially admiring your thighs when you looked over at me. I shrugged, "That's ok." I said, "We can hang out here until your phone is back on. And if it makes you feel better, I live over in Troy too." I know we've ran into each other multiple times already, that was probably why you hesitated to get into my car. I wouldn't want to get into a car that's been following me either. I took another hit and blew the smoke out of the window, then started some idle chat to help put you at ease. "SO," I started to get your attention, you looked like you were drifting back into your thoughts, "you said that you moved recently, how's that going for you?"

You took a deep breath, "It's stressful," you answered honestly, "but I'm working on making it work."

I watched you closely, memorizing the way you tucked your hair behind your ear, the way your throat worked when you swallowed. Everything about you, I need more of. You tried turning your phone on, but nothing happened, I took this time to further cement myself as a good guy in your pretty little head. "Hey," I said, demanding your attention. "Your friend shouldn't have ditched you like that. That was pretty low of her."

You scoffed and looked out the window. I couldn't stop myself from smirking, it was pretty cute seeing you like this. "Yeah, well Monday should be interesting." You spat, sarcasm dripping off every syllable. "I'm glad I only left my jacket in her car."

I bit my lip; I had a hoodie in the backseat but that will come later. I made more idle chat with you while we waited for your phone to charge up. Normal harmless things, such as "Do you have any pets?"

"No. I want a cat, but pets are against the lease." You replied.

Good, I thought. Dogs give you away, they always do, even when they like you. That's what happened with Alicia, her dog wouldn't stop yapping when I slid through her window. If it wasn't for that fucking dog...... I took the joint you passed back to me and took a hit. "What about roommates?" I wondered. "You can call them off my phone and ask if they can come pick you up." Again, I am such a nice guy.

You smiled sweetly at me. "It's just me. But thank you, that's kind of you to offer." I smiled back at you, the way you're looking at me is getting me higher than the joint. You turned away shyly, "What about you, any roommates wondering where you are?"

I shook my head no, "Nah, I live alone." I flicked the ashes out the window and handed the joint back to you. "How's your phone coming along?" Not that I was eager to get rid of you.

You pressed the power button, and it came on this time but then, "Why the fuck does this piece of shit choose now to update?" you started rambling about your outdated phone.

I wonder if I can talk you into letting me get you a new phone, it would be easy to keep tabs on you that way. Then I heard you say something about wanting to be dropped off at a McDonald's. I shook my head 'no'. "No way am I dropping you off anywhere by yourself at this time of night." I drummed my fingers on the steering wheel making a show of trying to act like I haven't been thinking of what I'm about to say since I first seen you at the store, "If you want, we can go back to my place." I suggested, like it wasn't the end game the entire night. "Just to use the Wi-Fi so your phone can update. Then I'll take you home."

You nodded your head and smiled at me. "Ok, sure."
When you started nodding your pretty little head, I had to lock my muscles to keep myself in place, I was almost sweating with the effort, stopping myself from pouncing on you.

I wanted to grab you by the back of the neck and push your head down onto my cock but now is not the time. But come on, do you blame me, you look so gorgeous sitting in my passenger seat, on the verge of tears. Since your hair was braided to the right, I had a clear view of your face. "Are you hungry?" I asked, food seems like a good distraction, "I know a taco truck that's open late, they have the best nachos."

The look you gave me, your eyes got really big, and you smiled brightly, I would have given you my car right then if you had asked; just then your face dropped. "I don't have any money on me." You looked so sad; you make it really hard for me not to pull you on top of me.

I felt my hand reach up, before I ran my fingers through your hair and covered your mouth with mine, I put it on the shifter. "No worries. I got you." You started to protest but I cut you off, "honestly, it's fine. It's not too far away from where I live so it's not out of the way if that's what you're worried about."

You took a deep breath in and let it out slowly, "Ok, let's go get some nachos."

I smirked and put my seatbelt on. I waited until you had your seatbelt buckled and put the car in reverse. "Ready?" I asked, already backing the car up, to drive us back to my place.

You tucked some hair behind your ear and gave a nervous laugh. "I'm at your mercy." You replied.

Oh, you have no idea, I thought. I smiled and took a right turn to get us on the freeway, putting on cruise control so I wasn't speeding to get us there quicker.

MELANIE (January 27 11:10)

The drive went by in a flash, Griffin kept the conversation going between songs. We had similar tastes in music, and I really enjoyed listening to some of the heavier stuff he showed me. When we finally made it back to town, and we kept going down streets I've never been on before, I started to get an unsettling feeling. By the time we pulled up to a house and Griffin steered the car into the connected garage alarm bells were going off. It was getting a little hard to breathe, I swallowed and looked out the windows, "I thought we were getting food?" I tried not to let my fear show but the tremble at the beginning fucked that up for me.

Griffin turned the car off and unbuckled his seatbelt, "We still are," he said, "I just don't like food in my car, especially if it's messy food." He winked at me and took off his seat belt. Then he twisted around so he was now facing me, and motioned out the window as he said, "It's parked just down the road; I figured the fresh air could do us some good."

The way he broke things down like that made me feel silly for feeling cautious, of course he wouldn't want to eat nachos in his car, that was asking to mess up the interior of his car, which he obviously holds to a very high standard. There wasn't a speck of dust to be seen anywhere. "I don't mind walking. But it's pretty cold out, and I don't have a jacket." I said with a shrug.

Griffin reached into the back and offered me a hoodie, "Here you can wear this."

I thanked him before I pulled it over my head. It smelled like him, his musky cologne wrapping around me as I flipped my hair out. The hoodie swallowed me, but it was so comfortable and smelled so good, I almost thought about asking him if I could keep it. It was just a plain black hoodie, there wasn't anything special about it other than it was keeping me warm.

"You ready?" Griffin asked, I looked over at him, and he was grinning at me.

I smiled back, "Yeah, I'm starving let's go." I opened the door and got out. Griffin walked on the outside next to the road.

While we were walking Griffin asked me more questions about myself. I appreciated him taking the lead on talking, I was an introvert at heart at hated small talk.

I found out that he was a mechanic, which was kind of hot. I was trying to smile but I failed, "a man who works with his hands huh?" I started imagining how his hands would feel on me. The wind started to blow, sending a cold chill down my body, I pulled the hood up over my head, "Isn't too much further, is it?" I pulled the hoodie around me tighter and crossed my arms, "I'm sorry it's just really cold."

"No, it's just down the street, see it?" Griffin asked, pulling me into him and pointing down the street.

There was a carwash that had a taco truck parked in front of it. I nodded my head, and we picked up the pace, Griffin kept his around me the rest of the time. His body warmth felt good against the night air.

When we walked up the truck Griffin rested his elbow on the counter, "Hey Alex! You in there buddy?"

A well put together man came up to the window shortly after and leaned out, "Well hello." He said looking me up and down. "Griffin who is this beautiful lady you bring to my truck tonight?" His tone and the way he was leering at me suggested that Griffin showing up this late with company was a common occurrence.

I looked up at Griffin, his body was tense, and he clenched his jaw before saying, "This is Mel," his tone was oddly flat, "We'll take 2 orders of nachos."

Alex put up his hands, "Hey ok." He laughed, "So, are you ok with nachos, or do you want something else?" He smiled and winked at me. Suggesting that Griffin was nachos, and he was the something else.

Griffin tightens his hold on me, and I leaned my head against his chest, "Nachos are fine." I said.

Alex slapped on the counter, "Coming right up," he said and disappeared to the back.

When he came back with our food Griffin dropped his arm to go pay. I could hear their tones, but I couldn't make out what they were saying. Griffin took the nachos off the counter, "Thanks man. Have a good one." He said, tuning to me with a smile on his face. He handed me nachos and led me away from the taco truck.

Having the nachos too keep my mind off the cold made the walk back to Griffins go by faster. Griffin was right, Alex made decent food. We both had finished our food before we got to his place, throwing our trash in someone's trash bin so we weren't carrying it the rest of the way,

Griffin walked up the porch steps to unlock his front door. It was too dark out to make out much of the outside of his house. If it weren't for the lingering effects of the alcohol, I'm sure I would have running in the other direction by now. The little voice in the back of my head was still going off but I shook it away and let the kind handsome stranger lead me into his house.

GRIFFIN (January 11:10)

The taco truck is usually parked a few blocks away from my place, so I took us there first. I figured we could walk there and back, not only to sober you up but I don't allow food in my car. I'd hate it if you dropped something in my car and made a mess. I pulled up the driveway and parked in the connected garage.

You were looking out the windows, "I thought we were getting food?" I heard a slight tremor in your voice, and I felt my dick start to stiffen. I wanted to lock the doors and claim you as mine right then but not yet, for now I need you relaxed not tense.

I turned the car off. "We still are, I just don't like food in my car, especially if it's messy food." I winked at you before I took off my seat belt and fully turned towards you, enjoying how you looked in my passenger seat. "It's parked just down the road; I figured the fresh air could do us some good." You said you didn't mind walking, but it was a little cold tonight, and you didn't have a jacket. I reached in the back seat and offered up the hoodie I was wearing earlier today, "Here you can borrow this." biting your lip you took the hoodie. When you pulled the hoodie on, I asked if you were ready.

You smiled at me, "Yeah, I'm starving let's go." I watched you as you opened the door and got out. We're going to have to talk about you getting your own door. You're a goddess Melanie, and goddesses don't open their own doors. But I have to admit, your ass is amazing from this angle.

We were walking side by side, me by the road because I'm a gentleman. I looked down at you and couldn't stop a smile. You looked adorable in my hoodie; I was tempted to tell you to keep it. I didn't want to walk the entire way to the taco truck in silence, so I decided to make some small talk to get to know you a little better. "Where do you work?" I asked. If you worked with the public, I'd make sure to frequent there after this.

"I work at the party supply factory." From the slight slur in your voice, I'm assuming you're still pretty drunk.

"Oh, that's downtown, right?" I know exactly where it's at, but I like hearing you talk.

"Yeah, we actually drove by it on our way here."

"Oh yeah, so are you on the day shift then?" I asked. Things would be so much easier if you were.

"Yep, I like a steady work schedule with weekends off."

"We're slammed with work, so they have us working Saturdays, but I agree. Weekends are nice to have off." I don't have a set schedule, I just show up whenever I'm called.

You looked over at me, "What do you do?" you asked.

I scratched my head, "I'm a mechanic." Half-truths are still truths. I'll tell you more about what I do, just not today. I looked down at you, it looked like you were fighting a smile. I wasn't sure if that was a good sign or a bad one.

"A man who works with his hands huh?" You pulled the hood over your head. "Isn't too much further, is it? I'm sorry it's just really cold."

"No, it's just down the street. See it?" I pulled you into me and pointed straight ahead and slightly to the right. There in an empty parking lot by a car wash was where Alex parked his truck every night between 8-3am. He owns the car wash too, but the truck is his main source. Well, that and the work we do at the garage. On this road he gets the nightly traffic of the people getting off and going into work on the night shifts. You nodded your head and picked up the pace.

Alex was a well put together guy, we all have a past and hobbies we don't like to talk about out loud, but we've bailed each other out of a few tight spots before, aside from him and Levi there's few people in this world I can trust. Growing up we all lived a couple houses away from each other, so we spent a lot of time together. We've been getting into trouble together for as long as I can remember. When we walked up, I hollered at Alex, he came to the window and looked you up and down, "Well hello. Griffin who is this beautiful lady you bring to my tuck tonight?" I didn't care for his tone.

"This is Mel. We'll take two orders of nachos." My tone was flat. I gave a warning look. I should have sent him a message. Usually when I showed up with a bitch this late at night, we all ended up in the back of the truck doing things better left in the dark. But I'm not sharing you Mel, you're all mine.

"Hey ok." Alex laughed putting his hands up. "So, are you ok with nachos, or do you want something else?" He said to you with a smile and a wink, Alex was naturally a smooth talker, and his charming demeanor seemed to be working on you.

I put my arm tighter around your shoulders to remind Alex that I wasn't fucking around. He looked at me and smirked, you rested your head on my chest and said to Alex, "Nachos are fine."

"Coming right up." He said and went to put our nachos together.

When I stepped up to pay Alex took my money and remarked, "So you're not sharing this one huh? I get it." He wasn't talking very loudly but I was still worried that you could hear him. "If she has a friend send her my way." That might work. I don't how close you and that bitch from the bar are, but I can use that to my advantage. Bitches are always letting their guard down when they have a friend with them.

The walk home went by faster than it did going to get the food. By the time we got to the door we had finished the nachos and threw the trash away in a random waste bin along the way. I unlocked the door and let you go in first. Now I hated myself for loaning you my hoodie, with it on I couldn't get a good view of your ass.

Seeing you standing in my living room wasn't something I thought would happen this soon. I have to play this smart, or you'll never willingly walk through that door again. I took a deep breath and walked up to you.

Melanie (January 27 12:15)

When I first stepped inside Griffins house the first thing that I noticed was the slight smell of weed. Then how clean it was. This place was spotless. It was small, the living room and kitchen was connected, there two doors, both closed. Griffin closed the front door as he walked in behind me.

I could tell I was still wasted when I tried to step to the side to let him through but ended up stumbling and laughing as he caught me. Griffin laughed as he steadied me, "You good Mel?"

I smiled, "Yeah, I'm alright." I was starting to get a little warm and tried to tug the hoodie off. It smelled so good, like motor oil and men's cologne. I wondered if he'd let me keep it but I'm sure that was just my drunk mind thinking. He's not going to give a stranger his hoodie. When I pulled it up over my head, I heard something fall out of the pocket. It was my phone. "Oh yeah, that thing." I tossed the hoodie over the arm of a small sofa and bent down to pick it up, bending at the knees so I didn't lose my balance, but when I tried to turn it on it asked for a Wi-Fi connection to download an update. "Right, the update." I squinted my eyes and tried to remember my Wi-Fi password. I wasn't sure why my phone didn't automatically connect when I walked through the door but when I looked around me and noticed Griffin checking me out, I remember I wasn't in my apartment. I was drunker than I thought. "Can you help me with this?" I asked, holding my phone out towards him.

"Of course." Griffins fingers brushed along my skin as he took my phone. I must have hit the power button cause when he showed me the screen it was black, "is there a code?" he asked.

I nodded and put in. "Sorry about that," I grinned not recalling pushing the power button but hey accidents happen. I put my pin in 1993 my birth year, and handed him back my phone, "I really appreciate this Griff. This really hasn't been a good time since I moved here." I looked around. This isn't the place for a breakdown. "Do you mind if I use your bathroom?"

"Yeah sure," he led me through one of the doors which opened up into a bigger room that had some workout equipment scattered around, a huge tv and couple of gaming chairs that was arranged around a small coffee table. There was also a long coffee table surrounded by comfortable chairs. This place is a lot bigger than I first thought. "Bathroom's over here," he said, reaching into a dark room to flip on a light switch. "Take your time and meet me back in the front room when you're done." He said with a wink. I bit my lip and smiled before I closed the door.

Ok so this place is definitely bigger than I first thought. I mean his bathroom has a fucking jacuzzi tub and a walk-in shower with natural stone walls.

Oh, I'm definitely in over my head. I thought, then looking at myself in the mirror and I shook my head, kicking myself for agreeing to go out tonight. This was too much stress. I used the bathroom and cleaned up the best I could. I'm sure Griffin had intentions set for the night, but I'm not sure one nightstands are a part of my personality. There's nothing wrong with having fun with strangers, it's just not for me.

Griffin wasn't that bag of a guy; I mean he did scare off that creep at the bar. He is such a sweet guy, even if he was stalking me through the store, which was once, and it was just a misunderstanding. He is so sexy, those blue eyes, devilish grin. I smirked and thought back to kissing him on the dance floor and wished I kissed him in the car, I smiled at myself and shook my head, thinking about the look he had when I caught him checking out my ass.

I washed my hands and after drying them I smoothed the makeup that had smeared and took out my braid to fix my hair which was a hot mess, I shook it out and ran my fingers through it a few times. Having it in a braid all day gave my long hair a nice wave, I ran my fingers through it a few more times and pulled it up into a sloppy bun. I readjusted my bra and jeans and smoothed out my shirt, with one last look over in the mirror to make sure my hair looked ok I made my way to the front room.

I sat down on the sofa and looked around as I bent over to take off my shoes. I caught Griffin in the kitchen looking down my shirt, I expected him to look away but instead he asked if I wanted anything from the kitchen. I bit my lip to keep from smiling too wide and stood up to put my shoes over by the door. "What do you have?" I asked. I walked up to him; he looked so causal leaning against the counter. Maybe I should let go for a change? He looked down at me, those blue eyes looked right into the darkest parts of me.

Griffin smirked, "What do you want?" he shot back.

"You" *Don't think about it just roll with it* I told myself as I stood up on my tip toes; but even then, I couldn't look him in the eye. I wrapped my arounds around his neck, pulling him down to me and kissed him. Kissing him was like nothing I had ever experienced with anyone else. It was exhilarating. Or maybe it was just the alcohol.

Griffin picked me up and I wrapped my legs around his waist, all while refusing to break the kiss. I couldn't get enough of him. I was kissing down his neck when he walked us through a door way and he tossed me onto the bed. Being throwing through the air was thrilling, yet terrifying. The way Griffin could just pick me up and toss me around like I weighed nothing was giving me a complex. I was a bigger girl, being tossed around like a rag doll didn't happen on a day to day.

When I hit the mattress, I started giggling, I was pushing myself toward the foot of the bed when Griffin grabbed my ankles and pulled me towards him. I sat up and he took the hem of my shirt and pulled it off, exposing my chest and my stomach rolls. I was about to move my arms to cover my stomach when he wrapped his arms around my waist and started kissing my chest. His lip ring was cold against my bare flesh, but it was his teasing kisses that sent chills down my spine. It was over too soon, Griffin leaned back and kneeled down in front of me.

"You sure you're ok with this?" He asked. I studied his face, the corners of his mouth turned downwards, eyes slightly narrowed. His tone gave him away more than anything, which sounded abnormally sweet. I was already in his bed, would backing out really be an option right now? Besides what's the worst that can happen? What's life without a few risks here and there?

I nodded once and he ran his hands up my back and unhooked my bra, "are you sure?" He asked, the lack of emotion made me think he was going through motions. I thought about the possible outcomes but was interrupted by a phone ringing. Griffin ignored the call and kissed my shoulders and along my collar bone, after a few rings it's stopped. He sat back, pulling my bra off and looked at me for a moment, like he was studying me or something.

Just when I was starting to get self-conscious again, he tossed my bra to the side and leaned forward and started kissing on me again. He sucked on my nipples and played with my breasts for a while. It felt good, I liked how he wasn't afraid to go for what he wanted.

"Lean back for me baby," he whispered, pushing me back gently. When I did, he leaned over me and took me in. "Mmmmm that's it," he said, tracing the tattoo under my breasts. His soft touch was ticklish, I tried not to laugh to kill the mood. Griffin must have realized he tickled me based off the grin that spread across his face just now. He ran his nails down my sides, switching from soft caresses to gentle scratching. He pushed my hips down and pinned me to the mattress. He unbuttoned my jeans and slid them down; I closed my eyes and bit my lip. Nervous yet eager for him to continue.

Griffin ran his hands up my thighs and hooked his thumbs under my panties to pulled them down, he started teasing me with kisses up my thighs.

RING, RING, RING. His phone started going off again. I looked down at Griffin, who was looking up at me just as confused.

I couldn't help but be a little suspicious. It was late at night, surely it had to be important. "Do, you need to get that?" I asked him.

Griffin pulled his phone out of his pocket, glanced at it and sat it face down on the bed after declining the call. He ran his hands up my thighs and grabbed ahold of my hips, "No" he said before he started kissing on my thighs again.

Then just as I was getting back into the mood, his phone started ringing. Again. I sat up, about to go looking for my clothes when Griffin silenced the call and started kissing on my neck.

I let myself melt into the sensation, Griffin nibbling on my jawline while massaging between my thighs. For the fourth time his phone started going off. "Griffin?" I tried shaking him off; but when he slid two of his fingers inside of me, I forgot what the problem was.

Griffin leaned back just far enough to look me in the eyes. The way he was moving his fingers inside me was making it hard to breathe. "Yeah, baby?" He asked, studying me. Then the phone rang again, bringing my attention back to his phone. Griffin sighed and pulled his fingers out. He put his fingers in his mouth before holding them up, "just give me 2 seconds." He said before standing up and leaving the room. "This better be fucking good," he growled into the phone.

I sighed and made myself comfortable on Griffins bed. I wasn't planning on falling asleep, but his bed was warm, and his pillows were so soft, plus they smelled incredible. I closed my eyes but just for a second.

Griffin (January 27 12:15)

I unlocked the door and let you go in first, I love watching you walk. I caught you as you stumbled, both of us laughing as I helped you steady yourself. I wouldn't mind knocking you down and fucking you right here, but I want to take my time. I asked if you were good and breathlessly you said, "Yeah, I'm alright."

Then you pulled my hoodie off. The effort it took not to rip it off of you along with the rest of your clothes had me sweating. The sound of your phone hitting the floor snapped me out of that daydream. My eyes traveled up and down you as you muttered to yourself for a moment. Are you trying to look seductive as you pick it up, dropping to the floor bending at the knees like a stripper picking up money? I was enjoying you being in my front room, focusing mainly on your ass when you turned around and held out your phone catching me checking you out red handed but you chose not to address it. "Can you help me with this?" You asked shyly.

Brushing my fingers along your skin, "Of course," I said, I can help you with so much more. I pushed the power button so I could watch you put the code in. "Is there a pin?" I asked, handing it back over to you.

You grinned sheepishly, "yeah, sorry about that," looking over your shoulder as you tapped on the screen, I noted 1993, "I really appreciate this Griff. This really hasn't been a good time since I moved here."

I smiled at the nickname you gave me. You seem to be feeling more comfortable with me by the moment. You took in a shaky breath, and for a second, I thought you were going to cry. Honestly, I wouldn't mind that, fucking a bitch who's crying has never bothered me. If anything, it helps get her pants off easier. A shoulder to cry on is a dick to ride on.

Then you asked for the bathroom.

I lead you through the gaming room and over to the bathroom, "Take your time and meet me in the front room when you're done." I gave you a smile and a wink that I knew made the ladies wet and based off that lip biting smile I knew I had your panties soaked.

I took your phone to my bedroom and plugged it in. Using the number combination 1-9-9-3 I got into your phone. That must be your birthyear. You're 9 years younger than me but I don't mind. We can use that age difference as kinky foreplay. I can already hear you moan "harder Daddy," and my dick started to ache. I rubbed the outside of my jeans, if I started jacking off now, you'd probably walk in on it. Would you scream and run? Or would you walk over and help me out? I shook my head and focused on the task at hand.

After connecting your phone to the Wi-Fi I started up the update, which took a lot longer than it should have. Mel, you really need a better phone; this piece of shit is so outdated I wouldn't be surprised if it became obsolete soon. But as long as your phone is connected to my Wi-Fi that means that I can get into your phone using my computer.

I went to the kitchen to pour a drink, just tea, and leaned against the counter. Trying to think of anything besides what I'm about to do to you. I heard the bathroom door open and waited for you to walk over to me. That's the hard part, waiting for you to come to me, even though you are right there. It would be so easy to pounce on you; but it's too soon. If I lunge now, you could run away. So, I took a breath to steady myself and waited.

I watched you walk over to the sofa and sit down; you were taking in your surroundings while you pulled off your shoes, bending over like that I got the perfect view right down your shirt. I didn't bother looking away when your eyes finally found me. "Do you want anything from the kitchen?" I asked, I almost expected you to sit back and politely decline but what you did next surprised me. Instead of being the shy awkward girl I pegged you to be, you walked toward me, setting your shoes aside along the way.

Your fluid like movements reminded me of a serpent, "What do you have?" you asked.

A hard on for you, I could almost taste those words coming out of my mouth instead I went with a safer approach, "What do you want?"

By this time, you were standing in front of me, the top of your head barely came up to my chin. You looked up at me "you," you whispered while wrapping your arms around me pulling me in.

Fuck, it felt good to kiss you. I thought of this moment a thousand times since I ran into you at the store. But none of them compared to actually kissing you. Feeling your body pressed against mine, set me on fire. Your chest started to heave as the kiss deepened.

I picked you up, your legs wrapped around my waist, and I walked us to the bedroom. You were kissing down my neck when I threw you on the bed. You squealed and started to push yourself towards me, laughing. Taking hold of your ankles, I pulled you to the edge. When you sat up, I took the hem of your shirt and tank top and yanked them both off of you and tossed them to the side. You went to cover your stomach with your arms, but I grabbed you around the waist and kissed the tattoo on your chest before you could hide yourself from me. You are beautiful, never be ashamed of how your body looks.

I asked if you were ok with this. I kept my eyes focused; I was worried what would happen if you rejected me at this point. Being turned down sucks. Much to my delight you nodded, just once. But it was all I needed.

I positioned myself in front of you like a king kneeling before his queen waiting for her to tell him what she wants. My heart raced and then my hands started to shake. I wanted to slap myself; I'm not going to let myself blow this.

Taking a deep breath, I ran my hands up your back and slowly and unhooked the clasps on your bra. "Are you sure?" I wanted it to come out reassuring, but it sounded robotic. You started to move but my phone ringing broke the moment. I ignored the phone completely, letting it ring while I kissed your shoulders, your collarbone. The phone stopped ringing when I leaned back to pull your bra off. I took some time just to admire you. I still had your black bra in my hands and noticed that I was twisting it nervously in my hands like a fucking teenage boy about to lose his virginity. I tossed your bra over to the side. You were leaned back on your elbows with your back arched, flowers decorated your skin, and I wished I were more patient so I could study them closer; but right now, I wanted a taste. I took your left nipple in my mouth and lightly pinched the other. You let out a sigh, and I teased your nipples some more. I sucked and nibbled on both of your breasts until I could feel your heartbeat on my lips.

"Lean back for me baby," I whispered pushing you back softly. You complied easily, almost as if I had you in a trance. I held my body over top of you, studying every curve and dip of your body. "Mmmmm that's it," I said lightly tracing the line work on the tattoo under your breasts with my fingers, you sucked in a quick breath. I could feel the laugh building inside of you, you're ticklish. I didn't fight the devilish grin, but I resisted the urge to explore this new discovery. Instead of lightly caressing you, I switched to running my nails down your sides and pushing your hips down.

You weren't skinny, I like that about you. I'm not a dog, boney women don't do it for me. I like my women to have a full figure, something for me to grab on to that doesn't feel like it's ready to break under my touch.

With slow deliberate movements I undid your jeans and pulled them off. I didn't want you to feel my trembling touch so every move I made was calculated. You sucked in a breath of air as I threw your jeans to the side. I looked up to your face, your eyes were closed, and you were biting your lip again.

I ran my hands up your thighs and hooked my thumbs under your panties and started to tug them down. Kissing up and down your thighs enjoying how all of this felt when, RING, RING, RING!

You looked down at me just as confused, "Do you need to get that?" you asked, suspicion creeping in your voice.

I looked over at the alarm clock on my nightstand, no wonder you were giving me that look, it was two in the morning. I pulled my phone out of my pocket and pressed the button on the side to silence the ringer. Setting the phone face down on the bed next to you I shook my head 'no' and went back to what I was doing. I kissed, licked, and bit my way back up to your pussy. I just got you moaning again when my phone started going off, again. I silenced the ringer again and started kissing your neck while gently rubbing your most sensitive area.

"Griffin?" The way my name fell off of your lips made me want to push you back and shove my aching dick inside that sweet slit. But I'm not done playing with you yet. I want to go slow with you, really enjoy it this time.

Sliding my fingers inside you I leaned back so I could look you in the eyes, "yeah baby?" I asked, you looked at my phone, which had started ringing again. I sighed; the mood was dying fast. I pulled my fingers out of you, sucking on them before holding them up, "Just give me 2 seconds." Leaving that room was easily one of the dumbest things I've done today but tasting you on my lips as I answered my phone almost made up for it. "This better be fucking good," I growled into the phone.

"You could be nicer you know? I was bouncing on your dick just last week." Fucking Natasha. This is one fucking cunt who can't take a hint. Pity fucking her probably doesn't help much but when I'm in a dry spell she's an easy lay. Besides as pathetic as she is, she's fucking hot. "I need a favor; I'm stuck at the club on fifth street, and no one will give me a ride home. I'll give you one if you come get me."

I rolled my eyes, never in a million years would I ditch Mel to go save some crusty bitch like Natasha. "Well good luck finding a ride I'm busy doing anything else." I could hear her protests as I hung up the phone. I walked back into my bedroom taking my pants off as I made my way back over to you.

Much to my disappointment you were fast asleep. You had pulled yourself up and was laying on your back, I could see all of you. My body was on auto pilot as I took my phone out and snapped a few photos. I was tempted to wake you up by ramming myself into you but I'm sure your dry by now and that wouldn't feel particularly good for either one of us. I thought about just laying down next to you and falling asleep but then I caught sight of your panties peeking out from under the bed.

I bent over to pick them up, they were a light blue. I was glad they didn't match your bra, which was a good sign that you weren't looking to get fucked tonight. before I knew it, I was in the bathroom, one hand aggressively tugging at my throbbing dick, the other pressing your panties to my face. I could still taste you on my lips, playing your moans back in my head and inhaling your sent from the underwear had me cumming in no time.

I walked quietly back in the bedroom. I bent down to untangle your tank top from your other shirt and picked up a sock. Walking over to the closet I folded your underwear and sock in the tank top and placed them under a stack of neatly folded shirts. I keep my clothes on shelves, I prefer that over digging around in drawers to find a shirt.

Walking over to the bed I was still amazed at how I managed to get you in my bed so easily. You came across smarter than this Mel, I was almost disappointed. In the time I was stashing your clothes away you had rolled over onto your stomach. You were almost hugging the pillow your head was on, and the other one was just under your shoulder. Gently tugging the latter out from under you the best I could without waking you up, but you shifted and mumbled something incoherent and nuzzled the pillow.

With the pillow now free I hovered over you and studied you. You are so beautiful, you had some hair hanging in your face, so I lightly brushed it back, you sighed smiled. My thumb was tracing the scar on your forehead, and I made a mental note of asking you about it when you woke up. But in the meantime, I forced myself to go to the living room before I woke you up.

I wasn't much of a sleeper, so I took my laptop out. It took a longer than usual, but I finally got into your phone. I went to your text messages but didn't see any male names in the most recent conversations. Your Facebook messages were another story, the edge of my vision turned red as I read through them. Although the majority were harmless, mundane conversations about work and school (why you didn't mention you were taking online classes I wasn't sure) there were some that had me shaking with rage. Looking at the dates, the messages were sent didn't make me feel any calmer, a few months ago you and Corey were exchanging pictures. I saved the pictures you sent him and went to his profile. This guy was a piece of shit, all over his feed were pictures of him smoking weed and drinking at parties. A few shots of him at work, apparently, he's a welder and likes to take pictures of himself welding something.

Then there was Jeff, you guys liked to talk about music and from the looks of it you two also liked to flirt. This mother fucker was a tattoo artist who was also in a band. The last time you guys talked was 10 weeks ago, he wanted to take you to a Slipknot concert and share a hotel room. You had agreed to the concert but needed a good reason to share a hotel room, wink. He said he had a few good reasons, but it was up to you. Your reply was, depending on how the concert went. I went through your pictures back 10 weeks ago. I flipped through a few pictures, and even though I didn't see any of you guys at the concert venue, it didn't do anything to calm me down. I continued to flip through your old photos, then I came across a picture of you in frame with what looked like a male arm around your shoulders, and I flipped my computer off my lap and went to lift some weights.

I knew this anger wasn't going away. I have a rage issue that has landed me in therapy, I go to the court ordered sessions, but I don't take the pills. After a few reps, I did a line of coke and took my phone out to look at my new obsession. Flipping through the pictures of your naked body made my dick twitch. But it was thinking of beating the shit out Jeff and Corey in front you that got me hard. I visioned standing over you, I could almost hear you crying. I closed my eyes and put my dick in my hand. I thought of pushing you down and taking you one last time, you screaming at me to stop and that you were sorry. They are always sorry near the end. I could feel you struggling under me as I ram myself into you. I had wrapped my left hand around your neck, the right had both of your wrists pinned down. Something I noticed tonight is that I can hold both of your wrists tightly in one hand. I was spilling cum all over when I thought of you finally slipping away while I finished inside you.

I went to the bathroom to wash my hands. Looking in the mirror, I started to laugh at myself, I know I'm sick, along with the medication to tame my anger I also refuse to take my antipsychotics. They make me so zoned out of my mind, I'm pretty much a fucking zombie. A lobotomy would be more humane than to stay on those pills.

Taking a deep breath through my nose, I got a whiff of pussy. And fuck it smelled good. I had almost forgotten that I was tongue deep inside you. If I weren't so mad at you, I would wake you up and put that smell all over me. But I know that if I go wake you up now, especially when I'm like this, you wouldn't come back. Instead of riding out the high while you ride me, I went and lifted weights. I put my playlist on shuffle, starting with Losing Control by Villain of the Story. I put my headphones on and started my workout. Usually, I would use the speakers, but I did not want to wake you up.

The next thing I knew, my alarm was going off. I was doing sit ups at the time, and I decided to stop collapsing onto the mat, I lay there panting. I was still a little mad at what I found on your phone, but I decided for the sake of our relationship I'll let it slide. I got up to take a quick shower.

You were still asleep by the time I got out. It was 5:50, I was on my way to the kitchen to make some coffee when the glow from my laptop sitting on the sofa caught my attention. I spotted my laptop still laying open on the sofa, your Facebook page was on full view. I casually walked over and closed the screen, which would look pretty suspicious if you were to see me creeping on your page. When the computer was closed and put on charge, I went to make my coffee.

MELANIE (January 28)

I woke up to the smell of coffee. I was sure I was in my apartment until I turned my face into the pillow, and the musky scent of man hit me. It was a clean kind of smell, like whoever this bed belongs to uses bourbon scented shampoo. It smelled good, I took one slower inhale through the nose, to get a last sniff before I pulled myself up and took in my surroundings. The room was clean, so I was able to locate my clothes easily. There were black metal band posters taped to the walls and a small bookshelf with actual books on it. I found that quite surprising, this guy just got more points added to his favor.

I put a hand on my head and thought back to last night. Being ditched at the bar. The handsome stranger who stopped me to tell me my slap was impressive. Smoking with him in his car. And that name, Griffin. That was a name I won't forget soon.

I looked over and seen my phone on the nightstand. Pushing the side button and squinting at the bright light the time read 6:06. Groaning, I got up and went to pull my clothes on. My head was killing me. The room started spinning when I bent over so I had to sit down to get dressed. My underwear and tank top were nowhere to be found, and I was missing a sock. I must have thrown my clothes around when I was getting undressed with Griffin. I don't remember what happened after he left to take that phone call, but what I do remember was enough to make me come back for more.

Walking out the bedroom door I seen Griffin over by the kitchen sink making a cup of coffee. "Mmm that smells good." I said. Griffins' shoulders tensed up before he turned to face me. There was a dark look in his eye that sent a cold shiver throughout my body.

Just like that, the look vanished and he smiled at me brightly, "I made enough for two. Want a cup?" I smiled and nodded, and he took a coffee cup down from the cabinets above him and offered it to me. I looked it over, it was red and had dragon scales carved into the ceramic, a black circle with a three headed dragon was in the middle. I couldn't help but smile, "Game of Thrones is the shit, you can't convince me otherwise." Griffin was grinning down at me sheepishly. Any hint of anger or hatred was gone, I made a mental note of that.

Taking the coffee pot and pouring myself a cup I laughed, "Don't worry I wasn't going to try to." Griffin had the milk and creamer out, so I poured some of both into the cup as well. "This is kind of embarrassing, but I'm missing some clothes." I admitted.

Griffin laughed, "Yeah you got undressed in a hurry. I'll be on the lookout." He's eyes roamed over me, something about his eyes were off. It was like he hadn't slept all night, and he was a little twitchy, every once in a while, he would scratch or rub his neck and arms. "When do you have to leave?" His voice was strained, he looked up and met my gaze. A smile that I couldn't read spread across his face, "I'd love to take you out for dinner tonight, if you're free."

My heart flipped. Was it normal for a guy to be so eager to meet back up with a bar hook up? I took a drink of coffee to hide my smile. This guy was giving subtle hints that he was unstable but then again, I did just meet him last night. Maybe I was over thinking the whole situation, waking up in a stranger's house is putting me on edge. Taking a breath, I put my coffee on the counter, I tucked some hair behind one ear and said, "yeah, that's sounds good," I pulled my phone out of my pocket, "I can text you later today so we can make plans. What's your number?"

Griffin rattled off his cellphone number. I put it in and saved it. While I had my phone out, I started scrolling through Facebook to see what was new, "Do you want me to give you a ride home?"

The idea that some random person would know where I live didn't sit well with me, but on the other hand I live in a pretty big apartment building, so the chances of him knowing exactly which one I lived in was a long shot. Taking a risky gamble (since I didn't have the extra spending money for an uber) I smiled politely and said, "That would be great!" Already kicking myself and trying to rationalize my decision. There were four stories to my building, sure I live on the first floor, but you wouldn't know that by dropping me off at the door. Griffin only needs the address to the building; he doesn't need to know the apartment number.

We both finished our coffee and poured second cups, Griffin led me to the workout/game room. We sat in the gaming chairs, and he pulled a rolling tray from under the coffee table and started rolling a blunt. "Nothing goes better with coffee than weed." While he was working the blunt in his hands, he looked at me, "wanna smoke?" he asked. I nodded my head and waited for him to light it.

While we smoked, we talked some more, I found out that Griffin was an only child and his parents split up when he was 2, leaving him with his dad who in turn relied heavily on his grandpa for support. I told him I hated my job but was having a tough time finding a new one. We talked about movies, we both like horror. We talked about interests such as I enjoy reading where he indulges in video games. Once in a while Griffin will help his dad out and do an odd job here and there, he didn't go into details just that every now and then he'd have to drive across the country.

We were still talking even when the blunt was spent and the smoke was dissipating. I was looking around taking in my surroundings. There were a few things on the wall, some posters, and sculptures of different masks; I recognized some of them, the Trivium demon mask, and some replicas of various Slipknot masks. I was looking over to the right studying a rather disturbing painting that was hanging on the wall. In it was a woman bound to a wooden post incased in flames, through the smoke you could see creatures flying around in the sky, the crowd was full of eyeless people; their mouths contorted in pain and oozing black blood. The woman was bent forward, her head hanging down, but her eyes were looking straight, as if she were looking at me. She was smiling.

My heart nearly leapt out of my throat when I felt a hand on my shoulder. Are you ready to head out, Mel?" Griffin was standing over me, looking down at me with a smirk. I nodded and followed him out the door.

It was around nine by the time we pulled up to my building. It was a shabby brick building four stories high surrounded by other mediocre apartment complexes. When Griffin put the car in park, I unbuckled my seatbelt and turned towards him, "Are we still on for dinner?" I asked.

"I'll be here at 8 to pick you up." Griffin replied, the authority in his voice leaving no room for debate. "Let me walk you in."

He was about to turn the car off but stopped short at my, "No," with his hand still hovering over the key, he turned his head towards me, anger swirling in his eyes. I rose an eyebrow and with a steady voice said, "the place isn't ready for visitors." I almost apologized but something my therapist and I been working on was to learning when not to apologize when I'm not really sorry. And I will not apologize for not wanting this man to know exactly which apartment I lived in. That and I don't want him to see the place in such disarray.

Griffin rested an elbow on the steering wheel so he could fully turn his torso towards me. The look in his eye softened but he still gave a pissed off vibe, he grinned at me, "Forgive me, I'm not used to being told 'No.'" he gave me a once over and his grin widened, "I'll see you at 8 then."

My hesitation melted at that grin, I returned a smiled and nodded, "Can't wait." I felt his eyes on me as I got out of the car. I looked back and waved before I pulled the door open and stepped inside. Once I was comfortably on my couch, I dialed Kendra's number. "Hey you busy?" I asked when she answered.

"Not at all, what's up?" Kendra's never too busy for some good gossip.

"Biiiitch, I had the wildest night." I ran a hand down my face, I already knew she was going to judge me, but I had to tell her. I tell her almost everything.

Kendra squealed and did her best impression of the matchmaker from Mulan saying, "Pour the tea." I laughed and summarized the events from last night as best as I could making sure not to go into too much detail; that and leaving out how Griffin went down on me like Pooh on a honey jar. When I was done the line was silent. I bit my lip worried that she had hung up. Just as I was about to say something I heard her take a breath. "Well…" she started and trailed off. With another deep breath she began again, "Well, I'm glad you're alive." I rolled my eyes, "Hillary sounds like a straight cunt, why the fuck would you ditch somebody at a bar when you're the one who drove?"

"Yeah, I don't know. Monday will be interesting for sure." I didn't want to think about how that would go down.

"So, what about all these red flags you're seeing with-what was his name?"

"Griffin." I sighed; she had a point. He was throwing a lot of red flags but it's hard to assess someone when you only know them drunk and hung over. "I don't know, I need to feel this out better. That's what the dinner tonight is for." If anything, the red flags seem to be turning into yellow caution flags.

"I just want you to be careful," I heard her shuffling some things around.

"Are you busy?" Looking for any excuse to jump off the phone now, I was trying not to back out of the dinner, and I was worried that she would talk me right out of it.

"Huh?" there was some muffled talking on her end, "No, I'm not busy. So, let's go over this one more time. The creep from the store, who you've seen following you around since, was at the bar. Then after you slapped the shit out of some handsy perv you ended up drinking with the stalker. He comes up with this half-baked theory that you look like some long-lost love then you go home with him because you were ditched at some bar out of town." She took a breath, "Yeah, I'm glad you're alive sis, why didn't you call me?"

I scratched my eyebrow. "My phone was dead, and I don't have your number memorized." I mouthed the words 'why didn't you ask the bartender if they had a charger?' along with her, "Dude I was stressed out and half-drunk by the time my phone died, I didn't think of it until I was waking up in a bed that wasn't mine. I'm glad I'm alive too, but I think this just might work out. Besides, this is small town, you've seen how big it is. I run into the same people all the time here, it's not that uncommon." I didn't want to start over-thinking this. If you go looking for shadows, you end up finding them. "I need to go; I still haven't finished unpacking. I love you."

"Be safe and call me when you get home. I love you too, bye." We said our goodbyes and hung up the phone. I glanced at the clock, I still had 5 hours until Griffin picked me up.

The hours crawled by; I tore through boxes of clothes looking for something cute to wear. There was a pair of jeans I've been looking for, the ones that fit perfectly all around, of course they had to be on the bottom of the last box I checked. Haphazardly putting my jeans in drawers and tossing the empty boxes in a corner, I went searching for a shirt. I had four laid out, a loose fit Tool band tee, a low cut plain black dress shirt, a black silk button up blouse, and silly graphic tee with aliens. I ran a hand through my hair and sighed. I was making this more complicated than it should be. Pulling my phone out of my pocket I checked the time, it was 4 o'clock. My indecisiveness cost me more time than I thought.

Walking past the closet that looked like it had exploded, I went to the kitchen to grab something to eat. I flipped on my comfort show and ate my sandwich, killing some time before I had to actually start getting ready. After the episode was over, I got up and put my plate in the sink. I checked the time, I still had three and half hours. I went to the bedroom and turned on the radio, hoping that the music would help put me in the mood to put my clothes away. I started by hanging up my nicer clothes. Once those were neatly put up, I refolded the rest of my clothes so they would fit in the dresser drawers better.

When I was satisfied with how the closet looked, I got up and went to the bathroom to get ready for my date. I had 2 hours and 45 minutes left. Starting with a quick shower that turned into a long one, my prickly legs made me self-conscious, doing my best to avoid getting my hair wet because it took too long for it to dry. When I stepped out of the shower, I opened my phone to put on some music while I dried off and put on my make-up. Seeing that I had three messages all from Griffin, I tilted my head to the side. I hope he wasn't trying to back out. I'd soon find out that it was the exact opposite.

Hey, mind if we meet a little earlier.

I'm ready to see you again ☺

I'm heading to your building now.

Ok I'm not sure if that's pushy or charming. I was typing out a reply when a drop of water splattered on my screen. My heart stopped and my face heated up, I knew if I looked at my reflection my face would be beat red. Griffin was on his way, right now. Probably pulling up and here I am soaking wet. I sat the phone down and dried off the best I could; but while I was frantically drying off my phone starting ringing. I froze. It was Griffin. I swiped the screen to answer "Hello?" My voice was so meek, sounding I wanted to laugh at myself.

Griffin however did laugh, "Hey, are we still on for tonight? You haven't answered any of my texts and I'm beginning to worry."

I cleared my throat, "Yes, we are. I'm sorry I thought I had more time. I just now stepped out the shower."

He let out a low moan. I bit my lip to stop myself from smiling. "Well, I'm right outside your building. Need me to come in and give you a hand?" Weighing my options quickly in my head, if I make him wait, will he stay outside? Or would he bail? My feet were already taking me to the door before I fully made up my mind. At the sound of the deadbolt sliding out of the lock Griffin spoke up, "Was that a, yes?" I can see the sly smirk on his face, a grin spread across mine.

"Yes, you can come in and wait for me, but no I don't need your help." I said, sliding the chain off the door.

"I'll take what I can get," over the phone I heard him open and close the car door.

"Frist floor, last one on the left. Apartment 1D. Come one in." Hanging up the phone I made a mad dash to the bedroom.

I dashed to my bedroom to get dressed. Pulling on my underwear and bra I was glad I didn't decide to wash my hair, if Griffin had stuck to seven then maybe it would have been ok, but since he's 2 hours early there was no way it would have been dry enough to go out to dinner. Putting on my jeans was a little difficult since my skin was still damp, but once they were buttoned, I grabbed a one of the four shirts that were still laid out on the bed, the black button up dress shirt. I shrugged already committed to putting it on. Griffin was in the bedroom waiting for me, I didn't have time to stand around trying to make up my mind. I brushed my hair and left it down; I've had it in a tight bun all day, so it had a nice wave to it. I put on some eyeliner and shoved my feet into my shoes, calling it good.

When I got to the living room Griffin was breaking down boxes for me. *He really is the sweetest,* I thought with a smile. "Oh, you don't have to do that." I said. "I appreciate it though." Not wanting his help to go unnoticed.

I must have startled him, he jumped and put the box in his hands on top of the pile, with the rest of the broken-down boxes. He took his time looking me over. I was starting to feel self-conscious when he grinned at me and said, "I wanted to do something to help." I looked down at my feet and grinned, I knew I was blushing. "You look stunning," he said, extending his elbow to me, "are you ready to head out?" He asked.

I picked up my purse and looped the strap over my body before taking Griffins arm. He smelled so good; he always smells great. Like aged bourbon. I smiled up at him and nodded, he was some handsome, his blue eyes looked into mine like he could straight into my thoughts. I felt my heart flutter as we walked out of my apartment together. I locked the door and flipped the charm over. Griffin waiting patiently for me and even held the door open for me as we walked out of the building.

It was starting to get dark out. I always found dark parking lots to be eerie. Walking up to Griffins black dodge charger, in a dark parking lot, was even more ominous. I still haven't quite gotten over him stalking who he thought was a past crush. My footsteps faltered as I started to reconsider going to dinner with him. What if he was lying? What if he's some crazy psycho and this is just some sick game he likes to play before he gets bored and murders me? A car drove by the headlights pulling me out of my true crime rabbit hole. Griffin walked ahead of me and opened up the passenger door.

I smiled at him, and at how ridiculous I was being. Do murderous psychos open doors for people? I'm not sure, but I highly doubt Griffin is a murderer. "Thank you," I said before getting in.

The grin he gave me made me swoon. Why does he have to look at me like that? Like he wants to devour and cherish me. I bit the inside of my cheek to stop myself from grinning too much. I couldn't help but follow Griffin as he walked around the front of the car to get in the driver seat. He was so gorgeous, the way he moved was so precise and calculated. When he got in, he looked over at me and winked, "You ready?" he asked.

I nodded, "Where are we going?" I asked.

Griffin laughed, "You'll see." He said putting the car in reverse.

The drive wasn't too long, he took me into the city and pulled up to a nice restaurant. I immediately felt underdressed. Griffin parked the car and unbuckled his seatbelt. He asked if I was ready. I took my seatbelt off and still looking out the window I asked, "There isn't a dress code is there?"

Griffin laughed, "No. And even if they do, you look like a Goddess. I'll take you somewhere else if they kick us out." He punctuated his promise with a wink and got out, rushing around the car to open the passenger door for me. I smiled at him, he made me feel special. It was the same way at the door to the restaurant. The only door I opened around Griffin was the door to my apartment, but I'm sure that if he had a key, I wouldn't even open that one.

The dinner was fantastic, a steak dinner with a side salad and a baked potato, we spilt a slice of red velvet cake for dessert. There were a few times during the dinner, I caught Griffin looking at me in an odd way. Like a dark shadow had passed over his eyes. But then he would blink and flash me with that disarming smile of his. I would smile back and then the conversation would go on like nothing happened.

I was really starting to like Griffin; we seemed to have a lot in common, and our views seem to mostly line up. We disagreed on some things, like someday he wants kids, but I wasn't planning on having any. I wanted to travel but he seemed ok with staying put.

After dinner Griffin took me home. He took a different path than usual, which turned out to be much longer, but I wasn't about to complain. I looked over at Griffin, he was smiling out the windshield, the corners of his eyes squinted slightly as he smiled and laughed. He glanced over at me and winked. He was so handsome. I was so wrapped up in his presence that I didn't notice that we were almost to my apartment building.

"What are you doing Wednesday afternoon?" Griffin asked, taking a right turn, and then pulled into the parking lot.

I wasn't sure if I had anything that needed to be on that day, other than going to work. "I don't have anything planned. What do you have in mind?" I was almost giddy with excitement that he wanted to spend more time with me.

Griffin took a long breath in through his nose before answering, he told me about how his grandpa had left him an old house, and he wanted me to go with him to take care of a few things.

I was intrigued, old houses always fascinated me, they hold so much history. And who knows, maybe we might see a ghost. I had to bite my lip from laughing at that last thought, I nodded and agreed. "That sounds like it could be fun. Sure, I'll go with you."

"Good, I'll be here at 3 to get you." He said, taking his seatbelt off. He got out and walked me inside. He held my hand in the parking lot and got the door for me. He wrapped an arm around my shoulders and walked me down the hallway to my apartment and then waited for me to unlock my door before saying, "This was a great night. Thank you for letting me take you out tonight."

I smiled up at him, "No, thank you. I had a wonderful time."

Griffin's smile was so wide I thought he was about to burst, "I can't wait to see you again," he leaned down and kissed me on the lips. "Good night, Mel."

"Good night, Griffin." I said. I watched him walk back down the hallway, he looked back at me and waved before opening the door and disappearing into the parking lot.

Griffin (January 28)

I was making my cup of coffee lost in thought when I heard you creep up behind and me and say, "Mmm that smells good."

My hands clenched, and I turned around to look at you, everything in me wanted to start screaming at you, demanding you tell me what the fuck is going on with these guys on your phone. But our relationship was still in the fragile stage, and I didn't want to cause a fight this early. I took a deep breath and forced my shoulders to drop. I smiled at you and asked if you wanted some coffee. I took down a cup I thought would impress you. A coffee cup from a popular tv show, it was actually supposed to be a Christmas gift, but shit happens.

You looked it over in your hands and I defended myself. The playful banter between us helped calm my rage. Your laugh is actually what brought me back down. I loved making you laugh. You nervously told me that you were missing some clothes. "Yeah, you got undressed in a hurry," I told you; I wasn't about to admit to taking them. The panties for obvious reasons, the other things were to make the missing panties less obvious. I licked my lips, "I'll be on the lookout." My eyes started to roam over you. I swiped a bug off my neck and took a drink of my coffee. I wasn't ready to let you go but I knew I couldn't keep you here, as much as I hated to, I asked, "When do you have to leave?" I was already thinking of different ways to keep you here. I realized I was still taking you in and drug my gaze up to meet those beautiful green eyes, eyes that could make me do anything. A hungry smile spread across my face, "I'd love to take you for dinner tonight." Then I added, "If you're free." I didn't want to be too assertive.

The confused look you got just then was almost too much to handle. You looked so adorable. After a moment you nodded and agreed, much to my delight. You put your coffee on the counter and brushed some hair behind your ear, my eyes followed your fingers as they tucked your unruly hair behind your ear. You had gauges, not excessively big, barely noticeable in fact. There was rose tattoo in your ear. Your voice pulled me out of my thoughts, "Yeah, that sounds good." You had your phone out asking me for my number.

I froze, I forgot I had already given you, my number. Well, 'Ryan' gave you, my number. Did you even save it? If you do, I'll use my 'job' as an excuse. I did tell you I was a mechanic. But relief washed over me when it turned out that you didn't save my number. Then I was hurt, why didn't you save my number? Who else would you call if you had car problems? I looked up at you, you were taking a drink of coffee looking through your Facebook newsfeed. "Do you want me to give you a ride home?" I asked. I don't like it when your attention isn't on me.

You looked me over and then smiled up at me, melting me to the core, and said, "That would be great!" I had to stop myself from punching the air in victory. With your permission, I know where you live. Now when I show up it won't be so suspicious. Because you willingly lead me to your apartment. I almost giggled, I was so excited at how perfectly this was playing out for me.

When we finished our coffee, I encouraged you to drink a second cup and to join me for a morning smoke session in the other room. I rolled us a decent blunt, one that would keep you here alone with me for a little while longer. I got to know you a little better, what are your work hours? What do you like to do after work? What kind of things do you do on the weekends? Innocent questions, really. I'm not at all trying to see when you'd be out of the apartment. I kept you talking even after the blunt was spent.

I smiled at you, so relaxed, and unsuspecting. You were looking around at things I had hung up on the walls. I noticed how you were studying the picture I painted of...... no it's not her. I reminded myself. The witch in the painting has no resemblance to her.

I put my hand on your shoulder, causing you to jump. That turned me on, I'm not going to lie. I leered down at you, "Are you ready to head out, Mel?" I loved the way your name fell off my lips. You nodded at me, and I helped you out of the chair. I wanted to scoop you up and take you back to the bedroom. Instead, I led us out to my car.

When we got into my car I waited until you told me the address to your apartment building. I already knew where it was, instead I just admired the way your lips formed the words.

When we pulled up to your building you beat me to asking if we were still on for dinner. I almost laughed, "I'll be here at 8 to pick you up." I said. "Let me walk you in." About ready to turn the car off, when you told me, 'No.' I turned my head toward you, furious. Who the fuck do you think you are telling me 'No.' I blinked and swallowed my anger. Not catching what you said, either way it doesn't matter. I put my elbow on the steering wheel and turned to face you and forced a smile. "Forgive me," I started, "I'm not used to being told 'No'." I looked you over again, memorizing how you look in my passenger seat. "I'll see you at 8." I reiterated and watched you as you walked inside, turning to wave at me before disappearing behind the door.

I sighed and put the car in reverse. I was on my way to Levi's but thought better of it. I didn't want to run into Natasha after our phone call last night. Instead, I called him over the Bluetooth. He answered on the fifth ring. "Yeah?" he asked, it sounded like I just woke him up.

"Hey man, what's going on today?" I asked. I needed something to occupy my time until our dinner tonight.

"Recouping from last night. I saw that girl you left with, nice catch." There was shuffling around on his end. A door opening and closing.

I chuckled, "Yeah," then I brought the conversation away from you, "Hey, is your sister around?" I asked.

"Nah man, she never came back last night. She kept blowing my phone up asking for a ride and bitching about how no one wants to help her." I heard a faucet turn on and water splashing. "Coast is clear if you want to come over."

"Bet, I'm on my way." I said hanging up.

—⚈—

I pulled up to Levi's house, it was a small two bedroom with a basement. Levi lived here with his older sister who had no sense of self-worth or will to be her own person. Which is what made her such an easy target for assholes like me to use for a night and ditch her in the morning.

I knocked on the door twice before walking in. The place wasn't clean, but it wasn't trashed either. You can tell the person who made most of the mess was a female. Natasha left her shoes, jackets, and bags (purses, shopping, fast food, things like that) all over the house. She had a bad habit of leaving fast food bags and wrappers just laying around and Levi refuses to pick them up until he snaps, then he gathers it all up and throws it on her bed. Honestly, it's hilarious to witness. Levi won't touch fast food with a 10-foot pole, getting him to eat anything covered in grease is like pulling teeth, so the chances of him leaving McDonalds nugget containers on the end table in the living room are slim to none.

"Hey Levi!" I hollered. I heard him yell back from the basement.

Levi turned the basement into a second hang out spot for us, the first being my gaming room. He was already smoking on a joint when

I came down the stairs. "What's up man?" He asked, handing me the joint when I sat down across from him.

I took a hit before I bothered answering, "Just killing time," I shrugged, passing it back.

He got up and turned on his Xbox. We played whatever first-person shooter was in for a few hours before Alex called and asked if there was anything that would pay going on today. I called my dad up but the only thing he had for us wasn't going down until tomorrow morning.

"I'm bored of this," Levi said, putting his controller down. Then we heard the front door open and close, "Guess the hag is back." He muttered lighting a cigarette.

We heard footsteps walking to the basement door and Natasha walked halfway down, her shapely legs appeared first then she poked her head in, "Hey Griff, I thought that was your car," she said. Her red hair falling down around her shoulders. Her shirt was cut so low her breasts almost fell out, not that I was complaining. "You should come up here and hang out with me." She said, licking her top lip.

Levi groaned, "Natasha, how many times do I have to fucking tell you. If you can't pick up your shit you're not allowed down here."

Natasha rolled her eyes, "Whatever, so Griffin what do you say? I'd love to show you what you missed out on last night," she said, pulling down her shirt.

Levi picked up a beer can and threw it at her. "Take a hint bitch, you're not wanted."

She pulled back and sneered, "I wasn't talking to you, dipshit."

I scratched my eyebrow. "Maybe some other time." I smirked at her, "I'll hit you up another time." I winked at her, and she pouted and stalked back up the stairs.

I watched her perfect ass sway side to side as she went up the stairs. I made a move to stand up when Levi brought me back to reality, "So that girl from the bar last night, how did you end up taking her home?" He asked. Standing up to retrieve the beer can that he had pitched at his sister.

I sat back down and smiled, oh little Mel, do you have any idea how many eyes were on you last night? I shrugged, "Right time, right place. How slim were the pickings after your show?" I asked.

Levi laughed, "I think you took the best one." Shaking his head, he went on to say, "The small town shows never turn out well for after parties." He shrugged, "That wasn't a huge priority last night anyway, I just wanted to come home and crash when we were done playing."

I smirked; I knew the real reason. He was upset over you. My grin got even wider when I said, "We have a date tonight, actually. I'm taking her out for dinner."

Levi nodded, "That's cool man. What happened with the blonde she was with?"

I shrugged, "Not sure. That's how it was so easy to pick Melanie up. Her friend left with some guy, leaving her there alone." I laughed, "Her friend was the one who drove."

Levi's jaw dropped, "Nooo," he said then laughed, "What luck for you man." He said and we high fived.

I glanced over to the stairs, "You think she's in her room or what?" I asked.

Levi shook his head, "I don't understand what you and Alex see in her. I mean even if she wasn't my sister," He mimicked strangling someone in front of him, "you've seen how she lives! It's fucking exhausting trying to get her to do anything around here! And you try asking her to do something simple, it's all attitude all the time. She thinks she deserves more in life but refuses to do anything to better it."

"Yeah, well that's why she's still your problem and not someone else's by now." I said, standing up and walking over to the stairs. "I think I'm gonna head out." I said grabbing onto the banister. We both knew I wasn't really leaving.

A sour look crossed Levi's face, "What about your date tonight?"

I shrugged, "That's tonight. This is now." Levi shook his head in disgust, "I'll give you 10 minutes," I said climbing the stairs. At least I'm giving him the chance the clear the house, so he doesn't have to hear me fucking his sister.

Levi followed me up the stairs, "If things start to fall through with this Melanie chick I'm taking my shot." He said before leaving.

For a split second I was torn on what to do. Follow Levi and make him eat those words, or- "Hey Griffin, I knew you couldn't resist. Come here, baby." I looked over to the open door on my left, looking into Natasha's room.

I grinned and walked in, closing the door behind me.

—⚏—

Back at my place I was pacing back and forth in the gaming room. It was just now 5 o'clock and I was losing my mind. Eight couldn't get here fast enough, I was ready to see you now. I had already took a shower and cleaned my house to its core. It wasn't messed up to begin with, I just like to keep the place clean, but I always feel like I have to take a shower and go home and clean after I spend time in Natasha's room. That bitch is a slob disguised as a pin-up.

Grabbing my computer, I sat down and lit a cigarette. I took a drag and logged into your Facebook account. Scrolling through I didn't see any new updates. You haven't posted anything recently, and there weren't any new messages to read through either. I smoked the rest of the cigarette while flipping through your pictures. I couldn't get enough of you, Mel. You were perfect in every way.

My phone pinged, letting me know that I had a new message. My heart soared, I knew deep in my soul that it was you, I bet you were asking if we could meet up right now. I smirked, loving the fact that you seemed to be just as obsessed with me. I picked up my phone to see what you sent me.

But much to my disappointment it wasn't you. It was my dad. He needed me to go to the garage later tonight to do a job. I sighed and typed out a reply. I wasn't expecting to be busy tonight, but I still had plenty of time. I checked the time, still five. I couldn't wait 3 more hours to see you. I sent you a message asking if we could meet up sooner and waited five torturously long minutes. When no response came I tried again, this time waiting 10 minutes, but still got nothing. Figuring you were in the shower or something I decided to just go over there. There wasn't much else to do here, so I grabbed my keys and locked up. I sent you a messaging letting you know that I was on my way over.

A couple minutes later I was turning onto your street when I called you up. The way you answered the phone made my heart smile, "Hello?" you sounded so small and confused. I couldn't help but laugh.

"Hey!" I said back brightly, it was good to hear your voice. "Are we still on for tonight? You haven't answered any of my texts and I'm beginning to worry."

You cleared your throat before answering, telling me that you were in the shower and just now stepped out.

Imagining you stepping out of the shower, dripping wet, made me step on the gas. I can see your building now. I involuntarily let out a moan, "Well, I'm right outside your building." I said pulling into the parking lot. I parked my car next to yours, "need me to come and give you a hand?" The line was so quiet I thought you had hung up then I heard the dead bolt *click* as you unlocked the door. The corners on my mouth pulled up into a victorious grin. "Was that a yes?" I asked, already taking off my seatbelt. I'll barge in there right now if I have to.

There was a slight giggle, sending my heart into overdrive, "Yes, you can come in, but no I don't need your help." You said coyly.

I opened the door and got out, "I'll take what I can get." I said with a huge grin, closing the car door and heading toward the front door of the building.

"First floor, last one on the left. Apartment 1D, come on in." Then you hung up. I couldn't get to your door fast enough.

I walked into the building and followed your directions. The last door on the left, apartment 1D. There was a small wind chime hanging on the door. I ran a hand through my hair and straightened out my shirt. Taking a deep breath, I reached for the doorknob; then my hand started shaking. 'What the fuck is this?' I asked myself, looking at my hand that was shaking like a fucking chihuahua. I cleared my throat, was I nervous? I wanted to slam my head against the wall, but instead I opened the door and stepped in.

At first, I was shocked. How can someone live like this? But then I remembered that you said you had just moved. Boxes were piled everywhere. There were a few that had been broken down and stacked neatly by the door, a couple empty boxes that was piled on top of them. Stacks of boxes still unopened, opened boxes half unpacked. Boxes fucking everywhere.

The place really wasn't ready for company, but I've been in worse places. I just hope that once you're settled in, I'll never see this place in such disarray again. I pulled out the knife I kept with me and made my way over to the empty boxes. I needed something to keep myself busy until you emerged from wherever it is that you are hiding. I felt a chuckle starting to build, and the nervous feeling I previously had formed to something else, in its place was that sweet familiar feeling of a hunt.

I scanned the room, the door to the bathroom was open and there were two other doors that were closed. Behind one of them you were naked and defenseless, mine for the taking. All I need to do is open the right door. 'No, not yet.' I told myself, 'Make this one last. Enjoy her for a while, don't make the same mistakes as last time.' I shook my head and flipped the knife around in my hand. I took a step towards the closed door that had wet footprints leading towards it. I forced myself to turn around and go over to the empty boxes instead.

I picked one up and sat it down in front of me. As I stood over it, the box morphed into you, Mel. I smiled as I pictured you tied up, crying. I gently touched your cheek, it was smooth and rough, the image of you slipped away and the box was in front of me again. I put the knife to the box and slowly dug the tip of the blade into the tape, slicing it open. With each new box I pictured you tied up in different positions, fuck this was fun.

My demented fantasy went on until all the boxes you had emptied were flattened. That one was your chest; this one was your thigh. The last box which was sitting in front of me now was your beautiful neck. I gently brushed my fingers down the tape, thinking instead of your soft flesh. My mouth twitched into a smile when the blade severed the tape holding the box together. I slid the knife back into its place on my belt. Then I picked up the box and opened the flaps to flatten it.

"Oh, you don't have to do that." The words came suddenly from behind, I almost jumped. I turned my head to look behind me. My mouth dried up. I threw the last box on top of the pile and turned around to fully look at you. You had your hair down, your jeans looked like they were painted on you, the black silk shirt will be fun to unbutton later tonight, if I didn't have to cut the night short that is; but I'll make up for that later. "I appreciate it though." You said with a smile.

I had to remind myself that this is where I'm supposed to interact back, if I keep standing here staring at you, you'll get creeped out. I need to keep you unaware. I put on my most charming smile. "I wanted to do something to help." I said. Your cheeks turned pink, ok that was cute. "You look stunning," I extended my elbow like the fucking gentleman that I am, "Are you ready to head out?" You picked up a purse and threw it over your head, so it crossed your body. Looping your arm through mine like the lady you are, you smiled up at me, so trusting and innocent. Your excitement flowed through you and soaked into me, I smiled back, and we walked out the door.

When we were in the hallway, I watched your ass as you bent slightly to lock the door. Not bothering to look away when you turned around, you didn't notice though, you were busy flipping over a charm on the door hanging that had turned it's self around. That was curious, my new plaything must be obsessive compulsive. So many layers to you Mel, I'll have a lot of fun with you.

I opened the door to the outside for you, when you walked by I smelled your perfume; it was sweet and flowery, kind of like roses in the woods. I followed you over to my car, the way the wind blew through your hair and the streetlight glowing dimly in the setting sun made you seem vulnerable. I could feel the knife held tightly in my right hand, my pulse quickened, and your scream was cut off by my left hand gripping your mouth shut.

A car drove by; the head lights casting us in a sudden blinding light. I blinked a few times and looked around me. You were almost to the car, untouched. I looked down in my right hand, the metal gleaming up at me was the key to my car. I shook my head and walked ahead of you to open your car door. You said something to me, but I was fighting the urge to shove you in and lock the door before you changed your mind. I grinned down at you and waited patiently until you put on your seatbelt before gently closing the door.

The dinner flew by. I took you to a nice restaurant and we both ordered a steak, medium rare. The conversations flowed naturally, and I found that I was genuinely enjoying myself. A few times I couldn't help but to think of different ways I could hurt you. Pushing those thoughts down I cut into my steak. I really was enjoying myself with you, although the urges are strong, I wanted to make whatever this was last. I went way too fast with the last two, I didn't want to do that with you Mel. I can tell you're a fighter, oh the fun we'll have.

The waitress came by and cleared the table. She asked if we wanted dessert, so I ordered a slice of red velvet cake for us to share. I checked the time, I still had some time before I had to meet my dad at the garage and it took 30 minutes to get there, forty-five if I did the speed limit. I wasn't ready to let you go just yet though Mel. On the ride back to your building we took a detour, just so I could have a few extra minutes with you.

I wanted more time with you, so I asked, "What are you doing Wednesday afternoon?"

It was a shot in the dark, but when my grandpa died he left me his old property that I like to visit, sometimes I'll even take someone with me. The last person I took up there was Ellie, she didn't like going up there but then again Ellie was never happy with me, sure she had her flaws, but she was a dime all the same. Speaking of what happens to a coin when you tossed it into a well? Ellie will be able to tell you, she's been swimming in one since we broke up 2 weeks ago.

But you Mel, I think you'll really like it out there. It's not as beautiful as you but it's a breath-taking sight. I took the last turn to get to your building, I pulled up, and I put the car in park. You chewed your bottom lip before answering, "I don't have anything planned. What do you have in mind?" Part of me loved how willing you were, but another part of me was disgusted at how willing you were. Why are women always putting themselves in dangerous situations? When you looked over at me a lock of hair fell into your face. I brushed it back into place and studied you for a moment, my hand lingering on the back of your neck.

I inhaled your perfume and dropped my hand, "There's a house that my grandpa left me that I need to clean out. I was wondering if you wanted to go check it out with me." I watched you closely, your expression was curious, and I knew you would agree. I didn't even hear the words that came out of your mouth but there was a big smile on your lips, and you were nodding. "Good, I'll be here at 3 to get you." I took my seatbelt off and got out to walk you in.

Melanie (January 28 7:00)

I felt like I was floating. Griffin was amazing, he opened the doors for me, he pulled my chair out for me at the restaurant, even paid the bill and left a huge tip. He walked me to the door and kissed me goodnight. I was almost expecting him to come in and was a little let down when he turned and walked down the hallway without a look back.

I went to the bathroom to brush my hair and braid it, and to remove my make up. Then I went to the kitchen next to grab a bottle of water.

I kicked my shoes off and threw myself onto the sofa. I had my phone out about to call Kendra when a text came through. It was from Griffin,

'I had a really good time tonight. Next time I'll stay longer.'

I bit my lip and smiled, my thumbs flew over the phone screen typing out, 'You better, 😊 I really enjoyed myself, thank you for such a great night.'

'Is it Wednesday yet?'

'I wish'

Turning on the speaker, I set my Spotify to a Pop Evil playlist, then I put my phone on the charger I had in the living room and went to the kitchen. I unpacked a few kitchen boxes while I let the music play. The music cuts in and out whenever I get a notification and right now it sounded like I was listening to a scratched cd. I checked my phone. There were six messages.

The first one was from Kendra 'call me when you get home' so I tried calling her, it rang and rang and went to voicemail. I'll try again later.

The other five were from Griffin 'We don't have to wait until then to see each other'

'I know tomorrow is Sunday but I'm free all day.'

'I'm not one of those church goers.'

'I'll go to church for you though.'

'But you'll have to ask nicely.'

I raised an eyebrow, 'no worries I'm not religious.'

Not sure what to make of his habit of blowing up my phone, I called my sister again. It rang a few times and went to voicemail. This is nothing new for Kendra, she's a busy lady. I made a mental note to call her again and went to change into pajamas.

I unpacked a few more boxes in the living room before turning off the speaker and turning on the tv. It was 9:00, I wanted to sit and watch some mindless tv before I went to bed. I picked up the remote and my phone started ringing. Not looking at the screen, I picked it up, "Hey! I was wondering if I'd get to talk to you tonight."

My whole body went rigid when a male voice spoke on the other end. "Who do you want to talk to Mel?" whoever he was, he sounded angry.

I pulled the phone away from my ear and looked at the name, Griffin. I relaxed a little, the wave of panic withdrew some, but I still felt the tingling sensation of a growing panic attack. "I've been trying to call my sister. I was expecting her to call me back." I went to Netflix to see if I could find anything to watch.

Griffin cleared his throat, "I didn't know you have a sister." His tone was now flat. "What are you doing?"

"Nothing really, just trying to find something to watch." I heard him take a deep breath and exhale. I pictured him sitting in one of his gaming chairs smoking. "What are you doing?"

"I'm helping my dad with something. I got a way for a quick smoke break and thought I'd give you a call."

I glanced at the time. It was pretty late: what would his dad need help with at this hour? Then the thought occurred to me that this is why he seemed so eager to rush our date. If he was busy tonight why didn't he just reschedule? I decided to pry. "What are you guys up to?"

He laughed, "Aren't you a curious little one? I'll tell you what, next time he needs help I'll swing by and grab you first."

My phone started beeping, I pulled my phone away and looked at the screen. Kendra was trying to call me, "Hey my sister is calling me, do you mind if I call you back?"

"What? No, we just started talking." He said in a flat tone. I laughed not really sure what to say, "Mel, I walked away from my father to call you," my phone beeped letting me know that Kendra was still trying to call me, "Come on, talk to me while I finish my cigarette." He sounded angry and annoyed.

I looked at my screen, the way Griffin is acting is a real turn off at the moment. Right now, I was tempted to hang up and talk to my sister. "Griffin-"

Over the phone I heard a loud crash and yelling, Griffin started laughing, cutting off what I was about to say he said to me "Oh man what a fucking idiot. You should really come with me next time Mel. So did you ever find anything to watch?"

I sighed when I heard the beep-beep letting me know Kendra's incoming call had gone to voicemail. "No, nothing looks good."

"What are you in the mood for?" He asked in a playful tone.

For one I was in the mood to talk to my sister, but that's not happening. And two if he really expected to be flirty/playful after that shitty interaction we just had he is delusional. I pulled my legs up and sat crossed legged. "I don't know, I'm getting kind of tired, so I think I'll go to bed soon." I said picking at a frayed string on the edge of my pajama pants.

Griffin was saying something on the other end, but I was zoned out on the tv screen displaying different choices for a horror movie, no longer in the mood to talk to him. "Hey Mel, are you still there?"

"Huh? oh yeah, I'm here." I turned the tv off.

"You sound distracted. What are you doing?"

I stood up and made my way to the bedroom. "Getting ready for bed."

"Oh? I thought you were watching tv?"

Through a yawn I said, "I gave up. Nothing sounded good."

"Alright. I'll let you go. Sleep well Mel, I'll talk to you later."

"Have a good night Griffin." With that I hung up. Sighing when I see the clothes that were on the bed still, I threw them off and into a pile near the closet. The whole time I was over thinking all the red flags Griffin was throwing up. He has great qualities too. I started thinking of all the red flags that I could give and decided to give Griffin the benefit of doubt. I'll give him a few more days to further feel him out, I don't have to commit to this right this second.

'Clean bedroom' moved to the top of my mental To Do list, I crawled into bed and just lied for a few minutes, my mind was racing, and I couldn't stop thinking about the moments that lead up to today.

I closed my eyes and tossed and turned until I found a comfortable position.

But I was soon staring at the wall over thinking things, I turned over and closed my eyes. But a few moments later when my eyes popped opened again I gave up on a good night's sleep and sat up. The book I was reading was still on the night stand, so I sat up and turned on my lamp, reached over for the book and read until my eyelids finally grew heavy enough to allow me to fall asleep.

Griffin (January 28 7:00)

I walked you back inside and kissed you one last time before I left, I'm not sure if I'll ever get used to kissing you. I didn't want to stop, feeling you against me is what I've been craving and now that I finally have it, I have to leave. I ripped myself away from you and turned to leave, not looking back. If I turned around to look at you, I knew I would just run back to you and scoop you up. So, without glancing back, I went to my car and called Alex. I would have called Levi too but he's busy with his band. The phone rang once before he picked up. "Need some money?" I asked him while texting you at the same time. I couldn't get enough of you. Seeing your name appear on my phone screen when you messaged me back was surreal.

I was typing out a reply to when Alex's voice over the Bluetooth brought me out of it. "Yeah I could use some quick cash, what's up?" He asked.

It was a 50/50 shot, he could be busy with his other side hustles but today must have been a slow one for him. So, I swung by his place to pick him up before heading over to the garage.

Dad gave us an address to go to, we didn't get many details. Just that everything needs to be cleared out. He also said that there were a few things he needed to do but he'll meet us there once it's done. I took down the address and Alex and I went to go get some easy money. These burn jobs don't come all the time, so when they do you gotta jump on it, in the span of 10 years I've only been recruited for a burn job three times.

It was dark by the time we got to the house, but the electricity was on for one more day, so the street light was on, illuminating the run-down two-story brick house. Crumbling chimney, porch falling apart, some windows where boarded up, others were completely shattered. "Fuck this place is a dump," Alex said stepping out of the car.

It was even worse when we got inside. The smell hit us first, when I pushed opened the door the smell of rot wafted over me. I took a few steps back and covered my mouth. From here we could see piles of garbage. That was the only way I could think to describe it. The items in the piles were normal everyday things, shoes, cups, shirts, and toys. But when they are all thrown together like this, covered in what the fuck ever that is, it all becomes trash. I don't want to think about it.

I shook my head and started back to my car. "Where you going?" Alex shouted behind me, jogging to catch up. "Don't think you're about to just ditch me here to do all the dirty work!"

I rolled my eyes, "Dude relax, I am just going to get something to cover my face. I'm not about to walk in there and have that smell rape my senses." When I got to the car I opened the trunk and shuffled around in the bag I kept in here for occasions like this. Disposable coveralls, shoe covers, some face masks, gloves. Basic things you'll need for a cleanup. I just hoped it would be enough to last until dad showed up. "Come on," I said handing him some things to put on, "don't act like this is your first time."

Alex started unfolding the coveralls and stepped into it, "Yeah, but none have been this fucked before." He said zipping up the front. "I feel like we just stepped into an episode of hoarders."

I nodded, "Yeah this one is…." I shook my head, "I've never had to deal with one like this." I said pulling on my own set of coveralls. "Go start a fire over there," I said nodding to the side yard that already had a decent clearing for a small bonfire. I gathered up some supplies that we would need inside, bags, gloves. Some bug spray, just in case. I don't do well around cockroaches, just the thought is enough makes me, I put a hand on my stomach and hunched over a bit trying not to heave. I took a few deep breaths and stood up when Alex came back over. He helped me haul everything to the porch for easier access. The smell from the open door was rancid. The first thing on my list was to open the windows when we got to them.

We shared a look and walked back to the car to get ready for the job ahead of us. No way we going in there without something covering our clothes.

"I thought they got rid of the bodies." Alex said. Putting on two pairs of shoe covers.

I shrugged. "They usually do. We're probably smelling something else."

Alex paused, "Fuck man, why do you have to say that. Is it too late to back out? These jobs are typically easy."

I laughed, "we only think that because we've only worked the easy ones." I pulled a face mask over my head and bent over the trunk to rummage around in the bag. Working in the garage I've heard some fucked up stories from the other guys. When I found what I was looking for I stood up and opened the small bottle and put a few drops of peppermint oil on my finger to dab on the inside of the mask. I closed and tossed the bottle to Alex. "This will help." I said.

Alex did the same as I did and then I tossed the bottle back in the bag and closed the trunk and headed towards the house. We propped the front door open, and Alex went to the right, and I went to the left so we could open the windows to air out the room. I tried not to look too hard at the random shit around me, but when Alex whispered, "Who the fuck would let kids live like this." I looked down at the floor. At the toy blocks covered in a dried yellow substance. I fought the urge to vomit.

I shook my head and looked up at the water damaged ceiling. Dad only told us the basics; this was a foster home that was only in it for the for money, kids would come here and some never left that my dad's employer caught wind of. I don't know the guy's name, I only heard him called "The Boss" I know, original I almost rolled my eyes. He sent his guys to come in and do the extermination; get rid of the 'rats'.

The kids are being taken care of, the ones who needed it are being hospitalized, they are all in therapy. For those kids who could go back to their parents did, but there were a few whose parents couldn't be located. Now that the bodies have been taken care of, it's now our job to go in and clean up. No big fires, just a small, controlled fire. So, we can't just burn the house down and be done with it. That would draw too much unwanted attention.

We set off to work. Not bothering to look through the contents of the house to see if there was anything worth saving. Instead, anything we came into contact with immediately went into a bag to be hulled outside to burn in the small brush fire that we started. We had just got the living room mostly cleared when two vehicles pulled up. My shoulders slumped; I was hoping he wouldn't show up so soon but looking around it only makes sense that he would come to oversee that this job got done quickly. I finished shoving the trash bag full and tied it shut aggressively. Standing up I turned to face Alex, "Hey, if you're done with that I'll take it outside and see what's up."

Alex looked out the window and sighed, "Yeah, I'm almost done." He said, filling his bag up some more. "There goes the party." He said sitting the bag down on the floor beside me. I only nodded before picking the bags up and walking outside.

Dad was standing behind the black SUV, the back hatch was open, and he and a couple of other guys were pulling on protective coveralls. I nodded over at them and continued on my way to burn the bags, one at a time so the flames don't get too big. I was watching the flames dance over one bag when footsteps approached me, and a shadow crawled across the grass. "How much have you got done?" dad's gruff voice was grating.

It took all I had not to roll my eyes or show any signs of annoyance. "Most of the front room is cleared out." I said, waiting until the bag was halfway burned before throwing the other one on top of it.

Dad nodded and walked inside. I watched him as he climbed the steps and disappeared through the door, covering his mouth before he went in. I looked over at the SUV, there were three other guys all suited up at this point walking towards the house carrying boxes of trash bags. I sighed and turned back to the fire; this was going to be a long night.

—⟡—

With the extra hands we had the top floors cleared out in a fraction of the time if it were just Alex and I alone. I decided that since we only had the basement left to do, and that was almost cleared out too, I could sneak away and smoke a cigarette, maybe get in a quick phone call.

The phone rang a few times and then you answered, cheerfully saying that you wondered if you were going to get to talk to me tonight. But we've already talked so you must have been expecting someone else. My grip on my phone tightened, I took a drag off my cigarette and tried to sound casual as I asked who you wanted to talk to you. But it came out as a snarl, I cleared my throat and took a breath.

The line was quite on the other end but a heartbeat later you said, "I've been trying to call my sister. I was expecting her to call me back."

I froze. A sister? And apparently you two stay connected. I started to panic a little. "I didn't know you have a sister." I wonder how close you are to her. "What are you doing?" I asked, walking towards the fire to throw another bag in the flames, the burning process is what's taking the longest.

You told me you were looking for something to watch. Something in the fire popped, making me jump. Over the phone you asked me what I was doing.

I smiled and told you that I was helping my dad with something, but I was on a smoke break and wanted to call you really quick. I couldn't stop the smile from spreading across my face as you asked what we were doing. "Aren't you a curious little one?" I teased, then I offered to get you next time we have a cleanup job to do. I didn't expect you to agree, but if I didn't offer it would lead to more questions and nothing good comes from asking questions.

Your phone beeped. I narrowed my eyes and glared into the fire. You were getting another call, but I wasn't ready to hang up with you. Not yet. "Hey, my sister is calling me, do you mind if I call you back?"

Rage pulsed through me, I clenched my jaw, "What? No, we just started talking." I lifted my cigarette up, you nervously laughed on the other end, but I wasn't joking. "Mel, I walked away from my father to call you," it was taking a lot for me not to yell at you. You were being really disrespectful right now. "Come on, talk to me while I finish my cigarette." I said flicking the ashes off.

"Griffin," The way you said my name, you almost sounded angry with me. My lips curled up into a grin. At the same moment Alex was walking out the door but wasn't paying attention to where he was at and ended up falling down the three steps.

I lost it, seeing him scrambling to stand up, and throwing blankets he had in his arms to the ground was priceless. "Fuck off Griffin!" He yelled at me. Kicking the blankets off to the side and disappearing back through the front door.

"Oh man, what a fucking idiot. You're definitely coming with me next time Mel." I said to you. You would be much better company than anyone else here. I knew we would work well as a team. "So, did you ever find anything to watch?" I asked.

You took a deep breath before answering me. I was making you mad; it was cute how you weren't trying to hide it. "No, nothing looks good."

I took the last hit off my cigarette and flicked it into the fire. "What are you in the mood for?"

"I don't know, I'm getting kind of tired, so I think I'll go to bed soon." Your tone was snippy. I liked it.

"I wish I could join you; we still have a lot to do here." I was going to say something else, but I noticed how the line was oddly quiet. Smirking I let the silence swell, trying to make out any noises through the phone, but it was dead. "Hey Mel, are you still there?" I asked, wondering if you had hung up.

"Huh? Oh yeah, I'm still here."

"You sound distracted. What are you doing?" I asked, picking up a bag and throwing it into the fire.

"Getting ready for bed." You said. That was strange, well you already said you were going to bed, but the way you're talking to me is strange. I asked you what happened to watching tv. "I gave up. Nothing sounded good."

I nodded my head, admitting defeat and gave up on this phone call as well, you weren't in the mood to talk to me and at this point I was just pushing you away. "Alright. I'll let you go. Sleep well Mel, I'll talk to you later."

"Have a good night Griffin." You said and quickly hung up. That could have gone a lot smoother.

It was good to hear Mel's voice. It still bothered me that you never mentioned having a sister, I tried not to obsess over what else you haven't told me, but the thought started to eat me alive. Fighting the urge to call you back I shoved my phone in my pocket in went back inside. Putting on a fresh apron and gloves at the door I picked up two boxes of trash bags and went back in the house.

Alex was walking out with a bag that looked like it was about to burst, "Few more bags to burn then we'll be ready to wipe everything down." Sweat was pouring down his face, we've been at this for hours, I told Dad this cleanup was too much, and we should just burn the place down, but he wasn't having it. Said it would draw too much attention. "I'm over this." He said, I watched him walk out the door and towards the fire.

I walked down the stairs to the basement. Dad was shoving towels in a bag, "Griffin. About time you showed back up."

"I stepped out for a smoke." I picked up some towels and started soaking up a puddle. Things between Dad and I have always been… tense.

"Faster we get this done, faster we go home." He tied the bag shut and made his way to the stairs. "No more smoke breaks." He said shoving past me.

—◆—

It was 3 on Sunday morning when we finally got the place clean.

Alex and I were currently sitting at my place smoking a joint. "After 2 scrubs I still feel like I need a shower." I said, in fact I know I still needed a shower. I still had shit under my fingernails.

Taking the joint from me, he said "I think I got a chemical burn from all that bleach." There was a rash on his hand. "Hey so what's the story with that bitch from the other night?"

I froze, not liking where this is going. "Why do you ask?'

Alex shrugged, "She was pretty hot, and I want to know why you won't share."

I knew this was coming, "She's nothing special." I lied. "She went a bar that Levi and his band were playing at the other night with a friend who ended up ditching her there. That's how she ended up with me that night."

"That's lucky. Is she still around?"

Taking the joint from him, I answered, "Yeah she's around. Seems to be pretty trusting, she agreed to meet up again on Wednesday." That made us both laugh.

"Oh man, I love the naive ones. Sometimes I run out of convincing things to say and when you can charm them the whole thing goes smoother." I had to agree, but even with the trusting ones you have to be careful. Mel already showed that she can fight. "You said she had a friend? Think there's a chance you can get her here?"

I thought for a moment and handed him back the joint. "Maybe." I got my laptop out and opened the tab that had your Facebook logged in. Scrolling through your friends list I found the cunt who ditched you at the bar. "Found her. Look up Hillary Summers."

Alex took no time finding people online, in 2 minutes he got ahold of her Snapchat and was able to use the friend locater to discover that she was at a bar 19 minutes away. "Hey Griff, you busy tonight?" He was smiling at his phone scrolling through Hillary's' Facebook pictures.

I laughed. "I need to wash off one more time, that cleanup was brutal. I still have blood under my nails."

"You have a point. I could use a nap." He stood up to leave. "What about tomorrow?"

I looked at the background of my phone; it was you laughing at the bar. You looked so happy sitting there across from me, it made me mad thinking of how easily your friend ditched you. I nodded my head, "Yeah. Yeah I can make time tomorrow."

Alex said he'll be here around nine in the morning. I had a good feeling about this. Getting some of these urges out on someone else will help our relationship last longer. And besides, you don't need a friend like Hillary, who lets her friends lift up her skirt at bars to take a picture for some likes on Facebook. You deserve better than that Mel. I'm doing this for you, for us.

When I got to bed I was pleased to find that everything still had your scent on it. My pillow smelled like your hair. I breathed in deeply through my nose and fell asleep pretending that you were lying next to me.

MELANIE (January 29)

Sunday morning was uneventful. I got my bedroom unpacked and organized. That took all morning and part of the afternoon. I messaged Griffin good morning, but he hasn't replied yet. I also sent Hillary a message being as nice as I could manage, 'Hey I hope you had a good time Friday. I think I left my jacket in your car. Could you make sure to bring it to work Monday?' That was around eight this morning, it's now 1 and still nothing.

I opened up Facebook messenger and seen that Hillary was online. Is she ignoring my text message? I sent her a quick message, 'Hey did you get my text?' I noted how she read the message but never responded. I was tempted to send another one, but something told me that one would be left on read as well. I don't understand what is happening here. She ditched me, not the way around. I felt myself starting to get angry.

Taking a deep breath to center myself I got on Facebook to scroll through my timeline, looking for some funny meme's to cheer me up. I was scrolling for a moment when I came across some posts from Hillary, she posted some recent pictures of her and some friends at a coffeehouse earlier this morning, and then a selfie of her and I'm willing to bet that was the guy she left with at the bar. The nosey part of me decided to go to her Facebook page. Her most recent post was from a few minutes ago. Something about how some people just can't take a hint. I tried not to read too much into it and went to put down my phone.

Then a message from Griffin came through. 'Good afternoon. Sorry for the late reply, I've been wrapped up.' I felt myself smiling. 'I've been thinking about you.'

'What have you been doing?' Maybe he was still helping his dad?

'Helping my friend out. He's been down lately, and I wanted to make sure he was ok.'

'That was really kind of you' It was a kind thing to do. A lot of people won't think twice about anyone else. Hillary was a good example of that. 'More people should be like you.'

I went to the living room, and a shadow in the window made me pause. For a moment it looked like someone was looking in my window. I jumped when I felt my phone vibrate in my hand. It was a message from Griffin. 'What are you doing?' he asked. I looked back up at the window, but the shadow was gone. I walked up to the window and looked outside. A few trees, some bushes. Plenty of places for someone to hide. My heartbeat sped up, and I double checked the locks. They weren't locked properly; sure, the lock was engaged but the window was installed crooked causing the lock and latch to not line up correctly. With some effort I was able to lock one side, but I wasn't able to get the other side to line up.

I closed the curtains and sat down on the sofa, not able to shake the feeling of being watched. My phone went off again. 'I wish I could see you.'

'We'll see each other soon.' I was really starting to like Griffin. Sure, he was a little rough at times but he's also really sweet. 'I'm about to watch a movie.'

'Did you ever get ahold of your friend from the bar?' He asked.

I rolled my eyes and typed out my response. 'No. I think she's ignoring me.' I was getting annoyed. Not at anything that Griffin did but at Hillary. I didn't do anything for her to be acting this way. 'I just want to move on from that.'

'As you should. You deserve better friends in your life.' Not long after he asked, 'What are you watching?' I put on Evil Dead Rise and told him just that. 'I've never seen that one. Is it scary?'

'I'm hoping.' I replied. I went on a whim and sent 'If I get too scared will you come hold me?'

'I'll do more than that 😊' I sat my phone and went to the kitchen, smiling like an idiot the entire way. I sat back down with a bowl of chips and wine cooler. My phone vibrated. I had three messages from Griffin.

'I love a good scary movie'

'I can come over now if you want some company.'

'Come on please say yes. I'll bring something special for us.'

I scrunched up my nose, what was *something special?* I thought, 'What are you bringing?' I asked.

'If I told you it wouldn't be a surprise.' Then he added, 'aren't you curious?'

It's true I was. I was starting to realize that being slightly pushy is part of his charm. I could see his wolfish grin. 'Ok fine. But only if you bring some more snacks with you.' I started the movie over and put it on pause. 'How long until you get here?' I asked.

'As fast as I can baby.' I bit my lip and pressed pause on the movie, it was only 4 minutes in. I walked to the bathroom to check my appearance; I quickly brushed my hair and threw on some eye liner and called it good. I went and sat back on the sofa. I was almost disappointed when I checked my phone and seen that Griffin hadn't messaged me during the time that I was in the bathroom. I scrolled through Facebook to kill some time. Hillary had made another post about getting a new job. I went to her page and unfriended her. There was a knock on the door making me jump. Surly that wasn't Griffin, it's only been 5 minutes. Looking through the peep hole, I seen that it was in fact Griffin.

I opened the door. "How did you get here so fast?" I asked.

He laughed and walked past me. Taking his shoes off he said, "I was in the neighborhood." He walked over to the coffee table and sat down a bag of Doritos, and I took note of the six pack of tall beers that was already missing 2. He laughed and opened one up. "Yeah sorry about that, I used one to get us this," He pulled out a blunt the size of my thumb. Griffin walked up and handed it to me, "Something special, for us." For a moment I thought he was going to kiss me, but then he asked, "Hey can I uh, put my beer in your fridge?" He pointed a thumb over his shoulder and shifted on his feet.

"Of course. I'll do that, you go sit down." I went over and picked the 3-remaining beers off the coffee table, wondering if all he had to drink was really just one beer.

While I was bent over, I felt Griffin walk up behind me. As he walked around I swore he ran his hand across my back. I stood up and we made eye contact as he sat down. His eyes were set on me, he tilted his head back and with a panty melting smirk he said, "you're sweet." I smiled and made my way to the kitchen. I could feel his eyes on me the whole time. "You've gotten a lot done around here, Mel. It looks really good." I thanked him and got another wine cooler before I sat down. Griffin scooted closer to me and threw an arm on the back of the sofa. "Do you need any help around here?" he asked while taking a lock of my hair and started twirling it around his finger.

I smiled at him. "I've got it covered but thank you." I leaned forward, feeling my hair pull out his grip, so I could get the remote. When I sat back it felt like Griffin had scooted closer to me. I looked over at him, yeah he was definitely closer. "You ready?" I asked.

He was so close. I could feel his breath on my cheek. Griffin glanced down to my mouth and back up. He licked his lips and leaned back just as I leaned in. Smiling he looked at the tv, "Let's do this," he said taking a long drink of beer.

Not long into the movie I was halfway through my second wine cooler. Griffin brought out my nervous side. I was giggly and a little clumsy around him so I was drinking faster than I would if I were by myself.

I felt Griffin run his hand through my hair. "You have gorgeous hair," he said wrapping it around his hand a few times. "It's so long and thick," he leaned in and pulled gently on my hair to tilt my head back. He brushed his lips along my jaw. "You smell so good," he mumbled into the crook of my neck, his words tickling my flesh. His hand was rubbing between my thighs, he easily moved my pajama shorts to the side and was rubbing the outside of my underwear. "I want you." His tone was sharp and firm. The authority in his voice made me pause. "Now." He said, and he took me by the side of my thighs and pulled me roughly to him. I fell onto my back, and then he was on top of me. His mouth covered mine, it all happened so fast I felt like the room was spinning.

Griffin wasted no time, he was already pushing my legs to the side and rubbing himself against me. "Wait, what about a condom?" I asked. Pushing myself up and scooting away from him.

With one hand, he pushed me on my back and kissed me gently on the lips, "Shhhh" he whispered, then he was inside me. The hand he pushed me down with slid up and wrapped around my throat. "Fuck," he groaned, pushing himself in harder. Griffin sat up just long enough to wrap an arm around me and to grab me by the shoulder.

The way I was laying on the sofa wasn't all that comfortable, and each time I tried to push Griffin off just enough to shift into a different position, he would tighten his grip, and his thrusts would get more aggressive. "Ow, not so rough. Griffin that hurts." I put my hand on his shoulder to push him back, but he swatted my hand off, grabbing both my wrists in just one hand he had my arms pinned above my head. I was on the verge of panic, my body started to shake, I swallowed the lump in my throat, "Griffin, let me up." Thankfully my fear didn't come out with my words.

With my hands still above my head he licked my neck and bit my ear lobe. Breathing in through his nose he then let go of my wrists. He pulled out of me slowly, and goddamn that felt so good. Brushing some hair out of my face he gently pushed back inside. I arched my back slightly, "I'm sorry Mel." Griffin breathed into my ear, he continued pushing inside me, gently this time. "Want me to stop?" I shook my head no, Griffin bent down and took my nipple in his mouth and moaned, "God you're so fucking sweet. I want to hear you say it." He said rubbing between my legs with his thumb. "Say you don't want me to stop Mel."

I wrapped my legs around Griffin's waist, "Don't stop," I moaned.

Grinning down at me Griffin pushed my hips down and started to move faster, "That's right, I want you to cum for me baby," his breathing turned into grunts, he took my right leg and threw it over his shoulder allowing him deeper purchase. "Say it again." He demanded.

I gritted my teeth and pushed back. The way Griffin threw himself into me was teetering more towards pain than pleasure. I got my leg off his shoulder and wrapped both of my legs around his waist, it was a little better but not by much. Clinging onto him, my nails dug into the flesh on his shoulders. Now that I wasn't being rammed into the sofa anymore, I could enjoy this moment a little easier. Then my body tensed.

"That's it, don't hold back baby," I could feel his chest rumble as he spoke, the vibrations going all the way down my stomach.

"Fuck!" moving my hips faster I felt the rush as I took him all the way in me.

Griffin's body tensed as he held onto my hips and pulled me closer to him. I didn't know if he could go any further in me. "Jesus Crist Mel."

106

After a few quick deep thrusts Griffin shuddered, he leaned forward and kissed me. Still inside me, he held himself over top of me. A sudden loud noise from the tv grabbed both of our attention laughing he said, "We missed our movie." Sliding out of me he sat up.

I laid there for a moment, my thighs screaming at me. "That's ok," I said sitting up.

We sat there for a moment, watching the last bit of the movie, naked. Griffin took a lock of my hair and twirled it around a finger, "Do you mind if I use your bathroom."

I nodded and got up to show him the way. When I walked back to the living room I kicked my clothes into a pile and got a dish towel from the kitchen to clean up the mess on the couch cushions.

Griffin snuck behind me. I jumped out of my skin when I felt him wrap his arms around me from behind. "You have some good pussy," he said kissing my neck. He moved around me to gather his clothes and started pulling them on. After he got his pants zipped he sat back down shirtless. "Ready to smoke?" He asked examining me standing naked in front of him.

"Let me clean up." I went to my bedroom to get some clean clothes. The whole way there my thighs ached like I ran a mile. I got some fresh clothes and went to the bathroom to clean up.

When I got back to the living room Griffin (still shirtless) was lighting the blunt. "We should get together again to rewatch this movie, Evil Dead is one of my favorite franchises." He said blowing out a puff of smoke.

"I'd like that," I said sitting down next to him. We ate the Doritos Griffin brought over, and we got to know each other a little better, we had similar tastes in movies, he wasn't much for reading, but we shared some favorite bands, and we both hate fish. I tried sitting crossed legged a few times, but my legs were hurting too much, the weed took the edge off, but I was still growing uncomfortable.

Griffin's phone dinged when he looked at the text; he got annoyed. "Fuck, I'm going to have to go. Alex can't seem to get his shit together." He looked at me, "Speaking of crappy friends; how are you going to handle tomorrow?"

It took me a moment to figure what he was referring to. "Oh, with Hillary? I don't have to worry about that, turns out she got a new job." I took a chip out of the bag, "I'm mad that my jacket was still in her car, and I'll never see it again."

Griffin chuckled "I can get you a new one if you want." He was looking at his phone but looked up at me when he was done texting.

This guy was so thoughtful, "I appreciate it but that's not necessary."

Pretty soon Griffin was putting his shirt back on and we said our goodbyes as he was walking out the door. I was picking up after the movie, throwing away the trash and cleaning up the cushions before I forgot. I gathered up my clothes to throw them in the washer and noticed that my underwear wasn't in the bundle. I went back to the living room, but I couldn't find it. Maybe Griffin had picked them up on accident? I shook my head, that didn't make sense, I didn't see him put anything in his pockets. I didn't think Griffin was the type of guy that would steal a pair of women's underwear. I shook my head, not wanting to put that thought in my head. Griffin was a good guy, he wasn't a creep who went around doing things like that, Griffin held himself to a higher standard; right?

Letting the mystery of the missing panties go I went to bed. I was excited for tomorrow knowing that I won't have to deal with the leftover awkwardness from Friday. I wasn't looking forward to working with Hillary after she ghosted me like Casper. I closed my eyes and drifted off to a sleep full of unsettling dreams and woke up exhausted the next morning.

GRIFFIN (January 29)

I woke up to my phone pinging. It was a good morning text from you. I smiled at my phone and sat up. After going to replying to your text I sent Alex a message telling him to get a hold of me when he's ready. Usually, we would include Levi in on these things but he's busy with his band.

I pulled on some clean clothes and went to start a pot of coffee. When I had a cup poured I sat down with my laptop and got to work tracking Hillary down. With the help of social media, I found out that she was still home getting ready for a day out with friends. And the group's first stop was the coffeehouse, that sells breakfast sandwiches. Which is great, I'm starving.

I was halfway through my third cup when Alex finally sent me a message telling me he was ready.

—✏—

When I pulled up Alex strutted out of his girlfriend's house. "Hey man," he said opening the door and getting in. "Too bad it's just us. I saw she had two friends tagged in that post."

I shrugged, "That won't be a problem. It's easy to turn a group on each other." I drove us to the coffeehouse and parked across the street.

Alex was scrolling on his phone, "It doesn't look like they've checked in yet. We might have to wait."

I turned the car off and got my phone out. Clicking on the names that Hillary tagged in her post earlier. 'Amy' was posting constant updates on her getting ready. Her hair was straightened and pinned up into a ponytail, she had done a full face of makeup and looked like she got her outfit off Pinterest. 'Ashely' on the other hand had her profile set to private.

"Well at least we know what 2 of them look like." I said. "I'm going to wait inside, I'm hungry." I said getting out.

"Right behind you, I need some coffee." Alex said stepping out and closing the door behind him.

I locked the car, and we went inside the coffeehouse. Just two guys having breakfast and using the cafés Wi-Fi. We waited for 20 minutes. I wasn't sure how slowly I could eat my sandwich before it got gross and cold, Alex had already gone up for another cup and a muffin. When he sat back he had a grin and a folded slip of paper.

I shook my head and laughed, "I swear, how do you do that?" I asked unfolding the paper and looking at the phone number with a scribbled name and heart on it.

"I'm just that good," Alex said brushing off his shoulder, "and the accent helps." He added with a laugh. From his chair he could see the front of the café. He sat up in his chair and nodded at the group of obnoxious females that walked in. "There they are." He said.

I turned around and looked at the three women, "I guess it's time to see just how good you are." I said turning back to Alex.

He scoffed, "Just watch." He said. The one who I recognized as 'Amy' looked over at the table. Alex nodded and winked at her. She smirked back and tapped Hillary on the shoulder saying something that got the other one's attention. I'm assuming that one was Ashley. She had mousey blonde hair that was cut short, it hung down to her jaw. They were all tall, Ashley was pretty thin, Amy was average, and Hillary had some weight on her. Ashely looked over at us and turned her nose up. But the other two kept looking over and getting all excited. Alex smirked and turned to face me. "The small one might be a problem." He said referring to Ashely.

When they walked by, Hillary was the one who stopped at our table and started talking to us. "Hey, I love your tattoos." she said, running her fingers across my arm.

I gritted my teeth, picturing myself yanking on her hair to slam her head into the table. I looked up at her and put on my most charming smile, "Thanks," I shifted in my seat to get a better look at the group. "What are you lovely ladies up today?" I asked.

Amy pulled at her ponytail, "Oh nothing really, just hanging out and catching up."

Alex looked her up and down, "You look like you're up to no good," he said, "would you like to join us?"

Amy sat her cup down on the table, she opened her mouth to say something but behind her Ashely spoke up, "We're actually out celebrating my podcast. After coffee we're going on a cave tour for the 100th episode. Which starts in 20 minutes." She said the last part looking right at Hillary, who was rolling her eyes sucking on her straw.

"Hey, don't worry, we'll make your cave tour." Amy said. "We're just having coffee with two really hot new friends is all." She said tossing her hair over her shoulder and shrugging.

I threw an amused look over at Alex. He picked up his cup and took a drink before saying, "Please, sit and tell us about this podcast of yours. It sounds fascinating."

Ashely perked up but Hillary sat down and said, "It's about the outdoors, nature, and stuff," she said waving her hand absently, "I'm Hillary; by the way." she said batting her eyes at me.

I put on a smile, "Griffin." I said, putting the last bite of my sandwich in my mouth before I lost my appetite.

"Hillary, come on. We really don't have time for this. The cave is 5 minutes away still." Ashely complained.

"It's ok, chill girl, you can always catch another tour." Alex said. "I'm Alex, join us please." He said pulling out a chair for Amy who was about to sit down but then looked at Ashely.

"Actually," Amy said picking her cup back up. "This is kind of important. Come on Hillary, we gotta go."

Hillary took a sip of her coffee, "I think I'll catch up with you guys later. I'm not really dressed for caves anyway; I mean what was I thinking with these shoes right?" She said laughing raising her foot to show off open-toed shoes.

Ashely dropped her shoulders, "Really Hillary?" I raised an eyebrow, so ditching her friends is a common thing.

Hillary shrugged and put her straw in her mouth, "Take lots of pictures." She said, taking a sip. "I'll take an uber home."

Amy waved at Alex, "See ya around." She said walking away.

"I am so glad you drove," Ashely said to Amy. "I can't believe her. Every time she does this…" her voice faded as they walked away.

Alex was watching them walk away and Hillary looked at me, "So Griffin, Alex, tell me about yourselves." She said leaning on the table.

I smirked at her and asked, "What do you want to know?"

She looked between us and smiled, "I guess I should start with…. are you single?"

Alex was the first to answer, "Are you?"

Hillary giggled and nodded, "Yeah, I don't want to settle down just yet. I'm just having fun, ya know?"

"Yeah me too." He said, and motioned to me, "Griffin has nothing serious going on either. Hillary was it?" She nodded again, "Mm lovely name. Tell me are you from here?"

Hillary shrugged, "Well kind of," she told some story about moving here few a years ago during school. But I wasn't paying attention. What did catch my attention was how she said, "but I don't talk my family anymore."

I looked over at Alex, we shared a pointed look. I turned my attention to Hillary, "Do you want to get out here? I know a place where we can go party."

"Yeah, let's go." She said getting up, "I love to party."

Alex wrapped an arm around her, "I bet you do."

—⚬—

We took Hillary back to Grandpas. We would normally be at the cabin for this but there was no way we would be able to talk Hillary into that. It's not like we can drive up to the cabin. So, we showed up at Grandpa's house.

Hillary scoffed and made off-hand comments about the old house when she got out of the driver's seat. I made Alex sit in the back seat, it made Hillary feel special. When we walked inside Hillary was quick to make sure we knew all her opinions about the interior design. I took a deep breath and looked over at Alex who was running a hand through his hair looking like he was growing tired of Hillary's high maintenance attitude as well.

With a small shoulder shrug, she turned to me and wrapped an arm around my neck. "But lucky for you, I've been in worse places with uglier guys." She smiled and kissed my neck. I smirked and let her go at it while Alex set out everything. "I can't wait for what's coming next." Hillary whispered in my ear then went to sit next to Alex.

—⚬—

Alex and I were sitting at the kitchen table discussing what to do with the body and doing lines of coke, when a phone chimed. I checked mine but I didn't have any notifications. Alex looked at his phone but shook his head, "Not mine, must have been hers." He said jerking his head toward the living room.

"Fuck, do you know where it is?" I asked getting up and going up the stairs, Alex got up and followed me. We looked around, but I couldn't find the thing.

"Think it's still on her?" Alex asked.

"Wanna look?" I asked him getting down and looking under the bed. Alex went over and patted the pockets. "Nope not here."

I stood up, "where the fuck is it? Never mind I see it." It was lying face down on the dresser. I tried to open it, but it needed a thumb print. I went over and sat down on the bed, "You don't mind do you darling?" I asked picking up a hand and pressing the thumb on the screen, laughing I said, "of course you don't." My mouth went dry as I seen your beautiful face on this phone screen, you were asking if your text earlier ever went through. I looked down at the body in disgust. So, this piece of human garbage not only ditches her friends when they need her the most, but she also ignores them when they reach out not once, but twice. I closed the messages and went to Facebook. I made-up a shitty post about how some people can't take a hint. Then I posted some pictures that were taken with the group at the coffeehouse, careful to check that Hillary didn't already post the pictures.

I got off the bed and followed Alex back down stairs.

If I knew females as well as I think I do, you would get upset over what Hillary just posted. I mean she's been ignoring you since Friday and after you reach out she's complaining how 'people' just can't take a hint? Come on that would hurt anyone's feelings right? You need a friend right now, and I'm willing to oblige.

In the kitchen I grabbed my phone, and I sat down. Alex handed me the joint, "Who was it?" he asked.

I opened my phone and sent you a message. "It was Mel. She was trying to get a hold of Hillary." I looked up at the ceiling and shook my head. Every that happened here I did for you, Mel. I hope you can see that.

"Do you think that's going to be a problem? Melanie is the only one who's messaged her since we left the café." Alex looked worried.

My eyebrows pulled together, rubbing my forehead I shook my head, "Honestly I don't know," I looked down at my phone, tempted to call you.

"Maybe you should go distract her. Drop the phone off somewhere on the way, we don't want it to lead to the body." Alex said, taking a drink. "My car is already here so I don't need a ride back."

"Good call," I said getting up. Taking a six pack out of refrigerator. I took one off the ring and handed it to Alex then I took one off for myself. "I'll make a few more post to ping different towers before ditching it. Keep me updated." I said walking out the door, cracking open the beer and slowly making way over to where my car is parked.

—⚬—

Instead of going right to go back to the city I took a left to go to the smaller town to make some updates on Hillary's timeline. I stopped at a gas station to post a selfie of Hillary and some guy from a few days ago that I noticed wasn't already posted, saying something about good times with a good guy can't wait for more memories. Then I drove 20 minutes outside of the town to compose another post about a new job and how excited I am for it. Then I sent some random texts to the last number that had flirty messages and called it before hanging up when they answered. I drove for a few more minutes before wiping the phone off and tossing it out the window. Then I turned around and started heading in your direction.

—⚬—

When I got into the city I parked my car at the store down the street from your apartment building. I needed to see how you were holding up during this. I mean your 'friend' did something shitty, it's time for a real friend to step up. I turned my car off and got my phone out and noticed that you had sent me a text a few hours ago, 'Good afternoon. Sorry for the late reply, I've been wrapped up.' I got out of the car and locked it, 'I've been thinking about you.' I sent before walking the short distance to your apartment building. Instead of going inside I went around back. Thanks to our date I now know that you're on the ground level in the back corner.

Your response was almost immediate, 'What have you been doing?' you asked. I smirked and told you that I was helping a friend who was down and wanted to make sure that he was ok. Apparently you found that admirable. I smirked knowing I had you in the palm of my hand. You told me that more people should be like me. I smiled and walked

114

up to the window that I knew looked into your living room. I asked you what you were doing before looking in to see if I could see you.

Funny enough you almost caught me looking in, I was able to slip back into the shadows before you walked up to the window. I watched as you struggled with the locks on the window and put that detail in the back of my head. Then to my disappointment you closed the curtains. I took out my phone and sent you a text. 'I wish I could see you.' I sent a little on the nose but I like mind games.

You messaged me back saying that we'll meet up again and then you told me that you were about to watch a movie. I wondered if I could talk you into letting me come over. I made my way back to my car making idle chat along the way. Casually asking if you ever heard from your friend from the bar. Turns out that she's been ignoring you. But thankfully you just want to move on from it.

I took a screen shot and sent it to Alex. 'Mel won't be a problem.' I said. Then I sent you a text saying that you deserve better. Then I took my shot. 'What movie are you watching?' It didn't matter what you said next; because that was my all-time favorite movie, and I could watch it all day. But when you said Evil Dead Rise I was actually interested. I told you the truth that I hadn't seen it yet and asked you if it was scary.

Your response was adorable. You said you hoped it would be, and then you hinted that you wanted me to come over, saying 'If I get too scared will you come hold me?'

I told you that I would do more than that. I said how I love scary movies, and that I could come over now if you wanted the company. I tapped on the edge of the screen; your replies were coming in so fast but now there was nothing. 'Come on please say yes. I'll bring something special for us.' I knew that last part would get you.

And just like that my little Mel grabbed the bait. 'What are you bringing?' you asked.

I opened the glove box and pulled out a small glass tube that had blunt rolled in keif in it. 'If I told you it wouldn't be a surprise.' Then for added effect I asked you 'Aren't you curious?'

When you told me that I could come only if I brought more snacks with me. I was in the middle of typing that you're the only snack I want, when you asked how long until I got there.

'As fast as I can baby.' I sent and looked around the car, I grabbed a bag of chips that Alex thought we left at the store and the rest of the beer and got out. Locking the car as I walked away.

I tried to play it cool when I got there but I was so hyped up I had no good excuse on how I got here so fast other than to say that I was already in the neighborhood. I noticed that you were eyeballing the missing beers, I laughed and grabbed one to drink. I know it's usually bad manners to bring a partial six pack to places but here we are, "Yeah sorry about that, I used one to get us this." I lied and walked up, handing you that glass tube. "Something special for us." I said almost going in for a kiss, but I wanted to talk first. I asked if I could put my beer in your fridge, I noticed this one was a little warm.

"Of course. I'll do that, you go sit down." I walked up behind you, you were such an easy target right now, bent over like that. I wonder if you know what's hidden underneath the façade I put on for you. I hovered my hand over your back as I walked by, not once taking my eyes off you as I sat down.

You looked up at me, with those big doe eyes. I tilted my head back and smiled at you, "You're sweet." I said. You blushed slightly and smiled at me. I watched your hips sway side to side as you walked to the kitchen to put my beer in the fridge for me. For the life of me I could not take my eyes off of you. You were just so captivating; I couldn't look away and risk you disappearing. I had to say something. I decided to complement how much you've gotten done by yourself. "You've gotten a lot done around here, Mel. It looks really good."

"Thank you, it's slowly getting there." You said grabbing a drink for yourself and sitting down.

I took that as an opportunity to get closer to you. I rested an elbow on the back of the sofa and started playing with your hair, it was so soft. "Do you need any help around here?" I asked. Mesmerized at how your hair slithered around my fingers.

You looked up at me and smiled, "I've got it covered thank you." You said then leaned forward. I closed my hand just as your hair pulled out of my grasp. As you were reaching for the remote I moved closer to you. You seemed surprised and asked, "You ready?"

I smirked and decided to toy with you. Glancing at your lips and acting like I was going to kiss you. Knowing what I was doing to you I looked at the tv and said, "Let's do this." Before taking a long drink of my beer.

I couldn't keep my hands off your hair, I kept playing with it, I was amazed at how many times I could wrap it around my fist. After all that went down today I was wound up. I wanted a release, and I wanted that release to be you. I started putting on the charm and tried to get in your pants. At first you were resistant, but with some persuasion the 'no' turned to a 'yes,' then the 'yes' turned in to 'I'm cumming.' I might have been a little too rough with you though. I noticed a bit of blood on me during the cleanup, but I shrugged it off.

When I got out of the bathroom you were cleaning up the sofa, to my delight you were still naked. I walked up behind you and hugged you. "You have some good pussy," I said into your neck. Then I moved around you and put on my pants. "Ready to smoke?" I asked. Opening up the glass tube and dropping the blunt into my hand.

"Let me clean up." You said walking away before I could protest. I looked down and seen your clothes in a pile. I reached down and picked up a trophy to be savored later. You wouldn't miss another pair of panties, right? If my therapist ever finds out about this, he would have the time of his life picking apart the 'why' of it all.

I spread out on the sofa waiting for you to come back. It was taking longer than I expected so I went ahead and lit the blunt. I told you that we should try to watch this movie again sometime. I would really like to sit down and focus on it; it looks fucked up.

As we smoked, we ate the chips and talked, there was no point in watching the movie at this time, it was almost over, and we missed all of it. I kept the conversation going asking about different movies and I thought it was funny how you thought I was big reader; I have a few books laying around my place maybe like 5 or 8. I read sometimes but honestly it's been years since I opened a book. I noticed how you kept switching positions and smiled to myself, knowing that you're uncomfortable because you're sore.

My phone went off; Alex was freaking out and wanted me to come back. "Fuck, I'm going to have to go. Alex can't seem to get his shit together." I glanced up at you and asked, "Speaking of crappy friends; how are you going to handle tomorrow?"

You tilted your head, confirming that you've already put Hillary behind you. "Oh, with Hillary?" Yep you're over it, "I don't have to worry about that, turns out she got a new job." Reaching for a chip you mentioned that you were mad you lost your jacket during all this.

I was telling Alex I would be on my way back in a minute. "I can get you a new one if you want." I offered. I would love to spend all of my money you. Just tell me what you want, and I will buy it for you.

You laughed and told me it wasn't necessary. I sighed and put my shirt back on, getting ready to go. "I guess I should get going." I said, walking to the door.

You got up to follow me. "Thank you for stopping by," you said. "It was a nice surprise."

I smiled down at you, you were so unexpecting of me. "Of course, anytime you need someone to watch a movie with hit me up." I said, leaning down and kissing you goodbye. "Have a good night, Mel."

"Good night, Griffin." You said closing the door. I wanted to tell Alex to figure it out and go back in, but I heard the lock click in place. Forcing me to focus.

I had my radio on, the lead singers growls blared through the speakers as Alex opened the door. I took the panties that were in the passenger seat and tossed them in the back. I didn't want him to sit on them. When Alex got in he tried to say something, but I kept my gaze out the wind shield. Not waiting for the door to close I sped off. "This better not be a waste of my time." I growled at him, my grip on the steering wheel tightened.

"Not unless you consider staying out of jail a waste of time." I looked over at him then back at the road. Turning down the radio letting him know I was listening. "I took her down to the ravine like you said, but when I came back with the bag she was gone." The more he talked the less I could see the road. "I looked everywhere. But I did see some bear tracks that weren't there when I first came through, with any luck the two are related." He shivered, "It's creepy thinking that I was this close to running into a bear."

I clenched my jaw, I shouldn't have left, I knew better than to leave Alex alone to handle a situation this extreme. I punched the steering wheel. I fucking knew better, and I still left. "Sorry man, I shouldn't have left you."

I wasn't paying attention to where I was driving, and we almost passed the turn off to get on the dirt road that leads up to Grandpas old house. I made a sharp left turn which had me driving my car through a shallow ditch. Alex was onto something with the bear theory, but I wasn't going to get my hopes up until he took me to the area where he last seen the cunt. I forced myself to slow down, I had two more roads to take until we were at the house and if I wasn't paying attention, I'll end up crashing my car into a tree.

Taking a deep breath to steady myself I said, "We'll see what we can find when we get there." Then I turned the music back up.

Taking one last right turn we drove through a tunnel of trees that opened up to a huge two-story house. Driving up to the house always gave me anxiety. At any moment that monster in human flesh would storm out of the front door and drag me into the cellar. Clenching the steering wheel, I parked in front of the house. Both Alex and I stared at the front door for a moment, although Alex had his own trauma we both shared nightmares that my grandpa inflicted on us. Shaking my head I forced myself to get out of the car. *He's dead* I reminded myself. "Ok, lead the way." I said when I heard the passenger door open and close.

There was a game trail that led from the side yard to a ravine that we used to explore when we were kids, the same trail that will eventually lead you to the cabin. I was half way across the yard when I stopped walking, I noticed that Alex had slowed way down. I turned around to face him. "Dude? What are you doing?" I asked.

"Man, I hate coming out here, it feels like someone is watching us." Alex was superstitious he thinks the place is haunted. I think it's the memories that taint the property, walking up to it not knowing what secrets the walls held, you'd say it's a beautiful house. I groaned and waited for him to catch up.

We made our way around the yard, and when we got to the well that was near the game trail I noticed that Alex had fallen behind again. I turned to face him and threw up my arms, "Come on man what's the hold up?" I asked.

"I hate that fucking thing," Alex answered, gesturing at the circle of stones.

I started laughing, "What? You think the chick from the Ring is down there or something?" I pushed him towards it, "Come on! Let's go see if she's there."

Alex started freaking out, "Dude! I swear I saw someone standing there last time I was here. Let's just get this over with so we can get the fuck out of here."

I laughed again, thinking of Ellie crawling her way out of the well, bloated and swollen from weeks of being down in the water. "The well isn't something to worry about. Let's go find our bear bait."

"I still feel like we're being watched." He said, taking the lead and rushing past the well and disappeared into the woods.

I shook my head and followed. "I wouldn't be surprised if a bear did come through and grab her, it's getting warmer, and they like an easy meal when they first wake up. Grandpa loved going out to hunt for bear at the northern end of the property, but the ravine isn't really all that close to where he hunted." The more I thought about it the more it made sense, but I still wanted to make sure. I also kind of felt like an ass for leaving Alex here by himself with hungry bears running around.

We walked for a few miles in silence, the ravine was a good hike away from the house it took us about an hour to get there. When we got close to the ravine Alex pointed out some tracks. "When I first came through these weren't here." He said pointing at a paw print and some drag marks in the dirt. The ground here was fairly soft, and it was easy to leave tracks behind. "Further up here there's some broken branches." We walked up further and came across some more drag marks. There was a shoe on the ground but nothing else to indicate that someone was here. "This is where I left her." Alex said nodding towards the shoe. The ground was definitely disturbed, there where claw marks in the dirt and you could tell something big was drug through the grass. Shrugging he said, "It's not like she walked away. I don't know, a bear is the only thing that makes sense."

I looked around. We weren't close enough to the ravine that gravity could have pulled her over the edge, but I walked over to look down anyway. Looking over I didn't see a body. "Well fuck." I said, looking around and playing out different scenarios in my head. Then I nodded in agreement, "I think you're right." Standing up I looked over at Alex and laughed. "A bear took care of our problem. Let's go get a drink!"

Melanie (January 30)

I woke up Monday morning with a headache, stuffy nose, and a scratchy throat. I couldn't afford to miss work, so I powered through the day taking cold medicine every hour or so. It was nice not having to hear about Hillary's conquests last weekend, although it was kind of lonely working by myself.

By the time lunch rolled around I couldn't breathe out of my nose which was chapped from the constant nose blowing and my throat felt completely raw. When I got home I took a large dose of NyQuil and went to sleep.

When I woke up, not sure of the time, I still felt like shit. I had developed a cough that only made my headache worse. I walked to the kitchen to make some hot tea. I put a pot of water on boil and sat down on the sofa. Turning on the tv for background noise I waited for the water to boil. After a few minutes had passed I got up and poured the boiling water into a tea pot, then I sat a basket of tea leaves in the pot and placed the lid on top.

I went to grab my phone to let the tea cool down. I had eight messages all from Griffin. I didn't even read them I just sent him 'hey sorry I don't feel good. I've been sleeping.' It was 2:55 in the morning and I still had another hour until my alarm went off to wake me up for work. My head felt like it was about to split in two.

I got down a coffee cup and made a cup of tea with honey and lemon and went to the living room. I kept nodding off and before I knew it my 4 o'clock alarm went off. My cough had gotten worse, and my head wasn't getting any better. I opened my call log and called into work. It wasn't hard to convince them that I was actually sick. Trying to talk was making me cough and by the time I got off the phone my voice was gone. I made a doctor appointment for 11 am online. I went to take a drink of tea, but it was ice cold. Instead, I took some more NyQuil and went back to sleep.

—⚋—

The rest of the day was a trainwreck. The doctor had tested me for an upper respiratory infection and told me to take the rest of the week off if I could. He sent me home with some antibiotics and cough medication.

When I got home I was about to unlock the door, but something made me stop and look at the charm I had hanging up. The little moon that flips over when the door opens and closes was backwards. That didn't seem right, I know I flipped it over when I left. I took a slow steady breath and unlocked the door. I pushed on the door, so it opens all the way and waited for it to hit the wall until I stepped in. Nothing looked out of place. I listened to see if I could hear any odd place noises, but other than the normal creeks and pops the place was quiet. I sat my keys, phone, and purse down on the coffee table and checked the apartment. I looked behind the doors and under the bed. I checked the closets and double checked that the windows were locked, the living room window needed locked again, but the others were tightly shut. Everything was normal, but I couldn't shake the feeling that something was wrong, it was probably because of all the cold medicine I've been taking.

I took a deep breath (which ended in a coughing fit) I was just being paranoid; I might have been too distracted to flip the charm over when I was on my way to the doctors. I went to the bathroom and got the water going for a hot bath. I added some salts and oils to help my body relax then for an added touch I poured in some bubbles. The steam mixed with the eucalyptus oil was already starting to clear up my nose. When the tub was full, I got in and lowered myself into the hot water. "Oh, that's nice," I said out loud. When I rested my head on the rim of the tub a loud sudden noise from the hallway made me sit up. I held my breath and stared out into the hallway. I didn't see or hear anything, but my anxiety had me on high alert. I sank down into the water and tried to clear my head, but I couldn't shake the feeling that someone was watching me.

The bath that was supposed to help me relax only elevated my anxiety. If someone was in my apartment with me, I didn't want to be caught off guard. Getting out of the tub I quickly dried off and pulled on a bathrobe. I drained the water and turned towards the doorframe. Times like these I hated living alone. I was pretty scared at this point. I peeked my head out the bathroom door and called out, "Hello?" Like anyone would actually answer back if they were here.

I rolled my eyes and told myself I was being overly paranoid and went to the kitchen to make some tea. When the tea was done, I went to sit down on the sofa. I reached down for my phone, but it wasn't there. I moved my purse thinking I might have sat it on top of my phone, but it wasn't there either. Looking around I seen it on the counter in the kitchen. I didn't remember putting it there.

I got up and picked up my phone, I had one new message from Griffin 'I hope you feel better. Let me know if you need anything' I felt myself smiling. I sent him back a reply saying thank you and I will. I wanted to call my sister but at this time her beauty parlor is usually busy so instead I stretched out on the sofa and took a nap.

The room was dark except for the shine from the projection room. The image on the screen was too dark to make out but it looked like someone was running through the woods. I heard whispering beside me. There was a shadow of a man in the seat next to me, he was facing me. He whispered something again, but I couldn't make out what he was saying.

"What?" I asked my voice barely audible.

"You're not safe." He said again.

"Safe from what?"

The man leaned forward, the shadow pulled back from Griffin's face as he grinned, "Me" he growled and shot his arm up and grabbed me by the throat.

I woke up gasping for air, which turned into a coughing fit. I sat with my elbows on my knees holding my head in my hands. I reached for my phone and called my sister. It rang a few times and went to voice mail. I sent a message instead; 'I just had the weirdest dream.'

I was burning up and drenched in sweat. I got up to go change into some pajama shorts and a tank top. I looked out the window and seen that the sun was starting to go down. A message came through. I almost expected it to be Griffin, but it was Kendra. 'Weird dreams are my HBO. Go on'

I typed out a summary of yet another theater dream. I don't have them as often as I used to, but the impression is still the same. I pulled the curtains close and sat back down. I felt like I was run over by a truck, I was exhausted. I took the last dose of cough medicine for the day and zoned out on whatever was playing on the Syfy channel.

My phone lit up, it was Kendra, 'Sounds like a warning. Maybe your subconscious is picking up on some bad vibes. Try distancing yourself from this guy. You said this dream took place in the theater room? Those dreams don't usually happen unless you're under a lot of stress. Moving to a new city can take a toll on you, take a break from guys for a while and focus on you.'

I love my sister; her advice is usually solid. We messaged each other back and forth for a while after that, catching up on what happened during the last month. Her business Beautiful You was going great, along with cutting and styling hair she's added a studio in the back for photography. I told her about my new job and failed attempt at making a friend.

It felt good to talk to Kendra, we haven't really had time to catch up since she helped me the first night I moved here. I ended up falling asleep on the sofa and woke up a few hours later just to move to my bed and fall asleep again.

Griffin (January 30)

I was pacing back and forth in front of my coffee table. My phone was sitting face up, I was waiting for a reply from you, a call or something. But my phone stayed quiet. *What are you doing Mel?* I thought as I stopped and picked my phone up. The last thing you sent was that you didn't feel good, but that was a few hours ago and it's been quiet since then. "Fuck this" I picked my phone up and grabbed my keys on the way out. I was going to go find out why you've been ignoring me.

When I pulled up to your building your car was gone. You must be at work; in that case I have about 4 hours until you get home. I parked my car a couple blocks away and looked for an easy way into your apartment. The only window that was unlocked was the small one in the kitchen but there was something from keeping the window from opening all the way. I'm going to have to pick the lock on the door, a simple task but the risk is high. This neighborhood gives the impression that the people living here won't go out of their way to call the police, but you can't be too sure.

Walking around to the main entrance of the building put me on edge but it was pretty quiet for a Tuesday. I walked inside the building like I was supposed to be there. When I got to your door I took a moment to study the locks. The bottom lock will be easy enough to deal with, but the dead bolt will be tricky. After a while I felt the bolt slide back into the unlocked position, I was out of practice. I stood up straight and took out my wallet, pulling out my I.D. I slid it between the frame and the door and popped it open with ease.

I watched as the charm on the door bounced and the bottom moon flip over. Smiling at the memory of you flipping it over before we left for dinner, it would be fun to mess with your head and leave it turned around. Shutting and locking the door behind me I scanned the apartment. The place was clean for the most part, there were tissues around the sofa and an empty cup on the coffee table. I shook my head in disgust, I know you're sick Mel but that doesn't mean you have to be a slob too. If you would have asked me to, I would have come over and look after you while you rested, I would pick up your tissues and wash your cup. I would brush your hair while we watched a scary movie.

Going to the kitchen I seen some dishes in the sink that needed to be washed and dishes that have been sitting on the drying rack that should have been put up by now. The counters were clean but cluttered, I went over and looked in the fridge, it was pretty empty except for some random condiments, half gallon of milk, and a Britta water pitcher. I shook my head and let the door swing shut; the cabinets were just as empty. If we were together I'd make sure the kitchen was always stocked.

I went around your apartment looking but not touching. Imagining how much better your life would be with me in it, your bathroom for one would have clean floors, you really need to mop the bathroom Mel. The sink had some toothpaste around the drain and there were water spots on the mirror. There was a towel hanging on the hook that smelled like your body wash, I wanted to wrap it around me and take it home.

I turned around and went into your bedroom, there were some clothes on the floor by the side of the bed, and the top of the dresser was cluttered. I sat down on your bed and laid back; your sheets smelled good. I pulled myself up and laid my head on your pillow, it smelled like your shampoo. I closed my eyes, and that's when I heard the door open. "Fuck." I breathed. What are you doing home so early? You should be at work. I peeked out the door to see what you were doing. You were putting your things down on the coffee table. You look tense, you knew something was wrong but didn't know what.

Making my moves according I slid out of the bedroom and into the bathroom as you went into the kitchen. It was heart pounding, you looked right me multiple times, it was almost like hide and seek, where you having fun Mel? I am.

I slipped into the living room and ducked behind the sofa when you were in the kitchen and waited until you went to the bedroom to swipe your phone and crouch behind the counter. No wonder I never heard back from you; you had typed a response to me; but you never pressed send. I went to your Facebook messenger but there was nothing new that I haven't already seen on my laptop. Hearing the water turn on in the bathroom I looked over in that direction, I couldn't see anything from here, but I could imagine you undressing to take a shower. *If I walked in there right now would you let me join you?* Yeah probably not. I opened up your text messages but there was nothing new there either. From the bathroom I heard the water turn off and thought you were stepping out the shortest shower ever when water splashing around you breathed out, "Oh that's nice."

My interest was piqued, I thought you were taking a shower, but you were getting ready for a bath. A grin spread across my face, and I started heading for the bathroom.

I went to walk around the counter when my foot caught the edge of the barstool and shoved it into the counter, it wasn't loud, but it was enough to make think that grabbed your attention. I almost put your phone back on the coffee table, but I wanted to play another trick. Just a small one, harmless really. I sat the phone on the counter and slipped out the door, just as I heard water draining from the bathtub and wet footsteps coming out of the bathroom, "Hello?" You adorably called out as I gently closed the apartment door and walked casually out the building.

Walking back to the car I didn't feel like I accomplished what I set out to do. I couldn't understand why we've been so out of touch the last couple of days. I don't care that you're sick, I can take care of you until you feel better and if you get me sick, then you can take care of me. You've been talking to your sister, but you can't talk to me? I thought better of you, Mel. My body tensed up, and the corner of my vision started to blur and turn red. Finally, my car came into view. When I got in my phone started ringing. "Hello?" I growled into the phone.

"Griffin I got a job for you. Get over here and we'll go over the details." It was my dad.

I rubbed my eyes and started the car. I called Alex up and let him know that we got called in. It was going to be another long night.

Melanie (February 1)

Wednesday was when Griffin wanted to hang out but instead I was curled up in bed trying not to cough up a lung. I rolled over and grabbed my phone, it was five in the morning. Being ill like this is really throwing off my sleeping schedule. I opened up the chat log between Griffin and I and sent him a message 'Hey I'm going to have to cancel today, but I still don't feel good.' I threw an arm over my eyes and sat like that until the phone in my hand vibrated to let me know I had a new notification.

It was Griffin. 'That's disappointing. I hope we can get together soon.'

I sat up and drug myself into the kitchen for something to drink. I opened the refrigerator and got out the water filter pitcher and poured a glass of water. Sitting down on the sofa I turned the tv on for some background noise and laid down quickly falling back asleep.

—⁓—

I woke up to a knock on the door. I wasn't excepting any company so I hesitant on answering it. Looking out the peep hole, I didn't see anyone there, so I opened the door and looked down the hallway. I saw someone walking out the front, I was about to shut the door when I spotted a Chinese takeout bag sitting on the floor. I picked it up and walked inside. I took off the receipt that was stapled to the outside about to call the restaurant to tell them they delivered to the wrong the apartment when a note written on the bottom caught my attention. 'I hope this helps make your day better -Griffin' I groaned. How am I supposed to push someone this kind away?

I couldn't ignore the fact that he went out of his way to send me food, especially since I haven't been to the store in a while. I took out my phone, no new messages. Not wanting to interrupt anything I sent Griffin a message asking if he was busy. I opened the bag and took out a container of egg drop soup, some fried rice and orange chicken. There was no fork, so I went and got one. When I sat back down my phone chimed. It was Griffin 'Hey, I'm not busy at all what's up?' so with that I hit call. He was quick to answer, "Well hello." His voice was a lot deeper over the phone.

"Hey, I wanted to thank you for the food. That was a nice surprise." I took the lid off the soup and took a drink, the hot broth running down my throat felt so good.

"Of course, how are you feeling? Any better?" He asked.

"Not much," I took another drink of the drink to stop a cough from creeping up and got up to get some more water. "I went to the doctor, and they put me on an antibiotic so I should get better in a day or two."

"Hopefully. Did I get the right food ordered? I wasn't sure what you liked so I just went for it."

I took a deep breath and sat down, taking a drink of water, "Everything is amazing, I really appreciate this Griffin." I took a small bite of chicken. "Where did you order this from? It is so good."

"China King. We should go when you get better. What did the doctor say you have, are you contagious?" his tone was playful.

I tried not to laugh, "I wouldn't want to hang around me right now if I could help it."

I was about to cough so I pulled the phone away from my face, so I wasn't coughing in Griffin's ear. When I put the phone back to my ear he was saying something but all I caught was "-so what do you say? I don't mind if you don't."

I rubbed my temple. I was starting to get a headache, "I'm sorry what did you say?" It came out all raspy.

Griffin laughed, "Nothing important, I'll let you go so you can enjoy your dinner. It was good to hear from you Mel."

"You too Griffin. Bye" I hung up first. I took a drink of water before I picked up the chicken to eat for the first time yesterday morning.

Griffin (February 1)

I woke up to a shrill chime from my phone. I looked at the time, who the fuck is messaging me at 5 in the morning. Figuring it was some addict looking for a quick fix, I was about to turn my phone off and go back to sleep when I happened to see the name of the person who messaged me. I almost couldn't believe it; I opened the text. 'Hey, I'm going to have to cancel today, I still don't feel good.'

"What the fuck?" I yelled. I almost threw my phone across the room. I've been looking forward to this day since we made the plans. This is bullshit. I wanted to call you and demand that we keep our plans, I wanted to drive over there and drag you out by the hair if I had to. Taking a deep breath, I typed out a thought-out response. 'That's disappointing. I hope we can get together soon.' "Fucking bitch." I muttered.

Well, I was awake now. I sat up with a groan and looked around the room not knowing where I was for a moment. I was in Alex's living room, I was too tall to fit comfortably on the sofa, and I definitely felt it this morning. When I stood up and stretched my back popped a few times.

I went to the kitchen and helped myself to some breakfast. I made some bacon, eggs, and toast, and put a pot of coffee on. I kept looking at my phone expecting a message from you, but there was nothing. I punched the counter and flipped the bacon that I almost burned.

Sitting down at the table I started eating. Alex shuffled into the kitchen yawning, "Cook any of my food for me?" He asked.

I laughed, "Fuck off, I left some crumbs for you in the pan." I actually made enough for us both, but we like to fuck with each other.

"Why are you yelling so early?" He asked making a plate.

I took a drink of coffee, "That bitch canceled on me today. We were supposed to go out to grandpas, but she got sick." It was a reasonable enough excuse, but it still made me mad that you didn't want to see me. "Fuck it, I'll find something else to do today."

"Is this that same chick we seen at Ryan's? She was pretty cute."

My body went rigid, I froze with my fork about to stab some eggs. I turned my head to look at him and growled, "What did you say?"

Alex held up his hands, "Hey man I'm not into that whole Addams family vibe. All I said was that she was cute. So, chill." He went back to eating.

I shook my head, letting it slide and finished eating. "Well, I'm out. I gotta go find something to do now that my day is suddenly free." I rinsed off my plate and went to put my shoes on.

"Alright man, hey let me know if anything comes up today."

"Sure." I held my hand up in a half wave and headed out the door.

—☓—

The drive home took me by your apartment. I pulled up and parked next your car. Not really knowing what I was doing here, I got out and walked around the building. Most of the curtains on the windows were closed, but I could see through the one in the living room. Looking in you were fast asleep on the sofa with the TV playing.

Peeling myself away from the window I went back to my car. At home I got out my laptop and opened your messenger. The only recent one was to your sister. Reading through it for the seventh time, it was intriguing to know that you've been dreaming about me. I didn't like how accurate your dream was though. I was going to have to up my charm. Also, I had to think of a way to get rid of your sister. I don't like how quick she was to tell you to toss me out like that, I mean come on it was just a dream.

I went to the other room and did an extensive workout to get this frustration out.

—m—

The day was dragging by it was after noon when I decided to order something to eat. I didn't feel like cooking, so I called the Chinese restaurant across town. I was about to hang up after my order was taken when I had a thought. "Hey, can you double that order but take it to another address for me?" It was a shot in the dark, but I figured sending you some food while you're down on the sofa will earn me some extra points in my favor. Thinking back to your empty refrigerator, I figured sending some food to you would be like a gift from God.

"Oh sure, what's the address?" The lady over the phone asked.

I recited your address, "One more thing ma'am, could you add a note to the receipt? So, she knows it's from me."

"Oh sure, she sounds like a lucky lady." The lady gushed. I laughed and told her what I wanted the note to say then she told me the food would be delivered within the hour.

I thanked her and made myself busy around the apartment until the food got here.

When the food finally arrived, I took it and grabbed some beer and a fork and sat down in the living room to eat. I was watching a random show on Netflix when my phone chimed. Just as I expected, you messaged asking if I was busy. I wiped my mouth and sat back smirking. I told you I wasn't busy at all. I expected a small back and forth before I called you, but you surprised me by calling first. I cleared my throat and answered the phone, "Well hello." I said in a low voice.

"Hey, I wanted to thank you for the food." You sounded breathless and your voice was husky. "That was a nice surprise." Even when you're sick you still do it for me.

I smiled and took a bite of chicken; this isn't how I wanted to have dinner with you, but I guess it'll have to do. "Of course, how are you feeling? Any better?"

"Not much." I could hear you trying not to cough, "I went to the doctor, and they put me on an antibiotic so I should get better in a day or two."

I winced. I didn't want to wait a day or two to see you. I took a drink of my beer, "Hopefully. Did I get the right food ordered? I wasn't sure what you liked so I just went for it." Meaning I just duplicated what I got, but it's the thought that counts right? I took another bite of chicken.

"Everything is amazing. I really appreciate this Griffin," *You better* I thought and pictured your empty fridge again. "Where did you order this from? It is so good."

I smiled and took a bite of rice. I told you where I got our dinner from and said that we should go together when you get better and joked about you being contagious. You wanted to laugh, I could hear it, but you turned me down saying you wouldn't want to be around you right now. I want to be around you. I could take care of you and made sure that you're eating and drinking enough to help you get better. "Well, I'm not afraid of getting sick. I can come over tonight, and we can watch a movie and just take it easy." I took a long drink of beer. "So, what do you say? I don't mind if you don't."

You took a deep breath that sounded raspy, "I'm sorry what did you say?" You sounded rough.

I sat back and stabbed a piece of chicken with the fork, "Nothing important. I'll let you go so you can enjoy your dinner. It was good to hear from you Mel."

"You too Griffin. Bye." I had so much more I wanted to say to you before we ended the conversation, but you already hung up. I drank the rest of my beer and got up to get another one.

Melanie (February 10)

My car started to make a strange sound, so I took it into the mechanic hoping that it was just a small and simple fix, but it ended up being something that required a part they didn't have and since my car was already apart, it was going to have to sit overnight. So, I was sent home with no car.

I had the windows open to let in a breeze. I was in the kitchen when a shadow passed by the window. Thinking nothing of it because I shared the yard with multiple other people, I got a glass of water and went to the sofa and sit down. A new text message came through from Griffin. 'What's up?' he asked.

'Not a lot, you?' I replied.

'Just hanging out, kind of bored.' I wasn't sure what to say to that, so I got up and made something to eat instead. When I got back, I had two messages from Griffin. 'So, I was wondering if you wanted to hang out? Maybe go watch a movie?' 'My treat.'

I heard a crashing from outside and went to the window to investigate, a cat or something must have knocked a trash can over. 'Not today. Maybe some other time.' I went and sat back on the sofa to eat my food.

'What about food?' he asked. 'I'd love to take you to that Chinese restaurant.'

I ran a hand down my face, 'Not tonight, I just want to stay in a relax.'

'I can come to you if that's the problem.'

'Alright; fine you win.' I knew he wouldn't let up until I agreed, he had a way of wearing me down to get what he wants. Not even 5 minutes later there was a knock on the door, well more like someone was banging on the door. As I was walking to answer it there was another set of rapid knocks. Whoever it was sounded frantic to get in. I almost ignored it, maybe if they waited long enough they would just go away. But I decided to see who was, if I didn't recognize them I'll just call the cops or something. After checking the peephole, I opened the door, "What the hell?" I asked Griffin.

He was bouncing on his feet, rubbing the back of his neck, and running his hand through his hair. Sniffing and swiping at his nose he smiled at me. "There she is!" He said, pushing past me. "Hey, where's your car? Man, it always smells good in here!" He turned around and looked at me, his eyes were blood shot, and his pupils were dilated.

"Fuck you look good, come here." He said pulling me in for a hug. "Hey, do you have any food? I'm starving." He let me go and went to my kitchen. Opening the refrigerator door he said, "You never have food. Good thing I'm here." He said laughing. Then he pulled his phone out to order a pizza.

"Griffin, are you ok?" I asked starting to get worried. I wanted to kick him out because he was making me uncomfortable, but I wasn't sure if it was safe for him to drive like this.

He rubbed his neck, "Never better." He said walking over and sitting down on the sofa, he picked up the remote pointing the spot next to him, "Come sit down Mel."

"So how did you get here so fast?" I asked sitting down.

"I was close by and wanted to see you. Where's your car?" He asked again, turning the tv on and started to scroll through Netflix. "I wasn't even sure if you were home."

"Yeah, my car is getting worked on. They didn't have the part to fix it today, but I'll get it back tomorrow." While I was telling him about my car situation he was turned to face me, giving me an odd look. "What?" I finally asked.

"You should have called me." He said. "I could have gotten your car fixed for you in an hour." He reached out and tucked some hair behind my ear, "Where did you take it?" He asked. When I told him he laughed, "That motherfucker will bleed you dry. Let me talk to him to make sure he isn't ripping you off."

A knock on the door caught our attention and Griffin got up to answer it. He sat back down carrying a pizza box. Grinning up at me, he took a slice and started eating. I got up to get some plates and napkins. By the time I sat back down, Griffin had turned on a Syfy movie about a killer alien.

I wasn't a fan of how Griffin seemed to like to invite himself over, I liked it even less how he came here high out of his mind. I'm all for smoking weed but this is completely different. He's been twitchy and he can't sit still. I got up to go to the bathroom, and he got up to follow me. "You don't have to follow me; I'll be right back." I said with a forced laughed.

"Where are you going?" he asked, still standing.

I sighed and put my hand on his shoulder, "I'm just going to the bathroom. Sit back down, I'll be right back." I said walking away. Grabbing my phone and going to the bathroom. I sent Kendra a brief run down on what was going on and asked if it would be unreasonable to ask him to leave. She advised me that if someone is making me uncomfortable in my own place then I have every right to tell them to get out.

When I sat back down, Griffin had his phone out and was angerly typing something on it. He looked up at me then back down to his phone, "That tweaker doesn't know how bad he fucked up. He never should have sold you that piece of shit vehicle."

I was confused for a moment, not really sure on what he meant, but then I remembered that day. Driving away after buying the car, and the man that I now know was Griffin making that threat. I took a breath. "This kind of thing happens a lot," I said, "if I had the money to get a more reliable car I would have." I shrugged. "It's fine, I'll take care of it." I bent over and took a slice of pizza.

Griffin typed out the last of the message he was composing and put his phone down to turn to me. "Yeah well, I can take care of it too." He said with a wink.

I looked at my phone for an excuse to look away from his gaze. "I have a long day tomorrow. I think I should get some sleep." I said standing up.

"Oh, I don't mind. I can sleep here." He said standing up with me.

I started closing up the pizza box, "No, I think you should sleep in your own bed tonight."

Griffin walked up to me and grabbed my hand, pulling me up and turning me so I was facing him. "Why do you want me to leave so bad?" He asked.

I searched for an excuse. "I just started my period and I'm not feeling well. I just want to lie down and go to sleep."

Griffin laughed and let go of my hand, "I'm not afraid of a little blood." He picked up the pizza box, "But I'll respect your request." He leaned in and kissed my cheek. "Have a good night, Mel. I'll see you later."

I walked him to the door and kissed him one last time. "Good night, Griffin. Drive safe." I said before closing and locking the door.

———m———

I woke up to the shrill ringing of my phone. Rolling over I picked up my phone to check the time and see who was calling me, it was Griffin. "Hello?" I answered.

"Hey!" Came an overly cheery voice.

I rubbed my eyes, "Griffin? Why are you calling so late?"

"No, it's not Griffin, it's Alex!" Came the cheerful voice again.

It took me a moment to place who 'Alex' was. "Oh well Alex, why are you calling so late?" I asked again, trying not to yawn.

Alex laughed, "Just wanted to see what was up. How you're doing?" It sounded like he was running.

"I'm ok," I laughed, "how are you?" Not sure what the fuck was going, I figured I would give this phone call a few minutes before I hung up.

"I've been better." He said.

Then I heard someone shout in the background, "He's being a fucking child!"

I giggled, "Tell Griffin it's not nice to call your friends names."

Alex laughed, "Sure Mel I'll let him know."

I heard some shuffling and loud scraping, like someone was rubbing something against the mouthpiece on the phone. Then what sounded like someone tripping over a chair? I don't know, I was so tired. I rubbed my eyes again and sat up. "Hey Mel." This time it was Griffin, his voice had more bass than Alex's, and as it turns out Alex had an accent. "I'm really sorry about that. My friend just got dumped and I took his phone away so now he's acting like an asshole." His words sounded slurred, which would make sense if they were drunk.

I laughed and pulled the covers up, switching the phone to the other ear before replying, "It's alright, you both sound really drunk, is everything ok?"

"Yeah we're ok," he said on the other end, "Alex is going through a hard time right now so we're trying to cheer him up."

The use of the word 'we' caught my attention. I wondered who else was there watching all this go down. "We?" I asked. I rolled my eyes at how it came out.

Griffin chuckled, "Yeah, 'we.' Levi is over here too. This isn't a one-man job, I needed back up to handle this."

I ran a hand through my hair, I forgot to braid before I went to bed so now it's just a wild mess, "Oh that's sweet of you guys," I said through a yawn, "You sound busy, I'll let you go. Try to keep Alex off the phone." I joked.

Griffin started to protest, "you don't have to hang up on the account of them, they can wait a little longer."

I yawned again and checked the time 12:46. "Maybe if it wasn't past midnight," I said stretching, "I gotta get some sleep, I have work in the morning. Have a good night Griffin, I'll talk to you later."

"Sleep well Mel." He said, his tone dropped a few octaves.

I almost stayed on the phone longer, but my eye lids got too heavy to keep open. I pulled the phone away from my ear and hung up. I tossed my phone on the other side of the bed and scooted down so I could put my head on the pillow. Not too much longer I was fast asleep, feeling much better about Griffin this time. If he is willing to stay up all night to help his friend through a breakup he can't be that bad, right?

I stretched and rolled until I found a comfortable sleeping position and drifted back off to sleep.

GRIFFIN (February 10)

It's been a few days since I last heard from Mel. The last time we talked she was backing out of our plans. I was currently at home, hanging out with Levi and Alex, we were doing lines and playing Halo in the game room I had set up. On the other side of the room there were a few other people that had come over with Levi. I didn't bother to remember their names. The two girls were dogs and guys were loud and obnoxious.

Alex was leaned back in one of the chairs scrolling on his phone and Levi was bent over the table, when he straightened up he wiped at his nose and said, "Hey, my sister has been asking about you. She wants to know why you're not returning any of her calls."

I rolled my eyes. Natasha was Levi's older sister. He warned me to not get involved with her, but I did anyway cause she was eager, willing, and so fucking hot. Later I found out that she's bat shit crazy, overly clingy and possessive, and even though she's easy on the eyes, she's the worse lay I've ever had. But during a dry spell she's always there.

From his chair Alex started laughing, "Have you not heard about the new bitch his been chasing? Fucker thinks he's in love." He said reaching for his beer.

Levi looked over me, "Yeah I've heard about her," he asked. Levi whistled, "Of all the times to be a part of the band. Where did you say you first seen her?"

Alex answered for me, "He ran into her at the store, and he's been stalking her ever since."

I shook my head and was quick to say, "I wouldn't call it 'stalking,' that makes me sound pathetic." I said laughing and taking a drink of my beer.

"What would you call it then?" Alex asked leaning forward in his chair.

I put an arm over the back of the chair I was sitting in and put a leg over the other to get more comfortable. "I prefer the term hunting. Stalking implies that they can get away."

Levi laughed and sat back, "That's fucked up man."

I took my phone out, but I still didn't have a new message from you. I've been giving you some space, but it seems like if I didn't reach out to you I wouldn't hear from you at all. I looked around at the four extra people in my game room, I would give anything to trade them for you to be here instead. Tossing my phone on my lap, I took another drink of beer. "Yeah well, when you know what you want, you go for it."

"Oh, shit I'm late for work!" One of the girls on the other side of the room shouted. She came over to us, and we all looked up at her impatiently, "Hey um Levi we gotta go I didn't realize how much time we've spent here."

Levi sighed and took a long drink of his beer. "Sounds like you guys should start walking." He shook his beer can at her. "I can't drive."

138

She huffed and stomped a foot, "I work on the other side of the town."

Alex sat back in his chair, "Call an uber." He said boredly and started scrolling on his phone again.

The girl looked over at me, and I just laughed at her. "You guys are assholes." She said turning away to walk back over to her group of friends.

"Hey sweetheart we didn't drag you here." I called to her. "Who the fuck are those jokers?" I asked Levi.

Levi laughed, "I only know Kyle, the rest came with him. He bought some pills off me that's why they came over." I nodded and we all looked up and watched as the group walked passed us and out the front door. One of the guys stopped as they walked by and exchanged a few words with Levi. "Hey man take it easy, I'll catch you later."

I was wondering why they were hanging back in the living room when they first got here. "Don't bring him back here if he's going to drag an entourage with him." I said. I kicked back in my chair again and pulled out my phone wondering for the thousandth time why you weren't reaching out to me. Running my hands though my hair I stood up, unable to take the silence any longer. "I gotta head out too."

Alex looked up, "Where are you going?" he asked.

"Don't worry about it." I said shrugging on a jacket. "You guys can hang here just lock up when you leave."

"He's probably going over to his is girls house," Levi replied, "hey man ask her if she has a sister for me." We all laughed, and I walked out to head over to your place.

When I drove by I was surprised to see your car was gone. I parked my car at the dollar store and walked back to your apartment building. I walked around the back and seen that you had your curtains opened. I went up your kitchen window and peered in, ducking to the side when you walked by. I chanced a peek and watched you walk into the living room and sit down with a glass of water. I pulled out my phone and sent you a 'what's up' message.

I watched you look at your phone and waited impatiently as you typed out a reply. You said you weren't doing a lot and wanted to know what I was up to. I told you that I was just hanging out and I was bored, I was hoping that would bait you into a conversation but instead you put your phone down and got up.

I ducked down out of sight when you walked back into the kitchen. I was squatting below the window sending you more texts, trying to get you to hang out with me. I stood up but stayed in a half squat so you wouldn't see me and moved to look through the living room window. I wasn't paying attention and knocked over a small patio table someone had set outside.

I pressed myself against the wall hoping you wouldn't come to the window and look outside. I slid down the wall and tried to keep out view as you appeared in the window, I could see you but thankfully you just looked out into the yard and didn't look any closer to the building like you should have. My elated state was quickly shot when you turned down my idea to go out and see a movie.

I clinched my hand into a fist and went to punch the side of the wall, but I stopped myself. Instead, I offered to take you out for food. I went to living room window and looked in. I saw you sitting on the sofa eating a sandwich. You ran your hand down your face, were you getting annoyed with me? I was hurt at that thought, my attention was pulled back to my phone. Apparently you wanted to stay in and relax. Ok I can work with that. 'I can come to you if that's the problem.' I told you. I mean I'm already outside, but you don't have to know that.

I looked in the window and seen your lips pull into a small smile and grinned myself. I knew I was in, and my assumption was confirmed when I read your text that said, 'Alright fine you win.' I know Mel, I always win. I stayed there for a moment watching you through the window getting impatient and wanting to see you now.

Pushing away from the window I sprinted to my car and drove it down to park it in front of your building. Getting out of the car I knew that not enough time had passed but I didn't care. I walked up to your door and knocked on it. Bouncing on my feet I knocked again. I wanted to just walk in, but I didn't want to freak you out. I started pacing, wondering what was taking so long I knocked again. You finally pulled the door open, "What the hell?" you asked.

"There she is!" I was so happy to see you, but you didn't seem happy to see me. I squeezed by you, "Hey where's your car?" I asked. Taking a deep breath in through my nose I could tell you had switched out the wax in your candle warmers. "Man, it always smells good in here." I looked around, the place looked nice, you had your stuff fully unpacked and there wasn't an empty box in sight. My eyes landed on you. "Fuck you look good, come here." I reached out and pulled you in for a hug. My stomach growled reminding me that I haven't eaten all day. "Hey, do you have any food? I'm starving." I went to the kitchen not surprised to find that the fridge was half empty. I started laughing and commented on how you never seem to have any food. I pulled my phone out and called the closest pizza joint to place an order.

When I hung the phone up you looked at me worried, "Are you ok?" You asked. I was touched that you cared enough to ask.

"Never better." I replied. I went to the living room and turned on the tv. "Come sit down, Mel." You sat down next to me and asked how I got here so fast. "I was close by and wanted to see you. Where's your car?" I asked again, since you never answered me the first time. I went to Netflix to turn something on for us to watch. "I wasn't even sure if you were home."

You sighed and told me how it was getting worked on.

I gave you sideways look, I thought I told you to call me if something went wrong with the car; I even gave you my number, why didn't you ever call? Not that you knew it was me who was talking to you, you thought that it was Ryan who was talking to you, not me.

"What?" You asked me when I had stared at you a moment too long.

"You should have called me." I said with a shrug, "I could have gotten your car fixed for you in an hour." I reached up and brushed some hair that had fallen into your face behind your ear. "Where did you take it?" I asked. When you told me that you took it to Markel Car Repair I laughed. "That old man is probably fucking around trying to get more money out of you." I told you, and I offered to talk to him to get you a better price.

I was about to reach out and pull you into me when there was a knock on the door. I got up and paid for the pizza and sat back down smiling like an idiot. I grabbed a slice and started eating, out of the corner of my eye I watched you get up and go to the kitchen. I turned my attention to the TV and sat back enjoying my pizza. This is much better than hanging out with Alex and Levi.

I thought we were having a good time, other than the bug or something that kept crawling on me, one that disappeared when I looked. You got up, I didn't want to leave your side, so I got up too. "Where are you going?" I asked.

You sighed and gently put a hand on my shoulder, "I'm just going to the bathroom." You said, "Sit back down, I'll be right back."

Reluctantly I sat back down and watched as you took your phone and disappeared into the bathroom. Maybe coming here wasn't the best idea. I tapped my fingers on the arm of the sofa and tried to focus on the tv instead. The alien on the tv was spitting acidic saliva into a half-naked woman's face.

My phoned dinged, Levi wanted to know if I had a job for him so he can get some extra money. He and his band just got done with their second state tour, they were starting to get more recognition, but it didn't pay enough for Levi. I thought about your car, sitting in a garage right now instead of out front. I had the perfect job for us tonight. I was mumbling to myself when you came back from the bathroom about Ryan and the car.

You sat down next to me, and I noted how our knees were touching. "I'm not too worried about what he's going to charge. This kind of thing happens a lot, if I had the money to get a more reliable car I would have." You said leaning over to grab a slice of pizza and said that you'll take care of it.

I told Levi to meet me at my house at 10, and looked over at you, "yeah well, I can take care of it too." I winked and grinned at you.

You reached for your phone and said that you were about to go to bed and stood up.

I stood up too, "Oh I don't mind, I can sleep here." I said. I just wanted a few more hours with you, I know I can get in your pants again if you just let me into your bed. You turned me down again, and the edge of my vision started to turn red, I want to know what your fucking problem is. I walked up behind you and caught you by the hand, careful not to grab you too hard. "Why do you want me to leave so bad?" I asked.

I studied your face; you looked really uncomfortable and told me how you had started your period and just wanted to go to bed. I laughed and joked about how blood didn't scare me, but if I kept pushing to stay and if you keep turning me down, I'm worried I might drag you to the bedroom anyway. I picked up the pizza box and kissed you on the cheek, telling you to have a good night before I walked to the door.

You surprised me by following me to the door and kissing me goodbye. I felt like a dick by not leaving the pizza with you, but I was hungry. I fished out a slice and ate it on the way to my car. I felt like an even bigger dick walking away with blue balls, but beating the shit out of Ryan and taking all that he has might make up for it.

When I drove up to my house I was surprised to see Alex's car sitting in the driveway. I got out and walked in knowing that if Alex was here my door was no longer locked. There was a duffle bag that was tossed on the sofa in the front room that wasn't there when I left. I heard music coming from the game room and opened the door.

Alex was laying on the sofa smoking a blunt, crying. "Kara kicked me out man. She found out about the dating apps and freaked out on me and then she kicked me out." He took a hit and sat up, "she said she never wants to see me again," some more tears ran down his face. He took another hit and handed it out to me. I took it and sat down. "Told me not to call her, blocked me on all social media. I don't know what I'm going to do without her man."

I shook my head and passed back the joint. Getting up I went to the freezer and grabbed the whiskey. I sat down and took a drink out of the bottle before I handed it to him. "I told you all that tinder bullshit wouldn't turn out good. Levi is coming over later, he's looking for a job."

"I could use a job, what do you got?" He asked, taking another drink from the bottle, and after wiping his mouth he handed it back to me.

"Nothing for the three of us. I was gonna throw some money at Levi to help me rob Ryan for selling Mel a crap car, but three people will draw too much attention. I'll ask dad if he has anything." I got up and went to call my dad. There was a shipment he wanted us to pick up but that wasn't until the 13th.

When I got back I went over the details with Alex and called up Levi to tell him that plans had changed, we had a lot of planning and a long drive ahead of us. Ryan will have to wait another day. Alex looked like a wreck, he was hunched over, and his usual swagger was gone. "You gonna pull through, man?" I asked him.

He shook his head and ran a hand through his hair, "I don't know. I just gotta keep my mind off it." I tried not to roll my eyes when he started crying again.

Not knowing what else to do I handed him back the bottle. By the time Levi came in we were laughing and singing pirate shanties. Levi laughed and grabbed the bottle from Alex, after a big swig he threw his arm over my shoulders and joined in on our off-key singing, there was a reason he was the drummer and not the lead singer.

After the song was over Levi turned to me and asked what the job was. I gave a slurred rundown.

Alex pulled his phone out, "I'm gonna call Kara, I know I can talk her into taking me back."

When he stumbled by me I caught him by the arm and took his phone away, "That's not a good idea man. Give her some space and she'll come back around sooner." I said putting his phone in my pocket.

Alex shoved me, "Fuck you man, what do you know about good ideas? As far as I know all your 'good ideas' turn to bear shit."

I clinched my jaw and gave him his phone back, "Fuck this. I was just trying to help you out dick."

Alex flipped the phone around and pressed the button on the side, laughing he pushed the screen a few times and put the phone up to his ear. "You gave me your phone ass hole." He said to me and then moved the phone to speak to whoever he had called. "Hey! No, it's not Griffin, it's Alex!" He said cheerfully.

"What the fuck is going on?" Levi asked. "I thought we were going to go over plans?"

I glared at Alex as he drunkenly pranced around the room thinking I was chasing after him to get my phone back. "We were, but Alex is being a fucking child!" I yelled loud enough so the person on the other end of the phone would be able to hear me too. To Levi, I explained how Kara, Alex's girlfriend of 6 years, finally kicked him out.

Alex laughed, "Sure Mel I'll let him know."

I had no intention of taking my phone back. I had figured that whoever Alex had called on my phone was better than him calling his ex who just broke up with him. But hearing your name out of his mouth triggered something in me. I felt my body pulse, walking up to him I grabbed my phone with one hand and shoved him to the side with the other. I looked at the phone screen and seen that the call was still connected and pressed it to my ear. "Hey Mel. I'm really sorry about that. My friend just got dumped and I took his phone away so now he's acting like an asshole."

Hearing you laugh doses the anger that was raging inside me. "It's alright, you both sound really drunk, is everything ok?"

I smiled despite myself, "Yeah we're ok Alex is going through a hard time right now so we're trying to cheer him up."

"We?" you had a jealous undertone, so I told you about Levi, who in turned looked over at the mention of his name, "oh that's sweet of you all. You sound busy I'll let you go. Try to keep Alex off the phone." You joked.

I laughed along with you, "You don't have to hang up on the account of them, they can wait a little longer."

You sighed, "Maybe if it wasn't past midnight. I gotta get some sleep, I have work in the morning. Have a good night Griffin, I'll talk to you later."

"Sleep well Mel." I waited for you to hangup, I put my phone in my pocket and turned around to face the guys "Alex man I owe you one." I knew I had messed up by showing up to your apartment unannounced tweaked out of my mind; I couldn't help it. I just can't stay away from you. But then my vulnerable friend drunkenly calls you up and now I bet you're thinking of how compassionate I can be, taking care of my friend in a desperate time. Just like that I went from annoying druggie, to caring friend. "Alright enough fucking around. We don't have a lot of time and there's a lot we need to go over still."

MELANIE (February 12)

I was in the middle of my shift when the reservoir for the ink went out, so I had to stop the machine to go fill it up. Usually when this happens the person who was checking the product and boxing them up would be the one to fill it up. But since they still haven't found someone to replace Hillary, I had to run the line by myself. While I was pouring the ink in, my phone chimed. It chimed again when I was putting the ink jar back, and it went off a third time when I went over and started the printer back up. Griffin was messaging me, he wanted to know if I was home. I told him I was at work and wouldn't be home for another 4 hours.

During the clean up so I could switch the ink from blue to green, an air bubble in the ink reservoir rose to the surface and popped, splattering me with bright green ink. I sighed and tried not to let it get to me, but this day wearing me down.

I didn't hear back from Griffin for the rest of the day. When I got home his car was in front of the building. I wasn't sure if I was in the mood for this, all I wanted was to find something to eat, take a shower, and go to bed. He was leaning against his car smoking. By the time I parked the car and took off my seat belt, Griffin was at the window. I gathered my things and opened the door, "Hi Griffin."

"Hey Mel!" Griffin replied cheerfully, then I noticed a gift bag in his hands with purple orchids poking out of the top. "I can't stay long. I'll be out of town for a few days, and since Valentines Day is coming up I thought I should drop this off early." He handed me the plain black bag, "You don't have to open it now, I just wanted to make sure you got it."

I looked up at him bewildered, "Thank you Griffin, this is really unexpected." I gave him a tight hug.

I felt Griffin chuckle as he returned the hug, kissing the top of my head he said, "Don't worry about it, I was just thinking about you is all. Let me walk you in." We linked arms and walked in the building. Griffin took the bag from me while I unlocked the door to my apartment.

"Thank you," I said when he handed me back the bag, I was eager to open it.

"You're welcome," He replied pulling me in for another hug. Griffin tilted my head up, so I was looking up at him, "I gotta get going." After a head spinning kiss, he turned around and left.

Smiling to myself like an idiot, I closed the door and went to sit down on the sofa. I gently pulled the orchid out first; it was planted in a black skull flowerpot that had a gold tooth. Sitting the plant down on the coffee table, I looked in the bag and saw that there was still a wrapped gift and chocolate. I reached in and pulled out the small, wrapped box. It had black wrapping paper, and a satin burgundy ribbon was tied around it. Tugging at the ribbon and letting it fall to the floor, I turned the box over and slide my apartment key under the tape that held the paper together. Now holding a plain white box, I took the lid off and revealed a silver bracelet with black and red stones. Taking it out of the box I went the kitchen to get a better look. It was gorgeous and looked stupid expensive.

I put the bracelet on the counter and took a picture to send to Kendra with the caption 'look at what Griffin got me.'

My phone chimed; I expected it to be Kendra, but it was my pharmacy letting me know that my prescriptions were due for a refill. I picked the bracelet back up and held it in the light, I don't think I've held something so expensive before, I put it back down, afraid I was going to break it. I picked my phone up and sent Griffin a text letting him know how much I appreciate his gift.

I went to find a place to sit the flower and settled for a spot on the side table next the sofa, then I went to my bedroom and changed into some sweatpants. When I got back to the living room I had no new messages, so I made myself busy around the apartment until I ran out of things to do, dishes to wash, and things to tidy up.

I had recently ordered a diamond painting that I had yet to start, but with it being the weekend and I had nothing to do, there was finally time to be able to sit down and crack it open. I took out the small card table I had and set it up in the living room so I could watch tv while I worked on the painting.

I had just sat down when my phone chimed letting me know that Kendra had replied to my earlier message. 'Is it real?' she wanted to know.

I didn't know, but to be honest I didn't care; it was pretty and sparkly, what more do you want? And I told her just that. She responded with a crying laughing emoji and asked if she could facetime me. I hit the call button instead of replying. "Hey what's up?" I asked when she popped up on the screen.

"Not too much, I just wanted to see you while we chat, make sure you're ok." Kendra said. She sounded concerned.

I smiled, "Yeah I'm fine."

"That is a really expensive looking gift from someone you don't know very well." Kendra said bluntly. "It kind of gives love bombing vibes."

I took a deep breath and nodded. "I was trying not to think about that, but it crossed my mind too." Out of the corner of my I seen the orchid and perked up a little, "Oh there was something else. Check out this orchid!" I got up and flipped the camera so she could see the flower in its skull pot.

"What!? That flowerpot is freaking cute! I want one, where did he find that?" she asked.

I flipped the camera back around and shrugged. "I don't know. But he said he was going to be out of town for a while and told me that it was an early Valentines Day gift. I didn't know that we were there yet but it's hard to say no when he shows up bag in hand."

"Please be careful Mel. This all kind of sounds like the beginning of a true crime podcast."

I laughed, "I'll be fine, there's nothing to worry about. You'll be the first one to know if things happen to get out of hand."

Kendra shook her head, "No the police will be the first ones. I'll be second in this case." She laughed, and then I heard the bell ring that she had above the door to her salon. "Be careful sis, I gotta go my client just showed up. I love you."

"I love you too. Bye." I said and hung up.

GRIFFIN (February 12)

I was in Levi's living room. Alex was sitting on the sofa next to me and Levi was in the other room gathering some things. "Man, my girl is really pissed I'm not gonna be around for Valentine's Day." Alex said.

I looked up at him confused, "Didn't she just kick you out?"

"Yeah but I went over there last night, and we talked things out. I told you man she's never gonna leave me for real." He said smiling.

I shook my head, "What makes you so sure?"

Alex shrugged, "Other than the fact that I pay all of her bills, and all of those gifts for her and those kids she's got. When I'm over there with them, that's all that matters and nothing else exists."

I laughed, "Wow for someone who's so infatuated, you sure do have a wondering eye."

Alex howled with laughter, "Yeah well you're one to talk," then he pulled out his phone "I picked up a few different pieces of jewelry, but I don't know which one to give her." He showed me some pictures, 2 necklaces, a pair of earrings, and a bracelet.

"Fuck I forgot Valentine's Day was coming up." I said rubbing my chin. "Give her a necklace." After a moment I asked, "What are you going to do with the rest?"

Alex shrugged, "Probably just hang on to them for future holidays."

"Can I buy that bracelet off you?"

He shrugged, "Yeah, sure. I'll take five for it." I pulled out my wallet and counted out the money. When I handed it over, I asked where he got the jewelry from. Alex looked at me and laughed. "What? You never keep anything when we clean up?" It took me a moment then it hit me. I shook my head and laughed. "It's not like anyone is gonna miss a necklace or a pair of earrings. I mean come on, whoever owned your chicks' new bracelet before, is dead now. What use is to the original owner? Do you know how much I've saved this way?"

I rubbed my eyes and laughed again. "I see what you mean. It's still fucked up."

"Do you want the bracelet or not?" Alex asked.

"Yes, I want the fucking bracelet." I said leaning back and looking up flower shops in the area I could hit up before we head out.

"I have it with me in the car. If I keep things like that around the house, Kara will find it real quick." He said standing up. We walked out and he opened the passenger door and got in. Fishing around the glove compartment he pulled out a bracelet and handed it to me.

I looked it over to make sure it wasn't fucked up or missing any stones, and most importantly there wasn't any blood on it. "Thanks man." I said putting it my pocket. "Tell Levi I'll be back in a few hours. I have somethings I need to do."

"I still need to take care of a few things myself before we leave." A car pulled up at that time, and we watched as Levi's sister opened the door and stepped out. Alex whistled and looked back at me and winked. "Maybe I'll stay a little longer." He said getting out and closing the door.

Natasha walked by us and ran her hand across my shoulders. "Hey guys." she said and glided into the house, her hips swaying back and forth as she moved.

I scratched the back of my neck. "I should get going before I do something stupid. Let Levi know I'll meet up with you guys at 4." I said standing up. "Enjoy that for me." I said nodding my head toward the house.

Alex nodded. "Won't be the same without you but you should leave before she comes back."

Walking over to my car I took my phone and checked the time. It was a little before noon, you were probably at work, but it didn't stop me from texting you. I unlocked my car and got in. I haven't heard back from you, so I sent you another message. I expected a reply by the time I got home but you didn't. Sighing I sent another text. I sat in the car staring at my phone for a while willing a text message to pop up, but nothing happened. Muttering under my breath I turned the car off and went inside to pack a few days' worth of clothes. When I got inside the house you finally messaged me back. You told me you would be home in 4 hours. I wanted to respond but I felt like you needed some space.

I threw some things in a duffle bag and zipped it closed then brought up the address to a flower shop on the other side of town.

—m—

The little bell above the door chimed when I stepped in. There was a wax warmer on the counter, the overwhelming smell of vanilla mixing with the flowers almost made me turn and leave. The little woman behind the counter turned around and greeted me warmly. "Good morning young man. Looking for some flowers for Valentine's Day?" she had short gray hair and huge glasses that magnified her light blue eyes.

I gave her my most charming smile. "Yes ma'am I am. I know I'm cutting it pretty close, but do you have any flowers available?"

She nodded her head and waved her hand, gesturing for me to follow her. She led me over to a cooler that was half full. "Is there anything in particular that you're looking for?" She asked.

I scanned the bouquet of cut flowers. None of them caught my eye. I shook my head no and looked at the bottom shelf that had some potted plants. Some purple orchids stood out. I opened the door and carefully pulled out the plant. To my delight it was in a skull pot with a golden tooth.

Behind me the shop owner groaned. "Oh, that thing is dreadful. My granddaughter talked me into ordering a few. Saying that 'skulls are popular.' All of them are still around. I sell the hard candy faster than I sell these. Take the roses dear, she'll appreciate those better." She said with a wink.

I shook my head. "No. These are perfect." On the wall by the counter, I picked up a white box, some wrapping paper and ribbon, and a bag to put it all in. "Thank you." I said when the lady handed me the receipt. When I got in my car I checked the time. I had one and a half hours until you got off work.

When I got home I put the last-minute gift together. Placing the bracelet in the box I then wrapped the box in the paper and tied the ribbon around to give the impression that this gift took time. After the plant was placed in the bag I tossed the wrapped box inside and waited impatiently for you to get off work.

Finding things to fill the 1 hour and 25 minutes was driving me insane. I started by just scrolling on my phone, then I got up to do some work out routines. That went on for a while.

151

Taking a break and wiping the sweat from my forehead I checked the time. I still had 20 minutes until you got home. Grabbing my keys and wallet, I went the gas station to fill up the tank. I went inside to grab a drink and while I was waiting in line I picked up a bag of chocolate hearts to toss in the bag.

Flowers, check. Jewelry, check. Chocolate, check. The perfect Valentine's Day gift. In the car I opened the bag and dumped some of the red foil hearts in the gift bag. Then I unwrapped one and popped it in my mouth before I turned the car on and drove over to your apartment building.

I was waiting for a while, getting impatient I got out and leaned against the car to smoke a cigarette. I watched as you pulled up and parked the car. Flicking the cigarette to the side I opened the car door and grabbed the black bag.

You didn't seem too excited to see me. But you also had bright green ink all over you, so you were probably just irritated from work. "Hi Griffin." You said flatly.

"Hey Mel! I can't stay long." I said, "I'll be out of town for a few days, and since Valentines Day is coming up, I thought I should drop this off early." I said holding up the bag. "You don't have to open it now, I just wanted to make sure you got it."

The surprised look on your face was kind of cute. Stumbling over your words you said thank you and gave me a tight hug. I never wanted to let you go.

Kissing the top of your head I told you not to worry about it. I hooked my arm through yours, "Let me walk you in." I said leading us inside. I held the bag as you unlocked the door and handed it back when you turned to face me. You said thank you and looked inside the bag. With a smirk I said, "You're welcome," and pulled you in for another hug. I cupped your chin to tilt your head up, "I gotta get going." After a quick kiss I forced myself to pull away and walk back to my car. If I stayed any longer, I would never leave.

I called up Levi and asked if he was ready to go. "Yeah, we're both waiting at your house. We got tired of hanging at my place, Nat wouldn't shut up, so we left. Where the fuck are you man?"

"I'm on my way." I said hanging up. When I pulled into my driveway, I had to park in the yard cause Alex parked his car like a douchebag, parking at a diagonal taking up most of the space. When I walked in the door, they were both in the front room watching something on the tv. "Nice parking." I said walking over to the kitchen to grab a bottle of water.

"Nice time management. We were supposed to be on the road 2 hours ago." Alex threw back.

Shrugging I went to the bedroom to grab my duffle bag. "I had to wait until Mel got off work to give her that bracelet."

Levi laughed, "you made us wait for that? Fuck man you're trying too hard."

I shook my head, "You don't try hard enough, maybe that's why your always single." That shut him up.

Alex had something to say though. "I just left my gift on the table with a heartfelt note telling her I'll make it up when I get back."

I rolled my eyes, "You're always pulling that shit. I don't know why she keeps taking you back."

Alex shrugged, "Ours is a complicated love but it's real." He stood up. "Are we leaving or what?"

"I'm waiting on you pussies now." I said walking over to the door. I waited for them to get up and walk out the door before I locked it up.

When Levi walked by me, he scratched his cheek. "You have green shit on your face."

Using my phone screen as a mirror I looked. I must have gotten ink on me when I was dropping the gift off to you. Laughing to myself I rubbed it off and got in the back seat of Alex's car. Levi was in the front seat and Alex was driving. "Let's get this over with," Alex said turning his car on.

Levi already had his phone out hooking it up to the Bluetooth. I stretched out in the back and pulled my phone out to keep me busy for a few hours of the drive.

Melanie (March 15)

I had just gotten off my lunch break and work when a message came through from Griffin, 'How's work?' he asked.

'Boring, what are you up to?' I sent back, putting my phone down and lining up a paper placemat under the printer. I pushed the button, and the machine whirred before a roller put a fresh coat of ink on the stamp and slammed down on the mat, leaving an image of a sleeping pink cat. I think this order was going to a child's birthday party.

Griffin sent me a text bragging about a nap that he just woke up from and how he never slept better. I quickly sent back that a nap sounded nice, and I was jealous that I wasn't there. 'You were with me in my dream.'

I put my phone down and went to the end of the line to seal up the place mats and put them in a box to be shipped out. On the way over to the computer to bring up a new order I asked Griffin what he was up to now that he was awake.

'Looking for some food but there's nothing to eat.' He messaged back. I read the text and put my phone in my pocket while I got the next order set up. After a while, my phone vibrated, 'Send me a pic?'

I smirked and finished up the prep work. Looking around to make sure no one was looking I snapped a quick selfie of me making a funny face and sent it. 'Your turn.' I typed out and pressed send.

After a while he sent me a picture of him eating a cheeseburger. I giggled and put my phone in my pocket to focus on work. About 10 minutes he sent me a text saying, 'You're so beautiful.'

I thanked him and joked about how that picture he sent me was going to be his new contact picture in my phone. He told me the same thing, and I laughed putting my phone down so the supervisor wouldn't catch me on my phone.

—⟋⟍—

After work I was out taking a walk around the neighborhood. I was walking down the road heading back to my apartment building when a red car pulled up next to me. It didn't stop, it just slowed way down matching my speed and driving next to me for a few feet. I stopped walking and the car stopped too, idling next to me. I refused to look at the car, instead I started patting my pockets and acted frustrated before turning around and walked in the direction I had just come from, not bothering to look back to see what the car ended up doing.

I took a left at the street corner and turned my head to see the car taking a right. I walked down the sidewalk for a moment, trying to push what just what happened out of my head. It was weird and creepy yes, but other than that I'm ok. Then I see the red car driving down the street toward me.

There was a busy gas station to my left that I went to, to get off of the street. When I pulled the door to the gas station open the clerk greeted me warmly. "Hello." I returned with a smile; I noticed right away that there were two exits right across from each other. I walked to the coolers that were lined against the back wall. Looking out the window, I watched as a handful of cars pulled in and out. When I saw the red car pull in and park at a pump I opened the cooler door, grabbed a water, and went to check out. My plan was to leave out the second entrance, I wasn't sure if that red car was actually following me, but I was nervous enough now that I didn't want whoever was driving to be able to see when I left.

"Hey Mel!" A deep voice called behind me.

My heart sank as I turned around not sure who to expect behind me. Relief flooded over me when I saw who it was. "Oh, hi Griffin."

Griffin gave me an odd look, "Were you hoping for someone else?" He asked doubtfully.

I shook my head, "See that red car out there?" I asked looking out the windows. Griffin followed my gazed and nodded, "I think they've been following me." I told him.

"What makes you say that?" He asked me. I quickly went over what happened while we waited in line to check out. "Yeah that is suspicious." He said once I was done talking, grabbing my water from me he went on to say, "let me pay for this. After I get some gas I'll drive you back home so you're not walking by yourself. Luckly I'm on the other side."

I agreed and followed him to his car, Griffin opened the passenger door for me. "Thank you, Griffin, you're amazing."

He grinned that wolfish smile of his, "I know."

On the ride back we made idle chat about our day, aside from work we didn't really have much going on. By the sound of it Griffin's work kept him a lot busier than mine did. When we pulled up the building Griffin asked what I had going on this weekend. "Nothing really. Did you have something in mind?" I replied.

"Well, you never did get to see my grandpa's property. We could go do that if you want to." He shrugged.

I pulled my phone to check the weather. "It's supposed to snow this weekend. How about something else?" I asked.

Griffin laughed. "The trees out there look beautiful covered in snow. I'd really love to show you."

I smiled. "I'm sure they do. But I don't have a pair of snow boots for that. Maybe some other time."

Griffin's smile dropped for a moment, "Ok then, how about I come here for a movie night instead. I'll bring coco."

"I like that plan a lot better." I reached for the door handle.

"Here let me. I'll walk you inside." Griffin got out and walked around the car to open the door for me. I noticed him staring hard down the street and turned my head to see what he was glaring at. I looked over my shoulder just in time to see a red car make a left. "Let me know if you see that car again." His tone was sharp.

"Do you know them?" I asked looking up at him.

Glancing down at me he said, "No" in an apathetic way and turned to walk me inside.

When I got my door unlocked, I turned to face Griffin. "I really appreciate you driving me home. I'm pretty sure I was just being paranoid, but you can't be too careful; right?"

Laughing Griffin agreed. "Yeah, can never be too careful. I can't wait to see you this weekend." He said tucking some hair behind my ear. "I've got to run Mel. Call me next time something like that happens, ok?"

I told him I would, and he gave me a quick kiss and left. In the apartment I paced back and forth trying to make sense of what happened, giving up I decided to call my sister and asked her opinion on what happened.

"Well maybe the person just missed their turn and slowed down to read the road signs?" I shook my head knowing she couldn't see me. "You've said that's a kind of smaller city so maybe people are still trying to figure you out? I wouldn't put too much thought into it, sis." I heard a bell chime in the background, "Hey I gotta go, my client just showed up. Love you."

"I love you too, thank you Kendra." I hung up my phone and ran my hand through my hair. Not feeling any better.

GRIFFIN (March 15)

I was bored out of my mind sitting at home. I've been playing a horror survival game, but it was quickly losing my interest. Sighing, I turned the game off and rolled a few joints. I messaged Levi and asked what he was up to today. It was too early in the day for Alex, and I knew you were probably at work. Levi on the other hand was hardly ever busy during the day unless he had something going on with his band.

A message came through from Levi telling me that he was busy today, something to do with a family get together. I leaned back in the chair and pulled my laptop out from the side pouch in the chair. I opened it up and got into your messages. You've been talking about me to your sister again, I seem to be a popular topic between you two. Good to know I'm still on your good side. I scrolled through your other messages but there wasn't anything worth looking at.

I got up and made my way to the front door. I wasn't sure what I was going to do but if I didn't get out of this house, I was going to lose my mind. Sitting down in the driver's seat I turned the key and put the car in reverse. Still not sure where I was driving, I made a few random turns and eventually pulled up to your apartment building. The parking lot was empty except for an old green Buick that I had never seen move.

I put the car in park and got out. Walking in the building was almost as easy as breaking into your apartment. It didn't take long before I popped the door open and stepped inside. Inhaling slowly through my nose I took in the pleasant smell of your apartment, today it was smelled like citrus. After I locked the door, I kicked my shoes off and made my way to your bedroom. I flipped the covers over and crawled into your bed, burying my face in your pillows, and breathing in deeply, taking in the smell of your hair wishing you were here. I pulled the covers up and closed my eyes, falling asleep.

I'm not sure what woke me up, but when I did, I sat straight up on high alert. I looked around me not sure where I was at first but relaxed and checked the time once I got my bearings. It was only 12:20. I still had a while before I needed to get out of your apartment. Stretching I sent you a message. 'How's work?' I laid back down with my arms behind my head looking around your room. Posters of different bands and a few Syfy movies covered the walls along with some random diamond paintings. There was a plant hanging in the window and clothes were scattered about.

I had my phone resting on my chest, it vibrated to let me know I had a notification. It was from you. 'Boring, what are you up to?'

I smirked, 'Just woke up from a nap. Can't remember the last time I slept so well.'

'A nap sounds nice. I'm jealous I wasn't with you.'

I smirked; how would you react if you knew I slept in your bed without you? 'You were with me in my dream.' Sliding back down into your bed I laid there for while with my eyes closed. My phone vibrated but I ignored it rolling over and sitting on the edge of the mattress getting ready to stand up. I reached over and looked at the message from you.

'So now that you're awake what are you doing?' You asked.

I got up and went to get something to eat. To my disappointment your refrigerator was almost empty. 'Looking for some food but there's nothing to eat.' I replied. Sitting down on the sofa I called the diner a few blocks over and ordered a double cheeseburger with fries for delivery. 'Send me a pic?' I asked you. I turned the tv on and no surprise it was on the Syfy channel. I let it play and waited for my food to arrive. Not long after I was getting up just to sit back down with a takeout bag, the fries were cold, but the burger was good.

My phone vibrated on the table. I wiped the grease off my hands and picked up my phone, laughing when I see the selfie you sent me. You had one eye closed with your tongue sticking out. 'Your turn.' You said.

I took a picture of me taking a bite of my cheeseburger, careful not to let anything in the background give my location away. After I sent the picture, I finished my lunch and cleaned up, putting all my trash in the plastic bag about to take it with me, when I had a thought to leave it behind. Would you notice if I just threw my trash away here? A grin spread across my face as I placed my takeout trash in the half full trash can. I slid my shoes back on and locked the doorknob before I pulled the door shut behind me. Flipping the moon charm over on the decoration that was on the door, so you didn't notice right away that anyone was in your apartment.

I walked out of the building, feeling refreshed and headed over to my car. When I got in, I looked at my phone, no new messages. 'You're so beautiful' I sent to get your attention. I started the car and drove back home.

'Thank you. You're not so bad yourself.' You replied. then you sent 'that's your new contact picture.'

Smirking, I told you the same thing. Setting the picture of you sleeping on the first night I had you in my bed to the one you just sent. When I got home I went to the backroom and turned on the Bluetooth speaker and pressed play on a heavy metal playlist before sitting my phone down and starting a strenuous work out.

I had sweat dripping down my back by the time I put the weights down. I picked my phone up, no new messages. I put the phone back down and went to the bathroom to take a shower, letting the music play in the background. I got out of the shower, dried off and got dressed. Sitting down in the backroom, I lit a joint and scrolled through my pictures just for something to do. Once the joint was spent, I got up to turn the music off. With nothing left to do I grabbed my keys and wallet to go fill up the gas tank.

I went to the nicer gas station across town, not only for the better grade gas but for the longer drive to fill up some time in the day. This gas station was bigger than the other ones in town with pumps on both sides, I parked next to a pump and went inside to prepay and get a drink. I was looking down and not really paying attention making my way to the drinks when I see a familiar figure in front of me. The shapely legs leading up to a nice round ass, a smile spread across my face. "Hey Mel!" I called out.

Nervously you turned around, "Oh, hi Griffin." You shifted uneasily.

I looked you up and down, "Were you hoping for someone else?" I asked, curious as to why you were acting like this. Shaking your head, you looked out the windows and told me how you think the red car is following you. "What makes you say that?" I asked looking out at Tylers vehicle. You quickly explained how Tyler creeped you out, so you came to the gas station to get away from him, but now it looks like he's waiting for you outside. I nodded my head. That seems like the kind of shit Tyler would pull, the fucking creep. "Yeah, that is kind of fishy." I grabbed the bottle of water from you, "let me pay for this. After I get some gas, I'll drive you home so you're not walking by yourself. Luckly I'm on the other side." Not really lucky, I wanted Tyler to see you with me, that way he'll leave you alone and if he doesn't, I had no problem making a public scene.

I opened the passenger door for you when we got to my car. You looked up at me and smiled, "Thank you Griffin, you're amazing."

I grinned down at you, "I know." I said and shut the door.

After I filled the tank, I got in and took you home. We talked about random things on the way back to your place, you asked me a few questions about my work, and I gave as little as possible. The less you knew about what I did the better. We pulled into the parking lot of your building.

"What do you have going on this weekend?" I asked. You said you didn't have any plans and asked if I had something in mind. "Well," I started, "you never did get to see my grandpa's property." I shrugged. "We could go do that if you want to." I'll drag you up there if I have to.

You pulled out your phone and looked at the weather forecast. Shaking your head, you said something about snow and asked to do something else.

I laughed, "The trees out there look beautiful covered in snow. I'd really love to show you." You turned me down again, I had to center myself before I locked the car doors and just drove us out there despite what you said. "Ok then how about I come here for a movie night instead." And since your so concerned about snow I added, "I'll bring coco."

Smiling brightly at me you said you liked that idea and reached for the door handle to get out. I stopped you and offered to walk you inside. When I got out and opened your car door, I noticed Tyler parked on the side of the road watching us. We stared each other down for a moment before he lost his nerve and drove off. I told you to let me know if you see that car again. I didn't like the idea of Tyler snooping around you.

"Do you know them?" You asked.

Glancing down at you then back to the road I said no in a flat tone and turned to lead you inside. While unlocking your door you were going on about how thankful you were that I drove you home and tried to play the whole thing like you were just being paranoid. I laughed and agreed that you can't be too careful. I tucked some hair behind your ear, "I can't wait to see you this weekend." I wanted to kiss you. "I've got to run Mel, call me next time something like that happens, ok?"

You said you would, and I gave in and kissed you. If I didn't have to deal with Tyler, I would take you inside, but this is something that can't be put off.

Tyler is a creep but he's also dangerous, when he sees something he wants, he'll just take it. Somehow, he's dodged multiple assault charges; rape is a hard thing to prove after all. A low life that wants to run with the big dogs and is always trying to do things he thinks will impress Levi, Alex, and me but something that he fails to understand is that he can't try to run with us and then go over to pull the same shit with Dan and his crew.

I called up Levi and asked if he was home. He was but so was Natasha and she was asking about me. I told him to meet me at my place instead. When he hung up I called Alex and told him what was happening and asked if he was down for a fight. When I got to my house Levi was already inside. "Hey man what's going on?" he said.

"Fucking Tyler is sniffing around my girl. I'm going to ask him to back off." I stated simply pulling out my laptop to track down Tyler.

Levi laughed, "Yeah, I'm sure you're going to ask him real nicely."

161

Shrugging I said, "I'll started out friendly and go from there." Alex walked in at that time. Nodding at him when he walked in I mumbled a "Hey man," and look back down at the computer screen.

"Hey guys what's happenin'? I heard Tyler is over at Ryans." Alex said when he got closer. "Whose car are we taking?"

"Mine." I said, closing my computer and getting up. When we pulled up to Ryans, Levi offered to go get Tyler. While he was walking toward the trailer, Alex leaned forward and asked what I had planned. I shrugged, "I don't have a plan. I'm just gonna drive around for a while, have a little chat." Then I added, "We'll see how that plays out and go from there."

Nodding Alex added, "What if the conversation doesn't go as planned?"

I took a deep breath and drummed my fingers on the steering wheel. "If Tyler starts to act dumb, and we all know he will, then I'll start taking us to grandpas."

I caught Alex's eye in the review mirror, a grin spread across his face. "And we all know what happens at grandpa's house."

Smirking, I watched as Levi strutted out the door, Tyler was looking smug behind him. Levi got in the front seat and Tyler got in the back with Alex. "Hey guys, I didn't know all of you were going to be here." I could hear a nervous undertone in Tylers voice.

Alex clapped him on the shoulder, "Relax buddy, we're harmless."

I put the car in reverse and drove out onto the freeway. "Yeah man, we just want to have a private chat with you. That's all." I said calmly.

Tyler stuttered, "Yeah sure ok. What's up man?"

Levi pulled out a joint and lit it. "I've started seeing this hot chick. She's kind of stuck up but she's a really good cook."

Passing the joint to Alex who replied, "Yeah, you need someone to cook for you. I still remember that dogshit you tried to pass off as food the last time we ate over at your house. Too bad your sister isn't as good at cooking as she is at sucking dick." We all laughed.

"I don't know what you guys see in her. Other than her looks she has nothing going for her." Levi retorted.

Tyler awkwardly laughed, "I've never had the pleasure of personally meeting Natasha but from what I hear she has plenty to offer."

There was a brief moment of awkward silence. Levi broke it, "I can set something up if you want to meet her." He said.

Tyler chuckled, "No that's cool man. I don't want to take advantage of that."

Levi turned around and stared hard at him, "What? You think you're too good for my sister?"

Tyler put his hands up, "No, I'm not saying that at all. She's just not really my type she's just too…. uh I can't think of the word."

Alex handed me the joint intentionally passing over Tyler, "you wouldn't be taking advantage of anything, Natasha isn't really the kind of girl who says no to an opportunity." I spoke. "Unless you already have a girl. Is that why you don't want a chance to sleep with Levi's lovely sister?" I asked, handing the joint over to Levi.

"Well, there is this new girl I have my eye on. I saw her walking around town, kind of gothic ya know. I think I might have seen you with her a few times but I'm not sure. Is that your sister?" Tyler asked me.

I glared at him in the rearview mirror, his smirk made me want to slam on the breaks to send him crashing into the passenger seat. "You know damn well I don't have a sister."

Tyler laughed, "Oh yeah that's right. Is she your friend, is it serious? I heard you guys like to tag team, mind if I get a taste?"

Alex barked out a laugh, "Yeah sure man. The next time we run a train on Melanie you'll be the first one."

That made Levi howl, "Oh man, can we please make that happen?" He aimed the question at me. I looked at him, I could slam his head into the dashboard.

I took in a deep breath, held it for a moment and gripped the steering wheel. "I'll set something up." I knew after this I would owe Levi and Alex a huge favor. I wasn't sure if you would be down for something like that, but I owed it them to at least try.

Alex handed me the joint. "You better man, after what we're doing for you today it would be appreciated."

Tyler took this as his moment to chime in, "What are we doing today?" He asked, "Why do you guys keep passing me?" He almost shouted and took the joint out of my hand.

Silence fell over the car again. Alex was the one to break it. "We told you. We're going to have a little talk."

—〰—

We finally pulled up to Grandpa's house. "Man, this place is creepy." Tyler said stepping out.

Levi walked up behind him and put his hands on his shoulders, causing Tyler to jump. "You have no idea." He said pushing Tyler forward.

Alex fell in step beside me, "Where to?" he asked.

I looked at him and then over at Levi who was watching us. "The cellar of course!" I said cheerfully. "Where else would good friends go for a chat?" I threw my arm around Tylers shoulders. "So, Tyler, talk to me. What do you have in mind for our beautiful Mel?" I didn't even hear what he was saying. I was nodding my head watching as he talked with his hands. I nodded and smiled along with him, "Uh-huh. Yeah man that all sounds really hot." Then I punched him in the gut. "I'm sure that'll really get her going!" I said as I punched him again and grabbed onto his left arm "Levi," I called out, "can you help me out? Alex can you get the doors?"

Levi grabbed Tylers other arm, and we drug him towards the house. Alex walked ahead of us opening the doors and Levi and I drug Tyler into the house, who was struggling to free himself. "What the fuck is going on?" Tyler yelled.

I leaned in and growled in his ear. "Do you really think I would share MY girl with you? I saw how you were looking at her. I know what you like to do. How you like to break the woman you're with. How you don't care if you don't even know their name and just grab them off the street. How you just laugh at them as they have a break down in the court room." By this time, we were at the door that led to the basement. Alex opened the door and Levi let go as I shoved Tyler down the stairs. We followed him down, me first then Levi and Alex was last.

We've all been down here enough times; we can easily pick our way through the dark. But Tyler would have a more difficult time. We stood in the dark laughing at him as he knocked things over trying to get away. "Fuck you man, you guys aren't any better."

I laughed, "Yeah, maybe you're right."

Levi added, "He has a fair point, we are pretty fucked up."

Alex joined in, "Completely psychotic. I'll go unlock the door." He disappeared into the cluttered maze.

Into the darkness I called out, "Come on Tyler don't make this harder on you." Although I couldn't see detail, I was able to make out the outline of shapes and objects, which made it easy to find Tyler.

Levi's eyesight was better than mine, he got to Tyler first. Tyler started pleading. "NO. No, guys I'm sorry. About everything. I'll leave you alone. I'll leave your girl alone, you won't even know I'm alive. I'm sorry just let me go!"

In a low calm voice Levi uttered one word. "No."

Both of us grabbed onto Tyler and wrestled him towards the room that at one point or another grandpa had locked each of us in.

We didn't do much to him. Tyler was able to walk on his own back to the car. We debated on what to do with him. Alex wanted to leave him; Levi wanted to dump him on the edge of town. I decided to drop him off at the entrance to the trailer park that Ryan lives at.

On the ride home we had the radio on, and we were joking over top of it. Alex sat up front this time. Levi lit a joint in the back and passed it to Tyler. "No hard feelings, right?" He asked.

Tyler grunted and took a hit then passed it up to me. "Yeah man, whatever."

Nodding Levi said, "Good. I don't know what your problem is with my sister, but I hope we settled it just now."

I handed the joint to Alex and looked at Tyler in the mirror. "How about you just stay away from all of our women, yeah? Don't talk to Kara. Don't message Natasha. And stop following Melanie around town."

Alex asked if anyone else was hungry. We all were but we didn't stop anywhere until we got to the trailer park. When we pulled up to the entrance, I unlocked the door.

"Nice talk Tyler. Don't do anything to initiate another one, alright?" Alex said when Tyler opened the door to get out.

Tyler looked back at us, and half glared half nodded. Muttering something he got out and shut the door. I didn't wait until the door closed before I drove away. Levi shook his head. "What do you think he meant by Natasha isn't his type? She's too, what?" He asked.

I laughed. "Why are you upset that someone like Tyler doesn't want to fuck your sister? You should be grateful."

Levi shook his head again, "I don't know, I just don't like people talking shit about my sister."

Alex leaned forward, "Hey can we go get something to eat? I'm starving." I nodded and started driving toward the closest fast-food restaurant that was still open. "Oh yeah, hey Griffin, I hope you were serious earlier. I mean after I got Kara to agree that one time I was wondering if you would show the same respect."

"Yeah, but that wasn't my idea. Levi came up with that one." I defended, lamely trying to back out.

"Hey, you're the one who wanted to start this when I was dating that blonde bitch back in the day." Levi said.

"Alex and I came up with that together." I defended.

"Whatever man. Don't try to back out of this." Alex said leaning back.

I shook my head and pulled into the parking lot. After putting the car in park, we all got out and went inside to get some food.

MELANIE (April 28)

I was at the grocery store in the alcohol isle trying to decide on what bottle of wine to throw in the cart. Making up my mind I reached for a bottle of semisweet red and turned around to put the bottle in the cart. Taking a few blind steps backwards I turned around but ended up bumping into someone instead.

I was horrified, "Oh my God I am so sorry! I didn't know you were standing there!" I said in a rush. I could feel my face heating up and I knew it was bright red.

The man chuckled. "It's my fault really, I didn't know I was in hitting distance." He cleared his throat. "I was waiting for the bourbon." He said motioning to the bottles to my right.

"Oh, I'm sorry I'll get out of your way." I said awkwardly and walked over to my cart to sit the bottle inside it, still dying from embarrassment.

I heard glass clinking behind me as the man took a bottle off of the shelf, "Have we met? You look familiar." The man said from behind me.

I turned and looked at him. He was tall with hair that you could run your fingers through, he looked like he hit the gym on a regular basis, and he had a few tattoos, there was one on his neck but without openly staring at him I couldn't make out what it was, if we have met before I didn't remember him. Shaking my head no I replied, "I don't think so."

"No, I'm sure I've seen you before." He said tapping his chin. "By any chance do you hang around a guy named Griffin?" he asked slyly.

I grabbed the handle of the cart I was pushing, "We're acquainted." I answered and took a few steps further down the aisle.

The guy fell in step beside me, "I'm Levi." He said.

I kindly smiled at him, "Melanie."

Levi grinned, "yeah, I know Griffin won't stop talking about you. Him and I go way back."

I looked over at Levi but kept walking. "That's cool." I said, I was not really sure what else to say to that.

Levi laughed, "He said you weren't big on small talk." I felt him hovering over my shoulder and looking into my cart, "What'd you have planned tonight?" He asked.

I ducked away and quickened my pace to get out from under him, "Not a whole lot. "I pulled my phone to 'check the time' and shoved it back in my pocket, "I'm really busy; I don't have a lot of time to linger at the store. So, if you'll excuse me, I have to get going." I said turning to walk to the registers even though I only picked up half of the groceries I needed.

"Hey, I'll walk with you. I only came in for this anyway." Levi caught up to me in two quick strides. "So how did you meet Griffin?"

I looked over at him confused on what his motives were. Is this the typical friend looking out for a friend? "We just kind of ran into each other." I shrugged.

Levi nodded his head, "Uh huh. Yeah, that's what he said too. I was hoping for a better version from you." He laughed. I gave a tight-lipped smile and went to stand in the line with the least amount of people. Levi stood behind me. "You know if you get bored tonight, you can always come over to Griffins and hang out. It would be cool to get to know the girl he's obsessing over."

Despite myself, I laughed, the thought of Griffin and his friends sitting in a circle and taking turns telling each other about their relationships was too funny not to picture. "Thanks, but like I said. I'm busy tonight." I started putting my groceries up on the counter so I could get out of here.

"Yeah looks like you're going to be real busy." He muttered eyeing the items I took out of the cart. I turned my focus to the cashier choosing to ignore his comment. I paid for my groceries and thanked the cashier before I took my bags and walked out of the store. I thought I was in the clear, but I wasn't even to the door when I heard, "Hey wait up." Levi was next to me before the automated doors opened. "I'm the drummer for the band Yesteryear and we're playing at The Frog next weekend. You should come."

At the mention of the band's name, I looked over at him again and tried to think back to when I saw them that night I was ditched. "I saw you guys once before. I wouldn't mind catching another show."

Levi grinned down at me. "Yeah? It's always nice to gain a fan. Hey, do you want a CD? We just put out a new album, and I keep some copies in my truck."

I shook my head. "That would be awesome, but I don't have any cash."

Levi laughed. "Honestly Mel, do you really think I would charge you?" He threw his arm over my shoulder, "Come on. I'll even sign it for you."

I shrugged his arm off, I caught a whiff of his cologne, it was intoxicating. I wanted to wrap myself in that sent. I shook my head. "I still need to put my groceries in the car." I said pushing the cart towards my car. Making a mental note to find that cologne so Griffin can wear it, would that be weird?

Levi followed me, in a few steps he was beside me. Laughing he said, "My truck is parked over here too," he pointed over to a silver truck that was parked in the row behind the one I parked in. "I'll be right back."

I opened the back passenger door and put my bags inside. By the time I got back from returning the cart Levi was walking over from his truck. He smiled at me and met me at my car.

"Let me know what you think. I'd love to hear some fresh feedback." He said with a wolfish grin. I noticed the tattoo on the hand that was holding the CD was the same spider and in the same place that Griffin had.

Making a mental note I took the CD and smiled up at Levi. "Thank you. I'll listen to it when I get home." I looked down at the CD, he had signed the cover with a silver sharpie.

Levi looked down at me, "Good deal, it was nice to officially meet you, Melanie." He walked back to his truck and got in.

I waved at him in case he was looking through the mirrors and went to my car, I was eager to go home to listen to the album while finishing my diamond painting and a bottle of wine.

—⁂—

Later that night I was halfway through the bottle, and I only had a corner the size of my hand left to do. I was watching an eighty's slasher movie and occasionally texting my sister, when my stomach growled so I went to the kitchen to make something quick to eat.

I heard my phone chime in the other room, *I'll get it when I sit back down*, I thought. I poured another glass of wine while I was in the kitchen, and I heard my phone chime again. By the time I had my sandwich made and a handful of chips laid out on a plate I heard two more chimes from my phone.

I sat back down at the card table and picked up my phone. One message from Kendra and 3 from Griffin. I replied to Kendra first then I opened Griffins messages.

'Hey Levi told me he ran into you at the store. Why don't you come over, and we can all hang out?'

'It's really boring here. Your company would really liven the place up.'

'I'll come get you if you need me to.'

'I'm busy tonight maybe next weekend?' I offered.

I really wanted to get this diamond painting done tonight and I have one more glass of wine before the bottle is empty. I put a napkin down,

169

so I didn't drop crumbs on the painting while I ate, good thing too; as soon as I took a bite of my sandwich, chip crumbs fell out of the bottom.

Griffin messaged back, 'Tonight is a better night though.' then soon after he sent 'It'll be fun I promise.'

I groaned and typed up another reason not to go. 'I'm a little drunk so I don't think I should be driving.'

Griffin had an immediate response 'I told you I would come get you.' I rolled my eyes and was about to type another message when I started to get an incoming video chat. Griffin was trying to facetime me; I tapped my finger on the side of my phone contemplating on whether or not I should answer it. I let the call ring a couple more times; taking another bite of my sandwich. After swallowing I answered the call.

Griffin looked completely wasted, "Hey! I thought since you won't let me come get you, I could see you this way." His words were slurred, his eyes were blood shot, and he was swaying slightly.

I smiled and put a chip in my mouth before saying, "I hope you don't mind me eating. I just made dinner before you called me."

Griffin grinned. "I don't mind one bit. What'd you make?"

I picked up my sandwich and showed him. "Nothing too special. Honey ham and Swiss, some fresh spinach and then I threw on some chips."

"That looks good. When I get there you should make me one." He winked.

I shook my head no, "Griffin you're in no better shape to drive than I am."

I heard a howl of laugher on Griffin's end. He looked past the camera then looked back at me. Grinning he flipped the view so I could see his buddies, Alex, and Levi. "One of these fuckers can drive then." He flipped the view back to him before I could make out what they were doing. There were bottles scattered about, and it looked like they were sitting around the smaller coffee table in Griffin's back room. "Or I can call an uber." He shrugged, "I'll walk if it comes down to it. Are you sure I can't see you tonight?"

I picked up my wine glass and took a drink, "I'd rather none of you drive, you all look pretty wasted."

In the background I heard one of the guys say, "Aww, she cares about us."

The other one replied, "Your girlfriend is the sweetest Griffin." Then another round of howling laughter.

Griffins wolfish smile got wider and to me he said, "What has you so busy tonight that you don't want to see me?" A dark look clouded his eyes, but that wide smile never left his face. "You don't have company, do you?" his words had a threatening undertone.

Not sure how to respond I flipped the view on my camera and showed him the tabletop. "No. I'm just working on this. It's almost done."

Griffin tilted his head to the side and laughed, "That looks extremely time consuming."

Levi appeared from behind Griffin, "Woah that's awesome. Is that really why you don't want to hang out?" I flipped the view back around and I shrugged. "Hey, did you get a chance to listen to my album?" He asked.

I nodded my head, I put it in when I got home and listened to it on repeat while I did some chores around the apartment, but they don't need to know that. "Yeah, you guys are amazing." I tried not to fangirl too hard, but I took a drink of wine then I started rambling. I couldn't shut up about the different things that I liked about their music. I listed the songs I liked, told him which ones I put on my playlist, even the songs I didn't care for. "Sorry, I guess I'm a little chatty tonight."

Levi grinned, "You're good. You should come over; we can hang and listen to some music…."

I shook my head no. "Not tonight."

Griffin glanced back at Levi and then turned back to me. "Honestly Mel I'm hurt," he said putting a hand to his chest.

I laughed. "I'm sure you'll be just fine." I propped my phone up so I could keep working on my diamond painting while we facetimed. When my phone was in place, I picked up my glass and took a drink.

"What are you drinking?" Griffin asked. I told him I was drinking wine and placed a few diamonds on the adhesive paper. "Oh? I've never been a wine drinker. I'm more of a whiskey guy myself. What kind of wine do you have?" We talked like that for a while, Alex and Levi joining in on the conversation once in a while.

Alex offered to go out and buy me a bottle of wine that I was drinking. I laughed awkwardly and turned down his offer. Then he offered to make some food, bringing up how I liked the food from his food truck. But honestly that was too long ago, I didn't remember if the food was all that good.

I shook my head and reminded them I was currently eating.

Levi came into view and offered to play video with me. That triggered an argument over cheat codes. I laughed and turned my focus on the diamond painting.

I was glad I stayed home instead agreeing to go over there. They looked like they were getting rowdy. For a while it was just them talking to each other, I was focused on the diamond painting looking up at the TV every now and then and eating my sandwich.

"What are you watching?" Griffin asked. I looked over at the phone screen and seen that the background had changed, it looked like he was now in his kitchen.

"Nightmare on Elm Street. There's a marathon on the Syfy channel." I replied.

I watched as he positioned the phone so he could sit down at the kitchen counter. "I can put that on over here and we can all watch it together. Come on it'll be fun. We can make it into a drinking game." He smirked at me. I watched him walk over and open the freezer door. He pulled out an ice cube tray and a bottle of whiskey. He put a couple ice cubes in a glass and poured a considerable amount of whiskey on top. After placing both the tray and the bottle back in the freezer, he sat back down. "Why don't you want to come over?" he asked.

I rose an eyebrow and tried not to let my aggravation show. I took a long drink before I responded. "It's been a long week, and I just want to stay home and relax."

"Then let me come to you. This isn't doing it for me." He said, waving a hand between him and the phone. "I want to be there with you." He said taking a drink. I shook my head, but he cut me off before I could speak. "I know, I know. But do you blame me for wanting to spend time with a beautiful woman instead of these two morons?" He gave me that wolfish grin of his.

I smiled and laughed. "I guess not. But the answer is still no." I shrugged.

Griffin looked down and scratched his eyebrow. "That's a shame. I was hoping to wear you down." He chuckled. "You look beautiful tonight." He said, taking another drink.

"Thank you," I said, biting the inside of my lip. The way he was looking at me made me blush. Good thing my face was already flushed from the wine.

A message reminder flashed across the top of the screen; Kendra had sent, 'last client of the day is finally finished! Now time to clean up and go to bed.' I sent her a good night message and told her I loved her.

"What's going on?" Griffin asked.

"Oh, I was just telling my sister good night." I took the last bite of my sandwich.

"Man, that looked like a good sandwich. I should get something to eat too, I'm getting hungry." Griffin got up and started going through his cabinets. He sat back down with a bag of chips and some queso cheese dip. I turned my focus back to the diamond painting; I was just about done. I heard some commotion in the background and glanced up. Alex was walking around in the background eating some chips. They started talking about something, but I was paying more attention to what was happening on the tv.

After about 5 more minutes the painting was finally completed, I sat back and took a drink of wine looking down at the completed project.

"Did you finish it?" Griffin asked.

I took the phone and flipped the view so he could see it. "Sure did."

"Does this mean you'll come over now?"

Alex came into view and chimed in, "Yeah come over, I'll send you an uber."

I flipped the view back over and held my phone out, "No. It means I'm going to get ready for bed."

"Hold on now. I'm not ready to say goodbye just yet." Griffin slurred.

I sighed and got up to take care of my plate and pour the last glass of wine. While I was pouring the glass, I told them, "I don't know how much longer I'll be able to stay awake. I'm getting pretty tired."

"Are we that boring, Mel?" Alex asked.

I shook my head no and took a drink. "It's not you." I said and yawned.

Griffin offered to make me some coffee.

I laughed, "Then I'll be up all night. I want to go to sleep at some point. We can hang out some other time."

Griffin smirked at me. "Alright fine. I'll let you go. But text me when you wake up, ok?"

I told him I would and hung up after we said good night. I sat on the sofa and watched tv until my glass was empty. Leaving my glass on the coffee table I turned the tv off and made my way to the bedroom.

I changed into some pajamas and crawled into bed. The covers were cozy and the soft glow from the wax warmer in the corner was so relaxing I was asleep before my head hit the pillow.

GRIFFIN (April 28)

Earlier that morning I got a call from Alex. Kara was spending the weekend with her mom, and he wanted to do some yard work that she had been asking him to do for a while. Mainly to try to stay on her good side. Kara had a nice house, two story with a front porch that had a swing, and a massive yard that her dog was always digging holes in. There was also some tree limbs that were scattered around from a recent storm that she wants picked up.

When I pulled up to the house Alex and Levi were gathered around the shed that was in the side yard. Alex nodded in my direction, "We were talking about loading up the tree limbs in Levi's truck and taking them out to your grandpa's old place to have a bonfire."

Nodding my head I replied, "Yeah sure, fine with me." Looking around the yard, I asked what all needed to be done.

Levi lit a cigarette and leaned against the shed, "Too much in my opinion."

Alex opened the shed and pulled out a rake and a shovel. "She wants the holes filled in, limbs picked up and then rake up the leaves and twigs." Handing me a shovel he added, "She also said that she wants the dog shit picked up and that there's a dead something in the back yard that needs gotten rid of; but I'm not doing that."

I scoffed and took the shovel, "Yeah you can fuck yourself. I'm not dealing with any of that. I'll fill the holes that's it."

"I'll start on the tree limbs," Levi said flicking his cigarette to the side.

Alex took the rake and flipped it in his hands a few times. "I'll take care of the dead thing, but the dog shit can stay. It's her dog; she can pick up after it."

—m—

Sweat was starting to roll down my back, I'm not sure how long we've been working on the yard, but I was ready for a break. I was still filling in the holes when Alex walked back around the house. His face was scrunched up, and he was holding his stomach.

I laughed, "Can't stomach a dead animal?" I yelled at him. He flipped me off and walked over to me. The smell that followed him made my stomach turn.

"Fuck you man, I fucking stepped in it. Ruined my fucking shoes!" he muttered raking some dirt back into a hole.

I laughed and patted a freshly filled in hole down with the shovel. After another half an hour most of the holes were filled in, sweat was dripping down my back.

Levi walked over, looking spent. "I got the ones worth burning in the truck. How's it going with you?" he asked.

I shrugged. "Alex stepped in the dead thing now he smells like shit. Other than that, I think we're almost done."

An hour or so later we had the yard mostly cleaned up. Alex decided to call it. "I need a shower." He said, pulling at his shirt.

"You need to throw away those shoes." Levi responded, brushing dirt off his jeans.

Alex flipped him off. "What are y'all doing after this."

"Not shit." I said with a shrug.

175

We agreed to meet up at my place in 2 hours. When I got home I stripped my clothes off and threw them in the washer. I turned the water in the shower on and waited for it to warm up before stepping in to wash the dirt and sweat off my body.

—⚬⚬—

I was in the kitchen pouring myself a drink when Alex walked through the door. Levi walked in shortly after, "I need to get my own place," Levi said running a hand through his hair. "I'm going crazy living with that psycho." Opening the refrigerator, he took out a bottle of beer.

"We have an extra room at our place," Alex piped up. "Maybe I can talk Kara into letting Natasha live with us." He joked, Levi punched him in the shoulder, Alex shoved him back.

Levi went to step toward Alex, but I stepped between them. "I got something new in the back." I said catching their attention. I went to the backroom and sat at the sofa on the far side. I pulled out the box underneath the coffee table. The guys were sitting down as I pulled out a tray and a bag.

"Where'd you get this?" Levi asked.

"New connections." I replied.

A few hours had passed, I'm not sure who turned on the TV but somehow we ended up playing Mario cart. Alex started bitching when he came in last. "Fuck this game. I'm over it." He said tossing the controller on the entertainment center.

Levi stretched, "You're just pissed cause you suck at this game." Turning to me said, "I'm getting hungry do you have anything to eat?"

I shook my head and got up to put the controllers back. "Not really, someone will have to go get something or order take out."

Shrugging Levi stood up. "I'll go get something."

I offered to go to, but he shrugged me off and walked out the door. A half an hour or so had passed, Alex was scrolling on his phone, it was quiet except for the radio that was playing for background noise.

"What the fuck is taking him so long, I'm starving." Alex complained, throwing his phone on the coffee table.

"How am I supposed to know, if you're that worried call him." I shot back. I got up to refill my cup. Alex said something behind me, but I didn't bother with it.

While I was putting the jug of tea back, Levi came through the door with a wolfish grin. He was carrying a bottle of bourbon and 2 boxes of pizza from the gas station that he sat on the counter. Turning to me he said, "I ran into your girl at the store." I took a drink and opened up the top pizza box, grabbing a slice I waited for him to continue. "We talked for a bit in the parking lot. Then I gave her a copy of the bands newest album."

I clinched my jaw, I was coming around to the idea of the possibility of sharing you, but I didn't want them trying to start anything behind my back. I took the bottle and put it in the freezer. "What else did you talk about?"

Levi smirked, "That's it really. I tried getting her to open up, but she wasn't budging."

I relaxed a little, this could be good. I nodded my head, "Yeah it took me a while to get her to drop her guard." I said. Almost laughing when I pictured Levi trying to charm you at the store.

Levi leaned against the counter. "I can see why you didn't want Tyler sniffing around her." There was a brief pause, "Do you think he got the point. He's not a fast learner. It might take some more convincing." I looked over at him, Levi shrugged.

Sighing I poured my glass of tea out and grabbed a beer from the fridge. "If I catch him near her again, especially after today, there won't be any more talking." I took a long drink of beer.

I had more questions about his encounter with you, but I didn't want to be the jealous over baring guy. I took another drink. Levi was talking about something, but I wasn't paying any attention. I was trying to drown out the image of you and him laughing in the grocery store parking lot. Levi took a beer out of the fridge and made his way to the back room.

I brought out some plates and looked inside the bottom pizza box. I closed the lid not bothering with the supreme pizza and put 3 slices of pepperoni on my plate. I shook my head to clear the idea of you and Levi, but the image kept creeping back in. I threw back the rest of my beer and poured a glass of bourbon with a few ice cubes and went to the back room.

—⚇—

All three of us ended up pretty wasted, we drank the bourbon along with most of the alcohol I had laying around. We had already ate the pizzas and now we were trying to come up with something to do. Levi suggested turning the PlayStation back on, Alex wanted to go to the bar, I could care less I was just getting tired of sitting here listening to music. I tapped the arm of the chair I was sitting in; I wondered if I could talk you into coming over. I would love your company, and I know the guys would appreciate it as well.

I picked up my phone. I was going to call you, but I wasn't sure how I would react if you didn't pick up. Instead, I sent you a text. I mentioned Levi and how you should come over to hang out. I sent another text saying how I was bored and that you would liven up the place. I even offered to come get you.

Alex threw something at me. It bounced off my shoulder and rolled off to the other side of the room. I threw my hands up, "What the fuck?!" I yelled.

"Pay attention next time. I said, next weekend we should hit up the concert that's playing downtown." He went over the details, what bands were playing, how much the tickets were, and if we wanted to bring anyone along and who we wanted to bring.

What felt like an eternity passed when you finally replied to my texts. You turned me down, saying you were busy and tried for next weekend. Smirking, I told you that tonight was better, I promised you a lot of fun. Almost immediately you told me that you were drunk and shouldn't be driving.

That got my hopes up. If you were already drunk when you got here it would be easier to talk you into fucking Alex and Levi. I reminded you that I would come get you. I was in no shape to drive myself, but you didn't need to know that. All you needed to do was come over and leave the rest to us. "Hey, I know what we can do tonight. I just need to talk Mel into coming over." The guys stopped talking and turned their attention to me.

"You're serious?" Levi asked, he pointed a finger at me swaying slightly.

I nodded and said, "There's a good chance she'll agree." I said pressing the button to video call you. It rang a few times, but when you answered I couldn't stop the grin that spread across my face when I saw you. "Hey! I thought since you won't let me come get you, I could see you this way."

You smiled and popped a chip into your mouth. You told me how you just made dinner and hoped I didn't mind you eating. I grinned and said I didn't mind at all. *I could watch you eat all day* I thought. Alex stood up and started making obscene gestures. I tried not to laugh.

"What did you make?" I asked you. You showed me the sandwich you made, "That looks good. When I get there, you should make me one." I said with a wink.

You shook your head, "Griffin, you're in no better shape to drive than I am." I thought I was doing a good job at hiding the fact that I was drunk, I guess not.

That made the guys bark out a laugh. I flipped the camera, "One of these fuckers can drive then," flipping the camera back around before they could do anything stupid, "Or I can call an uber." That was brilliant. I should have thought of that sooner, we could have been knocking on your door by now. Shrugging at the lost opportunity I went on to say, "I'll walk if it comes down to it. Are you sure I can't see you tonight?" I really wanted to follow through on my deal with the guys. Levi and Alex were taking turns throwing wads of paper at an empty bottle on the coffee table to see who could make it in first.

You picked up a glass, and I licked my lips as you brought it up and took a drink, "I'd rather none of you drive, you all look pretty wasted."

Alex put his hand to his chest, "Aww she cares about us."

Levi called out how sweet you were, and we all laughed. I smiled wider and asked what was keeping you from me, there was no way you had someone over. Anger rolled through me, but I kept the smile on for you, "You don't have company, do you?" I asked.

You picked the phone up and flipped the view around so I could see what you saw, and honestly I had no idea what I was looking at. It was a sparkly picture of the guy from the Scream movies, and you had tiny bits of plastic scattered around it. "No, I'm just working on this. It's almost done."

I laughed, "That looks extremely time consuming."

Levi came up behind me, "Woah," he said leaning over me, "That's awesome. Is that really why you don't want to hang out?" The view flipped back around to you, and you just shrugged at us. Taking the opportunity Levi took the conversation over. "Hey, did you listen to my album?"

You nodded and with a huge grin you started to talking about how amazing Levi's band was. While you were getting wet talking about your favorite songs, I bumped Levi's fist off screen. We both knew what was up.

Grinning Levi told you that you should come over, "We can hang out and listen to some music."

But again, you shook your pretty head no. "Not tonight." You said with a teasing smile.

I looked back at Levi and then to you, I put a hand on my chest, "Honestly Mel, I'm hurt."

Laughing, you told me that I would be fine and placed the phone in a position so you could still video chat with me and work on whatever it was that you were doing. I don't get it, usually girls' trip over themselves when we tell them to come over. You took another drink. I asked what you were drinking, and you told me wine and turned your focus back to your project.

"I've never been a wine drinker. I'm more of a whiskey guy myself." I asked what kind of wine you had, and you told me it was a red something, I wasn't really paying attention. I was too concerned with the way the light played with your features. The glow from your TV was casting shadows across your beautiful face in a way that was so hypnotizing I couldn't look away.

Alex flopped down next to me, causing me to jump. "We can get a bottle of that for you here."

"No, it's ok. One bottle is enough for the night." You laughed.

"Ok then we can get you something else." He suggested. Then he threw his arm up almost knocking the phone from my hand, "Oh I know! I can make some food! How about it, Mel? You liked the food from my food truck, just imagine what I can do in the kitchen."

You laughed, "Thank you but I'm still eating." You took a bite of your sandwich to further prove your point.

Levi appeared behind the sofa and leaned in between Alex and I, "We can play a game instead, I would love to go against you in Mortal Kombat."

Alex shoved Levi, pushing him into me, "He cheats at that game, you don't want to do that Mel. We can play together instead. That way it'll be a better match." He ended the statement with a wink.

I leaned around Levi, "How the fuck do you cheat at Mortal Combat?" I asked.

Alex looked at me like I was dumb, "There's combinations you can look up online to refill the health bar."

Levi and I both looked at him, Levi shoved Alex. "What the fuck ever dude. You're just mad cause you can't game for shit."

Alex got up and faced Levi, "I'm a better gamer than you bro. I'll wipe the floor with ya ass any day at any game."

Levi threw his arms to the side, "Then why do I eliminate you every time we play Mortal Kombat?"

Alex pointed his finger in Levi's face, "Cause you fucking cheat."

Slapping his hand away, "I don't fucking cheat, you just can't handle the fact that you fucking suck at that game."

I got up and went to the kitchen glancing down on the phone to make sure you didn't hang up. "What are you watching?" I asked. You told me about a movie marathon that was running on the Syfy channel. I sat down at the table and put my phone against the wall, so I didn't have to keep holding it. "I can put that on over here and we can all watch it together. Come on it'll be fun; we can make it into a drinking game." I smirked and got up to get another drink, whiskey on ice. I never fully run out of alcohol here there's a bottle hiding somewhere. I sat back down and took a drink, "Why don't you want to come over?" I asked.

You took a long drink of your wine before replying, "It's been a long week, and I just want to stay home and relax."

"Then let me come to you," waving my hand between me and the phone I said, "this isn't doing it for me. I want to be there with you." I took a drink. You shook your head and opened your mouth to speak but I quickly cut you off, "I know, I know. But do you blame me for wanting to spend my time with a beautiful woman instead of these two morons?" I gave you my most charming smile.

Smiling you said, "I guess not. But the answer is still no."

I scratched my eyebrow; this is harder than I thought it would be. "That's a shame. I was hoping to wear you down." I chuckled and took you in for a moment, "You look beautiful tonight." I took a drink.

You started to blush. I smirked as you said thank you. Something on your phone screen must have gotten your attention. Your blushing cheeks turned back to their original color as you picked up your phone and the screen when black for a moment. When you came back into view, I asked what was going on. "Oh, I was just telling my sister good night." You took the last bite of your sandwich.

My stomach growled at me at the sight of the food. I told you that it looked good, and that I should get myself something to eat too. I got up and grabbed a bag of chips and a jar of dip.

Alex walked in after I sat down and grabbed some chips, "I was coming in here to get something to eat too." After he ate a few chips he asked, "So she's not coming huh?"

I shook my head, "Nah. I can't convince her to come over. She thinks she's too drunk." I laughed and took a drink.

"Well now what?" He asked.

I shrugged. "Order some Chinese? I'll need more to eat than just chips."

Alex nodded, "Yeah some spring rolls sound good. I wonder if the Chinese joint is still open?"

"They should be." I said, "They changed their hours last week." I turned back to my phone and seen you looking triumphantly. "Did you finish it?" I asked.

You picked up your phone and showed me the picture you were working on. "Sure did!" You said excitedly.

"Does this mean you'll come over now?" I asked.

Alex looked over my shoulder, "Yeah come over, I'll send you an uber." he said hopefully.

You flipped view back so we could see you, smiling at us you said, "no. It means I'm going to get ready for bed."

"Hold on now. I'm not ready to say goodbye just yet." I said in a rush.

Sighing you got up. There was the clinking of dishes, "I don't know how much longer I'll be able to stay awake. I'm pretty tired." Alex asked you if we were that boring, you shook your head politely "It's not you." You said with a yawn.

"I can make you some coffee." I suggested.

You laughed, "Then I'll be up all night. I want to go to sleep at some point tonight. We can hang out some other time." You promised.

I smirked; you were so stubborn. "Alright fine," I finally said giving up, "I'll let you go. But text when you wake up ok?"

You smiled at me. "I will. Good night, Griffin." After a moment you added, "Good night, Alex, I don't know if Levi is in the kitchen as well, but good night to you too."

I laughed, "He's not but I'll tell him." the same time that Alex said, "Good night, Mel."

After we hung up I threw back the rest of my drink and went to the back room. "Melanie says good night." I said as I sat down.

"I take it she's staying home," Levi said. I nodded, "that sucks."

"Alex is ordering food." I said, taking the box out from under the coffee table.

"Still sucks. I was hoping to mess around tonight."

I shrugged, "I couldn't get her to leave her apartment. Next time we'll just show up."

Alex walked in and sat down. "Twenty more minutes and they would have been closed. Food will be here in fifteen." He said watching me cut up some lines. "Your girl is thick headed. Are you sure messing with her is a good idea?"

"Yeah, I'm sure. Besides, she's just being cautious. Give me a few more weeks and she'll be wrapped around my finger." I said and bent over to snort the white powder.

"Well in the meantime don't mind me if I swoop in." Levi said bending over the table once I sat up. "After all, I don't mind you fucking Natasha."

"You don't mind if anyone fucks her." I said, "you just want her out of your house, you don't care how."

Levi laughed, "But it doesn't work, she keeps coming back. Oh well, mom made me promise to keep a roof over her head, and I'm not about to dump money on her so she can get her own place. You know she's not good at keeping her bills paid."

I shrugged, "That's why I'm glad I'm an only child."

"Ya know, your sister would have better luck at finding a guy to take care of her if she would stop sucking off every guy who looked at her." Alex said.

Levi laughed, "Tell her that, not me."

A little while later there was a knock on the door and the food was delivered. The rest of the night went by in a smokey haze, Levi ended up crashing on the sofa in the back room and Alex took the one in the front room. I fell asleep in my bed looking at your Facebook page.

MELANIE (May 23)

It was a fairly nice day, a little breezy but it wasn't snowing. I checked the weather forecast and decided to take advantage of the nice day.

There was a park that had a 5-mile walking trail that looped through a wooded area and eventually took you to a lake; and then led you back to the parking lot. I've driven by it a few times and looked around on the internet to see what people had to say about the trail. It wasn't too far from the apartment, so I hopped into my car and drove the 20 minutes. I needed something to do, and it was a beautiful day outside.

When I pulled up to the parking lot there were three other vehicles, a blue SUV, a red truck, and a silver car. I parked in a shaded corner and grabbed my small hiking bag, in it I had a first aid kit, a peanut butter and jelly sandwich, some crackers, an apple, a water bottle, and my headphones. I made sure my belt knife was secure in its place before getting out. I put my phone in my pocket and double checked that I had everything one more time before locking the door and putting the car keys in the front pocket of the backpack. I stood in the parking lot at the trailhead doing some quick stretches, I wasn't planning on running but it didn't hurt to limber up before a long walk.

It was fairly nice out; out in the sun it was almost warm but once I got into the trees it cooled down significantly. I picked up my pace and took out my headphones, placing one in my ear and keeping the volume down so I was still aware of my surroundings. I loved being out in nature and reconnecting with the world outside of the city. I kept walking, taking in the sun rays cutting through the tree limbs and smiling at the squirrels chasing each other.

I made my way down the path, stepping over fallen trees that haven't been removed yet, and stopping to take a picture of a cool bug carrying a leaf. I stood up and was about to put my phone back in my pocket when a text message from Griffin came through.

'Wanna hang out?' He asked.

I typed out a message, telling him I wasn't home, but I would let him know when I got back. I heard a phone chime over to my left. I snapped my head toward the noise and froze, trying to see if anything stood out. My attention was pulled back to my phone. It was just a notification from Merge Dragons. I put my phone back in my pocket, along with the headphones and kept walking down the path.

It was quiet, other than my footsteps and the occasional bird, I didn't hear anything. I came up to the part of the path that forked, if I took a left, it would take me to a sculpture park, but if I kept going straight it would lead me to the lake. I decided to keep straight, I've seen plenty of pictures of the sculptures; the craftsmanship was stunning no doubt, but nothing manmade could ever compared to the sun reflecting off the water.

I saw an older couple walking hand in hand coming back from the lake. They both smiled at me as they passed and I returned gesture with a cheery, "Hello, beautiful day, isn't it?"

The woman agreed and they carried on down the path, and I kept going forward; eager to sit down and eat the lunch I had packed. It wasn't too much longer when the lake finally came into view, I could see the large gazebo that had benches facing the lake.

I adjusted my bag and took a step forward when I heard a twig snap behind me. I looked over my shoulder, but I didn't see anything. I couldn't tell if my heart was racing from the anxiety or from the walk. Turning back around I went over to the gazebo and took my bag off before I sat down. I pulled out my lunch and just sat there looking out onto the water, listening to the noises around me.

I picked up my water bottle and after a long drink I took out my phone so I could take a picture of the lake. I had a message from Griffin. 'I wish I could sit with you.' The hair on the back of my neck stood up, I felt like someone was watching me but when I scanned the area around me, I didn't see anyone. Other than a few chipmunks and a couple of birds I was the only one moving and making noise. My phone buzzed once in my hand, letting me know I had a new notification. 'What's wrong Mel?'

I started putting everything back in my bag. Once I had my arms through the straps, I asked him why he thought something was wrong. I looked back at the tree line but still didn't see anything suspicious. I put my hand on my belt knife and made my way back to the path that took me to the parking lot.

My phone buzzed again, 'You just seem quiet. Am I going to get to see you today?'

Typing out a fast, 'We can hang out when I get home.' I put my phone in my back pocket and focused on what was around me. I walked slowly, trying not to kick up too many rocks so I could hear if there were any footsteps coming from the woods.

When I got to the path that disappeared into the trees, I thought I heard a sigh, but it could have been the wind. I put my hand on my belt knife and picked up my pace. That's when I heard a whistle, it started low and ended on a high note. I'm not a bird expert but I'm certain that was human. "Is someone fucking with me!?" I shouted, pulling my knife free and turning around in a circle, looking in all directions. Of course, there was no answer.

On high alert I started walking again, keeping my knife out. It took longer than I wanted to get back to the parking lot, which was empty except for my car. That gave me some relief, knowing that in theory I was the only one out here. Walking by the trailhead I stopped to shrug my bag off so I could get my car keys out.

I was looping my arm back through the strap when from woods behind me I heard a masculine voice call out, "Bye."

Ice ran through me. I don't think I ever moved so fast in my life. In the blink of an eye, I was at my car ripping the door open. I threw myself inside and slammed the door shut, hitting the lock button. Jamming the key into the ignition, I put the car in drive and peeled out of the parking lot.

—◊—

When I got home I couldn't sit still. Every noise made me jump; every shadow turned into an intruder. I paced around the living room, I felt violated somehow. Thinking of someone following me and watching me through the trees made my skin crawl. I swiped at my arms like I was brushing off cobwebs, trying to shake the feeling that eyes were still on me. I looked around the apartment, something was still off.

I heard a noise coming from the bedroom. My heart pounded in my chest, and I started breathing heavily. I tried to swallow but my mouth was dry. I wiped my sweaty palms on my shirt and took a deep breath, I held it for 4 seconds and let it out slowly. I did that two more times, I was still on edge and terrified beyond belief but at least now I had control over my thoughts. Slowly I stepped toward the bedroom.

When I got to the door I poked my head into the room and looked around. I didn't see anything out of the ordinary, so I went and did a more thorough search. When I checked the closet I heard creaking above and behind me. Looking up at the ceiling, I realized the noises I heard was the upstairs neighbors. I let out a sigh of relief and felt my whole body relax as the tension melted away. I felt a little ridiculous but after what happened at the walking trails I'd rather be paranoid than dead.

I took a quick shower and messaged my sister. She thought I was being overly paranoid and that it makes sense to be on guard in a new place. I could see how that story would sound like the ravings of a madman but come on, that was horrifying. I sat my phone down on the coffee table and went to the kitchen to get something to drink.

I pulled a cup down from the cabinet and filled it with tea from the fridge. When I turned around my reflection in the window made my heart stop. Yeah Kendra was right, I was overly paranoid. I shook my head and put my cup down on the coffee table. Walking around the apartment I made sure that the windows were locked, and the curtains were closed.

When I sat down I picked my phone up. I was going to message Griffin, but he beat me to it. 'Are you home yet?'

I told him I was and asked him to come over. If that creep from the trails did follow me home there was no way he was going to try something with Griffin here. He told me to give him a half an hour, but he was knocking on my door 20 minutes later.

When I first heard the knocking I didn't know what to expect. My legs turned to jelly as I walked to the door and stood on my tip toes to look through the peephole. I took a breath to steady myself before I opened the door.

"Hey Griffin. Thanks for coming over." I said stepping to the side so he could walk through the door.

Griffin looked down at me with a wolfish smile. "No need to thank me, it's my pleasure really." He looked me up and down and then turned to take his shoes off and sat them by the door. "I'm glad you asked me to come over. I was just sitting at home watching TV, that's only entertaining for so long." He stood up and faced me. "I could never get tired of you."

I shook my head and tried to fight a smile. "You're something else." I laughed, "Do you want anything from the kitchen?" I asked to change the subject.

Griffin nodded his head. "What do you have to drink?"

I told him tea and water; he asked for some tea and went to sit down on the sofa. I walked over to the kitchen and poured Griffin a cup of tea and went to sit down next to him. Putting his cup down in front of him on the coffee table, I looked around the apartment focusing mainly on the windows making sure you couldn't see out the curtains. If you can see out, you can see in. A noise in the kitchen startled me but it was just the neighbors upstairs.

I had no intention of telling Griffin what happened. I already felt dumb that I let it play with my anxiety like this; but I was jumpy, and every little noise put me on edge. I was pulling at my hair looking down the hallway when Griffin nudged me to get my attention. "What's up, are you ok?" he asked.

I took a breath and fake laughed. "Yeah I'm fine, it's just been a crazy day."

Griffin side eyed me. "You're a horrible liar." He said leaning forward to pick up his cup. "What happened?" he asked casually taking a drink.

I shook my head and rubbed my temple. "Honestly nothing really."

"That can't be true if it's got you this messed up." He said. I could feel his eyes on me, but I kept mine down. "Melanie." I glanced up at him, his eyes were focused on mine. "What happened." His tone was stern, there was no detectible emotion on his face.

I flicked my eyes to the side and sat up straight. Sighing I ran a hand through my hair and went over what happened. "Well, I was out for a walk. Everything was going as you would expect." I stumbled over how to word this next part, but I just went with it. "Umm it was shortly after you messaged the first time, right after I replied I heard a phone go off in the woods beside me." I didn't look at him, "A while after that there was a twig that was snapped, like something heavy stepped on it. But other than me there was no one around. I didn't even seen any animals." I shook my head and reached for my tea. "It was so strange… the entire time I was out there I could feel someone watching me." I took a drink and prepared myself for the next part. "So, on the way back to the parking lot I was unsettled, to say the least. Then things got really weird, I heard heavy breathing and then there was this whistle that no way could have been from a bird. I was on guard and shouted, 'is someone fucking with me!' but of course I didn't get an answer. When I got to the parking lot I stopped to get my keys, and I know I heard someone say 'bye'." I didn't realize how fast I was speaking; I was out of breath when I got to the end of the story, and I know I heard a tremble in my voice.

Griffin put his hand on my knee, "Where there any other vehicles when you first got there?" he asked.

I nodded, "yeah, there was blue SUV, red truck, and silver car." I shrugged. "I didn't catch the make or model of any of them."

Griffin chuckled, "that's alright. What Park did you go to?" When I told him he kind of nodded. "There's three parking lots that have access to the trails you were on. There's no telling which parking lot that person came from." I look up at him almost surprised. "There's a lot of dangerous people in this area. If you're going to keep going out on your own, please promise me you'll be more careful."

I nodded and hugged him relieved that he was taking me seriously, "Can I stay with you tonight?" I mumbled. "When I got home I felt like someone was watching me, I'm just kind of creeped out." I gave an awkward laugh.

Griffin pulled me in tighter. "Of course."

I let the hug go on for a few more seconds then pulled away, "I need to get a bag together then."

In the bedroom I pulled a bag down from the closet and threw in some clothes, deodorant, a hairbrush, and some other things I might need for an overnight stay.

I was nervous about spending the night with Griffin, mainly because I didn't want to embarrass myself in front of him. But the thought of being here alone tonight when someone might have been lurking just outside the window was enough to make me want to puke. So, I put on a smile and went to the living room, where Griffin was waiting for me patiently on the sofa. He looked up at me over his phone and grinned, "Ready to go?" He asked.

I nodded and slipped on my shoes. "After you," I said, opening the door and getting my keys ready to lock up the apartment before we left.

GRIFFIN (May 23)

I drove by your place hoping that you would be home, but your car was gone. I went to go get something to eat and then drove by again, but your parking spot was still empty. I did this a few different times going to the store and coming back, but each time I passed your car still hadn't appeared. I pulled in and parked were you usually do and pulled out my phone. I checked out the social platforms I knew you had accounts on, but you hadn't posted anything on where you would be or what you had planned today, which was annoying. How was I supposed to find you if you didn't tell the world where you would be?

I went home and pulled out my laptop to see if I could get your phones location to pull up. It didn't take long to find out that you were at the state park just outside of town. I thought of driving over there to track you down on the trails, but I didn't feel like running around the woods today. I get enough of that at Grandpas.

Closing the laptop, I got up and turned on the radio. After a 20-minute workout I cleaned up and took out my phone. I sent you a text asking if you wanted to hang out. I hadn't heard from you all day and was a little disappointed when you told me that you weren't home but would let me know when you were. I was hoping you were going to tell me that you were already home and to come over.

I let a half an hour pass before I sent a message saying how I wish I could sit with you. I was getting bored and could use some company, but you were out running around the park; and I was here zoning out on a first-person shooter begging for something, *anything* else to do. After a few minutes I still hadn't heard back from you. So, I sent a message asking if something was wrong.

You asked why I thought something was wrong. I scratched my eyebrow. It's been 5 months, and you still don't seem completely sold on me yet. 'You just seem quiet. Am I going to get to see you today?'

'We can hang out when I get home.'

I raised an eyebrow and sat my phone down; we're going to have to have a conversation about your attitude. I picked the controller back up and played for a while longer, and before I knew it 2 hours had passed. Sighing, I picked my phone up and sent you a text asking if you were home. I thought you would have messaged me by now but I'm tired of waiting. When I read your reply, I couldn't fight the smile that spread across my face, not only were you home but you wanted me to come over. I told you I would be there in half an hour. I did a bump of coke and rolled a joint, I put on a fresh layer of deodorant and body spray and walked out the door, locking it behind me.

I made it to your place in record time. I couldn't get out of the car fast enough, practically tripping over myself getting out of the car. When I got inside the building I took a deep breath and smoothed out my clothes before I knocked on your door. When you opened the door and greeted me, I felt like I melted in your presence. "Hey Griffin," you said stepping to the side so I could come in, "thank you for coming over."

"No need to thank me," I said with a charming smile, "it's my pleasure really." Looking you up and down, my smile dropped. Something seemed off about you, I took my shoes off and sat them by the door. I said something about how I was glad you asked me to come over and how bored I was at home, "I could never get tired of you."

I smirked as you failed to fight a smile. "You're something else," you said, I laughed, "Do you want anything from the kitchen?" you asked, already walking around the counter that divided the kitchen from the living room.

I asked what you had to drink, hoping you would offer some form of alcohol but much to my disappointment you offered water or tea. I asked for some tea, went to the sofa, and sat down. You were acting really strange; every little noise made you jump, and you couldn't seem to focus on one spot for long. I watched you carefully as you brought my glass over to me and sat down beside me.

You were nervously tugging at your hair looking around the room. I nudged you to get your attention, "What's up, are you ok?" I asked once you looked at me. You forced a laugh and said that you were fine. "You're a horrible liar." I said leaning forward and grabbing my cup of tea. "What happened?"

You shook your head and rubbed your temples. "Honestly nothing really."

I sat my cup down and turned to face you, "That can't be true if it's got you this messed up." You avoided my gaze, you seemed tired. "Melanie, what happened?" I asked.

At first I didn't think you were going to answer me. But after a brief moment you went on to tell me about the experience you had while out on the trails. From the sound of it you got off easily. I put my hand on your knee and asked about the vehicles in the parking lot.

You gave me a typical answer, the color and style of vehicle but no make or model. Not very helpful but coming from you, it was kind of adorable. I laughed and asked what park you went to. When you told me were you went, all it did was increase the number of possible creeps that had stalked you through the woods. I hated to put this on you, but it was better that you were aware, "There's 3 parking lots that have access to the trails that you were on. There's no telling which parking lot that person came from. There's a lot of dangerous people in this area, Mel. If you're going to keep going out on your own, *please* promise me you'll be more careful."

You nodded and threw your arms around me. My heart skipped a beat when I heard you mumble, "Can I stay with you tonight? When I got home, I felt like someone was watching me, I'm just kind of creeped out." You forced another laugh.

I pulled you in tighter, you sounded so small and helpless. "Of course," I said burying my face in the top of your head and inhaling your scent.

You held on for a moment longer, I never wanted you to pull away. But when you did you said something about going to pack a bag, I let you go. Knowing you trusted me enough to seek comfort after a traumatic experience had me higher than any drug I've done in a while. I pulled out my phone to keep myself distracted while you got some things together. You following me out to my car so we could go back to my place was such an accomplishment you'd have a hard time taking this feeling from me. I opened the car door for you and then got in the driver seat to take us back to my place. Fuck, I felt like a kid on Christmas.

MELANIE (June 16)

It was a boring Saturday; I spent most of the morning cleaning and when I ran out of things to straighten up I decided to go get ready for a walk around town. I changed into a white tank top sporting a black metal band and put on a pair of black shorts, then I slipped a belt through the loops on my shorts to secure my belt knife for protection. I grabbed my phone and put in one ear bud, so the walk wasn't so quiet. Making sure the apartment was locked up I set out to walk over to the park that was on the other side of town. I've driven by it a few times; there's a walking path that had a few sculptures set around it.

The walk there wasn't too bad when the wind picked up, it was hot, and I was starting to sweat. I would need a shower when I got home but it was nice to get out of the apartment. When I got to the park it wasn't too busy, there were a few people milling about but not so many people that it made me want to turn around and leave.

I stepped on the walking path and followed it around the swings and slides and over to the sculptures. When I walked through the metal gateway it was like I stepped into a fairytale, there were sculptures of mushrooms the size of kitchen chairs, flowers that were taller than me, they had miniature trees that came up to my chin set up with tiny mushroom creatures going about what would be a normal day for them. I laughed and took my phone out, taking a picture of a tiny mushroom lady hanging out of a window next to a tree limb; she was shaking out a towel that looked like the artist made it to look like a leaf. I took a few more close-ups shots and stepped back to take another picture, flipping through them real quick I sent the best ones to my sister.

I continued down the path; it took me out of what I had now nicknamed the mushroom kingdom and down to a small hill by a pond that ducks were swimming in. I walked over and sat down on the bench to rest and take in my surroundings.

I was so wrapped up in enjoying myself and the song that was playing that I didn't hear the footsteps coming up on me. An arm was flung around my shoulders as someone sat down next to me. Reacting on instinct I shoved the person away from me and stood up, just to smash into the chest of another man who wrapped his arms around me and started to laugh. His laugh vibrated through me along with a wave of panic. I pushed myself away; but he just held me tighter.

"Chill out Mel, it's just us." The man holding me said. I took a couple wild breaths and looked up at the person who still had his arms around me and felt the tension drop from my body. Levi was looking down at me with a wolfish grin, "Didn't mean to scare you so bad little doe." He said, shifting so he was now standing beside me with an arm around my shoulders, like he was afraid I was going to run.

Alex was the one who had sat down earlier, the one I shoved away, he was laughing too. "I wish someone was recording that. That was hilarious."

I rolled my eyes, "Yeah so funny," I said sarcastically. My heart was still beating out of control.

"Oh. Come on, don't be like that," Levi said, his face was a little too close. I shrugged his arm off and took a step to the side. "Hey, I'm sorry we startled you." he said putting his hands up then he shoved them in his pockets, "What are you doing out here by yourself?" He asked.

I shifted uneasily and from the bench Alex chimed in, "You shouldn't feel threatened around us, Mel. We're harmless." I looked over at him, and he was taking a hit off a vape pen.

Levi shifted next to me drawing my attention back to him. I took the headphone out of my ear and put it back in the charging case. "Where's Griffin?" I asked, hoping he was going to show up soon. If these two are here he wouldn't be too far behind, right? I put my headphones in my pocket and looked around. But I didn't see him.

Levi shrugged, "Last I knew he was working on a car." His eyes flicked down then quickly back up, he cleared his throat, "Wanna go see him? We can drive you there."

I shook my head no, "If he's at work I don't want to bother him." I said walking back towards the walking path.

Alex got off the bench and quickly caught up to me. "Ok that's fair. We don't have to hang out with Griffin. That garage is dirty anyway, no place for a lady. We can go back to my place and chill there." He said with a sly smile.

I raised an eyebrow and shrugged, "I'm not sure your girlfriend would appreciate that."

Alex's smile shifted into almost a sneer.

Levi howled out in laughter, "Damn way to call him out like that." He reached for me, but I pulled back. Dropping his hand with an exasperated breath. "You act like we plan to hurt you," he ran a hand through his hair then he said lightly, "I promise you we have no ill intention." Looking over at Alex and back at me he continued, "We just want to make sure that you're safe. That's all," his gaze turned downward, and he slowly brought his eyes back up as he said, "There's a lot of dangerous people in this town, you shouldn't be out here alone."

I glanced from Levi to Alex. It was hard to read them, they both gave me funny vibes, but they haven't done anything to lose my trust.

Reflecting on to what Griffin was saying about the people in this city I nodded my head and agreed, thinking back that creep out on the hiking path the other day. "Yeah, maybe you're right." If I had Alex and Levi with me on the path I doubt that creep would have terrorized me the way he did.

Alex stepped over to me and asked, "Where did you park your car, we didn't even know you were here."

"Oh, I walked." Levi and Alex exchanged a glance and looked at me like I grew another head. "What?" I asked.

Levi shrugged, "Don't you live on the other side of town?" he asked.

I tilted my head to the side, "Yeah, and?"

Alex shook his head, "Just a long walk is all." He leaned over and said to Levi, "Should we tell Griffin? I don't think he'd be down with her walking through town."

I was taken aback, "Griffin will have to get over it." I said, "I'm a big girl, I can handle walking through town by myself." I said.

Levi smirked at me, "I'm sure you believe that." He said walking up to look down at me, he raised a hand as if measuring how tall I am, "you're pretty short," he said.

Alex stepped beside him, "Even though you have some meat on you, it would be easy to overpower you." he said.

"Especially if there were two." Levi added. A shock wave of anxiety washed over me.

I felt my soul leave my body as they both started laughing at the same time. "Relax, we're just making a point." Alex said.

Levi looped his arm through mine and started walking, "Sorry Mel, but it wouldn't be right if we left you alone out here. Come on, we were just about ready to head out and smoke."

I shook my head and pulled my arm away, "I don't feel good about smoking with y'all without Griffin."

Alex took out his phone and tapped on the screen. Turning the phone so I could read what he typed out, it was a text he sent to Griffin saying, 'Hey ran into ur grl at the park. Taking her to Levis to smoke.'

Griffin sent back a single 'k' then my phone started vibrating.

'Why are you at the park.' 'I thought we talked about you going places alone.' 'don't leave their sight.' 'This job is taking longer than I want. I won't get off until another few hours.' I sighed. Somehow, I feel like they just told on me, and now I was in trouble. Another one came through. 'Stay at Levis I'll come get you from there.'

Levi must have been reading over my shoulder, "Damn he blows your phone up. Griffin never shows us that much attention. Alex man look at this shit, she gets full on sentences, and all we ever get is one word. If that." Then back to me he said, "You heard the man, you're with me." he almost giggled as he started pulling me down the path.

Alex was on the other side of me, I almost felt trapped. "It'll be fun Mel," Alex said, "If at any time you feel uncomfortable we'll take you back to your place and we can wait for Griffin there."

I brought my shoulders up in a defensive motion, "Or you can drop me off at my place and go back to yours?"

Levi chuckled, "And pass up on this opportunity to have you all for us, to get to know you better? You're funny." Levi let my arm go and wrapped it around my waist to pull me closer to him, "Besides, Griffin said to stay with us until he gets off work." He slid his hand down and rested it on my hip, right on top of my knife. His jaw dropped and he pulled up the hem of my tank top just enough to expose the hilt, "My, my, my," He exclaimed, to Alex he said, "Our little Mel has claws," he laughed.

Alex (who had also seen the hilt) started laughing too, "Little doe? More like little kitten."

I rolled my eyes, "Don't call me kitten." I said disgusted.

Levi was the first to compose himself. "Joking aside it is nice to know that you're not *completely* defenseless. For some attackers, a little struggle is enough to deter them, having a knife on you increases your chances of fending off the more dangerous threats." He looked at me with admiration. "Good thinking Mel." He said smiling.

I gave a small smile in return.

Alex groaned, "Just fuck each other already so we can go."

My eyes got wide and I'm sure my face started to turn red. Levi laughed again, "Aww, he was just kidding Mel," He threw his arm around me again, "Although I'm down if you are."

I shrugged him off and went to walk on the other side of Alex, "Sorry I don't mess around with other people while I'm in a relationship." Alex chuckled, "What other people do is their business."

Levi smirked and changed the conversation, "Do you want to get something to eat before we go back to my place? Once we get there I won't want to get back out, besides it's hard to drive while I'm on that stuff."

Alex nodded, "Yeah we probably should."

I looked up at Levi then at Alex, "Hard to drive on what?"

The guys ignored me and started walking, talking about what sounded good to eat.

"Levi are you going to be good to drive?" I asked.

He laughed, "it's all good, I'm not the one driving. I just meant that I won't be the one who goes to get food if we wait."

I looked over at Alex, "Are you ok to drive then?"

Alex nodded and put his arm around my shoulders, "I'm always good to drive." He said then his foot caught the edge of the sidewalk, causing him to stumble almost pulling us down to the ground.

Levi laughed, "Yeah man, you are the definition of smooth."

We walked up to the parking lot and Alex led us over to his car. It was a nice vehicle, nowhere near as nice as Griffin's; but a hell of a lot better than mine.

Levi came up by me and said, "You can have front," then he opened the door for me and hopped in the back. These guys might give off weird vibes, but at least they have manners.

"Thank you." I said, getting in and closing the door.

Alex got in and started the car. Country music started playing, Levi leaned forward and said in my ear, "His taste in music is awful."

I turned my head, leaning backwards so I could see him, "You don't have to be so close to me."

Smirking he said, "You're right, I don't have to," He moved slightly closer and said, "But I want to."

I pulled the seat forward and turned my attention out the windshield. Alex turned the music down, "What sounds good for lunch Mel?"

I brushed some hair behind my ear, "Um, pizza?" I threw it out there. Not sure what else to suggest.

Alex nodded his head. "Yeah, that sounds good. Does it matter what kind?" He asked.

"No veggies or mushrooms, fish or fruit." I replied.

From the back Levi already had his phone out ordering a pizza, he laughed and said, "So nothing good." Then a wolfish grin broke on his face, "You'll get all the meat you can handle later."

I turned around in the seat and faced him, "What does that mean?" I challenged.

Smirking at me he winked, "It's just a joke." Then to Alex he said, "Got it ordered, usual place under my name."

I narrowed my eyes and turned back around.

"Yeah, his jokes aren't usually funny." Alex said from the driver's seat, "You'll get used to it," Glancing over at me he added, "maybe."

We pulled up to a pizza joint and Alex put the car in park, said he'd be right back and hopped out. When he closed the door Levi put his elbow on the driver's head rest. "My band is putting out a new song." I perked up and faced him, he laughed, "Want to hear it?"

"You guys have a new song out?" I took my phone out and opened Spotify.

Levi handed me a headphone, "It's still in the early stages of production so you won't be able to find it anywhere." My eyes widened, I was awestruck, how many people get this chance? Grinning like a fool, I took the headphone out of his hand and slipped it in my ear. "Go easy with your criticism, I'm sensitive."

I rolled my eyes and laughed, it was about that time Alex came back, he handed the pizza boxes back to Levi. "Alright let's go." Alex put the car in reverse, "I'm taking us to your place," he said glancing at me while looked over his shoulder to back up. "Mostly because Levi's sister is home."

I felt relieved and was about to tell him where I lived when Levi said from the back, "If that's that case we need to make stop at the liquor store."

Alex nodded, "Good call man."

"What's wrong with your sister?" I asked Levi.

Levi shook his head, "She's just a lot."

Alex laughed, "that and it was her turn to take out the trash, think she's done it yet?"

"Fuck no," Levi replied, "why do you think I haven't been home in days. If I go home and that trashcan is still over flowing; Alex man you better the cops I'm tired of dealing with her."

"I'll go scope out the place first if you want?" Alex offered.

Levi scoffed, "we could always send Griffin."

That part caught me off guard. "Why would you send Griffin?" I asked.

Alex looked at Levi through the rearview mirror. "He's just more assertive than us."

When that song was over, I handed Levi back the headphone, "So what did you think?" He asked.

In truth I forgot to pay attention, "It was pretty good, when do you think it'll be available for download?" I asked. I decided to drop the earlier topic, keeping it filed away in the back of my mind for later though. Something didn't feel right but I can obsess over it later.

Levi shrugged. "Give me your number and I'll let you know."

I raised an eyebrow, "Or you can just let Griffin know and then he can tell me."

Levi grinned and sat back in his seat.

Shortly after we were pulling up the liquor store, Levi tapped me on the shoulder and asked if I wanted anything in particular, I shook my head and told him that it was too early for me to start drinking. Levi smirked and said he'd be right back and hopped out the car.

I leaned my head back and wasn't aware that I was following Levi with my eyes until Alex cleared his throat, snapping me out of it. I looked over at him, and he was smirking at me.

"What's your address?" He asked. At first I thought he was going to call me out. "I'm pretty sure I already know where you live, but I want to double check." He nodded when I told him and laughed, "Yeah, I was so far off. I'm glad I asked."

I leaned my head back on the headrest and looked at him, "You know you guys don't have to babysit me."

"We're not babysitting you; we're just hanging out." He shrugged.

I rolled my eyes, "You can't honestly tell me that you two don't have anything better to do than 'hang out with me?' We wouldn't even be here I had walked to a different part of town."

Alex shrugged again, "But you didn't."

"What were you guys doing anyway?" I asked.

"Taking a shortcut. What were you doing?" he shot back.

"Enjoying the day and getting out of the apartment," I pushed some hair back from my face, "Speaking of, thank you for taking me back to my apartment instead of Levi's, I really wasn't a fan of going someplace I've never been to before, and to be honest I was thinking of just walking back home when we got out of the car."

Alex laughed, "Yeah that wouldn't have gone well. Besides, if we let you go home alone, you would have been walking through a bad part of town, again. And being the gentleman that we are, we couldn't let you do that twice in one day."

"I'm sure you do this for everyone." I said skeptically. Out of the corner of my eye I seen the door to the liquor store open and Levi came out carrying a brown paper bag.

Alex winked at me, "Only the pretty ones." Levi opened the back door and got in, "Do you need to go anywhere before we head back to your place?" he asked me.

I shook my head, "Even if I did, I didn't bring my wallet."

"What do you need? I can get it for you." Alex offered.

I started to stumble over my words, now embarrassed by my choice of words, "Oh no it's fine, that was more of a joke anyway. Besides, I couldn't let you do that."

Levi laid a hand on my shoulder. I looked at his hand and back up to him, '*what is it with this guy and touching me?*' I thought.

"You're so modest. Come on," he said running his hand down my arm before sitting back, "Let's get going, pizza's getting cold, beer's getting warm."

Alex pulled out of the parking lot and drove us to my apartment building. The guys mainly talked amongst each other. Every now and then Levi would scoot up and try to play with my hair while asking me a random question. "Hey Mel, what's your favorite movie?" "Do you think my band should add more drum solos?" "Hey Mel, what's your next tattoo?" He kind of reminded of that over friendly guy at the bar who's trying not to be a creep but at the same time is making it clear his into you.

"Well Levi, my favorite movie is Evil Dead. Griffin and I've watched it together a few times." "I think you're a pretty good drummer, a few songs could benefit from adding more percussion." "Griffin had a few cool ideas I'm considering…."

When we got to my building, Alex parked next to my car. I was the first to get out, eager to get out and be in the comfort of my home. "Wow, I didn't know this place was still livable." Alex said looking up at the building with its cracked windowsills, and broken fire escapes.

I grimaced, "Yeah I'm not really sure either." Thinking of all the repairs I've asked the landlord to fix but he never returns any of my calls.

Levi got out holding the pizzas, Alex had the brown paper bag. I went ahead to get the door, but Levi easily outpaced me and got to it first, he held the door open as I walked through and let it shut on Alex with a smug chuckle. Rolling my eyes, I walked down the hallway and unlocked my apartment door. I kicked my shoes off at the door and went over to turn the ac on. "Woah this place is tiny." Alex said looking around my apartment. "Still nicer than some of the places I've seen around here."

I shrugged, "Yeah, I'm not complaining, but it could be better." I went the kitchen and grabbed some plates and paper towels. "Bathroom is the door on right if you need it." I said pointing down the hallway when I sat the plates on the coffee table next to the open pizza box.

Levi got up and went the bathroom and Alex went the kitchen and sat the bag on the counter. "Mind if I put these in the fridge?" he asked, opening the bag.

"Go for it." I said, taking a plate and putting two slices of pizza on it. I sat down on the end of the sofa, not wanting to be sandwiched between them. All I had was the one sofa that was pretty big, we would all fit comfortably, but I still didn't want to be in the middle of them.

Alex sat down and handed me beer. I noticed the three shots of Jack that he also sat down. I raised an eye brow and looked at him, he shrugged, "There were 6 in there, but I put the other 3 in the freezer for later."

I shook my head, "No, I'm not comfortable drinking during the day." I looked at the time, "It's only 3 o'clock." I took a bite of pizza.

Alex laughed, "Oh come on, it's Saturday, what do you have to lose?"

I shook my head again, "I don't feel right drinking without Griffin."

"Not even a beer?" he asked, tapping the can he was holding to mine.

Levi walked down the hall, "Yeah I'll take a beer, where did you put them?" he asked, walking by us and into the kitchen.

"In the fridge. Really Mel? You won't have one shot with your two friends?" Alex asked, taking a drink of his beer.

Levi came in and was rolling a joint between his forefinger and thumb with his left hand and holding a beer is his right. "Can we smoke in here?" He asked.

I shook my head no. "But there's a patio we can sit on." After we finished the pizza I got up, walked to the bedroom and out to the patio that wasn't considered enclosed due to the broken wall. That was just one of the many repair requests that I've put in. "Sorry, I don't have much seating." I said. The patio was pretty small, just enough space for two bigger potted plants, a small table and 2 chairs. There was also a small ottoman that I could take the top off and store things in. I don't like sitting on it, because the bottom is warped and every time you move on it you feel like you're going to fall off.

When Levi walked through after Alex he winked at me and said, "There's plenty of room on my lap."

I pulled the ottoman closer to the chairs and sat down. "You just can't help yourself can you?" I said crossing one leg over the other.

Alex laughed and sat down in one of the chairs, "Don't mind him," he said, "he's overcompensating from a broken childhood."

Levi smiled sheepishly, "I'm sorry," he stated sarcastically, "I'll try to tone it down."

I didn't buy it, but I figured it wasn't worth getting into at the moment. Instead, I took the joint that Levi was handing me. I took a hit and coughed a little, then I passed it to Alex and took out my phone. I had one message from Griffin. 'How's it going?' he wanted to know.

While I was typing out a response Levi nudged my foot with his. I looked up and raised my hand with my palm up in the universal 'what!?' motion.

"Who ya texting?" he asked nodding at my phone. Taking a long drag off the joint and letting it slowly.

Raising an eyebrow, I stated plainly, "Griffin."

Alex clicked his tongue, "What's with the tone girl? We're all friends here."

Turning back to my phone I finished out my response, 'Are you getting off soon?' and said to the guys, "It's been a long day."

Alex leaned forward and rested his elbows on his knees, "Even more reason to day drink."

Levi passed me the joint. "Just one shot and we'll leave you alone about it."

Taking the joint, I shook my head, "Peer pressure isn't cool guys."

Alex laughed and took the joint when I handed it to him. "Good thing we're not cool."

Levi scoffed, "Whatever man, I'm cool." He said brushing off his shoulder.

I couldn't stop the laugh that bubbled up, "Like ice." I said rolling my eyes.

"Tell us about your day Mel." Alex said handing the joint to Levi, "what's bothering you?"

I rolled my shoulders back, "There's not a lot to tell really. It's just been a pretty boring day and I'm ready for the weekend to be over."

"Well, what better way to make the day go by faster than with a few a drinks?" Alex smirked with a small shrug.

Levi tried passing me the joint, but I shook my head. "You guys go ahead, I'm good." I stated standing up and heading back inside.

I heard Levi mumble something to Alex and they started laughing. I checked my phone, but I didn't have any new messages, Griffin must be busy. Shoving my phone back in my pocket I took the unopened beer, put it in the refrigerator, and poured myself a glass of tea instead. I leaned against the counter and took a drink. There was a sound behind me, and I turned around to catch Levi trying to sneak up behind me. He dropped his shoulders and complained, "How did you hear me? I was trying to scare you." I shrugged and took another drink. Levi walked up and stood in front of me, "What's in the cup?" he asked.

I looked up at him, being 5'4 I was used to feeling short around people, but Levi had to be 6', I had to lean back slightly so I wasn't tilting my head up at an odd angle, "It's just tea."

He nodded and moved to lean against the counter next to me. "Is there a reason why you don't want to drink with us?" he asked looking down at me.

I shrugged, "There's a few reasons. One, I don't like day drinking. Two, I don't feel good about drinking with the…" I never got to finish my sentence. Levi tilted my chin up and kissed me. My eyes grew wide, and I pushed him away, "Dude what the fuck?" I half yelled, stepping away from him.

Alex came walking in, Levi put his hands up defensively, "I'm sorry, you were giving mixed signals." Then he started to laugh.

Alex came over and grabbed a beer out of the fridge, "What's going on?" His question was punctuated by the hiss of the can opening.

"I kissed her and now she's freaking out." Levi said casually, my mouth dropped open.

Taking a long drink Alex caught my eye over the beer can, holding eye contact he brought the can down and swallowed. Turning his gaze to Levi he sighed, "Did you give any warning, or did you just go for it?"

I covered my mouth not sure what the fuck was happening as Levi just shrugged and stated simply, "You know how these things work."

I shook my head, "No this isn't cool. I'm calling Griffin." I took my phone out, but Alex quickly took it out of my hand. "Give me back. My phone. Now." It took a lot for me to keep my voice level, the last thing I needed to do was start yelling and draw the neighbors attention. Fire ran through me; I didn't care that there was 2 of them and only 1 of me, I didn't care that they could easily overpower me if they wanted to. I didn't care what was going to happen, I was mad; and I wasn't going to take this willingly.

Alex flipped my phone around in his hand, so it was facing him, he tilted the screen a few times, so the light reflected off the screen and then he tapped on it. The screen lit up as he unlocked my phone.

I blinked a few times in surprise, "How the fuck did you unlock my phone?" I asked.

"It's his thing," Levi said beside me. I glared over at him, and he held up his hands and grabbed a beer from the fridge and leaned against the sink.

Alex showed me a text he had typed up and was about to send to Griffin. 'Hey boo something crazy just happened, totally unexpected and nothing to worry about but I might have kissed your homeboy. Talk more when you get off work!' punctuated by a smile emoji.

I almost laughed. I shook my head and swiped my arm out to grab my phone, but he was too quick. I let out a frustrated breath, "I didn't kiss him, and I don't talk like that. Give me back my fucking phone."

Levi was still leaning against the sink smirking into his beer can. Alex showed me another text. 'Hey Griff, Levi got a little wasted and thought it'd be a good idea to kiss me. Alex said not to worry about it that he's going to keep things from going further. Can't wait to see you when you get off work.'

"This one sounds like you, right?" he said.

I shrugged, "Yeah I guess," watching in horror as he pressed send, "that doesn't mean you could send it!" I put my hands on top of my head. "Why couldn't I just call him?!" I brought my arms down and clenched my hands into fists, "you need to leave. Both of you, right now. Get out of my apartment."

Levi looked at me dumbfounded. Alex came up and handed me my phone, I swiped it out of his hand before he could pull it away again. He put a hand on my shoulder which I jerked away from. Holding the hand out in a disarming way, like you would when approaching an angry animal, Alex said, "You're not really supposed to bother Griffin while he's at the garage. He could get into a lot of trouble if he was caught during a phone call."

"So that gives you the right to steal my phone and send out text messages as me?" I shook my head and pointed at the door. "I meant it, I want you guys out."

Alex shook his head, and he and Levi started talking over each other. Alex held a hand out to Levi, "Dude just shut the fuck up for a second. Mel, why don't we talk about this outside?" He said laying a hand gently on my back between my shoulder blades, to lead me out the patio.

Again, I jerked myself away, "OK really, stop putting your hands on me." I directed that statement at both of them, but I was staring a Levi when I said it, who winked at me. I rolled my eyes in disgust and turned to go to the patio. I sat down in a chair and crossed one leg over the other. I rested an elbow on the arm rest and rubbed my temple.

Alex sat down next to me and lit a cigarette, the spider tattoo on his hand holding the cigarette flexed its legs as he brought his hand up and took a deep inhale. "You good?" he asked after breathing out the smoke.

I glared over at him, "No. I'm not *good*. Your 'homeboy' put me in a really shitty situation."

Alex took a drag off of the cigarette before he replied, "Yeah, he didn't think that one through." Leaning forward in his chair and putting his elbows on his knees he said, "Listen, Levi has a drinking problem. And when he drinks he gets a little friendly with the ladies. Especially the beautiful ones. I'm not trying to make excuses for him so stop looking at me like that." He laughed, pointing out how I was still glaring at him. My phone pinged, nodding at my phone he asked, "Is that Griffin?"

I nodded and read the text. 'That's Levi. I'll be at your place as soon as I can.' I shook my head and put my phone down.

"See? Everything is fine." I looked over at him, he was giving me a wolfish grin. Something in my stomach dropped. "How about that shot?" he asked.

I shook my head 'no' and turned to the side as Levi walked through the patio door; just so I didn't have to look at him. Childish; I know but even hearing his footsteps and smelling his cologne over Alex's cigarette smoke reignited my anger.

"I cleaned up the living room," Levi said apologetically, there was a brief moment of silence. I refused to look at him, keeping my head turned away from him. When it was clear that I wasn't going to respond, he went on to say, "I even washed the plates."

"Cool. Thanks." I said flatly and started inspecting my finger nails.

Levi cleared his throat, "Hey man, can I bum a cigarette?"

I heard Alex stand up and mutter to Levi, "Just fucking apologize." I looked over at them as they exchanged a few more quick words and then Alex went back inside.

I clenched my teeth and waited as Levi walked by me and stood in front of the chair Alex had just gotten out of. I uncrossed my legs and shifted in my seat.

"Before you run off, I'm sorry." Levi said around the cigarette in his mouth as he brought a lighter up to light the tip. Taking a drag and blowing out the smoke before he sat down. "I was out of line, and it was a shit thing for me to do. You're Griffin's girl and I had no right to kiss you without his permission."

My head snapped over in his direction so fast I thought I sprained my neck. "Um, ok; that started out great. That last bit could have been left out. I'm not Griffin's property, even if he said it was ok to fuck me, that doesn't give you the right lay a hand on me without MY permission." I said the last part pointing at myself to help drive my point across.

Levi shifted in the chair and cleared his throat, he almost looked amused. "I'm not good at apologizes." He said with a half-smile. I rolled my eyes. My phone pinged catching Levi's attention. Pointing with the hand that held the cigarette he asked, "Who are you texting?"

"It's just an email." I replied, irritation dripping off of every word.

Levi sat back in his chair and laughed, "Damn girl simmer down," I clenched my jaw and stood up, "Wait, Melanie come on don't go just yet."

I looked down at him, "What do you want Levi?" I asked crossing my arms.

Levi furrowed his eyebrows and took a drag off his cigarette; he looked around the patio awkwardly and then pointed at the potted plants. "Umm what kind of plant is that?"

I blinked a few times before answering, "Elephant ear." It came out as more of a question. I shook my head and looked down at the ground, "I'm sorry if I lead you on in some way. I have nothing against you, but I'm with Griffin, and you two seem close. You wouldn't want to ruin that with something as stupid as messing around your best friends girlfriend, right?" I looked up at him.

Levi was watching me, his head slightly tilted with a small smirk, his eyes flicked up and down so fast I thought I imagined it. He licked his lips and stood up, taking one last puff of the cigarette before putting it out on the small table. "Yeah, you make a few good points." He walked up and stood beside me, "We wouldn't want to get on Griffins bad side." He extended his arm towards the door, "after you."

Alex was tapping on his phone, sitting on the sofa when I came back into the living room. Levi went over to sit down, occupying the seat by the arm. Leaving the middle open for me, no way was I going to sit between those two. I went to the patio and drug in a chair.

"I would have gotten that for you if you had asked." Alex called out when I sat down.

"It's ok, I can take care of myself." I replied. Alex handed Levi his phone, they exchanged a look and with a chuckle Levi handed the phone back, soon after my phone pinged.

'Can I take a shower at your place?' Griffin wanted to know.

My fingers flew as I typed it out, 'of course when will you be here?'

'As fast as I can.' He answered.

I put my phone down in the chair as I stood up and went to get my drink. Looking around Levi was true to his word; the pizza was cleaned up, and the plates were in the drying rack. I almost felt bad for acting like a bitch now, but I had to remind myself that cleaning up after a meal doesn't excuse an unsolicited kiss.

About a half an hour later while we were watching some random show on tv when the door opened, and Griffin walked through. He had some dirt smeared on his face and up his arms. He came over and scooped me up out of the chair and kissed me. He smelled like motor oil, spicey cologne, and hint of sweat, I buried my face in his chest and fell into him. I felt more at ease now that he was here.

"Ready?" Griffin asked.

I leaned back to look up at him, confused. "Ready for what?"

Griffin chuckled, "For a shower. What else?" He answered smugly and pulled me into the bathroom. He looked over his shoulder and called out to the guys, "We'll be right back." He pulled the bathroom door closed behind us. Griffin went to turn the water on, "Man it's been a long day. I'm so glad to see you." he said, stripping his clothes off.

I was almost too confused to say anything, "What about your company?" I asked pointed at the door.

Griffin laughed, "I'd say they're your company. I mean this is your apartment and you've been hanging out with them all day."

"Not because I asked them too. Besides aren't you the one who wanted them to 'watch over me'?" I asked with air quotes.

Sighing Griffin ran a hand through his hair, "I was trying to look out for you. Look it's been a long day, and I just want to take a shower with you and relax for the rest of the night. Don't worry about the guys, they're either keeping themselves busy or they already left." He shrugged. Nodding his head to the shower curtain he went on to say, "I'm stepping in. I would really appreciate it if you came in with me."

—◊—

When we stepped out of the bathroom the place was quiet. Alex and Levi cleared out they even took the chair back to the patio. Griffin threw an around me, "We have the place to ourselves," he said grinning down at me. "What do you want to do?"

"I'm getting kind of hungry."

Griffin pulled me over to the sofa, "Yeah? What do you want to eat? I'll have it delivered." We settled on Chinese food. That seems to be a favorite of his.

While we were waiting for the food to get here, we watched whatever was on tv at the time. I was having a hard time focusing, "Hey this is kind of awkward, but I don't feel comfortable being left alone with Levi."

Griffin sat up and looked at me baffled, "What? Why what happened?" He asked then his eyes lit up, and he sat back in his seat, "Oh is this about that hug or whatever?"

"If it was just a hug we wouldn't be having this conversation," I said fully turning towards him, "this is about him kissing me in the kitchen."

Rubbing his eyebrow he said, "I'm sorry you feel that way; you should take it as a compliment, really. If you weren't so beautiful, he wouldn't have kissed you." he said cupping my cheek.

I blinked a few times and pull away from his touch, "So that was my fault?" I couldn't believe this.

Shrugging he went on to explain, "Well you can be flirty at times. I'm kind of shocked that it was only a kiss." My mouth dropped, laughing Griffin held up his hands, "I'm not mad at you, Mel. Levi is good looking for guy and hey so is Alex. Let's just say that if something other than a kiss were to happen, it still wouldn't be a big issue." He sighed and brought a hand up, running it through my hair and resting his hand on the back of my neck. "I know you care deeply for me; and something as small you kissing my friends isn't going to change that." He pulled my head towards him and kissed my forehead, "you could have fucked both of them today and I would still love you."

I shook my head so much of what he just said didn't make any sense, "I don't want to fuck them." I looked over at the tv and then back to him. "Wait did you say you love me?" I asked.

Griffin grinned at me and was about to say something when there was a knock on the door. Shrugging he stood up, "Well yeah. What's not to love?" Winking he grabbed his wallet and got the food.

I didn't like how casual he was being about all of this. I felt a sinking feeling in my stomach as he sat back down. "Are you seeing anyone else besides me?" I asked.

Griffin handed me a container of beef fried rice, he smirked at me before saying, "I only have eyes for you baby, what makes you ask?"

I stabbed into the rice with my fork, "If I found out one of my friends kissed you behind my back, I would be livid."

Griffin chuckled, "Would it have made things better if he kissed you in front of me? Do you want me to talk to him about it? I will." He said absently.

I took a bite of my rice, this conversation isn't going anywhere, "No you don't have to do that."

We ate the rest of the meal in silence, the tv was on but I was too lost in thought to care about what was happening on the screen. I was moving some rice around when out of nowhere Griffin said, "Hey." His deep voice demanding my attention with no room for argument. I looked up at him, his gaze was soft, he must have been thinking things over too, "I'm not taking anything that happened today lightly. Levi was out of line, and he'll hear about it, don't worry." Griffin then caressed my jawline, his touch setting my soul on fire. He tilted my head up and kissed me, I should have wiped my mouth when he started talking to me. "You're still my girl," the way he dropped his voice to say that was like ecstasy. Then he winked at me, and I was like putty in his hand. He said something else; but I was too distracted by the way his lips formed the words to hear what they were saying.

I bit my lip to control the grin that broke out on my face, "Alright fine," I turned my head away from him and took breath to get my shit together. Griffin had a way of making me feel giddy. I cleared my throat and asked how tired he was.

"Never too tired for you." He said. I leaned forward and put my container down before I stood up and faced him. The way he was looking me, taking me in from the feet up made me feel self-conscious, all of a sudden I was way too aware of how my pajamas fit over my stomach rolls. I grimaced and crossed my arms trying to hide my body.

Griffin made a face and stood up. He took my arms and moved them out of way so he could put his hands on my hips. Looking down while he slowly moved his hands up to my waist, my breath caught my throat. "Griffin.." I didn't even know what I was going to say after that. I felt weightless under his gaze.

Griffin met my eyes and in a blink of an eye he had me in arms, holding me like I really was weightless. "Don't hid your body from me." he said with a smile, and kissed me, "and now you're mine," he took us to the bedroom reassuring me that I wasn't too heavy without me even saying anything.

I looked up at him; he was incredible, just as I was doubting our relationship, he comes in a says all the right things to get us back on track. I squealed when he tossed me on the bed and pounced on top of me with a playful snarl.

GRIFFIN (June 16)

The morning started off earlier than I wanted. I woke up in Levi's house on the living room floor with Natasha wrapped around me. Groaning, I pushed her off so I could stand up. Bottles and cups were scattered across the room, Levi was crashed out on the sofa with Cassie.

There were a couple of other people laying around that I didn't recognize. My head started to spin as I was looking around, grabbing onto the arm of the sofa I kicked a beer bottle and it rolled across the floor, causing a noise so loud I thought my head was going to split in two.

I ran a hand down my face and tried to piece together last night but it was a fucking blur. I picked my way through the living room and to the kitchen, careful not to kick any more bottles. Alex was already sitting at the kitchen table when I stumbled through the door.

The strong smell of coffee hit me as the door swung close behind me, "Oh fuck yes, I need some coffee." I said going over to the cabinets and pulled down a coffee cup. It was a chipped white mug from a gas station that had a cartoon of a smiling wolf on it, I poured a cup and went to sit down in front of Alex.

"I can't find any aspirin; my head is fucking killing me." Alex mumbled, taking a slow sip of his coffee.

I patted my pockets, checking for my phone. "Hey man do you have the time?" I asked.

"Last time I checked it was 5:20, that wasn't too long ago." he answered, rubbing his eyes. I nodded a thanks and took a drink of the coffee, the bitter liquid helped take the edge off of the hangover but not near enough. "I gotta get Kara back home before her shift starts in an hour but I can't get her to wake up."

"Well, if she's late then that's her fault." I said, "Have you seen my phone?" Alex shook his head no. My wallet was still in my pocket, but my keys were missing too. I ran a hand down my face, "Alright, if you help me find my phone and keys, I'll help you wake Kara up."

Alex agreed and we drank the rest of our coffee in silence. When my cup was empty, I got up to put it in the sink and chuckled to myself when I see my phone laying on the counter next to the sink with my keys sitting on top.

"Well, that was easy." Alex muttered when I told him I found my shit.

If only waking up Kara was just as easy, I almost gave up after the second time she told us to fuck off and pulled the pillow over her face. Alex grabbed the blanket to pull it off her, but she clung to it, one more good tug and she let it go, Alex almost fell back but he caught himself, "This is fucking stupid." He said out loud.

I shrugged, "Well you tried, at this rate she's not going to make it to work."

Kara growled at us to go fuck ourselves and sat up looking around the room. "Where are we?" she asked, her voice coming out in a croak.

"Over at Levi's," Alex answered softly and sat on the bed next to her. "Come on babe, we gotta get going. You don't want to be late for work." he said, rubbing her back.

Kara shook her head, "I don't think I can go in today. I feel like shit. I drank way too much last night. I think I'm going to call in."

I scoffed, "I'm going to head out," and walked out the room, letting Alex deal with that. Calling into work because of a hangover is some weak ass, shit I don't take well.

On the way home I drove by your apartment, nothing seemed out of place in the parking lot and your windows were dark, you must still be sleeping. Further down the block I seen Tylers car parked on the side of the road. I drove around the block again so I could pull up behind him, but when I got to where he was, he had already pulled off. Not knowing where he went gave me a sinking feeling in the pit of my stomach.

Instead of looking for Tyler I just went home. I need a shower so I could wash the stink of Natasha off me. After I got out of the shower I pulled on some boxers and crawled back into bed. Hoping that when I woke up in a few hours my headache would be gone.

I didn't even get to close my eyes when I got a text from my dad. He wanted me at the garage in 1 hour. Groaning, I got up and got dressed. I put on a pot of coffee and went to the back room and pulled out the wooden box from under the coffee table. I cut up a line and with a quick inhale I was instantly awake, ready for anything. I did one more line and went to do some push-ups while I waited for the coffee to finish brewing.

I poured a to go cup and locked up the house behind me. When I got in the car, I sent a message to Levi asking him to keep an eye on you today, that Tyler was trying to move in, and he had been watching your apartment at night.

Levi said he would do what he could, and I opened my music app and started listening to my heavy metal playlist.

By the time lunch rolled around I was starving, Dad had a couple 'deliveries' that showed up during the night and he needed them swapped out before 10 o'clock tonight. I was covered in grease and sweat. I sat down at the table and started eating the food I had delivered, a French dip roast beef sandwich with Swiss. I was halfway through my food when I got a message from Alex. Apparently, he was out with Levi, and they spotted you walking down the street in Ryan's neighborhood. I shook my head, you just don't get the city you moved to, do you Mel? I asked the guys to pick you up and keep you with them until I got off work. I wanted to call you and let you know but my lunch was almost over I didn't have enough time to explain everything to you. So instead, I just let the guys handle it and scarfed down the last of my sandwich and went back to work.

About an hour later I was in the bathroom when Alex sent me a text saying that he picked you up at the park and you were heading over to Levi's. I didn't want you to run into Natasha but she would be at the club at this time so it wouldn't matter.

I sent you a message asking why you were walking around alone when I told you not to. I also told you to stay with the guys and the job was taking longer than it should, but I would pick you up at Levi's once I was done here.

The day was dragging by, just when we thought we were finished, Tony, my dad's right-hand man, and his crew just dropped off a new car. "Fuck man how many more are they bringing?" Elias asked as he popped the hood, "I'm ready to go home."

I shrugged, "Start it up," I said tapping on the side of the car. The engine purred to life.

I heard the office door open and close and dad's heavy footsteps on the metal stairs as he walked toward us. "Wednesday, I need you and the other 2 to go to this address and clean it up. No money but what you find you keep. Destroy the rest." He handed me a small slip of paper. He tapped the roof of the car to get Elias's attention; and handed him a piece of paper as well. "Keep an eye on this address for a few days and report back on Friday." As he walked away he yelled over his shoulder, "2 more and you can go home." He slammed the office door behind him.

I looked at the address, it was a few cities over. I rolled my shoulders and put the address with my phone in my toolbox, I pulled out my phone to check the time. I had 2 messages, one from Levi from a few hours ago, they took you back to your apartment instead to help you trust them more. Which is smart, I can see how you would be more at ease in your place over someone's house that you barely know. The other one was from you. I could tell you didn't write it, Alex had took your phone to tell me that Levi tried kissing you.

I started laughing and typed a quick reply before putting my phone back in the toolbox. I saw that coming, it was written all over Levi's face, ever since we talked about you that day after his show it was only a matter of time before he made a move. If Levi had gotten to you first you would be his girl; not mine. I can't wait to get off work now. I took out the small pouch I kept some coke in and put a small amount on my hand and in one swift movement I brought my hand up and sniffed the powder off the back of my hand.

Turning back to the car with a new burst of energy I clapped my hands, "2 more cars, that's it? I can go all night."

Elias shook his head, "I'm good, I'm ready to eat something that didn't come out of the vending machine."

I laughed, "We'll get you home in no time."

A few more hours later we were closing up the garage; exhausted, hungry, and covered in grime. "Man, if this job didn't pay so well I'd quit and find a cleaner one, where I don't have to work crazy hours. Don't have to drop everything and come running whenever the boss calls." Elias complained as he pulled the overhead door down, sliding the lock in place he made sure the pad lock was secure.

I shook my head, "Try having him as your father." I pulled my phone out of my pocket and sent dad a message letting him know that the place was locked up. I sent Alex a message telling him that I was on my way and depending on your mood we could have some fun when I got there. Then I sent one to you asking if I could take a shower. "Take it easy man. Go get a drink." I yelled over my car. Elias parked his jeep across from me.

"Plan on it. What are you gonna do?"

Shrugging I replied, "Hopefully get laid." I opened the driver door and waved at him before falling into the car. I put the key in the ignition and started it up. My phone connected to the Bluetooth and started playing a gore core playlist.

My phone vibrated in my hand, 'of course when will you be here?' you replied.

I smiled and typed up a reply, then Alex messaged me back saying you were acting cold towards them.

I wonder what all that is about? I shook my head and put the car in reverse. Throwing it in drive I sped to your place.

—⸙—

The drive to you was shorter than it would have been if I had drove the speed limit. But even going 40 over I still didn't get there as fast as I wanted. I parked my car next to yours and practically ran to your door. Taking a deep breath, I ran a hand through my hair and down my face and then I readjusted my shirt.

When I opened your door the first thing I noticed was Alex and Levi sitting on the sofa. Then I see you sitting on one of the chairs you kept out on your patio. It was cute how you were trying to distance yourself from Levi. I smirked and walked up to you, pulling you out of the chair and into a kiss. I couldn't stop myself from casting a triumphant look over at Levi. He was clenching his jaw scrolling on his phone.

"Ready?" I mumbled. You looked up at me confused and asked what for, it was kind of cute. I chuckled and took a step back towards the bathroom. "For a shower," I said and grabbed your hand and pulled you with me. "We'll be right back." After the bathroom door closed behind us I walked over to the shower to turn the water on, adjusting the knobs so the water wasn't freezing cold. I told you it was good to see you after a long day and started unbuttoning my work shirt.

You motioned to the door, "What about your company?" you asked.

I laughed and took my belt off, "I'd say they're your company. I mean this is your apartment and you've been hanging out with them all day."

You scoffed, "Not because I asked them too. Besides aren't you the one who wanted them to 'watch over me'?" You asked using air quotes.

217

Now naked I ran a hand through my hair. I don't know why you're acting like this, but I don't want to deal with it right now. "I was trying to look out for you. Look it's been a long day, and I just want to take a shower with you and relax for the rest of the night. Don't worry about the guys," I told you checking the temperature of the water, "they're either keeping themselves busy or they already left." I shrugged and flicked the water off my fingertips. Nodding my heads towards the shower I went on to say, "I'm stepping in. I would really appreciate it if you came in with me."

I smirked as you shook your head and started to pull your shorts off.

—⁓—

After the shower you had me look in the living room to see if the guys were still here. I wanted to tell you not to worry about them seeing you in just a towel, fresh from a shower. It took everything I had not to pick you up and throw you on the sofa.

But I walked out of the bathroom and with a quick look I seen that they had left. With the coast clear you walked to your closet and searched for some clothes. You handed me an old band tee. It was a faded black King 810 shirt. "Nice shirt." I said pulling it on, it was a good fit. Under my breath I started singing one of their songs that I liked to sing to you occasionally, "Coming back to you, my baby, coming back to you," I caught you by the hand and pulled you in for a kiss.

You playfully pushed me away so you could finish getting dressed. When we got to the living room, I put my arm around you. I just wanted to touch you; your skin was so soft. I pointed out that we were alone and asked what you wanted to do.

I was hoping you would suggest something sexual but instead you looked up at me and said, "I'm getting kind of hungry."

I lead us over to the sofa and offered to order us something to eat. After we agreed on what sounded good I called in an order at the Chinese restaurant. It was one of the only restaurants I knew that was open this late and would deliver.

While we waited on the food we just chilled on the sofa, you were leaning against me fidgeting, "Hey, this is kind of awkward," you said, pulling my attention away from the tv, "but I don't feel comfortable being left alone with Levi."

My jaw dropped slightly; I did not expect this. I scrambled to find something to say that would smooth this out. "Why?" I asked, "What happened?" Maybe if I brushed it off you would too. "Oh, is this about that hug or whatever?" You turned towards me; and I wish I could have listened to what you were saying but you were so cute, getting all flustered. After you stopped talking I took the opportunity to jump in, bitches like to be validated so I started off with that. "I'm sorry you feel that way, but you should take it as a complement. If you weren't so beautiful, he wouldn't have kissed you." I reached out and stroked your cheek with the back of my hand.

Based off the look on your face that was not the right thing to say. "So that was my fault?" you asked.

I could still sway your view on this, I have a few more tricks that I've picked up over the years. "Well, you can be flirty at times," I started, "I'm shocked that it stopped at a kiss," I know how persuasive the guys can be, when you know the right words it's easy to turn a no into a yes. I laughed at your expression; you were getting mad again. "I'm not mad at you, Mel. Levi is a good-looking guy and hey so is Alex." The look in your eye told me you agreed, "let's just say that if something other than a kiss were to happen it still wouldn't be a big issue." I don't see it as a big deal, you shouldn't either Mel. As long as it's ran by me first I don't care who sleeps with you. I tangled my fingers in your hair and grabbed you by the back of your head, "I know you care deeply for me and something as small as you kissing my friends isn't going to change that." As long as it's only my friends that is, if you started kissing on Tyler... I don't want to think about that. The hand on the back of your neck started to tense up, I pulled you close and kissed your forehead, "you could have fucked both of them today and I would still love you." I whispered, dropping my hand.

You shook your head and told me you didn't want to fuck them. Which I know is a lie, and even if it did turn out to be true you'll agree eventually. You have a hard time saying "no" to me. Then you perked up a little, catching the bait I laid out for you, "Wait did you say you love me?" You asked.

I was about to go further into it when a knocking on the door interrupted us. Shrugging as I stood up, I said, "Well yeah," I grabbed my wallet and winked at you, "what's not to love?"

I paid for the food and thanked the delivery driver with an extra tip due to his near perfect timing and went to sit the bags down on the coffee table. You had an odd look on your face. I tried to prepare myself for anything you were about to say.

"Are you seeing anyone else besides me?" you asked.

I made my hands busy by handing you a food container, I smiled at you before coming up with, "I only have eyes for you baby," I need to squash your suspicion of me, I don't understand I usually have the guard down by now; but you're determined to keep yours up. "What makes you ask?" If I knew the problem, I'll be able to fix it. You brought up the kiss again. I fought not to roll my eyes when you went on about how mad you would be if the roles were reversed.

I offered to talk to Levi about it, but you turned that down and started poking at your food instead. I watched you eat, wondering how you would react if you ever found out about my history with Natasha. I shook my head; you wouldn't understand that she is nothing more than something to pass the time with. She's only fun in the moment, you however are like oxygen. I can already tell I wouldn't be able to live without you. I need you. I thought of how I can turn this around. Once I was done eating I put the container on the coffee table.

"Hey." I said getting your attention. Your eyes snapped up to mine from your food, "I'm not taking anything that happened today lightly," I said changing up my tactic, "Levi was out of line, and he'll hear about it, don't worry." I reached out and ran my fingers softly across your jaw, relishing how soft your skin was. With my fingers under your chin, I tilted your face up and kissed you, ignoring the lingering taste of soy sauce, "You're still my girl." I said with a wink, "So don't let it get you down and let's enjoy the rest the night."

You smiled up at me and bit your lip, "Alright fine." I licked my lips and sat back in my seat smirking, enjoying how good this new victory felt. "How tired are you?" you asked, there was a sexual undertone to the question.

I raised an eyebrow and looked down at you, "Never too tired for you." I said, grinning from ear to ear.

You leaned forward to put your left-over Chinese food next to mine. I took you in as you stood up and turned to me. I studied you. Your feet were in black and white fuzzy socks, bringing my eyes up I admired your thick tattooed legs and your plaid pajama shorts hugging those hips. I loved how your tank top hugged your curves, but I hate how you fold your arms over your stomach while I'm enjoying you. I furrowed my eyebrows and stood up, taking your arms, and moving them out the way so I could put my hands on your hips and slowly slid them up your sides. I was looking down at your body as I did, "Griffin…" you whispered.

"Don't hide your body from me, you're beautiful." In one swift movement I scooped you up, holding you bridal style I smiled down at you and kissed you, "and now you're mine," I said taking us to the bedroom, "and no you're not too heavy and no I'm not putting you down. Not until I feel like it." I said grinning, enjoying how your face lit up.

MELANIE (July 19)

It was a Saturday morning; Griffin had sent me a text at 1 in the morning saying how he just got off work and was going to bed but wanted to let me know that he was thinking of me. I smiled to myself and got up. Changing out of my pjs I did some morning exercises and then took a shower to get ready for the day.

I was in the kitchen making some breakfast when Griffin sent me a text. 'What are you doing?' I told him I was about to eat breakfast, and he asked if he could come over.

I told him he could, and he said he would be here shortly. I had just sat down on the sofa with a plate of eggs and toast when there was a knock on the door.

I put down my plate and got up to answer it. I looked through the peep hole and opened the door, "Did you send me those texts from the parking lot?" I asked.

Griffin was standing before me looking down at with a wolfish smile. "Something like that. I was already on my way over." He walked around me and went to sit down.

"Are you hungry? I can make you something if you want." I asked before I sat down. I didn't want to eat in front of him if he hasn't had anything to eat yet.

Griffins eyes traveled across my body, he smirked rubbed the back of his neck, "Thanks but I already ate."

Nodding my head I grabbed my plate before I sat back down. I picked up the fork and shoveled some eggs into my mouth.

"What do you have planned today?" he asked.

I chewed and swallowed before answering, "Just some chores."

Griffin laughed and looked around, "What's there to do around here? Dust for cobwebs? Is it something that can be done a different day, I'd really love to kidnap you."

I furrowed my eyebrows, "And do what?"

He shrugged, "It's a nice day today, and if you're down for it we can go for a hike out on my grandpa's property."

"That sounds like a lot more fun than organizing my closet." I said, "I'll need to get ready I'm not hiking in this." I laughed, referring to the black tank top and blue plaid spandex shorts.

Griffin brushed some hair back from my face, "That's up to you, I see nothing wrong with what you're wearing."

I pushed him playfully and finished eating. "I won't be long." I said getting up. I put my plate in the sink first then I went to get dressed for a hike. I brought my belt and knife into the living room. Griffin watched me carefully and I threaded the belt through the loops on my shorts I wore for hiking. "What?" I asked him.

"What's with the knife?" He asked.

I looked down at the knife, "Many reasons, mainly for protection I guess."

Griffin chuckled, "You won't need it when you're with me. I'm all the protection you'll need."

Something in me wanted to protest. I cleared my throat, "Even so I'd like to bring it just in case. You never know when you'll need a knife, right?" I let out an awkward laugh.

Griffin stood up and walked over to me, grabbing my hands in his he said, "Melanie you don't need to protect yourself from me. It'll just be me and you; I have a knife on me if we happen to need one."

Reluctantly I agreed and left the knife lying on the coffee table as I finished putting on my belt. I picked my boots up from beside the door and went to sit down on the sofa to put them on.

Griffin looked down at his phone. "Ready?" He asked me, typing on his screen.

"Yeah. Is everything ok?" I asked.

Griffin put his phone in his pocket. Holding out his hand to help me off the sofa he said, "Yeah everything is ok. Levi is wanting to join us on our hike."

"What did you tell him?" I asked, grabbing my phone off the coffee table and putting it in my purse.

"I told him 'no' that today was more for you and me." He shrugged and walked over to the door, "Unless you don't mind him joining us. He can meet us there."

I shook my head no and closed the door behind me, I took my keys out of my purse and locked the door. "I'd rather not," I said tossing my keys back into my purse.

"Are you sure? He has a new a song he was hoping to get your opinion on."

I rolled my eyes, "Yes, I'm sure." I didn't mean for it to come out as harshly as it did.

Griffin took a step back and look down at me, "Hey hold up." He grabbed my elbow and held me in place, "I feel some tension here. I can't have my girl hating on my friends. What's going on?"

I tried pulling my arm out of his grasp, but he tightened his grip. I looked down at his hand and back up at him, not quite sure what was happening but not liking how he was holding me, it almost hurt. "Let me go." My tone was firm. Griffin met my hard gaze with his own for a split second. Then, he let go. My whole body went cold; but I kept the façade that I wasn't intimidated.

"Are you still hung up on that kiss." He said jokingly, "I thought you'd be over that by now." I looked down at the ground, I took a deep breath and was about to say something when Griffin cupped my chin and tilted my head up, "Look at me," he said softly, "You two are going to run into each other eventually. You might as well get it over with." He kissed me on the forehead and pulled his phone back out. "I'll tell Levi to meet us there."

"What about our 'me and you day'?" I asked. Tempted to just go back inside.

Griffin shrugged, "You two getting along is more important right now. Mel, he's practically a brother, I can't have bad blood between you two." He threw his arm around my shoulders and led me out of the building and to his car. He opened the passenger door for me and closed it when I sat down. Griffin smiled at me when he got in and started the car. "Don't look at me like that, it'll be fun."

"Fine but I'd like to go on an actual date after today, just you and me." I said putting my seatbelt on.

Griffin laughed and put the car in reverse, "Deal." He said pulling out of the parking lot.

—⁂—

The drive out to Griffin's grandpas took about an hour. When we started driving down a long dirt road the first thing that I noticed was Levi's truck. My heart started to sink as I saw him leaning against his truck smoking a cigarette. It sounds foolish but I did have a small crush on Levi, he was cute and charming but since I was with Griffin, I didn't dare try to take things further with him. I actually tried to avoid him after I ran into him at the store that first time. Him kissing me in my kitchen made me furious, I felt foolish that I let myself get that close to him in the first place.

Griffin pulled the car up to parked next to Levi, who was staring at me with a sly smile. "Where's Alex?" I asked unbuckling my seatbelt.

"He was busy." Griffin replied, opening the door, and stepping out.

He was busy? Did Griffin ask them both to come out? I'm beginning to think that he had alternative motives here. When I stepped out Levi took a drag off his cigarette and stepped up to Griffin, they greeted each other with a hand slap and fist bump. They started talking in hushed tones I couldn't make out what they were saying.

I looked around at my surroundings, the house we were at was a 2-story house with a wraparound porch. The paint was peeling off giving the house an unwelcome feeling. There were hanging pots lining the porch that held dead plants, the dried and shriveled vines hanging down like spider legs. The yard wasn't completely neglected, it looked like someone comes out every now and then to mow, but the grass along the house and the trees was much taller than the rest. Giving me the impression that weed eating didn't happen as often as mowing.

Movement out of the corner of my eye caught my attention. I turned my head in time to see someone disappear around the side of the house. I looked behind me, Griffin and Levi were still talking over by the car. I looked back to the house where the person disappeared and took a few steps; there was an old well and a shed that hung open. A shadow moved to my left; I looked up in time to see the curtain hanging in the window fall down. The way they would if someone was holding them open to look outside then let the curtains fall shut.

There was a splashing sound behind me. Turning around I surveyed the area. The guys were still talking I could hear them laughing, but now they were passing a joint you could smell the musky smoke in the air. I turned my attention back to the well and walked over to it. Something felt off about this. The wall of the well came up to my waist, it was made of stone. I put my hand on the edge and was about to look down in it when there was a sudden clap on my shoulder. I felt my soul leave my body.

"What are you doing?" Griffin asked, handing me a joint.

I took it and looked back at the well. "I thought I heard something." I said. "Is somebody here?" I asked, taking a hit.

Griffin shrugged. "Probably just a stone falling. This place is pretty old; nobody has lived here since grandpa passed. I come here to do some basic maintenance, just enough to keep the place from falling apart." He jerked his head toward the woods. "Are you ready?" he asked.

Levi came up to the other side of me and took the joint from me after I took another hit, dragging his fingers across mine and winking at me as he did. I looked over at Griffin, "Yeah I'm ready," I said threading my arm through his. I noticed he had a backpack on. "How long are we hiking?" I asked.

"I don't know." Griffin said, "Depends on when we want to turn around."

Levi walked up beside me and put his arm around my shoulder, I felt very uncomfortable and held onto Griffin's arm tighter. "There's a spot up here we like to hang out, it used to be a hunting cabin but now it's just a place to party." Levi said, his voice vibrating through me.

"There's also a lake out there that we can swim in if you want." Griffin said grinning down at me.

I shook my head, "I didn't bring a swimsuit."

The guys started laughing at me, "Sweetheart you don't need a swimsuit." Griffin said.

Then I started laughing, "I am not skinny dipping with you two. Nice try though."

Levi pulled me into him, "So that's a no to a three-way then." I glared at him and pulled myself away from both of them. Levi put his hands up. "I'm kidding! I'm just kidding."

Griffin chuckled and put his arm back through mine, "Honey you're going to have to get used to his humor." He said kissing the top of my head. "He means nothing by it. Come on, let's go." He pulled me down the path.

"Yeah Mel, I mean nothing bad about it." Levi said, once again appearing on my other side. I felt so small between these two men. Levi was slightly taller than Griffin, maybe by half an inch, but they both towered over me.

We walked like that for a moment, but something caught my eye ahead of us. It looked like a strappy sandal. I walked ahead of the guys and scanned the area I seen the shoe in, but I lost it. Close to the path a white butterfly landed on a blue flower. I bent down to look at it. I loved being out in nature. I should have come out here with Griffin sooner.

I stood up and looked around to see were the guys went. When I turned around they were both looking over at me. Griffin gave me that smirk of his and winked. I smiled back and he took that as his queue to start walking again, taking the lead and Levi walked beside him.

We walked for a while longer, Levi and Griffin mainly talked to each other, I was too engrossed in my surroundings to pay too much attention to them. The trees here were breath taking, we were walking along a ravine, the birds singing off in the distance. I stopped for a moment to look around, it was beautiful here.

The guys noticed I had stopped, and Levi walked up beside me. "What are you looking at?" he asked looking around too.

I shrugged, "Nothing in particular. It's just really peaceful here."

Griffin walked up on my other side and wrapped an arm around me. "It is, isn't it." He pulled me in and kissed me. "Come on the cabin is further up this way." He said tugging on me. Griffin kept me within reach the rest of the time we were walking. If his arm wasn't around my shoulders, it was looped through mine, and if our arms weren't linked, he was holding my hand.

A while later Levi held a joint in his mouth with a lighter up to it. I didn't see where he brought it out of, I didn't even know they had anything on them. I started to wonder what was in the bag that Griffin was carrying.

"Hey Griff?" I asked after he took a hit. "What's in the bag?"

He gave me a wolfish grin and watched with careful eyes when Levi handed me the joint, "You'll find out when we get to the cabin."

When I took a hit, it tasted weird. The effect it had was different than a normal joint. I shook my head and tried to hand it off to Griffin, "no I'm good." I said, it left an odd aftertaste in my mouth.

Griffin pushed my hand back, "It's fine, just take a few more hits." He urged, "It's a different strain than you're used to." He shrugged, I looked at him, and he just smiled at me. I took one more hit and tried again to pass it off. Griffin shook his head and laughed, "Come on girl, hit it like you mean it." I took a bigger hit and held my hand out to Levi. I almost gagged I was coughing so hard, Griffin laughed and rubbed my back, "That's a good girl." He said, the motion of his hand was making me dizzy, but it felt so good. I closed my eyes and focused on my breathing for a moment. Griffin's hand went from doing circles on my back to running down my arm and grabbing my hand. "Come on, we're almost there." He whispered in my ear, pulling me down the path.

We passed the joint around a few more times, I felt like the guys kept skipping each other giving me more turns at hitting the joint than they did. When I called them out on it they just laughed and Levi, who had the joint handed it to me when it was supposed to go to Griffin. I took it and passed it to Griffin who laughed and pushed the joint back, telling me I was just confused and that it was my turn.

The world started to warp, kind of like I was sinking in water. I stopped walking and looked down at my hands. Griffin, who had his arm around me, stopped too and asked if I was ok. His voice was kind of muffled, I looked over at him and nodded. I didn't want them to think I couldn't handle my weed.

Levi came into view, he smiled down at me, "That's some good shit huh?" he asked. I ran a hand through my hair and nodded, Levi glanced at Griffin, "Is the beer still going to be cold when we get there?"

Griffin nodded, "Yeah there at the bottom."

I shook my head, "No, I don't want to drink."

Griffin laughed and shook me a little bit, "Nonsense, you work too hard. You deserve to let loose once in a while."

I felt uneasy about this, "Just one beer," I said.

Laughing Griffin replied, "We'll see."

A few minutes later we came up to a cabin. Griffin let his arm fall off my shoulders as he walked up the 2 steps onto the porch, the wood creaking under his weight.

The cabin had a similar look to the house, you can tell whoever built one built the other, they had the same style of windows (the one on the left was broken), same shingles, the same door. The porch even wrapped around the cabin the same way it did the house. I tried to take a step forward, but I was frozen in place. There was a heavy feeling to the air, also similar to the house. I wasn't too keen on the idea of willingly stepping into the Evil Dead cabin.

Levi came up beside me, "Don't be scared Mel. Honestly, the cabin is less creepy than the house." He held his arm out to me, "Come on we can go in together." I looked up at him, our eyes locked, "Keep looking at me like that and I'm going to kiss you again." he warned with a smirked, then he rolled his eyes and shrugged, "Alex made me say that. He said that after the last time I need to start giving warnings."

I laughed despite myself. "Alex is right." I started walking up to the cabin, "I'm sorry. I didn't realize I was giving a look." I tried to swallow but my mouth was so dry. I purposely kept my gaze off Levi while I walked past Griffin and into the cabin.

It was a small open floor cabin. As I walked in the door there was a 4-person sofa against the wall to my right, in the corner across from it was a twin-size bed. There was a kitchen set up to my left, a wood stove and sink and a table with 4 chairs in the middle of the room. The place looked like it was decorated by a group of adolescent boys. Posters taped on top of posters, there were speakers hung up in the corners of the room. They turned the place from a hunting cabin to a mancave. From the looks of not a lot of female influence went to decorating.

Levi walked around me, his hand running across my lower back. I cleared my throat and looked around. Griffin was over by the table, so I walked over to him. When I was in front of him he handed me a cup. I took it and without thinking took a big gulp. My eyes went wide, and I started coughing, "Ugh! What was that?" I asked, grabbing onto the chair in front of me as the room started to spin. Warmth wrapped around my body and my thoughts started to blur together.

Griffin laughed, "That was whiskey, honey."

I mumbled a "What?" and looked at the table. Griffin had some cups out on the table, there was also a bottle of whiskey and a lock box.

I was about to ask him what was going on when Levi came over and took a cup and poured himself a drink. "You threw that back like a champ girl!" Picking up the cup and holding it out he looked over at Griffin, "I'm not going to let her out drink me."

I shook my head but when I did the room started to tilt again. I pulled a chair out and sat down. "I thought it was water." I said pathetically.

Griffin rubbed my shoulders and kissed my neck, "I'll get you some water honey." He said and walked over to the small kitchen. Griffin opened one of the cabinets and I saw a few different bottles of liquor on the top shelf. Griffin pulled 3 bottles of water off the bottom shelf and came back over to the table. He threw one at Levi and handed me the other one; loosening the cap for me before he handed it over.

"Thank you," I said with a small smile. The bottle tilted in my hand, almost dumping all over my lap. With some extreme concentration I took a few slow drinks, so I didn't spill water all over me. I didn't want to risk knocking the water over and making a mess, so I twisted the cap back on the bottle before putting it on the table in front of me.

Levi slid into the seat next to me, "How are you feeling after that walk?" he asked.

"Pretty good," I said with a shrug.

Griffin pulled a chair closer to me and sat down on my other side. "That was nothing for our little Mel." He said picking up some of my hair and started to play with it. With a look of admiration, he went on to say, "She could go all day and not get tired."

I blinked and smiled lazily; my eye lids started to feel really heavy. I shook my head slightly to clear the foggy thoughts, but it just made me dizzy. I reached for the water bottle (almost knocking it over) and tried to open it, but my movements were clumsy, and the bottle felt heavier than it should be. Griffin chuckled softly and took the bottle from me and opened it with ease.

I rubbed my eyes and when I dropped my hand Griffin held the bottle back out to me, his wolfish smile beaming down at me, the way the light was playing off his face made him look sinister. My mouth went dry, and I tried to swallow but it caught in my throat. I brought the bottle up to my lips and took a few long drinks. The water was tepid; but it was better than alcohol.

Griffin reached for the bag he was carrying and took out a bottle of Sprite and pulled the whiskey to him. He poured himself a drink and took the cup I had drank out of and poured me one too. Placing the drink in front of me, Griffin winked and grabbed his cup and held it up. Then he said, "To friendship."

Levi brought his cup up and repeated Griffin with excitement. They both looked down at me at the same time. I hesitantly held my cup and tapped it against theirs.

My stomach sank when the liquor hit it. *No more alcohol* I told myself.

Levi was lighting another joint. I must have been staring at him because when he glanced at me he smirked and blew out a smoke ring. *Fuck he made that look good*, I sat up straight and shook my head, *No I am not that girl*. I looked around and got up to stand next to Griffin who was back over by the cabinets. It looked like he was messing with the stereo.

"Hey, I don't feel good." I said. The room started to tilt at odd angles when I walked over to him, I turned around to lean against the counter.

230

Griffin stopped what he was doing and cupped my face in his hands. He studied my eyes for a brief moment, then put the back of his hand on my forehead. "What's going on?" he asked. Levi appeared behind him and handed him a joint.

I looked from him to Levi and then back at Griffin. "I'm getting a headache, and the alcohol is hitting too hard." I said.

Griffin took a drag and handed the joint to me. "Here, this will help." Then he went over to the table. I couldn't see what he was doing since his back was turned.

Levi came up beside me and hopped up to sit on the counter, "Can I hit that?" he asked.

"Sure," I said holding the joint out to him. He laughed and took it from me, I tried ignoring him, but his presence was almost too much next to me.

Relief washed over me when Griffin came back and held out a pill and my water bottle. "It's for your headache." He said and watched as I put the pill in my mouth and washed it down with a drink of water.

Levi handed Griffin the joint and I took the opportunity to stumbled my way over to the closest place to sit down. When I pulled the kitchen chair out it scraped across the wooden floor with a horrible screech. I rolled my shoulders and put my head in my hands.

Heavy footsteps approached me, and I heard another chair being pulled out. "This weed is a little harsh, it might be getting to you."

I sat up and looked over at Levi who was sitting down next to me. My head was spinning so fast just sitting up made me want to lie down. "No this is different." I said, my words coming out almost like mush. I cleared my throat, it felt like sandpaper. Levi said something but his words sounded like he was underwater. I blinked a few times, "What?"

Levi laughed and rubbed his hand on my thigh, "I said, do you want to lie down?"

I slapped his hand off, "No, and why do I have to keep telling you to stop touching me!"

Griffin came up behind me and put his hands on my shoulders, "Hey Mel, what's going on?" he asked, sliding into the chair on my other side. "We're all friends here."

I looked over at him, he was so beautiful, but something in him was ugly. I only see it on occasion. Like now, the way he was leering at me like a wolf staring down his prey. I looked down at my lap then back up to Griffin, "I don't like how he keeps making things sexual."

Griffin and Levi started laughing. Griffin stroked my cheek, "Oh little Mel, I've told you before that isn't a bad thing. You're an attractive woman." He sighed, "But fine." He pointed at finger a Levi, "Knock it off." he said mockingly.

I sighed and rubbed my temple, "Can you take me home? I don't feel right."

Griffin rubbed my back, "Maybe you should lie down," he said.

I shook my head, "No I don't want to lie down." Griffin got up and returned with the bottle of water I was drinking out of earlier. I took a couple long drinks.

When I sat the bottle on the table Griffin asked, "Are you sure you want to leave? It's a long walk back." I nodded my head, and the room bounced with me. I closed my eyes and put a hand on the table to steady myself. Griffin squatted down next to me and studied my eyes, brushing hair back from my face he said, "You're so beautiful." He smiled at me and stood up. "Well, I was hoping that you would have been more willing to make peace with my best friend, but alright. It's going to be awkward if you guys can't get along. I don't want to have to worry about keeping you guys separate. But since that's how it's going to be…" He trailed off and started to slowly gather up some of the things he pulled out of the bag.

A wave of guilt washed over me; I didn't want to be the girl who refused to be cordial with her boyfriend's friends. I reached out and put my hand on Griffins arm, "Wait," I said.

Griffin stopped and looked down at me with an eyebrow raised, "Yes?"

I tried to swallow but my mouth was so dry. "We can stay, but I really don't want any sexual advances from Levi. I'm not into that."

Griffin smirked at me, "I can't control him, but I don't see what the big deal is, it's just sex."

That comment kind of hurt, "Are you sleeping with other people?" I know we already went over this, but that comment was too suspicious not to question.

He pulled his chair closer and sat down, cupping my face in his hands he whispered, "Of course not," and kissed me. Dropping his hands from my face, he slapped the table causing me to jump, "Let me make you a drink!" He stated cheerfully and stood up.

"Not too strong?" I asked turning in my chair to face Griffin, and the motion made the room start to spin. I had to close my eyes and pinch the bridge of my nose for it to stop.

Griffin hollered something over his shoulder, but I wasn't paying attention.

When I looked back up I noticed that Levi wasn't at the table anymore. He was now over at the counter with Griffin, he was leaning with his back to the wall, facing me but his attention was on whatever Griffin was doing. I was about to reach in my pocket for my phone but then I remembered that I had left it in Griffin's car. I stood and clumsily walked over to the sofa. It looked more comfortable than the kitchen chairs.

I was right. As soon as I sat down I curled my legs up under me. Every time I blinked the room took longer to get back into focus. I rested my elbow on the arm of the sofa and held my head, I was staring at the floor when someone stepped in of front me, I followed the legs up to Griffins face, he was grinning down at me holding a cup in each hand. He held a cup out to me, "Drink this, you'll feel better." He took a drink out of his cup and waited for me to take a drink as well.

I took the cup and sipped it. It was slightly bitter, and I couldn't tell if it was gritty or if my mouth was just that dry, "I don't like it." I said shaking my head and handed it back.

Griffin smiled softly and sat down next to me. "One more drink," he coaxed, "there's not much there." He said pushing the cup back to me.

I tried one more drink, but I couldn't do it. I shook my head 'no' again, "I'm sorry, I can't do it." I said laughing.

Griffin laughed with me and threw an arm around me, he took the cup and threw the rest of the drink back, "That's ok." He said and then started playing with some of my hair, "I'm going to step out for a cigarette," he kissed my temple and got up to walk outside. Levi trailed after him.

I rested my head on the back of the sofa....

—〰—

And must have fallen asleep cause the next thing I remember I was waking up in the bed of the cabin with the sun glaring through the window.

My head felt like it was about to explode, every part of my body was protesting from just being awake. I felt like absolute garbage. I sat up and the room tilted as I did, I was on the side of the bed that wasn't against the wall, so I was able to put my feet on the floor to try to stop the room from moving.

I noticed Levi crashed out of the sofa, he was way too tall to be sleeping there, it was almost comical the way he was draped across the cushions. I looked behind me, Griffin was sound asleep next to me. Twisting my body around made my stomach start to turn and bubble. "Oh God," I said out loud and covered my mouth with one hand and wrapped my hair around the other. I got up and ran to the door, twisting the knob and flinging the door open, no concern about the men still asleep inside as the door slammed against the side of the cabin. I grabbed onto the porch railing and bent over it just in time for my stomach to empty itself. Luckily, I was able to keep my hair out of the way.

There was some shuffling around from inside, but I was too focused on not getting bile on me while still hanging over the railing to see who it was. He came up behind me and pulled my hair back for me. Then started rubbing my back, "It's ok, let it out," he mumbled, still half asleep from the sound of it. I went to turn my head to see who it was, but I had to look back at the ground before I ended up throwing up on whoever was trying to help me.

After a few more heaves I was able to stand up, gripping the railing, still breathing heavily. The brisk morning air helped cool me down after my stomach purged itself. I took a deep breath through my nose and let it out slowly through my mouth. I felt slightly better, but not much. Whoever had come outside also brought a water bottle with him, he held it out to me, the spider tattoo in full view. "Thank you," I said. He had already taken the cap off for me, so I didn't have to struggle with it. I rinsed my mouth out first, spitting the water over the railing before taking a few drinks.

"No problem." He said moving so he could lean with his back against the railing. I looked over and was disappointed to see Levi instead of Griffin. "You feeling ok?" He asked.

I shrugged, "Too much to drink I guess." I looked out at the view ahead of me. "Where's Griffin?" I asked.

"He's still sleeping." He said looking down at me. There was an awkward pause that Levi broke with a cough, "I'd really like it if we could be friends. You're really cool, and I feel like we vibe pretty well."

I kicked my toe on the wooden planks below my feet, "I can't be friends with someone who is constantly coming on to me even though I'm with his friend."

Levi rubbed his jaw, and looked up at the ceiling covering the porch, "I'll be honest..." He trailed off and just looked at me for a moment. I blinked and raised an eyebrow at him, waiting for him to finish. He blinked and went on to say "I've only had a few female friends and none of them can compare to you. They mostly look and act like guys, the rest of them I don't care enough about to keep around." He took an exaggerated breath, "I'll try harder to keep myself in check around you."

I looked out into the endless forest in front of me. I could easily get lost out there. The sun rising above the emerald leaves was so beautiful and relaxing to look at. I could feel Levi's gaze burn into me, "Ok." I finally said, turning my attention back to him.

A wolfish grin broke out on his face, "Really?" he asked. Putting his arms out and grabbing the railing. "After last night I wasn't sure if it was possible."

My eyebrows furrowed, "What do you mean?"

He cleared his throat in a poor attempt to cover up a laugh. "How much do you remember?"

I ran a hand through my hair, "up until y'all went outside to smoke."

"Yeah, that explains it. Well, you got pretty violent." He lifted his shirt up, exposing his stomach and some tattoos. On his ribs between an eagle and a skull was an angry bruise. I tried not to look at his abs. "You elbowed me when I came up behind you." He said, studying me.

My jaw dropped, "Levi...." I started to say something, anything but I was at a loss of words. Guilt gnawed at me. I shook my head and looked up at him, about to apologize.

Then footsteps came up behind me, "What's going on here?" Griffin asked, walking up, and stood over me putting his arms on either side of me to put his hands on the railing.

Levi lifted his shirt higher and looked at the bruise. "I was showing Melanie what she did last night."

Griffin laughed, "That was fucking hilarious." He said kissing the top of my head. "How are you feeling? It looks like your morning got off to a rough start."

I rested my back against his chest, "Like shit." Was my reply.

"Well, we have a good hike ahead of us. Think you can make it?" he asked, pushing off the railing. "Clean up won't take long, we'll head out once we're done."

"Yeah, I'll be fine." I said walking inside to help clean up. "Why did I elbow you?" I asked Levi who was picking up some darts off the floor.

"You just got tired of me." He said with a laugh. "But it's ok I forgive you."

—m—

The hike back was brutal. It took everything in me to keep up with the guys. By the time I got home I was exhausted. I washed my face, brushed my teeth, changed my clothes, and flopped in bed, falling fast asleep.

GRIFFIN (July 18)

I was just getting home from a long overnight at the garage. I needed a shower and a long sleep. I was unlocking the door when my phone pinged. Levi sent a text. I tried reading it, but it was all scrambled. I rolled my eyes and put my phone back in my pocket and went inside. My phone pinged again; it was Levi. I still could not read his text. I called him, and when he answered it sounded like there was a party going on. "Man, please tell me that you're home. I cannot stay here any longer." He said over loud pop music.

"Yeah," I said, kicking off my shoes and walking to the bathroom. "I just got home. Come on over I'll leave the door unlocked." I said hanging up the phone and turning on the shower. I took my clothes off, letting the water warm up before jumping in.

The hot water felt good on my back. I turned it up as hot as I could handle and let the steamy water envelop me. I almost didn't want to get out.

I stayed in the shower for a while longer. The only thing that motivated me to get out was that my stomach started to growl. Turning the water off I stepped out and reached for a towel. After I was semi-dry, I wrapped the towel around my waist and walked out to go to my bedroom, nearly pissing myself when I saw Levi sitting in one of the gaming chairs scrolling on his phone.

Looking him over you'd think he spent the last week sleeping in his truck. His eyes were bloodshot, and I couldn't tell if he was irate or depressed.

"Dude I forgot you were coming over." I laughed.

"Hey, why won't Mel accept my friend request?" He asked, he was still looking down at his phone.

Narrowing my eyes I studied him, the dark circles under his eyes, the stubble on his face. But his clothes looked clean and there was no stench coming from him. I shrugged my shoulders, "I don't know, want me to ask her?" I asked.

Levi glanced up at me and then shook his head no. "Nah it's not a big deal."

I rolled my eyes and walked away, heading to my bedroom to get dressed. I pulled on some pants and a white shirt then went to the living room to grab my laptop. I opened the tab that I kept your Facebook logged on to, it looked like you had more than just Levi waiting to be accepted by you. I looked up from the screen and saw Levi stumbling his way into the kitchen. "Hey, you good?" I asked.

He mumbled a reply and grabbed a cup down from the cabinet filling it up with water from the sink. Stumbling over, he sat down next to me and took a drink, "I am so fucked up." He said rubbing his hand down his face, then he looked at the computer screen. I had stopped at a picture you had recently posted. It was a selfie and fuck you were beautiful. "What are you doing?" He asked.

I shrugged and started flipping through your pictures. "Just some digging." I said. I rubbed the back of my head and tried to think of some different ways I could help persuade you to be more 'friendly' with my friends.

"It's just so fucked up." Levi muttered under his breath.

I cocked my head to the side and looked at him, "Don't act like you've never hacked into someone social media account." I said defensibly.

He shook his head, "No I mean, you and her." He said motioning between me and the computer screen.

I almost laughed, his demeaner makes sense now. "How so?" I asked flipping to your next picture.

"Every other day I go home, I have to hear Natasha bitch and moan about how you're ignoring her; or I have to hear you two fucking. Then I gotta deal with you obsessing over her," he swung his hand at the computer almost knocking it off my lap, "you talk about her like she's the only thing that matters, if that was true then why do you keep messing with my sister?" He shook his head and ran his hand through his hair. "It's fucked up how you and Alex think it's ok to have these incredible women who are loyal to you; and yet both of you still want to act like your single."

It took me a moment to get a grip on my anger, I clenched my hand into a fist, "So what, you're mad cause me and Alex have someone to go home to; and bitches act like you have a virus and want nothing to do with you?"

Levi laughed, adrenaline pulsed through me, and the edges of my vision started to turn red. "I have no problem with women. They just don't like coming over cause of that fucking whore who lives with me. I can't kick her out cause if she gets evicted from another place Grandma and Grandpa will cut me off completely."

When Levi was young his mom walked out on them, leaving his dad with two kids under 4. He couldn't handle it, so he dropped the kids off with his stupid rich but aging parents and went off to join the military. As an act of tough love, they kicked them out of their house once Natasha turned 18 and told her to take care of Levi. They set them both up with a bank account, but the rest was up to them to figure out. That is until Natasha irked them to the point of cutting off her funding. They keep the money flowing for Levi as long as he takes care of his sister and stays out of trouble. From what I hear they are this close to cutting him off too.

A bitter laughed escape me, "Why is that my problem?" I growled.

Levi glared at me, "why don't you take Natasha, and I'll take Melanie?"

"Not happening."

"Why not? I've seen you with my sister more than I have with Mel." I was about to say something when he cut me off, "Does Melanie know about Nat?" He asked.

My heart almost stopped. "She doesn't need to."

Levi snorted, "Cause if she did that would be it, and you know it." He laughed and shook his head.

"What's your fixation on her?" I asked.

"What's yours?" He shot back.

We sat there staring each other down. I forced myself to take a breath knowing that if it came down to it Levi could beat my ass. I would put up one hell of a fight, I might be able to hold my own for a little while, but I wasn't in the mood for a fight tonight. "Fine," I said through clenched teeth. "We'll get her alone and see who she wants." Levi asked how I planned on doing that. "She'll listen to me." I said confidently.

Levi raised an eyebrow, "You keep saying you can talk her into things, but you don't have a very good track record of that."

"Just trust me on this one," I said sitting my computer down and standing up to get myself some water and a quick bite to eat. On the way back from the kitchen I noticed Levi now had the computer in his lap. I flopped down next to him and took out my phone, it was still pretty early in the morning. I doubt that you'd be awake, I wanted to talk to you for a little bit before I crashed but it seemed today was just one of the many times that our schedules didn't allow it. "What makes you think you have a shot with Melanie anyway?" I asked. "I mean she obviously has a thing for you, and she fights herself on it," I laughed and shook my head, "you might have scared her off with that kiss though. She's still pretty pissed about it."

Levi smirked, "She talks about it?" He asked with an ear-to-ear grin.

I took a bite of my food chewing and swallowing before I answered. "Not in a good way."

He shrugged and brought up a picture of you from a few years ago. You were at a concert in a dark red lace up shirt looking like a gothic Instagram model. "I'll take my chances."

I finished eating and put the dishes in the sink. "I'm beat. You can chill here. Just put my computer away when you're done." I said, walking over to my bedroom.

Levi looked up from the computer screen, his eyes were bloodshot. "Huh? Yeah man that's cool." He nodded a few times and looked back down to whatever he was looking at.

I closed my bedroom door behind me, I wasn't worried that you would drop me to run around with Levi. I had you wrapped around my finger, sure I couldn't talk you into doing something that you didn't want to do. But if I could get you to think it was your idea….

A yawn took me by surprise, I was more tired than I thought. Flipping the covers over I fell into bed. Lying there never felt so good. I stretched out on my back and stared up at the ceiling, my phone was face up next to me. I picked it up and sent you a sweet good morning text before rolling over and falling asleep.

—⁂—

I woke up with a start. My heart was pounding out of my chest. I sat up and took a couple of long and deep breaths. Running a hand through my hair I squeezed my eyes shut, *a nightmare? When was the last time I've had one of those?* I thought. I tried thinking back to the dream that had just woke me up but all I got were flashes of chasing someone through the woods then tripping over, a wine bottle?

Shaking my head I swung my legs over the side of the bed and stood up, stretching. I walked over to the closet and pulled on some clean clothes. Gathering my phone up off the bed I opened my messages. One from you that read 'Sweet dreams, text me when you wake up.' I smiled and opened the other message. It was a nude from Natasha, I zoomed in on a few places and sent back a winking emoji.

Kicking the door open with my foot I walked over to the kitchen to make some coffee. The room behind me was empty but the door to the back room was open, I figured Levi had moved into there since the chairs there were better for sleeping.

That theory proved true when I walked through the back room to get to the bathroom. Levi was kicked back in one of the reclining chairs snoring his ass off.

In the bathroom I did my business and brushed my teeth. When I walked back through the back-room Levi was just starting to wake up.

"There's coffee." I told him on my way through. He muttered something and I heard the chair shift as Levi pushed the footstool back in place and stood up.

While I was pouring myself a cup of coffee, Levi came shuffling in to get himself a cup. "Mind if I use your shower?" He asked.

I took a drink of coffee before answering, "Sure man let me clear out first and the place is yours. I'll go over and pick up Mel. Meet you at the cabin?" I asked.

Levi nodded into his coffee cup. "Yeah that's cool. If you can get her there. How are you going to deal with her reaction to me being there? Are you just not going to tell her?"

I thought for a bit then shrugged, I had no idea really, "I'll make it up as I go along." I opened the freezer and pulled out some breakfast sandwiches. I tossed one at Levi and then threw mine in the microwave. "If you want to get somethings together to bring with us that would be cool." I said referring to some drugs and alcohol.

Levi nodded, "I'll see what I can do."

I finished my breakfast and then grabbed my keys and wallet. "I'm gonna head out, I'll let you know when we're on our way to the cabin." I shoved my feet into my shoes, "Lock up when you leave." I said over my shoulder and walked out the door.

I typed up a text to you asking what you were doing and got in the car, tossing my phone in the passenger seat, and then taking off. When I pulled up to your building I checked my phone, hoping for a response but had none. When I saw why I nearly lost it. I never hit send. I let the car run until you messaged me back. I was drumming my hands on the steering wheel to the music when you finally replied, you said you were about to eat breakfast. I asked if I could come over and you said I could so I told you that I would be there shortly.

I made myself sit there for a little while longer, listening to two more songs before I got out so you wouldn't think I was waiting in front of your building. But when I knocked on your door I realized I should have waited longer. You called me out, asking if I texted you from the parking lot.

"Something like that," I said laughing, "I was already on my way over." I walked around you and sat down on the sofa. On the coffee table there was a plate of cheesy eggs and some toast.

"Are you hungry?" You asked, getting my attention, "I can make you something if you want." It was sweet of you to offer but it wasn't your food I was interested in eating.

I looked you up and down, you were still in your pajamas a tight black tank top and form fitting blue plaid shorts. I smirked and rubbed my neck, "Thanks but I already ate." I watched as you grabbed your plate before you sat down and started eating. I asked what you planned on doing today.

"Just some chores," you said between bites.

I looked around the apartment. The place was cleaner than mine, I couldn't help but laugh. "What's there to do around here? Dust for cobwebs?" I teased. I asked if it was something that could be rescheduled, and that I really wanted to hang out with you. I was worried that you might be too set in your plans but then you asked what I wanted to do. I shrugged to seem casual, "It's a nice day, and if you're down for it we can go for a hike out on my grandpa's property."

You seemed to think about it for a moment, "that sounds like a lot more fun than organizing my closet. I'll need to get ready; I'm not hiking like this."

I reached up and tucked some hair behind your ear so I could see your face better. You could wear a ballgown and I would still take out to grandpas, "That's up to you, I see nothing with what you're wearing."

242

You pushed me with a shy smile and finished the last couple bites. Getting up you told me that you wouldn't be long. My eyes followed you to the kitchen then back through the living room and to your bedroom. Fuck those shorts look good on you.

I pulled my phone out and sent Levi a text that I got you to agree to go to the cabin.

He shot me back a text that he was at the store picking up some things and would be waiting at the house for us.

You came out dressed comfortably, I missed the shorts, but you look great no matter what you wear. You sat a knife down on the table and started putting a belt on. You noticed me watching you and called me out.

I nodded at the knife you sat down and asked what was up with it. Many reasons you told me, but mostly for protection? Protection against what? An amused chuckle fell from my lips, "You won't need it when your with me. I'm all the protection you'll need." Mainly I just don't want to risk you using the knife on me or Levi. I highly doubt you would but just in case.

You got a worried look in your eye, clearing your throat you said, "Even so I'd like to bring it..."

I stopped listening to what you were saying, I stood up and grabbed both of your hands in mine and said, "Melanie, you don't need to protect yourself from me. It'll just be me and you; I have a knife on me if we happen to need one." I said all the pretty little words to calm the inner voice that was telling you to run. I can see it in you, you're smart. But I'm smarter, I see that now as you hesitantly nodded and smiled up at me, saying that I was right and left the knife on the table as you went and got your boots and sat down on the sofa to put them on. I watched you, smiling at my small victory.

Levi sent me a text saying that he stopped at the last gas station on the way out to grandpas. I looked up to see how far you were from leaving. "Ready?" I asked you while telling Levi that we were about to leave.

"Yeah, is everything ok?" You asked me.

I panic for a moment, shoving my phone in my pocket I held my hand out to help you up, buying myself sometime, "Yeah everything is ok." I started, might as well get this next part out of the way, "Levi is wanting to join us on our hike." You asked what I told him, I wonder how easy it would be to trick you into inviting him. "I told him no," I lied, "that today was more for you and me." Then to turn it around I added, "Unless you don't mind him joining us. He can meet us there."

You shook your head no and started locking up your apartment, "I'd rather not." You said. It took me by surprise; I wasn't used to you acting this harshly.

"Are you sure?" I pressed, to cater to your interest I mentioned his band, "he has a new song he was hoping to get your input on."

"Yes, I'm sure." You snapped.

I backed up and looked down at you. Someone so tiny, filled with so much anger. Almost comical. Instead, I grabbed you by the elbow, forcing myself not to be rough with you, "Hey hold up," I said holding you there, "I feel some tension here. I can't have my girl hating on my friends. What's going on." I demanded.

You pulled on your arm, but I tightened my grip, your eyes flicked down to my hand and then back up to me, "Let me go," you said with mock courage.

You glared up at me, and I glared back, but just for a moment. I let go and joked about you still being hung up on Levi trying to get with you. "I thought you'd be over that by now." You looked down at the ground, embarrassed. I tilted your head, "look at me," I almost whispered, I had to turn on the charm to get out of this. "You two are going to run into each other eventually. You might as well get it over with." I kissed you on the forehead and pulled out my phone, "I'll tell Levi to meet us there."

"What about our 'me and you day'?" you asked looking at your door.

I shrugged, I was going to have to force this, "you two getting along is more important right now. Mel, he's practically a brother, I can't have bad blood between you two." I said throwing my arm around you and leading you out to my car. I opened the door for you, and you looked up at me skeptically, laughing to myself. I walked around the car and got in, you still had that look your face like you wanted to run back inside. "Don't look at me like that," I said starting the car, "It'll be fun."

"Fine but I'd like to go on an actual date after today. Just you and me." You said putting on your seat belt.

I laughed and put the car in reverse. "Deal." I said. If you decided you wanted me over Levi I'll give you anything you want. That's what this really all boils down to. Levi is jealous that I can have two bitches at my mercy, and he's stuck being by himself. I smiled at the thought of you choosing me over him, I know you will. I looked over at you in my passenger seat, you're so naive you'll forgive anything I do.

—m—

After the long ass drive we were pulling up to the house. Throughout the drive you seemed to switch between paranoid and chill. You seemed especially on edge when we pulled up the driveway and Levi came into view. I swear by your reaction you two dated in the past and had a nasty and awkward break up.

I noticed how you purposely avoided looking at Levi, I smirked at how this was all playing out in my favor. "Where's Alex?" You asked taking off your seatbelt.

"He was busy," it almost came out as a question. Why would you expect Alex to be here?

When we got out Levi came up to me, "Hey what's up man? What all did you bring?" I asked.

"Eh nothing too extravagant, some beer, some liquor, some drugs. There's some food in there somewhere in case we get hungry." He said.

"Good deal," I said looping my arms through the straps.

Levi turned his head and watched you as you wondered about the yard, "How did you get her here?" He asked, reaching into the bed of his truck, and pulling out two cooler backpacks. He handed me one and sat the other down on the ground.

"Charmed my way through it." I said. Levi shook his head, never once looking away from you. I wondered what would happen tonight if he hadn't kissed you, would you be as hateful toward him like you are now? The way he looks at you makes me want to put that cigarette his smoking out in his eye, but I knew he was faster than me and would have me on the ground before I could take the cigarette out of his mouth.

245

Melanie was still checking the place out, "Hey I brought some laced shit wanna hit it before we go up?" Levi offered, handing me a joint. But inside the rolled paper it looked strange, and it had a weird smell. I couldn't wait for him to light it.

"Hell yeah." I said, already pulling out a lighter.

"Think Mel would want a hit?" He asked, putting the joint to his mouth, and taking the lighter from me.

I shook my head. "Our little Mel isn't ready for this." I said taking the joint from him.

He shook his head, "Speaking of Mel, where did she go?" he asked looking around the yard.

"She's over there." I said pointing to the side of the house you were at. I've been keeping an eye you; I didn't want you to wonder too far.

Levi turned around and watched you as you walked around checking the place out. I narrowed my eyes, should I be worried that there could be a chance that you might choose him? I shook my head, which was crazy, I've spent so much time breaking down those walls you built, there is no way you'll pick Levi over me. But still the way he looks at you makes me want to punch him.

We passed the joint back and forth for a bit, getting a nice buzz. We hit it a few more times before Levi looked up and watched you as you started eyeballing the well, Levi picked his bag up off of the ground and put it on as he started walking towards you, "Hey," I called out. Picking up the last bag and throwing it on.

He stopped and looked back at me, "What?" He asked, aggravation dripping from the word.

"We're not at the cabin yet; besides, she's still pissed that you kissed her. She's not like the other bitches that we're used to dealing with, she won't fuck around with people behind my back." I walked ahead of him, making sure to reach you first. Just to insert my dominance.

"Yeah, but you fuck around on her just fine." He muttered loud enough for me to hear.

I bit back my words, now isn't the time to get into this. I needed to get you away from the well, and I needed to figure out how to secure you, so you won't go off with Levi.

I doubled my stride to get to you first, mostly to beat Levi there, but also I didn't want you to look too hard at your surroundings. I had a regular joint tucked behind my ear, I took it out and lit it as I walked up behind you and put my hand on your shoulder. You jumped and turned to face me, I grinned down at you, loving how skittish you can be. I offered you the joint, and asked, "What are you doing?"

You took the joint from me, our fingers bushing as you did. Fuck your skin is so soft, I almost didn't hear what you were saying. Apparently you heard something and wanted to know if anyone else was here.

I shrugged, there's been a couple different people who've said similar things, a small handful had even came out and said that they've seen ghosts here, but I don't believe in that shit. It made me want to laugh thinking that you believed in that crap. Instead of making fun of you; like I usually would, I went the safer approach and tried to put a logical explanation to it.

"Probably just a stone falling," I said, going on to explain that the property is pretty old, but no one has lived here since grandpa passed. I would know, I come out here to make sure that the place is still standing and that the yard doesn't get too over grown. I nodded my head towards the woods, "Are you ready?" I asked, eager to get you away from the well, I haven't looked down there recently so I'm not sure if Ellie's body is still hidden from view.

Levi then came up to us, stopping to stand on the other side of you, I watched you carefully as Levi took the joint from you, winking at you as he did.

"Yeah, I'm ready," you said. I wanted to punch the air in victory as you pressed yourself against me and lopped your arm through mine. I smirked at Levi and almost missed you asking, "How long are we hiking?"

"I don't know," I lied, "Depends on when we want to turn around."

Levi came up and put his arm around your shoulders, it took all I had not to yank you away from him like he just picked up and started playing with my favorite toy. He started talking about the cabin, telling you how we turned it from a hunting cabin to a party spot.

I mentioned the lake that was near the cabin and suggested we go swimming.

You shook your head and said that you didn't bring a bathing suit.

Levi was the first to laugh, I soon followed, "Sweetheart you don't need a swimsuit."

Then you started laughing. "I am not skinny dipping with you two. Nice try though." You said with little amusement in your voice.

Levi tightened his hold on you, pulling you away from me but just barely, our arms were still looped, he brought his face close to yours, "so that's a 'no' to a three-way, then."

You threw a glare at him and shoved him away. I was about to pull you into me when you shoved away from me too. Levi had his hands up saying something, but I wasn't paying attention to him. I was too focused on you. You were extremely agitated, I laughed softly and put my arm back through yours, "Honey, you're going to have to get used to his sense of humor," I said kissing the top of your head, your hair smelled amazing, I could stay like this all day. I mumbled some shit about how Levi didn't mean it and started gently tugging you down the path. I was too invested in you now to give up and turn around, you were too much fun to play with, all of the others gave in way too fast.

"Yeah Mel, I mean nothing *bad* about it," Levi said, coming up beside you once the path widened back up again. You looked up at him then over to me. I wonder what you're thinking right now, you clutched onto my arm tighter, you were probably just nervous.

I looked over you and at Levi, it was easy to do since you didn't even come up to my chin. I noticed how he wasn't trying to get too close to you, probably didn't want to push you any further than we already have. After five minutes of walking, you wondered ahead of us looking around at the trees and plants. You stopped and bent over to check out a butterfly that was on a blue flower, Levi walked around you, checking out your ass, making no attempt to be discrete about it.

You stood up and turned around, catching my eye. I winked at you and smiled. You shyly smiled back and with that we started walking again, me and Levi taking the lead and you not too far behind. As we walked Levi and I talked about random shit, mainly about how you kept falling behind to look at something. It didn't bother us, I thought it was cute.

Levi took this time to bring up his sister, "Nat wants to see you," he said.

I shook my head, "She always wants to see me." I said leaning against a tree while we waited for you to catch up.

Shrugging he said, "What's the big deal, you go with her, and I'll go with Mel, and everyone will be happy."

I clenched my jaw, "No offense but your sister won't make a very good house wife."

He shrugged again, "Yeah well you won't make a very good husband, so it fits."

I laughed and dropped it, mainly because Mel was walking up to us. You smiled up at me, and we kept walking. It wasn't too much longer when we came up to the ravine. I watched you as you walked up to the edge and looked out in the distance. I took my phone out and took a picture, I couldn't help it, you looked incredible out here.

I glanced over to where I last seen Levi, but he was gone, I looked around and saw him walking up to you, from here I could hear him say, "What are you looking at?"

I started making my way over to you at that point, you brought your shoulders up and I could see your lips move, but I didn't hear what you first said but I could make out the last part. "-really peaceful here."

Now at your side I put my arm around you, looking around I agreed, "It is, isn't it." Then to assert my dominance I pulled you in and kissed you, a feeling of accomplishment swelled inside me as Levi narrowed his eyes and looked away. I broke the kiss and nodded down the trail, "Come on the cabin is further up this way." I laced my fingers through yours and tugged you down the path.

I made sure to keep you next to me, keeping ahold of you so you wouldn't be able to randomly stop. I looked over my shoulder at Levi. He mimed smoking a joint and I nodded. Tilting his head to the side for a brief moment before he pulled out a small container that he took the laced joint from earlier.

You must have heard the lighter click, you looked over him then for some reason you looked at me with a doubtful look all over your face, "Hey Griff?" I love when you call me that, "What's in the bag?" I don't love when you do that though, how you pick up on something that most girls would just shrug off.

Levi leaned around you and held the joint out, I watched as you took it and brought it up to those perfect lips of yours, "You'll find out when we get to the cabin." I said in a light tone.

When you took a hit your face twisted up, you shook your head and held the joint out to me, "No I'm good." You said, your voice strained.

I pushed your hand back to you, "It's fine, just take a few more hits," I encouraged. "It's a different strain than you're used to." I explained with a shrug. We stared at each other for a moment. You seemed doubtful and I just smiled at you, you took a small hit and tried to hand it back to me again. I laughed, "Come on girl, hit it like you mean it." You gave me a half glare and took another hit sending you into a coughing fit. You passed the joint to Levi who looked like he was just as amused as I am. I started rubbing your back, muttering some comforting words, then I grabbed your hand and tugged you down the path with me. "Come on, we're almost there." I whispered in your ear.

Levi handed you back the joint, and after you took a hit you passed it to me. I handed it back to you and the rotation stayed that way until you caught on that we were trying to get you to smoke most of it. I stared down at you as you furrowed your eyebrows and asked, "What's going on here? Why do you keep skipping each other?"

Levi laughed, "We're not skipping each other, it's all even here." He held the joint out to you, after you just handed it to him.

You looked at him with a slight frown and then held your hand out to me. I chuckled and gently pushed your hand back, "We've taking hits, it's ok. You're probably just confused honey." My grin spread wider as you took a hit.

When the last of the joint was smoked I flicked off the cherry and stomped it out then tossed the roach to the side. I threw my arm around and we kept walking, I felt your footsteps start to slow down then eventually stop all together. You were looking down at your hands confused. I looked at Levi, and we shared a knowing look. I dropped my arm and looked down at you, "Are you ok, Mel?" I asked.

It took a second for you to find me, when your eyes met mine you lazily smiled and nodded. You looked down and over to the side. Levi stepped into your line of vision and grinned, "That's some good shit, huh?" he asked. Running a hand through your hair you nodded.

Looking over at Levi I asked, "Is the beer still going to be cold when we get there?"

Nodding he said, "Yeah they're at the bottom."

You shook your head and complained that you didn't want to drink. I laughed and put an arm around your shoulders, shaking you a bit as I said, "Nonsense, you work too hard. You deserve to let loose once in a while."

My grin grew wider as you frowned but nodded your head, "Just one beer." You said.

I couldn't stop the laugh even if I tried. "We'll see," I muttered under my breath.

Not much longer the trees gave way to the clearing that grandpa built the cabin in. The broken window was out of place here, I need to remember to bring a glass pane out here to replace it. I know grandpa has one somewhere in the house, the fucking hoarder never threw anything useful away.

I went to unlock the door, just basic precaution. If someone really wanted to get in here there was no stopping them, out in the middle of an ocean of trees, no cameras, no witnesses. It's hard to say what goes on out here. The steps to the porch groaned under me as I walked up to the door.

Behind me I heard Levi calming you down, "Don't' be scared, Mel." He said, this was a normal thing here, usually with the girls. *This place is creepy*, they like to say. I smirked and pushed the door open as I turned around to observe the interaction going on behind me. "Honestly, the cabin is less creepy than the house. Come on, we can go in together," he said holding his arm out so you could take it. You looked up at him, and he dropped his head, saying something that I couldn't quite make out. I narrowed my eyes and felt my body tense up. When you didn't say anything he shrugged his shoulders and said, "Alex made me say that. He said that after last time, I need to start giving warnings."

I made a mental note to thank Alex for that. You laughed, causing me to smile. "Alex is right." You said and then started walking toward me. "I'm sorry, I didn't realize I was giving you a look." You seemed slightly nervous as you walked past me and went into the cabin.

Levi was grinning like an idiot, watching you walk. I looked over my shoulder at you, you were looking around the cabin, taking in your surroundings. "This is going to be fun." He said.

I laughed, *fun indeed* I thought. You are so unpredictive, Mel, as soon as I think I have you figured out you prove me wrong. You've proven time and again that you're more loyal to me than you probably should be, I just hope you keep that up while under the influence.

I went in and put the bag I was carrying on the table. I took out the lockbox so I could get the bottle of whiskey and the cups and poured you a drink. I turned around in time to see Levi walking behind you. You looked unsure as you cleared your throat and looked around, when you found me you walked up, and I handed you the drink I poured.

I was about to tell you what was in the cup when you tossed it back, your eyes got wide and you coughed, "Ugh! What was that?" You grabbed the back of the closest chair. I laughed and answered you honestly. "What?" You mumbled, looking at what I pulled out of the bag so far.

You shook your head and was about to say something when Levi came over laughing, "You threw that back like a champ, girl!" he said while pouring himself a drink, he held the cup to me, "I'm not going to let her out drink me." He proclaimed and threw it back.

You pulled out a chair and sat down. I couldn't help thinking how small you looked when you shook your head and said, "I thought it was water," so softly I almost didn't hear it.

I *almost* felt bad, I rubbed your shoulders and bent over to kiss your cheek, "I'll get you some water honey." I went over to the cabinets; we keep cases of water on the bottom shelf and whatever alcohol is left over from a party goes on the top shelf. I got 3 bottles of water out and tossed one over to Levi. I opened the second one before handing it to you.

You smiled up at me, your eyes were glassy, and the smile was lazy, "Thank you," your words were starting to slur together.

"How are you feeling after that walk?" Levi asked sliding into the chair next to you.

I pulled a chair closer to the other side of you as you shrugged and said, "Pretty good."

"That was nothing for our little Mel," I said proudly, twisting some of your hair around my finger I looked down at you and told no one in particular, "She could go all day and not get tired."

You blinked up at me, the smile you gave me was a little lopsided but adorable all the same. You looked around the table confused at first then reached for your water just about knocking it over. I laughed softly, watching you struggle with trying to open the bottle, enjoying our handiwork before swooping into your rescue. I gently pried the bottle away from you, you gave zero resistance.

You rubbed your eyes, and I waited for you to drop your hand before handed the bottle back over. At this point your eyes were bloodshot and your pupils were extremely dilatated. I was starting to get excited. I grinned down at you and got to work pouring more drinks.

I brought some Sprite with us, I refused to drink straight alcohol. I was getting to old to deal with those kind of hangovers, especially when I'm this far away from the comfort of my own home. I poured myself a drink and made you one up too. I slid the bottle of soda over to Levi and he dumped some into his cup. I held my drink out and made a cheers to friendship.

Levi held his out, "To friendship," he repeated, and we both looked down you. You almost shrunk back into your chair, I smiled at how slow and sluggish your movements were getting. You picked up your cup and tapped it against ours, there was no emotion your voice, but I brushed it off. You were probably just wore out from the walk.

Levi took out another joint. A normal one this time. I noticed that he had one more laced one, just kept it separated from the others that he brought. I got up from the table, mostly to stretch my legs, and went over to the counter were we set the stereo up at it, we hung speakers up in the corners or the cabin so we could hear the music better. I was plugging my phone in, once again thankful that we followed Alex's suggestion and installed a solar panel out here so the cabin can get some power. Before it was all candles and trying to remember to keep fresh batteries for the radio out here.

You appeared at my side, turning around to lean with your back against the counter. You brought your hand up and grabbed your head, "Hey, I don't feel good." You slurred.

I turned all of my attention on you, cupping your cheek I looked into your eyes, even when they're unfocused and glazed over they are still the most gorgeous green eyes I've seen. I felt your forehead for show and asked what was going on.

Out of nowhere Levi came up and passed me the joint. Your eyes flicked between us, like you didn't know who look at, "I'm getting a headache, and the alcohol is hitting too hard." You told us.

I took a hit off the joint and held it out to you, "Here, this will help." I said, when you took it from me I went over to the table and grabbed the lockbox. I flipped the lip open and took out a small zip lock bag that had some random pills in it. They all had similar effects to varying degrees, I chose a white oblong pill, the most unsuspecting one of the bunch, and grabbed your water bottle before heading back to the counter. I held my hand out and offered you the pill and water, "It's for your headache," I said nonchalantly.

No questions asked you took the pill from me; after washing it down you made your way back over to the table and sat down. Levi watched you with a hungry gaze and in a fluid motion he hopped off the counter and stalked toward you. Curious to what was about to happen I hung back to observe.

You rested your elbows on the table and cradled your head in your hands. Levi slid into the seat next to you, "This weed is a little harsh, it might be getting to you."

You sat up and looked over him, closing your eyes for brief moment before saying, "No this is different."

"Why don't we go lie down?" He offered motioning over to the bed.

I rested my hands on the counter behind me, tapping my thumb against the edge of the wood, waiting on your response.

You blinked a few times, you looked confused, "What?" You asked, you must not have heard him.

Levi chuckled, "I said, do you want to lie down?" he asked leaning forward to rub your thigh.

You slapped his hand off, rather aggressively. I bit back my laughter as you freaked out on him, "No! And why do I have to keep telling you to stop touching me!" You all but shouted.

I grinned and took that as my queue to step in before things escalated. I put my arm around your shoulders before I took the seat on your other side, "Hey, Mel." I said, "what's going on?" I tried to make my tone as soothing as possible. "We're all friends here."

You looked up at me, your eyes flicked down to your lap but then you brought them up just as quick, "I don't like how he keeps making things sexual."

Levi tried to contain his laughter, I chuckled slightly reaching out to touch your cheek, "Oh little Mel," I said softly, "I've already told you before that isn't a bad thing. You're an attractive woman," I dropped my hand from your cheek and sighed dramatically, making a show of the whole thing I shrugged my shoulders, "But fine. Knock it off." I stated pointing at Levi.

"Can you take me home?" You asked rubbing your head. "I don't feel right."

I sat up and glanced over at Levi. I narrowed my eyes trying to figure out what that look on his face was about. It was almost one of concern. To be a good boyfriend I put my hand between your shoulder blades and started rubbing small circles, "Maybe you should lie down?" I suggested.

You shook your head, "No I don't want to lie down." You said sharply. I drew my hand back and looked down at you. You were acting like a real bitch right now.

I shook my head and walked over to get a bottle of water off the counter. I waited for you to finish drinking before asking, "Are you sure you want to leave? It's a long walk back." And it was almost sunset. It would be dark before too long. We've made the hike back to the house in the dark plenty of times, but I wasn't sure if that would be something you could handle right now. The woods could be scary at night, and in the state you're currently in there's no telling what would happen out there.

You nodded your head and then closed your eyes and grabbed onto the table. I grinned, knowing there was no way you were walking through that cabin door tonight. Squatting down in front of you, I brushed some hair back from your face. It won't be too much longer until the fun really begins, I just need to get you in a better mind set.

"You are so beautiful," I couldn't help but stating, I gave you a genuine smile and stood up. "Well, I was hoping that you would have been more willing to make peace with my best friend, but alright." If I couldn't convince you to stay maybe I could guilt you into staying. I mentioned how awkward things are going to be and I don't want to have to worry about trying to keep you two apart. Looking down at you I could tell it was working. I turned my back so you couldn't see the amused smirk, "But since that's how it's going to be.."

Levi rolled his eyes and took a few gulps of his drink. I started to gather some things up on the table and slowly put them back in the bag I carried in.

You put your hand on my arm, "Wait," you were still looking down at the table.

I waited until you looked up at me, my left eyebrow twitched up. "Yes?" I was eager to see the look on Levi's face when you tell us that you changed your mind.

You looked slightly uncomfortable when you said, "We can stay." Levi almost choked and I had to bite the inside of my cheek from shouting out in triumph. "But I really don't want any more sexual advances from Levi. I'm not into that." You added on stubbornly.

I almost shrugged my shoulders. We'll deal with that part later, you agreed to stay and that was the hard part. I smirked down at you, "I can't control him, but I don't see what the big deal is. It's just sex." I said pulling the items I placed in the bag back out.

"Are you sleeping with other people?" You asked.

I felt like the air was sucked out of me. I ignored Levi behind you, he looked like he was about loose it. I brought a chair close to you and sat down, cupping your cheek, my hand almost covered the entire side of your head, "Of course not." I punctuated the lie with a deep kiss. I dropped my hand from your face and slammed it on the table, making you and Levi both jump. "Let me make you a drink!" I needed a quick topic change. I didn't want to dodge that conversation again.

"Not too strong?" You called out as I got up and went over to the counter carrying the lockbox.

"I wouldn't make you a drink I wouldn't drink." I told you.

I put the box down on the counter and opened it up. Picking out a clear capsule with white powder in it. I twisted the capsule over a cup and dropped the powder in, pouring some sprite on top and a stirring in a shot of whiskey.

"She's going to be crushed when she finds out what you've been doing with Natasha." He taunted.

I poured myself another drink, without looking at him I replied, "That's why she's not going to find out." I shot back.

"She's not stupid, she's going to catch on." Levi stated.

I took a drink out of my cup and splashed in more alcohol. "Why do you plan on telling her?" I challenged and looked over at him.

We stared each other down for a few tense moments. Then he scoffed, "You're little secret is safe with me. But don't be surprised when this backfires on you."

I grabbed the cups and walked them over to you. You were now sitting on the sofa, your head in your hands, it looked like you were about to fall asleep. I stepped in front of you and handed you the one I made up first. Making sure there was no powder floating on top. "Drink this, you'll feel better." I coaxed. And to help you feel more at ease I lifted my own glass and took a drink.

You took a tentative sip and curled your lip. Shaking your head you held the cup out to me. "I don't like it."

I smiled and sat down next to you, "One more drink," I said gently pushing the cup to you, "there's not much there." I told you, encouraging you to drink the rest of it.

You took a bigger drink this time, but the reaction was the same. You shook your again and handed the cup to me. "I'm sorry I can't do it."

I took the cup from you and looked inside; you drank most of it. I swirled the cup in a quick circle, smirking and tossed the rest back. "That's ok," I twirled some of your hair around a finger, "I'm going to step out for a cigarette." I kissed your temple and got up.

Levi got up and followed me out to the porch. I turned around and rested my back against the rail and looked in to the cabin. The window in front of me gave me a good view of the bed and of you still on the sofa. I waited as Levi fished out his pack of cigarettes, took one out and tossed the pack to me. I got one out and put it to my mouth taking the lighter from Levi after he got his lit. "What happened to the window?" He asked looking over at the broken glass.

I took my time answering. "Remember when Alex and I came out here near the end of January?"

Levi looked back at me then out at the yard. He look confused for a moment, then his eyes lit up, "Oh, Alex was so pissed about that. I had to hear about that all Spring, how a bear almost attacked him."

We laughed for a bit at that. I looked ahead of me, through the closed window at you, your shoulders moved up and down rhythmically letting me know that you were passed out. "Yeah well, that was a result of that." I said pointing my cigarette and the cracked window. I shook my head and told him about that night. "I can't remember that bitches name, but she put up a hell of a fight, landed a few good hits on me and if Alex hadn't moved when he did the phone she launched at him would have hit him instead of the window. It wasn't until he tackled her and slammed her head against the floor when things finally calmed down." I laughed at how close she was to escaping.

Levi whistled, "Sounds like she's trouble all the way around," he said taking a hit off his cigarette and blowing the smoke out. He looked in the window at the back of your head.

I lowered my head and glared at him. If I could read minds now would be the time to do it. I didn't trust him to keep things between me and his sister quiet. He took another hit and said, "I don't know how you do it man."

Flicking the ashes off my cigarette I looked over at him, in a monotone voice I replied, "Do what?"

"Wrap these girls around your finger. You get them in a hold within the first few months and it's like they join the church of Griffin."

I laughed, "You just need to be more patient."

He shook his head and dropped his cigarette on the floorboards, stomping it out he said, "I'm going back inside. I don't want her to get lonely."

I nodded and hung back to finish smoking. The door was left open, so I was able to hear most of what went down. Levi walked in and sat down next to you. You lifted your head and looked over at him with a sleepy smile. Your lips moved but I couldn't hear what you said.

Levi ticked his head back, "He's still smoking, he'll be in a moment."

You looked over your shoulder, and then you both looked out the window at me. You smiled and I smirked back at you and winked. With your bodies twisted around like that, there wasn't much space between you and Levi. My breath was starting to get heavier, and my pulse started to quicken. I needed to calm down, the more you distracted Levi the less likely he was to tell you what I do behind your back. I forced myself to stay put, leaning back against the rails.

Levi leaned to the side and pulled out his phone and headphones, "Hey can I get your opinion on something?" He asked.

You turned away from me and gave him your full attention. "Yeah, sure." You said with a smile that was too big for the occasion.

He smirked at you and held out an earbud, "Awesome let me pull it up really quick." He put the earbud he still had in his ear and pressed on his phone screen times. He looked up at you and put an arm on the back of the sofa behind you, not quite making contact. "Ready?" He asked looking down at you.

You placed the earbud in your left ear and looked up at him. That look you gave him was none that I've never seen before. "Yeah, I'm ready."

Levi licked his lips and looked at his phone. "We just dropped this song so be nice." He said.

You nudged him with your shoulder, "I'm always nice." You laughed. I noticed how you didn't move away from him. Watching you two together made me nervous. What Levi had put on for you to listen to had you nodding your head. You got a big grin and looked up at him, "when are you guys gonna have another show?" you asked.

He shrugged and brushed your hair off your shoulders, "We're still trying to figure that out. If you want I can pick you up and bring you to practice sometime."

You nodded and said something I couldn't hear. I rested my hands behind me and gripped the railing.

"Hey, I got another song I want you to listen to. Not my band and not our song, but I think you'll like it." Levi said, now absent mindedly playing with your hair with one hand and messing with his phone with the other. He sat his phone to the side and looked down at you. You weren't paying him any attention, swaying side to side with what I'm assuming was the song he put on for you.

Levi leaned in to you and started kissing your neck. Fire shot through me, and you leaned into him. I gritted my teeth; you looked like you were into it for a moment. I thought you were going to kiss him by the way you turned to face him. But then your smiled slipped from your face and you stood up shaking your head. "Levi what the fuck?" you said.

Levi made a fist with the hand that was playing with your hair. He stood up and walked behind you, pulling your hair back to expose the side of your face and neck. "I'm sorry, but there's something here between us," he said taking your hand and turning you around, "I don't want to fight. Why are you?" he asked pulling you into him.

You put a hand on his chest and looked up him. Biting your bottom lip, you looked down and shook your head. "I'm happy with Griffin." You said, dropping your hand and turning around to walk away.

My chest almost exploded with pride. I punched the air in victory and laughed softly to myself. This couldn't be any better. Levi, however, wasn't giving up that easy. "But is he happy with you?" he called.

My face dropped and my heart stopped. *What the fuck is he doing?* I asked myself and walked to lean against the door frame to get a better look at what was going on. Since you moved off the sofa I could no longer see what was going on from the window.

"Of course, his is." You said confidently.

Levi walked and grabbed your elbow, "you know his fucking arou-" he groaned when your elbow came back and slammed into his side.

You whirled around, your eyes bright with anger, "Levi listen to me very carefully." You said eerily calm. "I am not the kind of girl to mess around on my boyfriend. I am dating your best friend. And while we are together, this isn't going to happen. Ok?"

Levi straighten up, rubbing the spot where you elbowed him he forced a smile. "Yeah I get it.

260

Griffin is lucky," he looked over at where I was standing in the doorway, and then back to you, "You could be a lot better, and I hope he knows it."

I smirked and pushed myself off the doorframe and strutted over to you, throwing my arm around your shoulder, and plucking the earbud out of your ear. "How was the song?" I asked you holding my hand out to the Levi so he can put his headphones away.

"It was incredible," you said smiling up at me like nothing happened. You leaned your head against my chest and looked up at Levi. "I'd love to watch it performed live if the offer to watch your band practice is still available?" you asked him.

"Yeah it's still available," he said with a chuckle and smiled down at you. He tilted his head side to side, cracking his neck, looking over to the right he seen the dart board hanging on the wall, "Hey Mel, are you any good at darts?" he asked walking over and pulling the plastic darts out of the peg board.

You shook your head with a smile, "No not at all."

I pulled you into me and kissed the top of your head, glad and relieved that you essentially chose me tonight and Levi is doing everything possible to ignore that. "We can be on a team," I said and tugged you over to were Levi stood. He handed me the blue darts; I passed one off to you and we stepped back to watch you take aim and throw the dart. It flew through the air for two seconds before taking a nose dive and bouncing on the floor a few times before it rolled in a circle.

Levi chuckled when you tossed your hands up and turned around, "I'm sorry," you said sheepishly at me.

I laughed and handed you another dart, "Try again," I said.

You took it from me and tried again, this time the dart hit the board at an angle and bounced off, landing on the floor. You bent over and laughed, "I'm no good at this, you guys play." You between giggles.

Levi shook his head and smiled, "Nonsense, it's all in good fun." He went to stand next to you. "Stand like this," he said with feet apart.

I walked up to the other side of you and put my hands on your hips, I moved you a little, "No more like this," I said. "There that's better." You caught my eye, and I winked at you.

"Ok, now close one eye and aim the dart at the center of the board." Levi trying to instruct you without crossing another one of your boundaries.

We tried for 20 minutes to help you hit a bullseye. You got the dart to stick a handful of times, but you were too inebriated to pay full attention. We were all laughing our asses off and decided to call it quits and moved on to a drinking game. It was a made-up game between Go fish and Bullshit. We made up the rules as we went, and it was a fucking disaster, we were all gone by the time the game was over. We lost track of who had the highest score, so no one was declared the winner.

Levi yawned and went to crash on the sofa, leaving the bed to us. I laid down first and pulled you on top of me. You laughed and curled up next to me. I nuzzled my face into your neck, and it wasn't too much longer after that I was fast asleep.

—◊—

I woke up to a loud bang. I groaned and rolled over reaching out to pull you into me, but the spot next to me was empty. I opened my eyes and lifted my head; Levi was walking out the door opening a bottle of water. I sighed and threw an arm over my eyes to block out the harsh rays of the early morning sunshine. I lied there for a little while longer wanting to go back to sleep but then I heard talking coming from outside. It wasn't until Levi started laughing that I got up.

When I got to the door, your back was to me, and Levi was standing next to you with his shirt pulled up. "What's going on here?" I asked, stepping up behind you and resting my hands on the railing.

Levi pulled his shirt up higher and looked down at his chest. "I was showing Melanie what she did last night." He said.

I furrowed my eyebrows and looked at him, there was a bruise from where you elbowed him. I laughed and kissed the top of your head, I couldn't be prouder, "Yeah that was fucking hilarious." I said. "How are you feeling?" I asked you. "It looks like your morning got off to a rough start."

You rested your back against me, "Like shit." You mumbled.

"Well, we have a good hike ahead of us. Think you can make it?" I asked and pushed myself off the railing. "The cleanup won't take long. We'll head out once we're done."

You nodded, "Yeah I'll be fine." You followed us inside and helped with the cleanup. You started stacking the empty cups, "Why did I elbow you?" You asked Levi, who was gathering up the darts.

He rubbed the back of his neck and laughed, "You just got tired of me. But it's ok, I forgive you."

I looked over you, there was a ghost of a smile on your lips. I narrowed my eyes and pushed the pang of jealousy away.

—⁂—

Hiking out always took longer than hiking in. Levi and I were both impressed at how well you kept up with us. When we got to the house Levi tossed the bags into the back of his truck. He said he'd catch up with us later and took off.

I asked if you were ready to go home, you looked like you could use some sleep. I didn't want to take you home, but I had things I needed to get done later today. I walked you to the door to your apartment and kissed you on the forehead goodbye. I'm not too about to kiss you until you brush your teeth. Morning breath I can handle, but not after you throw up.

When I got home I took a quick shower and set an alarm to wake up in an hour, so I wasn't late for the job I had to do.

MELANIE (August 2)

I was sitting on the floor in front of the sofa working on a dreamcatcher just taking some time for myself when my phone chimed. No surprise it was a message from Griffin.

'What's up?' He asked. I told him nothing much, he sent back 'I'm just now leaving the store.' 'I was picking up some things for tonight. Mind if I come over for a little bit?'

'What about your food?' I asked.

'Lol I didn't pick up any food.' His responses were always immediate. 'I can be there in 10 minutes.' He told me.

Sighing, I gave in. 'I'll see you in 10 minutes then.' True to his word, 10 minutes later there was a knock on my door. I put my project to the side and got up to go see who it was. With a quick look through the peep hole, I opened the door, "Hey Griffin." I said with a smile.

"There's my girl." He said and pulled me into a tight hug. "What are you doing tonight?" He asked, letting me go and stepping around me to go sit down on the sofa.

I sat down next to him and watched as he looked down at the dreamcatcher I was working on. "I don't have anything planned."

"Me neither," he said sitting back and turning towards me, "you should let me kidnap you tonight. We can just chill and put on a movie or something." He leaned towards me and picked up a lock of my hair and twirled it around in his fingers. "I'll let you choose what we watch." He said with a wink.

I grinned, "Alright, I need to go get ready." I got up to go get some socks.

Griffin followed me with his eyes, "Don't take too long." He said then pulled out his phone.

I did a quick look in the mirror, my eyeliner was a little smudged, I thought about putting on some more makeup as I fixed the eyeliner, but it's not like I was going to be around anyone else other than Griffin who had already seen me looking like a cave troll. I ran a brush through my hair and put on a fresh layer of deodorant and a spritz of perfume. I pulled on the first pair socks I took out of the drawer.

Griffin was scrolling through his phone waiting for me on the sofa. He looked up at me with that wolfish grin of his. "Ready?" He asked as I walked past him and to the kitchen.

"Yeah, I think so," I replied going to the kitchen counter to grab my purse. I slung the strap over my shoulder and walked to the front door to put my shoes on.

Griffin got up and followed me out the door.

—⚏—

At Griffins house I left my bag in his car and just took in my phone. I offered to help him carrying in some bags he took from the backseat, but he waved me off and asked if I would get the door instead. I took the keys he held out and went to unlock and open the door for him.

He dumped the bags on the counter and took me to the back room where we smoked and then went to the front room to curl up on the sofa. "What movie do you want to watch?" He asked me, handing me the remote.

I thought for a moment and typed 'Exorcist' in the search bar and pressed play.

"Good choice," He said put his arm around me.

About 15 minutes in Griffin was getting affectionate and pulled me closer to him when Alex walked through the door with a tall and thin woman in tow. She had shoulder length black curly hair and was a total bombshell. Alex nodded at Griffin who tapped on my hip and whispered, "Let's go smoke."

I looked back at him confused. I thought it was just going to be us. But I followed them, the woman looked me up and down then smile and introduced herself. "Hi I'm Cassie."

I smiled, she seemed nice, and Alex wasn't a horrible person to be around. I relaxed a little bit, "Hi, I'm Mel." I said and we followed the guys to the back room where Griffin was already rolling a blunt.

It was pretty relaxed. The guys were talking but I wasn't paying attention to what they were saying, Cassie was talking enough for the both of us which is ok because I'm socially awkward and talking to people I've just met isn't my strong suit. But Cassie was really cool, and she'd ask me a few questions about myself every now and then which helped me get out of my shell a little.

Then Levi walked in with 2 women following closely behind him; a red head with waist long hair and perfect curves and a short blond that had her hair pulled into a tight ponytail. Levi walked over to Griffin and Alex while the blonde walked over and sat down next to us. "Hey, Cassie I haven't seen you in forever..."

I looked over at Griffin and noticed that he was smirking at the red head who was heading to the bathroom. Alex nudged Levi and nodded over at my direction, they tried to cover up their laughs with fake coughs when I turned my focus on them. I felt my pulse quicken and my mouth went dry. The way that Griffin looked at her made me want to throw up, I crossed my arms to hide my stomach rolls all of sudden self-conscience of my body type.

Taking a deep breath, I tried to join in on the conversation that Cassie and the blonde where having but the two friends where too focused on the other. I pulled my phone out and checked the time for something to do when someone sat down next to me and handed me a blunt and lighter. Griffin smiled down at me, and I reluctantly took the blunt and lit it, handing the lighter back I took a drag and passed the blunt over to Cassie.

"Who was that?" I asked Griffin.

He shrugged, "No one special."

I didn't believe him and was about to call him out when more people started to show up. Random people kept coming up to the guys and greeting them like royalty. A guy in ripped jeans and a black shirt came up and started talking to Alex. Alex nodded his head and got Griffins attention who told me that he would be right back and just like that I was left surrounded by unfamiliar faces.

I took my phone out and started to message my sister. I felt someone sit next to me and looked over to see Levi, he threw his arm over the back of the sofa and leaned over to take the blunt from Cassie, which put his face next to mine. He smirked and winked at me, "How have you been Melanie?" he asked, sitting back in his seat.

"Can't complain." I said. "How about you?"

Levi laughed and handed me the blunt. "There's so much to complain about. But I won't bore you." He looked around the room that was now crowded with people. Someone had started some music and over all the people talking it was getting loud. Levi leaned in and whispered in my ear, "follow me to the kitchen." He said; his breath tickling my neck. "Let's get something to drink." Standing up he offered me his hand. I took it to stand up, but I let go once I was standing.

I saw the red head walk out of the bathroom; she had took the seat that Griffin had been sitting in. I wanted to ask Levi if he knew anything about that woman, but I was hesitant to start shit with all these people around us.

When we walked into the kitchen the group of people who were standing around got quiet. The guys in the group started to size Levi up but he didn't seem phased. These guys were pretty big if the tension turned into an actual fight I was worried how it would end up. The one guy who was wearing a hat spoke up, "Didn't expect to see your sorry ass here."

"Remember who's house you're in." Levi warned.

The guy smirked and glanced at me. "That your new play thing?" he asked.

I opened my mouth, a snappy retort on the tip of my tongue, but Levi beat me to it. "If you want to take this outside we can. Just keep in mind how it ended up for you last time."

The guy laughed and the group behind him followed. "I came out on top last time pussy."

Levi shook his head. "Only because the cops showed and put me in handcuffs." The two men both went rigid and stared each other down. "Why the *fuck* are you guys even here? This isn't your part of town."

The guy readjusted his hat. "I came to get my girl. I heard she was here."

"Then grab her and leave. You have 2 minutes before I drag your ass outside and we'll see who comes out on top this time." Levi growled. When the group made no move to leave he narrowed his eyes. "You really have forgotten where your at haven't you?" He took a few steps towards the group. The guys who were standing behind the one who was talking either lost interest in fighting or decided better of it. When Levi was within arm's reach the guy in the hat was standing alone.

The guy stood his ground, smirked at Levi, and patted him on the shoulder aggressively, "I'll be seeing you." He said.

Levi faked laughed, "HA!" Clapping him on the shoulder almost pushing him, "not if I see you first. Get your whore and get out." He watched as the guy walked into the living room and started arguing with a woman.

I pulled open the refrigerator and pulled out a beer bottle. "Hey Levi, did you want a drink?" He nodded but kept his gaze on the arguing couple. I pulled out another beer and let the door close on its own. I walked over to Levi and held out the bottle, waiting for him to take it.

Levi gave me a wolfish smile and took the bottle. "Thank you," he opened it and handed it back to me, then he took the unopened one from me and opened that one to take a drink. He watched as the guy in the hat eventually got the woman he was arguing with to leave, and they both walked out the door visibly mad. "Let's go sit down."

I followed him over to the sofa that was in the front room. I sat down next the arm and Levi sat down next to me, a little too close. I felt slightly awkward and after I took a drink I started to just ramble. "I started to follow your band on *YouTube*, you guys have really awesome music videos."

Levi laughed, "You flatter me, you should check out our Instagram we post a lot more content on there."

I told him I would and tried to ignore the red headed smoke show that walked out of the back room and looked around like she was lost. She leaned against the wall and started taking selfies. I got a weird feeling about her that only grew when Griffin and Alex walked out of his bedroom with the guy from earlier. The red head walked up to Griffin; and they started talking and laughing. She grabbed Griffin by the hand and pulled him into the back room.

Levi was talking but I cut him off, "Who is that?" I asked, motioning to the red head leading Griffin away.

Levi looked over and looked back at me. "She's a fucking idiot. You don't need to worry about her." He said almost annoyed. I just stared at him, Levi sighed and rolled his eyes. "She's my sister and wasn't even supposed to be here. Just a pain in the ass really." He reached out and gathered some of the hair the fell over my shoulder and twirled it around his fingers. I leaned back to pull my hair out of his hand. Levi looked up and met my eyes and dropped his hand. "Hang tight," he said and stood up, "I'll be right back." He winked at me before he left.

So, there I was, left alone on the front room sofa listening to crappy pop music and watching drunk people fall over themselves. I wasn't into the party scene, I was getting uncomfortable being surrounded by all these strangers who were either high, drunk, or both.

Standing up I went to try to find Griffin to tell him I was leaving, I was still working out on how I was going to get home since Griffin drove me here and my purse was in his car, I wasn't sure if it was locked or not and the last thing I wanted to do was set off a car alarm. Walking through the back room I wish I would have just went home and sent Griffin a text instead. I found him on the far side of the room sitting with Levi and Alex. Each of them had a woman on his lap.

Alex was the first who saw me, he started laughing and nudged Levi. When Levi looked over at him Alex nodded his head in my direction. Levi looked at me, and they both lost it, I wish I could hear what they were saying over the music, but I was still too far away to hear them. Griffin turned his head to see what his two friends where so amused by. He looked almost bored when he saw me, I have never been more humiliated. I should have just disassociated from all of this and went home in that moment, but like a fool I just kept walking over to the group of guys who were cracking up and having a good time.

My heart beat pounded in my ears. I forced a smile when I got to the group, and they all looked up at me. The girls looked annoyed; the one on Griffins lap looked enraged that I was there. Alex and Levi were hiding smiles behind their hands, at least they had the decency to stop laughing when I stopped in front of them. Griffin looked almost ashamed but mostly like he wanted to get this over with. "Hey guys." I said a little too sweetly.

Alex cleared his throat and through contained laughter he said, "Mel! Always a pleasure."

I looked over at Griffin who was rubbing his temple. The red head on his lap rubbed his chest and looked me up and down, the woman who was 'no one' and 'just a pain in the ass' with a perfect body and flawless skin. Levi was the next to speak. "Hey Mel, do you want a hit?" He asked holding out a blunt.

I shook my head no and smiled at him, "Thank you but I'm about to head out." I turned my attention to Griffin. "Can I talk to you for a moment?" That made the other two howl with laughter.

The girl on Griffin's lap started to say something but Griffin cut her off, "Yeah sure." Shoving her off his lap he stood up. He put his arm around my shoulders and led me away from the pack of laughing men. "So, what's this about, are you not enjoying the party?" He asked casually.

I shrugged off his arm and stepped away from him. "No not really. Who the fuck was that? Do you know what, that's not the point. Why was she on your lap?" I was shaking I was so mad. I shook my head and bit my tongue to keep from screaming.

Griffin looked down at me, "She doesn't matter, why aren't you enjoying yourself Mel?" He asked stepping towards me with his hand stretched out.

I took a step back batting his hand away. "To me it matters. How would you feel if you saw me sitting on some guy's lap?" I asked pointedly.

A dark look flashed across his face, sighing he said, "I didn't realize it would cause this much tension. But why are you getting so mad at this?"

I shook my head; *This is unbelievable* I thought. "I thought we weren't seeing other people?" my voice sounded strained. I felt really stupid.

Griffin clenched his jaw and looked at the air above my head, "I'm not seeing Nat. She had just sat down when you showed up." He looked down at me.

I looked away and shook my head. Ignoring that flat out lie. *This is worthless* I thought "Why did you even invite me over here if you were throwing a party tonight?"

Griffin reached out to me again, but I pulled away, "This wasn't our idea." He said dropping his arm. "It was just supposed to be us 6. You, me, and whoever Alex and Levi brought. But then Natasha jumped into Levi's car at the last minute and invited a bunch of people over."

I scoffed and rolled my eyes. There were too many questions, "So, then was it your idea or 'Nat's' to have her sit on your lap?" Griffin opened and closed his mouth, again I rolled my eyes and shook my head. "I'm going home. I don't want to keep you from your company."

At that moment I didn't care that my purse was in his car I just wanted to get away. I wasn't worried about my keys; I had an extra set back in the apartment and I left the bathroom window unlocked so I could get in that way. Breaking into my own apartment wasn't ideal but it outweighed the other option, which was going back in to face Griffin one more time. In a rage I walked outside to get an uber.

When I got off the phone, I heard the door open and close. It was just a random group of drunk guys who piled into a green car and drove away. I sat down on the porch stairs and waited for my ride. More people came and went as the minutes ticked by, someone sat down and cleared their throat. I looked over at Alex, "What are you doing out here?" he asked.

I shrugged my shoulders, "Why am I even here in the first place? I thought…" I trailed off and shook my head. *This is stupid* I thought, "It doesn't matter. I'm waiting for my ride." I said. I looked at my phone and checked the time on when my driver should be arriving.

Alex bumped me with his shoulder, "I can give you a ride home if you want."

I ran a hand through my hair, "Wouldn't they miss you in there?" I asked, venom dripping off every word. I don't know why I was being so hateful toward Alex; he didn't do anything.

Alex shrugged a shoulder, "Maybe, but they'll get over it." He grinned at me then he asked, "So why are you leaving so soon?"

"Why should I stay?" I asked him.

You could almost see the light bulb turn on in his head, Alex's jaw dropped slightly, "Oh I know what this is about. You're jealous." A wolfish grin spread across his face, "You're leaving because of Natasha."

My heart jumped. Even her name was gorgeous. Swallowing hard I asked, "Who is she?"

Alex rubbed his chin, "Well she's Levi's sister and a complete pain in the ass."

I scoffed, "Yeah, so I've been told. She seems to be pretty friendly with Griffin. I didn't know he was already wrapped up with another woman."

Alex took a little while to respond. "They've never been a 'thing.' Yeah, they might have messed around some; but other than Levi, who hasn't fucked Natasha. I mean you've seen her right?" He shook his head and laughed, "She's the type that's only fun in the moment. You don't have anything to worry about with her."

Rage boiled through me. I snapped my head to the side and glared at him. "Is that supposed to make me feel better?" I almost yelled. Alex put up his hands and started to defend himself, but I cut him off, "I don't fucking care what you're about to say next." At that moment, a car pulled up in front of us. I confirmed that it was my ride and stood up. "I'm going home. Tell Griffin, I hope he has a lot of fun tonight."

—⁂—

When the driver dropped me off at the front of my apartment building, I waited until he drove out of sight before heading to the back of building where my bathroom window was. I slid the panel up; the tricky part would be holding the window up while trying to crawl through. The window would slide down so I had to prop it open, but the "support beam" I used was a small tiki pole that had the ninja turtles carved on it and there was no way I could squeeze my fat ass through a 5-inch gap.

I looked at the bathroom window and decided to see if I could break in through the patio. The boards that made up the privacy fence were broken in places but none that would allow me access. Sighing I went back to the bathroom window and prepared myself for the worst.

I grabbed the ledge with one hand and slid the window pane up with the other. When the window was open as far as it could I put my head through the window and grabbed onto the ledge with both hands, pulling myself halfway in. When my stomach was through the window the pane slid down and hit my back. I twisted my body around kicking my feet as I did, hitting the side of the building with dull thuds. I was able to push the window up just enough for me to slide the rest of the way in. Falling onto the floor and banging my elbow on the bathtub. I stood up rubbing various places of my body, but I was glad I was able to get into the apartment without further embarrassing myself tonight.

I laughed as I shuffled my way to my bed room. I just wanted to forget that tonight ever happened, I kicked my shoes off and took off my bra and jeans. Flipping the covers over on my bed and I crawled in and was about to fall asleep when my head hit the pillow. Then my phone started ringing. Griffin was trying to call me. I ignored the call and turned my phone off, rolling over I closed my eyes and drifted in and out of sleep until morning.

—⁂—

I avoided turning my phone back on until midmorning. Missed calls and texts came flooding through. Griffin tried calling me 18 times and I had multiple missed calls from 3 different numbers. I had a few voice mails and the number of texts I had was unreal, most of it was just Griffin rambling, going back and forth on how sorry he was and switching to how ridiculous I was being and that he was just being a man. I have no reason to be jealous he kept saying.

I rolled my eyes and put my phone down. I walked to the kitchen to make a pot of coffee.

GRIFFIN (August 2)

I was in the middle of a workout, on my second set of 20 push-ups when my phone started ringing; cutting the music and replacing it with a shrill ringtone. I got off the floor and picked my phone up, "Hello?" I said turning off the speaker.

"Hey man, are you busy later tonight?" It was Alex.

"Not really, you have something planned?" I went to the kitchen and got a glass of water.

"Kara is out of town, and you know that means it's time to party!" He sounded too excited for that.

"Alright, we can throw one here. Don't let word spread around too much, I don't want cops showing up like last time." I said. Alex said something under his breath, "I mean it man, I don't have bail money."

"Ok fine. We'll keep it small." With that he hung up.

I should have said no and told him if he wanted to have a party he should have it over there. But if we did that, then Kara would know and throw Alex out again, and he's still trying to make-up for the last time she caught him messing around on her.

There was always the option of having it at Levi's house, but Natasha is over there I can't deal with her right now. The last time we were hanging out she tried to get me to tell her about you, Mel. But you are none of her business and if your name falls off her lips again they'll have to wire her jaw shut. Apparently Levi has been talking about you at home and Natasha thought she'd be cute and try to mock how bad you were at darts. While I was thinking about it I sent Levi a text stating that there was going to be a party here tonight but to leave Nat at home.

I looked through refrigerator and cabinets noting things I needed to pick up. Mainly just soda and alcohol. If people wanted to eat then they could leave and get food, I'm not feeding anyone. I walked from room to room cleaning up here and there. Then I went to the bathroom and made myself presentable before going to the liquor store and picking some things up for the night.

On the way out of the liquor store I unlocked my car and put the bags in the back. I slid into the driver seat and turned the car on. Before taking off I had a last-minute thought and decided to see what you were up to. I told you I was just picking some things up for tonight and was leaving the store and asked if it was ok to come over for a bit.

'What about your food?' You asked.

I laughed and typed out a reply, 'lol I didn't pick up any food.' Then 'I can be there in 10 minutes.'

I was already putting the car in drive and heading your way when you told me that you would see me in 10 minutes. I pulled up to your building, noting how Tyler's red car sped away when I put it in park. I got out and looked down the road where he disappeared too. I shook my head; *this is a problem* I thought as I walked into the building. I tried to push that to the back of my mind as I got closer to your door, but I didn't like Tyler lurking around you.

I let out a deep breath and knocked on your door. Almost worried that you wouldn't answer. But the door opened, and you greeted me with a big smile. "Hey Griffin!" You said cheerfully.

All thoughts of Tyler dissolved with that smile, "There's my girl," I said and pulled you into a hug. "What are you doing tonight?" I asked, letting you go and moving to sit down on the sofa.

I looked down at the mess of string on the floor, "I don't have anything planned." You said. There were beads threaded on the string, and you were looping it around in a circle. It took me longer than it should have to realize you were in the middle of making a dreamcatcher.

I leaned back and threw my arm on the back of the sofa so I could face you, "Me either," I lied. I knew you wouldn't want to go to a party, but I wanted you there. I wanted to show you off. And I knew that if

I wanted you at the party I had to lie to get you there. So, to get you over to my house before people started showing up, I offered up a movie night. I even told you that you could pick out the movie, isn't that sweet of me?

You grinned up at me, apparently that got you excited. "Alright, I need to go get ready." You said getting up.

I watched your hips sway side to side as you walked away, "Don't take too long." I said, pulling my phone to doom scroll until you came back. I grinned up at you when you walked through the living room to grab your purse from the kitchen counter. "Ready?" I asked. You fixed your makeup and brushed your hair, leaving it down, the perfume you put was driving me crazy, I was going to have to buy you more, so you didn't run out.

"Yeah I think so," you said going over and putting your shoes on. I got up and followed you out, I was eager to get this night started.

—⚬⚬⚬—

When we got to my house you offered to help me carry the bags in. It was really sweet and took me by surprise. I shook my head and smiled, taking my keys out and handing them to you, holding the one that unlocks the door up, "How about you get the door instead?" I asked.

You agreed and went to get the door. I watched you for a moment before dipping my head into the back seat and grabbing the bags from the liquor store, which I dumped on the counter so I could pull you into the backroom so we could smoke.

When we had a good buzz I took you back to the front room and turn the tv on to help distract you until people started showing up. I handed you the remote, "What movie do you want to watch?" I asked. You took a second to think about it and then put on the Exorcist. "Good choice." I would have said that to anything you put on. I put my arm around you to get closer.

I was paying more attention to you instead of the movie, playing with your hair and occasionally kissing on you. I had just pulled you closer to me when the door opened, and Alex walked in, followed by Cassie. I felt you tense up as they walked by, I nodded at Alex and gently slapped your hip. "Let's go smoke," I whispered in your ear. You looked up at me, confused and slightly angry. It was an adorable look. I thought you were going to refuse; but instead, you said nothing and got up to follow me in the back room.

The two girls exchanged pleasantries, at first Cassie was standoffish, you didn't really fit in with the bitches we usually keep around, but she warmed up to you. I sat down and started rolling a couple fat blunts for us to pass around. I could see you relaxing the more you and Cassie talked.

I brought the blunt up and lit it, passing it over to Alex, "I didn't know Mel was going to be here, how'd you manage that?" he asked.

In case you were listening to us I replied with a shrug, "you interrupted a movie night."

Alex laughed and shook his head, passing the blunt to Cassie. She was going on about a new pair of shoes that just went on sale, and you were feigning interest. You handed the blunt to me and I winked at you with a smile.

We passed the blunt around a few times when Levi came in through. He was shaking his head and looked like he wanted to punch something. I felt the blood drain from my face when I see Natasha walking in behind him, someone was behind her, but I couldn't peel my eyes off Natasha's chest. She was wearing that white crop top that I like so much. *Fuck this is going to be bad.* I was leering at her ass as she walked over to the bathroom.

I heard the guys laughing, they were looking over at you trying and failing at not drawing attention to themselves. I picked up another blunt and a lighter off the tray and went over to sit next to you. The first one was almost spent and since more people showed up I saw no harm in starting a new rotation with a fresh blunt.

I offered you the first hit, you took the blunt and lit it, handing me back the lighter and then passing the blunt off to Cassie. You blew out the smoke and tried to look casual as you asked, "Who was that?" You asked.

I didn't even bother asking who you meant, I just shrugged and answered as honestly as I could, "No one special."

You looked up at me skeptically, I braced myself for anything that was about to come out of that pretty mouth of yours when there was a sudden commotion from the living room. A group of people came walking and my head snapped over at the guys. They both looked around confused at the how many people all of a sudden showed up. Alex held his hands up and shook his head, Levi shrugged. *Who the fuck invited all these people to my house?* I thought. A couple people who buy off us came up and made small conversation before making themselves busy elsewhere.

One of Alex's usual buyers came up, nodding at him. Alex looked over at me and jerked his head towards the bedroom. There were too many bodies here, I needed to figure out who thought it would be a good idea to invite all of these people.

I looked down at you and told you I would be right back with a quick kiss on the top your head I got up and weaved my way through the crowd. Alex was already in my bedroom counting out the cash the tweaker handed him. I looked the guy up and down; he's seen better days. But then again haven't we all? I pushed the door halfway close; all these people made me nervous; I didn't want any prying to see in, but I wanted to hear what was going on out there.

Alex walked over to the closet and moved some things around to gain access to the stash I keep for situation like this. Then Alex paused, his back was still to me, but he looked over his shoulder holding up a pair of woman's underwear.

I shrugged, "Mel's." It was explanation enough.

Alex laughed and put the underwear back and flipped open the lid to what we call 'the candy store.' He took out a baggie and tossed it over to the guy who was looking at a Lorna Shore poster. Outside the door things started to get loud. More conversations started flowing through the door and worst of all someone started the radio.

Then we heard voices coming from the door, it almost sounded like a fight was about to break out. We heard a loud "HA!" I looked over at Alex who was staring at the door a look of concern was plastered on his face. He glanced over at me, and I held up a finger and focused on the commotion going on outside the bedroom door. It was definitely Levi; I couldn't tell if he was egging on the fight or trying to talk it down. I shrugged; Levi could hold his own in a fight. We'll finish up here and if things were still tense when we walked out then we'll deal with it then. Alex took the hint and turned back to what he was doing.

I shook my head and ran a hand through my hair. The noise level was getting out of hand, this was supposed to be to a quite night with just six people. This was not going according to plan. Alex was heading to the door when the tweaker said, "Oh wait hold up man! I forgot to ask if you had any Molly?"

Alex looked over at me, and I nodded, going over to the closet I dug some Molly out of the candy store and put your underwear back where I had them. Once Alex had the cash we left the bedroom. I made sure to close and lock the door. Thankfully, things between Levi and whoever he was talking to was already settled when we came out of the bedroom.

I looked around at all the people hanging around my house, about to start chasing people when I see Natasha was leaning against the wall, holding her phone out and taking selfies making sure to look fine as fuck. I licked my lips as she looked over and walked up to me. "Hey baby," She purred.

I smirked down at her, "What are you doing here?"

She pouted a little bit, "aren't you happy to see me?"

I grinned and laughed, "I'm always happy to see you."

Natasha giggled and grabbed my hand pulling me to the back room. And like a puppy dog I followed her. I let her drag me over to the other side of the room where the girls were passing around a joint and laughing. Cassie was practically sitting on Alex's lap laughing at whatever he was whispering in her ear. Bree looked up as we got closer, her smiling falling slightly as she said, "Hey you found him! Where'd Levi go? I haven't seen him since he took Morticia to get a drink."

Alex looked over at her confused, "Who's Morticia?"

She looked over him like he was stupid, "It's what we call the chick who's trying to steal Griffin away from Nat."

I looked down at Natasha who was smiling up at me innocently. I swallowed hard, "I told you not to worry about her." I said coarsely. "And why are you still telling people we're together?"

She ran her hand up my chest, "I can't help it. I don't like it when you hang around other girls."

I grabbed her hand, stopping it from moving so I could concentrate on what I was saying. Keeping her hand pinned to my chest I took her chin, forcing her to look up at me. Dropping my voice to a threatening tone I said, "What I do when I'm not around you is none of your concern, you got that. If you keep this up what we having going will end completely." I kissed her nose and let her go.

She leaned back pulling out of my grasp and looked at her feet. "You expect me to believe that she means nothing to you when you act like this whenever she gets brought up?" She asked in that whiney voice of hers.

I rolled my eyes and pushed her to the side to sit down on the sofa. I threw my arm over the back and looked at her. "I expect you to be a good girl and do what you're told. Now, do you want to come over here and sit on my lap; or do you want to stand there pouting like a child?"

Natasha looked embarrassed, good she's easier to control when she's worried what other people are thinking about her. She came over and sat down on my lap, wiggling slightly as a pathetic attempt to distract me from being mad at her.

I brushed her hair to the side; sure, it was long, and that red color is enough to make any man weak at the knees. But it was dry and felt like straw. All the hair dye she uses to keep that red color is ruining her hair, frying the ends to the point of no return. Not at all like your hair Mel, it's so soft and thick, and when I run my fingers through your hair it feels like strands of silk, not wool.

Natasha leaned back against me, bringing my focus back to the here and now. I leered at the side of her face. I never should have started messing around with her in the first place, but she is just one temptation I cannot say no to.

Alex reached around Cassie, grabbed a blunt off the tray, and lit it. He handed it to Cassie and said. "Man, this party really took off. Who invited all these people anyway?"

I shrugged my shoulders and took the blunt from Cassie, "I don't know I was trying to keep it contained." I took a hit and handed it off to Nat who started giggling. I blew the smoke out and tickled her sides, causing her to wiggle in my lap. I grinned and asked, "What's up with you?"

She looked over her shoulder at me, "I invited a few and they told a few of their people..." She shrugged and leaned forward handing the blunt to Bree, "As soon as I heard Levi talking to Bree over the phone about a private party tonight; I just knew I had to crash it." She turned to the side to throw an arm around me, "I had to get your attention somehow." She drug a finger down my neck, "I know you've been ignoring me."

I clenched my teeth and looked over at Alex. He was talking to Cassie ignoring what we were doing. Then someone came over and sat down in the chair, I wasn't surprised to see Levi glaring at me. He was shaking his head; I knew what he was thinking. That I was playing with fire sitting here with Nat wiggling around on my lap. I rolled my eyes at him. He was always worried about something.

"Hey, Levi, I was wondering if you were going to come back." Bree said scooting close to him.

He put his arm out stopping her from climbing on his lap. Her smile dropped as he said, "I'm not planning on being here much longer. This party sucks."

Alex nodded his head and handed him the blunt. "I know what you mean. If it wasn't for your sister this would have been a much better night."

Natasha perked up in my lap, "Hey that's not fair. If you guys would have just invited me in the first place this wouldn't have happened."

Bree tried to get Levi's attention again, but he shrugged her off. "What is your deal all of a sudden?" She asked, "You were just fine until you ran off with Morticia!"

Levi looked over at Alex, "Who's Morticia?" He asked, ignoring Bree again.

Alex rolled his eyes, "It's just a stupid nickname." He said.

Levi looked at me, and I rolled my eyes and said, "they made it up for Mel. I don't know what the deal with it is." Natasha laughed but I ignored it. "Speaking of, where did she go? I haven't seen her in a while." I said looking around making sure you didn't catch me under Nat, although this isn't the worst position to catch us in.

Levi said something about you being in the front room, but I was busy thinking of you, me, and Nat in a three-way. I was getting excited, and Nat noticed. She leaned back on me and started grinding her hips. I started rubbing her thigh and heard the guys chuckling to themselves. I ignored it and focused on how perfect Nat's ass looked moving around on my lap.

"Should we tell him?" Alex asked through uncontrolled laughter.

Levi took a breath and said, "Nah, I want to see how this plays out."

I shifted, pressing my erection against Nat, and looked over at them. They were looking at something going on behind me. I cast a glance over my shoulder and my heart dropped. You were walking towards us. With a look that chilled me. I shifted in my seat again tempted to push Nat off now, but I was worried how you would react to my now obvious boner. I rubbed my temple and tried to ignore the guys as they laughed their asses off.

You stepped up in front of us and gave a warm smile that clashed with the icy glare in your eyes. "Hey guys!" You said. Your tone reminded me of someone who worked in customer service.

Alex coughed, "Mel, always a pleasure."

I rolled my eyes and shook my head, this was bad. Natasha started rubbing my chest. Making things so much worse.

Levi took the blunt from Bree and after he took a hit he held it out to you, asking if you wanted a hit. But you shook your head no. "Thank you, but I'm about to head out." My attention snapped to you; you can't leave. If you leave now I was worried I might never see you again. Then you looked over at me, the look in your eyes switched from jealousy to hurt to hatred. "Can I talk to you for a moment?" You asked.

The guys started laughing and Nat opened her mouth to say something but before she could I spoke up first. "Yeah sure," I said. Shoving Natasha off my lap. You come before her, all day, any day. I hope you realize that, Mel. Nat is nothing compared to you but based off that look in your eye you don't see it that way. I put my arm around you and led you away from the group, the guys not even trying to contain their laughter. "What's this about? Are you not enjoying the party?" I asked as a group of drunk girls walked by talking over fits of laughter.

You looked up at me confused. I was just trying to ease the tension, but I see that I failed. You shrugged my arm off and stepped away. *Fuck you're really mad.* I thought.

"No, not really." You sneered. "Who the *fuck* was that?" You shook your head, "You know what, that's not the point. Why was she on your lap?"

I thought the easiest way to get out of this conversation was to shut it down as quickly as possible and change the topic over to you. "She doesn't matter," I said honestly, "Why aren't you enjoying yourself?" I asked. I reached my hand up to touch you, but you stepped back, away from me, batting my hand away. *Ouch, that hurt* I thought. I don't like it when you intentionally block me from touching you.

"To me it matters," You said stubbornly. "How would you feel if you saw me sitting on some guy's lap?"

It depends on the guy I almost said. I knew you were trying to make a point, but I just don't see how standing here fighting is going to help. "I didn't realize it would cause this much tension." I still don't see the big issue with this, Nat is just a mindless fuck, she is nothing to get worked up over. "But why are you getting so mad at this?" I couldn't stop the question from rolling off my tongue.

You shook your head, that question to seem to have caught you off guard. "I thought we weren't seeing other people?" I couldn't tell if you were going to start crying, or if you were going to start swinging on me.

I clenched my jaw and tried to explain the best I could. "I'm not seeing Nat. She had just sat down when you showed up."

You shook your head and refused to look at me. "Why did you even invite me over here if you were throwing a party tonight?"

I reached out for you again, but again you backed away just out of reach. I dropped my hand and sighed, "This wasn't our idea." I said, "It was supposed to be us 6. You, me, and whoever Alex and Levi brought. But then Natasha jumped into Levi's car at the last minute and invited a bunch of people over." I hoped that was enough of an explanation to talk you down. I hope that was enough to make you stay here with me, I don't want you to go.

You rolled your eyes and scoffed. My heart sank and I knew if you walked out that door I would have a hard time getting you back. "So, then was it your idea or 'Nat's' to have her sit on your lap." The way you said her name made me want to laugh. But now wasn't the time, I was about to say something about how you shouldn't feel threatened by her, but you rolled your eyes at me again. "I'm going home. I don't want to keep you from your company."

You walked away from me before I had the chance to offer to go with you. I took a few steps toward you to follow you out and take you home so we could be alone together, but someone grabbed me by the elbow and held me back. I looked behind me about to swing on them when Alex came into view and said, "Hey man, I don't think you should go after her right now. Let her chill for a moment. I'll go out there and make sure she gets home."

I swallowed hard and looked back to where you disappeared off into the crowd. I sulked back to the sofa where Levi was still trying to get Bree from getting on his lap. I sat down and looked over at her. "Hey doll, could you get us some drinks from the kitchen?"

She looked over at me and back to Levi. "Do you want anything?" She asked him batting her eye lashes.

He nodded, "Just grab me a beer." Bree eagerly got up and bounced away. Levi grimaced. "Is it just me or did she get clingy?"

Nat leaned forward in her seat, "No more clingy than that chick was. What's her deal anyway, what crypt did she crawl out of to be here tonight?" She laughed at her own joke but when she noticed that neither me nor Levi joined in her face dropped. "Oh, come on. What is it with you two?"

Levi shook his head, "It wasn't funny."

Natasha looked over to me and got up. As she walked over her hips swayed side to side. "What about you?" She asked, bending over in front of me and putting her hands on my thighs, "Do you think I'm funny, Griffin?"

The way she looked at me drove me insane. But then the look you had on your face before you left crossed my mind and I instantly felt guilty. I pushed Nat away by the shoulders and sat up, "No I don't. Now go find somewhere else to be or go sit back down where you were."

Nat stood up and scoffed, "You were just fine with me before Vampira came into the picture." She crossed her arms, "You know what? Screw you, Griffin. Fuck you, Levi. I'm out of here."

Levi held up his hands, "The fuck did I do?"

I shook my head, "You're sister is fucking nuts."

Natasha stomped her foot. "I am not crazy! Levi is just a tool, and I like to remind him of that." She turned on her heel and walked away holding her middle finger up as she did.

I slumped in my chair, not looking forward to a solo night. "I told you to leave her at home." I said rubbing my head.

Levi took a moment to answer. "Even if she did stay home it was only a matter of time before Mel caught you." He leaned forward and grabbed the rolling tray, "Nat is going to be hysterical when I get home. Mind if I crash here for a couple days until she calms down?"

There was a time when we were about 15 and Natasha was 18 and she was dating this older guy from college. They were hot and heavy for a few weeks then one day he left her in the dust. No explanation, nothing. She didn't take it very well, she took it out on everyone around her. She screamed and cried for days. Threw anything she could get her hands on. We would be better off putting her in a mental institution.

I nodded my head, "Yeah man, that's cool."

Bree came bouncing back looking confused. "Hey, Nat and Cassie just left. What happened?" She asked sitting down right next to Levi, who got up to sit in the chair next to the sofa.

I took the can of beer she brought me, "They decided to go do something else. If you're quick you might still catch them." I said cracking the beer and taking a big swing.

She looked over at Levi, "I was hoping we could go do something?"

Levi shook his head, "I'm just not in the mood. You'll have more fun with them." He said, taking the beer, she handed him.

Bree pouted, "Bu-"

Levi held out a hand, "I have a huge headache, and I won't make good company. Trust me, it's better for you this way."

Bree huffed and stood up. "Fine." And with that she was gone.

I watched her leave, "Maybe they're all getting clingy?" I suggested.

Levi shrugged. "I don't know man, maybe we're just getting too old for those kind of games."

I laughed, "You maybe. I kind of enjoy the games."

"You'd have to, the way you're going." He shot back. "Think Mel is over you yet?" He taunted.

Narrowing my eyes I looked over at him, "Why, are you going to swoop in and play shoulder to cry on?"

He took a drag off the joint and sized me up, "Why, think I have a shot?" He smirked and handed me the joint, "Nah, I'll give it a few days before I shoot my shot. Give her some time to heal, ya know?"

I shook my head, "She hasn't broken things off with me yet." I reminded him.

Alex came back in shortly after. He look slightly amused but mostly concerned. "Didn't go too well I see?" Levi asked when he sat down.

Alex shook his head and took the joint, "Nah she's pretty pissed. I told her about Nat and how she shouldn't see her as a threat, but she wasn't having it. She got an Uber to come pick her up."

I groaned and put my head in my hands. I was so fucking stupid. Why did she have to show up tonight of all nights?

I let the party go on for a while longer. The white noise was an easy way to drown out the thoughts that were swirling in my head. I wanted to call you, but I wanted to give you space to calm down like Alex suggested.

We sat there, drinking and smoking. Mostly talking about how fucked up it is how jealous bitches get. I lost track of time and didn't start chasing people out until Alex asked if he crash here tonight too.

I told him he could and got up to kill the music. The music cut off abruptly when I pushed the power button on the stereo. Multiple angry looks were shot in my direction as I held my hands up and shouted, "Alright! Time for you all to fuck off! The party is over!" Levi was in the back of the room ushering people out. I hung back and waved people on, "Come on guys, time to leave!" I yelled at some people who were still chilling over in a corner. They grumbled at me but got up and left all the same.

Levi poked his head in the bathroom and chased some people out of there. I went to the front room where Alex was already pushing people out the door. When things calmed down and everyone was out we looked around at the mess my house had become.

Levi shook his head, "Please don't tell me you're ocd ass isn't going to make us clean before we go to sleep." He complained.

"I thought about it." I said, but then I had a thought. "You guys mind if I use your phone to call Mel? I want to see if I can fix this."

Alex shook his head and handed his phone over, "That's not going to work, but knock yourself out." He said and went over to the sofa and plopped down, crossing his arm over his eyes. "Wake me up when's there coffee." He said.

Levi handed his over too, but when I went to take it he held on to it. "You know she just needs some space." He let his phone go. "Don't get mad at me when this time next year me and Mel are living together happy as can be."

I shook his comment off and went to my bedroom. I tried calling you off my phone, but it went straight to voice mail. I called you off Levi's phone and left a voice mail then got up to make a drink. I called you off Alex's phone and left a voice mail, then got up to do a line of coke. Then I sent you some text messages begging you to answer my calls. I went to the closet and took out the 'candy store' there was a burner phone we kept in there that I grabbed and called you on. Thinking that maybe you had the guy's numbers saved and that' why you didn't answer. But the call just went to voice mail. I sighed and went to do some sit ups. Then I left you another voice mail off my phone and downed the rest of my drink. I called you off my phone again and then got another drink. That's how I spent my entire night. I wish I could remember what I said during those voicemails but it's all a blur.

—∞—

I didn't wake up until midafternoon the next day. I was the first one up surprisingly and made a pot of coffee. I didn't try to be quite as I went around the kitchen with a trash bag cleaning up. Levi came shuffling into the kitchen and made himself a cup of coffee. "So did you ever get ahold of her?" He asked taking a sip.

I shook my head and threw some bottles into the bag, the glass clinking together echoing through the room, causing Alex to groan and yell from the sofa, "Could you douchebags be any louder?!" He was still face down, so his voice was muffled.

I laughed and tied up the bag. Shaking out a new one, making sure to be extra loud with it. With the guys help the house was clean within half an hour. I didn't like seeing all trash bags piled up in front of my house, but it was better than leaving the mess laying around. Alex left soon after the mess was picked up. Levi went to bring back some food, and I was left staring at my phone waiting for you to reply to any of my messages.

MELANIE (August 6)

During my lunch break I was scrolling through Facebook when a text from Griffin came through.

'Can we talk?' he asked. I tapped my thumb on the side of my phone debating on answering him at all. I haven't talked him since the party. 'At least let me return your purse in person.'

Before he could send another text I told him I wouldn't be home until 4. I could live without my purse. There wasn't anything important in there. For all I was concerned he could have it. But then again, it would be nice to have my main set of keys. And there was an expensive tube of ChapStick in there.

The rest of my work day drug by, and I was eager to get home and do nothing.

When I pulled into the buildings parking lot Griffin was leaning against his car smoking a cigarette. I could feel his eyes on me as I parked. I took a few deep breaths as I unbuckled the seat belt and got out, my hands were starting to shake. I just wanted to get this over with, I wasn't shaking because I was scared, I was shaking because I was starting to get mad again. Griffin gave me a small smile that I was reluctant to return. It was tight lipped and probably looked fake as fuck. Griffin took another drag off his cigarette before he dropped it on the ground and stomped it out. "It's been a while." He said.

"It has." I said flatly. "Can I have my bag back?"

Griffin chuckled, "Right down to it huh? Look, I'm really sorry about what happened; but there's nothing I can do to change that now. So, let's stop being children and go inside so we can talk about this." He put his hand on my shoulder and started to lead me to the door.

I pulled out of his grasp, there were too many things I wanted to say, but I was so angry I knew if I tried to talk I would just stumble over my words. I shook my head and walked ahead of him.

After unlocking the door, I stepped inside and left the door open for Griffin; who was following closely behind. I crossed my arms and turned to face him. "Let's talk." I said.

Griffin gave me that wolfish grin, "So feisty this evening. Did you have a bad day at work?" He asked walking over the sofa to sit down.

"No, work wasn't too bad actually. What do you want Griffin?" I wanted to keep this brief so he would leave.

He laughed and rested his elbows on the back of the sofa. "I want you to come sit down." Griffin raised his eye brows and stared at me.

There is no way I am going over to him and sitting down. Just to be defiant, I said, "I'm getting a drink. I can hear you just fine in the kitchen. Are you thirsty?" I walked into the kitchen and pulled down a glass.

Griffin let out a frustrated growl, "No. I'm fine."

I took my time taking the tea out of the fridge and pouring myself a glass. When I sat down, he was rubbing his temple.

"Are you done?" he asked, "I would really like to have a conversation with you." I nodded my head and took a drink. "I'm not sure why you're so mad at me. I was pretty wasted at the party. The last thing I remember was smoking with you and Alex, after that it's all blur." I just stared at him. Sighing he shook his head, "Are you going to say anything?" He reached out and put his hand on my knee, "Look Mel, I'm sorry, how many times do you want me to say that? I don't remember what happened, the guys said you left in a hurry, do you want to tell me what that was all about?"

I moved my leg, so his hand fell off my knee. "Your buddy Natasha showed up and decided that your lap was a better seat than an actual chair. You two looked pretty fucking cozy so I left." I stood up, "I actually have to get going soon; so, if you would give me my bag back, that'd be great." I forced a smile.

Griffin clenched his jaw. "It's out in my car." He stood up and I followed him out the door and to his vehicle. When we got to the door of the building, he held the door open for me, "Before I give you your purse back, would you want to smoke with me? It won't take long I promise." We walked over to his car, and he opened the passenger door for me, "What do you say?" he asked.

Reluctantly I nodded, "Sure." I slid in and sat down. I looked in the back seat, but I didn't see my bag.

When he got in the driver's seat, I asked him where my purse was. Griffin looked in the backseat and chuckled, "Well if it's not in the trunk, I might have left it at home." I started to say something, but his laughing cut me off. "Calm down. It's right here." He said, reaching behind my seat and pulling out my bag. Griffin lit a joint and handed it to me. "I really hope we can put that party behind us and move on."

I looked down at my lap, I wasn't sure if I could get over that. "I don't know." I pulled my phone out and checked the time. "I have to get going." I said, reaching for the door handle.

"Where are you going?" He asked.

"I have to run some errands." I opened the door and stepped out. "Thank you for dropping off my purse. I'll talk to you later." I closed the door before he could say anything else and headed over to my car. When I was inside I locked the door before I put the key into the ignition. Griffin was still sitting in his car when I pulled away, I felt bad for lying about being busy this afternoon, but I couldn't stand to sit there and listen to his bullshit any longer.

I know I left my apartment unlocked but right now I didn't care. I just wanted to get away, and since I had my other set of keys back I didn't need to go back inside to get my car key. I figured I could just walk around the store for a while to kill some time before going back home. So, I drove to the store on the other side of town and tried to think if there was anything I needed to get while I was out.

While pulling into the parking lot my phone chimed. I ignored it thinking it was Griffin. I parked next to a cart return and walked inside, and another text came through as I walked through the doors.

I grabbed a basket and started towards the crafting section; I could use some new paints. I was picking out some new blues when I heard a deep cheerful "Hey!" from down the aisle.

I looked up and Levi was heading towards me. I gave a half smile, "Hey Levi." I said, turning back to the paint.

He came up and stopped beside me. "I've been trying to text you, are you ignoring me?" He teased, nudging my arm.

I furrowed my eyebrows, "What? No. How could I ignore you? I don't even have your number?"

Levi laughed, "Yeah you do, Griffin took my phone to get ahold of you once and he didn't delete your number so…." He trailed off and looked around the aisle. "Are you going to do some painting tonight? That sounds cool."

I was so confused right now. I shook my head and took out my phone, "Um no, I'm just wasting time." I said going to the 2 new messages I had. They were from a number that Griffin had messaged me from after I had left the party. Since this number was Levi, I figured the other one that Griffin used must be Alex's.

I looked at the messages at the bottom, trying my hardest not to read any of the enraging texts Griffin sent me a couple nights ago to see what Levi had sent. The first one was him saying 'Hey I just wanted to see if you were ok' And the second one was 'Lol never mind I'll just ask you in person. I see you.'

Levi was holding a tube of purple glitter paint, spinning it around in the light, "So, are you ok?" He asked keeping his focus on the paint as the light bounced off the glitter.

"I'll be fine." I said, throwing a few tubes of different colored paints in my basket.

Levi put the paint back and looked at me, "That's not what I asked."

I clenched my jaw; I didn't want to get into this right now. "Honestly, I'm not surprised by what happened. It was all too good to be true, and I fell for it." I shrugged, "Time to move on I guess. Now if you'll excuse me, I should get going."

Levi looked taken back, "Just like that?" He asked and took a couple steps to walk next to me. "I thought you would be more tore up about it."

My breath hitched. Of course I was more tore up about it. But I'm not about to spill my guts out to one of the closest people to Griffin. I may be dumb, but I'm not that dumb. "What else is there to do?" I asked, "I could forgive him and risk getting hurt again. Or I could dwell on it and hurt myself even more." I contemplated going to the check out just to escape this conversation, but I was worried that Griffin would still be hanging around the apartment, so I turned and headed towards the book section.

"Yeah I know what you mean. Griffin didn't deserve you."

I almost stopped walking. I looked up at Levi, not sure what to make of him. "What makes you say that?"

Levi chuckled, "Well for one, if he was as in to you as he claimed to be he wouldn't have been fucking around with Natasha." He shook his head, "Alex and Griffin like to think that rules don't apply to them. But what they fail to realize is that they aren't as smart as they like other people to think they are. If you pay attention to them, they're kind of dumb."

Despite myself I smiled. I looked up at him and tried to see some resemblance between him and *Natasha*, but I just got too mad picturing her. "That's your sister." I said, not wanting to offend Levi by spitting out his sister names with venom.

It came out as a sneer anyway. Levi looked at me with amusement dancing in his eyes, "Yeah, she's my sister. It's exhausting to deal with her, it's like living with a toddler for the most part. She's always whining about something; she needs this, she wants that. I'm not even sure if she knows how to wash the dishes."

I wasn't sure if any of this was true, or if Levi was talking shit to make me feel better. But even so she was still a statuesque Goddess, and I am a hobbit. In fact, most of the female company that Griffin and his friends kept all looked like they stepped out of a Victoria's Secret catalogue. Thinking back to the beautiful women I had seen at the party started to make me feel self-conscious.

"You know, having you around has been refreshing. It's nice having a woman who's not so focused on herself that she doesn't care about anyone else." Levi looked around the aisle we stopped at, "Man I didn't know people still read books." He said picking up a random book and started flipping through the pages.

I laughed, "You should try it."

Levi hit the book in his palm a few times before putting it back. "Nah, I'm too busy. With the band and my other source of income, I need to be careful how I spend my free time. I'll just wait for the movie to come out." He joked.

"You don't know what you're missing." I said picking up a book I've been meaning to read, it was a fantasy romance novel, Kendra has been begging me to read it, so she had someone to talk about it with.

Levi followed me as I started walking towards the shoes. "You might be able to talk me into audiobooks." He stated when he fell in beside me.

I thought about it for a moment. "Yeah, maybe. You gotta be careful, sometimes they'll have a monotone person narrating and it'll put you right to sleep." I said. Looking around I saw a really cute pair of high heels that came up to the knee with red lace on the outside and a silver zipper on the inside. But when I looked at the price tag I winced.

"Those are hot. You should get them." Levi said over my shoulder. I shook my head and leaned away from him, putting them back on the shelf. "Ok fine, I'll pick them up for you. What's your size?" He asked looking at my feet.

"I'm not letting you get those. $90 is ridiculous for shoes." I said looking at a less appealing pair of boots.

"*You* don't be ridiculous. Would a size 7 fit?" he asked holding out a boot to see if it matched up to my shoe size.

My eyes widened in surprise. His prediction is spot on. "You're not buying those."

Levi grinned and put the boot back in its box. "I was right, wasn't I?" He put the box back on the shelf.

I shook my head, "Even if you were, I'm not going to tell you. I'm going to head out a get some food."

Behind me I heard Levi laughing, "Yeah I was right." He followed me halfway to the registers then said, "Well as fun as this has been, I have to take my leave my now."

I laughed, "I'll see you around Levi."

He licked his lips and grinned down at me. "Later, Mel."

I watched him walk away and round the corner, he looked back and waved with a huge smile when he saw that I was still looking at him. I blushed and waved back, turning around to go through the self-checkout.

—✺—

I went and got some food and took it to the park to eat. I didn't get back to the apartment until a few hours later. Griffins car was no longer there, thankfully, but I couldn't help but wonder how long he stuck around before he left.

I put my car in park and got out. I got my bags from the backseat and walked inside. The first thing to catch my attention was the big bag sitting in front of my door. I walked up to it, already suspecting what it was. Looking in the bag, I was right, Levi bought me those dammed boots. I smiled and went to open the door; but it was locked.

Narrowing my eyes I dug my keys out of my purse and unlocked the door. I put the bags on the coffee table and went to take my shoes off by the door and hung my keys up on the hook. Taped to the back of the door was a note from Griffin.

Mel,

I couldn't leave knowing your apartment wasn't secure. I hope you're not too mad at me for locking your door and I hope you can forgive me for being a selfish prick and letting my male urges get the better of me. You're all I want, and the only one I can see myself being with. Call me
  -Griffin

I could feel my eyes start to tear up as I balled the note up in my fist and threw it across the room. I took my phone out and scrolled through my contacts. I hit call and waited while it rang a few times. I almost hung up when they finally picked up. "I was hoping I wouldn't have to leave a voice mail." I said.

There was laughter on the other end as Kendra replied, "Yeah sorry I was pooping. Didn't think you'd want to hear all that. What's up?"

"Got a moment for some drama?" I asked. Sitting down and taking the shoe box out of the bag. I opened the box and there on top was a gift receipt.

"I always have time for drama, tell me everything!!"

I put the phone on speaker and told her what went down at the party, we both laughed as I went over how I broke into my apartment and bruised my elbow. And then I told her about Levi and how he dropped of the boots that fit like a glove.

"So, what's your question here sis? You already know that I'm going to say forget Griffin and see what Levi's all about."

I rolled my eyes and chuckled, "Not everything is about boys." I said, "I'm gonna give dating a break for now. Love is bullshit." I said, looking at how the boots looked on my feet from different angles.

Kendra sighed over the phone. "Love isn't bullshit. You're just hurt. Let Levi patch you up." Over the phone I heard her stomach growl, "Ugh did you hear that? I think my stomach is about to eat itself."

I laughed again, "I was wondering what that sound was. Thanks for listening, sis. Go find something to eat."

"Ok Mel. Love ya. Let me know how things work out." She said.

"I will, bye." I waited for her to say bye before I hung up. I looked down at the boots again and smiled. Getting up and walking into the kitchen was easier than I thought it would be considering how high the heels were. I felt like such bad ass in these boots, I went and got my phone to send Levi a thank you text.

It wasn't until a few hours later when I was in bed reading my new book when I got a reply from Levi. 'You're quite welcome. I'm glad they fit. I left the receipt in case they didn't. Or if you wanted to return them and pocket the money that's fine too.'

That last part was a little strange. Do people actually return gifts for the sole purpose of keeping the money and then tell the person who got them the gift that they did that?

'I would never do such a thing' I sent back.

'That's good to know. Next time I won't leave one.'

I smiled and put my phone down, I wanted to finish this chapter before I went to bed. My phone chimed and I picked up thinking it was a text from Levi. But it wasn't. 'Why is Levi buying you shoes?' Griffin wanted to know.

Furious I wanted to call him and bitch him out. Why am I supposed to be ok with someone sitting in his lap, but he wants to question why someone gets me a gift. I shook my head and typed a few different replies, each more hateful than the last. I deleted another draft telling him to get fucked and typed out 'We ran into each other at the store, and he saw me looking at them. He got them to help me forget about the party you threw.'

Griffin sent me a few more texts but I turned my phone off and finished reading the chapter so I could go to sleep.

GRIFFIN (August 6)

It's been a few days since the party, and you still haven't talked to me. I asked the guys if you ever responded to the texts I sent you from their phone but you're ignoring those as well. I stopped sending you good morning and good night texts, if you didn't bother putting in the energy to reply then why should I waste my time in the first place?

I got mad and went to the back room to work out my frustrations and didn't stop until I was out of breath and covered in sweat. Even still as the music pounded from the speakers and I was holding the 50 pounds weights up, anger coursed through me.

I've been ignoring Natasha just as much as you've been ignoring me. As much as I wanted to take all my anger out on her, I figured it would be best if I stayed away. If she hadn't have put that perfect ass on me in the first place I wouldn't be in this mess. I put the weights down and paced around the room.

"FUCK!" I yelled and punched the wall, leaving a hole that I'm going to have to patch up later.

Shaking my head I stalked to the bathroom and started the shower.

When I got out I checked the time. It was close to your lunch time. I thought about going to get some food and bringing it to you. Make you talk to me, but you were at work and if I caused a scene they could call the cops on me. Instead, I just sent another text that would just go ignored. It was nothing too extravagant I just wanted to talk. I waited a couple seconds, what could I use to get your attention? Then I remember that I still had your purse in my living room. I found it in my car the morning after the party. Of course, I took it inside to see what you kept in there. 'At least let me return your purse in person.'

'I won't be home until 4.' I blinked at the screen and waited for another longer and more pleasant response.

Wow, really? That's all I get? Short bitchy answers? I thought. I shook my head and squeezed my phone in my fist. *Fine, you won't be home until 4, that's cool. I'll be there when you show up.*

———

3:30 rolled around and I was eager to see you. I was still upset how easy it seems to be for you to brush me off but that all changes today. I went to the bathroom to make sure I looked presentable and locked up the house before I went on my way.

It didn't take long until I was pulling into the parking lot and going out of my mind waiting for you to get home. I drummed my hands on the steering wheel to the music for a couple of songs but eventually that got boring, so I got out and started smoking a cigarette. It wasn't a bad day outside and it beats making my car smell like an ash tray.

The cigarette was almost gone by the time you finally pulled up. I watched as you parked next to me. I took a few more drags, waiting for you to get out. I offered you a kind smile and you gave me a fake ass one in return. I almost sneered but I kept my façade friendly, so I didn't end up fucking this up. Today is supposed to be about making a truce, not to make things worse by losing my temper and scaring you away.

I took another hit off my cigarette before dropping it on the ground. "It's been a while," I said, putting the cigarette out with my foot.

You sounded over it already; your tone was flat and even when you agreed and then asked for your purse back. I guess that's it. I was disappointed you were still holding on to that little grudge of yours, but you'll come back around.

I let out an amused breath, how long can you keep this up? "Right down to it huh?" I tried apologizing and asked if we could go inside to talk, but when I put my hand on you to lead you inside you pulled away. My fingers curled into a fist and then I shoved my hands in my pockets to keep myself from lashing out.

You went in ahead of me, even your walk was tense. My eyebrow ticked up; this might be tougher than I thought. You unlocked the door to your apartment and went inside, where you stood by the door with your arms crossed.

"Let's talk." You said facing me.

I grinned at you, "So feisty this evening. Did you have a bad day at work?" I asked, that might explain why your being extra bitchy towards me. I went over to the sofa and sat down.

You told me work wasn't too bad and then demanded to know what I wanted. I felt my muscles flex as adrenaline started pumping through me. I don't like it when girls think they can be hostile, it's just not a good look.

I had to laugh otherwise I would kick over the coffee table. I put my arms out and rested them on the back of the sofa. "I want you to come sit down." That line always worked. There's no way that you could resist that female urge to be obedient. I smirked as you started walking towards me.

Then my smile fell as you turned and went to the kitchen instead. "I'm getting a drink," you said, "I can hear you just fine in the kitchen." You said. Then to try patch things up you offered me a drink as well.

Through clenched teeth I told you that I was fine. Each second you took pouring yourself a drink brought me closer to saying 'Fuck This' and leaving. I was getting a headache. I rubbed my temple to lessen the pressure when you finally sat down. "Are you done?" I asked almost too harshly, then I softened my tone, "I would really like to have a conversation with you."

I waited for an actual answer, but you just nodded and took a drink. I hope you know how childish you're acting.

I grasped for an explanation that you would believe. Something would smooth out this whole ordeal. The classic 'I was drunk and don't remember anything. This is what I heard happened; but it's all a blur.' I remember every second, Natasha is still blowing up my phone and Levi is still crashing on my couch. When I was done talking you just stared blankly at me. "Are you going to say anything?" I asked reaching out and putting my hand on your knee. I tried apologizing and asked for your side of the story. If I validate your feelings that would definitely help my cause.

You moved your leg to pull away from me, I let my hand slip off your instead of gripping it tight. You ranted about Nat sitting in my lap again, her name sounded poisonous when you said, I wanted to laugh but that would probably just piss you off. Then you stood up, "I actually have to get going soon; so, if you would give my bag back, that'd be great." You gave one those fake smiles your so fond of today.

I clenched my jaw to bite back a harsh comment. "It's out in the car." I got up and walked out the apartment, I held the door to the building open for you like a gentleman, even if your mad me at I will still treat you like a lady. On the way to the car, I asked if you wanted to smoke with me really quick. I opened the car door for you and waited for you to answer. "What do you say?"

You shifted from one foot to the other, I almost expected you to say no, but then you agreed and got in. I walked around the car and saw you looking around for your purse. You didn't take long to ask about it, I didn't even have the door closed when you asked, "Where's my purse?"

I looked in the back seat and laughed, just to mess with you I joked about leaving it at home. But you didn't find it very funny; so, I snuffed out the tension just as quickly as it ignited and reached behind the passenger seat to grab your bag. "Calm down, it's right here." When I handed you the bag I got out a joint and lit it. "I really hope we can put that party behind us and move on." I said sincerely.

You looked at your lap, either you couldn't be bothered to look at me, or you couldn't bring yourself to do it. "I don't know," you pulled your phone and turned the screen on. "I have to get going." You reached for the door handle.

My heart stopped. Why are you being so stubborn about this? "Where are you going?" I asked.

"I have to run some errands." You lied. And just like that you got out and closed the door before I could say anything else.

I forced myself to stay in the car. If I went after you now then you and Ellie would meet each other sooner than I want. I leaned my head back and stared at the dome light. The smoke swirled around in the sunlight, and I watched as it snaked in and around itself. I took a deep hit off the joint and slowly let it out.

This was supposed to fix things. We were supposed to be laughing in each other's arms right now. But instead, you're so eager to get away from me you forgot to lock your door before you left. I shook my head and finished the joint. I thought about just leaving, heading home, and letting you deal with coming back to a ransacked apartment. This is a hell of a neighborhood to leave your doors unlocked in.

"Fuck," I sighed and got out. When I got back in your apartment I looked around for a piece of paper and some tape. It took longer to find a pen but eventually I found one in a kitchen drawer, I scrawled out a note and hung it up on the back of the door. I made sure the bottom was locked before I closed the door and headed home.

Even if we're mad at each other I don't want you to be vulnerable. And unlocked doors to unattended apartments could land you into trouble.

On the drive home I zoned out. Not really sure where I was going until I was driving down the street that Levi lives on. His truck was gone but Natasha's cherry red Ford Escape was in the drive way.

I gripped the steering wheel slowed the car down, stopping in front of the house and thought about kicking his door in and dragging that fucking bitch out by her hair. I'd throw her in the car and take her out to grandpa's. She'd get all my attention then. I put the car in park and looked around. The neighborhood didn't look busy. I turned my head back to the house and studied the windows. If I knew Nat, she would be sleeping right now. My hand went for the keys to turn off the car.

But then I hesitated. This wasn't some random bitch from off the street. This was Levi's sister. I growled and punched the steering wheel. If it wasn't for that cunt inside I would be in your bed right now but instead you're off doing anything but me. I glared at the front door, wanting Natasha to come outside and see me waiting out here for her. It would be easier if she came to me anyway. But the seconds ticked by, and she never came out. I reached for the car keys again but couldn't force myself to turn the car off.

"You're being a fucking pussy just get out of the fucking car and get her!" I scolded myself, but I stayed put. "This is stupid." I growled, throwing the car in drive, and speeding off, my tires screeching at the sudden take off.

--

When I got home I just wanted to go to sleep and wake up sometime last week for a due over. I never would have agreed to that fucking party.

I kicked my shoes off and fell on the bed, I stared up at the ceiling wondering what you were doing and wondering when I was going to get back on your good side again.

—◊—

Sometime later I woke up to the sound of my front door opening and closing. I groaned and put a pillow over my head to block the obnoxious voices coming from the kitchen. I knew I should have closed the bedroom door. I waited for a few seconds, but the noise never died down, so I got up to see what the commotion was about. Levi was in front of the refrigerator putting some food away and Alex was leaning against the counter eating a bag of chips.

There was still more food to be put away, so I picked up a bag and went over to the cabinets. "Rough day?" Alex asked.

I shrugged and put a box of noodles in line with the rest. "Definitely didn't go as planned." I said, balling up the bag and reaching for another one.

"I went home to grab some shit and Nat was there; she tried taking my keys as leverage to get me to bring her here." He shook his head. "I'm surprised I still haven't gotten a phone call from Grandma yet."

Alex put his bag of chips down and got a drink. "Probably because Nat hasn't whined about it yet. Think about it man, how close is she to being out completely?"

Levi closed the freezer. "Last time Grandma called me she told me she was getting another will drafted. So, she's probably out now."

I scoffed, "Trust fund babies. Must be nice." I grabbed another bag and put the items away. At the bottom of the bag the receipt was folded up. I was about to crumble the bag up with the receipt and get myself a drink when the total caught my attention. I pulled the small strip of paper out and unfolded it. Who the fuck spends that much money on food. I scanned the side of the receipt with the list of the prices and stopped at the last item rung up which was $90, I matched the price up with the item which was a pair of women's boots. I held up the receipt, "Since when you do wear women's shoes?" I mocked.

An amused smirk spread across Alex's face. "Yeah, Levi. What's up with the boots?" He asked and started eating his chips again.

Levi gathered up the empty bags, when he stood up I took note of how tense he got. He shrugged his shoulders and pushed by me to get to the trash can. "They weren't for me. I ran into Melanie, and she looked really upset. I thought they would cheer her up."

I ran a hand through my hair and tried like hell to let it go. Levi could easily fold me in half. "What did she say?" I asked.

"We didn't talk for that long."

"But long enough to catch her shoe size?" Alex egged on. He was getting too much amusement from this.

Levi ignored him, he got himself a drink. I took out my phone, I had plenty of messages, mostly from Nat but none from you. I cleared my notifications and threw the receipt away.

I got myself a drink and went to the back room. Alex asked Levi if he was going to buy Kara a pair of shoes next. Levi told him to fuck off and followed me in to the backroom and sat down in the chair across from me.

I pulled out the wooden box from under the table and rolled a blunt. Alex came in and turn the radio on to start up some music. We shit talked for a while and passed the blunt around until I got hungry and got up to make some food.

I wasn't sure what to make so I just threw together a pasta dish with some garlic bread to go with it. That should be enough for 3 people. Alex stayed over, Kara was having a girls night and didn't want him to come home tonight so he's crashing in the front room.

Levi helped me clean up after dinner, after the dishes were done and we went to go sit down to smoke another joint. Levi asked Alex to call his phone cause he couldn't find it.

Alex made a big deal over it, saying if Levi was more attentive he would be in this situation. "Fucking Christ, I'll call it." I said and called his phone. We all got quiet and listened, but we didn't hear his phone ringing.

"It must be in the truck." Levi said and walked out to get it.

Alex leaned forward and continued scrolling on his phone. I looked over at him and asked, "What's Kara really doing tonight?" I asked.

He shrugged and sat up. "Beats me, all I know is that she's having a few of her friends over and I had to help her turn the living room into a 'fort.' I'm kind of jealous; it looked like fun. She was making food for it all day."

I laughed, "We could go crash it."

Alex smiled and shook his head, "She would kill me."

Levi came in at that moment looking like a cat that caught a canary. I narrowed my eyes, "What's up man?" I asked him.

"Just another day," He said sitting down. His phone went off, and he grinned while typing out a reply.

Alex leaned over his shoulder, "Good news Griffin, your girls new shoes fit her pretty well. Levi, ask her to send a pic." He nudged Levi's shoulder.

"Again, with these fucking shoes!" I growled. "What the hell kind of shoes did you get her that she's messaging you about them!" I took my phone out and sent you text in a blind rage. I immediately regretted it as soon as I hit send.

"I don't see what the big deal is. It's not like I took her to a fancy store in the city and got her a pair of custom heels. They came from fucking Target ok, calm down." He said bringing his shoulders up in a defensive gesture.

I knew I was over reacting, but I could feel you slipping away from me. I took a few deep breaths and read your message that just came through. 'We ran into each other at the store,' you said. Ok that checks so far, 'and he saw me looking at them. He got them to help me forget about the party you threw.'

I shook my head and put my head down. I wanted to throw my phone. 'It wasn't my party.' I sent. Then 'I'm so fucking sorry honey please don't do this.' I sent a few messages, but they all went unanswered. "Fuck!" I yelled. "Good job Levi. You fucking charmer you chased my girl away!"

Alex started howling with laughter.

Levi looked bewildered, "Are you seriously trying to blame this on me?" he shook his head, "Bro, don't get mad cause things caught up to you."

Alex started to say something, but I cut him off, "Alex you little shit stirrer just shut your fucking mouth." I closed my eyes and put my head in my hands. I heard a phone go off and my heart skipped a beat as I turned the screen on, then it dropped as I saw no new messages. I looked up and saw Levi looking at his phone, "Is that Mel?" I asked nodding at his phone.

He looked up at me, "What? No. Fuck man chill. If anything, *this*," he said gesturing to all of me, "is what's going to push her away."

"Then who's phone was that?" I asked.

"It was mine, man. Take a shot and relax bro. You're stressing out the room." Alex said.

"Fine," I got up and went for the kitchen. I brought back a bottle and some shot glasses. I sat them down on the table and poured some shots. I held one out to Levi. When he went to grab it I asked, "For real though, have you gotten anything back from Mel? I want to know if she turned her phone off or if she's just ignoring me."

"I haven't gotten a reply yet. Do you want to see?" He asked, taking his phone out and bringing up your guy's conversation. I glanced at the screen and was relieved to see he had no message from you. "The way you're acting is worse than you did with –"

"Don't say her fucking name!" I growled. The air room grew thick. I looked up at the painting of the burning Witch. I could feel her eyes on me. She was laughing at me. Her giggles echoed around me, and I took a shot glass and thew it back. Not once taking my eyes off the painting.

I forced myself to stay for one blunt and a round of shots before going to bed. I had that same dream of me chasing someone through the woods. I knew those woods well; I practically grew up there. I felt exhilarated as I ran faster and got closer to my skittish prey. Like a wolf pouncing on a doe, I tackled her to the ground and flipped her over. I knew that face all too well. It was you, Mel. But instead of looking terrified, you looked determined. You had a wine bottle and smashed it across my face.

I woke up in a cold sweat. I rolled over to look at the time and fell back on the bed. It was only 2 in the morning. I stared up at the ceiling, debating on getting up but the house sounded too quiet, and I didn't want to wake the guys up. So instead, I doomed scrolled until I eventually fell back asleep.

MELANIE (September 10)

I was heading out to the parking lot after a long day of work. The printer kept jamming up and I was covered in ink because of it. I just wanted to go home and scrub off what I could. When I checked my phone, I had a couple of messages; all from Griffin. He was wanting to take me out to see a movie tonight. We haven't seen each other since he dropped off my purse, and I haven't been keeping in touch like I used to. Every time I thought I was over it I would picture the tall slender red head with the perfect body rubbing on Griffin while he just sat there enjoying it.

I put my phone back in my pocket, taking a deep breath. *It's not worth it*, I told myself and got in my car and drove home.

After a really long shower and multiple times scrubbing I was finally ink free. I was walking out of the bathroom wrapped up in my black bath robe, drying my hair with a towel. I went over to the coffee table to get the remote so I could turn on the tv, but it was gone. I swear I left the remote right here in the little basket on the coffee table just this morning before I went to work. I looked over at the end tables, but they were empty. I looked on the bookshelves and on the entertainment center, nothing. I looked around the room, the place was clean so usually when I misplace the remote, I could easily find it by just looking around, but it was gone.

Shaking my head I went to get something to eat and drink from the kitchen, and looked around for the remote in there too, but no such luck. I went to the bedroom to grab my phone off the charger so I could use the app to control the tv. A text message came through from Griffin, 'we still have time for a movie if you want.'

Sighing I typed up an excuse to stay home. It wasn't a particularly good one and I probably would have been better off just ignoring his message completely, but here we are. Sitting back on the sofa I turned a movie on and started to eat. I wasn't even 10 minutes into the movie when the TV turned off. I stopped mid chew and just stared at the black screen. Using my phone, I turned the TV back on and brought the movie back up. 20 minutes later the TV switched over to the home screen. Adrenaline coursed through me; someone was messing with me. I put the movie back on, completely on edge. I lost my appetite, so I got up to scrape my plate off in the trash and put the plate in the dishwasher.

The movie was still playing when I crossed the living room and went to the bathroom. When I closed the door it muffled the volume of the TV, so I was unaware of what was happening on the screen. I washed my hands and walked out into the hallway. Something made me pause. The sounds coming from the living room didn't match up with the movie that I picked.

Music now drifted from the TV. I felt my body stiffen, the song that was playing was one that Griffin always sang to me. The singer was going on about the things he would do to get back to his love. I went over to the TV and grabbed the cord and yanked it out of the wall, cutting the music off abruptly. Silence fell around me.

Heart pounding, I forced myself to go through the apartment. Starting with the kitchen where I grabbed a knife, just in case. I checked the closets and under the bed. I scanned the yard, checked the patio, and made sure that the windows and doors were locked.

On a whim I called Griffins phone. I held my breath; listening, trying to see if I could hear a phone ringing. Griffins phone rang a few times before he answered, and I heard nothing in my apartment. "Hey Melanie! Did you change your mind about the movie?" he asked.

I rubbed my temple. I don't know what made me think Griffin was in my apartment fucking with me by stealing the remote and messing with the tv. I felt dumb, "Um no. I guess I just wanted to see what's up?" I said lamely.

Griffin chuckled, "You called because you miss me. Want me to come over?"

Keeping my breath steady I replied, "It's pretty late and I have to get up early."

"Oh yeah, mom doesn't like when you have company over on a school night." I rolled my eyes. "I can sneak in through the window, no one has to know I'm there."

"No. I have to be up at 3 in the morning. I'm worried that if you come over now and we watch something I'll wake up late for work."

Griffin laughed again. "I won't let that happen. Besides, I usually get up at 2. We'll be fine. Come on it'll be fun. Take control Melanie."

My heart rate jumped at the last statement. I forced that feeling down, thinking that I was being paranoid and putting things together that don't make sense. "I have plenty of control. I'm sorry I bothered you Griffin-"

"-wait it sounds like you're about to hang up. Please Mel, how long are you going to keep punishing me? I want to see you, I miss you."

I pinched the bridge of my nose and squeezed my eyes shut. Sighing I agreed to let him come over.

I sat down on the sofa and stared at the blank screen nearly jumping out of my skin when I heard knocking at the door. I got up and looked through the peep hole. Griffin was looking down at his feet with his hands in his pockets. When I opened the door he looked up at me. He stepped through the door and pulled me into a hug. "It's so good to see you." He said hugging me tighter. I must admit, the hug was nice.

I forced myself to pull away, I felt really awkward around him now. I wanted to move on, but how can I get over that? If it was someone closer to my body type would I still be this upset? Could this all just be my insecurities taking hold? I closed my eyes and took a breath; I don't know what to think. "Do you want anything from the kitchen?" I asked just to break the silence.

Griffin smiled, "Nah. I'm good, thanks though. What's wrong with your TV?" He asked nodding his head towards the television.

I looked behind me at the black screen and shrugged. "I don't know. I lost the remote and now it's being stupid, so I unplugged it." I turned around and walked over to the sofa to sit back down leaning on the arm rest.

Griffin walked over to the TV. "Mind if I take a look?" he asked already looking behind the screen to locate the plug.

"Go for it." I pulled my phone out and played Merge Dragons for a little bit.

Not too much longer Griffin was sitting down beside me with the remote in his hand, turning the TV on to whatever the Syfy channel was playing at the time. "I found your remote." He said and handed me the small plastic rectangle. "It was behind the entertainment center.

Something must have been pushing against it and pressing buttons." Shrugging, he threw an arm around my shoulders and pulled me into him.

I felt really stupid now. I didn't think to look behind the TV. I tried to relax into him; but I couldn't shake this odd nagging feeling in the back of my mind. I started fidgeting, picking at my finger nails, something was off. But I couldn't tell what it was.

Griffin was playing with my hair, picking up loose strands and twirling it around his fingers. Eventually the overwhelming feeling to get away was too strong to ignore, so I sat up and stretched, which was difficult because I was sandwiched between Griffin and the arm rest. "I'm about to head to bed. You should go home and get some rest too." I said, moving to stand up. I paused when Griffin chuckled.

"I thought I could sleep here." He said, wrapping his arm around my waist. I shook my head 'no' and he nodded his head 'yes.' "Please, it'll be fun." He said moving my hair off my neck. "Besides it's dark out there. It's dangerous to drive at night." He said running his fingers through my mostly dry hair. I looked up and met his eyes. The look behind them was dark and menacing, almost like predator eyes. I took a sharp breath in and then that look was gone, just like that. Griffin stood up and held his hand out to me. "Come on," he said grabbing my hand. "At least walk me to my car if you're going to kick me out."

I let him pull me up off the sofa. "I need to put my shoes on." I said going over to the door. I put one hand against the wall for support while I slid my shoes on. I was working on getting the left shoe on when Griffin walked over and pulled me into him. He leaned down for a kiss, but I turned my head, so he ended up kissing my cheek. "Griffi-" he cut me off by tilting my head up and kissing me.

He gently pushed me back against the wall, "I don't want to leave." He said, resting his forehead against mine. "But if you really want me to; I will."

We stared at each other for a few seconds. I searched for that dark look I keep getting glimpses of, but I didn't see it now. I looked down at my feet and all I could think of was how ridiculous I looked wearing only one shoe. Stepping on the heel of the shoe I pulled my foot out. Keeping my eyes down I stepped around Griffin and picked up my phone. "I'm going to bed." I told him over my shoulder, walking down the hallway.

I heard Griffin kicking his shoes off behind me. I was disappointed in myself for giving into him, again. But just because I'm letting him stay the night doesn't mean I've forgotten what he did at that fucking party. I put my phone on charge and put it down on the nightstand before turning the lamp off.

When I laid down Griffin was already making himself comfortable beside me grinning from ear to ear. I turned my back to him, and he put his arm around me, pressing me against his chest. "Goodnight Melanie." He said, his deep voice vibrating through me.

"Night Griffin." I mumbled. He kissed the side of my head and pulled me closer into him.

I had a hard time sleeping that night.

Griffin (September 10)

I was at home watching whatever was on the tv at the time. Just zoning out on screen, the sound from the show becoming a buzzing background noise. I glanced down at my phone again trying not to send you another text that would either get a short response or worse go ignored completely. I've been trying to give you some space but the more space I give you the further away from me you got.

I ran a hand through my hair and picked my phone up. I went to your Facebook, but you haven't posted anything since last week. I wanted to see you so badly, but I knew you were at work. I made myself busy for 20 minutes until the urge to go see you became too overwhelming. I grabbed my keys off the counter and headed out.

The drive there went by in a flash. I'm surprised I wasn't pulled over for how fast I was going. I pulled up to your apartment building and parked next to the spot your car is usually in. While I had your purse in my possession I was able to go make a copy of your key, making getting into your apartment so much easier. Breaking in with a key, no one would call the cops. They would think I was supposed to be here.

Looking around I wasn't sure what exactly what I was doing, so I went to the kitchen to get something to drink. I sat down on the sofa and took the remote from the basket on the coffee table and turned on a random movie to kill the time.

I checked the time, but I still had 4 hours until you got off work. Groaning I took my phone out and sent you some sweet texts, asking how your day was going, how you were feeling today, if I could take you out to see a movie tonight. But all my messages went unanswered. I was getting really annoyed with you at this point. I clenched my phone in a tight fist and stared at the tv, waiting until it was time for me to leave.

I had 20 minutes before you got home so I got up and put everything back where it was; except for the remote, which I slid into my pocket. I slid out the door and locked it up before casually walking outside, smiling cheerfully, and waving at an older lady who was waiting for the elevator. She smiled back at me before stepping onto the elevator that had just arrived.

I got to my car and unlocked it looking around. Narrowing my eyes at the red car down the street that took off once I walked out of the building. I waited to see which way it went before sliding into the driver's seat and moving my car a few blocks away so I could watch as you pulled in; but you couldn't see me.

It wasn't too much longer before you were pulling up and walking across the parking lot. You look exhausted. You were splattered with sky blue ink, every once in a while you would get off work with some ink on you, so that wasn't too unusual. Once you were inside I took my phone out to kill some time before making my move. I figured you would take a shower before you do anything else, so I gave you some time to clean up.

I parked my car back in front of the building and walked around back to see what you were up to. At this time, you were walking around looking a little lost, walking around in nothing but a bath robe and letting that long hair drip water all over the place. Your gaze slid across the windows, and I ducked out of sight. Waiting a few heart beats before risking another peak inside. But; I lost sight of you.

309

I went to a different window and found you in the kitchen putting together a quick meal. I watched as you sat your plate on the coffee table and went to the bedroom. I took out my phone, making sure it was on silent and sent you a text bringing up a movie once again. I wanted to spend time with you but for some reason you keep pushing me away.

A few drawn out moments later a text came through; you wanted to stay home cause you were waiting on the dishwasher. I gritted my teeth and shoved my phone back in my pocket. *Ok message received.* I thought and took out the tv remote. I waited until my breathing evened out and pointed the remote at the tv and pushed the power button.

I looked over at you, you looked confused, but you just picked up your phone and the tv turned back on like nothing happened. I smirked and watched you for a while. I was starting to get mad that I wasn't in there with you, eating food with you, laughing at the cheesy effects in the movie. But instead, I'm stuck outside like a dog. I pressed the home button and got a bigger reaction out of you this time, you hurriedly put your movie back on and then practically ran into the kitchen.

It took all I had not to laugh at how scared you looked right now. I watched you walk through the living room and disappear behind the bathroom door. Grinning like a fool, I switched the tv screen over to the music app and searched for my go to song. I turned up the volume a little so I could mumble the words along with the singer. "I don't wake up to your eyes any more, I don't wake at all." He growled through the speakers of the tv.

I sang the words under my breath until you came back in to view. You were going over to the tv, I watched curiously as you bent down and unplugged the tv. I took that as my queue to go back to the car.

The night was getting cold, I shoved my hands in my pockets and walked faster. My keys jingled as I took them out of my pocket and flipped the car key out so I could get out of the wind. I had just sat down and closed the door when my phone started ringing.

I couldn't help the smile that spread across my face as I read your name on the screen. "Hey Melanie!" I was so happy you called; I knew putting our song on would make you miss me. "Did you change your mind about the movie?"

I heard you take a deep breath on the other end. I should have stayed a little bit longer so I could see what you were doing right now. "Um no, I guess I just wanted to see what's up?"

I laughed how ridiculous that lie was. I knew why you called, you wanted to see if I was in your apartment fucking with you. "You called because you miss me. Want me to come over?" I almost added that I was already in the car, and it was no big deal, but that would raise too many red flags that I don't want to deal with.

You turned me down saying you have to get up early. I made a lame joke and told you I could sneak through the window, and no one will have to know.

Again, you had an excuse ready to go, but I quickly shot that one down too and told you that you need to take control. You took a quick breath and started speaking fast. My heart sank, and before you could hang up I started to spew some bullshit apologies. Telling you that I miss you, and I do. I would do anything to have you in my arms right now.

The line was quiet for a heartbeat. I held my breath worried that you already hung up but then I heard you exhale, "ok fine."

I was so fucking happy I could fly. I told you I would be there in a moment and hung up. I took a moment to soak up my victory, laughing at how that all played out. I smoked a quick cigarette to kill some time, not wanting to show up a few seconds after we got off the phone. That would be weird.

I knocked on your door and waited impatiently. When you opened the door I looked up and pulled you into a tight embrace walking us backwards and closing the door behind us. Your hair was still wet from your shower, it smelled like peaches. I was happy to see you were still in the bathrobe. "It's so good to see you." I said hugging you tighter. I never wanted to let go.

I felt you squeeze me for just a moment before you pulled away. The smile on my face fell, you wouldn't look at me, and you were doing that thing were you keep tugging at your hair and clothes. "Do you want anything from the kitchen?" You asked. Your voice sounded strained; but I looked past it.

Smiling I told you that I was good. Then I looked over at your tv and nodded at it asking what was going on with it. You shrugged and told me how you lost the remote and now it's being stupid. "Mind if I take a look?" I asked, already knowing that the solution was the misplaced remote that was in my pocket.

You told me to go for it and started playing a game on your phone. I got up and plugged the tv back in. Glancing over my shoulder to make sure that you weren't looking before I took the remote out of my pocket.

I went to sit down next to you and turned the tv on to whatever you were watching last. "I found your remote." I said handing it over to you. I made up some bullshit story about how it got stuck behind the entertainment center, and something was pressing against the buttons. I gave a half shrug and put my arm around you and pulled you into me.

I couldn't help but notice how twitchy you were. If I didn't know any better I'd swear you were on something. I looked down at you and picked up a lock of your hair, I loved how soft it was. I started twisting it around my fingers, wondering what you were thinking about that had you on edge. You took a shaky breath and sat up straight, stretching in a way that pulled your hair from my lose grip. I watched as the strands slid from my fingers, fighting myself from closing my fist around your hair and pulling you back to the sofa. I took in a deep breath and held it for 5 seconds before letting it out slowly.

"I'm about to head to bed." You said interrupting my violent fantasy. "You should go home and get some rest too."

I smiled and a laugh slipped out. It was funny how you think you can get rid of me that easily. I wrapped my arm around your waist and said. "I thought I could sleep here." You shook your head 'no' and I nodded. "Please," I begged, "it'll be fun." I brushed some of your hair back and tried to guilt you into letting me stay. Saying how dangerous driving at night can be. I ran my fingers through your hair, still a little wet from the shower. I was getting aggravated at how you keep trying to push me away, and I was thinking of telling you as much; then we locked eyes. I blinked and shoved down the anger, replacing it with something more welcoming. Swallowing down the biting insults I stood up and offered you my hand. "Come on," I said gently, "at least walk me to my car if you're going to kick me out."

You took my hand and told me that you needed to put your shoes on. I watched you carefully as you braced yourself against the wall. I walked over and grabbed you, pulling you in for a kiss. Your turned your head so I ended up kissing your cheek. I ignored your protests and grabbed your chin to properly kiss you. I moved you around to press you against the wall and leaned my forehead against yours. "I don't want to leave," I whispered, "but if you really want me to; I will."

We stared at each other for a few agonizing seconds. I'm not sure what you were thinking, but I kept my expression soft. Then you dropped your gaze and took your shoe off. I bit my lip to keep a victory cry from spilling out and stepped to the side as you walked around me to grab your phone off the coffee table. "I'm going to bed." You said, not bothering to look back or wait on me.

I chuckled quietly and took my shoes off. I was quick to undress and lie down as you turned off the lamp on the nightstand and got into bed. You turned your back to me, and I put my arm around you to pull you into me, "goodnight Melanie."

"Night Griffin." You mumbled. I kiss the side of your head and snuggled into you. I never want to leave this bed.

Melanie (October 31)

A few weeks ago, my sister got ahold of me and asked if I wanted to join her and a few friends in some Halloween shenanigans. I had nothing else planned so I told her that I would be there and started planning a costume. When she told me there was a theme I almost backed out, but then she told me that it was horror themed, and they wanted it to be with a sultry twist. I was back in.

It didn't take long to find a costume; black shoes, fish net stockings, black shorts, white tank top, black blazer, white gloves, red bow tie and do my make up. All I need was a little tricycle and I'm good. I took my inspiration from a little psychotic puppet.

The next couple days were long and felt like they would never end, but it was finally time to pack up a bag and make the drive back home. The drive was long and boring without someone there to keep me company but once I arrived at my sister's house it was like I never left. We spent the night watching horror movies and catching up, then we took the morning to get ready for the night ahead.

While we were getting ready, Kendra went over the plan for the night. We were meeting her friends at the bar, I wasn't sure how many people were going to be there or if I knew any of them, but I do know that there was a group theme of iconic horror movie villains, so it'll be easier to tell who's apart of the group tonight. Kendra dressed up as Freddy, and I was going as the puppet from the Saw franchise. I got red contacts just for this occasion. Kendra curled and styled my hair for me and by the time we were done we were pin-up versions of our horror movie counterpart. I got to admit it was kind of fun dressing spooky sexy.

We got in her car and put on some music to get us in a good mood for a night out. "Oh! Before I forget any longer and you're completely blindsided by this, there is a rule not to use names. Sue just got out of messy situationship and just in case he is here tonight she doesn't want her name being thrown around to catch his attention, ya know?" I asked her what she meant by a situationship, "Well they weren't official yet, but he turned out to be crazy, so she broke it off before things between them got too serious; and now he's kind of stalking her and being super creepy. She's already went to the police but there's not a lot that they can do in this situation."

"Ok that's understandable." If I was in her shoes, I wouldn't want a spiteful ex to ruin what was supposed to be a fun night out with friends.

We turned in the parking lot, it took us a moment to find a spot, the place was packed. We eventually found a spot near the back. Kendra put the car in park, and we got out to make our way to the bar. We heard the music before we got to the doors. I could feel my anxiety start to pick up, but I pushed it down and opened the door, I waited for Kendra to walk through before I let the door swing shut.

Looking around I seen all kinds of costumes. Some people went all out, some people just threw something together at the last minute, and there were a handful of people who didn't dress up at all. Kendra pulled me over to the middle of the bar and joined a group of girls who were also dressed up like slutty killers. We said our hello's and complimented each other's costumes.

I was introduced around the group as Jigsaw, I didn't want to be that person and say, 'Well the puppets name is actually Billy, Jigsaw was the alias that the killer John Kramer used.' So, I was 'Jigsaw' tonight. There were 4 other girls. A Michael Myers, a Jason Vorhees, and a lesbian couple dressed as Chucky and Tiffany who went to get a round of drinks.

When they got back Tiffany handed out shots. "Happy Halloween Bitches!" She said holding up her glass. We all held up our shots to clinked them together and throw back the bitter liquid. It was warm going down, sending a slightly fuzzy feeling to my limbs.

We all seemed to get along well enough, Michael and Jason kept mostly to themselves, but Chucky and Tiffany were nice. We went to get a table in the back, we had idle chitchat, well I more listened to them talk about work and chimed in when I could. "Hey Freddy, I'm going to get a drink do you want one?" I asked Kendra. She took my offer and ordered a Midori and monster.

"Oh, Jigsaw wait! I'll go with you." Jason said, getting off the stool she was sitting on. "Micheal, do you want anything?"

"I'll take a Carona." She said handing a 5 to Jason. Tiffany also got up to get her and Chucky a drink.

Now a group of 3 we went to the bar to get our drinks. Weaving through the crowd was a journey in itself. We got compliments right and left, mostly from horny drunk men but the ones from the ladies made it worth it; and the ones who wanted to take their picture with us, that was cool too.

We finally made it to the bar, Tiffany ordered first. I was looking at my phone when the hair on the back of my neck stood up. Looking around to see if anyone was looking at me didn't really do any good, there was a lot of people looking over in my direction, I was dressed provocatively standing next to two other beautiful women who were also dressed provocatively. I swallowed the lump in my throat and waited as Tiffany grabbed her drinks and turned to us. "Hey, I'm gonna take these back, are you guys ok up here?"

We told her that she was fine to go back. We weren't talking for too long I didn't think, just a quick exchange of words and she was gone. But when we turned to step up to order our drinks a couple of guys had pushed in front of us and were already ordering. Ok fair enough, we waited until it was clear to step up and get our drinks. I was looking back down at my phone again when I got that same prickly feeling as if someone were watching me, I put my phone in my back pocket and looked around the room taking in my surroundings. "Hey, are you ok?" Jason asked and she sounded concerned.

"I keep getting this feeling like someone is staring at me." I told her.

She scanned the room around us, "Well you look hot, but that is no excuse to make you feel uncomfortable," she shook her head, "I don't see anything unusual. Let me know if you see anything and we'll leave, ok." I nodded my head and then the guys cleared out, so she stepped up to order her drinks. When the bartender sat 2 glasses in front of her, she paid and picked up the almost overflowing glasses, she turned to me a said, "I really hate to do this to you, but I promised Micheal I wouldn't leave her tonight. She's been going through some hard times, and I don't want her to feel like she's being ditched."

Figuring that Micheal was Sue I nodded my head. "It's all good I get it. Don't worry I'll be fine."

She smiled at me a said 'thank you' before disappearing into the crowd. I turned to step up to order my drinks, but a group of 6 slutty animals had slithered their way up to the bar. They kept stepping backwards causing me to take a step back as well. The mouse kept flipping her hair to try to hit me to get me to back up, and the cat was whipping her tail around. Keeping my comments to myself because I didn't want to start shit with a group of 6 when it just me; that didn't sound like it would be a fair fight.

The bunny took a step back almost pressing herself against me until I took a step back as well and ended up bumping into the side of someone, "Oh I am so sorry!" I said turning around.

The guys laugh was deep, and it vibrated through me. "No sorry needed just don't ask me to play a game." He spoke.

It took me a little bit to get what he was talking about but then it hit me, he was referring to my costume. I forced laughed, "Good one." I said awkwardly, not really knowing what to say now. I went to turn back around so my place didn't get taken again.

The guy stepped up beside me, "Hey I'm Trevor. Let me buy you a drink?"

"No thanks Trevor, I'm here with my friends." I smiled at him. He wasn't in a costume, just jeans and a Megadeath t-shirt.

"How about a picture then? Saw is one of my favorite movies." he said, pulling his phone out and wrapping an arm around me.

"Please don't touch me." I said shrugging his arm off, "You can take a picture but don't put your arm around me." I said and then smiled up at his phone. He gave me a sideways look, snapped the picture, and slinked off.

I willed the bartender to hurry up with the group in front of me so I can get my drinks and get back to my group. I felt oddly exposed. There was that tingly feeling again but this time when I looked around, I saw him. He was wearing dark blue jeans and a black hoodie. He had a silver demon mask on with a smooth surface where the mouth should be. He was leaning against the wall, motionless. I wasn't sure if he was actually looking at me, but it was just a feeling I couldn't shake.

The group of girls finally cleared out, and I stepped up before anyone else could get in front of me. I paid and tipped the bartender when she put my drinks in front of me. Before I walked away I put napkins over the top of the glasses to make sure nothing was dropped in them as I made my way back to the killer group of girls I was with. I glanced over to the wall, but that guy was no longer there.

It took some time, but I was able to make it back to the table without spilling the drinks or bumping into anyone. Which was surprising since the place was packed. When I got to the table I noticed it was just Kendra.

I sat a glass down in front of my sister and we cheers'ed to finally getting our drinks. While we enjoyed them, she filled me in on where everyone went. Chucky and Tiffany were dancing and the other two went to the bathroom. Kendra looked over my shoulder and made a face, "Someone is walking straight towards us, and I have no idea who it is."

I looked behind me. I had to do a double take. "Hey Mel. What are you doing here?" Griffin (of all people) asked sliding into the seat next to me. His words slurred together, and he had look about him was that too relaxed. He took his time looking me up and down and I took note of the dark blue jeans and black hoodie he was wearing but didn't see a mask anywhere. Maybe he sat it down? "I like this." He said gesturing towards my costume, he was fidgety and scratched at his neck and arms occasionally. He was definitely on something.

Confused and stuttering I stumbled over my words thanking him and introducing him to my sister at the same time. "Wh-what are you doing here?"

Griffin laughed, "I asked you first." He said smirking and put a hand on my thigh and leaned into whisper in my ear, "I have a game I want to play later." I turned my head to the side, the alcohol and smoke on his breath was overpowering. Leaning back, he threw his hands up, "But fine I'll answer, I'm here acting as moral support for my friend Alex, you remember him, don't you?" He asked me, he was swaying and talking with his hands. "He's around here somewhere with a tinder date." His eyes snapped to me, and he got really serious, "I only drove him here cause his license is suspended, not because I'm cheating on you. I'm a one-woman man."

I laughed, "It's good to know you've changed your mind on that." I took a drink to help make it less awkward. I looked over at Kendra, who was looking at Griffin assessing the situation, I didn't want to cause a scene and ruin her night. I took another drink, not sure what was happening here. Why was Griffin *here?* I found myself wondering.

"Come dance with me, Mel." He said getting up and taking my hand.

I pulled my hand away. "No, Griffin. I'm sorry but I'm here with my friends." I noticed Kendra start to get a defensive stance.

He stiffened and looked at me, "Mel please, of all the people I could have run into tonight I ran into you." He ran his hand down my arm and grabbed my hand again, "It's fate. Dance with me."

I started to shake my head 'no' when Jason and Micheal walked up and saw us holding hands. Jason smiled from ear to ear. "Oh, is this your boyfriend! He's cute!" She exclaimed.

Griffin stood up and extended his hand, "Yes, I'm her boyfriend. Griffin." Smiling, they shook hands. My mouth dropped open, and I looked over at Kendra, who looked more confused than I had ever seen her. I was about to protest when Griffin went on to say, "I was trying to get her to dance but she wants to stick with a girl's night." He shrugged trying to play this off as casual. I narrowed my eyes and looked him up and down, I found myself wondering again who would go to a town 5 hours away from where you live for a tinder date? This wasn't adding up.

The girls started talking at the same time, saying how I should go ahead and dance with my boyfriend; and that's how I was pulled away from my sister and her two friends, and ended up on the dance floor. I looked around while Griffin put his arm around my waist. "Where's Alex? I don't see him." I didn't know what he was playing at but this whole thing just seemed to weird.

Griffin laughed and pulled me closer, grinning down at me he said, "What Mel, you don't trust me?" He licked his lips and looked up. "Oh look," he said, spinning me around and pulling me in, so my back was pressed against his chest. Leaning over me to press his cheek against my temple, he pointed over to a couple dancing on the other side of the room. I followed his finger and seen Alex, who had on a Halloween shirt (his attempt at being festive I guess) dancing with a young woman dressed as a genie. Spinning me back around he laughed, "You look amazing by the way." He said, "I'm glad I let Alex talk me into this, someone would have surely snatched you away from me tonight."

"Tonight was supposed to be a girl's night." I said getting aggravated. This still didn't make sense to me and all I wanted was to sit down and have a drink with my sister.

Laughing he spun me around, "Lighten up sweetheart, I just want one dance, and I'll let you go back to your friends." He pulled me into him, "Although let's be honest, you could do better."

I turned my head to the side, so he wasn't breathing right on my face, the alcohol on his breath mixed with cigarette smoke made me want to gag. "Griffin how much have you had to drink?"

He was swaying us to the music, "I wasn't counting." He mumbled.

"One dance." I sighed, "How are you going to get home if your drunk and Alex can't drive?"

Griffin pulled back, he had a look that I couldn't read and then just as quickly he smiled like a wolf that finally caught the doe. "Well since you put it that way, I guess we should stay in town for the night. To sober up. Guess that's what happens with the D.D. decides he wants to drink too. How well do you know the area?" He asked.

"Well, enough, I grew up here." I gave him a sideways look when he laughed, "Why did you drive 5 hours away for a Tender hookup?"

"What makes you think that it's a hookup? He could really like this girl." He said laughing, I could tell even though *he* didn't believe that. "Ok so maybe it is a hookup, but we were on our way back from Canada and when we pulled over to eat he got on Tinder." Griffin shrugged like it was an everyday thing but something in his story caught my attention that just raised more questions.

"What were you doing in Canada?" I asked.

Griffin paused and looked me up and down, "I really do like this get up Mel. We can make a movie later if you're free."

I rolled my eyes; I really didn't like this side of Griffin. "No. Griff, you seem pretty drunk, you should probably think about going and getting a room or something. Some place where you can sleep it off."

The grin on his face somehow got wider, "I like how much you care about me. I can sleep with you tonight. Where is that by the way?"

"At my sisters. And no, I'm sorry but you can't crash there tonight."

"Why? Are you gonna have 'girl time' and boys aren't allowed." He used air quotes and laughed at his own joke. I shook my head and went to leave when he caught me by the arm. At first his grip was harsh; he immediately loosened his grip but still had a firm hold on me. "I, am. Sorry." He said slowly. "I'm pretty drunk, you're right. We didn't think this out fully. It just seemed like a good idea at the time." Griffin let my arm go to scratch the back of his neck. "Honestly, Alex is more than likely going to sleep over at his dates place, and I'll just sleep in the car. I don't want to sleep next anyone who isn't you."

I sighed, "I'm sorry too." Taking a step back, I wasn't sure what to do.

"Can I have another dance? Please?" Griffin asked sheepishly.

I looked over to the table that my sister was sitting at. They looked like they were having a good time. "One more." I said.

1 song later he talked me into doing shots and got me a strong drink. I asked him what it was, but it was a mixed drink that I had never heard of. It was strong, bitter, and went down like liquid fire. When we got back to the dance floor the room started to look funny, like everything had a double outline. I swayed a little and grabbed onto Griffin, he steadied me, "Are you feeling alright Mel?" he asked in my ear. I looked up at him and nodded, smiling. "Good, let's go meet up with Alex and his date. See what they're up to." He gently led me to the opposite side of the bar where my sister and her group of friends were.

When we sat down at the table Alex and his date were at, there was already 4 shots of dark liquid waiting for us. Thinking nothing of it, I took the shot when Griffin handed it to me.

"Hey Mel. Fancy seeing you here." Alex said with a wink when he finished his shot.

"What are the odds right?" I agreed laughing.

"Must be a smaller world than we think." He said sharing a look with Griffin.

The song switched to a pop song and the genie that was hanging on Alex started begging for a dance, so he let her pull him back to the dance floor. Griffin held a handout. "Come on, let's dance." I put my hand in his; and followed him like he was the only one there. I felt like I was floating, my head felt hazy.

3 songs later we were doing more shots with Alex and his date for the night, who's name turned out to be Jenny. I wish I was joking. My dancing was getting clumsy, so Griffin led me to the table, he was talking to me about something but his hand on my thigh was distracting me. His hands were rough with calluses, and his grip was firm, he moved his hand up and fingered the hem of my shorts. I looked up at him, but his eyes were looking down at his hand that was on my thigh. After a moment his eyes flicked up and met mine, he was leaning and just as we kissed, Kendra came up behind us. "What the fuck! Did you seriously ditch us?" she almost yelled.

I looked over at her, and the room started to spin. "What!! Kendra! When did you get here!" I said raising my arms and going to stand up but ended up stumbling over my feet.

Kendra pushed some hair out of my face and looked at me, studying my eyes. Snapping her head towards Griffin she narrowed her eyes, "Did you fucking drug my sister?" She gathered me in her arms, and I fell into her like a doll laughing.

I touched her hat, "Griff wouldn't do that to me. He's a nice guy."

Griffin grinned that wolfish grin and held his arms out, "Yeah Kendra, I'm a nice guy! I wouldn't do anything to your sister that I wouldn't want done to mine. We just had a lot to drink. Make sure she gets home safe." He came up and kissed me on the forehead. "I'll call you in the morning."

Stumbling, I let Kendra lead me back over to the group. "Guys I have to cut this short; I need to get her out of here."

"Is she ok?" I heard one of them ask. I lazily nodded my head.

Kendra took her phone and wallet from a girl dressed like a Tiffany doll, "Thanks," she said, "Yeah, I think she's fine. Just too much to drink."

The girl with the hockey mask asked if she needed any help and Kendra accepted. She came over and looped her arm around my waist.

I tried to raise my head, but it just lulled back down. "I'm tired." I mumbled.

I felt my hair being smoothed back and heard some muffled voices, but I couldn't focus on what they were saying.

Griffin (October 31)

Alex and I were on the way back from a drop off. Levi was supposed to come with us; but his band had ended up getting booked for a Halloween show so he couldn't make it.

We've been on the road for almost 10 hours straight. Alex was in the passenger seat scrolling on his phone, "Man I'm starting to get hungry." I said, we still had over 6 hours to drive, and I was ready to get out of the car and take a break.

"Same, I'll look for a place to eat." Alex said.

Seeing what town was coming up was like fate, all the times you've talked about your hometown and now here I was, getting ready to drive through it. And it just so happens that I remember you telling me that you were going to be going back home for a visit this weekend. I took the exit already planning on how to find you.

We found a Dennys to stop and eat at. "Hey, do you mind if we stop here for a while? We're already way ahead of schedule, you're dad isn't expecting us back until tomorrow night anyway."

I watched as the waitress sat my plate in front of me. She was pretty cute for that small town look. I watched her walk away and started eating, "Yeah we can stop for the night. So, get this, Mel talks about this town a lot. She said she grew up here, I'll see if she's around." I took out my phone and opened up the Facebook messenger app. I logged on into your account on my phone so I could keep better tabs on you while I was away. You've been making plans with your sister for a night out for a while now. I knew the time you were meeting, where you were meeting and with a little help from Alex, we were able to figure who all was going to be meeting you there. Social media is all connected, and people like to share what's going on in their lives. Making it all too easy to find out how Angela is 'so excited to dress up as Tiffany and Chucky and go out drinking with my besties #HappyHalloween' had tagged your sister, and she even tagged the bar they were going to be at. You weren't tagged in the post, but you are going to be with your sister.

Alex had set up a Tinder date to meet him at the bar for some drinks. I booked a room for the night at the Super 8 and started thinking of different ways tonight could go down, every ending seemed to go my way. Alex reached into his pocket and handed me a small baggie with a pill. "Never know." He shrugged.

I shook my head I knew I wouldn't need it. You couldn't resist me, all I needed was a little alcohol and some smooth compliments and you're putty in my hands. But I slipped the pill in my pocket anyway.

It was just now 5 o'clock and you wouldn't be at the bar until 9. We stopped at the liquor store and picked up some Jack and went to the hotel to kill sometime. I went to the bathroom and when I got out Alex was cutting up lines.

It seemed like I had just sat down to do a line when the alarm I set for 9:20 went off. I went to pour a drink, but the bottle was empty. I ran a hand down my face, "fuck it's already time to go." I said over to Alex who zoned out on the TV. He nodded and got up to get ready. I slipped into the bathroom before pretty boy could and fixed my appearance. I splashed water on my face and ran my fingers through my hair a few times. When I got out of the bathroom Alex was still obsessing over his reflection. "I'm leaving in five minutes whether you're ready or not." I told him putting my shoes on and then rolled up a joint. I got up and went over to the door, I waited for a few moments while Alex smoothed the hair on the side of his head.

Getting impatient I opened the door and stepped out. "Hey fucker wait up!" He yelled and got to the door just as it closed. He yanked it open and closed it behind him. "Couldn't wait 10 more minutes?" He asked.

I shrugged. "You'll be fine. There's a mirror in the car if you're that worried."

When we walked out of the building I lit a cigarette and got the keys out of my pocket. "Jenny is at the bar, look at the pic she sent." He showed me picture of a chick dressed as a genie. She was nothing special just another slut dressed up in a costume.

I got in the driver seat and set GPS up to take us to the bar. When we got there we split up, Alex went to go find his date and I went to go get a drink. When I had my beer I picked a spot along the wall that gave me a good view of the bar. Walking through the crowd of people I picked up a random mask and leaned against the wall. You'll come up here eventually. I'm patient, I'll wait.

I was about to pull my phone out and message you when I saw a slutty puppet with swirls on her cheeks walk through the room up to the bar. There was a female Jason Vorhees and a Tiffany too, looking over at the puppet I noticed some familiar tattoos, and my heart sped up. I found you. You had on black flat shoes and fishnet tights. The black shorts you had on were practically underwear; you had a low-cut white tank top and a black blazer that buttoned just below your breasts. You wore a red bow tie around your neck, and your hair was curled. Your makeup looked like it took a while, it'll be a shame to see it all smeared later.

I watched you for a while, waiting to see if I'd get an opportunity. One girl from your group left and after a while the other one left leaving you alone. I watched as you bumped into a guy and he tried to get handsy, I was moving to step in when he glared at you and walked away. Laughing I leaned back and admired you some more. When you got your drinks you looked right over at me. Behind the mask I licked my lips.

When you moved out of sight I took off the mask and got another drink. Throwing it back and feeling invincible I made my move. You were sitting at a table with your sister. I knew I should wait until she got up leaving you alone, but you were so beautiful I couldn't help myself. I sat down in the chair next to you. "Hey Mel, what are you doing here? I like this." I said looking at your chest.

You pushed some hair back from your face, you're cute when your frustrated, "Th-thank you? Um Griffin this Kendra, Kendra, Griffin." You scratched your eyebrow. "Wh-what are you doing here?" You asked.

I laughed and turned on the charm. "I asked you first." I put a hand on your thigh and whispered, "I have a game I want to play later." Pulling back, I put my hands up, explaining how Alex has a Tinder date and that I drove because he doesn't have a license. My drunk tongue threw out how I was staying a one-woman man. I expected you to be impressed, flattered, grateful even. But instead, you just looked annoyed and threw a snappy comment at me. I winced and tried to think of a way to cheer you up. You were looking over at your sister, who was staring me down. I needed to smooth this all out before she took you away. "Come dance with me, Mel." I said getting up and grabbing a hold of your hand.

You pulled your hand away, "No Griffin I'm sorry but I'm here with my friends." You looked so cute trying to be firm. But one day you'll learn that you don't tell me 'no.'

"Mel, please of all the people I could have ran into tonight. I ran into you." I slid my hand down your arm to grab your hand. I just wanted to touch you at this point. "It's fate." I said, "dance with me."

Just then your other friends came up and giving you no time to react I introduced myself as your boyfriend and with their help I got you on the dance floor. I was growing less confident in my skills to talk you into leaving with me. I hooked my arm around your waist, you were looking around the room, "Where is Alex? I don't see him."

I laughed at how smart you thought you were. "What Mel, you don't trust me?" *You shouldn't* I thought and looked around the room. I saw Alex and his date not too far away, "Oh look!" I said and spun you around and pressed my chest to your back. I rested my head against yours and pointed over at Alex. I waited a moment enjoying how easily I could wrap you up and spun you back around, so you were facing me again. I told you how amazing you looked and that I was glad I was here because someone else would have grabbed you up before I could.

You were getting mad at me at this point. I tried to smooth things over, but you just turned your head in disgust. "Griffin how much have you had to drink?"

I bounced on my feet; debating on snatching you up and having my way with you in the bathroom. "I wasn't counting." I mumbled.

I'm not sure what I did but you agreed to one dance. That's all I need. You asked how I was going to get home if I was drunk, and Alex couldn't drive.

I looked down at you surprised you would ask that; it threw me off. I guess that means I finally got to you, I grinned and agreed that it would be better if I stayed in town for the night to 'sober up.' And for added measure I asked how well you knew the area and even acted surprised when you said you grew up here. You asked why we would drive all this way just for a hook up and we joked at how it couldn't be anything else cause Alex is more for one-night stands than staying loyal to Kara. My drunk tongue told you more half-truths.

You raised an eyebrow "What were you doing in Canada?"

Not knowing how to answer without you asking more questions I said the first thing that came to mind, "I really do like this get up Mel. We can make a movie later if you're free." Please tie me down and torture me dressed like the puppet from Saw, I'll play all the games with you.

You rolled your eyes and said that I should go sleep it off. But the only thing I heard was you calling me Griff. I love when you call me that, it lets me know that you're not really mad. I asked where you were staying but all you said was your sisters house. Fair enough. I made a joke about boys not being allowed at your girls night. I guess that struck a nerve because you tried to turn away. I grabbed your arm to keep you here. When I had your attention I let go but kept my hand on your arm, so you can't try to walk away again. "I'm sorry." I made some half excuse about being drunk, saying *anything* to keep you here longer.

You took a step back and apologized too. I asked for one more dance. And to my surprise you agreed. Wanting more time with you I asked if you wanted a shot.

You shook your head, "No that's ok."

"Come on. One shot, it can't hurt. My treat."

I gave you a cheesy smile and reluctantly you smiled back, and then you agreed. "Fine. One shot."

Taking your hand, I pulled you up to the bar with me. Not letting you go I got a shot for each of us and a rum and coke for you (with something extra) and a beer for me. I got my phone out while you weren't looking and sent Alex a text asking him to get 4 shots together for us and the girls. After we drank our drinks I lead you back to the dance floor, you started to sway, and I asked if you were feeling ok. Say the words and we'll go back to the hotel room. You looked up at me smiling lazily and nodded. I grinned and took us over to Alex and 'Jenny.'

We sat down at the table that Alex and his date were sitting at. Nodding at Alex with a knowing smirk I picked up a shot glass and slipped it into your hand. Like a good girl you drank it without question.

"Hey Mel. Fancy seeing you here." Alex said when you put the shot glass on the table.

You were much more relaxed than you were a few minutes ago. You were smiling and laughing, actually enjoying yourself with us. When Alex was pulled away for a dance I coaxed you into one as well. I wanted to feel you against me. I could tell you were feeling the effects of the drinks now, you were beginning to lean against me, and your eyes were glazing over. I got us another round of shots.

We were feeling each other and the music, I didn't want this to end. I took us to the table, so I could hopefully talk you into leaving with me tonight. I was sure it wouldn't be that hard. I had my hand on your thigh, enjoying how soft your skin was. "I think you should come with me tonight; I got a hotel room, so we'll have plenty of privacy. I have plenty of weed and I can pick up some more alcohol. Or I can order us a pizza, and we can just…relax." I fingered the hem of your shorts and looked up at you. Your eyes were blood shot, and you had a lazy smile still on your lips. I leaned in to kiss you but then some bitch dressed like Freddy Kruger came up behind us and started yelling.

You got up and tripped over your feet in the process, your sister caught you and then started yelling at me for drugging you. You reached up and played with her hat coming to my defense saying, "Griff wouldn't do that to me. He's a nice guy."

Almost laughing at the irony. I gave a wolfish grin and held out my arms. "See Kendra? I'm a nice guy. I wouldn't do anything to your sister that I wouldn't want done to mine." The only difference here is, I don't have a sister. "We just had a lot to drink. Make sure she gets home safe." I got up and kissed you on the forehead, "I'll call you in the morning." Furious, I watched as your sister dragged you away from me. I was so fucking close.

I sat back down and tried to control my breathing. Alex and his date came back a few minutes later, "Hey where's Mel?" Alex asked.

I clenched my hands into fists and through gritted teeth I growled, "Her sister came and got her." Not bothering to wait for his response I said, "I have to get out of here." I got up and pushed my way to the exit, shoving people out of my way when necessary. When I got to my car, I lit a cigarette and got in. I punched the steering wheel a few times, "FUCK!" I yelled. You should be sitting next to me right now. I should have pushed for us to leave earlier. I was about to put the car in reverse when I saw you and your sister walking through the parking lot. Someone dressed like Jason Vorhees was with you. I sat back and watched to see what vehicle they put you in and waited until they got in too and took off. I put the car in reverse and followed to see where you went.

After a few turns I decided to give it up. I didn't have a plan on what to do once the car came to stop. I felt so cheated. Everything was going so perfectly, I almost fucking had you. Punching the steering wheel again I went back to the hotel and stalked your profile until I fell asleep.

Melanie (November 1st 10 AM)

I woke that morning with a pounding headache. The sunrays coming in through the window was like a spot light right in my eyes. I groaned and rolled over, putting the pillow over my face. There was a bird outside the window that kept singing, it's shrill chirps sliced right into my eardrums. I squeezed my eyes shut and pinched the bridge of my nose.

"Oh good, you're awake." I heard someone say, rather loudly, and then something was sat down heavily not too far from me.

With tremendous effort I sat up and looked around but had to close my eyes and wait for a wave of nausea to pass. When I felt like I wasn't about to dry heave I looked at table in front of me, then it came back to me. Well parts of it. I was in my sister's living room, and she looked mad as hell. "Good morning to you too." I said, rubbing my neck. Sleeping on a sofa was all fun and games when I was younger, but now days it's just torture.

"Who was that at the bar last night? He said he was your boyfriend, but last time we talked you had the exact opposite of a boyfriend." She uncrossed her arms and went over to open the curtains on the window.

I turned my head from the sudden burst of blinding light. "That was Griffin. It's kind of hard to explain." I stood up and twisted my back, giving it a good crack to stretch out from a night of questionable sleep.

"Well start talking. I want to know what last night was about."

I rolled my eyes and grabbed my overnight bag, "Let me wake up first." I went to the bathroom to wash my face and brush my teeth.

After some toast and coffee, I explain the best I could to Kendra things between Griffin and me. Her face was scrunched up, and she was just looking down at the table between us. Then she started shaking her head, "I don't like him." She said plainly. "He sounds sketchy, and the way you were acting last night.... That wasn't just from alcohol. Are you sure he wouldn't put anything in your drink?"

I furrowed my eyebrows and shook my head, "I'm pretty sure he wouldn't do that." At least I hoped that he wouldn't.

"What about the couple he was with? The other guy at the table gave some creepy vibes."

I paused for a moment too long, then slowly shook my head, "that was Alex. And I can't vouch for him. I don't know that much about him."

Kendra made a face. "And you believe that bullshit story he gave for *why* they were here last night?"

I shrugged, "I don't know, weirder things have happened."

"I don't trust him. I mean he's obviously playing some sort of game. I hate to see you fall for it."

I sighed and put my head in my hands. "I know, but he makes it so easy to forgive him."

"Don't fall for it." Kendra warned. "He sounds like a fuck boy, you deserve better."

I was about to say something, but my phone started ringing, I groaned.

"That him?" She asked taking a sip of her coffee. I nodded. "Oh, answer it! Put it on speaker, I wanna hear."

I snorted and answered the phone, putting on speaker. "Hey Griffin." I answered.

"Hey Mel!" He said cheerfully, "How are you? I hope you're not too hung over."

Kendra rolled her eyes. I covered my mouth to stifle my laugh, "I feel like shit." I answered truthfully. Kendra started mouthing something and pointing at the phone. I raised an eyebrow at her, and she did it again. I blinked and raised my hand up in the 'what?' gesture. She sighed and raised up her coffee cup and fluttered her eyes while swaying from side to side. "Hey umm, are you still in town?" I asked, finally catching on to what Kendra was doing. "If you want, I'd like to meet up for a coffee."

"Yeah I'm still in town. Just say where and I'll be there." He said over the phone.

I gave him the name of the coffee shop that was just down the street from Kendra's house. We agreed to meet in 20 minutes, and I hung up first. I ran a hand down my face and stood up to get ready.

"Want me to come with you?" Kendra asked from the table.

I shook my head no. "That's ok. I can handle it." I said while brushing out my hair and putting it in a quick bun. I pulled a hoodie to keep warm, "I'll be back in a little bit." I said opening the door.

"Call me if you need me." She called out to me.

"I will." I replied before closing the door and headed out to make the short walk to the coffee shop.

When I got there Griffin was already waiting for me. He got out of his car and smiled warmly at me. "Hey Melanie! It's so good to see you!" He said.

"Hey Griffin." My voice coming out in a fake cheery way.

His smile fell, "Are you ok?" He reached out to touch me, but I stepped around him and went to walk in to the shop.

Over my shoulder I said, "Yeah, I'm fine. Come on I need some coffee."

Griffin ordered his food, and I tried to order mine separately, but he wasn't having it, and I didn't want to waist the effort in arguing over $8. The order didn't take long and once we had our food and coffee we took it outside for some privacy. It wasn't too cold outside and sitting in the brisk morning air with a hot coffee was oddly relaxing.

"What's wrong?" Griffin asked after a while of sitting in silence.

"This isn't easy to ask but I wanted to see your reaction in person, instead of asking over the phone."

Griffin took a drink of his coffee then smiled at me, "Mel, you can ask me anything."

I looked down and picked at the cheese Danish I had ordered; he was being really sweet and here I was about to accuse him of something awful. "What happened last night?" I asked looking up at him.

"We had too much drink," he said with a shrug, "trust me, I'm pretty hung over too." He joked about not spending another Halloween with Alex again.

I smiled weakly, but it quickly dropped. I shoved a small bite in to my mouth for something to do before I asked, "did you see anyone put anything in my drink?" I asked. If someone did spike my drink I would rather it have been a complete stranger over someone who claimed he cared for me, or his friend. Actually, I would just prefer not getting drugged in the first place, maybe it was just too much alcohol.

Griffin shook his head, "No I didn't. I wouldn't let something like that happen to you while you're around me." He reached out and took my hand, "Melanie, you're safe with me."

I took a deep breath and subconsciously squeezed his hand and explained why I was asking about last night.

Griffin took another bite of his sandwich and after a drink he said, "you're sister doesn't like me does she." I shook my head 'no' and swirled my coffee. "Mel look at me." Griffin said softly. I looked up at him, and he leaned forward, not breaking eye contact, "I didn't drug you. I would never do anything to hurt you."

I almost laughed, "No she doesn't like you." I took another bite out of my Danish. "I'm sorry Griffin, this is all just too weird. Did you follow me here?" I asked.

Griffin sat back in his seat. He looked offended as he told me how he was on his way back from Canada. "Where is all of this coming from?" He asked, a confused look was plastered on his face. He got up and sat back down in the seat next to me.

I turned to face him, "I don't know, this morning Kendra was telling me what happened last night, and she saw-"

"Mel." Griffin cut me off and laid his hand of my thigh. He leaned in so close I could feel his breath on my face. "Do you believe I would ever do that to you?" He asked.

His gaze was so intense. I searched his eyes but found nothing sinister. I was so confused I didn't know what to do. I rested my forehead against his and Griffin pulled me in for a tight hug. I took in a deep breath, "I want to believe you, but a lot of what she was saying makes sense."

Griffin started rubbing my back and told me how we did a lot of shots and that can fuck you up. Convincing me that it was just a nasty hangover he lifted my chin; so that I was facing him. Looking me in the eyes he said, "Mel, I care about you way too much to put you in a situation where you don't have full control." He pulled me in for another hug, "I'm sorry your sister is trying to put these thoughts in your head. I'm not a bad guy, Mel. You can trust me."

I really wanted to believe him. I made myself nod. "I'm sorry Griff." I pulled back and kissed him. And then I apologized and kissed him again.

Griffin smiled into the kiss and told me it was ok and kissed me back. "Let me drive you back?" He offered.

I took him up on it and followed him back to his car. I gave him directions, and he was soon pulling up to Kendra's house. I got out and waved at him before going inside.

Kendra was already at the door asking me how it went and what he said. I shrugged my shoulders, "He just kept saying that it was too much drink." I rubbed my temples. "Can I steal some Tylenol from you: this headache won't go away."

"Yeah sure." I followed Kendra to the kitchen where she tossed a small bottle at me. While I was getting a drink she grilled me for more details. I gave her a quick rundown of the conversation I had with Griffin. "Yeah he's full of shit. You're not falling for it, are you?" She scolded.

I swallowed the pills and took a couple drinks of water. "Not really. Too much isn't adding up and I'm tired of it."

Kendra nodded, "Good for you. Keep your head up you got this."

I put my cup in the sink and shook my head, "why do guys have to suck?"

She laughed at me. "To give us something to talk about and look out for I guess." Then she got serious, "when are you heading out?" She asked.

My shoulders dropped. "I should get going soon. I don't want to get home too late." I ended up hanging around for another hour before packing up the car and making the long drive back home.

Griffin tried calling and texting a few times while I was driving but I didn't want to deal with that, so I waited until I was pulling up to my apartment building. I put my car in park and debating calling him back but decided against it. I grabbed my bag and walked inside. While I was unlocking the door to my apartment my phone starting going off. I almost let it go to voicemail but answered it at the last minute. "Hey Griffin." I answered.

"Hey Mel. I haven't heard from you and wanted to see if you were ok."

"Umm yeah, I'm ok." I said hanging my keys up. "I'm just getting home and I'm really tired." I said, hoping he would hang up after hearing that.

No such luck. "I've been home for a while now." He went on to say how good it is to be in his own bed then how he was lucky to have Alex for company on the ride.

"It was pretty boring; all I want is a hot shower and a long sleep." I said. Griffin asked if I wanted company. I laughed, "maybe tomorrow. For now, I just want to relax. It was nice seeing you at the bar." It was, I could have done without the drama that followed but I liked dancing with him.

"It was nice." He agreed, "I just wish we had more time together."

I grimaced, "Kendra can be protective. But she's my sister and she means well."

"Yeah you're real lucky to have someone to watch over you." He said. "Are you sure I can't come over? Seeing you would make my night."

"No, I just want to go to bed, I'm not really in the mood for company." I said,

"Oh, come on, what else do you have going on? I'll be there in 30 minutes" He said and hung up before I could say anything else.

Griffin (November 1st 10 AM)

I woke up around 10 the next morning. I had an hour until check out. I got a quick shower and called you while I dried off. I was expecting to get your voicemail, but my heart skipped a beat when you answered. "Hey Griffin." You sounded off.

"Hey Mel. How are you? I hope you're not too hung over."

"I feel like shit." The phone went quiet for a moment, I was about to ask if you were still there when you started to speak again. "Hey umm, are you still in town? If you want, I'd like to meet up for a coffee."

I punched the air in victory, "Yeah! I'm still in town. Just say where and I'll be there."

"Perfect. There's a coffee shop called 'Cold Brew;' can we meet there in 20 minutes?"

I'd meet you there now if you'd ask. I put the coffee shop into gps and saw that it was only 5 minutes away. I didn't want to wait 15 minutes to see you again. "Yeah 20 minutes sounds great. I'll see you then Mel."

After you hung up I finished getting ready and gathered my things to leave. Once in the car I sent Alex a message saying that I was meeting you for coffee and I'll get ahold of him when we were done.

I got to the coffee shop with 5 minutes to spare. I was sitting in my car waiting for you to pull up and a few minutes later I seen you walking up on the sidewalk. I got out of my car to greet you. "Hey Melanie! It's so good to see you!"

You smiled at me awkwardly, "Hey Griffin."

My face dropped; we were back to my full name? What happened with 'Griff'? "Are you ok?" I went to put my hand on your shoulder, but you walked around me to go in the coffee shop. *Fuck, this isn't starting out well.* I thought.

You looked over your shoulder at me. "Yeah I'm fine. Come on I need some coffee."

I got a black coffee and a breakfast sandwich, and I got you a medium hazelnut coffee with a cheese Danish. You tried paying for yourself, but I wasn't having it.

We took our order and sat outside were no one else was sitting. It was a little chilly, but it wasn't too bad. You look troubled. I took a bite of my sandwich and asked what was wrong.

"This isn't easy to ask but I wanted to see your reaction in person, instead of asking over the phone."

My blood ran cold. I didn't like this. Picking up my coffee so I could get ready myself, I took a slow drink. I smiled warmly at you and said, "Mel, you can ask me anything."

You looked down and picked at the Danish sitting in front of you. I swallowed the lump in my throat and waited for you to ask your question, "What happened last night?" You looked up at me with doubts written all over your face. I know you knew what happened, but would I be able to convince you otherwise?

"We had too much to drink." I shrugged, "Trust me, I'm pretty hung over too. That's the last time I let Alex talk me into going to the bar on Halloween night." I laughed.

You didn't seem amused. You picked up your Danish and took a small bite. I watched you carefully as you then asked, "Did you see anyone put anything in my drink?"

You looked up at me, I kept my breathing slow, "No I didn't. I wouldn't let something like that happen to you while you're around me." I reached out and took your hand in mine. "Melanie, you're safe with me."

You took a deep breath and squeezed my hand, "Kendra swears my drink was spiked last night. A lot of it is a blur and I can't remember a time that someone could have slipped something in my cup. I'm not blaming you, and I'm sure you wouldn't bring me around people that would do that to me, but-" you trailed off and took a drink of your coffee.

I froze. Slipping my hand out of yours so I could take another bite of my sandwich. Washing it down with coffee I chuckled. "You're sister doesn't like me does she? Mel look at me." When I had your attention I looked in your eyes and said, "I didn't drug you. I would never do anything to you to hurt you." I didn't like this at all. I need to do something about this.

"No, she doesn't like you." You said bluntly. You looked down and took another bite of your Danish. "I'm sorry Griffin, this is all just too weird. Did you follow me here?"

I leaned back in my seat. "What? No. Mel I told you I was on my way back from Canada. Where is all of this coming from?" I got up to sit next to you instead of in front of you.

You turned to look at me. "I don't know, this morning Kendra was telling me what happened last night and what she saw-"

"Mel." I cut you off. I didn't want you to take anything that your sister was saying to heart. I put my hand gently on your thigh and leaned in, our foreheads almost touching. "Do you believe I would ever do that to you?"

You were searching my face for something to tell you otherwise. But I kept a calm façade and kept my breathing level, then you finally cracked and rested your forehead against mine. I wrapped my arms around you and pulled you all the way in for a hug, I felt you take a deep shaky breath, "I want to believe that. I really like you, but a lot of what she was saying makes sense."

I rubbed your back; worried that my racing heartbeat would give me away. "We were doing a lot of shots. That will fuck you up quick."

As much as it killed me I pushed you away and held you at arm's length to look in your eyes. "It's a nasty hangover from a night of heavy drinking." I cupped your chin and looked into your eyes, "Mel, I care about you way too much to put you in a situation where you don't have full control," I pulled you in and hugged you tight. "I'm sorry your sister is trying to put these thoughts in your head. I'm not a bad guy, Mel. You can trust me."

I felt you nodding your head, and I almost laughed. I couldn't believe that worked. "I'm sorry Griff." You pulled back slightly and kissed me. "I'm sorry." You said and kissed me again.

I smiled in the kiss and pulled away to say it's ok and kissed you back. "Let me drive you back?" I wanted to know where your sister lived.

You nodded and followed me back to my car and following your directions I dropped you back off at your sisters house. I watched you as you walked away, when you got to the door, you turned around and waved at me before going inside.

I gripped the steering wheel and went to get Alex. "What happened to you last night?" He asked when he got in.

"Nothing, I just went back to the hotel. But she did ask me for coffee this morning." I started laughing. "Apparently her sister is trying to convince her that I'm trouble. I think I was able to sway her back in my favor, but the sister might be a problem." I tapped the steering wheel thinking. "Where did you end up?"

Alex told me about his night with the bitch from Tinder. She had a dog that kept barking from the kennel so she had to put it in the bathroom, but he could still hear it. Then her boyfriend came home early, and he had to sneak out the bedroom window. He spent the morning at the truck stop drinking coffee and waiting for his phone to charge.

The ride home felt longer than it actually was. We got back an hour before schedule and dad was actually impressed. He gave us our cut plus and extra 10%.

When I got home I called you, but you didn't answer. I sent you a text asking you to call me when you got this. I waited a few hours, but I still heard nothing. So, I tried calling you again one last time. I was about to hang up when you answered. "Hey Griffin."

I love hearing you say my name. "Hey Mel. I haven't heard from you and wanted to see if you were ok."

"Umm yeah I'm ok." I heard keys jingling in the background. "I'm just getting home and I'm really tired."

"I've been home for a while now. It's good to be in my own bed ya know. Man, that drive is insane right? I can only imagine what it was like for you, at least I had Alex to keep me company."

"Yeah it was pretty boring." I tried to pictured what you were doing. "All I want is a hot shower and a long sleep."

I licked my lips picturing you in the shower. "Do you want company?" I asked ready to walk out the door shirtless and no shoes.

You laughed, "Maybe tomorrow. For now, I just want to relax. It was nice seeing you at the bar." I could the hear the smile in your voice.

I went back to that night. Trying not to think of how close I was to having you all for myself, I thought of dancing with you instead, the way we moved together. I agreed. "It was nice. I just wish we had more time together." I hated how you were snatched away from me like that.

You sighed. "Kendra can be protective. But she's my sister and she means well."

I said something about how you're lucky to have someone to watch over you, and then I turned the conversation back to us. "Are you sure I can't come over? Seeing you would make my night." You turned me down again, "Oh come on, what else do you have going on. I'll be there in 30 minutes." I hung up before you could you turn me down again.

I raced to get presentable. I threw on some deodorant and sprayed on some cologne. I fixed my hair and grabbed a couple joints I had rolled when I got home and locked up before I got in the car and raced to your apartment.

Melanie (November 1st 11 PM)

I was in the bathroom when I heard knocking on the door. I was annoyed that Griffin just invited himself over. I was washing my hands when I heard knocking again, a little louder this time. I dried my hands and checked my reflection. If he was going to rush over here uninvited he could stand in the hallway until I feel like answering. Another knock on the door, more urgent this time.

I took my time walking to the door. I looked through the peep hole and seen Griffin looking around the hallway. I opened the door, and he turned his attention to me and grinned. "Hey Mel." He said.

"Hi." I pushed some hair behind my ear. "What are you doing here Griffin?" I asked impatiently.

Griffin licked his lips, "I'm here because I wanted to see you." He held up some bags from the Chinese restaurant that's open late. "I got us some dinner. I was hungry when I got home, so I can only imagine how you're feeling."

I looked at the bags in his hands, I could smell the teriyaki chicken, and my stomach started to growl. I rolled my eyes and stepped to the side to let him in. I went the kitchen and got us some utensils and plates. "Do want anything to drink? I have tea and water." I looked over my shoulder, and from here I could see him pulling out food containers and sitting them on the coffee table. He agreed to some tea, and I got down two glasses and filled them up and sat down next to Griffin on the sofa. Looking at the food made my stomach growl again, "This looks really good, thank you Griffin." I scooped out some rice and put it on my plate.

Griffin furrowed his eyebrows then took a drink of tea. Sitting the glass down he looked at me and grinned. "Yeah well any excuse to have dinner with a beautiful woman." We talked about random things while we ate.

When we were done eating, I gathered up the trash "Thank you Griffin, I really appreciate you bringing me food."

Griffin got up and took the trash to the kitchen for me. I picked up the dishes and followed him to the kitchen. Griffin leaned against the counter and smirked at me. "I wanted to make sure you ate today." He said with a shrug then gave me that lopsided grin.

I sighed feeling myself giving into him, again. "It's getting kind of late," I said. "If you want you can stay here for the night."

"I was hoping you'd ask." He said pushing himself off the counter and walking towards me. "I'm exhausted, let's go to bed." Throwing his arm around me, we went to the bedroom. Griffin took his shirt and jeans off and sat them on top of his shoes and socks. I changed into a loose shirt and pajama shorts. "Come here." Griffin said, I turned around, and he was already lying down in bed.

I crawled into bed and pressed my back to him; he wrapped his arm tightly around me and pulled me closer into him.

—◦◦◦—

I woke up a few times through the night, I got up to go to the bathroom and when I got back Griffin was awake waiting for me to come back. When I laid down he asked where I went. "I had to pee." I answered putting my head on the pillow. Griffin looked down at me, I couldn't make out his expression, "Griff, you ok?" I asked sitting up.

He shook his head slightly and pulled me in to kiss my forehead, then he kissed me and pulled me on top of him, "Kiss me." He whispered, so I did.

Griffin moved some hair of my face and pulled me into him.

"What's wrong?" He asked.

There was a lot of things that were wrong. But finding the words to explain why I feel this way was beyond me. So, I just shook my head and looked away from him.

He kissed me on the lips and then laid back down, pulling me with him. "I'm not ready to wake up," he nuzzled the top of my head and started singing, "Coming back to you, my baby, coming back to you," it was the song he liked singing to me during times like this. When it's just us wrapped up in each other.

A tickle in the back of my mind brought me back to the night when I lost the remote, I squeezed my eyes shut and pushed the thought away. It was just a crazy coincidence, that song must have been the last one to play on the music app so when the remote was jammed behind the tv it was the song to play when the music opened?

Griffin started playing with my hair while he sang, lulling me back to sleep, his deep voice vibrating through me, it wasn't long before my eye lids started to get heavy and I fell fast asleep.

Griffin (November 1st 11 PM)

On the way to your apartment, I stopped at a small Chinese restaurant and picked up some food for us. I'm not sure if you were hungry but we could have the left overs for lunch tomorrow. When I got to your building I scanned the parking lot. It was dark, and nothing seemed out of place. I dropped the cigarette I was smoking on the ground and stomped it out before I grabbed the food and walked inside.

I ran my hands through my hair and tugged at my clothes before knocking on your door. I waited a few minutes, checking out the decoration you had on the door. The bottom moon was flipped over so I flipped it like I've seen you do every time you leave. I looked to my left, down the hallway and then back at your door, irritated that you haven't answered yet. I took a deep breath and knocked again, louder this time. Maybe you didn't hear me the first time.

I glared at the door wondering what was taking you so long to get to the door. I knocked again louder and longer and took a step back. I looked down the hallway, at the door that lead outside and thought about looking in your windows to see if you had someone over. But then the door opened.

I looked over at you and grinned, "Hey Mel."

"Hi," you said flatly and pushed some hair out of your face, "what are you doing here Griffin?" You asked.

I had to bite my lip from snapping at you, I don't know why you're acting like such a bitch right now, but I can turn it around. "I'm here because I wanted to see you." I held up the bags saying how I was hungry and thought you might be too.

Your eye roll didn't go unnoticed, but you let me in anyway. While you went to the kitchen to get plates I sat the food out on the coffee table. You asked me if I wanted anything to drink, offering me tea and water. I knew I should have brought some beer with me. I asked for some tea and sat down to wait on you. From here I had a good view as you stretched to get two cups from the cabinet above the counter.

Not much longer you came over with the drinks, plates, and silverware. If we were at a restaurant I would have to speak to your manager about your attitude.

341

At least you had the decency to take the time to thank me for the food before you started filling your plate.

I had to take a drink before responding so I didn't say anything to ruin this. I told you that I would use any excuse to have dinner with a beautiful woman. We talked about random things while we ate, and when we were done you thanked me for the food again. This time your tone was actually appreciative.

You had already gathered the trash and put it into a pile, so I got up and took it to the kitchen for you. You followed me with the glasses and forks. I leaned against the counter and smirked at you, "I wanted to make sure you ate today." I shrugged and gave you a look that I knew you found irresistible.

And just like that the ice wall melted, and you were inviting me to stay the night.

I pushed off the counter and walked towards you, "I was hoping you'd ask." I put my arm around your shoulders and lead us to the bedroom. "I'm exhausted. Let's go to bed."

I took my time getting undressed, watching you move around the room was more of a priority. I got in bed and memorized the way you slid your shorts over your hips.

I waited until you had your shirt on before calling you to bed. It was so surreal having you crawl into bed and press your ass against me. If I wasn't so tired I would take full advantage of this moment. Instead, I wrapped my arm around you and pulled you in closer.

I'm not sure how long I've been asleep or even when I fell asleep. But when I woke up you were gone. I sat up and looked around the room, waiting for you to come back. When you finally came back to bed I asked where you went.

You said something about going to the bathroom and laid down. I looked down at you, "Griff, are you ok?" You asked sitting up.

I grabbed the front of your shirt and pulled you in to kiss your forehead, I kissed your lips and pulled you on top of me. "Kiss me," I whispered.

You did but it was so, hardly more than a brush of your lips of mine.

I moved some hair out of your face and asked you what was wrong. Your eyes flicked downwards.

I brought my lips to yours and pulled you down with me as I laid back down. I was still tired, and I wanted to get more sleep before I had to get back to my normal schedule. "I'm not ready to wake up," I said burying my nose in your hair and inhaling your scent. I started singing a song that often remind me of you. "Coming back to you, my baby, coming back to you."

I started playing with your hair as I sang to you. I loved your hair; it was so soft and slid through my fingers like silk. I would do anything to keep you by my side. I don't care what happens; you are mine.

I played with your hair and sang our song until you fell asleep. Then I nuzzled up to you and let myself drift off as well.

MELANIE (November 11)

I was setting up the coffee pot, I should have checked to make sure there were coffee grounds before I filled up the water and got a filter out. When I pulled the container of coffee down and opened the lid, there wasn't even enough grounds at the bottom to make a full cup. I tossed the mostly empty container away and slipped my shoes on to walk down to the gas station to get a cup of cappuccino. I had nothing else to do today, I was heading back to my hometown for the weekend but that isn't until tomorrow and I was already packed so a quick walk down to the gas station was no big deal. I know I had just visited during Halloween; but with the seasons changing I wasn't sure when the next time I would be able to visit.

Making sure I had everything before I locked my door and headed down the hallway to go outside. When I pushed the glass door open, the wind picked up my hair and blew it in my eyes, blinding me for a moment. I tucked some strands of hair behind my ear and pulled the hood of my jacket over my head to block the wind.

At this time of day, the building was usually empty except for 3 or 4 people, me included. So, when I saw a red car parked in the buildings parking lot I did a double take. I could tell the car was still running from the fumes coming out of the exhaust pipe, but it was parked too far away for me to make out the driver. Griffin and his friends haven't stopped warning me about Tyler, they say he wasn't the type who'd make good company. They told me the make and model of his car; but I had no idea what they were talking about, only that it was a red car.

I brushed it off thinking maybe the car could be someone visiting one of my neighbors and continued on my way to get my gas station coffee. The walk was short but cold, the wind was brisk and bit into my cheeks. I would need to get a scarf soon if I wanted to keep my face warm during these coffee runs.

On the way back it was nice having the hot coffee cradled in my hands to warm me up, every drink was like a warm hug going down. But my blood ran cold when my building came into view, and I saw a strange man pacing in front of the building smoking a cigarette. I slowed down and pulled my phone out to call Griffin. From here he looked like that guy Tyler. But I still wasn't sure.

My thumb hovered over the call button, but I hesitated. Rolling my eyes I figured I was being overly paranoid. But just in case, I kept my phone out and walked to my car. It wasn't parked too far away; and if it did happen to be that Tyler guy I was warned about, I didn't want to enter the building and risk him following me inside. So instead, I was going to go get some breakfast and if he was still here when I got back I'd deal with it then.

The car was about 20 feet away when I heard a man call out behind me. "Hey, wait up!" I looked over my shoulder, no surprise that guy was heading towards me with a cocky smirk on his face. He took a few more drags off his cigarette as he walked over and flicked it to the side when he got closer. "I'm uh, wondering if you could do me a huge favor?" He clapped his hands together and pointed at me. "I've been stuck out here for a while, my buddy is leaving me hanging and I really gotta go, ya know?" he winked at me and gave an awkward chuckle, "I was hoping you could let me in so I could use your bathroom?" He brought his shoulders up and smiled sheepishly at me.

I looked at my phone, Griffins call log was still open. "I'm really sorry, I wish I could help you but I'm running late as it is." I pushed call and brought my phone up to my ear.

It rang twice and Griffin picked up the same time Tyler was calling my bluff. "If you're so busy then why did you decide you have time to get your little coffee? But when it comes to helping someone other than yourself, you're all of a sudden in a hurry to leave? Who ya calling?"

Over the phone Griffin starting yelling, "Who is that? Mel, what's going on?" He sounded agitated.

To Griffin I said, "I don't know, he was in the parking lot when I came back from the gas station." To the guy I said, "I'm really sorry but I have to go." Pivoting I hurried to my car.

Over the phone Griffin started to scold me, "Why are you apologizing? Mel, where are you?"

I opened the driver door and slid inside, making sure to lock the doors. Tyler was still trying to get my attention, but I just kept shrugging and saying that I have to go. I put the keys in the ignition and started the car. There was a knock on the window making me jump "Hey come on, I'm sorry I scared you, how about I make it up to ya, huh? Let me buy you a drink, yeah?" He said pulling on the handle trying to open the door.

I shook my head and yelled out another lame apology and then he slammed his palm on the window. I don't know when my phone connected the call over to the Bluetooth, but Griffins voice made me jump too, thinking someone was in the car with me, "What is going on?" He asked.

"I'm in the car now, I'm just about to leave." I said putting the car in reverse and started to slowly back up.

Tyler slammed his fists on the hood of the car as I was backing up, "Fucking bitch! I just need the bathroom!" He yelled throwing his middle finger up at me.

"Fucking psycho." I muttered.

"Melanie, please tell me you're ok." Griffin said over the speakers.

My head was spinning, my heart was pounding, I wasn't sure what to make of all of that, but it was unsettling to say the least, "I'm not 100% sure but I think that was that guy Tyler," I told Griffin about how I seen the red car on my way out to get coffee and when I came home he was standing by the door smoking.

"What'd he say to you?" He asked, I told him how he wanted to use my bathroom, "what are you doing now?" I told him that I was going to get some breakfast. "Why don't you come over here for a while. Just in case he's following you." He said.

I agreed and hung up. The drive there was uneventful, and I wasn't surprised to see that Levi's truck was in the driveway. I parked the car and got out. I walked up to the front door and knocked a few times. I didn't have to wait long before Levi opened the door and leaned against the frame.

He nodded and grinned down at me. "Hey, this is a nice surprise."

I smiled awkwardly, "Where's Griffin?" I asked and walked inside when Levi moved to let me in.

He sighed and threw an arm around my shoulders. "Always about Griffin with you. Yeah he's in the back, I'll walk you there." His words were a little slurred. "I like this color on you," He said, tugging on the sleeve on my shirt.

I furrowed my eyebrows. "It's just a white shirt."

Levi kind of shrugged his shoulders, pulling me in a little, "It still looks good on you." He said as we walked through the door that separated the backroom from the rest of the house. I shook my head and laughed.

Griffin and Alex were playing a street fighter game, Alex ignored us as we walked in; but Griffin did a double take causing him to lose the fight. Alex punched the air with his right hand, "Fuck yeah! I'm still the king bitches!" He gloated.

Griffin tossed his controller down, "Whatever man, it's just a game." He growled, eyeballing Levi's arm that was still around me. Griffin walked up and pulled me from under Levi's arm and into a tight hug, "How was the drive, did you see anyone following you?" He asked. His breath smelled like he's been drinking.

I shook my head returning the hug, "Not that I noticed."

I felt Griffin nodding, then he put his hands on my shoulders and leaned back so he could look down at me, "Tyler is a fucking rat. I'll take care of it for you." He said brushing some hair behind my ear.

I didn't know what he meant by 'take care of' but the atmosphere in the room got really heavy. Alex was the first to break the silence. "Hey Mel, you wanna play?"

I looked around Griffin, Alex was holding up a controller. I smiled nervously, "I'm not very good at those games."

Griffin laughed, "Nonsense, you just push a bunch of buttons," he led me over to the game chairs.

Levi came up from behind me and leaned on the back of the chair I was sitting in. "There's more to it than that," he said as the character screen pulled up. "There's 4 different types of fighters, I like to wait to see what fighter my opponent picks before I choose mine."

I turned slightly in the chair so I was facing Griffin, he was half glaring at Levi who was still going on about the style of fighters and which one I should choose. I laughed to myself and pulled my focus back to the tv screen. Levi slapped my shoulder excitedly and told me I should select the fighter in the top row second from the right, I picked the fighter on the third row in the middle. I shifted in the seat to sit on the edge; mostly to get him to stop touching me without seeming like a bitch.

The fight only lasted 5 seconds, Alex completely destroyed me. I laughed and handed the controller to Levi who was shaking his head trying to hold in his own laughter. Taking the controller from me, he said, "you might have won if you took my advice."

I shrugged and got up to sit by Griffin who immediately put his arm around me to me pull in, "Have you ate?" I asked him. I was getting hungry.

Griffin shook his head, "Are you hungry? We could go and get something if you want." I nodded and he stood up holding out a hand to help me up. "We're going to go get food, want anything?" The guys called out their order, but I don't think he was listening. Griffin was staring at my mouth biting his lip. I smirked as he told them to text it to him.

In the car Griffin took his time scrolling through his playlist. I looked over at Levi's truck. "Levi is really friendly," I stated pulling my seatbelt over my shoulder and clicking it in place.

Griffin kind of shrugged and replied, "He's a friendly guy." I furrowed my brow and faced the window. It seems weird to me how he just brushes things off that should be a concern, maybe I'm just making too much of it.

I nodded, "Yeah he doesn't come across as a bad guy." Griffin kind of chuckled in response. "Where are we going?" I asked as he put the car in reverse. We started heading to a part of town that I haven't been to yet.

"There's a diner that serves breakfast over this way. I think you'll like it. We'll put in the order to go and take it back to my place." We pulled up to a shabby diner that looked like it hadn't been updated since the 60's. Griffin got out and got my door for me. "The biscuits and gravy's the best thing on the menu. It's all pretty good but stay clear of anything that needs lettuce." He said as we made our way to the front door of the diner.

The little bell above the door chimed as we entered, the interior matched the exterior down to the water-stained drop tile ceiling. There was a group of older gentlemen drinking coffee at the back table, a young mother and her two children were getting up to leave and there was an elderly couple sitting at a table in the middle of the room who looked like they were halfway done with their meal. The waitress was a middle-aged woman in a pink dress, she didn't wear a nametag and greeted us with a cold, "I'll get to you in a minute."

I followed Griffin over to the counter where we sat down and waited for the waitress to finish tending to the coffee pot. Griffin handed a menu to me so I could choose what I wanted to eat. There wasn't a lot of choices, they had the basic menu of pretty much every diner out there. When the waitress finally got around to taking our order my stomach was ready to eat itself. I settled on a bacon egg and cheese breakfast sandwich on a croissant. Griffin ordered the biscuits and gravy and read off the order from Alex and Levi.

Our food took longer to order than it did to cook. On the way out to the car I asked Griffin is the waitress was always like that. I was surprised to find out that she was actually in a good mood, I was even more surprised when he told me that she owned the diner. It still doesn't explain the way she treats her customers. I shrugged it off and got in when Griffin opened the car door for me, he handed me the bag of food before he closed the door.

It wasn't long before we were back at Griffins sitting in the back room eating breakfast with his friends. It was pretty fun, Alex and Levi made for good company. The way the guys fed off each other had my sides hurting from laughter. I'm not sure if it was my imagination but I thought I kept seeing Griffin casting glares in my direction, not all the time mainly when I laughed at something stupid that Levi had said. When I was done with my food, I got up to throw my trash away and offered to take Griffins trash as well.

I heard footsteps come up behind me, I expected Griffin, but Alex was there instead. "I didn't mean to scare you." he said stepping around me to throw his Styrofoam container away. "How long have you lived here?" he asked crossing his arms and leaning against the counter.

I shrugged. "Almost a year I guess."

He nodded. "That's cool. How are you liking it?"

I smiled and kind of shook my head, "Well enough I suppose."

Alex smirked and tilted his head, "Yeah, I get that." I raised an eyebrow as he eyed me up and down. "So how long has Tyler been bothering you?"

I shrugged, "I never really talked to the guy before now, I've only seen him from a distance and from the picture Griffin showed me a while ago." Alex nodded and pulled his phone out. He tapped on the screen a few times and held his phone out for me to see. On the screen was a picture of the guy from the parking lot. It was a candid photo of him yelling and pointing a lit cigarette at someone who was almost out of shot. I nodded, "yeah that was the guy in the parking lot this morning."

Alex put his phone back in his pocket. Nodding he said, "I know we keep saying this but he's not the kind of guy to let your guard down around." He scratched the back of his neck, "a few years back there was a 16-year-old that went missing. Her body was found in a trunk of a car that had been abandoned. Turns out that the car was one of Tylers, but there wasn't enough evidence to tie him to the crime, so he was let go." He looked down at me, "He has a long list of fucked up shit he's gotten away with."

Levi walked into the kitchen to throw his trash away and leaned against the counter next to Alex, shoving his hands in his pockets. He grinned at me. "Don't worry Mel. We'll protect you."

I laughed, "My hero." I said sarcastically and turned around and went to the back room. I heard Levi mumble something to Alex and they both laughed. I rolled my eyes and went over to sit next to Griffin.

A few hours later Alex got a call from his girlfriend. She wanted him to pick up some things from the store and since he showed up with Levi, Levi had to go too. He didn't want to leave at first offering Alex his keys instead, but Levi's truck is a stick shift, and Alex doesn't know how to drive a stick. Grumbling Levi left with Alex. The guys did their fist-bump on their way out, Alex pulled me into a hug before he walked out, and Levi did the same.

Griffin shrugged at me, "What do you want to do?" He asked when the guys cleared out.

"We could watch a movie?" I asked. That's how we spent the rest of the afternoon, cuddling on the sofa in the front room, watching random movies and enjoying each other's company with no distractions.

It was starting to get dark, so I got ready to leave. "Are you sure you don't want to stay?" Griffin asked pulling his shoes on so he could follow me home. He wanted to make sure that Tyler wasn't hanging around still.

I smiled, "I'm sure. I have to be up early tomorrow; I'm heading back home for a weekend visit, and I want to head out as soon as possible."

Griffin stood up and grabbed his phone off the coffee table. "Oh yeah I forgot about that." He said gruffly. We walked out the door together and I waited as he locked up. Griffin opened the car door for me and kissed me before I sat down. "I'll be right behind you." He said before closing the door and heading over to his car.

I thought him following me home was a little overkill, but it was sweet that he wanted to make sure I was safe. I waited until I seen his car turn on before I pulled out of the driveway and headed back to my apartment building.

—m—

When I pulled into the parking lot it was fairly empty save for the normal 4 cars that were always parked there at this time. I pulled into my usual spot and Griffin pulled up and parked next to me. I got out and walked over to his car, he rolled down the window, and I leaned in through it to kiss him. "Thank you for following me home," I said with a big smile.

Griffin smirked, "I'd follow you home any day," then he added, "text me before you leave in the morning." I kissed him again and told him I would. Griffin turned the car off. "I'm going to walk you inside. I don't like how that front door doesn't lock; he could be waiting in there."

I rolled my eyes, "Oh, I'm sure." I stepped back so Griffin could get out and walk me in. "I appreciate this, Griffin." I said, linking arms with him and letting him lead me into the building.

Griffin was scanning the parking lot, "you can't be too sure." He said letting me go to open the door for me. When we got to my door, Griffin pulled me in for one more kiss. "Have a good night, Melanie." He said when I unlocked my door and opened it.

"You too Griffin." I said.

"Make sure you lock this when I leave," he told me knocking his middle finger on the door to my apartment. I told him I would, and we kissed one last time before he left.

I locked the deadbolt, the lock on the doorknob, and after sliding the chain into place I went to the kitchen to pour a glass of water. I picked up the book I was reading and went to get ready to lay down in bed to read until I fell asleep. I sat the book down on the bed and put the glass of water on my nightstand. Flipping the lamp on I went over to the closet and changed into a pair of green plaid pajama shorts and baggy Tool band t-shirt. I closed the door and turned the bedroom light off and slid into bed, getting comfortable. I read a few chapters and when I couldn't hold my eyes open anymore, I sat the book down, turned the lamp off and went to sleep.

—⊷—

I was having trouble sleeping, I thought I kept hearing a knock coming from the living room, but my upstairs neighbors are heavy footed, and they seem to be night owls. So, I brushed it off as people walking around upstairs and tried to go back to sleep. But I just kept tossing and turning, eventually I gave up and just laid there glaring at the ceiling. This isn't the first night loud noises kept me up, I made a mental note to pick up some earplugs next time I was at the store.

Out of the dark I heard a deliberate tap, tap, tap, on the window. I turned my head and stared at the closed curtains. *Was I hearing things?* I wondered. Then I heard it again a little louder this time. I sat up in bed debating on what to do. I looked around and picked up the first thing I thought would make a suitable weapon, not sure how much damage a hairbrush will do but I'm about to find out.

I had no idea what time it was, but even if it was in the middle of the day *nobody* should be knocking on your bedroom window. I took a deep breath to prepare myself for the worst.

I slid out of bed, firmly holding the hairbrush in my hand. Putting one foot in front of the other, I reached out and pulled the curtain back. The first thing I seen was the outline of a man, I took a step back, still holding the curtain to the side so I didn't lose sight of the figure standing outside of my bedroom and shouted some stupid threat at him to make him leave. I should have grabbed my phone so I could call the cops, I wanted to turn around and grab it; but I was afraid what would happen if I turned my back.

Then the man pressed his hand against the glass, I felt my soul leave my body, and he stepped closer to the glass. I could just make out Griffins features in the dark. Standing there confused I put the brush down and unlocked the window so I could push it open, "Griffin, what are you doing?!" I asked backing away as he crawled inside.

There was just enough light coming from the wax warmer, too much light for what was about to happen next. His fingers were bloody, and his knuckles were busted. He had blood splattered all over him, there was a wild look in his eyes. "I knocked on your door; but you weren't answering." He swallowed hard and his shoulders dropped. Sighing he reached out and to my horror he pulled me into him, "I'm so glad you're ok. Don't worry about the blood; it isn't mine." He laughed.

I shook my head and tried to push him away. "What?" I asked even more confused.

He tightened his hold around me and said in a cool even tone, "there was a rat, snooping around in your car. So, I took care of him." Sticky blood smeared on my cheek. Horrified, I shoved myself away from him. Griffin smiled down at me and brushed some hair back from my face. "Don't worry," he said softly, "you won't see him around here anymore. I made sure of it." My mind went back to this morning when Griffin called Tyler a rat; and that look he had when he said that he would take care of it for me.

I shook my head again, I brought my hand up and I touched my face, looking down I barely registered my red fingertips. I shook my head and tears started to blur my vision, "What did you do?" I asked. My voice hardly more than a whisper.

Griffin held his hands up and shook his head, his mouth was moving but I couldn't hear what he was saying. A loud ringing in my ears overtook his words. He reached out and put a hand on my shoulder, I looked down at it. The spider tattoo looked like it was spinning a web of blood, he had so much of it splattered up his arm. I looked up at him; I was almost afraid to look past the wolfish grin hovering over me. His smile looked so much bigger than I remember it being. With my heart pounding in my ears, I made myself look into his eyes. They were black and focused. Like a predator he held me under his gaze. My breath caught in my throat; I noticed the small specs of blood across his face.

I forced myself to act normal, swallowing my fear and reminded myself that part of acting normally was breathing. Slowly I took a breath in through my nose and out through my mouth and started to think about what to do.

I looked around the room, my phone was on the nightstand charging, I looked over at the bedroom door that was closed, then over to the window that was slowly sliding shut and at the bloody handprints on the wall. Then back up to Griffin who was talking in a hushed tone, but I couldn't focus on what he was saying. I covered my mouth but then went to wipe my hands off on my pants, but I just slid my sweaty palms across my bare legs. I forgot I was wearing shorts. I didn't know what to do in that moment my mind was racing too fast, and I felt a panic attack coming on. I was definitely not acting normal.

Griffin reached out and put a finger under my chin, "Mel, look at me." I blinked and looked up at him holding my breath. He was calm, how was he so calm? "I need you to get some towels." He said in a soothing tone. "And then we need something to clean up with, do you have any bleach?"

I shook my head and took a step back, running my hands through my hair I turned around, there was a high-pitched ringing in my ears. At first I stood there, covering my mouth, and tugging at the end of my hair. Then I started pacing, I didn't know what to do. My heart was pounding in my ears.

Griffin was talking behind me, I felt him put a hand on my shoulder, but I shrugged it off and made for my phone. I don't know how, but Griffin got to it first. Calmly he unplugged it and looked at the screen as it flashed on, it was a picture of us making silly faces. Griffin swallowed and looked at me, my chest felt heavy, "I think I'll hold on to this for now."

"Please, give back my phone," my voice came out in a hushed tone barely above a whisper.

Griffin flipped my phone around in his hand. Keeping his head down he looked up at me, "Why?"

The look he gave me chilled me to my core. I opened my mouth, but nothing came out.

Griffin shook his head, he looked defeated. Putting my phone in his coat pocket he said, "I thought I could count on you." He readjusted his coat and popped his neck. He took a breath and ran a hand down his face. While his attention seemed to be else where I took a step toward the bedroom door. "Where are you going?" His words were cold and came out almost like a growl.

"Just going to the bathroom." I managed to breathe out.

Griffin materialized beside me and with a tight grip on my upper arm he grinned down at me, "Good, while you're in there grab the towels." He ripped open the door and shoved me out of the bedroom and followed me over to the bathroom. I stepped in and closed the door behind me, but he threw it back open. The door hit the wall with a loud BANG, it bounced off the wall and started to swing shut. Griffin laughed and put a hand out to catch it, "No, no, no sweetheart, the door stays open, or I go in there with you."

I didn't answer, instead I just walked to the toilet and did my business. I looked over at the door, but he was no longer there. I didn't know where Griffin went to, but I knew he didn't go far. I got up, flushed the toilet, and washed my hands. I just caught my reflection in the mirror and jumped out of my skin when I saw Griffin leering over my shoulder. He just stared at me through the reflection, that dark look in his eyes was still there. I turned and stepped around him to grab a stack of towels off the shelf that was above the toilet.

Griffin took the towels from me and said, "Now the bleach." I bent down and opened the cabinet doors under the sink and pulled out a half gallon of bleach. Griffin took the jug and shook it, sighing he said, "It'll have to do." He looked down at me, "I packed you a bag, it's on your bed. Can I trust you to go get it?" I stared up at him and nodded. "Good." He waited for me to walk out of the bathroom before he followed.

When I got to my bedroom I looked behind me, he didn't follow me in here. I looked at my bed, the duffle bag I used for the trips back home was sitting on there. It looked like Griffin dumped out what I already had packed, all the clothes and bathroom supplies I had in it where scattered on the floor.

I walked past it and went to the patio door, but it was locked. "Shit," I mumbled, I thought about unlocking it; but, then what? The door is loud when you open and close it, Griffin would surely hear that and come running. And if I happened to make it to the patio before he could make it to the bedroom, then what? Well, I could try to squeeze my way out between the broken planks that make up the wall; but that would never work. The gap is too small, and my ass is too big.

I went over to the window Griffin had crawled through, doing my best to ignore the red handprints. I grabbed the bottom of the window expecting it to slide up with ease, but it stayed put. My heart plummeted.

My hands were trembling as I fumbled with the locks. I had the left one undone and was trying to get the right one unlocked when I heard footsteps behind me and Griffin growled out, "God dammit!" I caught his reflection in the window as he swung his arm up and brought something heavy down to smack me across the back of the head.

I was able to duck down in time; but as I scrambled to stand up, to dash to the bedroom door, he pounced on top of me, pushing his knee into my back and grabbing me by the hair. He pulled my head back, "I'm sorry about this," he kissed my cheek and slammed my head against the floor. A bright light exploded in my vision and then my world went black.

Griffin (November 11)

I can't remember the last time I went to sleep, but I felt more alive than I ever had in my entire life. I swiped at my nose with the back of my hand and sat up as Alex threw his fist in the air gloating about another win on the game we were all playing. Levi challenged him to yet another round, Levi and I taking turns at getting our asses handed to us. Every once in a while I'll get a win, and Levi won a handful of times, but Alex spends more time with a controller in his hands than we do.

We left a party at Ryans a few hours ago to come back to my place and unwind. I reached over for my cup but ended up knocking it over, good thing it was empty. I stood up and stretched, popping my back and my neck. I looked over at the window confused at when the sun came up. Shrugging it off I went to the kitchen to make another drink. I poured some Coke in my glass but when I went to grab the Rum the bottle was nowhere to be found. With a quick search I spotted the empty bottle in the trashcan. Frustrated I took a drink of the soda immediately spit it out in the sink; it had gone flat. I dumped the rest of the soda down the drain and went to grab a beer, but they were all gone too.

I went back to the back room and shouted, "Which of you fuckers drank the last beer!?" The guys just shrugged and went back to their business. On the coffee table my phone lit up and started vibrating. Your contact info was displayed on the screen. A grin broke out on my face as I picked it up and answered it, but it fell as soon as the call connected.

"-hurry to leave? Who ya calling?" A male voice shouted.

Confused and worried for your well-being my mind started racing. What was going on? "Who is that? Mel, what's going on?"

Levi turned his attention away from the tv causing him to lose the fight.

Over the phone you said, "I don't know, he was in the parking lot when I came back from the gas station," I could tell you were scared, there was a slight tremble in your voice, "I'm really sorry but I have to go."

I ran a hand through my hair, "Why are you apologizing? Mel, where are you?!" I wanted to jump through the phone and pull you away from whatever had you scared.

I had the guys full attention now. Levi was already standing up looking like he was ready to head to a fight, Alex put his controller down and was looking between me and Levi ready for our next move.

There was some commotion over the phone, I furrowed my eyebrows and put my phone on speaker. I sat my phone on the coffee table so we could all hear what was going on. Over the phone we heard a man shouting at you to come back and talk for a while. Then there was the sound of a car door opening and closing then you said. "No, I have to get going. As I said I-" The call was interrupted as you started the car.

Alex sat back in his chair, "Who is that?" He asked, "It's hard to hear him."

Levi shook his head; he looked like he was about to say something when we heard a knocking coming from over the phone. Then a male voice said, "Hey come on, I'm sorry I scared you, how about I make it up to ya, huh? Let me buy you a drink, yeah?" Then it sounded like he was trying to open the door.

My eyes shot up to Levi as it hit me. The accent was a dead giveaway, there was no question about it. Levi nodded his head, coming to the same conclusion I did.

Alex chuckled to himself and sat up, "Say what you want man, Tyler has a set of huge balls to pull something like this."

Levi's head snapped in his direction. "The fuck did you just say? Stand up and say that again."

I ignored them and pulled the phone closer to me, you were tossing another apology at Tyler and then there was a loud thud shutting the guys up. My heart sank as I feared the worst, "What's going on?" I asked.

"I'm in the car now," You said, your words came out all at once, "I'm just about to leave."

Tyler hit your car again, I started counting the seconds until I could get my hands on him. "Fucking bitch! I just need the bathroom!" He yelled. My blood boiled at that.

"Fucking psycho." You muttered.

That made me smile. Knowing you were in your car and driving away from him made me feel better, but I hate how you had to go through that. I can only imagine how scared you must be. "Melanie, please tell me you're ok." I almost begged.

"I'm not 100% sure but I think that was that guy Tyler." You replied, not exactly answering my question but I'll look past that. "I walked down to the gas station to get some coffee, and I saw his red car, I didn't think too much of it at the time. But when I got back he was smoking by the door to the building."

I rubbed my eyes, wondering why you didn't call me sooner. "What did he say to you?" I asked.

"He said he wanted to come in and use the bathroom."

The room stilled. I was relieved that you weren't dumb enough to let him inside your apartment. "What are you doing now?" I asked.

"I was thinking about getting some breakfast now that I'm out driving around. This isn't really how I planned my morning."

"Why don't you come over here for a while. Just in case he's following you." There is no doubt in my mind that Tyler jumped in his car to try to follow you to see where you went. Chances of him coming here are slim to none.

"Yeah, ok. I'll see you in a bit." You said and hung up.

Levi was the first to speak, "What are we going to do about Tyler?"

I shrugged and leaned back in my chair. "Same thing you do with the rest of the vermin you catch in your house."

Alex started shaking his head. "Dude if that was Kara there is no way he would make till the end the week."

"He won't last the day." Levi said. I noticed how he had his keys in his hands. "Did she say how long till she gets here?" He asked.

I shrugged, "Shouldn't be too long, maybe 10 minutes at most."

He nodded and tossed his keys back on the coffee table. "Fuck. I feel so useless right now." He said.

Alex agreed, "yeah that was fucked up. I'm glad Mel has a good head on her shoulders. Who knows what would have happened if things went differently."

I shook my head. I didn't want to think about that.

Alex blew out a breath. "Levi, let's do a rematch while we wait."

Levi shook his head, "Nah man I'm good. I'm gonna get something to eat." He stalked out of the room and closed the door behind him.

Alex turned his chair towards me. "How about you man, wanna rematch?"

I debated on that for a moment, I thought about going to meet you outside, but I wanted to redeem myself. I hate how smug Alex gets when he wins. I grabbed the controller Levi sat down, "You're on."

A few matches later the sound of laughing pulled my attention long enough for Alex to win the fight. A fire lit up my insides as I took in Levi's arm around your shoulders. "Fuck yeah! I'm still the king bitches!" Alex shouted, but I barely heard over the pounding in my ears.

My vision pulsed and I put the controller down, "Whatever man, it's just a game." I said and turned to look at you but all I could see was Levi's arm where mine should be. I walked up and pulled you away from him, bringing you into me. I smirked at Levi over your shoulder, he scratched his eyebrow and walked around us. I watched him triumphantly and asked you if anyone followed you here.

You shook your head no, "Not that I noticed." You said.

I put my hands on your shoulders so I could look you over again, I reassured you that I would take care of it. The guy's got the hint at what I had planned, you could feel it in the air.

"Hey Mel, you wanna play?" Alex suddenly asked, holding a controller up to you.

You moved to see around me and smiled sheepishly, "I'm not very good at those games." You said timidly.

I laughed; you looked so cute right now. "Nonsense," I said, and just to piss Levi off I added, "you just push a bunch of buttons." He hates it when people don't know how to actually play these games, I find it comical. I took you by the hand and led you over to the gaming chairs and sat down myself.

Levi took the opportunity to step behind you and lean on the back of your chair. That anger flared up again as he guided you through the character screen. I should have had you sit on my lap. I hated how he kept stealing every opportunity to touch you. I almost jumped out of my seat when he tapped your shoulder and kept his hand there. The way you scooted to the edge of your seat made me question if you did that to better focus on the game, or if you did that to get away from Levi?

I was so lost in thought I didn't see what happened on the screen. All I cared about was how you got up and sat next to me. I immediately wrapped my arm around you and pulled you into my side. You asked me if I had ate yet.

I shook my head no, trying not to focus on how I could smell the deodorant that Levi uses on you. "Are you hungry?" I asked, "We can go get something if you want." I waited for your answer and when you nodded your head I got up and turned to help you off your seat. I shouted over to the guys that we were leaving to go get food and asked if they wanted anything, but I was too focused on your smile to listen to what they said. "Just text it to me," I said, enjoying how the corner of your lips pulled into a coy smirk.

When we got to my car I scrolled through my playlist until I found our song. I'm not sure why you felt the need but for some reason as you pulled on your seat belt you said, "Levi is really friendly," your tone was tight. I wasn't sure where you getting with this.

I almost started to panic, where you going to break things off with me, so you could get with Levi? I took a breath and shrugged, "he's a friendly guy." I said mostly as a dismissal. I don't want to talk him up to you, but I don't want to smear his name either. I couldn't help but laugh when you said he didn't come across as a bad guy. *Oh, darling if only you knew.* I thought.

"Where are we going?" You asked.

I told you about the diner and how we were going to put the order in to-go. I also gave you a quick run-down on the food, the place has good food, but the owner also likes to cheap out on expenses, so you have to watch what you eat here.

When we walked through the door the old hag of a waitress gave her usual flippant welcome. I usually walk out when I see her working, but I wanted some of their biscuits and gravy so today I'll deal with it.

We waited for about 10 minutes while the waitress went about doing mundane tasks that could wait until after she took our order. She just got done with the coffee pot now she was cleaning off the sugar jars. I rolled my eyes and pulled out my phone to make sure that I had the guys order ready, then I leaned over the counter and grabbed a menu so you could look it over while we waited. I watched you as you read the food options, you looked so unsuspecting. I could stay like this all day; sitting next to you, memorizing the way the lights reflected off of your eyes as they scanned the menu.

A couple of minutes later the old hag must have gotten tired of looking at us, she came over with a scowl and took our order. I let you order first; I loved the way your mouth moved when you spoke. I smiled to myself and read off the guys order before I gave her mine.

"It'll be right out," the waitress muttered as she tore the ticket off of her pad and shuffled over to the window to the kitchen.

I rolled my eyes and kept my comments to myself. I looked down at you, you were taking in the place. I looked around too, trying to see the place through your eyes but all I could see was a rundown diner that should have been closed down a decade ago.

A few more minutes ticked by then the waitress was tossing our food down in front of us and slapped a receipt Infront of me without a second glance.

I shook my head when you looked up at me confused. I put a 50 on the receipt, grabbed the bag and walked out.

You waited until we were out in the parking lot before asking if she was always like that. I laughed and shook my head, "That was actually her on a good day. We don't eat there very much because of that. BUT it is her diner so I guess she can do what she wants?" I shrugged and opened the car door for you.

I waited until you sat down then I handed you the bag and closed the door. I flipped the keys around in my hand, scanning the parking lot and passing cars as I walked around to the driver's side. There was a red car that was driving down the road, but when I looked harder it was an elderly woman being driven around by her granddaughter. I shook my head and got in.

I made it back home in record time. It helps to know which streets to avoid, at this time of day the main roads are always a nightmare to cross. When we got back the guys flocked you, Alex took the bags from you and started to tear into the food. Levi hung back and questioned you on what food you got. My vision pulsed as you laughed at whatever Levi said to you. I shook my head to clear my thoughts and pulled our food out of the bags, I couldn't stop myself from looking back over at you and Levi. He was smiling down at you and before he could say anything else I walked up to you; my arm pulled back, but instead of catching Levi in jaw, I took you by the elbow and lead you away.

I had our food containers in my hand, I sat them down on the coffee table before sitting down on the sofa, making sure that you were next to the arm, so I was the only one sitting next to you. I leaned over and gabbed the food as Levi walked in and pulled one of the gaming chairs over and sat down across from you. Alex came in shortly after and followed suit, pulling the other gaming chair over to sit down and eat.

Surprisingly enough the noise level was still loud, despite the tv and radio being off, and everyone eating. I loved these moments when you were relaxed and laughing. I just wish that it was only you and me, I really can't stand the way Levi keeps looking at you. I looked over at you fully expecting you to be making googly eyes back at him but instead you were looking at me, with eyes so full of love and the corners of your perfect mouth pulled up into a flirtatious smile. I was too distracted by the way your mouth moved to listen to the words that you were saying but based off the way you pointed at my left-over food and held your hand I guess you were offering to take my trash.

I leaned back in my seat and dead-eyed Levi as he watched you leave the room. Out of the corner of my eye I saw Alex shake his head.

Levi took the last bite of his food, after washing it down he set his jaw and looked up at me, "What the fuck is your problem? You've been looking at me like you wanna fight, got something to say?"

Alex sighed and got up, gathering up his trash before disappearing from the room.

My vision started to pulse again. I squeezed my eyes shut and pinched the bridge of my nose. You walking into a fight between me and Levi was the last thing I wanted. I forced the air out of my lungs and sucked in a breath through clenched teeth. I shook my head, "Nah man, we're cool."

"Really? Cause I don't think we are." He said casually. "You're starting to do it again, man."

I didn't think it possible, but my heartbeat sped up. I clenched my hand into a tight fist and gritted my teeth. I shook my head, "Doing what?"

Levi rolled his eyes, "Getting all primal over a woman. The last time you got this aggressive over your girl, she was gone within a month."

I shook my head. "No this is different. I'm not going to hurt Mel." My palms started to sweat.

"Isn't that what you said about La-"

"Don't say that fucking cunts name." I growled. "She never felt the same way about me that I did for her."

Levi sighed, "Listen man. You're like family to me, we're practically brothers. But you have to get to a hold of yourself before your 'bad habit' lands you into some deep shit." He threw up air quotes around bad habit, he let out a deep breath and leaned forward, resting his elbows on his knees, "I bailed you out last time. Literally. If Grandma and Grandpa ever find out the reason why I needed to make such a large withdraw from my account, they would never speak to me again. When that happens everything I've worked for would be for shit. Do you even know how much your fucking bail was set at? You do realize that money is supposed to be for bills and shit, right?" He rolled his eyes and shook his head. "Whatever that's not the point. Don't go pulling you're old shit. This one is pretty cool. I want to see her around for a while."

I took in a slow steady breath and nodded. I didn't know what to say other than 'go fuck yourself' but that wouldn't help in this situation. I clenched my teeth and watched as he gathered up his trash and left the room. All I could think of was how to put distance between you and Levi without it being too obvious.

I was still lost in thought when you sat down, I didn't notice you walking back into the room until you were nuzzling up against me. I grinned down at you and pulled you in. You said something but I was still thinking of ways to keep you for myself. I laughed and agreed with whatever you said, thanking Whoever was listing that I answered correctly.

The guys walked back in the room shortly after and I took note of all of Levi's glances he threw in your direction. We passed the time smoking a few joints keeping it light since you were here now. Alex talked Levi into another match on the fighting game. When Alex won the game Levi turned to you and held out the controller asking if you wanted to play. You politely declined the offer and Levi turned away with a wink and a smile. I knew he did that just to piss me off; and it fucking worked.

I turned your face towards me with a finger under your chin and kissed you, just to remind everyone here who you belong to.

When Levi won the next round I took the controller from Alex and got ready to go against Levi. It was a weird power move I know but I would feel so much better if I could get this aggression out, and since I can't do anything physical (because you are here, and I don't want to get my ass handed to me) I'll settle on kicking Levi's ass in a video game. Which is exactly what I did. There's only been a handful of times were I felt this triumphant. I handed Alex back the controller and took my seat next to you.

"Good game man." Levi said as I was leaning back.

I smirked and nodded. "Better luck next time." I gloated and kissed the side of your head. I wasn't sure if I was talking about the game or my woman, but it felt pretty good to have both.

Levi just shook his head and turned to face the tv screen again.

We played a few more rounds on the game until Alex got a phone call. He answered it and almost lost the round but made a quick come back. "Hey, baby what's up?" He said into the phone. He had it pinched between his ear and shoulder so he could still play the game. "Nah, I'm at Griffins… Just playing some old video games… Um, what? Ok, yeah sure… Yeah, just text it to me, I can't remember all of that… Yeah, ok… Sure… Alright, love you too… I'll see ya soon… Bye." When he hung up the phone and put it down is when Levi made a finishing move and won the round. "What the fuck! That was a default win, it doesn't count."

Levi laughed, "Hell yeah it still counts. Maybe you should call back next time, if winning is more important than your girl."

"Whatever, we gotta go anyway. Kara wants me to pick a few things she forgot at the store." Alex said and looked at a text that just came through. He shook his head, "Man, I'm glad I had her text this to me, there's no way I could have remember all of this." He showed me the text, there was at least 15 different things.

I shook my head, "She's probably just fucking with you."

Alex took his phone back. "Either way I should still go. Hey, Levi man come on, we gotta go."

Levi shrugged, "How is that my problem. She didn't send to the store." He stood up and fished the keys out of his pocket. I noticed how you glanced over at Levi before looking up at me with sly smile.

I tilted your head up and kissed you.

"Just take my truck. I'll come and get from you later no big deal." Levi said holding out his keys.

Alex went to take them but then he flipped Levi off. "Nice try asshole. Who the fuck still drives a stick shift?"

"I've offered to teach both of you fuckers." Levi shook his head and muttered something under his breath. "Whatever, let's go." He said pushing himself off the chair.

I tapped you twice on the hip, letting you know I wanted to get up. When I stood up I held a hand out to help you up, together we walked the guys to the door. Alex pulled you into a hug after he said bye to me, it took some effort not to yank you away and pull you behind me. I tried to act normal like everything was fine. Levi was right, I was starting to do it again. Now the only question is do I fight it and let you go? Or do I embrace and keep you for myself?

When the guys left I wanted to scoop you up and carry you to the bedroom. I asked you what you wanted to do, kind of hoping you'd suggest that. But instead, you wanted to watch a movie. Not sure how much of the movie we actually watched though.

After the movie you started to get up to leave. I pulled you in and started kissing on your neck. "Stay just a little longer?" I begged.

You smiled at me, "I have to get up early tomorrow." You said.

I nodded my head and kissed that spot under your ear. "I won't keep you here long. Just for a few more minutes." I lied. It took some convincing, but I got you to agree. An hour later when sun started to set I finally let you go. "Let me follow you home," I said pulling on my jeans. "Just to make sure you get to bed safely."

"If you think it's necessary…" you trailed off as you leaned over to put on your shoes. There was something about the way your hair fell over your shoulder that set me on fire.

"Are you sure you don't want to stay?" I asked, pulling my shoes on.

You smiled up at me. You brought up your trip back home that you had planned this weekend.

I wasn't really listening to you; I mumbled a reply so you wouldn't think I was ignoring you. We walked outside together, I quickly locked the door and walked ahead of you so I could open your car door for you. When you were seated I reassured you that I would be right behind you. You smiled at me again before I closed the door.

You blew me a kiss before putting your seat belt on and starting the car.

Something in my heart ached while I was walking over to my car. The feeling only got heavier as I sat down and put the key in the ignition. The radio was blaring when the car came to life, I turned it down and put the car in reverse so I could follow you home.

I was on edge the entire way to your building. I started to get hot, so I rolled the window down when we came to a red light. When the light turned green I just caught a glimpse of the 2nd car waiting to turn left onto the road we were now driving on. Tyler was looking down so he didn't see as we passed, I couldn't help but wonder if he noticed us driving by.

I kept one eye on the road in front of me and one eye at the cars behind me. I didn't like how I kept losing sight of Tylers car. When we got your building I pulled up and parked beside you. You got out and walked over to me. I rolled down the window, and you leaned in to kiss me.

"Thank you for following me home." You said with a smile.

I grinned back you, "I'd follow you home any day. Text me before you leave in the morning." You kissed me again. It was when you pulled away that I saw Tylers car creep by. When you stood up I turned the car off. "I'm going to walk you inside. I don't like how that front door doesn't lock; he could be waiting in there."

The way you teased me was both cute and infuriating. I was tempted to just let Tyler have you, but the thought of him touching you was enough for my vision to start to turn red. But then you looped your arm through mine, and your touch was enough to calm the rage bubbling in me. "I appreciate this, Griffin." I was glad my effort to keep you safe tonight wasn't going unnoticed.

I got out and scanned the parking lot. "You can't be too sure." That was all I said while we walked across the parking lot. I only let you go so I could open the door for you. When we got to your door I had to force myself to leave. I waited until you had the door opened before I pulled you in for a last kiss goodnight. "Have a good night, Melanie." I said, loving the way your name tasted on my tongue.

"You too Griffin." Hearing my name roll out of your mouth was better than extasy.

I gently tapped on the door, telling you to make sure you locked it when I leave.

"I will," you said. You stood on your tip toes to kiss me before watching me walk down the hallway to leave.

While walking out the door I pulled a pack of cigarettes out of my jacket pocket, tapping the pack on the heel of my palm a few times I scanned my surroundings. I pulled out a cigarette and fished around for a lighter. Leaning my back against the brick wall I smoked the cigarette and watched the cars go by, taking closer looks at the red ones as they passed.

I waited around for 20 minutes; I was hoping to wait around longer but my stomach started to growl. I decided to go get something to eat, grab a few things from the store, then come back here to check up on things.

—⁂—

When my stomach was full I drove back to your building. The streets were dark at this time, the street lamps casting eerie shadows, turning everything into a potential threat. My grip tightened on the steering wheel, I'm not sure what it was but something felt off. I pressed down on the gas pedal, speeding down the road almost hitting a cat that ran out in front of me.

I slowed down when I turned onto your road. My heart was beating out of my chest as I drove past your building. Tylers red car almost blended in with the shadows, but I've been here enough times during the night that I know when something is out of place here. I turned my attention back to the road and started thinking of a plan as I parked my car down the street. I didn't want to give Tyler the chance to get away. I had put everything I would need for tonight in small black bag that was in the passenger seat, I made sure to grab it before I pulled into the parking lot of the dollar store. If I left the bag, tonight wouldn't go as planned.

The walk was short, either that or I was too lost in thought to pay attention to how long I was walking. Your building was coming into view, so I started looking around for something to use a weapon. From here I could see your car, I could also see that somebody had the passenger door open and was sitting inside of it. My breathing slowed down, but I could feel my pulse quicken. It was like the world had stopped when I bent down to put the bag on the ground and pick up a brick from the pile next to the door.

Tyler was going through the papers in your glovebox, smoking some dirt weed and flicking the ashes on the floor of your car. He didn't notice me until I was already in arms reach.

His eyes went wide, and he trapped himself in your car, scrambling to climb in the backseat. "Hey man, this is just a misunderstanding!" He yelled out as I opened the back passenger door. He was doing everything to try to fight me off but there wasn't much he could do; he was still twisted up between the driver and passenger seat.

I was able to get my hands on him and pull him into the back seat. He was pleading and spewing some bullshit about how he had the wrong car. I got tired of hearing his mouth, so I fed him the brick that was still in my hand.

By the time I was done with Tyler, sweat was running down my neck. Breathing heavy I stretched around the front passenger seat and unlocked the doors so I could walk around to open the trunk. The bloody brick was tossed in first. Then I drug Tyler's body out of the car and stuffed him into the trunk.

I brought my arms over my head and stretched; my back cracked in a few places. I went back to my car to smoke a quick cigarette before going inside to grab a few things to help me clean up the mess.

I flicked the cigarette butt to the side and walked back to your building. Feeling much lighter now that I know for a fact that Tyler will never be showing his arrogant face around here again. I cleaned off the windows the best I could, I'll get the rest later. There was some blood on the concrete that would need cleaned, pouring some bleach on it should do the trick; most of it is inside of the car.

Calling it good I went inside the apartment building to wake you up. I just wanted to make sure you were ok. When I got to your door I knocked softly a few times, not wanting to wake up any of your neighbors. I let some seconds tick by again, admiring the moon phase charm hung up on your door. I flipped over the bottom one before knocking a second time, a little louder and little longer this time. As 3 seconds turned into 15 I could feel the edges of panic start to creep in on me. I took a deep breath and ran a hand through my hair. I refuse to think that something happened before I got back, but images of your lifeless body started flashing in my mind. I blinked them away and knocked again. I tried the door knob, but it was locked tight. I scratched the back of my neck and knocked once more before dashing out of the building and sprinting around the back.

I went around to see if I could squeeze through the broken wall that surrounded your patio, but my shoulders were too broad, there was no way to get through. *It would have to be the window.* I thought. I went over and peered inside, but the curtains were closed. I couldn't see shit. I tried to slide it open, but it was locked; I muttered under my breath and tapped on the window. I gave it a few seconds and knocked with my knuckle; I didn't want to break the glass, but I would if I had to.

Thankfully it wouldn't come to that. The curtains were pulled to the side. The soft glow from the wax warmer you kept in your bedroom wasn't enough light for you to see that it was me knocking at your window.

"Get out of here before I call the police!" You shouted.

I laughed. Even if you did we both know they wouldn't get here in time. I pressed my hand against the glass and stepped up to the window so you could see. I didn't want to talk through glass, I didn't want to risk waking someone else up.

You looked at me confused, then you put something down and opened the window for me. I grabbed the window frame and pulled myself inside.

"Griffin, what are you doing?" Your voice was shaky, I couldn't tell if it was because you had just woken up, or if you were scared.

I didn't like the way you were looking over at me. It wasn't admiration. It wasn't gratitude. You looked horrified, almost disgusted. "I knocked on your door; but you weren't answering." I reached out and pulled you into me, wanting to make sure that you were real. "Don't worry about the blood. It isn't mine."

I felt you shake your head. My heart beat quickened as you tried to push yourself away from me. "What?" You asked. The tone in your voice was definitely panicked.

I felt something in me click. I tightened my grip on you and explained how I found Tyler rifling through your car. I let you push yourself back, but not too far. I smiled at you and brushed some hair so I could see your beautiful face light up when I told you that you wouldn't have to worry about him anymore.

But you just shook your head, wiped some blood off your face and whispered, "What did you do?" It was so quiet I almost didn't hear it.

I brought my hands up in a disarming way, "I didn't do anything uncalled for. Melanie he was going to hurt you." My words seemed to have fallen on deaf ears though. You were starting to panic. I put a hand on your shoulder. You looked down at it and then your gaze slid up my arm and then to my face. I smiled down at you. "Everything is going to be ok. You're just going to have to trust me." I don't think you were listing.

You took a few forced breaths and looked around the room. My body tensed as you checked the exits. I wasn't sure what was going on in that pretty head of yours, but I didn't like how this was turning out.

"Mel, honey. I need you to relax for me. It's going to be alright; I need your help but first we have to clear our heads." I'm not sure how much of that you actually heard. Judging by the way your eyes kept dilating and how your breathing has become shallow and erratic, I figured that my words just fell on deaf ears. With a finger under your chin, I tilted your head up, "Mel, look at me." When our eyes finally locked I went on, "I need you to get some towels. And we need something to clean up with, do you have any bleach?"

Your eyes somehow widened even more. You shook your head and took a step back, my heart dropped to the floor the same time you turned your back on me. I already knew the outcome when you started pacing. But I was still hoping there was time to fix this mess.

"Melanie baby, you know I would never do anything to hurt you. What happened outside will never happen to you, I made sure of that." I waited for a few seconds, before reaching out to you. "Baby, please," I begged, reaching out and putting a hand on your shoulder. I wanted to comfort you, to hold you and kiss you. But instead, you pulled out of my reach. Thinking that you would be slick and dive for your phone. But much to your surprise I already knew what you were planning. Unplugging your phone, I looked at the screen. The picture caused an ache to form in the middle of my chest. I wanted to go back to that day we took the picture, back to when we could stick our tongues out and bare our teeth at the camera. I swallowed my hurt and looked up at you. "I think I'll hold on to this for now." I said.

Your voice came out so quite I almost didn't hear you ask for your phone back.

I wanted to laugh. I almost did. I kept my head down and flipped your phone around my hand, taunting you with it. "Why?" I asked. When no answer came I looked up at you. Already knowing that you wanted to call the police with it. I set my jaw and waited for your next move.

You couldn't find the words. You just stared at me with those big doe eyes wide with fear.

371

I shook my head and dropped my shoulders. I put your phone in my coat pocket. "I thought I could count on you." I pulled at my coat and popped my neck. While I was taking a moment to reconsider, you tried to leave. Making a move for the door. "Where are you going?" I growled.

"Just to the bathroom." You breathed out.

I closed the distance between us and seized your arm, grinning down at you I told you to grab some towels while you were in there. Then I yanked the bedroom door open and shoved you out first. You went straight for the bathroom; at first you tried closing the door behind you, but I put my hand out and pushed it back open. It hit the wall harder than I intended, bouncing off the wall with some force. I laughed and put a hand out to catch it. "No, no, no sweetheart," I taunted, "the door stays open. Or I go in there with you." Either way it didn't matter to me.

You didn't bother answering me. Instead, you just walked over to the toilet. Backing out of the room I went to pack you some clothes. I hope you appreciate this; I didn't bother gathering anything for the other bitches that I drug up to Grandpas for an attitude adjustment. I took the backpack you typically use for walks through the woods and shoved some clothes into it. It would be a little chilly up at Grandpa's, you'll want some warmer clothes. I shoved your hairbrush you threatened me with earlier along with some extra socks on top.

Nodding to myself I walked over to close and lock the windows then I went to check up on you. It's been pretty quiet since I heard the toilet flush. You were washing your hands when I walked into the bathroom. When you looked up in the mirror your pupils dilated and your nostrils flared, other than that you were calm as you walked around me and grabbed the stack of towels.

I grabbed the stack from you, "Now the bleach." I said and watched as you bent down and grabbed a jug from under the sink. You handed me the jug, and I shook it. Sighing when I realized it was only half full. "It'll have to do." I said and looked down at you. "I packed you a bag, it's on your bed. Can I trust you to go get it?" I asked.

You didn't say anything, just nodded.

"Good." I said and stepped to the side so you could leave first. I went to the kitchen to see if you had any other cleaning supplies that I could use for your car. I made quite the mess out there. I didn't find anything that would work better than what I already had for a rush clean up. So, I went to check up on you, you should be out here by now.

I started to panic and ran to the bedroom. Glad I came back here when I did, you were at the window fumbling with the locks, happy that I had locked them when I did. You would have been long gone otherwise. I cursed at myself for trusting you to be back here alone. I picked up a decorative rock that you had on your dresser, the one that fit in my fist and walked up behind you. You ducked just as I brought my fist down.

I dropped the rock and pounced on you before you could get up. Grabbing a fist full of your hair I pulled your head back. "I'm sorry about this." I said and meant it too. I kissed your cheek before I pulled your head back a little further and slammed it on the floor. Knocking you out cold.

I took a breath and stood up. Rolling my shoulders I twisted my head to the side, popping my neck. I almost grabbed the bag that was still sitting on the bed, but since you thought you could be slick and try to get away while my back was turned, I don't think you deserve it. I scanned the room and put a few things in my pocket that would make transporting you a little easier on me. I scooped you up and carried you out of the room. I grabbed your keys on my way through the living room.

I didn't lock the door I would be right back. I carried you down the hallway and placed you in the back seat of your car. Fishing around in my pocket I took out the crafting cord you used to make a decorative basket for the bathroom and tied your ankles together, then I did the same with your wrists. Then I took out the bandana and sock. Brushing the hair out of your face I admired how beautiful you looked. Almost like you fell asleep in the back seat. I sighed and traced your lips with my fingers before I pulled your bottom jaw down and shoved the sock inside. Then I tied the bandana around your head and crawled out.

In record time I grabbed the bleach and towels and did what I could with the minimum light in the parking lot. The I tossed the used towels and empty bottle in the back, grabbed the black bag from where I dropped it and drove off.

Obeying the speed limit until I got out of town and off the highway. It took longer than usual because of that but I didn't want to risk getting pulled over. Every once in a while I look in the back, to make sure you weren't trying to pull some bullshit again; but you were still out like a light. I furrowed my eyebrows and looked out the windshield just in time to swerve around a rather large raccoon. I turned the volume up a little louder, hoping the music would wake you up. I didn't want to dispose of you so soon.

I didn't like the song that was playing so I turned it a few times before I found one I could get lost in. I turned the music up a little louder and let the drums and bass chase my worries away. When the singer started in with the vocals I didn't try to fight the urge to act like I was right on stage with him. I dropped my voice and growled out a demonic yell right along with the recorded song and punched the steering wheel in time with the drummer. Music therapy always makes things better. I glanced behind me and seen that my trick worked. You were starting to move around. I knew I didn't hit your head hard enough to do any real damage, but you've been so still I was almost worried. I laughed at myself and went back into the song.

Melanie (November 12 12:20am)

Loud music woke me up, I couldn't tell if the singer was screaming a weird note or if the radio was losing single. Was I right next to a speaker? Bass pulsed through me; every drum beat, and every scream was like a hammer on my head. I looked around me, but it was so dark at first I couldn't tell what was happening. I squeezed my eyes shut, hoping this was just a bad dream. I opened my eyes and tried to make sense of my situation. I was on my side, and it felt like I was moving. My head hurt so bad I thought I was going to throw up. Wherever I was, it was almost too dark to see, and it was too loud to hear anything over the music. I went to rub my head; but I couldn't move my arms. My heart nearly stopped when I noticed that my wrists were bound together behind me, I panicked but the cloth tied around my mouth made it hard for me to breathe. I closed my eyes and forced my breathing to slow down. I can't panic right now, that won't help me. I tried moving my hands around to free myself, but the binds were too tight, and I was just making them tighter. My ankles were tied together as well and there was something shoved in my mouth, but I couldn't spit it out due to the bandana around my head.

It was hard to think over the music. It was too loud. Someone had the music turned all the way up, the bass was like a hammer on my head and the singers growling vocals sliced through me, making me want to die. I opened my eyes again and it took a second to figure out what was happening. I was in the back of a car, and it was still nighttime. It was hard to make out the details around me, but from the necklace I could see swinging from the rear-view mirror I assumed we were in my car.

I looked at the driver. Of course it was Griffin. He was pounding on the steering wheel yelling along with the music. It didn't seem like he knew I was awake, how long until he noticed? It was difficult to sit up, I didn't try to be sneaky about it, there was nothing I would be able to do right now anyway. When I finally pushed myself into a sitting position, I looked into the rear-view mirror and Griffin was already staring back at me.

His mouth curled into a sneer, and he turned his head to glance back at me. "Hey, look who's finally awake," he said over the music and laughed, "I was beginning to think that I might have hit you too hard."

I looked out the window, this had to be a horror movie. There was no way I was actually tied up in the back of my own car that was driving down a country road in the middle of the fucking night. My vision started to blur as tears formed, I blinked them away. Crying wouldn't do anything right now. In fact, he might even like it. I shook my head and tried to control my breathing. I moved my jaw around to see if I could free my mouth, but nothing happened.

Griffin reached back to rub my leg; it took everything I had not to flinch away from him. "Don't worry honey, we're almost there. If you keep being a good girl, I'll untie you." It was hard to hear him over the music, I looked out the front windshield, at the old house crawling out of the darkness as Griffin slowly drove us down the driveway.

When Griffin put the car in park and opened the door I was momentarily blinded by the light. I heard the trunk pop open before Griffin stepped out. When my eyes readjusted I wished I was still unconscious, blood was splattered all over the back seat. It was like a small bottle of red paint exploded. My eyes went wide, and I started to hyperventilate but I couldn't breathe cause my mouth was still gagged and covered. I squeezed my eyes shut and shook my head. I heard Griffin grunting and something heavy hit the ground. The car bounced violently as Griffin closed the trunk.

The cabin light faded off, and the back door never opened, I looked out the window to see what he was doing. Griffin was dragging something big across the yard. I couldn't hold back the tears anymore. They started streaming down my face in hot torrents.

The side door was yanked opened a moment later, and Griffin reached in. I flinched away from him and awkwardly scooted away, he smiled softly at me. "What's wrong honey?" he asked. "Why are you crying?" He brushed a tear off my cheek with his thumb, "Tears, a waste of good suffering," he quoted and started chuckling and then brought his hand to his mouth to suck the tip of his thumb, "Mmmm, you'll have time for that later." He grabbed me by the arm and pulled me out of the car.

There wasn't much I could do but wiggle and thrash around. I yelled at him, but it just came out in muffled huffs. All I was doing was wearing myself out and amusing him. I threw myself forward at him; almost smacking my head into his, but he pulled back before I could make contact.

"Melanie!" He barked, "calm down. I can't get you inside if you keep throwing yourself around like that." He growled at me.

I narrowed my eyes, "Fuck you." I said, but through the gag it just sounded like angry groans.

Griffin gritted his teeth and elbowed me in the nose, rocking my head backwards. I could feel the bandana soaking up the blood pouring out of my nostrils. I blinked a few times in surprise, Griffin took in a deep breath through his nose and through clenched teeth he said, "you're just going to make things worse for you."

I held his gaze a moment longer before casting my eyes downward, at the blood-stained seats. It was getting harder to breathe, especially now that he broke my nose. I moved my jaw around thinking of my next move. This guy is a psycho, he obviously has no problem hurting people and at the current moment I can't do much being tied up. I tried to swallow but the thing in my mouth prevented me from doing so.

Griffin shook his head and sighed, "I really thought you were different," he said. Once again grabbing on to my arm but this time he wasn't as gentle. He yanked me out and threw me onto the ground. With my arms tied behind my back I couldn't put my hands out to catch myself. I twisted my body the best I could, so my head didn't bounce off the ground, the landing was rough but didn't hurt near as bad as the elbow to the face. Griffin closed the car door and picked me up, throwing me over his shoulder with ease. He slapped my ass and started walking us to the house.

Griffin walked inside and took us to the living room. He threw me on the sofa and sat down on the coffee table, watching as I struggled to push myself up into a sitting position. We stared at each other for what felt like an eternity. A heavy silence fell down around us, I wondered if he was able to hear my heartbeat. I heard some footsteps above us and flicked my eyes towards the ceiling. When I looked back Griffin was leaning forward, our faces a couple inches apart.

He put a hand on my neck and with the other he reached around and untied the knot holding the bandana around my head. The folded material fell away, and I spit whatever was in my mouth out. I didn't even get a chance to take in a proper breath, once the gag was out of the way Griffin had his mouth on mine, kissing me with such fervor I almost forgot what was happening.

Griffin leaned back licking his lips, "your kisses are so sweet." He had some of my blood smeared on his mouth, when he smiled that wide grin his teeth were red. I felt like I was staring at a wolf that had just taken his first bite out of me. "Can I get you anything?" he asked.

The question was so normal. I blinked a few times, stumbling over my words I replied, "Um my umm my head really hurts."

I swallowed the lump in my throat as he ran the back of his tattooed hand down my cheek. "Of course it does. Let me go get something to take care of that for you." He kissed my forehead and got up, disappearing behind a door that swung shut behind him.

I looked around me working my hands behind my back, trying in vain to undo the cord wrapped around my wrists. The room was old and out dated, dust coated most of the items except for the frequently used appliances, such as the tv screen and the record player. The lamps gave off a soft yellow glow, the overhead light had a burnt-out bulb casting half of the room in a shadow. I looked down at my feet, at the cable tied around my ankles. He had wrapped the cord around so many times I couldn't tell where the end was.

A loud bang caused me to flinch as the door was kicked open, and Griffin strolled through carrying a glass of water in one hand. "What? No fight left?" He asked sitting down next to me and put something between my lips, "open," he said, I barely opened my mouth before he shoved the pill between my teeth and brought the glass to my lips, tilting it up so I could get a drink of water.

"What was that?" I asked.

Griffin chuckled, "Codene, for your head. I don't want you to be in too much discomfort." He said stroking my hair.

Griffin (November 12 12:20)

It took all I had not to pull the car over once you started moving around in the back. I forced myself to keep facing forward, to keep screaming the lyrics along with the radio. I didn't want to scare you anymore than you probably already are. I waited until you were sitting up until I spoke; which to be honest took a lot longer than I thought it would. I've been in similar circumstances before and by the time it took you to sit I would have already been out of the binds and at the persons throat. But I guess that's a good thing for me. I laughed at myself and pounded on the steering wheel as the music pulsed through the car.

I looked back in the mirror, and you were now in an upright position. We locked eyes for a moment, the corners of my mouth twitched into a tight smile. "Hey, look who's finally awake." I said, "I was beginning to think that I might have hit you too hard."

In the mirror I could barely make out what you were doing. You shook your head in a way that made it seem like you were about to cry.

Taking it slow down the dirt road that took us to the house I reached back and rubbed your leg. I assured you that we were almost there and that I would untie you once we were inside.

I parked the car and popped the trunk before I got out. Walking around to the back of the car I looked in the backseat; I knew I was putting more faith into you staying put than I should, but where would you go out here? Tied up? In the dark? In the middle of fucking nowhere? I laughed and pulled Tylers body out of the trunk and drug him over the well. Maybe Ellie was lonely down there, this would give her someone to talk to. Getting Tyler over the wall of the well was a lot easier that it was to get Ellie in there. Once he was edge I stood up and stretched, thankful that that part was finally done with.

I turned back to the car, almost expecting a chase. But you were still there, in the back seat. I smiled to myself, *You keep surprising me, Mel.* I thought, just when I think I know what's going on in that pretty little head you switch it up on me. *Where was that fight you had back at your apartment?* I almost wanted to ask you. I jogged back to the car and opened the back driver's side door. I reached in to help you out; but you pulled away from me. Tears were streaming down your face. My eyes followed a tear as it welled up in your bloodshot eye and cascade down your cheek to be soak up by the bandana I tied around your mouth. You might be cooperating now, but I know there's more fight in you.

I smiled at you, "What's wrong honey?" I asked, almost in a whisper. "Why are you crying?" Another tear fell, but this time I caught it with my thumb. I never understood why some people waste their time and energy with crying, it's not like it helps. I muttered a quote from one of my favorite movies and licked the tear off my thumb. I couldn't help but think back to Grandpa in these moments. He always did hate to see people cry. I took in a deep breath and focused myself. I need to get you out of the car, I grabbed you by the arm, assuring you that you'll have time to break down later.

As soon as I grabbed your arm, the fight I knew was still there kicked in. You brought your knees and elbows in tight before stretching out violently making it hard to get a hold on you. You were saying something but all I could understand was muffled huffs. I thought it was kind of funny, slightly adorable, but mostly exhausting. Honestly how long can you keep this up before you wear yourself out?

I was all for letting you struggle for a while longer but when you threw your head forward and just about got me in the face I wanted to throw you out on the ground and kick you in yours. "Melanie, calm down!" I barked, "I can't get you inside if you keep throwing yourself around like that."

You narrowed your beautifully bloodshot green eyes and tried to say something tough, but how intimidating are you really; all tied up? It was time to stop being so gentle. I clenched my jaw and brought my elbow up. Your head rocked backwards, your eyes widened, and blood immediately started running down your face. I wanted to feel bad, but I had time for that later. I had to focus on getting you inside. I took a deep breath to center myself. "You're just going to make things worse for you."

We stared each other down for a moment longer. Then you cast your gaze downward, your eyes moved back and forth like you're debating something in your head. I wanted to ask what you were thinking when you started moving your jaw around. Looking anywhere but at me. That got under my skin. If you really wanted me to remove the gag you could at least show me the decency and look me in the eye.

I shook my head no, "Not until we're inside." I made that mistake once. And I wasn't the one who untied......I shook my head again. I grabbed you by the arm, not caring how rough I was being, and yanked you out of the backseat and tossed you on the ground. I closed the car door before I picked you up and tossed you over my shoulder. I'm not sure where the fight in you went, was it still there? Or did it go away when I bloodied your nose? I slapped your ass to see if I could get a reaction; but you just let me carry you inside.

It used to be a struggle getting inside, but I've gotten this down pat. I kicked the living room door open and dropped you on the couch. I sat down in front of you on the coffee table and watched in amusement as you struggled to push yourself up. It wasn't long until you were upright, glaring at me. You're breathing was labored, heavy and shallow. I studied you, waiting for you to do something but we just stared at each other.

There was some heavy thudding from upstairs. Your eyes flicked up, and I took the opportunity to lean forward, to get a closer look at you. When you looked away from the ceiling your eyes widened in surprise but just for a moment, I brought my right hand up and held you by the side of the neck as I untied the bandana with my left. As soon as you spit the sock out of your mouth, my lips were on yours. I kissed you like it was our first time; like it was our last time.

I leaned back and licked my lips, savoring how the kiss felt. "Your kisses are so sweet." I said, smiling at how the blood smeared around your mouth looked like ruined lipstick. I smiled wider at the horrified look you gave me. I can only imagine what *I* look like after that kiss. I could feel the blood already drying on my chin. "Can I get you anything?" I asked.

It always amazed me how much that question threw people off. You blinked in surprise and tripped over your words as you told me that your head hurt. I brushed your cheek with my knuckles, your skin still damp with tears. I was hoping for a smart-ass comment or a pathetic plea to let you go. In truth I wasn't actually expecting you to ask for anything other than that.

"Of course it does," I answered, "Let me go get something to take care of that for you." I kissed your forehead as I stood up and left the room.

Out in the hallway I held my breath and listened, waiting to see if you would try anything. I was pretty confident in the knot around your wrists but the one I tied at your ankles was iffy. A few heart beats later when I didn't hear any shuffling around I went to go get you something for your head out of the box that was in the cabinets above the kitchen sink. I flipped through some small baggies and pulled out one with oblong white pills. Fishing out a single pill I tossed the baggie back into the box and went to get some water. I took a glass out of the cabinet and poured some bottled water into it.

When I got to the living room I kicked it open; but was let down when I saw you still sitting on the sofa like a good girl waiting for me. I smirked at how well this was going. "What? No fight left?" I asked sitting down next to you. When you turned your head to me I put the pill between your lips and brought the glass up, so you could wash it down.

You asked me what I gave you, I told you truthfully, "Codene, for your head. I don't want you to be in too much discomfort." I brushed your hair back from your face and smoothed it out. If you keep behaving this well you'll be back to your old life in no time.

We sat like that for a moment until you couldn't fight the effects any longer and fell fast asleep. I picked you up and carried you up the stairs, the wooden steps groaning as we went. I flipped on the hallway light and headed towards the open door to the extra room up here. I couldn't help that tickle of fear I got when I turned my back to the closed door that led to Grandpa's room. People keep telling me that he's still around, but I refuse to acknowledge the superstations. Ghosts aren't real, weird noises happen in old houses.

In the bedroom I gently laid you down on the bed. I slid an arm under your shoulders, so I lift you up just enough to pull your hair from under you. I took my phone out and snapped a few pictures. I went to go get a wet rag from the kitchen to wipe the blood off your face, humming to myself as I went about my business; gently removing most of the dried blood and undoing the binds. I had just got your wrists free and was working on freeing your ankles when a faint creak made me pause. I lifted my head and stared out into the hallway.

I blinked a few times. Grandpas bedroom door was halfway open. I quickly finished untying your feet and stood up. I shook my head and rationalized it as old hinges, worn out door knob, there was an air current that pushed the door open. I walked out of the bedroom, closing the door behind me and turned around. Not giving myself long enough to over think it, I shut his door and went down stairs.

I went outside to grab somethings I left in your car. I pulled my phone out to make a call. I opened the driver side door and got in, shuffling through the black bag I threw in the passenger seat. I grabbed a small zip up pouch and opened it just as the call was answered.

"You do know what time it is right?" Alex said.

I took out a plastic tube and popped it open, dumping out a joint and lighting the end before I replied. "Yeah, I know. But I kind of fucked up and I need your help."

I heard a door open and close, "Really, what did you do this time?" He asked, I heard a lighter click on. He didn't sound too concerned.

I took a long hit off the joint and held it for a moment, debating on how much I should tell him over the phone. I wasn't sure who was around Alex right now but just in case I decided to keep it vague. "I need one last thing from you." I brought the joint up, "I've already delt with the rat but I need help with the traps."

Alex let out a frustrated groan, "Fine, what do you need me to do?"

"Nothing too extreme. I'll tell you more off the phone, for now can you get my car from the dollar store down the street from Mel's apartment and drive it to the shop?"

"Man, those are words I don't like hearing together. What did you do?" I could be tripping but I think I heard actual concern in his voice.

I took a hit and looked up at the house, There were no windows upstairs that looked out onto the front yard, but I could picture you up there. I narrowed my eyes and took a long drag. "She's fine. I just need you to bring me my car." I said after flicking some ashes on to the floor.

There was a long pause on the other end. I took a couple hits and still no response.

"Alex?" I heard some noises on the other end. The door opening and closing, and a chair being pulled out. "Come on man, don't let me down. I already did the hard part. I just need you to drop off my car, so I have a way back tomorrow."

"Fine," he finally agreed, "I'll get it done as soon as I can." Then he hung up.

I finished the joint and headed back inside, bag in hand. It wouldn't be much longer until the sun started to come up.

Frist, I went to the kitchen to put the food away. It wasn't much, just some things for breakfast. When the food was up, I went to the living room to unwind from the hectic day. I'm pretty sure I pulled a muscle in my shoulder dumping Tylers body in the well. I know Tyler won't mind being down there with Ellie but I'm pretty sure she would hate me for it. I laughed and sat down on the sofa and started looking through the bag, Ellie always hated me deep down, she just never wanted to admit it.

I finally found the metal pill bottle at the bottom of the bag and dumped a few random pills into my hand and tossed them into my mouth. Then I got up to put on some music to fill the quiet. I laid out on the sofa, letting the music carry me away. I don't know how long I stayed like that, but the next thing I knew I heard footsteps coming from upstairs.

I waited for you to make it to the bottom of the stairs before I got up and went to the living room door. Eager to see what would come next for us.

Melanie (November 13)

When I woke up, I was laying on a bed. I was no longer tied up, red welts still showed where he had tied the cord around my ankles and wrists. I sat up looking around me, the room was bare except for a small dresser. There was a window, pale sun light reaching through the curtains. There were also 3 doors, 2 of which stood open. 1 was an empty closet, the other one took you to a bathroom. I swung my legs over the edge of the bed, the floor creaked under me as I walked over the closed door and twisted the knob.

Music came up from downstairs. It was so loud; the bass vibrated the floor beneath me. I peeked my head out of the doorframe and looked into the hallway. To my left was a wall, to my right was the stairs. Directly in front of me was a closed door, the light underneath shining brightly. I had a bad feeling in the pit of my stomach when a shadow appeared, like someone had moved to stand on the other side of the door.

I went downstairs, following the music, my legs were shaking under me. I grabbed onto the polished wood of the banister and made my descent. Every step I took was louder than the last, or at least that was what it had felt like. I stopped at the foot of the steps and looked around, in front of me was the front door, another door to my left, a matching one to my right that was slightly open, that was the room where the music was coming from. I looked behind me, a hallway that was shrouded in darkness with more closed doors. I looked back to the front door and was greeted by Griffin, leaning against the door frame to the living room with his arms crossed.

He was smirking at me. "Good morning. You must be hungry." He shouted over the music. He held his hand out to me, "I have a few things laid out for breakfast." He said grabbing my hand and pulling me into the kitchen. He let go when we got to the table and started pulling things out of the grocery bag that was sitting there. There was a bag of bagels, a box of honey nut cheerios, and a box of cherry pop tarts. "There's milk and cream cheese in the fridge." He went over to the cabinet and pulled down a toaster. He looked at me over his shoulder, "So what sounds good to eat?" he asked plugging the toaster in.

I opened the box of pop tarts and pulled out a package. "Is there anything to drink?" I asked, breaking off a corner of the pop tart and forcing myself to chew and swallow it.

Griffin drummed his hands on the counter, "I could make some coffee if you want."

I pulled out a chair and sat down, confused at what was happening. "Coffee sounds good."

I watched him cross the room and pull out a coffee pot, he took a bag out of the refrigerator and pulled a small bag of coffee and some cream cheese out and placed the rest back in the fridge. When the pot was set up, he came over to the table and sat down next to me. He was about to say something when the toaster popped, he got up and returned shortly with his bagel and a butter knife. While he was spreading some cream cheese on his bagel he started talking, "I hope you can forgive me for how things played out." He said, taking a bite. "I didn't want to hurt you, but I thought you were going to turn me in." He started chuckling, and took another bite, "I know how dumb that sounds." He laughed, "I mean you wouldn't call the cops on me. I killed him for you." He said winking at me.

My mouth went dry, sure I suspected he did something along those lines last night, but to hear him say it so casually was horrifying. I kept my eyes down refusing to look anywhere but at my barely eaten 'breakfast.'

Griffin started tapping the butter knife on the table, piercing the silence with metallic tings. Sighing he said, "We're going to have to do something about your car. We can't just leave it in the driveway. So, here's what we're going to do." He leaned forward and pointed at me with the butter knife, cream cheese smeared on the edge, "You're going to be a good girl and stay here while Alex and I take care of it for you. Then when I get back, you'll thank me for what I did."

I shook my head, "I never asked for this." I whispered, still looking down at the table.

"No, but you should be grateful." He said, putting his hand on my cheek and turned my head so I had to look at him, "Do you want to know what happened?" He asked with a sly smile.

He looked crazed; his hand was still cupping my face. His fingers were tangled in my hair, and his thumb was rubbing up and down my cheek. I couldn't speak, I couldn't even breathe. I felt frozen under his cold stare.

Griffins smile spread wider across his face, "When I got to your building last night; Tyler was in the passenger seat of your car; going through the glove compartment. He seen me coming and closed the door trying to buy himself sometime." I tried to pull away as he told me this. His grip on my head tightened when I moved backwards, and he pulled me closer and held me there. "I picked up a brick and got to the door before he could lock it." His breath was hot, that wolfish smile plastered on his face matched the predatory look in his eyes. "He tried to get away by crawling into the backseat but that only made it easier to pin the rat down." He closed his eyes and sighed, "Nothing feels as good as that first hit. When that brick came down on his face," he laughed and opened his eyes, "The only thing that feels better than that is you writhing under me." I felt sick. Griffin kissed my forehead and let me go. "I'm going to meet Alex shortly, we'll get rid of the car and come back here, then we can discuss how you will thank us."

My stomach turned in the most painful way, "I'm gonna be sick." I breathed out. Griffin stood up and helped me over to the sink.

He pulled my hair from my face and rubbed my back as I threw up stomach acid into kitchen sink. "Don't be ashamed, this a normal reaction." He said. Hunched over the sink, my eyes started watering, then I started to sob. Tears were streaming down my face, Griffin pulled me into a hug, "It's ok honey," he said, "we'll get through this." The sound that came out of my mouth was unreal. I shook my head 'no' and pushed at his chest, but he just held me tighter, "This isn't the kind of behavior that lets me know that I can trust you." Again, his grip got tighter, I gasped as he squeezed the air out of my lungs. I started to panic and kicked my legs. "I'm sorry to do this," He turned me around and picked me up so fast the room started to spin, then he began to drag me out of the kitchen.

I struggled against him, kicking my feet, and throwing my head around. "No, just let me go!" I yelled.

Grunting he started climbing the stairs. I screamed and put my feet out to push against the stairs, the wall, anything that might help. "Stop struggling Melanie," he growled, turning around, and walking up the stairs backwards. When we got to the bedroom he threw me inside and slammed the door shut. I ran at the door and yanked on the knob, but it wouldn't move. Griffin must have been holding onto it. "I'll let you out when I come back." He said through the door. I heard a lock click in place, then his heavy foots steps as he walked down the hallway, the floor boards creaking under him as he went.

I punch the door, "FUCK!" I screamed. How am I going to get out of this?

The day drug by locked in that room with nothing to do but pace and try to ignore my growling stomach. Every now and then I would hear the floor boards creak as someone walked around in the other room. Every time I thought it was Griffin coming back to let me out, but the door remained shut.

With nothing better to do I searched the room. I opened the closet first, there was a pull string to turn the light on; but when I tugged it, nothing happened. There was lightbulb screwed in; but I figured it was just old and burnt out a while ago. No one bothering to change it out. There were some cheap plastic hangers but other than that the closet was empty.

I went to the bathroom and flipped the switch, but the light didn't come on in here either. I swallowed down my panic and went over to sit on the edge of the bed. *Why aren't the lights coming on? What the hell is happening? Why aren't the lights coming on? Why did he lock me in here?* My mind started racing and I felt the cold embrace of a panic attack coming on. Taking a few deep breaths, I put my head in my hands and tried to figure out my next move.

I got up and started pacing the room. I couldn't let myself crumble. Once I was on my way out of this town and far away from that psycho then I can break down and feel bad. But for now, I have to hold on.

I went to the dresser and started going through the drawers, most of them were empty nothing but dust and an old price tag from Victora's Secret. I flipped the tag around in my fingers feeling my stomach twist and drop; I wondered what the tag went to, just for something else to focus on. I put the tag on top of the dresser and pulled the drawers out, wondering if whoever the tag belonged to left something else behind.

The dresser had 7 drawers, and all 7 held nothing in them but on bottom of 3 drawers were carvings. One was a rough looking flower, but the other 3 held initials and warnings. EM CR LK, I ran my fingers over the carved letters, wondering who these people were and tried not to think of where they were now. The carved warnings were hard to read in the dying light, I could just make out one. 'His promises are empty; he will never let me go' I ran my fingers over the words. I felt defeated as I slid the drawers back into place.

I sat down on the floor and rested my back against the dresser, looking up at the sky thinking of how to get out of here.

It wasn't until the sun had gone down that I heard a car pull up. There were 3 car doors that slammed shut. I must have fallen asleep on the floor. I pulled myself off the floor and looked around. The house was almost pitch black by this time. The only light was the soft glow from the moon coming in from the window. I sat on the bed and scooted against the wall to bring my knees up to my chest.

Almost like an explosion the lights came on. I closed my eyes and buried my face in my arms. The sudden change of light hurt my eyes.

The front door of the house burst open, slamming against the wall. Then the sound of yelling and laughter, whoever Griffin brought back with him sounded like they were having the time of their lives. Awhile later after most of the yelling died down I heard someone coming up the stairs, the heavy footsteps approaching the bedroom door accompanied by the creaking floor. I tried to sink down in the bed, but I couldn't make myself any smaller.

There was a faint click as the door was unlocked, and the knob slowly turned. Griffin pushed the door open just far enough to see inside. "Mel?" he asked softly. I kept quiet. He pushed the door open the rest of the way and stepped inside. I buried my face in my arms that were crossed over my knees. The bed shifted as he sat down next to me and started rubbing my back. "You must be hungry. Come downstairs with me, we brought back some food."

There was a hollow feeling in my stomach when he mentioned food. I picked my head up and looked at him, "Who is we?" I asked.

Griffin chuckled and brushed some hair back from my face, "Who else? Levi and Alex. They're excited to see how grateful you are that they helped get you out of your sticky situation."

"Did they both come back with you just now?"

Griffin nodded, "Yeah, why?" he asked, his brow furrowed.

I looked over at the door, "It sounded like someone else was here while you were gone."

"No, honey you've been alone this whole time. No one else is in this house besides us and the guys downstairs." He nudged my arm, "Come on. Let's not keep them waiting, your food is getting cold."

"I don't want to." I said.

Griffin froze and robotically turned to face me. "What?" he growled.

My heart was beating in my ears. I swallowed and repeated, "I don't want to."

Griffin sighed and ran a hand down his face, "don't be ungrateful." He warned.

"I am not going down there dressed like this." I said, pulling at my shirt. I was still in the same pajamas as the night when Griffin stole me from my apartment. How long ago was that?

Griffin started laughing, "They wouldn't care if you walked down there naked. Now get your ass off the bed and follow me down the stairs."

I took a breath to steady myself, looking him straight in the eyes I said, "No."

Griffin took a step back, laughing, "Ok, if that's how you want to play. Fucking starve," He turned on his heel and walked out the door, he slammed the door shut and the faint click of the lock was followed shortly after, then his footsteps retreated back down stairs.

I didn't see or hear from anyone for the rest of the night. In fact, after the sound of the party died down the house got eerily quiet. The house shook as the front door slammed shut and not soon after the electricity was turned off; and like a heavy blanket, darkness fell down around me.

My heart sank as I heard a car drive away. My stomach growled and I never felt as dumb as I do now. I should have just went downstairs so I could eat something. My stomach growled again at the thought of food; and I banged my head against the wall in frustration.

Footsteps on the other side of the door caught my attention, "Hello?" I called out. But no one answered. I shrugged it off as the house settling.

Griffin (November 13)

When you reached the bottom of the stairs I thought you were going to run for the door. But you just looked around, not even glancing in my direction. I crossed my arms and leaned against the doorframe, wondering what you were thinking of doing next.

You looked behind you, down the hallway at the closed closet doors. I tried to view the house how you were probably looking at it; old, outdated, could use some more lighting. This house was always shrouded in darkness. You turned back around, eyes widening slightly when they landed on me.

I smirked at you and shouted over the music, letting you know that I had food waiting for us. I held my hand out to guide you to the kitchen. I let go of you at the table and started unloading the grocery bag I left on the table. I told you about the food in the fridge and asked what you wanted to eat. I grabbed the toaster from the cabinet and plugged it in so I could warm up a bagel.

Instead of answering the question you asked if there was anything to drink. I cast a glance behind me, to see what you were doing. You have gotten a pop tart out and was picking at the corners. I drummed on the counter, trying not to run out of patience so soon. I offered to make some coffee.

Once I had the coffee pot set up and brewing I went to sit down to go over a few ground rules. But then the toaster popped, letting me know that my bagel was ready. I got up to fetch my breakfast and a butter knife. I sat back down and started smearing some cream cheese on the bagel while spewing some bullshit about forgiveness. I don't need forgiveness; I need reassurance that you won't go around town stringing together lies about how last night went down. I took a bite and swallowed. "I didn't want to hurt you, but I thought you were going to turn me in." That part was true, I laughed and took another bite, "I know how dumb that sounds, I mean you wouldn't call the cops on me," I looked right at you, studying every little twitch you made as I said with a wink, "I killed him for you."

The blood drained from your face and your breathing faltered and you dropped your gaze. I smiled to myself and took another bite. It was so quiet here, I could hear the hum of the refrigerator, the creaking floors upstairs.

I started playing with the butter knife, tapping it on the table and trying to figure out what to do with your car once we got it to the shop. I let out a breath and started thinking out loud.

I was appalled when you started shaking your head 'no' and said, "I never asked for this," hardly above a whisper. I almost didn't hear it.

I got up and pulled a chair over to sit next to you, "No, but you should be grateful," I said putting a hand on your cheek to make you look at me. "Do you want to know what happened?" I asked, grinning at the wide eye look you gave me. I held you there and savored every moment as I told you in detail what happened. I never felt more alive.

But the moment as ruined when you told me that you were going to get sick. I stood up and led you over to the sink, where I held back your hair as you gagged over the sink. And since I'm such a nice fucking guy I started rubbing your back and reassured you that it was a normal reaction and not to feel embarrassed.

Your shoulders shook in an odd way, and you let out a choking sound. It took me a moment to realize you were crying.

I pulled you into me and wrapped my arms around you, "It's ok honey, we'll get through this." I told you and kissed the top of your head.

A wale came out of you instead of words of gratitude. You shook your head 'no' and tried to push away from me; but I tightened my grip.

Through gritted teeth I said, "This isn't the behavior that lets me know that I can trust you. I'm sorry to do this." I said with little meaning and started dragging you out of the kitchen.

You panicked and began thrashing around. Screaming for me to let you go.

It was a struggle, but I finally got you to the stairs. I had to admit, you were putting up one hell of a fight, you kept throwing your head back; I lost count of how many times you almost hit me in the face. You kicked your feet out, making it hard to do anything. I could feel my heart rate start to speed up, you were wearing me out, but I wasn't sure if you were just that desperate to get away or if I was just that tired. I turned around and went up the stairs backwards so it would be harder for you but easier for me. I growled at you to stop struggling, I loved yet hated how hard you were fighting against me, why can't you just do what your told?

Finally, we made it to the top of the stairs, I used the last bit of my energy to get you to the room. I threw you inside and quickly closed the door, holding the knob in place as I reached up and grabbed the key from on top of the door frame. I felt you trying to twist the knob and held on to it tighter. "I'll let you out when I come back." I said while locking the door and placing the key back in its spot.

On my way to the front door, I heard a smack and a loud angry yet desperate, "FUCK!" I shook my head and locked the door on my way out.

When I got to your car I took a moment to catch my breath. I stared up at the house and tried to picture what you were doing. After a few moments I started your car and put it in drive, eager to get this over with. I wasn't looking forward to the long drive to the shop after yesterday's events. I was exhausted and I just wanted to lie and take a nap.

—⚬—

Somehow I made it to the shop in one piece. When I pulled up the garage door was already opening, like someone was inside waiting for me to show up. My pulse quickened for a moment, but I quickly relaxed when Alex came into view. He was looking behind him talking to someone. I pulled the car into the garage and got out, tossing the keys on the dash before closing the door.

"Where's Mel?" Levi asked.

I sighed and turned around. I was hoping he wasn't going to be here. In fact, I was hoping no one would be here. I was planning on going up and crashing on the sofa that dad has up in his office. Why does everything have to be so difficult?

Alex walked up and shrugged, "He overheard the phone call." He moved around me and went up to the car, peering into the back seat. "The fuck man?"

Looking straight at Levi I said, "Yeah that's what happens when someone fucks with something that doesn't belong to them."

Levi shook his head, "I can't believe this."

Narrowing my eyes I said, "Your girl is fine, she's cooling down at Grandpa's. She's kind of messed up in the head right now but give it a couple of days and we'll have her back to her old self."

I didn't get a response, instead Levi walked past me to look at the car; shoulder checking me on the way. I didn't like the way that the guys kept their voices low as they talked amongst themselves. I studied them as I slowly made my way over to them.

Levi looked over at me, "I think we should just burn it." He motioned to the car, "it looks like more work than I want to deal with."

I tilted my head and looked at the car, "We'd still have the frame to take care of. You really think a charred-up car frame will go unnoticed?"

Alex shook his head, "Things go unnoticed here all the time. There's that scrap yard a few miles out of town, you could drop it off there. After hours."

I shook my head, I didn't care how we got rid of the car, just as long as we got rid of the damn thing soon. "Fine," I said, "we can rip the fabric out and burn it out back. I'll drive the car out to the scrap yard, but I need someone to pick me up."

Alex looked over at Levi, who was looking down at me. Levi crossed his arms and said, "Fine, we'll meet you there."

With that said I grabbed some tools and began to remove upholstery on the backseat. I had gotten a good amount of the fabric cut away when I decided to take a quick break. I went up to dads office and took out the bottle of Jack I keep up here in the filing cabinet. I took it down and poured out three glasses, by the time the back seat was stripped we had made-up and were back on good terms with each other. It's easy to piss Levi off but give him some alcohol and he's back to being your best friend.

In a few hours we had the fabric stripped out of the car. Levi went out back to start a fire, leaving Alex and I to gather up everything that could be burned.

"It's going to suck driving the car like this." I said, dragging a bundle of what used to the be the passenger seat over the back door.

Alex shrugged, "You've been through worse."

I scoffed, then nodded. "True enough."

"How did you get rid of Tyler?" He asked, tossing the carpet on top of the growing pile.

I went over to the corner of the garage that was used a breakroom, where the mechanics hang their coats and sit down to eat and grabbed a broom, and Alex gathered the rest of the fabric. "Threw him down the well, I need to get out there when it warms up and pour some concrete in it." I started sweeping around the car to clean up the mess.

"Yeah, good luck with that." He said, opening the door to let Levi in.

"Ok, we're good to start burning now." He looked over at the pile Alex and I made, "what you couldn't put this on a pallet or in a wheelbarrow?"

Alex threw his hands up, "Does it look like either of those are laying around?"

Levi scanned the garage and raised an eyebrow. "Fair point." He bent over and grabbed some foam padding. "Ok, let's get this over with."

Alex propped the door open and followed Levi out with some fabric. I swept the pile out the door and went to put back the broom, nearly jumping out of my skin when a woman with shoulder length hair appeared out of nowhere. I blinked and she was gone. I laughed when

I noticed that it was just the coats on the wall. I must have had more to drink than I thought. I shook my head and put the broom back. A shiver went down my spine, I couldn't remember if this part of the garage was always cold. There must be a breeze from the open door, I told myself. Something fell behind me. I looked over my shoulder, expecting to see one the guys messing around, but no one was there. I looked on the floor and went over to pick up the clipboard that usually hangs on the hook in the front lobby. I looked around one more time, still seeing nothing I put the clipboard on the table and went to help burn the upholstery.

Burning everything was easy and took no time at all, after the ashes had died down we went over to my place to have a mini celebration. I was wide awake now, ready to take on anything. I was on top of the fucking world.

We piled into Levi's truck and went to get some food before going back to grandpas. I didn't realize how hungry I was until that first bite hit my mouth. Levi turned the radio on and started up a metal playlist, much to Alex's displeasure.

"Ugh, not this shit again. I can't understand a fucking thing these guys are saying!" He shouted over the music.

I scoffed, "like your music is any better. I can't understand yours either, but you don't hear bitching about it."

Alex turned back and looked at me like I was stupid. "If you would bother to learn some Spanish you might be able understand it. There's no language lessons on how to speak demon."

Levi laughed, "I like to think I'm fluent in both."

"Well, aren't you just God's favorite." Alex spat.

Levi chuckled and cleared his throat, then proceeded to growl out something in Spanish. I had seen it coming but apparently Alex didn't; he was bringing his cup up, about to take a drink but ended up jumping and spilling some in the process.

"Dude, what the fuck." He signed the cross over his chest, "Abuelita was right, my friends are el diablo."

"Aw your grandma is sweet." Levi said.

"I always knew she liked us." I chimed in. Which was such a lie, back in the day she banned us from stepping foot in her house. She tried to keep Alex from hanging with us; saying we're no good for her grandson. But you can't keep someone from doing something that they really want to do. So, she did the next best thing; if she even caught us on her porch she would call the police on us for trespassing.

A while later Levi was taking the turn to get on the dirt road that lead to Grandpas. Alex took long sip out of the crown bottle and handed it back to me. I took a drink and passed it back. When Levi put the truck in park he grabbed the bottle and downed the rest.

"Fuck, man. That was last of the alcohol." Alex complained.

Levi shrugged and turned the truck off, putting the keys in the sunglass holder.

"There should still be some in the kitchen inside." I said, opening the door on the driver's side and getting ready to hop out. "I'll look after I get Mel."

As I was closing the door I heard Levi and Alex exchange a few words in Spanish. I took out a little bag with 3 joints and took one out. I placed the bag back in my pocket and took a few hits. Levi got out first and looked up at the house. Alex was hesitant just sitting there with his door open.

"What's his deal?" I asked, pointing with my chin at the truck and handing Levi the joint.

He shook his head and laughed, "he said he saw a woman encased in black flames," he looked down and took hit off the joint, "that would be a bad ass album cover." He nodded a few times and handed me back the joint.

I shook my head and studied him for a moment. Nothing seemed off, but I didn't believe that's what they were talking about. I heard a faint click before Alex got out the truck.

"Alex, buddy!" I shouted; he jumped causing Levi to laugh. "Hey man, you good? What's going on?" I didn't wait for him to join us. I walked over and put my arm around his shoulders. "What's this I hear about women on fire?!" I took a drag off the joint and held it out for Alex.

He shot Levi a look, who wasn't paying attention. "It could have been a shadow caused by headlights? I don't know. But it looked like there was a woman on the porch surrounded by black fire."

I nodded and let him go. I took a few steps to the house and looked back at him. "Kind of reminds me of a few years ago. You said you saw the same thing." I narrowed my eyes at him and looked over at Levi. He still wasn't paying attention. I looked back at Alex. He didn't seem nervous. I raised an eyebrow and forced a laugh. "Maybe you guys are right. Maybe this place really is haunted." And maybe I am paranoid. I haven't slept since……. I couldn't remember. But I am so full of energy!

I shook my head and chuckled, for a moment I really thought that the guys were turning against me. Levi was still looking around when he walked up to us, he was shaking his head, "I'm going inside, is it locked?" He asked.

I shook my head 'no' and started to head for the door. I was about to say something when I saw something duck into the well from the corner of my eye. My head shot towards the well and I stared at it for a moment. Alex noticed me staring and turned his attention to the well also.

"The fuck are you two doing?" Levi asked nudging me on the shoulder, almost knocking me off balance.

I shook my head, "Nothing, it was just a bat or something." I looked at Alex who was still glued to the well. "If we stay out here any longer the Grudge will come out and drag you away."

Levi made a noise, "The Grudge didn't come out of a well, they were in the attic dumb ass. You're thinking of the Ring."

I rolled my eyes, "Whatever, I'm going inside."

Behind me I heard Alex saying something, I caught a few words like house but most of it I didn't understand. I waited until I was at the porch before turning around. I threw my hands up and yelled, "BOO!" Scaring the shit out of Alex. Levi and I started dying. Alex started cussing me out in Spanish.

I opened the door, and we piled inside. Alex shoving his way in first. "Aww I think you hurt his feelings." Levi joked.

I laughed, "He makes it too easy." I looked around and listened for any out of place noises. Not for ghosts that shit isn't real. I was trying to tell if I could hear you in the house. But other than the noises we were making, the house was quiet.

I nodded at the stairs, "I'll be down in a moment, I'm going to go get Mel."

Levi's jaw flexed. "Ok, cool," then he disappeared behind the living room door.

Taking a breath to steady myself I went up the stairs. I was a little nervous at the state I would find you in. When I got to the door I reached up and took the key off the door frame. I unlocked the door and immediately put the key back. Opening the door just a crack I called out your name, but I didn't get a response. My heart began to sink. I pushed the door open further and stepped in, preparing myself for the worse. But then I saw you, curled up on the bed.

I went over and sat down next to you. I gently rubbed your back and said, "You must be hungry. Come downstairs with me, we brought back some food."

I could hear your stomach growl as you lifted your head and looked at me, I seen no more fight in you, that was a good sign. "Who is we?" You asked.

I laughed and brushed back the hair that fell into your face. "Who else?" I asked, "Levi and Alex." I studied your expressions as I told you how eager the guys are for you to go downstairs. But you threw me off when you asked if they had arrived just now. I nodded, "Yeah, why?" I was curious at where this was going. Slightly amused that everyone around me seems to believe in ghosts. Everyone I bring here says the same thing about footsteps and how creepy the place is.

Just as I was thinking that; you told me how it sounded like someone was here while I was gone.

I shook my head and told you that you've been alone the entire time until just now, then I nudged your arm, "Come on. Let's not keep them waiting, your food is getting cold."

"I don't want to." You said flatly.

Something in me click. I turned to face you and through gritted teeth I asked, "What?"

You swallowed and replied, "I am not going down there dressed like this." You tugged on the hem of your shirt.

I laughed, I know the guys wouldn't care. You still smelled clean and that's what they care about. "They wouldn't care if you walked down there naked. Now get your ass off the bed and follow me down the stairs."

You took a deep breath and said, "No."

So much for that. I thought. I started walking backwards laughing. "Ok, if that's how you want to play. Fucking starve." I turned around and slammed the door shut behind me. I locked it before you had time to run over and open it while you could.

At the bottom of the steps, I ran a hand through my hair and took a deep breath. I shook my head and walked to the living room. Levi and Alex were throwing around a wad of newspaper talking about ghosts. Alex looked over at me and ended up getting hit in the face with the paper ball.

"The fuck, man?" He complained and bent to pick up the ball, he chucked it at Levi, but it bounced harmlessly off Levi's shoulder. Alex turned back to me and looked behind me, "What happened? Is she getting ready?"

I shook my head and scratched at my eyebrow. "No, she doesn't want to come down."

Levi took a step and looked up at the ceiling, "If she doesn't want to come down, why don't we go up?"

I shook my head, "I don't think that's a good idea. She's pretty pissed off right now."

Levi scoffed. "I wonder why?" He asked sarcastically.

My attention snapped to him; I opened my mouth to say something but a loud bang from the kitchen distracted me. My heart stopped and I darted out of the room. I threw the door open and sprinted down the hallway. All I could think of was how did you get out of the room so easily? I couldn't breathe as I pushed the kitchen door open and looked around, no one was in here. My breathing was so loud I didn't hear the guys walking in behind me.

Alex walked over and picked the cast iron skillet up off the floor. "Doesn't this usually just sit on the stove?" He asked, flipping it over in his hand. "Damn, this thing weighs a ton."

Levi shuddered, "I hate this place," he looked around the room and back up at the ceiling, "are you sure she's still up there? That could have been Mel running through here. I'll go up and look."

I put my arm out. "No, it's fine. She's up there. Let's turn off the lights and get out of here. Give Mel some time to cool off." The kitchen door had a padlock on the inside that was still in place, and the way the latch works on the basement door, it wouldn't be latched still.

Levi shook his head, "I don't like the thought of her being here alone."

I looked at him sideways, "Well get over it, if I let her out now she'll just run straight to the police."

Levi looked back up at the ceiling. He shook his head and walked out of the kitchen.

As the guys were making their way out to the truck, I walked around the house to turn off the electric. Mostly out of habit, what's the point of paying utilities on a house that hardly gets used?

I got to the truck and climbed into the back, Levi was drinking a beer and Alex was scrolling through his phone. I didn't have the door closed before Levi put the truck in drive and sped down the dirt road.

—⁂—

When I got home, I went straight to the bedroom. I kicked my shoes off and collapsed on the bed. My head wasn't even on the pillow before my eyes closed.

I'm not sure how long I was out but when I woke up; covered in a layer of sweat, I wasn't sure what I needed most, food or a shower. I opted for taking a shower, the hot water felt so good. I let the hot water beat down on me until it ran cold. Begrudgingly I got out and dried off and went to the kitchen to get something to eat.

While I was eating I heard a phone go off. It wasn't a ringtone I was immediately familiar with. But when I tracked down the phone it made more sense. It was your phone; I had almost forgotten I took it. Your sister was trying to call you. I ignored the call and sent a text, telling her to fuck off. She tried calling again, and again I ignored it and sent more texts each more insulting than the last telling her that you never wanted to hear from her again. I turned your phone off and tossed it on the sofa and finished eating.

MELANIE (November 29)

I was pacing back and forth from the bathroom to the bedroom, every now and then I would go over and try to open the bedroom door, but every time it was still locked. I rubbed my eyes and paced back to the bed, going over my failed attempts at escaping.

The first night Griffin left he didn't come back for 3 days. When he finally showed up with food, I made a break for the door while he went to the bathroom. He caught me out on the porch and pulled me back and held me in the doorway for a moment, grabbing my right wrist he brought my hand up and held it by the frame.

"Grab it." He demanded. I tried pulling out of his grip, shaking my head in a panic. Griffin rolled his eyes, "Just grab the door frame, the longer you make me wait the worse it will be." My heart felt like it was about to stop. I clenched my teeth as his grip on my wrist tightened, he slammed my hand against the threshold and held it there as he slammed the door closed. I screamed and fell to the floor; Griffin picked me up and took me back up the stairs. Scolding me for trying to leave. I wasn't able to do much with that hand for a few days. But little did I know I wouldn't see him for another 5 days.

The next time he showed up I waited until he was asleep. As quiet as I could, I fished the keys out of his pants pocket and tiptoed out of the room. I went fast, trying to keep my steps light so the floorboards wouldn't creak under me. I was halfway down the stairs when I made a wrong move and the wood beneath my feet let out a groan. Panicked I flew down the rest of the stairs; but once I hit the bottom step, arms wrapped around me and pulled me back up the stairs. I couldn't see out of my left eye for a while.

The next time Griffin showed up I played the sorry 'Good Girl' he wanted. I had a plan on how to get down the stairs without them creaking and I was ready to do *anything* to get his guard down and get out the front door. I did everything he wanted to that night, he took so many pictures and videos of us doing things that I don't ever want to think about again. I pushed past the indecency of it all, figuring if I could get through these hours of humiliation I was sure I could get out of here. We took a shower together and while I was drying off I noticed that he was getting dressed. I swallowed the lump in my throat and got in bed. I asked if he was leaving. He pulled his shirt over his head and asked me if I wanted him to stay; I wanted him as far away from me as possible but in order for me to get out I needed him here. So, I begged him to stay; but he shook his head and laughed. He congratulated me on my performance today; but he knew that I was faking it. I was jumping off the bed as he closed the door and locked it. I screamed and yelled for him to come back. Through the door he told me that if I didn't start acting right I would see less of him. I almost took that as a challenge, but if Griffin wasn't here then there was no food. If Griffin wasn't here, there were no lights, no heat. He's been turning off the breaker when he leaves, to give me time to 'reflect' he likes to say. Another sick game of his, I'm sure.

I stopped keeping track of the days between his visits. It was starting to drive me mad knowing how long I've been here.

I ran my hands through my hair and went to get a drink of water. As gross as it is, I've been drinking small handfuls of water out of the back of the toilet. I guess it's a good thing I don't eat while I'm here alone, one flush and my drinking water would be gone.

I should ask Griffin for something to help pass the day. The only thing I have here for any sort of entertainment is the window that only changes when the sun moves. I've told him once before that I was bored throughout the day, and he said he would fix it. The next time he showed up he brought me a few different lingerie sets; laughing and saying that his entertainment is more important than mine. He could at least get a matching pair of socks; the nights are starting to get colder. The comforter helps keep the chill out, but it does nothing for the cold floor.

The heavy footsteps on the other side of the door were just white noise now. I used to call out to it, but I never got an answer just stomps and bangs.

I curled back into the bed and pulled the thick blanket over my head, squeezing my eyes shut trying to make myself fall asleep.

—⁂—

I was woken up by someone gently shaking my shoulder. I rolled over and sat up, rubbing the sleep from my eyes. Griffin was sitting on the bed grinning down at me. "I have something for you." he said with a wink.

"What is it?" I asked, my voice coming out in a croak from lack of use and lack of water.

"Ah-ah," he said wagging a finger at me, "don't I get a kiss a first?" I gave him a tight-lipped peck. He sighed, "I guess you don't want your surprise then." I gritted my teeth and kissed him again, longer, and more relaxed. Griffin shook his and pulled back and licked his lips, "I'll take it." He looked at me with that same longing look he had when we first met. I used to love it when he looked at me like that, now days it just makes me sick. He brushed his hand over my hair, "Let's go downstairs and eat first."

My stomach started growling at the promise of food. Griffin had me go down first, I guess he was worried I would push him down the stairs; a worry that wasn't too far-fetched. The smell of rosemary chicken filled my nose, coaxing me to go down the stairs faster. Griffin held the kitchen door open for me. I walked by ignoring the heat of his gaze and went straight for the table. Griffin had already laid out the food and set the table up. It smelled amazing; chicken breast, green beans, and a salad, served on paper plates with cheap plasticware. There was also the customary bottle of wine (the only thing that was sturdy enough to do damage when used as a weapon, but he kept it close to him) served in plastic cups.

Griffin pulled out my chair for me. "Eat up, honey." He sat down across from me, looking at his plate, he smiled and said, "I'm starving, I haven't ate all day. I've been so busy..." His voice faded off into the background as I took the first bite of the chicken. It was so fucking delicious; I tried to savor it, but I was so hungry I almost swallowed the bites whole. When I finished the last bite Griffin offered some more. "There's more food if you're still hungry, but keep in mind there is dessert."

"I'm ok for now," I said and added, "thank you," as an afterthought, not trying to 'disrespect' him. "That was really good, thank you Griffin." I got up to throw my plate away, holding my hand out to take his plate too.

"You're welcome baby. Do you want your surprise now?" He asked, handing me his trash.

I painted on a smile, "whenever you're ready." I said sweetly and turned to discard the paper dishes.

Griffin pushed himself back from the table and stood up. "It's in the living room," he said. I followed him out of the kitchen, he held the door open for me, and I crossed the hallway and into the living room. There was a silver gift bag sitting on the table. Griffin grabbed me by the elbow, his tight grip made me clinch my teeth, "Wait. I want a dance first." He said pulling me into him. He took out his phone and tapped on the screen a few times, the speaker that doubled as a record player came to life and started playing a slow melody. The piano was haunting and when the cello came in a cold shiver ran down my spine. Griffin tucked his phone in his back pocket and pulled me in close and twirled me to the music. "I've missed you," he said, brushing the back of his fingers down my cheek.

I looked up at him, there was an odd look in his eyes. I sucked in a breath, "I missed you too." I said flatly.

Griffin looked up at the ceiling and chuckled, "You've always been a horrible liar." Sighing, he looked down at me. "I know this is all a little crazy, honey but it'll get better soon. I promise." He held me out at arm's length and dropped his hands, letting them fall to his sides. "Time for gifts." He whispered with a small smile.

I followed him over to the sofa and sat down, waiting for him to make the next move. Griffin was standing at the coffee table; he picked up the bag and held it out for me to take. "Thank you," I said sitting on my lap and looked inside. Inside there looked to be a box wrapped in black silk. I pulled it out and sat the bag on the floor. I unwrapped the bundle and at first I thought I was hallucinating. Griffin had picked up three books and wrapped them in a black silk robe. Based off the cover and quick summary on the back they were all dark fantasy novels. I looked up at him, "You got me some books," somehow that was unnerving. I don't know what else I was expecting, it's not like he would have gifted me something that would physically help me escape and not just mentally.

404

"Of course, I'd do anything for you." He sat down next to me and picked up the bag, "there was one more thing in there," he said tightly and handed me something.

I was shocked when I looked down and saw a pair of grey wool socks. I was afraid if I touched them they would disappear. I shook my head, he would do anything he said, "then let me go."

With a chuckle he said, "I'd do *almost* anything for you." He wrapped a hand around the back of my neck, "I don't trust that you won't go straight to the police just yet. I need you to prove yourself before I let you go."

It was all pointless. He is never going to let me leave, I thought of the carved messages underneath the drawers. I looked down at the books in my lap. At least I have some entertainment now. "How do I prove myself?" I asked.

Griffin brushed some hair back over my shoulder, "just be a good girl," he shrugged, "it's not that hard."

'Just be a good girl?' I wanted to throw one of these books at him. Instead, I just put on the socks. They were so warm and soft.

When I didn't say anything he sighed, "do what you're told, don't make me ask twice. Don't talk back, don't destroy the house while I'm gone." He took a breath, "stop doing things that make me hurt you," he said taking my hand; the one he slammed in the door frame, and brushed his lips across my knuckles. Still holding my hand, he stood up. "Let's go upstairs." He said pulling me off the sofa.

Griffin left a few hours ago. I was on the bed laying on my back, staring up at the ceiling, holding my cheek that was still throbbing. I needed an ice pack but that wasn't happening. Griffin had punched me before he left. He got mad at me when I told him I was hungry, and I wasn't going to let him do anything else until I ate again. He said I was being a greedy pig and the meal he brought early today was more than enough to satisfy him so it should have been enough to satisfy me. I brought up how I have been locked in a room for days with no food and I was fucking hungry. That's when he pulled his arm back and slammed his fist against my face before he threw the door shut behind him. The floor creaking under him adding to all the noise he was making. He was yelling the whole way to the door, even after the house shook when he slammed the front door close I could still hear him going off outside.

I took the books and threw them at the door. It didn't do anything except make me feel a little bit better.

—⚬—

I tossed and turned, by now I was used to the noises of the woods that surrounds the house but tonight there was something in the cacophony of nature's night time lullaby, something that grabbed my attention and pulled me from sleep. I sat up and looked around. The room was so dark, if it wasn't for the moonlight peeking through the window I don't think I would have been able to see a thing.

A screech from outside pierced the silence. I got up and walked unsteadily over to the window. At first I didn't see anything, just when I was about to go back to bed I seen a glow coming from the trees. There was another screech, this time it was longer and sounded more like a woman screaming. I blinked a few times, unable to step away from the window as the glow came closer to the house. I could make out bright orange flames just on the other side of the tree line, and inside that fire was a woman. There was another scream as she stepped out of the trees and walked onto the grass. She grabbed her head and wailed, the sound so full of sorrow and pain. The flames danced around her as she stood there crying.

I put a hand on the glass, and she immediately turned to face me. She covered her mouth with one hand and pointed at me with the other. The scream she made was so deafening I had to cover my ears. I closed my eyes and stepped backwards away from the window. My feet collided with something, and I fell to the floor. Scrambling back until I hit the bed, I crawled up and pulled the cover over my head like a scared little girl.

The next thing I knew the sun was up. I groaned and pushed my face into the mattress and fell back asleep.

GRIFFIN (November 29)

I was in my room with the lights off, I don't think I've ever had a migraine this bad before. I've been pulled in so many different directions the past few days I wasn't sure when that last time I actually sat down was. Dad has been keeping us busy at the shop, and I've been keeping myself busy with parties chasing away my problems with a line a white powder and endless bottles of booze. I was lying in bed on my stomach, with a pillow over my head. Occasionally, I would hear a 'ping' from the other room, sending waves of pain radiating through me with each shrill note. Even though I tossed my phone on the sofa in the front room and my bedroom door was half closed I could still hear it when it went off.

The guys have started to turn against me, they say I'm paranoid, and I get in these moods from time to time; but I can see it. It was just a suspicion at first, a weird tugging feeling at the back of my head. It wasn't until the day that I brought back the pictures and videos when my paranoia was brought to light. The guys and I used to show off our conquests all the time; hell, we would even upload a video or two if one of us thought it was worth it.

But something must have changed, I noticed it in Levi first. His expressions while going through the pictures were neutral, then I heard the 'Good Girl' video start playing. Levi looked up at me, shaking his head he started telling me how I went too far. Alex's eyes were glued to the phone, I couldn't tell what he was thinking. Levi covered his mouth and stared at the back wall. I followed his gaze, the painting of 'The Burning Witch' grinned back at me.

Levi then turned to me and asked, "you're not still turning the power off when you leave, are you? Man, it's getting below freezing at night."

"Relax. She's fine. We've been through worse. At least it hasn't snowed yet." I said going to get a drink.

I heard Levi walk up behind me and turned around. "I don't give a fuck what *we* went through. *NO ONE* should be treated like that."

I took a step back and looked at Alex. He was just scrolling, keeping his focus on his phone, pretending to ignore us.

"It's not that cold yet, the frost is gone by the time the sun comes up." I shot back.

Levi laughed and pushed by me. "I can't deal with this right now," he said. Over his shoulder he yelled, "At least get her a pair of fucking socks!" He made sure to slam the door shut when he left.

Now every time I walk in a room, they're talking in Spanish knowing I can't understand what they're saying.

I pinched the bridge of my nose. Maybe they're right. Maybe it's all in my head. Or maybe they are hiding something, maybe they're planning something. Thinking about them just made my headache worse.

I grabbed the pillow and pressed it down on the back of my head. Nothing was making this headache go away, I almost wanted to eat a bullet to make the pain stop. My phone started ringing, I covered my ears and waited for it to stop. I stayed like that for what felt like hours, in all reality it could have only been a minute; but my phone wouldn't stop ringing. So, I pulled myself out of bed and went to turn it off. But when I picked it up, I had no missed calls or messages. I put my phone down and went to sit on the sofa when my phone started ringing again.

I turned and looked down at my phone, but the screen was still black. Confused I looked around, and my eyes landed on the top right drawer of the entertainment center; where I had put your phone all those days ago. Hesitantly I walked over and pulled the drawer open. And, sure enough your phone was lit up and a picture of you and your sister flashed across the screen.

I grabbed the side of my head and closed my eyes. I know I turned that phone off before I put it in the drawer. I shook my head in confusion and ripped the phone out of its hiding place. I hit the ignore button and sent your sister a long message, using whatever insult I could think of before taking your phone in the kitchen and hitting it a few times with a meat tenderizer.

With my headache now a thousand times worse, I went to the backroom and took a few random pills I hoped would make me feel better and drifted off in one of the gaming chairs.

—⁂—

I had a pleasant dream for once. I was in the backroom sitting in the chair I had fell asleep in. There was some noises in the kitchen, so I got up to check it out. You were in the kitchen, wearing black high heels and classic black dress with white polka dots on the skirt. Your hair was held back with a bright red head band, and you were humming our song while stirring something in a mixing bowl. I came up behind you and kissed your shoulder. You turned and smiled up at me, taking your left index finger and dipping it in the batter. Bringing your batter dipped finger up to my lips I sucked it clean. I don't know what shined more brightly, your eyes or the ring on your finger. I grinned down at you and kissed your lips. I took your left hand in mine and admired the ring. This is all I wanted. Someone to love me, someone who will never leave. You look up at me and mouthed 'I love you.' I bent down to kiss you on the lips.

—◊◊—

I groaned and opened my eyes. The house was quiet. There was no one in the kitchen baking anything. I ran a hand down my face and looked over at the window. It looked like it would be a cold one tonight. I figured I should pick up a few things and go check on you. I hoped giving you a few extra days away from me will be enough for you to realize how much you need me. I forced myself to get up and take a quick shower, hoping the warm water would help chase away the headache.

I got up to get ready, starting some coffee before getting dressed. While I pulled my jeans up I went over a list in my head of things to pick up at the store. When I poured a cup of coffee to go I thought of few more things I should get while I was there and smiled to myself. After tonight things will get better.

I locked the house up before I left, kicking myself for not starting the car to let it warm up. I drove to the store and practically ran through the isles. I kept double checking the basket making sure that I didn't forget anything. While I was grabbing a silk robe off the hanger, Levi's words echoed through my head. 'At least get her a pair of fucking socks!' I gritted my teeth; out of spite I didn't want to get any dammed socks, but the fucker had a point. I grabbed a pair grey wool socks on my way to the registers.

—∿—

When I got the old house it seemed less dark, somehow more cheerful. Like it knew that everything was going to change for the best. I put the car in park and pulled out a few things to put together as a gift for you. First I took the silver gift bag and put the socks on the bottom. Then I got the 3 random books I had grabbed off the shelf, the covers were mostly black with pops of dark colors with animals etched in bronze, silver, and gold. I stacked the books and wrapped the black silk robe around them and placed the bundle in a silver gift bag.

I got out of the car and went around the house to flip on the breaker. When I got everything inside I went to the kitchen to turn everything back on and got to work heating up the food. I went over and set the table then dropped the gift bag off in the living room. I went back to the kitchen to check on the food and make the plates, I wanted to make sure there wouldn't be a moment were my back was turned to you.

When everything was perfect, I went upstairs to bring you down so we could eat together. I unlocked the door and peered inside. You were curled up on the bed, sleeping. I walked over and sat down next to you, gently shaking your shoulder to wake you up. You rolled over and sat up. I couldn't fight my grin, "I have something for you." I teased with a winked.

Your voice was horse as you asked what is was. I scolded you, asking were my kiss was first. You gave me a tight-lipped kiss; well, it was more you pressing your lips against mine; it wasn't a kiss at all. I sighed, "I guess you don't want your surprise then." Your jaw tensed as you leaned in and kissed me again. I almost laughed at the dramatic difference, this one was longer and much more relaxed, but it was still fake as fuck. In a way you kind of reminded me of.... I shook my head at the flash of flames and pulled away from the kiss. I licked my lips; you two are so similar, but you taste so different. "I'll take it." I studied your face, the more I look at you the less I see of *her* and more I see of *you*. And how much I love you, and how I would do anything to keep this. To keep you. I brushed some of your hair back, it was starting to get greasy, but I could get past that. I wanted to ravage you, but I was hungry for actual food. I haven't eating all day. "Let's go downstairs and eat." I said, getting off the bed and walking towards the door.

Out of habit I had you go downstairs first; I learned that lesson the hard way. But it was my first my time and I never made that mistake twice. Since you resemble *her* so much I'm gonna have to be on guard. Keeping you in sight I opened the kitchen door and held it for you as you went in and looked at the table. I know you wouldn't pull the shit that *she* did, you're better than *her*. But you can't be too sure, that's why I keep the bottle of wine next to me.

I walked in and pulled a chair out for you. "Eat up honey." I said sitting down in the chair in front of you. I looked down at the food on my plate, it smelled amazing, and I couldn't wait to eat. "I'm starving, I haven't ate all day. I've been so busy; it's like as soon as I sit down my phone's going off. I need to go pick up this car then I need to go drop off these parts." I rolled my eyes, "it never ends." I cut up some chicken and popped it into my mouth. "Then when I get home the guys want to hang out. And I can't say no to the boys. We've been through too much to do that to them." I wasn't sure if you were listening, but it was nice to talk to someone who didn't need anything from me. When you had finished your plate I offered you more food but told you to keep in mind that there was dessert.

You shook you head, "I'm ok for now, thank you." Then you looked up at with a small smile, "that was really good, thank you Griffin." You got up and held your hand out to take my plate.

I relaxed, your attuited taking a pleasant turn. Handing you my trash I said, "you're welcome baby. Do you want your surprise now?"

You smiled at me sweetly and said, "Whenever you're ready," and turned to throw away the paper plates.

I got up from the table "It's in the living room," I said, and took a chance by turning my back to you to cross the hallway and open the living room door. You walked right by me and started heading for the sofa. I grabbed you by the elbow to stop you and ask for a quick dance first. Still holding onto you I took out my phone and started playing some Peter Gundry. His music never fails to sooth my dark side. I tucked my phone back into my pocket and pulled you in to me and moved us with the music. Brushing your cheek with back of my hand I whispered how much I missed you.

"I missed you too," you said, unconvincingly.

I looked up at the ceiling and laughed, "you've always been a horrible liar." Sighing I looked back down at you. "I know this all a little crazy, honey but it'll get better soon. I promise." I held you out at arm's length and dropped my hands to my sides. "Time for gifts."

We walked over to the sofa, you just a step behind me but could still see you. You sat down and waited patiently for me to hand you the bag. "Thank you," you said, looking inside. I watched you untied the robe and look at the books. You looked like you were ready to cry. "You got me books?" You said in disbelief.

"Of course." I said sitting down next to you. I picked up the bag and took out the socks. "There was one more thing in there." Handing them to you I said. "I'd do anything for you."

You took the socks from me, running your fingers over them like they might disappear. Then you looked up at me, instead of gratitude, you only shook your head and said, "then let me go."

I couldn't help but chuckle. "I'd do *almost* anything for you." I put my hand on the back of your neck, "I don't trust that you won't go straight to the police yet. I need you to prove yourself to me before I let you go."

I expected a smart-ass remark, some witty comment. But instead, you looked down at the books and asked, "How do I prove myself?"

I brushed some hair behind your shoulders. "Just be a good girl. It's not that hard." You looked at me, I waited for a moment, but you still hadn't spoken so I elaborated. "Do what you're told, don't make me ask twice. Don't talk back, don't destroy the house while I'm gone." I took the hand I slammed the door on and kissed the scars on your knuckles. "Stop doing things that make me hurt you," I stood up, still holding your hand I said, "Let's go upstairs."

We were having an amazing time, breathing each other in. Tasting every inch of each other. It wasn't until your growling stomach made you stop and start complaining about how hungry you still were. I just wanted a few more minutes to enjoy you but you couldn't let me have that. You wanted to eat something before we did anything else. Which was absurd. I was still full from when we ate, you should be too, and I told you so. But that only made you mad, and you started crying about how you've been locked up here for days with no food, and you were hungry. I didn't like the tone you starting to get and the next thing I knew my knuckles were stinging and you were on the floor holding your cheek.

I threw the bedroom door closed. Words just flew out of my mouth before I could stop them. I was so furious, all I saw was red. I was on auto pilot as I turned off the power to the house and got into the car, peeling out of the drive way. Eager to get home and drink this all of this away.

At the end of the driveway, I could have sworn I saw someone standing there. But it was just some bushes. I shook my head and fished around for my cigarettes. A nicotine buzz wouldn't fix the stress of the day, but it was a good start. I would have to stop at the liquor store before I get home. My alcohol consumption as doubled in the last couple of days.

MELANIE (December 7)

I could see my breath this morning. It's snowed a few times the past couple of days but only a little. It would only get colder from here, so far last night was definitely one of the coldest nights here. I wrapped the blanket around me tighter and closed my eyes again, trying to remember those days during the summer when it was suffocatingly hot.

I brought my legs up to curl into a tighter ball. There was those damned footsteps again, pacing around, taunting me. I know that no one is there, but hearing those footsteps always gave me a false since of hope. Like someone had finally figured out that something very bad has happened to me and they found out where I was and now, they are coming down the hall to save me.

My mind took that thought and just rolled with it. The mysterious footsteps belonged to my sister and she's looking for a key to unlock the door. A tear rolled down my cheek, I wiped it away furiously. Crying isn't going to help. Waiting around for a savior isn't going to help. I closed my eyes and focused on my breathing.

—m—

Then the strangest thing happened. KNOCK, KNOCK. I sat up straight and looked at the door. I opened my mouth, but nothing came out. KNOCK, KNOCK again. I moved the cover aside and got out of bed. My legs felt like jelly underneath me, I couldn't breathe as I put a hand on the door trying to feel who was behind it. KNOCK, KNOCK. The sudden rapping made me gasp and step back, my hand falling away from the door.

"Melanie?" A male voice ask. I blinked in confusion, that voice didn't belong to Griffin, I couldn't tell who was behind the door. "Melanie, are you in there?"

"Who's there?" I called out.

"Ouch, that kind of hurts." His tone was light, edged with laughter, "come on out, we're going to be late for the movie."

I shook my head, "what movie?" I asked. What was going on, I was so confused. I put a hand on my head, this must be one of Griffin's sick games.

"I know," the voice sighed, "you're not a fan of comic book movies, but it's either superheroes or a kid show." He laughed, "come on, we'll get the big popcorn bucket, and you can take it home. Come on out, I've got the car warming up; so, you won't be cold."

I shook my head, "I can't."

"Why not?" The voice asked.

"The door's locked." My voice was barely above a whisper.

"Why would you lock the door?" There was a scraping sound, a shiver went through me. "There, now open the door Melanie. I want to get some good seats."

I took a step towards the door, but it seemed further away somehow. It felt like I was moving in slow motion as I reached up and twisted the knob. I took a deep breath and held as I opened the door.

"Wow, you look incredible." I looked up at the man and was horrified. Tim was standing in front of me, blood running down his neck from the gunshot wound under his chin and soaking into his shirt.

"Are you ready to go?" He asked holding out his arm for me to hook mine through.

———m———

I gasped and shot up straight in bed. Panting I looked around the room. I untangled the cover from my legs and ran a hand through my sweaty hair. My heart was beating so fast I thought I was going to have a heart attack. I fell back on to the bed and covered my face with the pillow; willing myself to just die right here. But of course, it wouldn't be that easy.

GRIFFIN (December 7)

I tossed and turned, every time I drifted off to sleep the nightmares over took me. Every night my dreams haunt me; they seem to get worse on the nights I don't party. I sat up in bed and ran a hand down my face. I reached over to pick up my phone so I could check the time; but it was dead.

Dragging myself out of bed I went to get dressed but there were no clean clothes. I forgot to get the clothes out of the dryer and start a new load, so I threw on yesterday's outfit and went to the front room to plug my phone in, but there was already a phone on the charger. I furrowed my eyebrows then I heard the toilet flush and turned towards the noise. I looked back at the phone and tried to remember who it belonged to. Looking around the room for clues I saw a duffle bag and a jacket on the floor by the sofa. I shook my head even more confused.

"Hey man, you're out of toilet paper." Levi said walking into the front room.

I tilted my head still looking around, still confused. "Yeah, I'll pick some up next time I'm at the store."

Levi looked at me through narrowed eyes, "you ok?"

I rubbed the back of my head, "Haven't been getting much sleep." I mumbled and headed to the kitchen to grab something to eat. Levi must have started a pot of coffee already; the pot was halfway done brewing. I opened the refrigerator but there was only some condiments, an empty carton of milk and a 12 case of beer with only one can left. The cabinets weren't any better. I settled on some toast and tossed some bread in the toaster.

"You sure you're alright man?" Levi asked, "When was the last time you ate?"

I shrugged, and opened the refrigerator door again, "I eat, just not at home." I said taking out the butter.

Levi's eyebrow twitched, "Alright. Since I'm gonna be crashing here for a while I'm going to pick up some actual food. Unlike you I value my body and what goes in it."

"Whatever Gandi." I said, grabbing the bread from the toaster and tossed the slices on a plate. I grabbed a butter knife and smeared some butter on the toast. It was a better breakfast than whatever I could get out of the vending machine at the shop. Which I was late for. I brushed some crumbs off the front of my shirt before pulling on my jacket. I took out my wallet and handed Levi some cash, not bothering to count it. "I won't complain about you stocking the cabinets though."

Levi shoved the money in his back pocket. "When was the last time you went out there?"

My mouth went dry; to buy some time I poured some coffee. "It's been a few days." I didn't hear anything behind me, so I looked over my shoulder to see what he was doing.

Shaking his head, Levi was walking over to the sofa. "Dude, she needs to eat. I know you're not leaving food when you leave."

"We eat together all the time." I stated in my defense.

"Don't give me that bullshit. You just said it's been a few days." He shot back.

I rubbed my temple; this wasn't helping my headache. I seem to be getting a lot of those lately. "She's fine." I said turning and grabbing my coffee. "I don't need this shit. I'm late for work." Levi was saying something behind me, but I tuned him out. I focused on getting my boots on. "You know where the spare key is, make sure you lock up when you leave the house." I told him, gathering up my things before pulling my jacket on. Today was going to be a long day.

—◊—

When I got home the house was dark. I almost expected the front door to be unlocked but Levi wasn't that spiteful. The first thing I wanted to do was to take a shower and wash the motor oil and sweat off of me. I flipped the lights in the front room on and noticed that Levi had left his things here, the duffle bag was on the floor by the sofa and there were some things thrown on top like he was looking for something before he left. Since his truck was gone I figured that he went back to his place. I shrugged and went to take a long shower.

I didn't turn the water off until it ran cold. When I stepped out I went over to the dryer and shuffled the clothes around looking for something clean to wear. I took the basket off the dryer and sat it down on the floor, so I wasn't putting clothes on the now wet bathroom floor since I was dripping water everywhere. I used the towel I dried off with to wipe up the water up off the floor and threw the towel in the washer.

I felt much better. Actually, in a good mood, I made my way to the kitchen to see if there was any food. All the cabinets were full. Levi really went all out. I made myself something to eat and sat down in the front room.

Turning on the tv for some background noise, I kicked my feet up on the coffee table and savored my dinner. I was halfway done with my plate when Levi's truck interrupted the scene on the tv. Not bothering with any formal greetings Levi came through the door and went straight to the backroom. I scoffed and went back to eating.

A few minutes later Levi came back in and went to the kitchen. I heard glass clinking and figured he was making a drink.

"Hello to you too." I called out sarcastically.

Levi grumbled something and took a long drink from his glass.

I watched him for a moment. He seemed agitated. "What's up man?" I asked.

"'What's up' is that your ass is on my fucking pillow." He spat, turning around to face me.

I looked down at the cushion under me and laughed. I didn't even notice I had sat down on it. "So, fucking what? I just got out of the shower." I took a bite out of my dinner and turned my attention to the tv.

Levi came over and kicked my feet off the coffee table. "Get up." He stated.

I rolled my eyes and pulled the pillow out from underneath me without getting up. I tossed the pillow aside, "there, happy?" I said absently.

"No," he stated. "I said, *get up*." I paused mid chew and drug my gaze over to him. He looked drunk, swaying slightly, eyes blood shot.

I sat my plate down on the coffee table and stood up. "What's this ab-" Levi cut me off by sucker punching me in the mouth. Caught off guard, I took a step back to catch myself. "What the fuck man?" I asked, running a hand down my face and checking my fingers for blood. Levi struck out again, this time catching me in the shoulder. I blocked a side swing and brought my knee up to get him in the stomach, but he stepped out of my reach and slapped me across the face. "You're really starting to piss me off." I yelled.

"Good motherfucker." He shouted back and lunged for me. Knocking me backwards with him on top. He started punching down at me, I blocked most of them but a few landed. I was able to knock him over, it was easy since he was wasted. Sober Levi wouldn't have been so easy to fend off. I pushed myself up and kicked him hard in the ribs.

He grabbed my foot on the second kick and threw it to the side, causing me to lose my balance and fall over. Levi laughed and pushed himself up. Anger pulsed through me, I pushed myself back up and lashed out. I got a few good hits in, catching him pretty good in the jaw and splitting his lip. Levi started retaliating, he was getting the better of me when Alex came through the door.

"Hey, what the fuck is going on!?" Alex yelled and started pulling Levi off me.

Levi pointed a finger in my direction, "I get so tired of his bullshit." He swiped the back of his hand across his mouth, smearing blood and saliva across his face.

"We all do, man. But you don't see me picking fights." He held a hand out to me and helped me up. Adrenaline was keeping the pain away; I knew I would feel it tomorrow. "What did you do?" Alex asked me when I stood up.

"I didn't do shit! I was sitting here eating my food-" I started but Levi cut me off.

"Oh, fucking blah, blah bitch! You know what you're doing!" Levi tried lunging for me but with Alex now in the way he started pacing.

"Is this about your stupid pillow?" I asked motioning to the pillow I threw to the side moments before all this started.

"No, you fucking idiot!" Levi shouted. "You think you're so slick don't you. You got away with it how many times? Now it's just a sick fucking game to you! Isn't it!" He started rambling, his words slurring together making it hard to understand him. But he made his point loud and clear. Alex and I let him ramble on, most of it didn't make any sense. "So fucked up. Here I am just an enabler." He said flopping down on the sofa and covering his face with his hands.

I rolled my shoulders and popped my neck. I could already feel some bruises forming but the adrenaline still coursing through me kept most of the pain away. I would feel it once the rush of the fight died down.

"I picked a bad time to come over." Alex stated before he started going through the refrigerator.

I walked over to him and grabbed a beer, holding it on my left eye for a few moments before cracking it open and taking a long satisfying drink. "It's never a bad time. What's up man?" I asked.

Alex looked into the front room at Levi who was now staring at his phone, pinching the screen as if he was zooming in and out on a picture. "I needed to get out of the house. Kara gets weird this time of year."

"It's just the holidays." I stated. "It messes with people's heads."

Alex nodded and took a drink. "Maybe so." He looked back into the front room. I could practically see the thought swimming around in his head.

I could feel the anger starting to boil inside me again. I furrowed my eye brows and took another drink before asking, "do you agree with him?"

Almost startled Alex looked over at me. "About what?"

"About me and my relationships."

Alex swirled his beer can and took a long drink. He was stalling. I studied him until he spoke, "it is kind of messed up how you end things."

"I don't end things. I never, not once broke up with any of them. I did everything for them!" I could tell I was starting to yell. Taking a deep breath, I pushed myself off the counter and went to the back room.

I sat down in one of the gaming chairs. I could hear Levi and Alex start talking in Spanish. I cover my ears and squeezed my eyes shut, trying to drown them out. But I could still here them blabbing. Angerly I got out of the chair, sending it rolling backwards and hitting the wall behind it. I went to the bathroom and took something for the headache that was sinking it's claws into my brain.

When I came out of the bathroom Alex was rolling up a blunt and Levi was staring up at the ceiling. When he heard the door open he popped his head up and looked at me. "You're taking me to go see Melanie."

I paused, looking between him and Alex. "I'll take her back to her apartment in a few days. You can see her then."

Levi shook his head. "Now."

"No. I have her in a good spot, she's almost to that breaking point I can feel it."

"And what is the 'breaking point'?" Alex asked, reaching for a lighter.

"It's when I know she won't rat us out to the police."

Alex kind of laughed. "What did we do? This was all you."

I took a breath and sat down. "Yeah well, a few more days and she'll be back to her normal life."

Levi shook his head again, "I'm not waiting a few days. A 'few days' never run out. We're going now." He stood up. "I'm not asking permission. I'll go myself if I have to."

Amused I tilted my head to the side. "Then go."

Levi clenched his jaw and looked down at me. "I don't know the way. There are too many dirt roads. I'll just get turned around."

I laughed and took the joint from Alex. "Yeah. If I'm not paying attention I get turned around too."

Levi said something else, but I was too busy checking a notification that just came through on my phone. It was a flirty text from Natasha, I smirked and was about to reply when my phone was ripped out of my hands. "What the fuck?" I yelled.

Levi looked at my phone; he curled his lip in disgust and threw it back at me, hitting me in the chest. "You're not even listening, you prick!" He yelled.

"I'll fucking take you tomorrow. Get off my back!" I got up and went to my bed room. Closing and locking the door behind me. I sat down on the bed and thought about what I was going to do about you and Levi. But then my phone started to ring. I smirked and answered it, "Hey, Nat I was just about to call you."

MELANIE (December 9)

I was in the bathroom getting a handful of water from the toilet tank when I heard a truck pull up.

A truck? That was odd. It was too loud to be Griffins car. I went the window and pressed myself against it, trying to see the driveway from here but it was useless. 2 car doors opened and shut, there was laughing, and then the front door opened and closed shaking the house a little as the door slammed shut. There was some muffled noises, and then footsteps coming up the stairs. They were a little heavier than Griffins steps. The creaking floor letting me know who it was, was getting closer.

Is this another dream? Or is this actually happening? I thought as I stared at the door. The jingle of keys and the tink of metal-on-metal rung through my ears. The lock slid out of place and the doorknob twisted. My dreams have felt so real lately I am half convinced I'm still asleep.

"Mel?" It was a male voice, but it wasn't Griffin.

I could almost choak on my fear as my heart leapt up into my throat. I pressed my back against the dresser and reached behind me, grabbing onto a book to throw at whoever was behind the door. A useless weapon really but any fight is better than being a willing victim.

Whoever it was pushed the door open and stepped into the room, I had to be dreaming, there was no way this was real. My heart was beating too fast, I had no time to process what was happening before adrenaline took over and then the book went sailing across the room.

Levi swatted the book away before it hit him and closed the door, leaning against it casually. "I'm glad to see you still have some fight." He crossed his arms over his chest and tilted his head to the side, examining me. We stared at each other for a minute. My eyes were drawn to his mouth, more specifically his healing split lip. Then he cleared his throat and looked down at his feet.

I tried to speak but all that came out was a weird croak. Levi looked up at me confused. I swallowed what saliva I could work up and tried speaking again, "What are you doing here?" I asked, still not convinced this wasn't just another dream my psyche made up to torture me with.

Levi looked up at me and chuckled, "Getting my 'Birthday gift' from Griffin." Then he walked over to the bed and sat down, patting the spot next to him. I just stared at him, refusing to move. Levi scratched his chin and laughed. I noticed his knuckles were scabbed up. "We all kind of thought that's how it was going to be. What is it about me that repulses you so much?" He asked. He almost looked hurt; I wanted to laugh.

Instead, I rolled my eyes and shook my head. "It's the situation I find repulsive."

Levi tilted his head and looked at me. I couldn't tell if the concern on his face was real; but I decided it was fake. "Come here, let's talk about it." He said, wincing slightly as he sat up on the bed and leaned forward.

I shook my head again, "I can hear you from here." I said, my eyes flicking to the door.

Levi looked over at the door too and laughed, "No one else is going to show up if that's what you're waiting for." He hissed as he stood up and started walking toward me. "I don't want anything sexual from you, although I won't object." He grinned. "I just want to talk to you." He said, stopping a few feet in front of me and shoving his hands in his pockets. "I wanted to see how you were holding up. Based off what Griffin was saying it would be any day before you cracked." He looked me up and down, nothing covering my legs, a tank top that didn't even go to my butt, I felt completely exposed. I noticed how his gaze lingered on my feet with the grey wool socks covering them. He smiled and looked up at me, "Other than missing some pounds and a few bruises here and there you seem fine to me."

I seemed *fine?* My jaw dropped; I was anything but 'fine.' I looked up at Levi and shook my head, weighing my options. I crossed my arms in a way to cover as much of me as possible. My eyes went back to his lip, "What happened?" I asked.

Levi rubbed the back of his neck and shrugged. "Got into it with Griffin a few days ago." He started laughing but quickly stopped. "It was a dumb fight, nothing to worry about."

I nodded my head, not sure what to say.

"I won; in case you were wondering."

I felt myself starting to smile. Picturing Levi beating the shit out of Griffin was a nice thought, but if it doesn't get me out of this house then I don't care. I looked back at Levi and wondered again how much of him really cared, and how much of him was just here looking for an easy lay. My stomach turned at the thought of being used like that, being handed over to someone as a 'gift.' I took a step back unconsciously.

Levi took a breath and stepped back as well. "I'm not here to hurt you, Mel. Please look at me." I forced my eyes to meet his. Silence fell down around us, I just stared at him waiting for him to speak. After a few moments he took a step forward and held his hand out. "I'm sorry this happened to you, I'm doing all I can to make it easier for you." He looked at my feet as he said this, I couldn't help but wonder if he was responsible for them, I doubted that Griffin would have thought of it.

I shook my head, deciding that he was full of shit. Levi dropped his hand and let out a frustrated sigh. He ran a hand through his hair and turned to sit on the bed. My stomach twisted again but I wasn't sure if it was nerves or because I was hungry. My mind started thinking about food, and my stomach let out a growl. I crossed my arms over my stomach and walked over to the dresser. I touched the handle of the drawer with the warnings carved on the bottom. I started to wonder if I could get Levi to break me out of here. It wouldn't hurt to try, right?

"Have you heard from my sister?" I asked. "I was supposed to go visit a while back, what does my family think happened to me?" I kept my back turned to him, I could feel my eyes start to water and I didn't want him to see me any weaker than I had already appeared.

"Your sister isn't worried about you. Maybe a little mad but she won't be sending a search party any time soon."

My shoulders dropped; I opened my mouth, but no words came out. I shook my head 'no.' *What happened?* I thought *Griffin must have sent some messages acting like he was me.*

"Hey, cheer up. Be happy that she's not hurt." I heard the bed shift as he stood up. "I can get you some food and something to drink but that's as much I can do for you right now."

I looked down and closed my eyes, nodding my head 'yes' because too afraid if I started to speak I would cry. And that won't help me.

Levi left closing the door behind him. I stared at the door noting how I didn't hear the lock slide back into place. How fast can I make it down the stairs and out the front door? Did Levi leave his keys in the truck? Where was Griffin? I know I heard two car doors. Would I be able to secure the keys and get to the truck before Griffin caught me? If Levi had the keys on him I think I might be able to distract him long enough to pick his pockets.

I was so wrapped up in my thoughts I jumped when the door suddenly opened. I didn't even hear the footsteps coming up the stairs. Levi walked in with a deli meat sandwich and some beers. He handed me the food. "Made it myself," he beamed down at me.

"Thanks," I muttered and looked down at it in suspicion. I didn't hear his footsteps, was I that lost in thought; or is this going to turn into a nightmare soon? I looked at Levi, he seemed hurt that I wasn't eating.

"What's wrong?" He asked.

I shook my head and took a small bite. My shoulders dropped and I felt my whole body relax. The food was real, or it seemed real. I took another bite, even if this was a dream I was going to savor it. I forced myself to take smaller bites, I wanted to make it last as long as I could.

Levi talked about random things while I ate, mostly about his band and ranting about how his sister is getting on his nerves. He mentioned how he pretty much swapped houses with Griffin to get away. That last part caught my attention.

I was about to ask him for more details on that, but I took a drink instead. Why do I care if Griffin is shacking up with Levi's sister? It should be a good thing that he has another woman to distract him that isn't me. Maybe if things go good with them, he'll let me go? That thought made me laugh.

Levi looked over at me and tilted his head to the side with an eyebrow raised. Smirking slightly, he asked, "What'd I say?" He asked, "let me know so I can say it again. I missed seeing that smile."

I shook my head, "It's nothing," I looked down at the bottle in my hand, "just been awhile since I've had a beer."

Levi furrowed his eyebrows and looked around the room. "I had to do a lot of favors to be here today." He said.

The bite I took of my sandwich turned to ash in my mouth. I forced myself to swallow and chased it with the last of my beer.

"Hey, like I said before I just wanted to see how you're doing." Levi handed his beer over, "I can get another one downstairs." He said with a shrug and a half smile. I didn't think twice, I took the bottle from him.

It was half drank but still cold. "Is anyone else here?" I asked.

Levi shook his head, "No just me and Griffin. I don't know what he's doing but he said he wouldn't be far."

I nodded and took a drink. "Is there more food?" I asked.

Levi rubbed the back of his head. Why was he hesitating? After a while of debating silently with himself he got up and held out his hand. "Let's go see."

I grabbed his hand and followed him down the stairs. Our footsteps paired with the creaking floors were almost deafening. The house was quiet. Levi led us to the kitchen; the door squeaked on its hinges. I watched as Levi walked over to the refrigerator and opened it up. I walked around him and thought about slamming the door on his head and making a break for it; then I saw Griffin walk by the kitchen window. I went over to the table and sat down just as Griffin walked through the front door. My back was to the kitchen door, so I only heard when he came in. Flinching when I heard the door swing open.

"What's going on?" He asked. I couldn't tell if he was confused or angry.

Levi took the food he got out and went to the counter. "She was hungry," he said casually, "so I'm getting her some food."

Griffin made a noise and came up behind me. My soul left my body when he suddenly clapped his hands on my shoulders. He leaned down and asked, "So, was our girl everything you imagined?" His hot breath tickled the side of my face; his breath was sour from alcohol. My skin crawled as he kissed my temple.

Levi laughed, "We didn't get that far. I can't get off with her stomach growling like that."

Griffin started to rub my shoulders; it was rough and almost hurt. He laughed and whispered in my ear, "and to think I was out there being jealous over nothing." He shook me a little before sitting down next to me. "But be careful turning your back to this one. I wouldn't put it past her to try something stupid."

Levi laughed and brought the food over and sat it down in front of me. "Fair point, she's not a wilting flower." They kept talking like I wasn't there. Which was fine with me, I ate my food and listened to them talk.

After a while Griffin got up to go to the living room to smoke. He wrapped a hand around my arm and pulled me up out of the chair, "You either come smoke, or you go back to your room." He said to me. "Your choice, but you're not staying in here by yourself."

There was no way I was going to get high around these two. They don't trust me and that's fine, I don't trust them either. "I'll go back upstairs." I spoke.

Griffin laughed, "You hear this?" He said to Levi, "This is the shit I'm talking about. Just when I think she's starting to learn." He shoved me through the door, "get your ass in the living room."

Levi said something to Griffin as I stumbled into the hallway and caught myself on the banister. When the door swung closed, I overheard Griffin telling Levi to stay out of it. A noise from upstairs caught my attention, the same time that the guys were coming out of the kitchen.

Levi stood next to me and looked up the stairs. "This place is haunted." He stated casually.

Griffin laughed, "No it's not. It's just an old house with bad history."

I looked over at Griffin who shrugged and went to the living room. I looked back at Levi who had a haunted look about him. When he seen me looking at him, he grinned and held his arm out, "Let's not keep him waiting."

I walked past him and pushed the living room door open. Griffin was bent over the coffee table, snorting a line of white powder up his nose. "I thought we were smoking." I spoke.

"This is better." Griffin replied. Waving me over. I sat down on the sofa but didn't get any closer. "Trust me honey, you'll like it." I shook my head 'no'. Griffin gave me a disappointed look. "Mel, stop being stubborn and loosen up. It'll do you some good."

Levi sat down next to me, "Just once?" He asked.

I looked over to him and scooted away, shaking my head again, "I don't want to." I said pointedly.

Levi and Griffin shared a look. Levi clicked his tongue, "Well in that case, let her smoke, Griffin." He said bending over the table.

"Fine," Griffin growled, pulling out a bag from his coat pocket. There were three joints rolled up in it. He opened the bag and took one out. He handed it to me along with a lighter and said, "That one is all yours."

Looking it over it looked like a regular joint. The taste and smell from the smoke reminded me of the joint they gave me that night at the cabin. I smoked slowly but the effects still hit me like a freight train. Frist my eyes started to get heavy then it was like a someone threw me into a pool of water, sounds were muffled, and my limbs felt heavy.

I leaned forward to flick the ashes on the tray that was on the table, but it felt too far away. Levi chuckled and helped me out, taking the joint and flicking the ashes for me. He threw his arm around my shoulders before handing it back. Glancing over my heart sank deeper and deeper into my chest. Griffin was glaring at me, a look so full of hate.

I subconsciously pressed myself closer to Levi. He rubbed my arm, "Are you cold?" He asked. "You're shaking."

—⁓—

That was the last thing I remember from that night. When I woke up the next morning, I was naked and alone, there were some fresh bruises along with bite marks on me. My whole body was sore; it was my right side that made me cry out when I went to stand up. I found my clothes on the floor at the foot of the bed. My panties were ripped and the strap on my tank top was no longer attached. I grabbed a new tank top out of the closet and a pair of underwear from the dresser and went to the bathroom. I couldn't find the socks anywhere. The floor felt like ice under my feet.

Looking at myself in the mirror I had an angry bruise on my shoulder in the form of a line. A flash of memory came to me. I was crawling across the bed getting away from someone, and they grabbed at the tank top, getting ahold of the fabric that was over my shoulder blade, he was pulling back as I was pulling forward, the strap digging into my skin before the stitches on the seem gave away, sending me sprawling on my stomach and colliding with the headboard.

I closed my eyes and pinched my nose, willing the memory to go away.

When I got out of the bathroom I didn't bother trying the door, I just grabbed a book off the dresser, curled back under the blanket and started reading the book; again; for the 6th time.

GRIFFIN (December 9)

I'm not sure why every morning needs to come with a headache. I yanked the pillow from under my head and pressed it down on my face. Mostly to stop the pounding in my temples but partly to cut off my breathing. I was exhausted, what I wouldn't give for just 2 more hours of sleep.

But I knew that wasn't going to happen; not with the banging going on in the kitchen just outside of my bedroom door. I removed the pillow from my face and turned my head to glare at the door. I wasn't in a hurry to investigate, instead I reached over and unhooked my phone from the charger.

I was scrolling through social media, enjoying all the desperate pick-me girls that came across my for you page. I clicked on one who was wearing nothing but a leather jacket in her video and scrolled through the rest of her pictures.

Then my bedroom door swung open, it bounced off the wall with loud THUD. "What the fuck man!" I yelled.

"Get your ass up!" Levi came into the room and ripped the phone out of my hand. "Classy Griffin." He said sarcastically and tossed my phone in my lap, hitting me just in the right spot to send a wave of blind agony through me.

I gritted my teeth and cupped my balls gently, "Fucking prick, what's your problem."

Levi shrugged, "I got tired of waiting for you to wake up," he turned around and walked out, flipping the light on as he left.

I bared my teeth and pulled myself out of bed. I wasn't eager to start the day, but the sooner we get this done the sooner I don't have to deal with it; or at least until the next time it drops below 25 degrees. I don't like going out to grandpa's house unless I really have to; and I guess today is one of those days.

I pulled on the first outfit I came across, running a hand through my hair I went to get some coffee, luckily Levi already had a pot going. Levi was sitting in the living room, drinking his own coffee and doing something on his computer.

When he heard me move around in the kitchen, he set his computer to the side and stood up. "You have 5 minutes before I leave."

I scoffed at the empty threat. I pulled down a to-go cup and filled it with coffee. I turned to him and shook the cup at him. "I'm ready when you are." I said sarcastically.

Levi glared at me, he took a deep breath and said, "let's go," before walking out the door.

I took a sip of coffee and cringed as it went down, it was way too hot still. I blew out a frustrated breath and walked out the door, locking it behind me.

When I jumped in the truck Levi was puffing on a small joint. "I can't deal with you sober right now." He said, taking a long drag.

I laughed and pulled out a joint from my jacket pocket. "That makes two of us." I said, lighting the tip and taking a hit. I rolled the window down and blew the smoke out, coughing a bit I turned to Levi, "How long are you going to be pissed off at me?" I asked waving some smoke out the window.

Levi shrugged and took another hit before answering, "Until I'm over it." He tossed the roach out the window and backed the truck out of the driveway.

—⚋—

When we hit the highway, we were yelling over each other. Each trying to make his own point before the other. I gave up trying to speak over him, the mother fucker has demon lungs. Eventually we calmed down enough to speak to each other at a level that didn't strain my vocal cords.

When we reached the dirt roads, we were back to laughing and joking around. "Hey Levi," I said when we were about halfway to the house, when he turned to me, I tossed him the keys, "I got some things to do, it's all the same key." I said before veering to the right to turn on the breaker to the house.

The hum of electricity chased away the quiet of the woods. I took out a cigarette and watched a squirrel climb up a tree and run across a few branches, not eager to go inside and hear whatever Levi is doing to you right now. I tried to act casual about this, but I can't help the anger building inside me. I knew that me messing with Natasha rubs Levi the wrong way, the way I use her and toss her aside when I'm done. I knew if I acted on my anger or jealousy at this moment then that would be the last of me and Nat.

I blew out a cloud of smoke before I set off for a walk around the perimeter of the house, to make sure everything was still intact and nothing needed repaired. Then I made my way over to the tool shed. Sun came in through the grimy windows, giving the place a sepia effect. I made my way through rakes and shovels, heading to the back wall where a tool bench was still set up. I opened the top cabinet and took out the last jar of Grandpa's moonshine he stashed away. There was 1 jar left, it was a little under half full. He never told me where he got the liquor from so, I tried to drink it sparingly. I kept it out here in the shed, with less chances of someone else finding it a drinking it.

I unscrewed the jar lid and took a whiff. The fumes burned my eyes, but it smelled so fucking good. I brought the jar up to my mouth and took a small sip at first, letting myself get used to the burn before taking a bigger drink.

As I brought the jar up for another drink the shed went dark, like something big was blocking the window. I turned to see what it was but as I moved the place lit up again. I shrugged, figuring that a cloud must have blowen over the sun. I took a drink of shine and rested against the tool bench, looking around at the shed. How many times have I ran out here as kid to escape the old bastard inside. I took another drink and memories started coming back. I looked over at the corner of the shed by the door and saw a kid's drawing of 3 little boys by a tree. I chuckled and took my phone out to snap a picture. The guys would get a kick out of this throwback.

I took one last drink out of the jar and put it back in its hiding place. When I stepped out of the shed I lit another cigarette and paused; for a brief moment I thought I saw someone walking in the trees. I shook my head and made my way to the well and leaned against the rock wall. I looked down into the tangle of branches and flicked the ashes off the end of my cigarette. I watched them drift down, like dirty snow. I popped my necked and looked around me, puffing on the cigarette lost in thought. When I got down to the filter I put it out on the rock wall and dropped the butt into the well. I took out and lit another cigarette.

Birds started chirping around me. First it was just a few, then more chimed in. I brought the cigarette up and took a long hit, listening to them chirp and squawk back and forth. It wasn't until the wind started to pick up that the birds got quite. I leaned back and closed my eyes, enjoying the feeling of the wind on my face. I took deep breath, then "Griffin!" A female whispered.

My eyes went wide. I tried to stand up but something cold and wet wrapped around my wrist. I looked down at was holding on to me, my blood ran cold as my eyes took in pale and bloated fingers gripping my wrist in a tight hold. I forced myself to look down further; at the arm and eventually at the face. My vision pulsed, Ellie was baring her teeth at me, her eyes so full of hatred. She yanked on my arm pulling me down; I yelled in horror and started to shake my arm. I finally broke free from her grip and fell backwards tripping over something and landing hard on my ass.

I sat there for a moment and rubbed my wrist, trying to get the feeling of her cold dead grip from me. Everything in me screamed at me to get the fuck away from the well, I shook my head and pushed myself off of the ground. "Stop being stupid!" I said out loud and took a hesitant step towards the well, but I couldn't make myself go any further. "It's all in your head, she's dead. It's not possible," I gritted my teeth and closed the distance between me and the well and looked down. All I could see was the tree limbs. I rubbed my forehead and made my way inside.

When I opened the front door I could hear some commotion in the kitchen. I couldn't think of a good reason why Levi would let you out. So many things ran through my head as I threw the kitchen door open and looked around. "What's going on?" I demanded.

You were sitting at the table with your back to me. Levi was standing at the counter messing around with the food, he glanced over at me and went back to what he was doing. He mentioned something about you being hungry, but I wasn't listening. I was too focused on the back of your head.

I walked over to you and put my hands on your shoulders. I leaned over you and asked Levi if he had fun.

Levi laughed and made a joke about how your growling stomach kept ruing the mood. I laughed and started rubbing your shoulders, "and to think I was out there being jealous over nothing," I whispered in your ear. "But be careful with this one," I said shaking you, "I wouldn't put it pass her to try something."

Chuckling he gathered up the food and brought it over to the table. "Fair point, she's not a wilting flower."

I grabbed a chair and sat down, keeping an arm on the back of your chair in case you tried to leave. While waiting for you to finish eating Levi and I continued to talk, mostly about random shit; whatever to fill the silence.

"Man, this week has been really crazy," Levi said, "Our lead singer is trying to pull some sketchy shit, I know he's taking money from the band."

"Just kick him out already, no one really likes the guy anyway." I picked some lint out of your hair and watched it fall to the ground. You were so focused on the sandwich; Levi and I could talk about anything, and you wouldn't care.

Shrugging Levi responded, "the guy can scream. Once we can find someone who can growl out lyrics like him then he's out."

"Or you could take it over yourself." I suggested.

Levi laughed, "we'd still be down a lead singer. But good thought."

"I brought some good shit with us to help us forget." I said.

"Well, what are we waiting for? Let's go."

I looked over you, you were almost done eating; so, I stood up, grabbed your elbow and pulled you up. "You either come smoke, or you go back up to your room. Your choice but you're not staying in here by yourself."

You looked up at me, I couldn't tell what you were thinking but I wasn't all that surprised when you said you'll go back upstairs.

I scoffed and turned to Levi, "You hear this? This is the shit I'm talking about. Just when I think she's starting to learn," I shoved you out the door, "Get your ass in the living room." I snapped.

"You don't have to shove her like that." Levi complained.

I shook my head, "Stay out of it." I warned.

Levi walked up to me, "you need to chill." He said, shoulder checking me on the way out. Out in the hallway you looked like a trembling deer looking around for a predator. Levi walked up next to you and looked up at the ceiling. There was no denying the thumps coming from upstairs. "This place is haunted." He said like he was telling you what color his shirt was.

I rolled my eyes; I was so sick of the ghost talk from him and Alex. I shook my head, "No it's not. It's just an old house with bad history."

There was a time, back when we were little kids, when grandpa had gotten stuck with watching us. He had gotten pissed off that Alex left his shoes in the hallway, so like any other rational adult, he took 6-year-old Alex and locked him in the closet under the stairs; then he left. Leaving 8-year-old me in charge, Levi would have been 5 around this time. Grandpa had left strict orders not to let Alex out until he came back, which little did we know wouldn't be until later the next morning. Things were quite; you could hear Alex crying. Levi wanted to let him out, but the door was locked, and we couldn't find the key.

We would pass things under the door, pieces of unwrapped candy we found in one of Grandma's old purses things like that. We stayed by the door, keeping Alex company, it went fine for the first few hours; then somehow the already silent how went completely still. Levi looked up at me, then Alex started screaming. He was pounding on the door so hard, begging to be let out, yelling how there was someone in there with him. I told him the same thing grandpa would always tell me; stop being stupid there's no one there. Levi was losing his mind at this time; in a few months he would soon understand. We all took turns being locked in the closet. And yes I will admit that at times it did feel like someone was in there with you. But the closet was tame compared to the horrors of the basement.

I only realized I was staring at you, when you looked over at me. I shrugged and went to the living room, to escape the memories that were starting to come back. And the best way to clear your mind was waiting for me on the coffee table.

When you came into the room you didn't get further than the couch and just stood there, "I thought we were smoking," you said.

I waved you over, "this is better," I said as you sat down, "trust me honey, you'll like it." But you just shook your head. "Mel, stop being stubborn and loosen up. It'll do you some good."

Levi plopped on the couch next to you, "just once?" He asked.

I felt a triumphant smile creep up as you scooted away from him and said that you didn't want to.

Levi looked over at me, I raised an eyebrow and pulled a bag out of my coat pocket. "Fine," I took out one of the laced joints and handed it to you along with a lighter, "that one is all yours." I said with morbid curiosity as I watched you put the joint between your lips and brought the lighter up.

The effects were almost immediate, after a few hits you started to sway a little. When you leaned forward to flick the ashes on the tray. Levi, the little fuck, took the joint and flicked the ashes off for you. When he handed it back he put his arm around you, I glared at you as you sunk into his side. We locked eyes, you must have felt my anger in that moment.

Levi ran his hand up and down your arm, you pressed yourself closer to him when he asked, "Are you cold? You're shaking."

You took a long hit and nodded your head, "It's a little cold in here," you muttered.

Levi tightened his grip around you, "get closer."

I shook my head and bent over the table again, loving the way the sudden adrenaline took over the anger. "Your socks should be enough to keep you plenty warm." I spat out at the couple on the couch.

Levi scoffed. "Took you long enough to get those for her. When are you going to get her a decent pair of pants? Her legs are like ice." He said rubbing your outer thigh.

Rolling my eyes I stood up and pulled off my jacket. I threw it over your lap and turned my glare to Levi, "Happy?" I asked and sat down.

Levi laughed, "Dude you need to chill."

I squeezed my eyes shut and rubbed the bridge of my nose. I could feel a headache starting to come on. "Sorry man, I'm just tired."

He shrugged and changed the subject to something else. I didn't hear a word of what he said, all I could focus on was that persistent tug at the back of my mind. The feeling pulsed in time with the headache making things much worse. I shook my head, trying to shake off the creeping feeling that was starting to overcome me.

Levi kicked the table to get my attention. "Hey man, you good?"

I rubbed the back of my neck and nodded. I looked over at you, you were watching the smoke swirling around in the light. "Just a headache." I answered.

Levi was fortunate enough that he never ran out of things to talk about. Unlike Alex who was just as talkative Levi never seemed to annoy me with his constant chatter. Alex never seemed to want to talk about anything other than pussy, his side hustles, and his hair. Right now, Levi was talking about a podcast one of his band mates was into, a conspiracy podcast; I nodded my head and glanced at you, I thought you would be hanging onto his every word but I don't think you were really listening to him. You were so focused on chasing dragons to know what was going on.

"I'll have to check it out, we can listen to it on the way back if you want." I said absent mindedly.

Nodding his head Levi went on to say something else. Something big going by the window caught my attention, apparently it caught your attention too. We both snapped our focus to the window, then you turned your head to look at me; eyes wide in fear, "was that her?" you asked me, barely above a whisper.

"Who?" I asked, confused and angry. Confused on who you would be talking about and angry that someone was out here, and I didn't know about it.

"The woman on fire. Sometimes I can hear her screaming."

Levi looked down at you, horrified. "And you're just now telling us this?" He asked.

You shrugged, "I thought it was a dream," you said almost wistfully.

I don't know why but ghost talk always went straight through me, grandpa always got irrationally angry whenever anyone would mention the dead or something slightly paranormal, dad would just make fun of you until you left the room. I could see grandpa now, swiping his arm across the coffee table and yelling until his face turned purple that ghosts don't fucking exist. You and Levi were talking about footsteps when I slammed my hand down on the coffee table. "Guys, come on all your doing is making yourselves paranoid."

"Yeah, you're probably right," Levi said, he took a few strands of your hair and twirled it around his fingers. "hey, have you guys heard the crazy theory about sky quakes?" I couldn't think about anything other than your silky soft hair sliding through Levi's fingers.

You shook your head and looked at him like he was the most interesting thing on the planet. Levi started going on about sky quakes, never once letting your hair drop from his hand, "Wow," you breathed, "that's crazy."

Levi looked at you and laughed, "that's some good stuff huh?" He asked, nodding at the joint in your hand. You offered it to him, but he shook his head, "I don't want to take it from you, I'll get my own," He said with a wink, "Take another hit, smoke some more."

I squeezed my eyes shut, and when I opened them Levi still had his arm around you, at that was enough to set off the dark side in me. My vision pulsed red, and I stood up.

—⚏—

The next thing I knew I was shutting the passenger door to Levi's truck. He was shaking his head lighting a cigarette. "Have you ever thought of going to get that checked out?" He asked.

I shook my head, confused. "Get *what* checked out?"

He looked over at me bewildered, "The black outs; we were just talking about them a few seconds ago. You told me you could feel them getting worse." He shook his head and took a drag off his cigarette, "man that's unsettling." He laughed and put the truck in reverse.

I rubbed my forehead; I still had a splitting headache, but that nagging feeling was gone. "I think it's genetic. Dad mentioned them a few times growing up, I think that was one of the reasons why mom dipped." I fished around in my coat pocket, but I was out of cigarettes. "Hey, can I bum a cigarette?"

"Yeah, sure." He handed me his pack.

—⚏—

When we pulled up to my house, I was eager to head inside and grab the bottle of migraine relief, I planned on taking 3 Pm tablets and not waking up until this headache went away.

Levi kicked his shoes off and sat down on the sofa, "Hey man, I appreciate what you did tonight. I know you don't like seeing someone playing with your girls."

I nodded tensely, "yeah well, you share with family; right?" I went to my bedroom and closed the door. I rummaged around in the drawer of my nightstand before finally finding the half empty bottle of Pm migraine relief. I closed my eyes and sent a silent thank you to whatever higher power was looking out for me, opened the bottle and dumped 3 pills into my hand. There was a bottle of water by the bed, so I didn't have to go back to the kitchen to wash down the pills. I kicked off my shoes and threw myself into the bed, it took a while for the pills to kick in; I just lay there with my eyes closed until I fell asleep.

MELANIE (January 2)

I felt the bed shift. Griffin let out a groan as he stretched. I heard him get up and walk to the bathroom. I had about 10 minutes before he got out, he didn't like it when I woke up before him, he liked it even less if I was still in bed by the time he came out of the bathroom. I slipped out of bed and tugged on a silk black robe over my black panties and red tank top. My feet were freezing, I missed the wool socks. I couldn't go far because he always locked the door before we went to bed keeping the key on a hook that just out of my reach, so I just sat on the edge of the mattress and waited for him.

I heard the water turn on and then off. I sat still, staring at the bottom of the bathroom door watching his shadow move back and forth. The door opened and I watched Griffins feet as he walked towards the bed. I kept my gaze down looking at his tattooed legs as he stood in front of me, staring down at me. I could feel his gaze burning into me and kept as still as possible and waited.

"Look at me." He whispered. I flicked my eyes up at him keeping my head down. Griffin tilted my head up with a finger under my chin, "I said look at me." He squatted down in front of me and looked me up and down. He ran his hand down my arm and rested it on my thigh. "I don't like keeping you locked up like this, but I have to know that I can trust you." His hand was gripping my thigh tightly. "But I can't come back here for a few days; and I can't take you with me."

Whenever he leaves it's always a gamble when he'll come back. Sometimes it was 2 days, sometimes I wouldn't see him for a week. Griffin squeezed my thigh tighter.

I kept my face emotionless; he liked knowing I was in pain, he tried to deny it, but you can tell. I painted a smile on and reached up to caress his face, he caught my wrist in a tight grip. "You can trust me." I said, leaning in so my forehead was resting on his. "I won't do anything I promise, I won't tell anyone. I'll keep my head low and keep to myself. I'll move away-" The next thing I knew I was on the floor. I laid there, eyes wide, mouth open, stunned. I tasted blood and could feel it start to drip from the corner of my mouth.

I heard Griffin sigh. "Get up," his voice was flat.

I took a breath and picked myself up.

Griffin looked me up and down and whistled. He took a hold of the left side of my robe and used it to pull me closer. "You look like royalty," he purred licking the blood off my chin. He pulled back and sighed, "Mel, you are so incredible, and you do so much around here."

He started rocking us back and forth, the fastest way out of this was to smile and play along. With an actresses smile I wrapped my arms around his neck and rocked with him.

"I know you try, but darling you're not trying hard enough."

Inside I rolled my eyes, he was impossible to please, I winced as he kissed my cheek. I could already tell that it was bruised, then he kissed my jaw.

"My love, I understand how badly you want to leave," he kissed my neck. "But you're mine."

He kissed me on the lips then shoved me on the bed. Taking a hold of my legs, he flipped me over on my stomach and climbed on top of me.

"You're not going anywhere."

My heart was pounding, I hated this. If I fight back he'll beat me until I black out again. I can fight him off for a little bit but ultimately he's just too big and too strong, he usually always wins. I heard his pants unzip, and I was pulling at the mattress trying to get away when his phone started to ring.

"Hello?" He answered.

I started to scream, and he laughed and put the phone to my ear.

"Go ahead and beg for help honey, he doesn't care about you!"

I pressed my face into the mattress and tried to get my shit my together.

"Oh that's no one, just some bitch. No, she won't get in the way." Griffin started playing with my hair, he was quiet for a while; kissing on me and listening to whoever was on the other end of the phone. "Fine. I'm on my way." He hung up the phone and got off me.

I pushed myself into a sitting position on the bed and rolled my shoulders. Griffins feet appeared in front of me. I shook my hair out of my face and looked up at him.

He bent over and kissed my forehead. "I gotta go, baby," he said, and cupped my chin in his hand so he could tilt my head back, bathing my face in light. "You are so lovely," he breathed and gently kissed the new bruise that was forming on my cheek, "I'll see you in a few days my love." Griffin released his hold and left. I waited to move until I heard his car pull away.

I don't know how long he's kept me here, a few weeks perhaps, I could feel myself breaking down. I needed to find a way out, but I couldn't think of one. This house was in a remote part of the area, nothing but trees around me. It was so quiet out here when Griffin left, it felt like he took all the sound with him. I had nothing but what was in this room to keep me busy. The house used to belong to an elderly man but from what I've seen laying around there wasn't anything useful. There was the basement that I've never been in before, maybe I could find something useful down there? I could feel myself going mad here. My cheek started to throb, and the craziest thing crossed my head. 2 words that seemed so simple. 2 words that could really fuck my life if things went wrong.

Looking out the window I could see snow starting to fall. It was so cold in here, but it was just going to get colder. I had a thick blanket but for how long will that be enough to keep me warm? I already had goosebumps up and down my arms and legs.

I went to the mirror and looked at myself. I inspected the bruise from where he backhanded me in the kitchen. There was an almost healed bruise on my temple from when I was being disrespectful in the living room. A necklace of bruises wrapped around my neck. My legs had finger marks and teeth imprints poking from under the hem of my robe.

Shaking my head in disgust I turned away and went back into the bedroom. 2 other words came to mind instead but what if I didn't succeed? I couldn't even begin to think what he would do if he came home before I was gone. I couldn't kill myself, if he'd come home before I could slip away, then where would I be? Knowing Griffin, he'd probably keep us both locked up here to keep an eye on me after that.

I went to the bedroom door and tried the handle, but it didn't move. My heart dropped to my stomach, and I turned the handle again but still nothing, "No, no, no, no," I said jiggling and pulling on the door, but it didn't budge. I punched the door and slid down it crying. I should have known it was locked, but I thought that since I didn't hear the lock click in place, that he had left in too big of a hurry and had forgotten to lock it. I guess I was too lost in thought and missed hearing it.

He didn't tell me when he'd be back. He didn't even say where he was going. The last time I ate was yesterday morning, Griffin had just came back from a party and high out of his mind, he brought me a breakfast sandwich from McDonald's. I had no food in the room; Griffin liked the place spotless, and food belonged in the kitchen. Even then there wasn't anything there. He only brought enough food for when he was here. I was getting hungry, my stomach growled, I need to stop thinking about food.

I looked around the room to see what I could use to help me in any way, but there wasn't much. A few clothes on plastic hangers, a dresser that was falling apart, bed with a metal frame. There were a few books on the dresser, but there's not much I could do with a paperback book. The bathroom was just as bare, an empty medicine cabinet, the towel rack was already taken down when I got here, and the curtain rod was attached to the wall.

Still sitting on the floor, I started banging my head against the door, my eyes kept going back to the bed. I got up and turned to the door, looking at the hinges I wondered if I could pop them out of place with something. Pacing around the room, going over different plans in my head on how I could get out of here. If I managed to get out of this room I still had to get out of the house. It should be as easy as walking out the front the door, but I needed backup plans in case Griffin did something to the front door. The windows were barred from the outside, the back door was nailed shut and there was no exit from the basement that I could see, even if I did manage to get out of this room I still had to get out of the house before Griffin got back.

My gaze went back to the bed, more specifically the bed frame. It was raised and looked like the metal was sturdy enough. I got on my belly and looked under the bed, there was smaller metal bars keeping the mattress flat, so you didn't need a box spring. My heart fluttered as I stood up and pushed the mattress off the frame. The metal bars just slid down in place and there was 11 running down each side of the frame giving me 22 metal bars to work with. I tried not to get too hopeful I wasn't out yet; I had a long way to go.

Testing the durability of the bars I took one and started messing with it, trying to see how easy it was to bend. They seemed strong enough, so I took one to the door, and wedged the end of the bar under the head of the pin in the middle hinge and pushed up. It took longer than I wanted but I was finally able to pop the pin just out of place, when the pin was halfway out; the bar slipped, just a scratch no blood.

My shoulders were getting sore, but I pushed through the pain in my arms and sting on my hands; I didn't have time for a break. After a few more good pushes I was able to get the pin out. Without pausing I started on the top one, it looked like it would take longer to get that one out, I would get the bottom one last.

I took a breath, I had to stand on my tiptoes to reach the hinge with the bar, but once it was in place I pushed up as hard as I could. The bar slipped and sliced into my palm; but the pin fell onto the floor and rolled away. The bottom pin was a little tricky, but eventually I was able to pop that one out as well.

I didn't bother trying to catch the door as it fell into the hallway. I welcomed the loud thud as it echoed through the house. I was about to head out to the hallway but then I remembered the cut on my hand. I took a moment to look it over. It wasn't too bad; but it was bleeding steadily.

I took a tank top that was hanging up and ripped a piece off of it to tie around my hand. There wasn't a lot of clothes in this room. I had no pants here, no shorts, a few different pairs of underwear, some tank tops, and the robe that I was currently wearing. I didn't even have socks. I wiggled my toes and wondered what happened to the grey wool socks.

With the bleeding on my hand taken care of I stepped up to the door, with it no longer blocking the way I felt that false since of freedom. but that was only one lock on this cage. There was still one more to go. I took a breath and stepped out into the hallway.

I looked to my right, where the stairs led down to the first floor. I was almost terrified to look over to my left, at the end of the hallway. I took a deep breath in and held it. Turning my head slowly I looked down the hallway and seen nothing but the wall and the window that looked out to an endless sea of trees. I shook my head, if Griffin was here there was no way he would let me break a door down just to 'test me' as he calls it.

It was a couple days after he had brought me here. He told me one day that he was heading out and would be back in a few hours. I thought I was going to get out that day. I opened the bedroom door and ran out into the hallway, bolting to the stairs just to be tackled to the floor from behind. Griffin laughed at me, telling me that he was disappointed that I would try to leave him so soon but was happy that I wanted to amp things up.

I shook my head to erase the memory. All the more reason to get the fuck out of this house.

The hallway was freezing. I wrapped the robe around me as best as I could to get the most warmth from it and looked to the door in front of me; Griffins grandpas room. I took a breath and opened the door. I remember the first time I was here, walking through the front door and hearing distinct footsteps coming from this room. You could hear the door open, the atmosphere turned heavy and ominous, and then the door slam shut, feet were stomping down the hallway towards the stairs. It all sounded so aggressive and *real*. I remember watching the top of the stairs expecting someone to charge down at us, but no one ever came. I turned to Griffin and asked him who else was here, but he told me we were alone.

In here was the best chance I had for a decent pair of clothes. Griffin told me about his grandpa, I knew he was a big guy but with any luck I would be able to find something that would fit. I went over to the dresser and pulled open the bottom drawer but there was nothing in it. The middle drawer had some different pairs of jeans, thread bare and torn long johns, and a pair of sweat pants that I pulled on. They were way too big for me, but I pulled the draw-string tight and rolled up the legs, so I wasn't tripping over them. I looked ridiculous but I was already warmer and that's all I cared about.

In the top drawer I found a couple pairs of socks, I took a bundle and sat on the bed to pull them on. They were white tube socks and came up past the knee, but they would keep my feet warm. I was putting the left sock on when I felt the bed shift like someone sat down on the other side of the bed behind me.

My body tensed, this *was* a trap, and I fell for it. Griffin is right behind me, he never left, he just wanted to see if I would try to escape again. I flinched as fingers caressed the side of my neck as he pulled my hair back. I took in a breath, "Griffin-"

I could feel his breath as he "Shhh"ed next to my ear. He wrapped my hair around his hand and then yanked his hand down, pulling my head backwards, the pain of my hair being ripped out of my scalp made me close my eyes. When I opened them to look up at him, there was no one there. I scrambled off the bed and turned around in circles looking around the room like a wild animal. I was alone.

The back of my head hurt, tenderly I ran my fingers through my hair and a handful of strands fell out. My heart was beating out of my chest as I backed out of the room waiting for Griffin to come out of the shadows, but he never did. When I was in the hallway I pulled the door to the room shut and hurried down the stairs.

I ran to the front door hoping that since I was locked in the bedroom Griffin would have left the front door unlocked, but I was lying to myself. Of course, the nob didn't turn. Of course, I was still stuck in this house.

My stomach started to growl again, the last time Griffin brought groceries was a few days ago and it was only a couple of bags. I decided to go try my luck in the kitchen. Most of the cabinets were empty but I found a half box of apple jacks cereal, I ate a handful and sat the box on the table. At least being out of the room I'll be able to eat something. Griffin never left food with me when he locked me in the bedroom.

I turned around and went to the living room. It was a spacious room that had 2 large windows both of them barred up from the outside. I sat down on the sofa trying to think. The room was getting darker, the sun must be setting. Breaking out of the bedroom took more time than I had thought. I didn't bother with the lights; I knew that the power would be off. When Griffin left he would turn off the breaker. I got up and went to the window that looked out over the side yard. Every now and then I would see someone out there, hopefully they were there today, hopefully I could get them to help me.

I pressed my hand against the cold glass and peered out into the yard. It was getting hard to see but I could make out the tree line, and part of the shed. I was scanning the tree line when movement caught my eye. My hopes sky rocketed when I saw a woman standing with her back to me looking up at the sunset.

"Hey!" I shouted and pounded on the window so hard I was sure I was going to break it, but she didn't move. "HEY!! LOOK BEHIND YOU!" I yelled. She turned her head but didn't turn around. Instead, she just walked past the shed and out of view. "What the fuck?" I asked out loud. A cold chill ran through me, tonight was going to be cold. And with the power out there would be no heat. I thought of the thick comforter that was on the bed upstairs, but I didn't want to go anywhere near *that* room, especially not in the dark.

With limited visibility I went to the coat closet that was in the living room and pulled out whatever I could get my hands on. Feeling around I was able to find a small throw blanket on the floor and grabbed that for my legs. I curled up on the sofa and waited for the sun to rise.

The night droned on, every time I felt myself drifting off to sleep I was woken by loud bangs from upstairs. I tried to tell myself it was just an old house settling, but after my hair was pulled you'd have a hard time convincing me that this house isn't haunted. I was always hearing noises, but I was never touched. I was always seeing things out of the corner of my eye, but they never 'shh'ed me. That felt like a living person. I got goosebumps thinking of that again and tried to think of anything else, but the throbbing on the back of my head kept bringing me back.

Griffin (January 2)

We had the perfect weekend together. I wanted to relax for a few days before I had to make a run for dad. I wasn't sure what was all in store for that, but I wanted to make sure everything was tight and secure at grandpas house before I had to leave. The guys wanted to come with me, mainly for the easy money that we get from these runs; but I didn't want to think of that right now. All I wanted to do was hold you close and sleep until I had to leave.

But that wasn't going to happen. I sat up and stretched, groaning. After just a few hours of sleep I was still aching all over. The floor felt like ice this morning, I almost felt bad for taking away your wool socks, but for some reason I hated the fact that Levi was the one who was behind that. I shook my head and went to the connecting bathroom. I was always surprised at how well you maintained the place while I was gone, Ellie had the place trashed, it took forever to get the smell out of the bathroom. But with you here, I could almost sleep on the bathroom floor and not think twice about it.

I finished my morning ritual and went out to have some fun before I got the call that it was time to go. Like the perfect girlfriend that you are, you were sitting at the foot of the bed waiting for me. It used to bother me when you got up before me, I didn't trust that you weren't trying to leave while I was still sleeping. And there is just no excuse for you to still be asleep once I was up. That was just lazy.

I walked up and stood in front of you, you kept your eyes down too shy to look up at me. I tilted my head to the side and studied you for a moment, the bruises blending in with the tattoos on your skin, the way your hair was getting tangled at the ends giving you a wild and unruly look. I made a mental note to bring you back a hairbrush; I think you would really appreciate that.

I waited for a moment longer, "look at me," I said calmly. You looked up at me through you lashes, I smirked and lifted your head with a finger under your chin, "I said, look at me," I squatted down in front of you, so our eyes were level, I studied the way you were sitting there, memorizing the curves and angles; truly a work of art. I ran my hand down your arm enjoying your soft skin and rested my hand on your thigh. I started to tell you how I had to leave and that you couldn't come with me. I felt my grip on your leg tighten as I explained all of this to you, but the more I talked about leaving you, the more I could feel that tugging at the back of my mind.

I was taking some steady breaths to make it go away but when I heard you say something about moving away I lost it. I felt the predator break free and lunge forward as my hand swung around and collided with your cheek. I sighed and shook my head. Sometimes it's hard to keep that beast in its cage. Sometimes I'm not sure who was really in charge, me or that genetic evil that over took grandpas life.

Shaking my head I looked down at you, "Get up." The back of my hand stung, I shook it out as you pushed yourself up. When you were on your feet I grabbed your robe and pulled you to me. You are so fucking beautiful, like a goddam Queen and I told you so. I licked the blood that was starting to run down your chin.

I started to praise you, rocking us back and forth to a song that plays on repeat in my head. I kissed the fresh bruise on your cheek then I kissed your jaw, muttering "my love, I understand how badly you want to leave," I kissed your neck softly. "But you're mine." I stated simply, that's when I knew that I wasn't in control anymore. I let go of my self-control and let the beast come out to play. Who knows how long I'll be able to keep that part of me on a tight leash, if I don't get it out of my system now it'll be pounding to get out later.

You play well with that dark side of me. I think that's why he's kept you around for so long; he gets bored easily and he doesn't know when to stop sometimes. But today the shrill ringing from my phone grabbed the beasts attention long enough for me to regain control.

Still on top of you I reached for my phone and answered it. It was my dad, "hello?" I said the same time you screamed. I laughed knowing what you were doing, I put the phone to your ear so you could talk to him. I taunted you, "go ahead and beg for help honey. He doesn't care about you!" I took the phone away and brought it back to my ear.

"Who was that?" Dad asked, just as a formality. His tone was distracted, I could hear some people talking in the background.

"Oh that's no one, just some bitch." I didn't want to tell him the truth. He has a way of using girlfriends against you, that's why Levi is still single; and Alex goes for the flavor of the week to keep attention away from Kara. Dad asked if you would be a distraction. "No, she won't get in the way." I said truthfully, hard to get in the way when you're locked up. I laughed to myself and started to twirl some of your hair through my fingers. Dad was droning on about details, places and times. I nodded absently and kissed your back; we've already been over this a hundred times. I knew every detail by heart.

"Grab the guys and meet us at the garage, we need to get going while time is still on our side." Dad said then hung up.

I rolled my eyes, "Fine. I'm on my way," I said to no one. I climbed off the bed and stretched; not ready for the days ahead of me.

I studied you as you pushed yourself into a sitting position. I stepped in front of you, shaking some hair out of your eyes you looked up at me. I smiled to myself at the defiance that was still in those captivating eyes.

Bending over, I kissed your forehead and told you I had to get going. I took a hold of your chin and tilted your head so I could see your face in different angles of light. "You are so lovely," I brushed my lips across your cheek, "I'll see you in a few days my love." I stood up and walked out of the bedroom, making sure to lock the door. I put the key in its usual spot, resting on top of the door frame.

When I turned around I noticed the door to grandpas room was slightly ajar. Without missing a beat, I went over and closed it then made my way downstairs and out the door.

—m—

I stopped by Alex's place first; he was on the way home and I didn't feel like back tracking. I called him when I was few minutes away, told him to be ready when I got there. I wanted to take a quick shower before we left and if I had to pick up Alex up I'd better do that first.

I parked at the end of the driveway and honked. Not long after, Alex was leaving the house, before he closed the front door he leaned in and kissed Kara goodbye. Kara leaned around him and waved at me, I absently waved back.

"Man, you look rough, bad weekend?" Alex asked when he got in.

"Quite the opposite. Mel and I spent the whole weekend together just hanging out." I put the car in reverse and started heading home.

Alex nodded, "Everything is still going good between you two?"

"Never better." I answered. "Honestly, I think it's improved. We have a special bond, Mel and I. Kind of like you and Kara."

Alex whipped his head in my direction, "yeah, we really have something special, huh?"

I looked over at him and back at the road. "When you find something you love, hold it close." I said and turned on the radio.

When we got to my house I pulled into the driveway and parked next to Levi's truck. He was laid back on the sofa in the front room, watching something on the TV. I told them I would be ready in 10 minutes and went to the bathroom to clean up; hoping like hell the clothes I put in the dryer were still there, I was pushing time with the shower, I didn't want to waste anymore by running around looking for clothes. I started the shower and went to find some clean clothes. Levi must have done some laundry while I was gone, and thankfully he just tossed my clothes on top of the dryer. I took a quick shower and pulled on clothes, I rushed through brushing my teeth and only ran my hands through my hair.

In the front room Alex and Levi were talking back and forth, at first it sounded like they were speaking in Spanish, but when I walked into the room Levi glanced at me and asked what the plan was once we got there.

Shoving my shoes on I grabbed my phone and keys from the kitchen table. "I'll tell you guys in the car." As I reached the door my phone vibrated, it was a text from Dad giving me an address. He said some things have changed and that we needed to go here first and to wait for further instructions. When I got in my car I plugged my phone in and set GPS to take us to the new address. "Slight change of plans." I said putting the car in reverse.

"What's happening now?" Alex asked from the back seat.

"Not sure," I answered honestly, "he said change of plans and sent a different address."

Levi took out a pack of cigarettes, "I'm just ready to get this over with." He rolled his window down, "What all *do* you know?"

I looked over at him then back at the road, "Just the address and to wait for more details."

"Helpful." Levi scoffed and took a drag off his cigarette.

The new address took us a half an hour longer than the original meet up location. GPS took us to a bar in a small city. I double checked with Dad to see if we were in the right place, he told me to go inside and wait; that someone would be coming to get us in a moment. I scratched my head and put my phone down.

Swallowing I looked around the parking lot. It was pretty busy; I wasn't sure what I was looking for, but something didn't feel right.

"Man, you're freaking me out." Alex said looking out his window.

I shook my head and held my phone out so they could read the messages. Levi looked at me, "Well, it's up to you. One of us could stay here, as a look out; while the other two go inside and see what's up."

I shook my head and held a hand out, "hold on," I looked out the windshield down the street we just came from. Something in me told me to drive; so, I did.

Levi was silent but Alex wouldn't shut up, he started muttering in Spanish, Levi turned around and told him something, but I couldn't understand what he was saying. When we turned out of the parking lot that gut feeling was proven correct. When we stopped at the stop light and waited for the light to turn green you could see red and blue lights heading down the street behind us. When the light turned green we slowly took off and watched as the cops started flooding into the bar we were supposed to go into.

My heart was pounding, I couldn't control my breathing. Thoughts ran through my mind so fast they started colliding with each other. Setting cruise control so I wasn't speeding down inner-city roads I took us to the other side of the town and pulled over at a gas station. I gripped the steering wheel and took a few deep short breaths, "Man, I don't think I can drive us back." I said looking down at my feet. The edges of my vision was turning red, and I couldn't stop shaking.

Levi was saying something beside me, but I couldn't hear him over the ringing in my ears. I shook my head and looked over at him. Alex was talking in the back, but he sounded miles away. I closed my eyes and rubbed my forehead.

I couldn't believe what just happened. I picked my phone up, I wanted to call Dad to see what the hell is going on but if he set us up like that I shouldn't go making calls letting him know it didn't work.

I was pulled out of my thoughts by a door closing. I looked over, Levi was walking towards the gas station building; "What's going on?" I asked Alex.

"He's going to pre pay for some gas. Said something about you getting out to clean the windshield then when he gets back he'll drive us somewhere to hang back for a few days to see what happened."

I nodded and got out to wash the dirt and salt from the windshield. The frigid wind felt good, but it quickly became too much. I see the price on the pump flash and zero out, then the prompts came up to start pumping gas. I quickly set it up and hurried to sit in the passenger seat.

When Levi came back he put the hose back up and got in the driver seat. I hated seeing someone else driving my car, but my nerves are so shot right now there was no way I could drive us anywhere safely. Levi pulled the car around the pumps and started driving towards the bar, which was crawling with police by now. I started to panic for a moment.

"Bro what are you doing?" Alex said, I looked back at him, he looked really pale.

Levi shook his head.

How the fuck did he keep so calm? I thought.

"Relax," Levi said, "we're not going to stop. I just want to see what they're doing."

At the moment we could see two police officers escorting two men out of the bar. Other officers had random people doing sobriety tests but the guys in cuffs kept pulling my attention as we drove past. I recognized one of them, he worked at the garage during the weekend. Maybe Dad didn't set us up? I fished around for my phone again but put it back down. If I called Dad and the police answer; then what?

"This is so fucked." I said, rubbing my hands on my jeans. "I can't believe that just fucking happened."

"Where are you taking us Levi?" Alex asked.

Levi shook his head. "I have no clue. We can't really go home right now. Not until we know what is going on. How much battery do you have left on your phone?" He asked looking in the review mirror.

Alex opened his phone, if felt like a beacon in the backseat. "It's at 63%" He answered.

Levi nodded, "Can you start digging around, see what you can find on a police raid at the bar." He looked over at me, "There's no way that could be a coincidence."

I nodded, "I was thinking that too. Did you see who they had cuffed?"

"Yeah, they must have been setting this up for a while. Do you think they've been watching us? Or just them?"

I shrugged, "It's hard to tell, they have more blood on their hands than we do, but you can't be sure." I ran a hand down my face, "fuck, what are we going to do?"

Levi shook his head, "lie low until we have more answers. Guys, mind sharing a hotel room?"

"I'll share a room, but I'm not sharing a bed." I told him.

"I am *not* sleeping on the floor." Alex shot from the back seat.

Levi looked over at me then back at the road. "Look for a hotel in the next city over, I doubt this one has a hotel with a room big enough for us."

"Isn't that going to look suspicious?" Alex asked.

Levi shook his head, "I don't fucking know! We'll just tell them it's my bachelor party."

Alex started laughing, "you getting married, that would be the day." He sat up and rested his elbow by the head rest of my seat. "Who's the lucky lady Levi? Ya know, in case they ask."

"I don't fucking know Alex, just make a name up." Levi snapped.

We both looked at him then shared a look, "Someone's pissy," Alex said, sitting back. "Did you find anything yet?" Alex asked me.

I looked at my phone and scrolled through some different options. "There looks like a good one 60 miles away." Levi nodded in agreement, so I hooked my phone up to my car and sat back as Levi drove us even further away from the shit show that was going down behind us.

It was quiet for a while until Alex asked, "Should we give fake names."

"That's actually a good idea," I said turning to look at him. "I'll be Brian."

"I've always like the name Anton," Alex leaned forward again, "if Kara ever has a boy we agreed to name him that."

"I'll think of one when we get there." Levi said. "I'll get us the room for 2 nights. Even if we don't hear anything by then we should probably move around and lie low for a while. You never know."

Alex sat back again and started scrolling on his phone. "That was fucked up man. You don't think it was a set up do you?"

The guys turned their attention to me. I held my hands up, "How the fuck should I know? I was there too; I was just about to walk into all of that, same as you. My Dad doesn't tell me shit other than what cars to tear down and where I need to go he'll tell me more when I get there. That fucked me up just as much as it did you." I clenched my jaw and looked out the window. "Just take us to the fucking hotel."

—⁓—

The rest of the ride was pretty silent, aside from the radio none of us talked until we were in the hotel room. There was a sofa which Alex took since he was the smallest, and the 2 twin sized beds went to me and Levi. I stretched out on the bed and closed my eyes.

"Alex have you found anything?" Levi asked.

"I'm still looking," was Alex's reply.

I threw my arm over my eyes, "let us know when you fine something." I said.

A few hours later Alex was sitting on the edge of my bed. "Guys, I think I found something. Check this out," Alex held his phone out. Levi got up and sat next to Alex, I looked over at his shoulder as he hit play.

On his screen was a shaky first-person video. You could see people running around beside the person filming. "Ready? On three." Someone off screen whispered. They counted down then you could hear the splintering of wood and people started shouting. "FBI! hands up!" "Get down!" "Drop the weapon!" The screen flashed, pops echoed through the phone speaker, people cried out, and you could hear someone hit the ground with a loud thud. "Watch your back!" Someone yelled. Then there was a loud grunt and the camera recording fell to the ground, an arm clad in black appeared in front of the camera, the angle now showing the room from the floor. We watched as agents ran around trying to avoid getting shot while at the same time trying to take out whoever was shooting at them. The shooting started to dwindle down, and you could see agents move forward and grab people, putting them in cuffs. I recognized some of the faces that were being escorted out; Dad being one of them. Then someone stepped in front of the screen.

"Fuck! We got a man down here, weak pulse. Where the fuck is the medic!" Somone else in the background started yelling at the same time, "Put your gun down! Put it down!" Then POP, POP, POP! "Back up! I need help!" POP, POP, POP! The agent on screen fell forward and the screen went black.

I swallowed as Alex got up and started pacing. Levi was quiet. I ran a hand over my face, "fuck" was all I could say.

Melanie (January 3)

Rays of sun finally poked through the living room windows. I sat up with a groan, stiff and cold after a night of restless sleep on the sofa. If I was still trapped here tonight I was going to make sure to be in the bedroom before nightfall.

I drug myself to the kitchen and got another handful of cereal. I couldn't remember what was in the refrigerator and I wasn't about to open it. Griffin didn't bring many groceries here, he said he didn't want to risk an infestation. My stomach growled, god I was so hungry. No, I shook my head to clear my thoughts, I couldn't think like that.

I went back to the living room to grab one of the jackets I pulled out of the closet last night. One of the jackets stood out from the rest, I picked it up and studied it, wondering why it looked so familiar. I went through the pockets and felt something in the left one. When I pulled my hand out and looked at what I found; I had to sit down. A tube of chap stick, the type and brand I use. This is my jacket, and most importantly this is the jacket I left in Hillary's car. Did Griffin do something to Hillary? Something in me clicked. I put my jacket on and steadied my breathing. This all played out to his psychotic plan, didn't it?

I have to get out of here. I went to the kitchen and stood in front of the door to the basement. I've never been down there, but I was hoping I would be able to find a way out. I opened the door and looked down into the darkness. From the top of the stairs, I could see shelves lined up like a convenience store, full of totes and boxes. I took a couple steps down and tried to look further into the basement, I couldn't see anything, so I took a few more steps down. I felt like a little kid who was sent downstairs alone, I was terrified. I knew it would be dark down here, but I just wanted to see if there were any windows that I could crawl out of.

Standing at the bottom step I looked around. From what I could see the place was used as extra storage, small paths cut through piles of totes and there were rows of shelves that filled up most of the basement. I couldn't see a window but on the far wall I could see what looked like a door, what I hoped was a door. Tapping my fingers on my thigh I decided to try to navigate my way through the darkness and see where that door lead to.

The stone floor was cold beneath my feet, the worn-out socks not doing much to keep the soles of my feet warm. I put my hands out in front of me and slowly walked forward. My left hand felt the lid of a tote, and my right hand knocked over a can; that made a loud clang as it banged off different surfaces until it finally hit the floor and rolled off into the dark. I rubbed my eyes; they were starting to hurt.

I pushed forward, bumping into chairs and knocking over what felt like a lamp in the process. I couldn't tell how far I had left to go; but looking behind me at the light that was coming from the kitchen door; it didn't seem like I had made it that far.

Sighing, I turned around and went back upstairs. For this I'd need a flashlight. Slowly I made my way back to the stairs, once I reached that first step I ran up them as fast as I could, closing the door quickly behind me and pressing my back against it. I leaned my head back and laughed at how childish I must have looked.

I started going through the kitchen drawers looking for anything useful. Keys, screwdrivers, a flashlight. So far I only found some spoons, a couple of forks, some batteries, but nothing that could help in the current situation. I put the batteries in my pockets and checked the cabinets again, eating another handful of cereal when I came across the box.

When I had combed through the kitchen I went to check the hallway closets. In the first one I was surprised to find a flashlight, but it was dead and the batteries I had in my pocket didn't fit. I sat the flashlight aside and kept digging. I found a pair of shoes that were a couple of sizes too big, even if I tied them as tight as they would go they just slid right off, more of a hazard than anything.

I was about to give up and move on to a different closet when I found another flashlight, its light was dim, but it was better than nothing. Racing to the kitchen I threw open the door and hurried down the stairs. Sweeping the light across the basement I seen that it was more cluttered than I thought. I could barely see the back wall through the shelves that was set up. Griffin's grandpa must have been a hoarder. With the flashlight I was able to slowly make my way to the back wall. The basement was a maze of totes, boxes, and shelves, even with the dim light to help me navigate I was still bumping into things.

After what felt like an hour a wood panel wall was in front of me, better yet so was the door. I took the knob in my hand and turned it. At first it didn't move, I pushed and pulled but it was either stuck or locked from the other side. Looking for hinges but seeing none I figured that the door pushed to open from this side. Taking a few deep breaths, I gave the door one last good shove, using my whole body I shoved myself forward and it finally gave way, swinging open and I almost fell in but caught myself. My shoulder and hip were throbbing but at least I got the door open.

My heart lifted and I was expecting to see stairs leading up and the bright blue sky above me, but that daydream was quickly squashed when I realized that I was just in a different part of the basement. There was a chair in the middle of the room, and a single light hung from the ceiling. "What the fuck?" I asked out loud. The floor was discolored and the smell in here was awful. I swept the light across the room, bugs where scattering across the floor and what looked like claw marks could be seen on the walls. I swallowed and turned my attention to the small window to my right. I ran up to it, it was too high for me to reach even when I jumped. I went to grab the chair so I could stand on it to get a better look at the window, but when I grabbed it and pulled, to drag it across the floor; it didn't move. I pulled my hand back as if the chair had shocked me. Why would somebody bolt a chair down?

Not wanting to know the answer I went to go find a chair. The first one I came across was a metal-folding chair, taking that back to the window I was able to get high enough to see out. The first thing I noticed was that I could still see daylight. The second was the 3 metal bars blocking the window. Looking closer at the bars I noticed the bottom of them was rusted. I wondered if they were rusty enough to break free from the window sill. To get to the bars I would have to break the window first. Shaking the sleeve of my jacket down far enough to cover my fist I was able to punch out the glass without getting cut up.

Looking closer at the bars on the window I was surprised to see that it looked handmade. Someone had taken a bar about an inch thick and cut it into 3 pieces, from there they welded the bars in between 2 pieces of metal and screwed that to the window. Someone went to great lengths barring up the windows of this house, I thought; thinking back to the bars that covered the outside of the living room windows and the ones on the inside of the bedroom window. I ran my finger along the bottom of the middle bar and my assumption at it being partially rusted through was correct. I took the flashlight and aimed it at the bars, the weld on the bottom of the left bar was completely gone and the middle bar was only connected by half a weld on the bottom. The rest of the welds still looked like they were holding. I look back to the bottom of the middle and left bar. With any luck I'd be able to break those 2 free and wiggle myself to freedom. I laughed, it wouldn't be easy, but it would be easier than sitting here waiting for Griffin to come back.

As I was stepping off the chair, the flashlight started to flicker. My heart rate spiked as I slapped it in my hand, frantically trying to bring it back to life. But my effort was worthless, the flashlight died leaving only a sliver a daylight shining through the broken window. I looked out the door into the dark basement. Somehow I was supposed to make it through a hoarders maze by feeling my way through the basement. I ran my hands through my hair and made my way to the stairs.

It was a tedious task. Every few steps I'd bump into something. I kept knocking things over making so much noise I was worried that if Griffin happened to come back while I was down here I wouldn't be able to hear him. That thought made me move faster.

Then my foot got caught under something, it was solid and about a foot high. I was sent sprawling forward. I panicked and waved my arms in front of me trying to catch myself; but I landed hard on my left wrist, I felt a snap and a wave of nausea went through me, but I didn't want to think about that right now. Pushing myself to get up, I knocked more things over, causing random objects to fall down around me.

By the time I finally made it to the stairs I was crying. I sat down on the bottom step and sobbed, cradling my wrist that now had a deep throbbing pain. I cried for longer than I should have, but I was tired, my shoulder was throbbing, and my wrist was starting to swell up. I wasn't sure how much longer I could ignore my growling stomach. And my sister.... I started crying again. Would I ever get to see her again?

I sat there until I got my breathing under control. I don't even care how much time I wasted wallowing in self-pity. I sat for a moment longer holding my head in my right hand thinking of my next move. My wrist was starting to get to me, and my fingers were getting tingly, I tried not to move it around too much, when I did a sharp pain shot up my arm.

Shaking my head, I pulled myself up and went back upstairs, not surprised to see that the sun had set while I was down in the basement. I was getting better at seeing in the dark though, getting to the sofa was a lot easier than walking to the other side of the basement that's for sure. I grabbed the box of cereal on my way through the kitchen and fell down on the sofa, getting as comfortable as I could.

While I ate what little cereal was left, I thought of different ways I could break the bars off the window. The obvious choice would be a prybar or something similar but there is no way Griffin would leave something like that where I could find it. I wonder if I could use a piece of the bed frame upstairs, I could get a longer piece and put it behind the bar sideways and push to pop the bar out of place. That might work. If it didn't, I would need a backup plan. I don't want to cross over that pile of random shit any more than I needed to. I wanted to have at least 3 different ideas before I went back to the window.

Griffin (January 3)

The guys and I didn't do much. We decided to stay in the hotel room, getting food delivered and keeping an eye on the news. There was a brief segment on the local news. I was hit with a wave of emotions, mostly regret, as dads mugshot flashed across the screen. Along with the guys who worked at the garage and a few other familiar faces. There was no mention of me Levi or Alex. After a quick discussion we decided it would be best to go home and pretend like nothing happened.

Melanie (January 4)

I didn't get much sleep, so I was up in time to see the sun just start to rise. My wrist was bruised, the swelling had gotten worse overnight, and I couldn't bend it without crying out. I was fairly certain it was broken but I couldn't think about that right now. I needed to get out of here. I went to the closet in the living room and started pulling everything out. I went through every box and every bag. I found more batteries of different sizes, I took a wire hanger and thought I might be able to use it to get under the bars, to help break away the weld that's holding it in place... maybe? I took one of the bags and tossed in the batteries and the hanger.

Going to the closet in the hallway I did the same thing, tearing through it looking for anything useful. A loud thud upstairs made me pause; a thought crossed my mind to check the grandpa's room. I stood up and looked up the stairs, weighing my options when I heard another thud. I thought I would have been scared, but I felt nothing. I gripped the banister and started up the stairs.

When I got to the top and seen the door standing half open, I started to get angry. I walked to the door frame and stopped, looking into the grandpa's room.

"Are you here?" I asked. The bedroom door was pushed open and slammed against the wall. I looked over at it, "Your fucking grandson is the reason I'm stuck in here." I heard something in the room fall and hit the floor. "Oh, shut up." I said walking in and going for the closet.

I pulled everything out, ripping open boxes and pulling all the clothes out going through the pockets. In the back of the closet, I found a long barrel shot gun. Looking around I didn't see any bullets, but I could use the gun to help pry the bars out of place...maybe?

I took the gun and went into the other room to see if I could find a piece of the frame that might help me out.

Once I had what I was looking for I went downstairs to see if any the batteries matched the flashlights. One took C batteries, and I only had AA and AAA. But the other flashlight took AA, and I had plenty of those, only to find out that most of them were dead. After trying battery after battery, I was finally able to get the flashlight to work.

Grabbing everything, I made my way to the basement. At the bottom of the stairs, I turned on the flashlight and aimed it at the far wall. Stepping down on the stone floor felt like I was stepping on ice. The cold bit into the bottom of my feet with razor sharp teeth, I was thankful for the socks I had found but I wish I had found a pair of shoes that stayed on my feet. I probably should have put on another pair of socks over these but it's too late to turn back now, not when I'm so close to the end.

There was a path of destruction in the middle of the room but the rest, even though it was all tightly packed together, was neat and organized. It was a wonder I didn't stumble into one of the shelves that was reaching across the room. I almost felt like I was in an antique shop.

With the flashlight I was able to weave around all the crap that was stacked up down here, being careful to step over everything I had knocked over last night. I saw a footstool on its side that had been sat down on the floor at the end of one of the shelves and figured that's what I had tripped over.

On the last set of shelves, I happened to see a toolbox, I felt butterflies in my stomach as I stepped up to it. Feeling relieved I pulled out a hammer. Holding it in the light I turned it over, not believing my eyes for a moment. It look sturdy enough, throwing it in the bag with the rest of my makeshift tools I hurried to the window.

The room was a lot colder than yesterday, snow trickled in from the broken window. The flakes melting halfway through their journey turning into a puddle of water on the grimy floor. The dampness increased the smell in the room making me want to gag.

I rested the shotgun against the wall and took the bag off and sat it on the floor beside it, trying to avoid stepping on broken glass. It was impossible to avoid stepping in the water as soon as I walked over to put my things down the socks had already soaked through. I could see my breath as I stepped onto the folding chair and looked out. The snowflakes falling down were another reminder that I needed to stop wasting time and get the fuck out of this house.

Stepping off the chair I emptied the bag on the floor, stray batteries rolled off in different directions, the metal bar from the bedframe making a hollow ting as it hit the stone floor. I put the bag on the chair, so I wasn't standing on the freezing metal. I grabbed the gun and stepped backwards, getting ready to go start on the window. A sudden sharp pain made me sit down, I looked down at my foot and saw a piece of glass sticking out of the sock. After carefully pulling off the sock, I reached for the flashlight, so I could see how bad it was. Blood dripped off my heal as I twisted my foot around to aim the light at the shard of glass sticking out of the center of my foot. "Just fuck me, right?" I muttered out loud as I pulled the glass out of my foot. I gritted my teeth and held my breath as it slowly slid out, with the blood around it I thought it was smaller than it originally looked.

Breathing out I tossed the piece of glass to the side and tied the tube sock around my foot to try to stop the bleeding. "This is fucking great." I said furiously wiping tears from my eyes, taking the gun, and shoving the barrel behind the leftmost bar on the window. My wrist was screaming at me, I couldn't put a lot of weight on my foot, and my stomach felt hollow, but I couldn't think of any of that right now.

I don't know how long I was pulling and shoving on the shotgun to loosen the bar, but after a good shove the gun slipped and clattered on the floor. My arms fell to my sides, my shoulders were numb, and I was sweating which wasn't good because the cold wind sliced right through me. I couldn't move my wrist anymore, it hurt too bad to ignore at this point.

I looked at the bar preparing myself to be let down, there was no way that worked. But to my surprise the bar was sitting at an angle, the weld at the top had given way when the bar shifted, and I was able to pull it off with a small tug. I held the bar in my hand in disbelief and stepped off the chair, I looked at the pile of tools I had and seen the wire hanger. Dropping the bar and picking up the hanger I went back to the window. If I was smaller, I would be able to squeeze through the window like this. But there is no way my hips would allow me to do that, so one more bar needed to go. I wedged the hanger under the

461

middle bar where it had partially rusted out, bending on the window seal to put a 90-degree bend in it. I stepped off the chair to grab the hammer. I held the hanger as best as I could with my left hand and swung the hammer with my right to drive the hanger further under the bar. I watched in amazement as the hanger poked out through the other side. It didn't take long to clear the rest of the weld from the bar.

When the weld around the bottom was broken off, I could see a 1/8-inch gap between the bar and the piece of metal it was attached to, which is why I was able to break it away so easily. I took the hammer and started swinging at the bar wildly, I was so close. I could see the bar start to move which made me swing faster and harder. Sweat was running down my back and my breath came out in white puffs; my feet were so cold they were starting to hurt but the only thing I was focusing on was the crack in the top of the middle bar that was blocking my way to freedom.

Laughing manically as it finally broke away and fell to the floor. I clawed at the side of the window and pulled myself up and out of the dark room. I grabbed at the snowy edge of the window well and pulled while I kicked my legs to get out, but my ass was stuck. "Shit!" I yelled and twisted myself and put my hands on the side of the house. I could feel myself starting to slip back in. I rotated my hips and pushed with my arms, "No, no, no, no, no." My legs were too short to reach the back of the chair but while my left leg was stretched out, that positioned my hips just enough for me to slip the rest of my body through the window. I scrambled out of the window well, my foot catching the stone edge sending me falling and landing roughly on the snow-covered ground; but I made it.

I rolled over onto my back and looked up at the grey sky. Taking deep frantic breaths, I was exhausted. I looked at the sky, at the setting sun turning the clouds orange, it wouldn't be too much longer before it would start to get dark, but there was still enough time left to make it to the highway and get help.

"There's still time," I whispered and got up, and took a step towards the driveway. An odd feeling in my right arm pulled my attention away. The sleeve was cut open, and the fabric was wet with blood. While I was swinging the hammer, I must have sliced it on the broken window.

I took off the other sock and did the best I could at tying it around my arm, the cut was long, but it didn't look deep enough to concern me right now. I was getting light headed, I shook my head to clear my thoughts, I don't have time to worry about that now. I gathered myself and pushed forward, I was out of the house now and I need to get to the road and find help before Griffin catches me.

Taking a deep breath, I started limping down the driveway. I couldn't remember how long the road was, but it felt a lot shorter when I was first brought here. The rocks were hurting my feet, and the snow was picking up. I pulled my jacket around me tighter, but it didn't do much to keep the cold out especially with the giant rip down the arm. I was looking down at my feet trying to keep my mind off the cold, thankful that the sun hadn't gone down yet. Rays of sun light still peaked over the trees.

Something in the distance caught my attention, I slowed down so I wasn't kicking rocks up so I could hear better. I couldn't tell if that was the wind or a car engine I heard. I took a few more steps forward when the familiar sound of a car driving on gravel overtook my senses. My mouth automatically dried up, and my heart pounded in my ears. I froze like a deer in headlights as the black dodge charger came to a stop a couple of yards ahead of me.

I tried to breathe but every breath got caught in my throat. I heard the engine kick off and I took a step back too afraid to blink. The door opened and Griffin stepped out. He rested an elbow on the roof of the car and looked at me.

He shook his head and shouted, "Honey what are you doing, it's freezing out here."

I shook my head and started to turn around.

"Mel, come on, I'm sorry. You must be hungry. Here I brought some food."

I paused and looked over my shoulder at him. He smirked at me and held up a takeout bag from Olive Garden. My stomach started growling.

"Come here, let's eat." Griffin flashed a smile that used to make me melt.

I took a step toward him, then the light shifted, and his smile turned wolfish, and I noticed how he started to tense up. I took another step to him and then darted off to the left and disappeared into the trees.

I heard him hit the roof of his car, "Fuck! MEL!" He growled, then softer, he shouted, "Melanie honey I'm sorry, please come back and let's talk through this over dinner."

I could hear him starting to chase after me. The ground was frozen, but the trees kept most of the snow from hitting the ground.

Behind me I heard Griffin talking out loud, "What happened here babe? Did you hurt yourself? Let's go back to the house and I'll fix you up while you eat."

I looked down at my foot, the sock fell off. Now he knew I was hurt, that wasn't good.

I ignored him and pushed myself harder. I thought of going back to the road and stealing his car but then I remembered that he had turned his car off, the keys were probably in his pocket. I looked around me trying to think of a place to go, somewhere to hide. I started running in a random direction that I hoped would take me to the highway. The frozen ground was siphoning all my body heat, the cold rocks jabbed into my feet and thorned branches grabbed at me as I ran. My foot got caught on a root, "Shit!" I yelled and the ground quickly came up and slapped me hard against the face.

I moaned and rolled over on my back, the trees above me came into focus first. Then Griffin came into view, he was kneeling over me grinning from ear to ear, "Looks like you could use some help." He offered me his hand.

Groaning I pushed myself up into a sitting position and started scooting away.

Pulling his hand back Griffin laughed, "You're a determined little one, aren't you?"

His words fell on deaf ears, I rolled over on to my side and pushed myself up with my right arm, trying not to give away my broken wrist. He already knew I was hurt; he didn't need to know how badly.

While I was stumbling to get up Griffin called out behind me, "What did you do to your arm babe? That looks pretty bad, come here, and let me clean that for you."

I shook my head and started walking away faster, he followed me.

"Mel," he started calmly, "I would really appreciate it if you STOPPED IGNORING ME!" He reached out and grabbed me by the elbow.

I spun around and yanked my arm from his grip, "Fuck off Griffin!" I yelled.

He smirked and with lighting fast movements he grabbed me by both wrists and twisted my arms down to hold them at my sides. Pain radiated from my left wrist causing me to scream out in pain, "What's your plan now sweetheart?" He growled into my ear. I threw my head towards him, but he seen it coming and pulled back laughing, "Ooo so feisty." The way he had my arm twisted caused the gash to start bleeding again, Griffin squeezed my wrists, I wanted to throw up from the pain. Studying my eyes, a dark smile started to spread across his face. "Time to go home." His tone was flat, and he started dragging me back the way we came.

My eyes went wide, I dug my heels in the ground and tried to pull my arms out of his grip, ignoring every part of my body that screamed at me to stop. "No, no. No, I'm not going back there!" I yelled. I was moving around like a madwoman, throwing my body back and forth trying to shake off his grip. I started kicking at him, bringing my knees up to hit him wherever I could.

Griffin spun me around and crossed my arms over my body and held me in a tight bear hug. He didn't even seemed phased; I however was growing tired. I was panting heavily; sweat was dripping down my neck. Griffin picked me up and tossed me over his shoulder, my arms dangled down his back, and I watched as blood dripped off my fingertips and hit the leaves below.

"Stop fighting Mel," he said slapping my ass, "the food is getting cold, it's time to go." At the mention of food my stomach growled making Griffin laugh, "Don't worry, I'll fill you up soon my love."

A wave of panic went through me. I started kicking my legs and pounding my fists at his back. I managed to kick him in the balls, and he dropped to his knees throwing me to the ground in the process.

"You little bitch," He groaned. I rolled onto my side and propped myself up and was about to stand when I was shoved back down to the ground. Griffin rolled me onto my back and crawled on top of me. Taking my arms and pinning them above my head he bent down and licked my neck, "Oh little Mel. Look at what you've done to yourself. You must be in so much pain." He squeezed my broken wrist and laughed at my reaction.

"Fuck you." I said through clenched teeth and then I spat at him, spraying his face with saliva.

Griffin smiled and shook his head. "Things would be so much easier if you'd stop struggling." He took my wrists in one hand and with the other he wiped my spit off then he slapped me across the face, rocking my head to the side. My entire world went black.

Griffin (January 4)

Alex was the first to wake up that morning. The sound of him taking a shower woke me up. I groaned and checked my phone for the time. 9 o'clock in the morning.

I threw a pillow over my face and tried to get that weird dream out of my head, I was chasing something through the woods, I could just make out the back of someone disappearing through the brush. I followed whoever it was to the side of a road. I chases after footsteps, running across the pavement keeping my focus straight ahead at the figure getting further away. Then, the world grew bright. Almost too bright. And the deafening blow of a semi horn shattered the silence.

I rubbed my eyes figuring the door to the bathroom closing is what pulled me from the dream. I pressed the pillow tighter over my face and stayed like that for a while.

Then I heard the shower turn off and waited for Alex to exit the bathroom. I tossed the pillow to the side and went to take a piss. A shower sounded nice but none of us had clean clothes, I didn't see the point in showering just to put dirty clothes back on, I'd wait until I got home for that. I did my business and went to sit on the bed.

Levi was still sleeping so I turned the TV on and put it on mute.

"Think it's safe to go back today?" Alex asked from the sofa.

I shrugged my shoulders. "Haven't seen anything else on the news. What about you? Have you came across anything online?"

He shook his head.

"I don't see why not then. As long as we keep our heads low we should be fine."

Alex nodded and started scrolling on his phone.

"I wouldn't mind sleeping in my own bed for a change." Levi said. Startling me for a second. I wonder when he woke up.

I scoffed, "You're going back home? I thought you loved crashing at my house."

"Only when you're shaking up with Nat. Whatever mattress you have, I want 5." Levi said stretching and crossed his arms under his head. "What time are we leaving today?"

"I don't know, probably closer to noon. I don't want to be in a hurry." Alex said, "I'm still freaked out."

"Don't start acting all twitchy, that'll just draw more attention." Levi said.

I glanced at the tv. It had changed over to the weather; it looked like there was supposed to be a snowstorm later tonight. I rubbed the back of my head to help ease that tugging feeling, but all that did was make it worse. I tried not to think of grandpa's house while I was out, in fact I hated going there. I'm counting down the days when I can just light the whole thing on fire and dance in the ashes. But I couldn't do that until Dad was out of the picture, which wouldn't be too long depending on how his trail goes.

That tugging feeling got more persistent as I watched the colors on the map swirl around. I would have to go back to that house tonight; there was no way I could leave you there alone; especially knowing that there was going to be a snowstorm. I had strict rules whenever I had company at grandpas house; always clean up after yourself, don't leave food that will attract vermin, keep the doors locked, and if it dropped below 10 degrees I stayed with them until it got warmer. Grandpa was the one who taught me that, the first thing I did when I was put in charge of the property was tear that fucking shed in the side yard down. God it felt so good to take a sledgehammer to that thing. I grinned thinking about how liberating it felt to watch it crumble.

"You're in a chipper mood, share your secret man. I'm dying over here!" Alex complained.

I shook my head, "I was just thinking about tearing the shed down at Grandpa's."

Levi stood up and started heading for the door.

"Where are you going?" Alex asked.

"Out for a smoke." He said.

Levi never liked dredging up the past. Can't blame him. I stood up and stretched. "I gotta go back to grandpas tonight. It looks like it could get rough."

Alex looked over at the tv. "You should just let her out."

My head snapped over to him. He was right, but I didn't want to let you go. You would never come back. Not after all of this. Not after what I've done. I can try to distance myself from that darker part of me, the one that is always tugging at me, trying to get control. But if I'm being honest, that's when I feel the most alive.

I shook my head and looked back at the tv. "You're probably right. But then what?"

"Melanie is a good girl. I don't see her going too far." Alex replied and got up making himself busy by gathering empty beer cans.

I raised an eyebrow. I wish I knew what would happen if I just let you go. I don't see you going to the police. But I don't see you hanging around, either. If I let you go, I don't think I would ever see you again.

When Levi came back, we chilled for a little while longer then made our way out to the car. The ride back home was pretty quiet. After Alex was dropped off we went back to my house where Levi hopped in his truck and left. I took a quick shower, got dressed, placed an order for pick up and a random restaurant and went the store to pick up a few things for tonight.

I was trying to shake off the feeling that something wasn't right. Nothing has been right since yesterday. By the time I got out of the store the temperature had dropped a few degrees. I pulled my hood up and loaded the bags into the backseat. When I got into the driver's seat I checked my phone. The food still had 24 minutes until I could pick it up. So, I drove to the restaurant and sat in the parking lot until it was ready.

The drive out to grandpas old house always took more effort than it was worth, mostly because of how slow you had to drive through here; there's no telling what kind of animal is going to jump out in front of your car. Levi has already totaled 2 trucks on this road. One was because of a deer; the other was just us being drunk and stupid.

My stomach growled, the food smelled so good, I can't remember when I last ate. It took a lot of restraint not to start picking at the food sitting in the passenger seat; it smelled so good, and I was starving.

I was almost to the house, taking the final turn to get on the long ass dirt road was both a relief and a warning to turn around and go back. Something moved on the road up ahead, just out of the reach of the headlights. I slowed the car to a stop and put it in park. I almost didn't believe it. How in the *fuck* did you get out of the house? You looked magnificently wild and terrified standing in the middle of the drive way. I was to impressed that you managed to get out of the house to be irate that you managed to get out of the house. I noticed the jacket you were wearing, I would have to answer for that, I'm sure; but how could you be mad at me for bettering your life by getting rid of the toxic people in it.

I readied myself for anything that was about to come next. I twisted the dial to keep the headlights on and turned the car off. Stuffing the keys in my pocket before opening the door and hitting the lock button. If this ended in a chase, I didn't want you circling back and try to steal my ride.

I stepped out of the car and rested an arm on the roof. I almost laughed, shaking my head I called out to you. But instead of running to me like I had hoped, you just turned around. Where you thought you were going I had no idea. I called out an apology and tempted you with some food. Reaching in the car but not taking my eyes off you in case you darted into the woods. I grabbed the bag of take out and held it up. You looked over at me.

Got you, I thought. Smirking I held the bag higher, "Come here, let's eat." I gave you my best smile.

Like trusting prey, you started to walk to me. I was thinking about what I was going to do once I got you in car. I just had to get you close enough, you're still too far away. Then you suddenly darted to right and I could feel the anger over take the awe.

I slammed my fist down on my car, "fuck, MEL!" I knew screaming at you like this wasn't going get me anywhere, but I am I so fucking mad, you should probably run faster little doe.

I tossed the bag into the driver seat and slammed the door shut. Shaking my head I took a calming breath and jogged after you. I kept shouting out apologies and asking you to come and eat. I knew you had to be hungry, when was the last time you ate?

Something white stood out on ground. I walked up to it and picked it up. It looked like one of grandpas socks, covered in blood. I turned it around in my hands and called out asking what happened and offered to play doctor while you enjoyed your dinner.

I wasn't sure how long I could keep this calm demeanor up. You were starting to really piss me off. I was able to track where you went by half foot prints and fresh drops of blood. You were being careful not make too much noise; if I stopped to listen I could just make out your heavy breathing ahead of me. If you kept going in this direction you'll eventually end up at the cabin. Which is fine, at least you didn't go the other way, which would have taken you straight to the highway. I grinned and continued going after you.

My grin got even wider as I heard you yell, "Shit!" soon followed by a SMACK. A few yards ahead of me I saw you sprawled out on the ground; you must have tripped over a root.

I walked up to you and kneeled down. "Looks like you could use some help," I said, offering my hand out to help you up. Instead, you just pushed yourself up and scooted away. I watched half amused as you struggled to stand. I shouted out some bland words of encouragement, noting how little you were using your left arm. You're right arm wasn't any better, blood was running down your arm. "What did you do to your arm babe? That looks pretty bad, come here let me clean that for you." Your arm did look nasty, if we didn't get it clean soon there's no doubt that it'll get infected.

By this point you were starting to walk away from me.

Where are you going? I thought with a chuckle. "Mel, I would really appreciate if you STOPPED IGNORING ME!" I reached out and grabbed ahold of your elbow. I was done playing around.

Yanking your arm from my grasp, you spun around and told me to fuck off.

I smirked and lunged forward. Grabbing both of your wrists I twisted your arms down to your sides. The sound you made was almost unreal; I thought the door frame made you hit a new octave but here you are breaking records. I was impressed that you were able to stay on your feet for so long, you look like you've been drug through hell. I leaned forward and whispered in your ear, yanking back when you almost head-butted me. I couldn't help the sadistic laugh that followed. I taunted you and squeezed your wrists tighter, taking note of how your pupils dilated.

"Time to go home." I said.

If I thought you were struggling before; fuck that was nothing compared to the hell cat you turned into now. You started screaming, begging me. I easily restrained you; you seemed like you were running low on whatever fuel was keeping you going at the moment. You were breathing heavy and sweating like you just ran 5 miles, I toss you over my shoulder and started to take us back to the car.

I slapped your ass and taunted you some more. When your stomach growled I told you not to worry, thinking it would help get you out of this frantic mood that you're in; but then pain exploded between my legs. I threw you to the ground and dropped to my knees.

"You little bitch." I hissed through my teeth. I looked up, just as you almost had yourself in a good position to make another run for it.

I didn't even think, I just pounced. Landing on top of you I pinned you to the ground. You squirmed beneath me.

"Oh, little Mel, look at what you've done to yourself." I smiled at the blood that was starting to run over my fingertips, "you must be in so much pain." I said with mock sympathy and applied more pressure than necessary to your left wrist.

How you still have some fight left in you; I'll never know. You looked up at me with eyes full of hate, "fuck you," you hissed through gritted teeth then you spat at me.

I closed my eyes and smiled softly when saliva hit my cheek. "Things would be so much easier if you'd stop struggling." I shifted my hold on you. Your wrists were so small they both easily fit in one hand. With the other I wiped your spit off my cheek and slapped you as hard as I could across the face.

I took a breath and slowly stood up. Being slow and gentle I picked you up and carried you back to the car. The way the final rays of sun lit up your sleeping face made me want to lie you down right here and wake you up by making love to you. You were so beautiful, even with the dirt, blood, and sweat smeared all across you. Like some twisted fairytale.

Smiling I nuzzled you closer and hurried back to the car. My thick coat was doing nothing to keep me warm in the cold wind.

When we got to the house you were still out. Brushing some hair back I took the time to admire you. I pressed two fingers to the side of your neck and waited. You've been so still and quite; you haven't moved since I picked you off the ground. Smiling when I found a pulse I started dragging things inside. I would have to be quick about this, I wasn't sure how much time I had until you woke up.

My mouth dropped open when I saw the condition you let the house go to while I was out. We would have to talk about your housekeeping once you woke up. I could feel myself getting angrier as I went in to the kitchen, the house was truly a disaster. There was an open box of cereal I forgot to get rid of left out on the table. I swiped my arm across the table clearing all that was left on it and sending everything clanging to the floor. I dropped the food off and went back to the car. Half hoping you were awake and attempting another useless escape plan.

But you were still out like a light in the passenger seat. I went over to the car and opened the door, reaching in and sliding my arms under you so I could carry you inside like it was our first night being married. Gently laying you down on the sofa I went back to the kitchen to grab the first aid kit.

In the cabinets on the far side of the kitchen is were Grandpa kept a fully stocked first aid cabinet. One of the only useful things that man left behind. I shook my head, I didn't want to think of him right now. I had to focus. I took out a bunch of supplies that I would need to fix you up and closed the doors.

When I turned around I was genuinely shocked to see the basement door standing wide open. I stared at the entrance to the basement for what felt like a lifetime. I tried to fight back the memories of being drug down there. The small room in the back that grandpa called the cellar. My mouth went dry, and I hurried over to close the door before any more memories decided to crawl out of the dark.

I couldn't believe I missed seeing that when I was bringing in the bags. "What the fuck do you do when I'm gone?" I asked out loud, even though you were still knocked out in the other room. I shook my head and walked up to close the basement door.

I still could not wrap my head around how you got out. When I got the living room I dropped the medical supplies on the coffee table and drug it closer to the sofa. I started to undress you so I could see how badly you hurt yourself.

Shaking my head at the number of cuts, I started bandaging you up. You would look like a mummy when I was done, and I couldn't help but laugh at the image. Once I got the brace on your broken wrist I went to get the clothes I bought for you. Nothing too spectacular, I was on a time crunch at the store, so I only picked up the first things I saw in your size. When I was done playing doctor on you I got up and went to prepare our dinner.

Melanie (January 5)

When I woke up I was laid out on the sofa. I felt my heartbreaking; I lost. I was back in that fucking house with that fucking psychopath! At least now that Griffin was here the power was back on. My broken wrist was in a brace, and my right arm was all bandaged up. My foot was wrapped up too. On top of bandaging me up, Griffin had changed my clothes, I was now in a pair black sweatpants that fit me and a purple t-shirt. I tried sitting up, but my head started to spin, making me lie back down. I heard noises coming from the kitchen and then footsteps started approaching me. The living room door swung open.

"Oh hey, you're finally awake." Griffin sat down the food he was carrying on the coffee table in front of me. He leaned over me and gently

473

helped me into a sitting position, laughing he said, "I don't know what happened in here, but you really fucked up babe." I just glared up at him. "Oh, come on don't look at me like that, I'm not the one who did all of this to you." He said pointing to my wrist.

My jaw dropped opened, I shook my head not believing what he just said. "You're the one who keeps me locked in this fucking house."

Griffin scratched his head, "Yeah you got me there, but you didn't really leave me a choice honey. You were going to leave me." He got up and pulled the coffee table closer. He had warmed up the food and put it out on a plate for me. Picking up a plate he started eating. "Come on now, let's eat before the food gets cold, again."

After a moment when he realized that I wasn't eating he sat his plate down.

"I'm not going to poison you sweetheart, that wouldn't be any fun." He picked up my plate and fork, scooping up some food he held it close to my mouth, "You said you were hungry. Now eat." His tone was dark, but that look in his eye was darker. He let out an aggravated sigh, "Baby, you're starting to piss me off."

I narrowed my eyes and took the fork from him, knocking the food off of it, he watched me while I forced myself to eat.

"That's not so hard, now is it?" He asked.

We glared at each other while we ate.

When the food was gone, I asked, "What are you going to do to me."

Griffin laughed and got up. "Nothing bad if you're a good girl." He took my plate and went to the kitchen.

My heart beat pounded in my ears, I felt sick. I heard Griffin whistling in the kitchen, and then the 'pop' of a wine bottle being opened. I looked around me for something heavy to hit him with, but the room had been cleared out of everything except for the furniture. I waited on the sofa until Griffin came back in.

When he did he was carrying 2 wine glasses and an opened bottle of wine. "I'm slightly disappointed, I thought for sure you would have been waiting for me by the door." He poured a glass and handed it to me. I looked at the glass and back up to him. "Honestly Mel?" He took a drink and handed it back out to me.

I watched him pour himself a glass and then he topped off my glass before setting the bottle back on the table. "Is this supposed to be romantic?" I sneered as he turned to me with his glass held up. "Because it lost its charm a month ago."

Griffin took a deep breath. "Why are you being such a bitch tonight? Don't you know how much trouble I've gone through to get here tonight to be with you?!" He was leaning forward yelling at me, I had to lean backwards to keep him away. "You have the fucking nerve to sit there and treat me like I've done something wrong. Everything I've done was for you. IT WAS ALL FOR YOU! Drink your fucking wine you ungrateful cunt!" He took my wine glass from me and brought it up trying to force me to take a drink but ending up pouring it all over me instead. I swiped at the wine dripping off of my face and tried to stand up. "Sit back down!" Griffin yelled as he pulled me back down to the sofa by my left wrist.

My head spun as I fell back down. My stomach turned and I bent over, I took a couple of deep breaths and felt Griffin put a hand on my back. Leaning away I pushed him off, "Don't fucking touch me."

Griffin looked shocked at first. Then it was as if a shadow had passed over him. He glared at me and almost bared his teeth as he growled, "I'll touch you all I want, little Mel."

It all happened so fast. Frist he pounced on me, pinning my right arm to the arm of the sofa while his right hand went around my throat. I took my right knee and drove it into his side. Griffin coughed and loosened his grip enough for me to get my arm free. I clawed at his hand around my neck, my nails digging into his flesh and mine. I pushed myself up with everything that I had, over powering him just enough for me to get off of the sofa and slip away.

I scrambled around the sofa, pulling away when Griffin almost grabbed my elbow. I wanted to go out the door, but I knew if I did I would be screwed. This needed to end. I darted for the coffee table, but I had hesitated too soon. Griffin tackled me from behind. I kicked my feet, "Get off!" I screamed.

Griffin laughed and roughly turned me over, "Plan on it." He said and pulled me towards him.

I brought my foot up and kicked him in the stomach, he pushed my leg aside and back handed me across the face. I slid back a little and brought my other leg up to kick him between the legs. Griffin collapsed on top of me, groaning. I shoved him off and pushed myself up. I had no time to think. I took the bottle of wine by the neck and swung it in an arch behind me in case he was already there, but he was just now standing up. I took 3 steps towards him and swung the bottle down on his head. Griffin fell to the floor in a heap, I kicked his shoulder, so he was on his back looking at me. He seemed to be in a daze.

Still gripping the bottle, I got down on the floor and started searching his pockets for the car keys. My heart stopped when I heard Griffin start to cough out a laugh. "Get it girl." He said grinning. "I knew all this was just roleplay."

I looked at him disgusted, "Griffin," I said tightening my grip on the bottle. We locked eyes for the last time. I brought the bottle up and swung it down. Griffin brought his arm up a half a second too late, I hit him over the head, once knocking him back down, and again for good measure. Then one last time, cause if horror movies taught me anything it's that they always come back. I sat the bottle down on the floor next to me and patted him down, looking for the keys the he had in his front right pocket. After fishing them out I went to the front door not bothering to look back.

Griffin

After I got you all wrapped up I went to the kitchen to get our dinner ready. My stomach was starting to growl. I watched the paper plate spin around in the microwave, trying to remember the last time I had an actual meal. Fuck the food smelled really good. The kitchen wasn't as torn up as the living room or hallway, you must have gone crazy and started digging through the place looking for something.

I drummed my fingers on the counter; how in the fuck did you get out? I looked over my shoulder at the now closed basement door. Why was it open? It's not like there was a door that led outside down there, fuck there isn't even a window in this house that hasn't been seal shut.

The microwave finally dinged, snapping me out of my thoughts. I pulled the plate out and sat it down with the other one. I gathered up some plastic utensils, grabbed the plates, and headed for the living room. Meals are better when shared with people you care about.

When I walked in the living room I was relieved to see you moving around.

"Oh hey, you're finally awake." I said, sitting the food down on the coffee table. Leaning over I helped you into a sitting position. I couldn't stop the elated laugh that bubbled from somewhere deep within me. You looked so defeated; I wanted to take a picture of how gorgeous you look right now. But still that was no excuse for the mess you made in the living room. Or the hallway. I haven't even gone upstairs yet but I can only imagine what it looks like up there. "I don't know what happened in here, but you really fucked up babe."

You just glared up at me.

I bit back a smile, "oh come on don't look at me like that. I'm not the one who did all of this to you." I motioned to your wrist.

You're jaw dropped like you've just been offended. "you're the one who keeps me locked in this fucking house." You snapped.

Rubbing my jaw to cover my amusement I agreed. "Yeah you got me there, but you didn't leave me with much of a choice honey. You were going to leave me." I pulled the coffee table close and sat down so I could eat. "Come on now. Let's eat before the food gets cold; again."

I took a few bites. You never made a move to even touch your plate which was so fucking stupid.

"I'm not going to poison you sweetheart, that wouldn't be any fun." I put my plate down and picked up yours. I didn't like how stubborn you were being. I scooped some food onto the fork and held it out for you to take a bite, "you said you were hungry. Now eat." I held the fork close to your mouth, expecting you to take the fucking bite of food already. Why don't you ever just do what your told? I let out a breath, I was getting so tired of these mind games. "Baby, you're really starting to piss me off." I said flatly.

You narrowed your eyes and swiped the fork from my hand. I could feel the anger radiating off of you; I almost wanted to laugh. Would you still have this much attitude if you knew how close to death you were?

You stabbed some food with the fork, if I didn't have such a good hold on the plate we would both be wearing it by now. Shoving the food into your mouth you glared at me; in the fakest tone I could manage I spat out, "That's not so hard, now is it?"

The rest of the dinner we ate in silence, staring each other down. I forgot how beautiful your eyes are. Even now with fire burning in them I found myself lost under the intensity of your gaze. We sat quietly for a moment, then you broke the serenity of the moment by asking what I was going to do to you.

I laughed and got up, gathering up the trash I said, "Nothing if you're a good girl." Then I turned my back and went to the kitchen. I'm not sure what's come over me; but I was in a really good mood. I started whistling and tossed the trash into a bag. Looking around I could only imagine how many bags we'd need to clean this mess up.

Taking my time, I took the bottle of wine out of the refrigerator and went over to the table to open it. I grabbed the plastic wine glasses and went back to the living room. I fully expected you to be off of the sofa and doing anything other than just sitting there.

Walking over to the coffee table I couldn't keep my eyes off of you. I told you how disappointed I was that you weren't waiting by the door for me. It almost took some of the fun out of it; but I kept that part to myself. I smiled at you and poured a glass of wine. I held it out for you to take. You hesitated but then you took it and just stared up at me.

I rolled my eyes and sighed, "honestly, Mel?" I grabbed the glass from you and took a drink. I gave a 'there, see?' look and handed it back. When you took it I poured a glass and topped off yours before sitting the bottle on the table, close to me because I'm not stupid enough to let you get a hold of it.

"Is this supposed to be romantic?" You suddenly asked, I was hurt you didn't find any spark in what I was doing for you, for us. I looked over at you, my glass half raised. You kind of shook your head and simply stated, "because it lost its charm a month ago."

I took a deep breath to calm down that darker part of me that wanted to backhand you across the face for saying that. Instead, I asked, "Why are you being such a bitch tonight?" I leaned forward subconsciously as I spoke, "don't you know how much trouble I've gone through to be here tonight, to be with you?!" We were practically nose to nose at this point. "You have the fucking nerve to sit there and treat *me* like *I've* done something wrong." With each word I just got madder. "*Everything* I've done was for *you*." It was like someone left the door open and the hound just bolted out the door, one minute I was in full control then the next I was leaning over you screaming in your face. "IT WAS ALL FOR YOU!" I yelled, I glanced down at the wine glass you were holding, mad at how you haven't even took a sip and amazed that it hasn't spilled yet. I yanked it out of your hand and brought it up to your lips. "Drink your fucking wine you ungrateful cunt."

The wine poured all over you, soaking the front of your shirt. You brushed the wine off your chin and tried to stand up to shake the rest of it off.

I reached out and grabbed your broken wrist and yanked you back down to the couch, "Sit back down!" I demanded.

The blood drained from your face as you collapsed back onto the sofa, sweat broke out along your hair line as you doubled over and took a few deep breaths. I started to rub your back; to help comfort you but instead you pushed me away.

"Don't fucking touch me." You spat at me.

My eyes went wide. Then I mentally took a step back and let the beast have its way. I narrowed my eyes and grinned down at you. "I'll touch you all I want, little Mel." Lunging at you I easily pinned you to the sofa.

I almost had you until you drove your knee into my side in a way that made me cough. That was just enough for you to get one hand free. Clawing at me like a hellcat you managed to get yourself free. The back of my hand and up my arm was covered in bleeding scratches but so was your neck and jaw line. I shook my head and laughed, reaching out to grab your elbow but you were too quick.

You moved for the living room door, but something made you hesitate. Which was fine, that gave me enough time to tackle you from behind. You kicked at me and tried to crawl away from me, but you couldn't get away.

"Get OFF!" You screamed.

Laughing I roughly turned you over, so you were facing me. "Plan on it." I pulled you towards me and climbed on top of you. The things I was going to do to you.

My thoughts were quickly interrupted when you tried to kick me in the stomach. I pushed your leg to the side and back handed you across the face. Somehow you were able to get the upper hand when you slid yourself back and kicked me right in the balls. Light exploded in my vision, and I fell down on top of you, and you pushed me to the side.

I was in too much pain to even begin to worry about what you were doing. I took a few deep breaths and pushed the pain down, but it took longer than it usually does to regain composure and move on. When I finally got myself into a good position to stand up something hit me over the head, sending me back to the floor.

Something, I'm guessing your foot; dug into my shoulder and pushed me over on my back. Then you came into view. Like a fucking Angel.

I smirked when I felt you feeling me up, moving your hands around my hips. I laughed, "Get it girl." I said. "I knew all this was just roleplay." I laughed at your disgusted expression.

"Griffin," You said softly. It was almost a whisper. We locked eyes for a moment. Then you brought the wine bottle up, when did you grabbed that? I wasn't sure, but you brought it down and hit me across the temple; turning out the lights.

Melanie (January 6)

It was dark out now, but it had stopped snowing. I almost went back in the house to grab a jacket, but I would warm up in the car. The snow-covered gravel bit into my bare feet as I walked up to the driver side of Griffins car. I was thankful when I saw that he had pulled it up to the house and hadn't left it halfway down the long ass dirt road. I got in and started the car.

The smell of weed hit my nose. Opening the center console hoping that Griffin had put a joint in there like I've seen him do plenty of times before and was relieved when I see one sitting in there on top of the car charger along with a lighter. I lit the joint and sat there staring at the front door waiting for the car to warm up.

I glanced at the clock, just now 3 in the morning. I looked back to the door of the house, making sure that no one would come stumbling out. I took a hit and thought about my next move. I really just wanted to go home. Not back to the city but somewhere else, I took another hit and winced when I moved my wrist wrong. I smoked until the joint burnt my lips, flipping the roach out the window I put the car in drive and followed the dirt road away from the house; away from that nightmare.

I wasn't sure where I was going, it was so dark I couldn't see past the headlights. I just kept taking right turns until I seen a sign that pointed towards the interstate.

By the time I hit the highway that took me back to the city it had started snowing again, the snowflakes zooming at me were hypnotizing. It all felt surreal, I was worried that I was going to wake up at any moment and find myself tied to the bed again. Running a hand through my knotted hair I tried to keep it together, I couldn't unravel right now. I was driving, and it was snowing. I shook my head and stepped on the gas, turning on the radio to distract myself.

After a few moments I heard a siren behind me, I looked up and seen red and blue lights in the review mirror. I pulled the car off to the shoulder and looked at my reflection. I was covered in little scratches, my right eye was dark purple and swelling shut, my lip was split, and I had Griffin's blood splattered across my face. My hair and clothes still smelled strongly of wine, the cut on my right arm was bleeding again, soaking the white bandage in blood, and I still had the brace on my left wrist. To put it nicely I looked rough.

Laughing I shook my head and rolled the window down when the police officer walked up. "Good morning, Officer." I said, "I need your help."